KURT VONNEGUT

Kurt Vonnegut

NOVELS & STORIES 1950–1962

Player Piano

The Sirens of Titan

Mother Night

Stories

Sidney Offit, editor

THE LIBRARY OF AMERICA

The paper used in this publication meets the
minimum requirements of the American National Standard for
Information Sciences—Permanence of Paper for Printed
Library Materials, ANSI Z39.48—1984.

Distributed to the trade in the United States
by Penguin Group (USA) Inc.
and in Canada by Penguin Group Canada Ltd.

Library of Congress Control Number: 2011928612
ISBN: 978-1-59853-150-3

First Printing
The Library of America—226

Manufactured in the United States of America

Contents

PLAYER PIANO

For Jane—God Bless Her

Consider the lilies of the field, how they grow:
They toil not, neither do they spin;
And yet I say unto you,
That even Solomon in all his glory
Was not arrayed like one of these. . . .

Matthew 6:28

Foreword

THIS BOOK is not a book about what is, but a book about what could be. The characters are modeled after persons as yet unborn, or, perhaps, at this writing, infants.

It is mostly about managers and engineers. At this point in history, 1952 A.D., our lives and freedom depend largely upon the skill and imagination and courage of our managers and engineers, and I hope that God will help them to help us all stay alive and free.

But this book is about another point in history, when there is no more war, and . . .

Chapter I

ILIUM, NEW YORK, is divided into three parts.

In the northwest are the managers and engineers and civil servants and a few professional people; in the northeast are the machines; and in the south, across the Iroquois River, is the area known locally as Homestead, where almost all of the people live.

If the bridge across the Iroquois were dynamited, few daily routines would be disturbed. Not many people on either side have reasons other than curiosity for crossing.

During the war, in hundreds of Iliums over America, managers and engineers learned to get along without their men and women, who went to fight. It was the miracle that won the war—production with almost no manpower. In the patois of the north side of the river, it was the know-how that won the war. Democracy owed its life to know-how.

Ten years after the war—after the men and women had come home, after the riots had been put down, after thousands had been jailed under the antisabotage laws—Doctor Paul Proteus was petting a cat in his office. He was the most important, brilliant person in Ilium, the manager of the Ilium Works, though only thirty-five. He was tall, thin, nervous, and dark, with the gentle good looks of his long face distorted by dark-rimmed glasses.

He didn't feel important or brilliant at the moment, nor had he for some time. His principle concern just then was that the black cat be contented in its new surroundings.

Those old enough to remember and too old to compete said affectionately that Doctor Proteus looked just as his father had as a young man—and it was generally understood, resentfully in some quarters, that Paul would someday rise almost as high in the organization as his father had. His father, Doctor George Proteus, was at the time of his death the nation's first National Industrial, Commercial, Communications, Foodstuffs, and Resources Director, a position approached in importance only by the presidency of the United States.

As for the Proteus genes' chances of being passed down to

yet another generation, there were practically none. Paul's wife, Anita, his secretary during the war, was barren. Ironically as anyone would please, he had married her after she had declared that she was certainly pregnant, following an abandoned office celebration of victory.

"Like that, kitty?" With solicitousness and vicarious pleasure, young Proteus ran a roll of blueprints along the cat's arched back. "Mmmmm-aaaaah—good, eh?" He had spotted her that morning, near the golf course, and had picked her up as a mouser for the plant. Only the night before, a mouse had gnawed through the insulation on a control wire and put buildings 17, 19, and 21 temporarily out of commission.

Paul turned on his intercom set. "Katharine?"

"Yes, Doctor Proteus?"

"Katharine, when's my speech going to be typed?"

"I'm doing it now, sir. Ten, fifteen minutes, I promise."

Doctor Katharine Finch was his secretary, and the only woman in the Ilium Works. Actually, she was more a symbol of rank than a real help, although she was useful as a stand-in when Paul was ill or took a notion to leave work early. Only the brass—plant managers and bigger—had secretaries. During the war, the managers and engineers had found that the bulk of secretarial work could be done—as could most lower-echelon jobs—more quickly and efficiently and cheaply by machines. Anita was about to be dismissed when Paul had married her. Now, for instance, Katharine was being annoyingly unmachinelike, dawdling over Paul's speech, and talking to her presumed lover, Doctor Bud Calhoun, at the same time.

Bud, who was manager of the petroleum terminal in Ilium, worked only when shipments came or went by barge or pipeline, and he spent most of his time between these crises—as now—filling Katharine's ears with the euphoria of his Georgia sweet talk.

Paul took the cat in his arms and carried her to the enormous floor-to-ceiling window that comprised one wall. "Lots and lots of mice out there, kitty," he said.

He was showing the cat an old battlefield at peace. Here, in the basin of the river bend, the Mohawks had overpowered the Algonquins, the Dutch the Mohawks, the British the Dutch, the Americans the British. Now, over bones and rotten palings and cannon balls and arrowheads, there lay a triangle of steel and masonry buildings, a half-mile on each side—the Illium Works. Where men had once howled and hacked at one another, and fought nip-and-tuck with nature as well, the machines hummed and whirred and clicked, and made parts for baby carriages and bottle caps, motorcycles and refrigerators, television sets and tricycles—the fruits of peace.

Paul raised his eyes above the rooftops of the great triangle to the glare of the sun on the Iroquois River, and beyond—to Homestead, where many of the pioneer names still lived: van Zandt, Cooper, Cortland, Stokes . . .

"Doctor Proteus?" It was Katharine again.

"Yes, Katharine."

"It's on again."

"Three in building 58?"

"Yessir—the light's on again."

"All right—call Doctor Shepherd and find out what he's doing about it."

"He's sick today. Remember?"

"Then it's up to me, I guess." He put on his coat, sighed with ennui, picked up the cat, and walked into Katharine's office. "Don't get up, don't get up," he said to Bud, who was stretched out on a couch.

"Who was gonna get up?" said Bud.

Three walls of the room were solid with meters from baseboard to molding, unbroken save for the doors leading into the outer hall and into Paul's office. The fourth wall, as in Paul's office, was a single pane of glass. The meters were identical, the size of cigarette packages, and stacked like masonry, each labeled with a bright brass plate. Each was connected to a group of machines somewhere in the Works. A glowing red jewel called attention to the seventh meter from the bottom, fifth row to the left, on the east wall.

Paul tapped the meter with his finger. "Uh-huh—here we go again: number three in 58 getting rejects, all right." He glanced over the rest of the instruments. "Guess that's all, eh?"

"Just that one."

"Whatch goin' do with thet cat?" said Bud.

Paul snapped his fingers. "Say, I'm glad you asked that. I have a project for you, Bud. I want some sort of signaling device that will tell this cat where she can find a mouse."

"Electronic?"

"I should hope so."

"You'd need some kind of sensin' element thet could smell a mouse."

"Or a rat. I want you to work on it while I'm gone."

As Paul walked out to his car in the pale March sunlight, he realized that Bud Calhoun *would* have a mouse alarm designed—one a cat could understand—by the time he got back to the office. Paul sometimes wondered if he wouldn't have been more content in another period of history, but the rightness of Bud's being alive now was beyond question. Bud's mentality was one that had been remarked upon as being peculiarly American since the nation had been born—the restless, erratic insight and imagination of a gadgeteer. This was the climax, or close to it, of generations of Bud Calhouns, with almost all of American industry integrated into one stupendous Rube Goldberg machine.

Paul stopped by Bud's car, which was parked next to his. Bud had shown off its special features to him several times, and, playfully, Paul put it through its paces. "Let's go," he said to the car.

A whir and a click, and the door flew open. "Hop in," said a tape recording under the dashboard. The starter spun, the engine caught and idled down, and the radio went on.

Gingerly, Paul pressed a button on the steering column. A motor purred, gears grumbled softly, and the two front seats lay down side by side like sleepy lovers. It struck Paul as shockingly like an operating table for horses he had once seen in a veterinary hospital—where the horse was walked alongside the tipped table, lashed to it, anesthetized, and then toppled into operating position by the gear-driven table top. He could see Katharine Finch sinking, sinking, sinking, as Bud, his hand on the button, crooned. Paul raised the seats with another button. "Goodbye," he said to the car.

The motor stopped, the radio winked off, and the door slammed. "Don't take any wooden nickels," called the car as

Paul climbed into his own. "Don't take any wooden nickels, don't take any wooden nickels, don't take any—"

"I won't!"

Bud's car fell silent, apparently at peace.

Paul drove down the broad, clean boulevard that split the plant, and watched the building numbers flash by. A station wagon, honking its horn, and its occupants waving to him, shot past in the opposite direction, playfully zigzagging on the deserted street, heading for the main gate. Paul glanced at his watch. That was the second shift just coming off work. It annoyed him that sophomoric high spirits should be correlated with the kind of young men it took to keep the plant going. Cautiously, he assured himself that when he, Finnerty, and Shepherd had come to work in the Ilium Works thirteen years before, they had been a good bit more adult, less cock-sure, and certainly without the air of belonging to an elite.

Some people, including Paul's famous father, had talked in the old days as though engineers, managers, and scientists were an elite. And when things were building up to the war, it was recognized that American know-how was the only answer to the prospective enemy's vast numbers, and there was talk of deeper, thicker shelters for the possessors of know-how, and of keeping this cream of the population out of the front-line fighting. But not many had taken the idea of an elite to heart. When Paul, Finnerty, and Shepherd had graduated from college, early in the war, they had felt sheepish about not going to fight, and humbled by those who did go. But now this elite business, this assurance of superiority, this sense of rightness about the hierarchy topped by managers and engineers—this was instilled in all college graduates, and there were no bones about it.

Paul felt better when he got into Building 58, a long, narrow structure four blocks long. It was a pet of his. He'd been told to have the north end of the building torn down and replaced, and he'd talked Headquarters out of it. The north end was the oldest building in the plant, and Paul had saved it—because of its historical interest to visitors, he'd told Headquarters. But he discouraged and disliked visitors, and he'd really saved Building 58's north end for himself. It was the original machine shop set up by Edison in 1886, the same year in which he opened another in Schenectady, and visiting it took the edge off Paul's periods of depression. It was a vote of confidence from the past, he thought—where the past admitted how humble and shoddy it had been, where one could look from the old to the new and see that mankind really had come a long way. Paul needed that reassurance from time to time.

Objectively, Paul tried to tell himself, things really were better than ever. For once, after the great bloodbath of the war, the world really was cleared of unnatural terrors—mass starvation, mass imprisonment, mass torture, mass murder. Objectively, know-how and world law were getting their long-awaited chance to turn earth into an altogether pleasant and convenient place in which to sweat out Judgment Day.

Paul wished he had gone to the front, and heard the senseless tumult and thunder, and seen the wounded and dead, and maybe got a piece of shrapnel through his leg. Maybe he'd be able to understand then how good everything now was by comparison, to see what seemed so clear to others—that what he was doing, had done, and would do as a manager and engineer was vital, above reproach, and had, in fact, brought on a golden age. Of late, his job, the system, and organizational politics had left him variously annoyed, bored, or queasy.

He stood in the old part of Building 58, which was now filled with welding machines and a bank of insulation braiders. It soothed him to look up at the wooden rafters, uneven with ancient adze marks beneath flaking calcimine, and at the dull walls of brick soft enough for men—God knows how long ago—to carve their initials in: "KTM," "DG," "GP," "BDH," "HB," "NNS." Paul imagined for a moment—as he often imagined on visits to Building 58—that he was Edison, standing on the threshold of a solitary brick building on the banks of the Iroquois, with the upstate winter slashing through the broomcorn outside. The rafters still bore the marks of what Edison had done with the lonely brick barn: bolt holes showed where overhead shafts had once carried power to a forest of belts, and the wood-block floor was black with the oil and scarred by the feet of the crude machines the belts had spun.

On his office wall, Paul had a picture of the shop as it had been in the beginning. All of the employees, most of them recruited from surrounding farms, had stood shoulder to shoulder amid the crude apparatus for the photograph, almost fierce with dignity and pride, ridiculous in stiff collars and derbies. The photographer had apparently been accustomed to taking pictures of athletic teams and fraternal organizations, for the picture had the atmosphere, after the fashion of the day, of both. In each face was a defiant promise of physical strength, and at the same time, there was the attitude of a secret order, above and apart from society by virtue of participating in important and moving rites the laity could only guess about—and guess wrong. The pride in strength and important mystery showed no less in the eyes of the sweepers than in those of the machinists and inspectors, and in those of the foreman, who alone was without a lunchbox.

A buzzer sounded, and Paul stepped to one side of the aisle as the sweeping machine rattled by on its rails, whooshing up a cloud of dust with spinning brooms, and sucking up the cloud with a voracious snout. The cat in Paul's arms clawed up threads from his suit and hissed at the machine.

Paul's eyes began to nag him with a prickling sensation, and he realized that he'd been gazing into the glare and sputter of the welding machines without protecting his eyes. He clipped dark glasses over his spectacles, and strode through the antiseptic smell of ozone toward lathe group three, which was in the center of the building, in the new part.

He paused for a moment by the last welding-machine group, and wished Edison could be with him to see it. The old man would have been enchanted. Two steel plates were stripped from a pile, sent rattling down a chute; were seized by mechanical hands and thrust under the welding machine. The welding heads dropped, sputtered, and rose. A battery of electric eyes balefully studied the union of the two plates, signaled a meter in Katharine's office that all was well with welding-machine group five in Building 58, and the welded plates skittered down another chute into the jaws of the punch-press group in the basement. Every seventeen seconds, each of the twelve machines in the group completed the cycle.

Looking the length of Building 58, Paul had the impression of a great gymnasium, where countless squads practiced precision calisthenics—bobbing, spinning, leaping, thrusting, waving. . . . This much of the new era Paul loved: the machines themselves were entertaining and delightful.

Cursorily, he opened the control box for the welding-machine group, and saw that the machines were set to run for three more days. After that, they would shut down automatically until Paul received new orders from headquarters and relayed them to Doctor Lawson Shepherd, who was second-in-command and responsible for Buildings 53 through 71. Shepherd, who was sick today, would then set the controls for a new batch of refrigerator backs—however many backs EPICAC, a computing machine in Carlsbad Caverns, felt the economy could absorb.

Paul, calming the anxious cat with his long, slender fingers, wondered indifferently if Shepherd really was sick. Probably not. More likely, he was seeing important people, trying to get transferred out from under Paul.

Shepherd, Paul, and Edward Finnerty had all come to Ilium together as youngsters. Now Finnerty had moved on to bigger things in Washington; Paul had been given the highest job in Ilium; and Shepherd, sulky and carping, but efficient, had, in his own eyes, been humiliated by being named second-in-command to Paul. Transfers were an upper-echelon decision, and Paul hoped to God that Shepherd got one.

Paul arrived at lathe group three, the troublemaker he had come to see. He had been agitating a long time for permission to junk the group, without much luck. The lathes were of the old type, built originally to be controlled by men, and adapted during the war, clumsily, to the new techniques. The accuracy was going out of them, and, as the meter in Katharine's office had pointed out, rejects were showing up in quantity. Paul was willing to bet that the lathe group was ten per cent as wasteful as it had been in the days of human control and mountainous scrap heaps.

The group, five ranks of ten machines each, swept their tools in unison across steel bars, kicked out finished shafts onto continuous belts, stopped while raw bars dropped between their chucks and tailstocks, clamped down, and swept their tools across the bars, kicked out the finished shafts onto . . .

Paul unlocked the box containing the tape recording that controlled them all. The tape was a small loop that fed continuously between magnetic pickups. On it were recorded the movements of a master machinist turning out a shaft for a fractional horsepower motor. Paul counted back—eleven, twelve, thirteen years ago, he'd been in on the making of the tape, the master from which this one had been made. . . .

He and Finnerty and Shepherd, with the ink hardly dry on their doctorates, had been sent to one of the machine shops to make the recording. The foreman had pointed out his best man—what *was* his name?—and, joking with the puzzled machinist, the three bright young men had hooked up the recording apparatus to the lathe controls. Hertz! That had been the machinist's name—Rudy Hertz, an old-timer, who had been about ready to retire. Paul remembered the name now, and remembered the deference the old man had shown the bright young men.

Afterward, they'd got Rudy's foreman to let him off, and, in a boisterous, whimsical spirit of industrial democracy, they'd taken him across the street for a beer. Rudy hadn't understood quite what the recording instruments were all about, but what he had understood, he'd liked: that he, out of thousands of machinists, had been chosen to have his motions immortalized on tape.

And here, now, this little loop in the box before Paul, here was Rudy as Rudy had been to his machine that afternoon—Rudy, the turner-on of power, the setter of speeds, the controller of the cutting tool. This was the essence of Rudy as far as his machine was concerned, as far as the economy was concerned, as far as the war effort had been concerned. The tape was the essence distilled from the small, polite man with the big hands and black fingernails; from the man who thought the world could be saved if everyone read a verse from the Bible every night; from the man who adored a collie for want of children; from the man who . . . What else had Rudy said that afternoon? Paul supposed the old man was dead now—or in his second childhood in Homestead.

Now, by switching in lathes on a master panel and feeding them signals from the tape, Paul could make the essence of Rudy Hertz produce one, ten, a hundred, or a thousand of the shafts.

Paul closed the box's door. The tape seemed in good condition, and so were the pickups. Everything, in fact, was as ship-shape as could be expected, considering the antiquity of the machines. There were just going to have to be rejects, and that was that. The whole group belonged in a museum, not a production setup. Even the box was archaic—a vaultlike affair bolted to the floor, with a steel door and lock. At the time of the riots, right after the war, the master tapes had all been locked up in this way. Now, with the antisabotage laws as rigidly enforced as they were, the only protection the controls needed was from dust, cockroaches, and mice.

At the door, in the old part of the building once more, Paul paused for a moment to listen to the music of Building 58. He had had it in the back of his mind for years to get a composer to do something with it—*the Building 58 Suite*. It was wild and Latin music, hectic rhythms, fading in and out of phase, kaleidoscopic sound. He tried to separate and identify the themes. There! The lathe groups, the tenors: "*Furrazz-ow-ow-ow-ow-ow-ak! ting! Furr-azz-ow-ow* . . ." The welders, the baritones: "*Vaaaaaaa-zuzip! Vaaaaaaa-zuzip!*" And, with the basement as a resonating chamber, the punch presses, the basses: "*Aw-grumph! tonka-tonka. Aw-grump! tonka-tonka* . . ." It was exciting music, and Paul, flushed, his vague anxieties gone, gave himself over to it.

Out of the corner of his eye, a crazy, spinning movement caught his fancy, and he turned in his delight to watch a cluster of miniature maypoles braid bright cloth insulation about a black snake of cable. A thousand little dancers whirled about one another at incredible speeds, pirouetting, dodging one another, unerringly building their snug snare about the cable. Paul laughed at the wonderful machines, and had to look away to keep from getting dizzy. In the old days, when women had watched over the machines, some of the more simple-hearted had been found sitting rigidly at their posts, staring, long after quitting time.

His gaze fell upon an asymmetrical heart scratched into the old brick, and in its center, "K.L.—M.W.", and the date, "1931." K.L. and M.W. had taken a liking to one another, then, in the same year that Edison had died. Paul thought again of the fun of showing the old man around Building 58, and suddenly realized that most of the machinery would be old stuff, even to

Edison. The braiders, the welders, the punch presses, the lathes, the conveyers—everything in sight, almost, had been around in Edison's time. The basic parts of the automatic controls, too, and the electric eyes and other elements that did and did better what human senses had once done for industry—all were familiar enough in scientific circles even in the nineteen-twenties. All that was new was the combination of these elements. Paul reminded himself to bring that out in his talk at the Country Club that night.

The cat arched her back and clawed at Paul's suit again. The sweeper was snuffling down the aisle toward them once more. It sounded its warning buzzer, and Paul stepped out of its path. The cat hissed and spat, suddenly raked Paul's hand with her claws, and jumped. With a bouncing, stiff-legged gait, she fled before the sweeper. Snatching, flashing, crashing, shrieking machines kept her in the middle of the aisle, yards ahead of the sweeper's whooshing brooms. Paul looked frantically for the switch that would stop the sweeper, but before he found it, the cat made a stand. She faced the oncoming sweeper, her needle-like teeth bared, the tip of her tail snapping back and forth. The flash of a welder went off inches from her eyes, and the sweeper gobbled her up and hurled her squalling and scratching into its galvanized tin belly.

Winded after a quarter-mile run through the length of the building, Paul caught the sweeper just as it reached a chute. It gagged, and spat the cat down the chute and into a freight car outside. When Paul got outside, the cat had scrambled up the side of the freight car, tumbled to the ground, and was desperately clawing her way up a fence.

"No, kitty, no!" cried Paul.

The cat hit the alarm wire on the fence, and sirens screamed from the gate house. In the next second the cat hit the charged wire atop the fence. A pop, a green flash, and the cat sailed over the top strand as though thrown. She dropped to the asphalt—dead and smoking, but outside.

An armored car, its turret nervously jerking its brace of machine guns this way and that, grumbled to a stop by the small corpse. The turret hatch clanged open, and a plant guard cautiously raised his head. "Everything all right, sir?"

"Turn off the sirens. Nothing but a cat on the fence." Paul knelt, and looked at the cat through the mesh of the fence, frightfully upset. "Pick up the cat and take her to my office."

"Beg your pardon, sir?"

"The cat—I want her taken to my office."

"She's dead, sir."

"You heard me."

"Yessir."

Paul was in the depths again as he climbed into his car in front of Building 58. There was nothing in sight to divert him, nothing but asphalt, a perspective of blank, numbered façades, and wisps of cold cirrus clouds in a strip of blue sky. Paul glimpsed the only life visible through a narrow canyon between Buildings 57 and 59, a canyon that opened onto the river and revealed a bank of gray porches in Homestead. On the topmost porch an old man rocked in a patch of sunlight. A child leaned over the railing and launched a square of paper in a lazy, oscillating course to the river's edge. The youngster looked up from the paper to meet Paul's gaze. The old man stopped rocking and looked, too, at the curiosity, a living thing in the Ilium Works.

As Paul passed Katharine Finch's desk on his way into his office, she held out his typewritten speech. "That's very good, what you said about the Second Industrial Revolution," she said.

"Old, old stuff."

"It seemed very fresh to me—I mean that part where you say how the First Industrial Revolution devalued muscle work, then the second one devalued routine mental work. I was fascinated."

"Norbert Wiener, a mathematician, said all that way back in the nineteen-forties. It's fresh to you because you're too young to know anything but the way things are now."

"Actually, it is kind of incredible that things were ever any other way, isn't it? It was so ridiculous to have people stuck in one place all day, just using their senses, then a reflex, using their senses, then a reflex, and not really thinking at all."

"Expensive," said Paul, "and about as reliable as a putty ruler. You can imagine what the scrap heap looked like, and what hell it was to be a service manager in those days. Hangovers, family squabbles, resentments against the boss, debts, the war—every kind of human trouble was likely to show up in a product one way or another." He smiled. "And happiness, too. I can remember when we had to allow for holidays, especially around Christmas. There wasn't anything to do but take it. The reject rate would start climbing around the fifth of December, and up and up it'd go until Christmas. Then the holiday, then a horrible reject rate; then New Year's, then a ghastly reject level. Then things would taper down to normal—which was plenty bad enough—by January fifteenth or so. We used to have to figure in things like that in pricing a product."

"Do you suppose there'll be a Third Industrial Revolution?"

Paul paused in his office doorway. "A third one? What would that be like?"

"I don't know exactly. The first and second ones must have been sort of inconceivable at one time."

"To the people who were going to be replaced by machines, maybe. A third one, eh? In a way, I guess the third one's been going on for some time, if you mean thinking machines. That would be the third revolution, I guess—machines that devaluate human thinking. Some of the big computers like EPICAC do that all right, in specialized fields."

"Uh-huh," said Katharine thoughtfully. She rattled a pencil between her teeth. "First the muscle work, then the routine work, then, maybe, the real brainwork."

"I hope I'm not around long enough to see that final step. Speaking of industrial revolutions, where's Bud?"

"A barge was coming in, so he had to get back to work. He left this for you." She handed him a crumpled laundry slip with Bud's name on it.

Paul turned the slip over and found, as he had expected, a circuit diagram for a mouse detector and alarm system that might very well work. "Astonishing mind, Katharine."

She nodded uncertainly.

Paul closed his door, locked it silently, and got a bottle from under papers in a bottom drawer. He blacked out for an instant under the gloriously hot impact of a gulp of whisky. He hid the bottle again, his eyes watering.

"Doctor Proteus, your wife is on the phone," said Katharine on the intercom.

"Proteus speaking." He started to sit, and was distressed to find a small wicker basket in his chair, containing a dead black cat.

"This is me, darling, Anita."

"Hello, hello, hello." He set the basket on the floor gently, and sank into his chair. "How are you, sweetheart?" he said absently. His mind was still on the cat.

"All set to have a good time tonight?" It was a theatrical contralto, knowing and passionate: Ilium's Lady of the Manor speaking.

"Been jumpy all day about the talk."

"Then you'll do it brilliantly, darling. You'll get to Pittsburgh yet. I haven't the slightest doubt about that, Paul, not the slightest. Just wait until Kroner and Baer hear you tonight."

"Kroner and Baer accepted, did they?" These two were manager and chief engineer, respectively, of the entire Eastern Division, of which the Ilium Works was one small part. It was Kroner and Baer who would decide who was to get the most important job in their division, a job left vacant two weeks ago by death—the managership of the Pittsburgh Works. "How gay can a party get?"

"Well, if you don't like that, I have some news you will like. There's going to be another very special guest."

"Hi ho."

"And you have to go to Homestead for some Irish whisky for him. The club hasn't got any."

"Finnerty! Ed Finnerty!"

"Yes, Finnerty. He called this afternoon and was very specific about your getting some Irish for him. He's on his way from Washington to Chicago, and he's going to stop off here."

"How long has it been, Anita? Five, six years?"

"Not since before you got to be manager. *That* long." She was hale, enthusiastic about Finnerty's coming. It annoyed Paul, because he knew very well that she didn't care for Finnerty. She was crowing, not because she was fond of Finnerty but because she enjoyed the ritual attitudes of friendships, of which she had none. Also, since he'd left Ilium, Ed Finnerty had become a man of consequence, a member of the National Industrial Planning Board; and this fact no doubt dulled her recollections of contretemps with Finnerty in the past.

"You're right about that being good news, Anita. It's wonderful. Takes the edge off Kroner and Baer."

"Now, you're going to be nice to them, too."

"Oh yes. Pittsburgh, here we come."

"If I tell you something for your own good, promise not to get mad?"

"No."

"All right, I'll tell you anyway. Amy Halporn said this morning she'd heard something about you and Pittsburgh. Her husband was with Kroner today, and Kroner had the impression that you didn't *want* to go to Pittsburgh."

"How does he want me to tell him—in Esperanto? I've told him I wanted the job a dozen different ways in English."

"Apparently Kroner doesn't feel you really mean it. You've been too subtle and modest, darling."

"Kroner's a bright one, all right."

"How do you mean?"

"I mean he's got more insight into me than I do."

"You mean you don't want the Pittsburgh job?"

"I'm not sure. He apparently knew that before I did."

"You're tired, darling."

"I guess."

"You need a drink. Come home early."

"All right."

"I love you, Paul."

"I love *you*, Anita. Goodbye."

Anita had the mechanics of marriage down pat, even to the subtlest conventions. If her approach was disturbingly rational, systematic, she was thorough enough to turn out a creditable counterfeit of warmth. Paul could only suspect that her feelings were shallow—and perhaps that suspicion was part of what he was beginning to think of as his sickness.

His head was down, his eyes closed, when he hung up. When he opened his eyes, he was looking at the dead cat in the basket.

"Katharine!"

"Yessir."

"Will you have somebody bury this cat."

"We wondered what you wanted to do with it."

"God knows what I had in mind." He looked at the corpse

and shook his head. "God knows. Maybe a Christian burial; maybe I hoped she'd come around. Get rid of it right away, would you?"

He stopped by Katharine's desk on his way home and told her not to worry about the glowing jewel on the seventh meter from the bottom, fifth row from the left, on the east wall.

"Beyond help," he said. Lathe group three, Building 58, had been good in its day, but was showing wear and becoming a misfit in the slick, streamlined setup, where there was no place for erratic behavior. "Basically, it wasn't built for the job it's doing anyway. I look for the buzzer to go off any day now, and that'll be the end."

In each meter box, in addition to the instrument, the jewel, and the warning lamp, was a buzzer. The buzzer was the signal for a unit's complete breakdown.

Chapter II

THE SHAH OF BRATPUHR, spiritual leader of 6,000,000 members of the Kolhouri sect, wizened and wise and dark as cocoa, encrusted with gold brocade and constellations of twinkling gems, sank deep into the royal-blue cushions of the limousine—like a priceless brooch in its gift box.

On the other side of the limousine's rear seat sat Doctor Ewing J. Halyard, of the United States Department of State, a heavy, florid, urbane gentleman of forty. He wore a flowing sandy mustache, a colored shirt, a boutonniere, and a waistcoat contrasting with his dark suit, and wore them with such poise that one was sure he'd just come from a distinguished company where everyone dressed in this manner. The fact was that only Doctor Halyard did. And he got away with it beautifully.

Between them, nervous, grinning, young, and forever apologetic for his own lack of éclat or power, was Khashdrahr Miasma, the interpreter, and nephew of the Shah, who had learned English from a tutor, but had never before been outside of the Shah's palace.

"*Khabu*?" said the Shah in his high, frail voice.

Halyard had been with the Shah for three days now and was able to understand, without Khashdrahr's help, five of the Shah's expressions. "*Khabu*" meant "where?" "*Siki*" meant "what?" "*Akka sahn*" meant "why?" "*Brahous brahouna, houna saki*" was a combination of blessing and thanks, and *Sumklish* was the sacred Kolhouri drink which Khashdrahr carried in a hip flask for the Shah.

The Shah had left his military and spiritual fastness in the mountains to see what he could learn in the most powerful nation on earth for the good of his people. Doctor Halyard was his guide and host.

"*Khabu*?" said the Shah again, peering out at the city. "The Shah wishes to know, please, where we are now," said Khashdrahr.

"I know," said Halyard, smiling wanly. It had been *khabu* and *siki* and *akka sahn* until he was half out of his mind. He leaned forward. "Ilium, New York, your highness. We are about to cross the Iroquois River, which divides the town in two. Over there on the opposite bank is the Ilium Works."

The limousine came to a halt by the end of the bridge, where a large work crew was filling a small chuckhole. The crew had opened a lane for an old Plymouth with a broken headlight, which was coming through from the north side of the river. The limousine waited for the Plymouth to get through, and then proceeded.

The Shah turned to stare at the group through the back window, and then spoke at length.

Doctor Halyard smiled and nodded appreciatively, and awaited a translation.

"The Shah," said Khashdrahr, "he would like, please, to know who owns these slaves we see all the way up from New York City."

"Not slaves," said Halyard, chuckling patronizingly. "Citizens, employed by government. They have same rights as other citizens—free speech, freedom of worship, the right to vote. Before the war, they worked in the Ilium Works, controlling machines, but now machines control themselves much better."

"Aha!" said the Shah, after Khashdrahr had translated.

"Less waste, much better products, cheaper products with automatic control."

"Aha!"

"And any man who cannot support himself by doing a job better than a machine is employed by the government, either in the Army or the Reconstruction and Reclamation Corps."

"Aha! *Khabu bonanza-pak?*"

"Eh?"

"He says, 'Where does the money come from to pay them?' " said Khashdrahr.

"Oh. From taxes on the machines, and taxes on personal incomes. Then the Army and the Reconstruction and Reclamation Corps people put their money back into the system for more products for better living."

"Aha!"

Doctor Halyard, a dutiful man with a bad conscience about the size of his expense accounts, went on explaining America, though he knew very little was getting through. He told the Shah that advances had been most profound in purely industrial communities, where the bulk of the population—as in Ilium—had made its living tending machines in one way or another. In New York City, for instance, there were many skills difficult or uneconomical to mechanize, and the advances hadn't liberated as high a percentage of people from production.

"*Kuppo*!" said the Shah, shaking his head.

Khashdrahr blushed, and translated uneasily, apologetically. "Shah says, 'Communism.'"

"No *Kuppo*!" said Halyard vehemently. "The government does not own the machines. They simply tax that part of industry's income that once went into labor, and redistribute it. Industry is privately owned and managed, and co-ordinated—to prevent the waste of competition—by a committee of leaders from private industry, not politicians. By eliminating human error through machinery, and needless competition through organization, we've raised the standard of living of the average man immensely."

Khashdrahr stopped translating and frowned perplexedly. "Please, this *average man*, there is no equivalent in our language, I'm afraid."

"You know," said Halyard, "the ordinary man, like, well, anybody—those men working back on the bridge, the man in that old car we passed. The little man, not brilliant but good-hearted, plain, ordinary, everyday kind of person."

Khashdrahr translated.

"Aha," said the Shah, nodding, "*Takaru*."

"What did he say?"

"*Takaru*," said Khashdrahr. "Slave."

"No *Takaru*," said Halyard, speaking directly to the Shah. "*Ci-ti-zen*."

"Ahhhhh," said the Shah. "*Ci-ti-zen*." He grinned happily. "*Takaru—citizen. Citizen—Takaru*."

"No *Takaru*!" said Halyard.

Khashdrahr shrugged. "In the Shah's land are only the Elite and the *Takaru*."

Halyard's ulcer gave him a twinge, the ulcer that had grown in size and authority over the years of his career as an interpreter of America to provincial and ignorant notables from the backwaters of civilization.

The limousine came to a stop again, and the driver honked his horn at a crew of Reconstruction and Reclamation Corpsmen. They had left their wheelbarrows blocking the road, and were throwing rocks at a squirrel on a branch a hundred feet overhead.

Halyard rolled down his window. "Get these damn wheelbarrows out of the way!" he shouted.

"Ci-ti-zen!" piped the Shah, smiling modestly at his newly acquired bilinguality.

"Drop dead," called one of the rock throwers. Reluctantly, surlily, he came down to the road and moved two wheelbarrows very slowly, studying the car and its occupants as he did it. He stepped to one side.

"Thanks! It's about time!" said Halyard as the limousine eased past the man.

"You're welcome, Doc," said the man, and he spat in Halyard's face.

Halyard sputtered, manfully regained his poise, and wiped his face. "Isolated incident," he said bitterly.

"*Takaru yamu brouha, pu dinka bu*," said the Shah sympathetically.

"The Shah," said Khashdrahr gravely, "he says it is the same with *Takaru* everywhere since the war."

"No *Takaru*," said Halyard apathetically, and let it go.

"*Sumklish*," sighed the Shah.

Khashdrahr handed him the flask of sacred liquor.

Chapter III

DOCTOR PAUL PROTEUS, the man with the highest income in Ilium, drove his cheap and old Plymouth across the bridge to Homestead. He had had the car at the time of the riots, and among the bits of junk in the glove compartment—match cards, registration, flashlight, and face tissues—was the rusty pistol he had been issued then. Having a pistol where some unauthorized person might get at it was very much against the law. Even members of the huge standing army did without firearms until they'd disembarked for occupation duty overseas. Only the police and plant guards were armed. Paul didn't want the pistol but was forever forgetting to turn it in. Over the years, as it had accumulated a patina of rust, he'd come to regard it as a harmless antique. The glove compartment wouldn't lock, so Paul covered the pistol with tissues.

The engine wasn't working properly, now and then hesitating, catching again, slowing suddenly, catching again. His other cars, a new station wagon and a very expensive sedan, were at home, as he put it, for Anita. Neither of the good cars had ever been in Homestead, and neither had Anita for many years. Anita never needled him about his devotion to the old car, though she did seem to think some sort of explanation to others was in order. He had overheard her telling visitors that he had had it rebuilt in such a way that it was far better mechanically than what was coming off the automatic assembly lines at Detroit—which simply wasn't true. Nor was it logical that a man with so special a car would put off and put off having the broken left headlamp fixed. And he wondered how she might have explained, had she known, that he kept a leather jacket in the trunk, and that he exchanged his coat for this and took off his necktie before crossing the Iroquois. It was a trip he made only when he had to—for, say, a bottle of Irish whisky for one of the few persons he had ever felt close to.

He came to a stop at the Homestead end of the bridge. About forty men, leaning on crowbars, picks, and shovels, blocked the way, smoking, talking, milling about something in the middle of the pavement. They looked around at Paul with an air of sheepishness and, as though there were nothing but time in the world, they moved slowly to the sides of the bridge, leaving an alley barely wide enough for Paul's car. As they separated, Paul saw what it was they had been standing around. A small man was kneeling beside a chuckhole perhaps two feet in diameter, patting a fresh fill of tar and gravel with the flat of his shovel.

Importantly, the man waved for Paul to go *around* the patch, not *over* it. The others fell silent, and watched to make sure that Paul did go around it.

"Hey, Mac, your headlamp's busted," shouted one of the men. The others joined in, chorusing the message earnestly.

Paul nodded his thanks. His skin began to itch, as though he had suddenly become unclean. These were members of the Reconstruction and Reclamation Corps, in their own estimate the "Reeks and Wrecks." Those who couldn't compete economically with machines had their choice, if they had no source of income, of the Army or the Reconstruction and Reclamation Corps. The soldiers, with their hollowness hidden beneath twinkling buttons and buckles, crisp serge, and glossy leather, didn't depress Paul nearly as much as the Reeks and Wrecks did.

He eased through the work crew, past a black government limousine, and into Homestead.

A saloon was close to the end of the bridge. Paul had to park his car a half-block away, for another crew was flushing out the storm sewers with an opened fire hydrant. This seemed to be a favorite undertaking. Whenever he had come to Homestead when the temperature had been above freezing, he'd found a hydrant going.

One big man, with an air of proprietorship, kept his hands on the wrench that controlled the flow. Another stood by as second-in-command of the water. All around them, and along the course of the water to the sewer mouth, a crowd stood watching. A dirty little boy caught a scrap of paper skittering along the sidewalk, fashioned it into a crude boat, and launched it in the gutter. All eyes followed the craft with interest, seeming to wish it luck as it shot perilous rapids, as it snagged on a twig, spun free, shot into the swift, deep main flow, mounted a crest for a triumphant instant, and plunged into the sewer.

"Uh!" grunted a man standing by Paul, as though he had been aboard the boat.

Paul worked his way through the crowd, which was continuous with the clientele of the saloon, and got to within one rank of the bar. His back was against an old player piano. No one seemed to have recognized him. It would have been surprising if someone had, for, in line with policy, he kept pretty much to his own side of the river and never permitted his name or picture to appear in the Ilium *Star-Tribune*.

Around the bar were old men, pensioners, too old for the Army or the Reeks and Wrecks. Each had before him a headless beer in a glass whose rim was opaqued by hours of slow, thoughtful sipping. These oldsters probably arrived early and left late, and any other business had to be done over their heads. On the screen of the television set behind the bar, a large earth mother of a woman, her voice shut off by the volume knob, beamed, moved her lips excitedly, and broke eggs into a mixing bowl. The old men watched, occasionally clicking their dentures or licking their lips.

"Excuse me," said Paul self-consciously.

No one made a move to let him get to the bar. A fat, whitening collie, curled beneath the barstool of an old man blocking Paul's way, showed its toothless gums and growled fuzzily.

Futilely, Paul waved his hand for the bartender's attention. As he shifted from one foot to the other, he recalled the fully mechanized saloon he, Finnerty, and Shepherd had designed when they'd been playful young engineers. To their surprise, the owner of a restaurant chain had been interested enough to give the idea a try. They'd set up the experimental unit about five doors down from where Paul now stood, with coin machines and endless belts to do the serving, with germicidal lamps cleaning the air, with uniform, healthful light, with continuous soft music from a tape recorder, with seats scientifically designed by an anthropologist to give the average man the absolute maximum in comfort.

The first day had been a sensation, with a waiting line extending blocks. Within a week of the opening, curiosity had been satisfied, and it was a boom day when five customers stopped in. Then this place had opened up almost next door, with a dust-and-germ trap of a Victorian bar, bad light, poor ventilation, and an unsanitary, inefficient, and probably dishonest bartender. It was an immediate and unflagging success.

He caught the bartender's eye at last. When the bartender saw Paul, he dropped his role of highhanded supervisor of morals and settler of arguments and became an obsequious host, like the bartender at the Country Club. Paul was afraid for a moment that he'd been recognized. But when the bartender failed to call him by name, he supposed that only his class had been recognized.

There were a few men in Homestead—like this bartender, the police and firemen, professional athletes, cab drivers, specially skilled artisans—who hadn't been displaced by machines. They lived among those who had been displaced, but they were aloof and often rude and overbearing with the mass. They felt a camaraderie with the engineers and managers across the river, a feeling that wasn't, incidentally, reciprocated. The general feeling across the river was that these persons weren't too bright to be replaced by machines; they were simply in activities where machines weren't economical. In short, their feelings of superiority were unjustified.

Now, the bartender had sensed that Paul was a personage, and he made a show of letting everyone else go to hell while he gave service to Paul. The others noticed, and turned to stare at the privileged newcomer.

Paul ordered the bottle of Irish in a quiet voice, and tried to become inconspicuous by bending over and petting the aged collie. The dog barked, and its owner turned on his barstool to confront Paul. The old man was as toothless as the dog. Paul's first impression was of red gums and huge hands—as though everything were sapped of color and strength but these.

"He wouldn't hurt nobody," said the old man apologetically. "Just kind of edgy about being old and blind, and never sure of what's going on, is all." He ran his big hands along the dog's fat sides. "He's a good old dog." He looked thoughtfully at Paul. "Say, I bet I know you."

Paul looked anxiously after the bartender, who had disappeared into the cellar after the whisky. "Really? I've been in here once or twice before."

"No, not here," said the old man loudly. "The plant, the plant. You're young Doctor Proteus."

A lot of people heard, and those closest to the two studied Paul with disturbing candor, and fell silent in order to hear whatever was being said.

The old man was apparently quite deaf, for his voice was erratically loud, then soft. "Don't recognize my face, Doctor?" He wasn't mocking, he was frankly admiring, and proud that he could prove himself on speaking terms with this distinguished man.

Paul colored. "I can't say I remember. The old welding shop, was it?"

The old man swept his hand over his face deprecatingly. "Aaaah, not enough left of the old face for my best friend to recognize," he said good-humoredly. He thrust out his hands, palms up. "But look at those, Doctor. Good as ever, and there's not two like them anywhere. You said so yourself."

"Hertz," said Paul. "You're Rudy Hertz."

Rudy laughed, and looked about the room triumphantly, as though to say, "See, by God, Rudy Hertz does know Doctor Proteus, and Proteus knows Hertz! How many of you can say that?"

"And this is the dog you were telling me about—ten, fifteen years ago?"

"Son of the dog, Doctor." He laughed. "I wasn't no pup, then, though, was I?"

"You were a damn fine machinist, Rudy."

"I say so myself. Knowing that, knowing smart men like you say that about Rudy, that means a lot. It's about all I got, you know, Doctor? That and the dog." Rudy shook the arm of the man next to him, a short, heavy, seemingly soft man, middle-aged, with a homely, round face. His eyes were magnified and fogged by extremely thick glasses. "Hear what Doctor Proteus here said about me?" Rudy gestured at Paul. "Smartest man in Ilium says that about Rudy. Maybe he's the smartest man in the country."

Paul wished to God the bartender would hurry up. The man Rudy had shaken was now studying Paul sullenly. Paul glanced quickly about the room and saw hostility all around him.

Addled Rudy Hertz thought he was doing a handsome

thing by Paul, showing him off to the crowd. Rudy was senile, remembering only his prime, incapable of remembering or understanding what had followed his retirement. . . .

But these others, these men in their thirties, forties, and fifties—*they* knew. The youngsters in the booth, the two soldiers and three girls, they were like Katharine Finch. They couldn't remember when things had been different, could hardly make sense of what had been, though they didn't necessarily like what was. But these others who stared now, they remembered. They had been the rioters, the smashers of machines. There was no threat of violence in their looks now, but there was resentment, a wish to let him know that he had intruded where he was not liked.

And still the bartender did not return. Paul limited his field of vision to Rudy, ignoring the rest. The man with thick glasses, whom Rudy had invited to admire Paul, continued to stare.

Paul talked inanely now about the dog, about Rudy's remarkable state of preservation. He was helplessly aware that he was hamming it up, proving to anyone who might still have doubts that he was indeed an insincere ass.

"Let's drink to old times!" said Rudy, raising his glass. He didn't seem to notice that silence greeted his proposal, and that he drank alone. He made clucking noises with his tongue, and winked in fond reminiscence, and drained his glass with a flourish. He banged it on the bar.

Paul, smiling glassily, decided to say nothing more, since anything more would be the wrong thing. He folded his arms and leaned against the keyboard of the player piano. In the silence of the saloon, a faint discord came from the piano, hummed to nothingness.

"Let's drink to our sons," said the man with thick glasses suddenly. His voice was surprisingly high for so resonant-looking a man. Several glasses were raised this time. When the toast was done, the man turned to Paul with the friendliest of smiles and said, "My boy's just turned eighteen, Doctor."

"That's nice."

"He's got his whole life ahead of him. Wonderful age, eighteen." He paused, as though his remark demanded a response.

"I'd like to be eighteen again," said Paul lamely.

"He's a good boy, Doctor. He isn't what you'd call real bright. Like his old man—his heart's in the right place, and he wants to do the most he can with what he's got." Again the waitful pause.

"That's all any of us can do," said Paul.

"Well, as long as such a smart man as you is here, maybe I could get you to give me some advice for the boy. He just finished his National General Classification Tests. He just about killed himself studying up for them, but it wasn't any use. He didn't do nearly well enough for college. There were only twenty-seven openings, and six hundred kids trying for them." He shrugged. "I can't afford to send him to a private school, so now he's got to decide what he's going to do with his life, Doctor: what's it going to be, the Army or the Reeks and Wrecks?"

"I suppose there's a lot to be said for both," said Paul uncomfortably. "I really don't know much about either one. Somebody else, like Matheson, maybe, would . . ." His sentence trailed off. Matheson was Ilium's manager in charge of testing and placement. Paul knew him slightly, didn't like him very well. Matheson was a powerful bureaucrat who went about his job with the air of a high priest. "I'll call Matheson, if you like, and ask him, and let you know what he says."

"Doctor," said the man, desperately now, with no tinge of baiting, "isn't there something the boy could do at the Works? He's awfully clever with his hands. He's got a kind of instinct with machines. Give him one he's never seen before, and in ten minutes he'll have it apart and back together again. He loves that kind of work. Isn't there someplace in the plant—?"

"He's got to have a graduate degree," said Paul. He reddened. "That's policy, and I didn't make it. Sometimes we get Reconstruction and Reclamation people over to help put in big machines or do a heavy repair job, but not very often. Maybe he could open a repair shop."

The man exhaled, slumped dejectedly. "Repair shop," he sighed. "Repair shop, he says. How many repair shops you think Ilium can support, eh? Repair shop, sure! I was going to open one when I got laid off. So was Joe, so was Sam, so was Alf. We're all clever with our hands, so we'll all open repair shops. One repairman for every broken article in Ilium. Meanwhile, our wives clean up as dressmakers—one dressmaker for every woman in town."

Rudy Hertz had apparently missed all the talk and was still celebrating in his mind the happy reunion with his great and good friend, Doctor Paul Proteus. "Music," said Rudy grandly. "Let's have music!" He reached over Paul's shoulder and popped a nickel into the player piano.

Paul stepped away from the box. Machinery whirred importantly for a few seconds, and then the piano started clanging away at "*Alexander's Ragtime Band*" like cracked carillons. Mercifully, conversation was all but impossible. Mercifully, the bartender emerged from the basement and handed Paul a dusty bottle over the old heads.

Paul turned to leave, and a powerful hand closed on his upper arm. Rudy, his expansive host, held him.

"I played this song in your honor, Doctor," shouted Rudy above the racket. "Wait till it's over." Rudy acted as though the antique instrument were the newest of all wonders, and he excitedly pointed out identifiable musical patterns in the bobbing keys—trills, spectacular runs up the keyboard, and the slow, methodical rise and fall of keys in the bass. "See—see them two go up and down, Doctor! Just the way the feller hit 'em. Look at 'em go!"

The music stopped abruptly, with the air of having delivered exactly five cents worth of joy. Rudy still shouted. "Makes you feel kind of creepy, don't it, Doctor, watching them keys go up and down? You can almost see a ghost sitting there playing his heart out."

Paul twisted free and hurried out to his car.

Chapter IV

"DARLING, you look as though you've seen a ghost," said Anita. She was already dressed for the party at the Country Club, already dominating a distinguished company she had yet to join.

As she handed Paul his cocktail, he felt somehow inadequate, bumbling, in the presence of her beautiful assurance. Only things that might please or interest her came to mind—all else submerged. It wasn't a conscious act of his mind, but a reflex, a natural response to her presence. It annoyed him that the feeling should be automatic, because he fancied himself in the image of his father, and, in this situation, his father would have been completely in charge—taking the first, last, and best lines for himself.

The expression "armed to the teeth" occurred to Paul as he looked at her over his glass. With an austere dark gown that left her tanned shoulders and throat bare, a single bit of jewelry on her finger, and very light make-up, Anita had successfully combined the weapons of sex, taste, and an aura of masculine competence.

She quieted, and turned away under his stare. Inadvertently, he'd gained the upper hand. He had somehow communicated the thought that had bobbed up in his thoughts unexpectedly: that her strength and poise were no more than a mirror image of his own importance, an image of the power and self-satisfaction the manager of the Ilium Works could have, if he wanted it. In a fleeting second she became a helpless, bluffing little girl in his thoughts, and he was able to feel real tenderness toward her.

"Good drink, sweetheart," he said. "Finnerty upstairs?"

"I sent him on over to the club. Kroner and Baer got there early, and I sent Finnerty over to keep them company while you get dressed."

"How does he look?"

"How did Finnerty always look? Awful. I swear he was wearing the same baggy suit he wore when he said goodbye to us seven years ago. And I'll swear it hasn't been cleaned since then, either. I tried to get him to wear your old tuxedo, and he wouldn't hear of it. Went right over the way he was. I suppose a stiff shirt would have been worse in a way. It would have showed how dirty his neck is."

She pulled the neck of her dress lower, looked at herself in a mirror, and raised it slightly again—a delicate compromise. "Honestly," she said, talking to Paul's image in the mirror, "I'm crazy about that man—you *know* I am. But he just looks awful all the time. I mean, after all, a man in his position, and not even clean."

Paul smiled and shook his head. It was true. Finnerty had always been shockingly lax about his grooming, and some of his more fastidious supervisors in the old days had found it hard to believe that a man could be so staggeringly competent, and at the same time so unsanitary-looking. Occasionally, the tall, gaunt Irishman would surprise everyone—usually between long stretches of work—by showing up with his cheeks gleaming like wax apples, and with new shoes, socks, shirt, tie, and suit, and, presumably, underwear. Engineers' and managers' wives would make a big fuss over him, to show him that such care of himself was important and rewarding; and they declared that he was really the handsomest thing in the Ilium industrial fold. Quite possibly he was, in a coarse, weathered way: grotesquely handsome, like Abe Lincoln, but with a predatory, defiant cast to his eyes rather than the sadness of Lincoln's. After Finnerty's periodic outbursts of cleanliness and freshness, the wives would watch with increasing distress as he wore the entire celebrated outfit day in and day out, until the sands and soot and grease of time had filled every seam and pore.

And Finnerty had other unsavory aspects. Into the resolutely monogamous and Eagle Scout–like society of engineers and managers, Finnerty often brought women he'd picked up in Homestead a half-hour before. When it came time, after supper, to play games, Finnerty and the girl would generally take a highball in either hand and wander off to the shrub-walled first tee, if it was warm, or out to his car, if it was cold.

His car—in the old days, anyway—had been more disreputable than Paul's was today. In this direction, at least—the most innocuous direction, socially—Paul had imitated his friend. Finnerty had claimed that his love of books and records and good whisky kept him too broke to buy a car and clothes commensurate with his position in life. Paul had computed the value of Finnerty's record, book, and bottle collections and concluded that the Irishman would still have plenty left for even two new cars. It was then that Paul began to suspect that Finnerty's way of life wasn't as irrational as it seemed; that it was, in fact, a studied and elaborate insult to the managers and engineers of Ilium, and to their immaculate wives.

Why Finnerty had seen fit to offend these gentle people was never clear to Paul, who supposed the aggressiveness, like most aggressiveness, dated back to some childhood muddle. The only intimation as to what that childhood had been like had come not from Finnerty but from Kroner, who took a breeder's interest in his engineers' bloodlines. Kroner had once remarked, confidingly and with a show of sympathy, that Finnerty was a mutant, born of poor and stupid parents. The only insight Finnerty had ever permitted Paul was in a moment of deep depression, during a crushing hangover, when he'd sighed and said he'd never felt he belonged anywhere.

Paul wondered about his own deep drives as he realized how much pleasure he was getting from recollections of Finnerty's socially destructive, undisciplined antics. Paul indulged himself in the wistful sensation of feeling that he, Paul, might be content, if only— and let the thought stop there, as though he knew vaguely what lay beyond. He didn't.

Paul envied Finnerty's mind, for Finnerty could be anything he wanted to be, and be brilliant at it. Whatever the times might have called for, Finnerty would have been among the best. If this had been the age of music, Finnerty would have been, and in fact was, a top-flight pianist—or he might have been an architect or physician or writer. With inhuman intuition, Finnerty could sense the basic principles and motives of almost any human work, not just engineering.

Paul could have been only what he was, he thought. As he filled his glass again, he supposed that he could only have come to this moment, this living room, into the presence of Anita.

It was an appalling thought, to be so well-integrated into the machinery of society and history as to be able to move in only one plane, and along one line. Finnerty's arrival was disturbing, for it brought to the surface the doubt that life should be that way. Paul had been thinking of hiring a psychiatrist to make him docile, content with his lot, amiable to all. But now, here was Finnerty, pushing him in the other direction. Finnerty had seemed to see something in Paul he hadn't seen in the others, something he'd liked—possibly a rebellious streak that Paul was only now beginning to suspect. For *some reason* Finnerty had made Paul his only friend.

"In a way, I wish Finnerty'd picked another day," said Anita. "It raises all sorts of problems. Baer's supposed to be on my left, and Kroner on my right; but now, with a member of the National Industrial Planning Board blowing in unexpectedly, I'm not sure who goes where. Is Ed Finnerty bigger brass than Kroner and Baer?" she asked incredulously.

"Look in the *Organization Directory*, if you want," said Paul. "I think you'll find the N.I.P.B. is listed ahead of the regional people—but it's more brain trust than brass. Finnerty won't care. He'll probably eat with the help."

"If he sets foot in the kitchen, the Board of Health will throw him in jail." She laughed uneasily. It was evident that she found it trying to be a good sport about Finnerty, to pretend that his eccentricities were amusing. She changed the subject. "Tell me about today."

"Nothing about today. One more, like all the rest."

"You got the whisky?"

"Yes. I had to go across the river to get it."

"Was it such an awful ordeal?" she chided. She couldn't understand why he hated to run errands into Homestead, and teased him about it. "Was it so awful?" she said again, bordering on baby talk, as though he were a lazy little boy coaxed into doing a small favor for his mother.

"Pretty bad."

"Really?" She was surprised. "Nothing violent, I hope."

"No. Everybody was very polite, in fact. One of the pensioners recognized me from the old days and threw an impromptu party for me."

"Well, that sounds like downright fun."

"Does, doesn't it? His name is Rudy Hertz." Without describing his own reactions, he told her what had happened. He found himself watching her closely, experimenting.

"And that upset you?" She laughed. "You *are* a sensitive

darling, aren't you? You tell me you've been through a nightmare, and nothing happened at all."

"They hate me."

"They proved they loved and admired you. And, what's more, they should."

"The man with the thick glasses as much as said his son's life wasn't worth living on account of me."

"You said that. He didn't. And I won't have you saying ridiculous things like that. Do you get some sort of pleasure out of making things up to feel guilty about? If his son isn't bright enough for anything but the Reeks and Wrecks or the Army, is that your fault?"

"No; but if it hadn't been for men like me, he might have a machine in the plant—"

"Is he starving?"

"Of course not. Nobody starves."

"And he's got a place to live and warm clothes. He has what he'd have if he were running a stupid machine, swearing at it, making mistakes, striking every year, fighting with the foreman, coming in with hangovers."

"You're right, you're right." He held up his hands. "Of course you're right. It's just a hell of a time to be alive, is all—just this goddamn messy business of people having to get used to new ideas. And people just don't, that's all. I wish this were a hundred years from now, with everybody used to the change."

"You're tired. I'm going to tell Kroner you need a month off."

"I'll tell him, if I feel like it."

"I wasn't trying to run your life, darling. But you never ask for anything."

"Let me do the asking, if you don't mind."

"I don't. I promise you I don't mind at all."

"Did you lay my things out?"

"On your bed," she said primly. She'd been hurt. "Tuxedo, shirt, socks, studs, cuff links, and a new tie."

"New tie?"

"Dubonnet."

"Dubonnet! For Christ's sake."

"Kroner and Baer are wearing dubonnet ties."

"And is my underwear like theirs?"

"I'm sure I didn't notice."

"I'm wearing a black tie."

"Pittsburgh, darling—remember? You said you wanted to go there."

"Hi ho, dubonnet." He climbed the stairs to their bedroom, stripping off his coat and shirt as he went.

"Ed!" Finnerty was stretched out on Anita's bed.

"So there you are," said Finnerty. He pointed at the tuxedo laid out on Paul's bed. "I thought this was you. I've been talking to it for half an hour."

"Anita said you'd gone to the club."

"Anita expelled me out the front door, so I came in the back and up here."

"Well, I'm glad you did. How are things?"

"Worse than ever, but there's hope."

"Fine," said Paul, laughing uncertainly. "Married?"

"Never. Shut the door."

Paul closed it. "How's the Washington job?"

"I've quit."

"Really? Something bigger yet?"

"I think so, or I wouldn't have quit."

"Where?"

"No place. No job at all."

"Not enough pay, or worn out, or what?"

"Sick of it," he said slowly. "The pay was fantastically good, ridiculously good—paid like a television queen with a forty-inch bust. But when I got this year's invitation to the Meadows, Paul, something snapped. I realized I couldn't face another session up there. And then I looked around me and found out I couldn't face anything about the system any more. I walked out, and here I am."

Paul's invitation to the Meadows was carelessly displayed by Anita in the front-hall mirror, where no one could fail to notice it. The Meadows was a flat, grassy island in the St. Lawrence, in Chippewa Bay, where the most important men, and the most promising men ("Those whose development within the organization is not yet complete," said the *Handbook*) in the Eastern and Middle-Western Divisions spent a week each summer in an orgy of morale building—through team athletics, group sings, bonfires and skyrockets, bawdy entertainment, free whisky and cigars; and through plays, put on by professional actors, which pleasantly but unmistakably made clear the nature of good deportment within the system, and the shape of firm resolves for the challenging year ahead.

Finnerty took a crumpled pack of cigarettes from his pocket, offered one bent at almost a right angle. Paul straightened it out, his fingers unsteady. "Got the shakes?" said Finnerty.

"I'm chief speaker tonight."

"Oh?" He seemed disappointed. "Then you don't ordinarily have the shakes these days? What's the occasion?"

"Thirteen years ago today, the Ilium Works was placed under the National Manufacturing Council."

"Like every other plant in the country."

"Ilium was a little earlier than most." The union of the country's manufacturing facilities under one council had taken place not long after Finnerty, Paul, and Shepherd came to work in Ilium. It had been done because of the war. Similar councils had been formed for the transportation, raw materials, food, and communications industries, and over them all had been Paul's father. The system had so cut waste and duplication that it was preserved after the war, and was, in fact, often cited as one of the few concrete benefits of the war.

"Does that make you happy, that this has been going on thirteen years?"

"It calls for comment, anyway. I'm going to keep it factual. It isn't going to be like Kroner's evangelism."

Finnerty fell silent, apparently uninterested in pursuing the subject. "Funny," he said at last, "I thought you'd be pretty close to the edge by now. That's why I came here."

Paul twisted his face as he struggled to get his collar button moored. "Well, you weren't completely wrong. There's talk of my chatting with a psychiatrist."

"So you *are* in rough shape. Wonderful! Let's get out of this damn party. We've got to talk."

The bedroom door opened, and Anita looked in from the hall. "Oh! Ed. Who's with Baer and Kroner?"

"Kroner's with Baer, Baer's with Kroner," said Finnerty. "Close the door, please, Anita."

"It's time to go to the club."

"It's time for *you* to go to the club," said Finnerty. "Paul and I'll be along later."

"We're going together, and now, Ed. We're ten minutes late as it is. And I won't be bullied by you. I refuse." She smiled unconvincingly.

"Let's go," said Paul.

"Anita," said Finnerty, "if you don't show more respect for men's privacy, I'll design a machine that's everything you are, and *does* show respect."

She colored. "I can't say I find you screamingly funny."

"Stainless steel," said Finnerty. "Stainless steel, covered with sponge rubber, and heated electrically to 98.6 degrees."

"Now, look—" said Paul.

"And blushes at will," said Finnerty.

"And I could make a man like you out of a burlap bag filled with mud," said Anita. "Anybody who tries to touch you comes away dirty!" She slammed the door, and Paul listened to her heels clicking down the staircase.

"Now, why in hell did you do that?" said Paul. "Do you mind telling me?"

Finnerty lay motionless on the bed, staring at the ceiling. "I don't know," he said slowly, "but I'm not sorry. Go on with her."

"What are your plans?"

"Go on!" He said it as though Paul had suddenly intruded just as he was giving form to an important, difficult thought.

"There's Irish whisky for you in a brown bag in the front hall," said Paul, and he left Finnerty lying there.

Chapter V

PAUL overtook Anita in the garage, where she was starting the station wagon. Without looking directly at him, she waited for him to climb in beside her. They drove to the club in silence, with Paul feeling let down by the coarse, irrational reality of Finnerty. Over the years, he supposed bitterly, he must have created a wise and warm Finnerty in his imagination, an image that had little to do with the real man.

At the club door, Anita straightened Paul's tie, pulled her cape down to bare her shoulders, smiled, and pushed into the brightly lighted foyer.

The far end of the foyer opened into the bar, and there two dozen of the Ilium Works' bright young men, identical in their crew cuts and the tailoring of their tuxedos, surrounded two men in their middle fifties. One of the older men, Kroner, tall, heavy and slow, listened to the youngsters with ponderous affectionateness. The other, Baer, slight and nervous, noisily and unconvincingly extroverted, laughed, nudged, and clapped shoulders, and maintained a continuous commentary on whatever was being said: "Fine, fine, right, sure, sure, wonderful, yes, yes, exactly, fine, good."

Ilium was a training ground, where fresh graduates were sent to get the feel of industry and then moved on to bigger things. The staff was young, then, and constantly renewing itself. The oldest men were Paul, and his second-in-command, Lawson Shepherd. Shepherd, a bachelor, stood by the bar, somewhat apart from the rest, looking wise, and faintly amused by the naïveté of some of the youngsters' remarks.

The wives had congregated in two adjacent booths, and there spoke quietly and uneasily, and turned to look whenever the volume of voices rose above a certain level, or whenever the bass voice of Kroner rumbled through the haze of small talk with three or four short, wise, wonderfully pregnant words.

The youngsters turned to greet Paul and Anita effusively, with playful obsequiousness, with the air of having proprietorship over all good times, which they generously encouraged their elders to share in.

Baer waved and called to them in his high-pitched voice. Kroner nodded almost imperceptibly, and stood perfectly still, not looking directly at them, waiting for them to come up so that greetings could be exchanged quietly and with dignity.

Kroner's enormous, hairy hand closed about Paul's, and Paul, in spite of himself, felt docile, and loving, and childlike. It was as though Paul stood in the enervating, emasculating presence of his father again. Kroner, his father's closest friend, had always made him feel that way, and seemingly wanted to make him feel that way. Paul had sworn a thousand times to keep his wits about him the next time he met Kroner. But it was a matter beyond his control, and at each meeting, as now, the power and resolve were all in the big hands of the older man.

Though Paul was especially aware of the paternal aura about Kroner, the big man tried to make the feeling general. He spoke of himself as father to all of the men under him, and more vaguely, to their wives; and it was no pose. His administration of the Eastern Division had an emotional flavor about it, and it seemed unlikely that he could have run the Division any other way. He was cognizant of every birth or major illness, and heaped blame on himself in the rare instances that any of his men went wrong. He could also be stern—again, paternally.

"How are you, Paul?" he said warmly. The quizzical set of his thick eyebrows indicated that this was a question, not a salutation. The tone was one Kroner used when inquiring into someone's condition after a siege of pneumonia or worse.

"He's never been better," said Anita briskly.

"Glad to hear it. That's fine, Paul." Kroner continued to hold on to his hand and to stare into his eyes.

"Feel good, do you, eh? Good? Good, eh? Wonderful," said Baer, clapping him on the shoulder several times. "Wonderful." Baer, the Eastern Division's chief engineer, turned to Anita. "And, oh my! Don't you look nice. My, yes. Oh! I should say so." He grinned.

Baer was a social cretin, apparently unaware that he was anything but suave and brilliant in company. Someone had once mentioned his running commentary on conversations to him, and he hadn't known what they were talking about. Technically, there wasn't a better engineer in the East, including Finnerty. There was little in the Division that hadn't been master-minded by Baer, who here seemed to Kroner what a fox terrier seems to a St. Bernard. Paul had thought often of the peculiar combination of Kroner and Baer, and wondered if, when they were gone, higher management could possibly duplicate it. Baer embodied the knowledge and technique of industry; Kroner personified the faith, the near-holiness, the spirit of the complicated venture. Kroner, in fact, had a poor record as an engineer and had surprised Paul from time to time with his ignorance or misunderstanding of technical matters; but he had the priceless quality of believing in the system, and of making others believe in it, too, and do as they were told.

The two were inseparable, though their personalities met at almost no point. Together, they made an approximately whole man.

"Did someone tell you Paul had been sick?" said Anita, laughing.

"I'd heard Paul's nerves had been bothering him," said Kroner.

"Not true," said Paul.

Kroner smiled. "Glad to hear it, Paul. You're one of our best men." He looked at him fondly. "In the footsteps of your father, Paul."

"Where did you hear about Paul's nerves?" said Anita.

"Can't imagine," said Kroner.

"Doctor Shepherd told us," said Baer brightly. "I was there this morning. Remember? It was Shepherd."

"Now listen," said Kroner with unaccustomed quickness, "that was something else Shepherd was talking about. You know it was, if you'll just think back."

"Oh sure, that's right, that's right; something else, something else," said Baer, looking puzzled. He clapped Paul on the shoulder again. "So you're feeling better, eh? Well, that's what counts. Wonderful, wonderful."

Doctor Shepherd, his neck blazing red above his stiff collar, moved quietly away from the bar toward the French doors that opened onto the golf course.

"By the way," said Kroner heartily, "where's your friend Finnerty? What does Ed look like? I imagine he's found life in

Washington a little less—" he searched for a word—"informal than here."

"If you mean, does he wash?—the answer is still no," said Anita.

"That's what I meant," said Kroner. "Well, none of us are perfect, and darn few of us perfect enough to get a place on the National Industrial Planning Board. Where is he?"

"He may be along later," said Paul. "He's a little tired from his trip."

"Why, where's Mom?" said Anita, ditching the subject of Finnerty. Mom was Kroner's wife, whom he always brought to social functions, deposited with other wives, and ignored until the affectionate moment when it was time to retrieve her and cart her hundred and eighty pounds home.

"That intestinal thing that's been making the rounds," said Kroner gravely.

Everyone within hearing shook his or her head compassionately.

"Dinner," said a Philippino waiter. There had once been a movement to have the service done by machines, but the extremists who'd proposed this had been voted down by an overwhelming majority.

As Paul, Kroner, Baer, and Anita walked into the candlelit dining room, followed by the rest, four of the youngest engineers, the most recent arrivals, brushed past and turned to block the way.

Fred Berringer, a short, heavy, slit-eyed blond, seemed to be their leader. He was a wealthy, extroverted, dull boy from a good family of engineers and managers in Minneapolis. He had squeaked through college, and was just barely acceptable to the personnel machines. Ordinarily, nobody would have hired him. But Kroner, who knew his bloodlines, had taken him on anyway and sent him to Ilium to be trained. The break had done anything but teach him humility. He took it as evidence that his money and name could beat the system any time and, paraphrased, he'd said as much. The hell of it was that his attitude won grudging admiration from his fellow engineers, who had got their jobs the hard way. Paul supposed, gloomily, that beaters of systems had always been admired by the conventional. At any rate, Kroner still believed in the boy, so Paul had no choice but to keep him on, and to pair a smarter man with him to backstop his mental apparatus.

"What is this, Fred, a stickup?" said Paul.

"Checker champion," said Fred, "I hereby challenge you for the championship immediately after dinner."

Kroner and Baer seemed delighted. They were forever suggesting that teams be formed and games be played as a method for building morale in the Eastern Division's family.

"Just you, or all four of you?" said Paul. He was in fact the club checker champion, though there had never been any sort of official playoff. No one could beat him, and, wearily as often as not, he had had to prove his invincibility to each new group of engineers—like these four. It was a custom, and the close little society on the north side of the river seemed to feel the need of customs, of private jokes, of building up social characteristics to distinguish themselves—in their own eyes—from the rest of society. The checker game of the new engineers with Paul was one of the hoariest traditions, now in its seventh year.

"Me, mostly," said Berringer. "But all of us, in a way." The others laughed like conspirators. Apparently something special had been cooked up, and one or two of the older engineers seemed to be sharing in the high expectations.

"All right," said Paul good-humoredly; "if there were ten of you, and each one blowing cigar smoke in my face, I'd still win."

The four parted to let Paul, Anita, and the two guests of honor get to the table.

"Oh," said Anita, studying the place cards at the head of the table, "there's been a mistake." She picked up the card to her left, wadded it up, and handed it to Paul. She moved another card into the vacant position and sat down, flanked by Kroner and Baer. She called a waiter to take away the now extra place setting. Paul looked at the card and saw it was Finnerty's.

The assemblage was a practical, earthy one, and the shrimp cocktails, consommé, creamed chicken, peas, and mashed potatoes were enjoyed for their own sake. There was little talk, and much pantomimed savoring and beaming to show the hostess that everything tasted first rate.

Periodically, Kroner would comment on this dish or that, and he would be echoed by Baer, and then by nods about the table. Once, an argument broke out in loud whispers at the far end of the table, among the four youngsters who had challenged Paul to the checker game. When all eyes turned in their direction, they shut up. Berringer frowned, sketched a diagram of some sort on a napkin, and thrust it at the other three. One of them made a slight correction and handed it back. Understanding, then admiration, showed on Berringer's face. He nodded vigorously and went back to eating.

Paul counted around the table—twenty-seven managers and engineers, the staff of the Ilium Works and their wives, less the evening shift. There were two vacant places: one, the bare square of tablecloth once reserved for Finnerty; the other, the untouched setting for Shepherd, who had not come back from his hurried trip onto the golf course.

Finnerty was probably still lying in the bedroom, staring at the ceiling, perhaps talking to himself. Maybe he'd left soon after they had and gone on a bender or whoring expedition in Homestead. Paul hoped they'd seen the last of him for another few years. The brilliant liberal, the iconoclast, the freethinker he had admired in his youth now proved to be no more than sick, repellent. The quitting, the uninvited attack on Anita, the glorying in neuroses—all had a frightening cast to them. It was an awful disappointment. Paul had expected that Finnerty would be able to give him something—what, he didn't know—to assuage the nameless, aching need that had been nagging him almost, as Shepherd had apparently told Kroner, to the point of distraction.

As for Shepherd, Paul felt completely charitable, and even embarrassed that the man should be so upset at having been discovered as an informer. Paul stood.

"Where are you going, dear?" said Anita.

"To get Shepherd."

"He didn't say you were having a breakdown," said Baer.

Kroner frowned at Baer. "No, really he didn't Paul. If you like, I'll go after him. It was my fault, bringing up the subject. It wasn't Shepherd, and the poor boy—"

"I just *thought* it was Shepherd," said Baer.

"I think it's up to me," said Paul.

"I'll come, too," said Anita. There was a promise of vengeance in her voice.

"No, I'd rather you wouldn't."

Paul headed through the bar quickly, and heard her coming after him.

"I wouldn't miss this for anything."

"There isn't going to be anything to miss," said Paul. "I'm simply going to tell him everything's O.K., I understand. And I do understand."

"He wants that Pittsburgh job, Paul. That's why he told Kroner you were having a breakdown. Now he's scared stiff for fear of losing his job. Good!"

"I'm not going to get him fired."

"You could keep him worrying for a while. It'd serve him right."

"Please, Anita—this is between Shepherd and me."

They stood on the turf of the golf course now, in a muffled world of blues and blacks under the frail light of a new moon. Seated on the bench by the first tee, his legs stretched out and far apart, was Shepherd, with three cocktail glasses lined up beside him.

"Shep," called Paul softly.

"Hello." It was flat, with nothing behind it.

"Beat it," whispered Paul to Anita. She stayed, clenching and unclenching her hands.

"Soup's getting cold," said Paul, as kindly as possible. He sat down on the bench, with the three glasses between them. "I don't give a damn whether you told them I was going to pieces or not." Anita stood a dozen yards away, silhouetted against the French doors.

"I'd rather you'd get sore as hell about it," said Shepherd. "I told them, all right. Go ahead and can me."

"Oh, for Christ's sake, Shep, nobody's going to can you."

Paul had never known what to make of Shepherd, had found it hard to believe that any man really thought as Shepherd did. When Shepherd had first arrived in Ilium, he had announced to his fellow new arrivals, Paul and Finnerty, that he intended to compete with them. Baldly, ridiculously, he talked of competitiveness and rehashed with anyone who would listen various crises where there had been a showdown between his abilities and those of someone else, crises that the other participants had looked upon as being routine, unremarkable, and generally formless. But, to Shepherd, life seemed to be laid out like a golf course, with a series of beginnings, hazards, and ends, and with a definite summing up—for comparison with others' scores—after each hole. He was variously grim or elated over triumphs or failures no one else seemed to notice, but always stoical about the laws that governed the game. He asked no quarter, gave no quarter, and made very little difference to Paul, Finnerty, or any of his other associates. He was a fine engineer, dull company, and doggedly master of his fate and *not* his brother's keeper.

Paul, fidgeting silently on the bench, tried to put himself in Shepherd's place. Shepherd had lost a round, and now, grimly respectful of the mechanics of the competitive system, he wanted to pay the forfeit for losing and get on to the next episode, which he was, as always, determined to win. It was a hard world he lived in, but he wouldn't have it any other way. God knows why.

"Wanted to do me out of the Pittsburgh job, eh?" said Paul.

"I think I'm a better man for it," said Shepherd. "But what difference does that make now? I'm out of it."

"You lost."

"I *tried* and lost," said Shepherd. It was a vital distinction. "Go ahead and fire me."

The surest way to needle Shepherd was to refuse to compete. "I don't know," said Paul, "I think you'd be a good man for the Pittsburgh spot. If you like, I'll write a recommendation."

"Paul!" said Anita.

"Go back in, Anita," said Paul. "We'll be back in a minute." Anita seemed to be itching to give Shepherd just what he wanted, a rousing fight, something he could use as a starting point for another, as he saw it, cycle of play.

"I forgive you," said Paul. "I want you to go on working for me, if you will. There isn't a better man in the world for your job."

"You'd like to keep me right under your thumb, wouldn't you?"

Paul laughed bleakly. "No. It'd be just as before. Under my thumb? How could—"

"If you won't fire me, I want a transfer."

"All right. You know that isn't up to me. But let's go inside, shall we?" He held out his hand as Shepherd stood. Shepherd refused it, and brushed by.

Anita stopped him. "If you have any opinions on my husband's health, perhaps he or his doctor should be the first to hear them," she said huskily.

"Your husband and his doctor have known for months what I told Kroner and Baer. He isn't in any shape to be trusted with a foot-treadle sewing machine, let alone Pittsburgh." He was warming up now, getting his spirit back, and perhaps seeing the possibilities of having their voices carry into the dining room.

Paul seized them both by their arms and propelled them into the bar and in view of the dinner party. All were looking questioningly in their direction. Paul, Anita, and Shepherd smiled, and crossed the bar to the dining room, arm in arm.

"Under the weather?" said Kroner to Shepherd kindly.

"Yessir. Scallops for lunch did it, I think."

Kroner nodded sympathetically and turned to the waiter. "Could the boy have milk toast, do you suppose?" Kroner was willing to go to any lengths to preserve harmony in his family, to give a man in a tight spot a way out. For the rest of the evening, Paul supposed, Kroner would be keeping alive—as with the milk toast now—the polite fiction of Shepherd's illness.

After coffee and a liqueur, Paul gave a brief talk on the integration of the Ilium Works with other industry under the National Manufacturing Council fourteen years before. And then he went into the more general subject of what he called the Second Industrial Revolution. He read the talk, rather, taking pains to look up from his manuscript at regular intervals. It was, as he had told Katharine Finch in the office that afternoon, old stuff—a progress report, a reaffirmation of faith in what they were doing and had done with industry. Machines were doing America's work far better than Americans had ever done it. There were better goods for more people at less cost, and who could deny that that was magnificent and gratifying? It was what everyone said when he had to make a talk.

At one point, Kroner raised his big hand and asked if he might make a comment. "Just to sort of underline what you're saying, Paul, I'd like to point out something I thought was rather interesting. One horsepower equals about twenty-two manpower—*big* manpower. If you convert the horsepower of one of the bigger steel-mill motors into terms of manpower, you'll find that the motor does more work than the entire slave population of the United States at the time of the Civil War could do—and do it twenty-four hours a day." He smiled beatifically. Kroner was the rock, the fountainhead of faith and pride for all in the Eastern Division.

"That *is* an interesting figure," said Paul, searching for his place in the manuscript. "And that, of course, simply applies to the First Industrial Revolution, where machines devalued muscle work. The second revolution, the one we're now completing, is a little tougher to express in terms of work saved. If there were some measure like horsepower in which we could express annoyance or boredom that people used to experience in routine jobs—but there isn't."

"You can measure rejects, I'm here to tell you," said Baer, "and the darnedest, stupidest mistakes imaginable. The waste, the stoppages, the lemons! You can express it in dollars all right, dollars that went into bad workmanship."

"Yes," said Paul, "but I was thinking of it from the worker's point of view. The two industrial revolutions eliminated two kinds of drudgery, and I was looking for some way of estimating just how much the second revolution had relieved men of."

"I work," said Baer. Everyone laughed.

"The others—across the river," said Paul.

"They never did work," said Kroner, and again everyone laughed.

"And they're reproducing like rabbits," said Anita.

"Somebody telling dirty jokes about rabbits reproducing?" said Finnerty standing in the doorway. He swayed slightly, and his breathing was shallow. He had evidently found the whisky. "Which one was it? Where the little girl rabbit went into the rabbit hardware store, and the clerk—"

Kroner was on his feet. "Well, Finnerty—how are you, my boy?" He summoned the waiter. "You're just in time for coffee, my boy—a big cup of black coffee." He put his huge arm around Finnerty and steered him to the place that Anita had had cleared. Finnerty picked up the place card of the engineer next to him, squinted at it, then at the man. "Where's *my* goddamn place card?"

"Give him his place card, for heaven's sakes," said Anita.

Paul took it from his pocket, smoothed it out, and set it before Finnerty. Finnerty nodded, and fell into a morose silence.

"We were just talking about the Second Industrial Revolution," said Kroner, as though nothing were amiss. "Paul was talking about how there is no real measure of the kind of drudgery it has eliminated. I think the story can be told in terms of a curve, perhaps—as most stories can be presented most clearly."

"Not the one about the little girl rabbit in the rabbit hardware store," said Finnerty.

Everyone, following Kroner's example, ignored him. "If we plot man hours worked against the number of vacuum tubes in use, the man hours worked drop as the tubes increase."

"Like rabbits," said Finnerty.

Kroner smiled. "As you say, like rabbits. Incidentally, Paul, another interesting sidelight your father probably told you about is how people didn't pay much attention to this, as you call it, Second Industrial Revolution for quite some time. Atomic energy was hogging the headlines, and everybody talked as though peacetime uses of atomic energy were going to remake the world. The Atomic Age, that was the big thing to look forward to. Remember, Baer? And meanwhile, the tubes increased like rabbits."

"And dope addiction, alcoholism, and suicide went up proportionately," said Finnerty.

"Ed!" said Anita.

"That was the war," said Kroner soberly. "It happens after every war."

"And organized vice and divorce and juvenile delinquency, all parallel the growth of the use of vacuum tubes," said Finnerty.

"Oh, come on, Ed," said Paul, "you can't prove a logical connection between those factors."

"If there's the slightest connection, it's worth thinking about," said Finnerty.

"I'm sure there isn't enough connection for us to be concerned with here," said Kroner severely.

"Or enough imagination or honesty," said Finnerty.

"Oh, honestly! What are you talking about?" said Anita. She wadded her napkin nervously. "Come on—shall we leave this gloomy place and have the checker championship?"

The response was sighs and grateful nods all around the table. With little regret, Paul laid the remainder of his speech aside. The party, save for Finnerty, swept into the club's game room, where a checkerboard had already been set up, and where a battery of floor lamps ringed the table on which it rested, immaculate and glaring.

The four challengers trotted ahead, held a hurried conference, and three of them went to the checkroom. The fourth, Fred Berringer, sat down at the board and grinned mysteriously.

Paul took the chair opposite. "Play much?" he said.

"A little, a little."

"Let's see, Fred, you're from Minnesota, aren't you? Is the Minnesota checker championship by any chance at stake, Fred?"

"Sorry, I've got the club championship to win, and nothing to lose."

"You're going to lose, going to lose," said Baer. "They all do, all do, all of them do, eh Paul? All lose to you."

"Modesty forbids that I answer," said Paul. "My record speaks for itself." He permitted himself a mild sort of elation over his invincibility. There would be some bizarre twist to tonight's game, judging from the activity in the checkroom, but he wasn't worried.

"Make way for Checker Charley! Make way for Checker Charley!" shouted Berringer's seconds from the foyer.

The crowd in the gameroom parted, and the three rolled in a man-high box that was shrouded in a bedsheet and grumbled along on casters.

"There's a man in there?" said Kroner.

"A brain, a brain," said Berringer triumphantly. "Checker Charley, world's champion checker player, and looking for new planets to conquer." He grabbed a corner of the bedsheet, and unveiled Charley—a gray steel box with a checkerboard painted on its front panel. In each square that could be occupied by a checkerpiece were a red and a green jewel, each with a lamp behind it.

"Pleased to meet you, Charley," said Paul, trying to smile. When he realized what was going on, he felt himself reddening and getting a little mad. His first inclination was to walk the hell out.

Baer had the back of the box open. "Oh, oh, my, yes indeed," he said. "Look, look, look, and that goes over to there —and oh! Ha! Oh, my, I believe it's even got a memory. Isn't that what the tape's for boys, huh? Memory? Tape memory?"

"Yessir," said Berringer uncertainly. "I guess so."

"You built this?" said Kroner incredulously.

"Nossir," said Berringer, "my father. His hobby."

"Berringer, Berringer, Berringer," said Baer, frowning.

"You know—*Dave* Berringer; this is Dave's boy," said Kroner.

"Oh!" Baer looked at Checker Charley with new admiration. "By George, no wonder, no wonder, no wonder." Fred's father, one of the top computing-machine men in the country, had built it.

Paul slouched in his chair resignedly and waited for the comedy to begin. He looked at young Berringer's dull, complacent face, and was sure that the youngster didn't know much more about the machine than its external switches and signals.

Finnerty strolled in from the dining room, eating from a plate he held at chin level. He set his plate atop the cabinet and stuck his head into the back, alongside Baer's. "Any money on this?" he said.

"Are you crazy?" said Paul.

"Anything you say, boy; anything you say," said Berringer. He laid his fat billfold on the table.

The other three youngsters had plugged a cord from Checker Charley into an outlet in the baseboard; and now, as they flicked switches on and off, the box hummed and clicked, and lights on the front panel winked off and on.

Paul stood. "I concede," he said. He patted the box. "Congratulations, Charles, you're a better man than I am. Ladies and gentlemen, I give you the new club champion." He started out toward the bar.

"Darling," said Anita, catching his sleeve. "Oh, come on now, that isn't like you."

"I can't win against the damn thing. It can't make a mistake."

"You can at least play against it."

"And prove what?"

"Come on, Paul," said Finnerty, "I've looked Charley over, and he doesn't look so all-fired bright to me. I've got fifty dollars on you with Goldilocks here, and I'll cover anybody else who thinks Checker Charley's got a chance."

Eagerly, Shepherd slapped down three twenties. Finnerty covered him.

"Bet the sun won't rise tomorrow," said Paul.

"Play," said Finnerty.

Paul settled into his chair again. Dispiritedly, he pushed a checkerpiece forward. One of the youngsters closed a switch, and a light blinked on, indicating Paul's move on Checker Charley's bosom, and another light went on, indicating the perfect countermove for Berringer.

Berringer smiled and did what the machine told him to do. He lit a cigarette and patted the pile of currency beside him.

Paul moved again. A switch was closed, and the lights twinkled appropriately. And so it went for several moves.

To Paul's surprise, he took one of Berringer's pieces without, as far as he could see, laying himself open to any sort of disaster. And then he took another piece, and another. He shook his head in puzzlement and respect. The machine apparently took a long-range view of the game, with a grand strategy not yet evident. Checker Charley, as though confirming his thoughts, made an ominous hissing noise, which grew in volume as the game progressed.

"As of now, I am offering odds of three to one against Checker Charley," said Finnerty. Berringer and Shepherd both took him up on it for another twenty apiece.

Paul exchanged one man for three.

"Say—now wait just a minute," said Berringer.

"Wait for what?" said Finnerty.

"Something's wrong."

"You and Checker Charley are being beaten is all. Somebody

always wins, and somebody always loses," said Finnerty. "That's the way it goes."

"Sure, but if Checker Charley was working right he couldn't lose." Berringer arose unsteadily. "Listen, we'd better call this thing off while we find out what's wrong." He tapped the front panel experimentally. "Jesus Christ, he's hot as a frying pan!"

"Finish the game, Junior. I want to know who's champ," said Finnerty.

"Don'tcha see!" said Berringer furiously. "It isn't working right." He looked pleadingly around the room.

"Your move," said Paul.

Berringer looked helplessly at the lights, slid a man forward.

Paul took two more of Berringer's pieces and made his own piece a king. "This must be the trickiest booby trap in history," he laughed. He was enjoying himself immensely.

"Any minute now, Checker Charley's going to see his opening, and then it's going to be bye-bye championship," said Finnerty. "Hop, hop, hop, hoppity hop. Curtains, Paul."

"Calculus is a wonderful thing," said Paul. He sniffed. The air was getting heavy with a smell like burning paint, and his eyes were beginning to smart.

One of Berringer's seconds jerked open the back of the box, and smoke, colored a poisonous green by the glare from within, poured into the room.

"Fire!" cried Baer.

A waiter came running with a fire extinguisher and sent a jet of fluid into Checker Charley's entrails. Steam billowed up as the jet fizzed and sputtered on the glowing parts.

The lights on Charley's steel bosom were skittering about the board wildly now, playing a demoniacal and swift game according to rules only the machine could understand. All the lights went on at once, a hum swelled louder and louder, until it sounded like a thunderous organ note, and suddenly died. One by one, the little lamps winked out, like a village going to sleep.

"Oh my, my, oh my," murmured Baer.

"Fred, I'm so sorry," said Anita. She looked reproachfully at Paul.

The engineers crowded around Checker Charley, and those in the front rank probed through the ashes, melted tubes, and blackened wires. Tragedy was in every face. Something beautiful had died.

"Such a lovely thing," said Kroner sadly, resting his hand on Berringer's shoulder. "If you like, perhaps things would go easier if I told your father what happened."

"It was practically his life—away from the laboratory," said Berringer. He was shocked and scared. "Years and years. Why did it have to happen?" It was one more hollow echo to the question humanity had been asking for millenniums, the question men were seemingly born to ask.

"The Lord giveth, and the Lord taketh away," said Finnerty.

Berringer bit his lip and nodded, until it began to dawn on him just who it was that had spoken. His round, stupid face slowly took on a mean, threatening cast. "Uh-huh," he said, licking his lips, "the wise guy. Almost forgot about you."

"Well, you'd better not. I've got a lot of money bet on who's going to win."

"Now, see here, Finnerty," said Kroner placatingly, "let's call it a draw, shall we? I mean, after all, the boy's got a right to be upset, and—"

"Draw, hell," said Finnerty. "Paul beat Checker Charley fair and square."

"I'm beginning to see, I think," said Berringer menacingly. He gathered Finnerty's lapels in his hands. "What'd you do to Checker Charley, wise guy?"

"Ask Baer. His head was in there with mine. Baer, did I do anything to Charley?"

"What, eh? Do anything, do anything? Damage, you mean? No, no, no," said Baer.

"So sit down and finish the game, fat boy," said Finnerty. "Or concede. Either way, I want my money."

"If you didn't do anything to Charley, how come you were so sure he'd lose?"

"Because my sympathy's with any man up against a machine, especially a machine backing up a knucklehead like you against a man like Paul. Besides, Charley had a loose connection."

"Then you should have said so!" said Berringer. He gestured at the ruins of the machine. "Look—just look, will you? Look what you did by not telling me about the connection. I ought to mop this place up with your dirty face."

"Now, now, now—there, there," said Kroner, stepping between the two. "You should have said something about that connection, Ed. This is a shame, a real shame."

"If Checker Charley was out to make chumps out of men, he could damn well fix his own connections. Paul looks after his own circuits; let Charley do the same. Those who live by electronics, die by electronics. *Sic semper tyrannis.*" He gathered up the bills from the table. "Good night."

Anita dug her fingernails into Paul's arm. "Oh Paul, Paul, he's ruined the whole evening."

On his way out, Finnerty paused by Paul and Anita. "Nice going, champ."

"Please give them their money back," said Anita. "The machine wasn't working right. Be fair. Isn't that right, Paul?"

To the amazement of the whole somber group, Paul lost control and burst out laughing.

"That's the spirit, champ," said Finnerty. "I'm going home now, before these gentlemen sportsmen find a rope."

"Home? Washington?" said Anita.

"Your house, dear. I haven't got a place in Washington any more."

Anita closed her eyes. "Oh, I see."

Chapter VI

"WHAT was his expression like when he said it?" said Anita.

Paul had the comforter pulled up over his face and was trying to get to sleep tightly curled in the dark, muffled womb he made of his bed each night. "He looked sad," he murmured. "But he always looks sad—real sweet and sad."

For three hours they had been going over the events of the evening at the club, coming back again and again to what Kroner had said by way of farewell.

"And he didn't take you aside for a couple of words at any time?" She was wide awake.

"Scout's honor, Anita, all he said was what he said at the last."

She repeated Kroner's words judiciously, " 'I want you to come see me and Mom sometime next week, Paul.' "

"That's all."

"Nothing about Pittsburgh?"

"No," he said patiently. "I tell you, no." He tucked the comforter more snugly around his head and pulled his knees up higher. "No."

"Haven't I got a right to be interested?" she said. He'd evidently hurt her. "Is that what you're telling me, that I haven't the right to care?"

"Gladja care," he said thickly. "Fine, wonderful, thanks." In the quasi nightmare of being only half asleep, he visualized the notion of man and wife as one flesh—a physical monstrosity, pathetic, curious, and helpless Siamese twins.

"Women *do* have insight into things that men don't have," she was saying. "We notice important things that men let go by. Kroner wanted *you* to break the ice about Pittsburgh tonight, and you just—"

"We'll find out what Kroner has on his mind when I call on him. Now, please, let's sleep."

"Finnerty!" she said. "He's the one who threw a monkey wrench into things. Honestly! How long is he going to stay?"

"He'll get sick of us in a couple of days, the way he gets sick of anything."

"The N.I.P.B. mustn't leave him much time to go traipsing over the country to insult old friends."

"He quit. Hasn't got a job."

She sat up in bed. "They fired him! Well, good for them."

"Quit. They offered him a raise to stay. His idea." He found himself awakened by a subject that interested him. Anita's hammering at the subject of Pittsburgh had tended to make him curl up tighter and tighter. Now he felt himself relaxing somewhat, straightening out like a man. Finnerty was a magical name again; Paul's feelings about him had swung a full circle. Morale and *esprit de corps*, which Paul hadn't felt in any undertaking for years, had sprung up between them in the course of the exhilarating humiliation of Checker Charley. Moreover—Paul's thoughts were coming alive as though refreshed by a cool wind—there was enchantment in what Finnerty had done, a thing almost as inconceivable and beautifully simple as suicide: he'd quit.

"Paul . . ."

"Hmmmm?"

"Your father thought you'd be manager of Pittsburgh someday. If he were alive, nothing would make him happier than to know you got the job."

"Umm hmmmm." He remembered how Anita, shortly after their marriage, had dug up a picture of his father from a trunk and had had it enlarged and framed as her first birthday present to him. The picture was over on his bureau now, where she had put it—where he could see it the first thing in the morning and the last thing at night. She had never met Paul's father, and he hadn't said much about him to her; yet she'd built up a kind of mythology about the man that could keep her talking knowingly for hours. The myth had it that Paul's father in his youth had been just as easygoing as Paul, and that the strength that got him to the top job in the economy came in the middle years of his life—came in the years Paul was just beginning.

Kroner, too, kept alive the notion that Paul could be expected to follow in his father's footsteps. This faith of Kroner's had had a lot to do with Paul's getting to be manager of Ilium; and now that faith might get him the managership of Pittsburgh. When Paul thought about his effortless rise in the hierarchy, he sometimes, as now, felt sheepish, like a charlatan. He could handle his assignments all right, but he didn't have what his father had, what Kroner had, what Shepherd had, what so many had: the sense of spiritual importance in what they were doing; the ability to be moved emotionally, almost like a lover, by the great omnipresent and omniscient spook, the corporate personality. In short, Paul missed what made his father aggressive and great: the capacity to really give a damn.

"What are you going to do about Shepherd?" said Anita.

Paul started to curl up again. "Do? I've already done it. Nothing."

"If somebody doesn't clip his wings, he's going right over everybody's heads one of these days."

"Welcome to."

"You don't mean that."

"I mean I want to sleep."

Her bedsprings creaked as she lay down once more. She shifted her weight about restlessly for several minutes. "You know, it's a funny thing," she said.

"Hmmmm?"

"I've always noticed that when Shepherd turned his face a certain way, he looked an awful lot like somebody else. And it wasn't until tonight that I figured out who it was."

"Mmmm."

"When you see him at just the right angle, he's the spitting image of your father."

Chapter VII

PRIVATE FIRST CLASS Elmo C. Hacketts, Jr., approached the Shah of Bratpuhr, Doctor Ewing J. Halyard, of the State Department, Khashdrahr Miasma, their interpreter, General of the Armies Milford S. Bromley, General William K. Corbett, camp commander, Major General Earl Pruitt, division commander, and their aides.

Private First Class Hacketts was in the middle of the First Squad of the Second Platoon of B Company of the First Battalion of the 427th Regiment of the 107th Infantry Division of the Ninth Corps of the Twelfth Army, and he stayed right there, and put his left foot down every time the drummer hit the bass drum.

"Dee-veesh-ee-own—" cried the Division Commander through a loudspeaker.

"Reg-ee-ment—" bawled four regimental commanders.

" 'Tal-ee-own—" cried twelve battalion commanders.

"Cump-neeee—" shouted thirty-six company commanders.

"Batt-reeee—" shouted twelve battery commanders.

"P'toon—" muttered a hundred and ninety-two platoon commanders.

"Hacketts," said Private First Class Hacketts to himself.

"Halt!"

And Hacketts did, hut, two.

"Ri-yut—" said the loudspeaker.

"Right, right, right, right, right, right . . ." echoed two hundred and fifty-six voices.

"Right," said Private First Class Hacketts to himself.

"Fay-yuss!"

Hacketts faced right, hut, two. And he stared into the small, bright eyes of the Shah of Bratpuhr, spiritual leader of 6,000,000 people somewhere else.

The Shah bowed slightly from the waist.

Hacketts did not bow back because he wasn't supposed to and he wasn't going to do a goddamn thing he wasn't supposed to do and he had only twenty-three more years to go on his hitch and then he was through with the Army and the hell with it, and in twenty-three years if some sonofabitching colonel or lieutenant or general came up to him and said, "Salute me," or "Pick up that butt," or "Shine your shoes," or something like that he'd say, "Kiss my ass, sonny," and whip out the old discharge and spit in his eye and walk away laughing like crazy because his twenty-five years was up and all he had to do was hang around with the old gang in Hooker's in Evansville and wait for the old pension check and to hell with you buddy because I don't have to take no crap from nobody no more because I'm through and—

The Shah clapped his hands delightedly and continued to stare at Private First Class Hacketts, who was a huge, healthy man. "*Niki Takaru*!" he cried, exhaling a strong effluvium of *Sumklish*.

"No *Takaru*!" said Doctor Halyard. "Sol-dee-yers."

"*No Takaru*?" said the Shah in puzzlement.

"What's he say?" said General of the Armies Bromley.

"Said they're a fine bunch of slaves," said Halyard. He turned to the Shah again and waggled his finger at the small, dark man. "No *Takaru*. No, no, no."

Khashdrahr seemed baffled, too, and offered Halyard no help in clarifying the point.

"*Sim koula Takaru, akka sahn salet*?" said the Shah to Khashdrahr.

Khashdrahr shrugged and looked questioningly at Halyard. "Shah says, if these not slaves, how you get them to do what they do?"

"Patriotism," said General of the Armies Bromley sternly. "Patriotism, damn it."

"Love of country," said Halyard.

Khashdrahr told the Shah, and the Shah nodded slightly, but his look of puzzlement did not disappear. "*Sidi ba*—" he said tentatively.

"Eh?" said Corbett.

"Even so—" translated Khashdrahr, and he looked as doubtful as the Shah.

"Lay-eft—" shouted the loudspeaker.

"Left, left, left, left, left, left . . ."

"Left," said Hacketts to himself.

And Hacketts thought of how he was going to be left alone

in the barracks this week end when everybody else was out on pass because of what happened in inspection that morning after he'd mopped and squeegeed the floor and washed the windows by his bunk and tightened up his blankets and made sure the tooth-paste tube was to the *left* of the shaving-cream tube and the tube caps both pointed *away* from the aisle and that the cuffs on his rolled-up socks pointed *up* in his foot-locker and that his mess kit and mess cup and mess spoon and mess fork and mess knife and canteen were shining and that his wooden rifle was waxed and its simulated metalwork blackened and his shoes shined and that the extra pair under his bunk were laced to the *top* and tied and that the clothes on his hangers went: two shirts, O.D.; two pants, O.D.; three shirts, khaki; three pants, khaki; two shirts, herringbone twill; two pants, herringbone twill; field jacket; dress blouse, O.D.; raincoat, O.D., and that all the pockets were empty and buttoned and then the inspecting officer came through and said, "Hey soldier your fly's open and no pass for you," and—

"Fay-yuss."

"Hut, two," said Hacketts.

"For'd—"

"For'd, for'd, for'd, for'd, for'd for'd . . ."

"For'd," said Hacketts to himself.

And Hacketts wondered where the hell he'd go in the next twenty-three years and thought it'd be a relief to get the hell out of the States for a while and go occupy someplace else and maybe be somebody in some of those countries instead of a bum with no money looking for an easy lay and not getting it in his own country or not getting a good lay anyway but still a pretty good lay compared to no lay at all but anyway there was more to living than laying and he'd like a little glory by God and there might be laying *and* glory overseas and while there wasn't any shooting and wasn't going to be none either probably for a good long while still you got a real gun and bullets and there was a little glory in that and sure as hell it was more grownup than marching up and down with a wooden one and he'd sure like a little rank too but he knew what his I.Q. was and everybody else did too and especially the machines so that was that for twenty-three more years unless one of the machines burned out a tube and misread his card and sent him to

O.C.S. and that happened now and then and there was old Mulcahy who got ahold of his card and doctored it with an icepick so the machines would think he was qualified for a big promotion but he got restricted to barracks instead for having clap twenty-six times and then transferred to the band as a trombone player when he couldn't even whistle "Hot Cross Buns" and anyway it was better than the frigging Reeks and Wrecks any day and no big worries and a nice-looking suit only the pants ought to have zippers and in only twenty-three more years he could go up to some sonofabitching general or colonel or something and say, "Kiss my—"

"Harch!"

"Boom!" went the bass drum, and down came Hacketts' left foot, and off he went in the midst of the vast, tractable human avalanche.

"*Takaru*," said the Shah to Khashdrahr above the din.

Khashdrahr nodded and smiled agreement. "*Takaru*."

"What the hell am I supposed to do?" said Halyard unhappily to General of the Armies Bromley. "This guy thinks of everything he sees in terms of his own country, and his own country must be a Goddamn mess."

"*Amerikka vagga bouna, ni houri manko Salim da vagga dinko*," said the Shah.

"What's eating him now?" said Halyard impatiently.

"He say Americans have changed almost everything on earth," said Khashdrahr, "but it would be easier to move the Himalayas than to change the Army."

The Shah was waving goodbye to the departing troops. "*Dibo, Takaru, dibo*."

Chapter VIII

PAUL breakfasted alone, while Anita and Finnerty, in widely separated beds, slept late after a busy evening.

He had difficulty starting his Plymouth and finally realized that it was out of gas. There had been almost a half-tank the afternoon before. Finnerty, then, had gone for a long ride in it after they'd left him alone on the bed and gone to the Country Club without him.

Paul rummaged about the glove compartment for a siphon hose, and found it. He paused, sensing that something was missing. He stuck his hand into the glove compartment again and felt around inside. The old pistol was gone. He looked on the floor and searched behind the seat cushion without finding it. Perhaps some urchin had taken it while he'd been in Homestead after the whisky. He'd have to tell the police about it right away, and there'd be all sorts of forms to fill out. He tried to think of a lie that would get him out of accusations of negligence and not get anybody else in trouble.

He dipped the siphon hose into the station wagon's tank, sucked and spat, and plunged the other end of the hose into the Plymouth's empty tank. As he waited for the slow transfer to take place, he stepped out of the garage and into a warm patch of sunlight.

The bathroom window above clattered open, and he looked up to see Finnerty staring at himself in the medicine-cabinet mirror. Finnerty didn't notice Paul. He had a bent cigarette in his mouth, and there it remained while he washed his face with a cursory and random dabbing motion. The ash on the cigarette grew longer and longer, and, incredibly, longer, until the coal was almost at his lips. He removed the cigarette from his mouth, and the long ash fell. Finnerty flipped the butt in the direction of the toilet, replaced it with another, and proceeded to shave. And the ash grew longer and longer. He leaned close to the mirror, and the ash broke against it. He pressed a pimple between his thumb and forefinger, seemingly without results. Still squinting in the mirror at the reddened spot, he groped for a towel with one hand, seized one without looking at it, and swept Anita's stockings from the towel rack and into the bathtub. Finnerty, his toilet complete, said something to his reflection, grimaced, and made his exit.

Paul returned to the garage, coiled the siphon hose in the glove compartment, and drove off. The car was hesitating again—catching and slowing, catching and slowing. At any rate, it took his mind momentarily from the inconvenient matter of the missing pistol. On the long grade past the golf course, the engine seemed to be hitting on no more than three cylinders, and a squad from the Reconstruction and Reclamation Corps, putting in a spruce windbreak to the north of the clubhouse, turned to watch the car's enervated struggle with gravity.

"Hey! Headlamp's busted," called one of the men.

Paul nodded and smiled his thanks. The car faltered, and came to a stop, just short of the summit. Paul set his emergency brake and got out. He lifted the hood and tested various connections. Tools being laid against the side of the car made a clattering noise, and a half-dozen Reeks and Wrecks stuck their heads under the hood with his.

"It's his plugs," said a small, bright-eyed, Italian-looking man.

"Aaaaaaah, in a pig's ass it's his plugs," said a tall, ruddy-faced man, the oldest of the group. "Lemme show you where the real trouble is. Here, that wrench, that's the ticket." He went to work on the fuel pump, soon had the top off of it. He pointed to the gasket beneath the cap. "There," he said soberly, like an instructor in surgery, "there's your trouble. Sucking air. I knew that the minute I heard you coming a mile off."

"Well," said Paul, "guess I'd better call somebody to come and get it. Probably take a week to order a new gasket."

"Five minutes," said the tall man. He took off his hat and, with an expression of satisfaction, ripped out the sweatband. He took a penknife from his pocket, laid the cap of the fuel pump over the sweatband, and cut out a leather disk just the right size. Then he cut out the disk's center, dropped the new gasket in place, and put the pump back together. The others watched eagerly, handed him tools, or offered to hand him tools, and tried to get into the operation wherever they could. One man scraped the green and white crystals from a battery connection. Another one went around tightening the valve caps on the tires.

"Now try her!" said the tall man.

Paul stepped on the starter, the motor caught, roared fast and slow without a miss as he pumped the accelerator. He looked up to see the profound satisfaction, the uplift of creativity, in the faces of the Reeks and Wrecks.

Paul took out his billfold and handed two fives to the tall man.

"One'll do," he said. He folded it carefully and tucked it into the breast pocket of his blue workshirt. He smiled sardonically. "First money I've earned in five years. I oughta frame that one, eh?" He looked closely at Paul, for the first time aware of the man and not his motor. "Seems like I know you from somewhere. What's your line?"

Something made Paul want to be someone other than who he was. "Got a little grocery store," he said.

"Need a guy who's handy with his hands?"

"Not just now. Things are pretty slow."

The man was scrawling something on a piece of paper. He held the paper against the hood, and twice punched his pencil through the paper as the pencil crossed a crack. "Here—here's my name. If you've got machines, I'm the guy that can keep them going. Put in eight years in the works as a millwright before the war, and anything I don't know, I pick up fast." He handed the paper to Paul. "Where you going to put it?"

Paul slipped the paper under the transparent window in his billfold, over his driver's license. "There—right on top." He shook the man's hand and nodded to the others. "Thanks."

The motor took hold with assurance and swept Paul over the hilltop and up to the gate of the Ilium Works. A watchman waved from his pillbox, a buzzer sounded, and the iron, high-spiked gate swung open. He came now to the solid inner door, honked, and looked expectantly at a thin slit in the masonry, behind which another guard sat. The door rumbled upward, and Paul drove up to his office building.

He went up the steps two at a time—his only exercise—and unlocked two outer doors that led him into Katharine's office, and beyond that, his own.

Katharine hardly looked up when he came in. She seemed

lost in melancholy, and, on the other side of the room, on the couch that was virtually his, Bud Calhoun was staring at the floor.

"Can I help?" said Paul.

Katharine sighed. "Bud wants a job."

"Bud wants a job? He's got the fourth-highest-paid job in Ilium now. I couldn't equal what he gets for running the depot. Bud, you're crazy. When I was your age, I didn't make half—"

"Ah want a job," said Bud. "Any job."

"Trying to scare the National Petroleum Council into giving you a raise? Sure, Bud, I'll make you an offer better than what you're getting, but you've got to promise not to take me up on it."

"Ah haven't got a job any more," said Bud. "Canned."

Paul was amazed. "Really? What on earth for? Moral turpitude? What about the gadget you invented for—"

"Thet's it," said Bud with an eerie mixture of pride and remorse. "Works. Does a fine job." He smiled sheepishly. "Does it a whole lot better than Ah did it."

"It runs the whole operation?"

"Yup. Some gadget."

"And so you're out of a job."

"Seventy-two of us are out of jobs," said Bud. He slumped even lower in the couch. "Ouah job classification has been eliminated. Poof." He snapped his fingers.

Paul could see the personnel manager pecking out Bud's job code number on a keyboard, and seconds later having the machine deal him seventy-two cards bearing the names of those who did what Bud did for a living—what Bud's machine now did better. Now, personnel machines all over the country would be reset so as no longer to recognize the job as one suited for men. The combination of holes and nicks that Bud had been to personnel machines would no longer be acceptable. If it were to be slipped into a machine, it would come popping right back out.

"They don't need P-128's any more," said Bud bleakly, "and nothing's open above or below. Ah'd take a cut, and go back to P-129 or even P-130, but it's no dice. Everything's full up."

"Got any other numbers, Bud?" said Paul. "The only P-numbers we're authorized are—"

Katharine had the *Manual* open before her. She'd already looked the numbers up. "P-225 and P-226—lubrication engineers," she said. "And Doctor Rosenau's got both of those."

"That's right, he does," said Paul. Bud was in a baffling mess, and Paul didn't see how he could help him. The machines knew the Ilium Works had its one allotted lubrication engineer, and they wouldn't tolerate a second. If Bud were recorded as a lubrication engineer and introduced into the machines, they'd throw him right out again.

As Kroner often said, eternal vigilance was the price of efficiency. And the machines tirelessly riffled through their decks again and again and again in search of foot draggers, free riders, and misfits.

"You know it isn't up to me, Bud," said Paul. "I haven't got any real say about who's taken on."

"He knows that," said Katharine. "But he has to start somewhere, and we thought maybe you'd know of some opening, or who to see."

"Oh, it makes me sore," said Paul. "Whatever got into them to give you a Petroleum Industries assignment, anyway? You should be in design."

"Got no aptitude for it," said Bud. "Tests proved that."

That would be on his ill-fated card, too. All his aptitude-test grades were on it—irrevocably, immutable, and the card knew best. "But you *do* design," said Paul. "And you do it with a damn sight more imagination than the prima donnas in the Lab." The Lab was the National Research and Development Laboratory, which was actually a war-born conglomeration of all the country's research and development facilities under a single headquarters. "You're not even paid to design, and still you do a better job of it than they do. That telemetering arrangement for the pipeline, your car, and now this monster that runs the depot—"

"But the test says no," said Bud.

"So the machines say no," said Katharine.

"So that's that," said Bud. "Ah guess."

"You might see Kroner," said Paul.

"Ah tried, and didn't get past his secretary. Ah told her Ah was after a job, and she called up Personnel. They ran mah card through the machines while she held the phone; and then she hung up, and looked sad, and said Kroner had meetings all month."

"Maybe your university can help," said Paul. "Maybe the grading machine needed new tubes when it went over your development aptitude test." He spoke without conviction. Bud was beyond help. As an old old joke had it, the machines had all the cards.

"Ah've written, asking them to check my grades again. No matter what Ah say, Ah get the same thing back." He threw a piece of graph paper on Katharine's desk. "Theah. Ah've written three letters, and gotten three of these back."

"Uh-huh," said Paul, looking at the familiar graph with distaste. It was a so-called Achievement and Aptitude Profile, and every college graduate got one along with his sheepskin. And the sheepskin was nothing, and the graph was everything. When time for graduation came, a machine took a student's grades and other performances and integrated them into one graph—the profile. Here Bud's graph was high for theory, there low for administration, here low for creativity, and so on, up and down across the page to the last quality—*personality*. In mysterious, unnamed units of measure, each graduate was credited with having a high, medium, or low personality. Bud, Paul saw, was a strong medium, as the expression went, personality-wise. When the graduate was taken into the economy, all his peaks and valleys were translated into perforations on his personnel card.

"Well, thanks anyway," said Bud suddenly, gathering up his papers, as though embarrassed at having been so weak as to bother anyone with his troubles.

"Something will turn up," said Paul. He paused at his office door. "How are you fixed for money?"

"They're keepin' me on a few more months, until all the new equipment gets installed. And Ah've got the award from the suggestion system."

"Well, thank God you got something out of it. How much?"

"Five hundred. It's the biggest one this year."

"Congratulations. Is that on your card?"

Bud held the rectangle of cardboard up to the window and squinted at the nicks and perforations. "Think thet little devil raht there's it."

"That's for your smallpox vaccination," said Katharine, looking over his shoulder. "I've got one of those."

"No, the little triangle next to thet one."

Katharine's phone rang. "Yes?" She turned to Paul. "A Doctor Finnerty is at the gate and wants in."

"If it's just to shoot the bull, tell him to wait until late this afternoon."

"He says he wants to see the plant, not you."

"All right; let him in."

"They're shorthanded at the gate," said Katharine. "One of the guards is down with flu. What'll they do about an escort for him?"

The few visitors that did get admitted to the Ilium Works were taken about by guides, who only incidentally pointed out the wonders of the place. The guides were armed, and their main job was to see that no one got close enough to vital controls to knock them out. The system was a holdover from the war, and from the postwar riot period, but it still made sense. Every so often, antisabotage laws notwithstanding, someone got it into his head to jimmy something. It hadn't happened in Ilium for years, but Paul had heard reports from other works—reports of a visitor with a crude bomb in a briefcase in Syracuse; of an old lady in Buffalo stepping from a group of sightseers to jam her umbrella into some vital clockwork. . . . Things like that still happened, and Kroner had stipulated that visitors to plants should be watched every second. The saboteurs had come from every walk of life—including, in at least one hushed-up instance, the brass. As Kroner had said, you never could tell who was going to try it next.

"Oh, what the hell, let Finnerty in without an escort," said Paul. "He's a special case—an old Ilium man."

"The directive said no exceptions," said Katharine. She knew all of the directives—and there were thousands of them—cold.

"Let him roam."

"Yessir."

Bud Calhoun watched the interchange with far more interest than it merited, Paul thought. It was as though they had been putting on an absorbing drama. When Katharine hung up she mistook his gaze for adoration and returned it warmly.

"Six minutes," said Bud.

"Six minutes for what?" said Katharine.

"Six minutes foah nothin'," said Bud. "It took thet long to get a man in through the gate."

"Well?"

"Three of you tied up for six minutes—you two and the guard. Eighteen man minutes in all. Hell, it cost over two bucks to let him in. How many people come to the gate a year?"

"Ten a day, maybe," said Paul.

"Twenty-seven hundred and fifty-eight a year," said Katharine.

"And you pass on each one?"

"Katharine usually does," said Paul. "That's the biggest part of her job."

"At a dollah a head, thet's twenty-seven hundred dollahs a year," said Bud reproachfully. He pointed at Katharine. "This is ridiculous! If policy is iron-clad, why not let a machine make the decisions? Policy isn't thinkin', it's a reflex. You could even build a gadget with an exception for Finnerty and still get away foah less than a hundred dollahs."

"There are all sorts of special decisions I have to make," said Katharine defensively. "I mean, all sorts of things come up that require more than routine thought—more than any old machine could do."

Bud wasn't listening. He held his palms apart, marking the size of the box being born in his imagination. "Either a visitor is a nonentity, a friend, an employee, small brass, or big brass. The guard presses one of five buttons in the top row on the box. See it? Either the visitor is sight-seein', inspectin', makin' a personal call, or here on business. The guard pushes one of four buttons in thet row. The machine has two lights, a red one for no, and a green one for yes. Whatever the policy is, bingo!—the lights tell him what to do."

"Or we could tack a memo about policy on the guardhouse wall," said Paul.

Bud looked startled. "Yes," he said slowly, "you *could* do thet." It was clear he thought it was a pretty drab man who would think much of *that* solution.

"I'm mad," said Katharine, her voice small. "You have no right to go around saying a machine can do what I do."

"Aw, now honey—there wasn't anything personal in it."

She was crying now, and Paul slipped into his office and shut the door.

"Your wife's on the phone," said Katharine brokenly on the intercom set.

"All right. Yes, Anita?"

"Have you heard from Kroner?"

"No. I'll let you know if I do."

"I hope he had a good time last night."

"He did—or firmly believes he did."

"Is Finnerty there?"

"In the plant somewhere."

"You should see the bathroom."

"I saw it in the making."

"He had four cigarettes going, and forgot about every one of them. One on top of the medicine cabinet, one on the window sill, one on the top of the john, and one on the toothbrush rack. I couldn't eat my breakfast. He's got to go."

"I'll tell him."

"What are you going to tell Kroner?"

"I don't know yet. I don't know what he's going to say."

"Pretend I'm Kroner and I've just said, sort of casually, 'Well, Paul, the Pittsburgh spot is still open.' Then what do you say?"

This was the game she never tired of—one that took every bit of Paul's patience to play. She was forever casting herself as a person of influence and making Paul play dialogues with her. There would then be a critique, in which his responses were analyzed, edited, and polished by her. No real dialogues ever came close to her phantasies, which served chiefly to show how primitive a notion she had of men of affairs and of how business was done.

"Go on," she prodded.

"Pittsburgh, eh?" said Paul. "Holy smokes! Wow!"

"No, now, I'm serious," she said firmly. "What will you say?"

"Darling, I'm busy now."

"All right; you think it over and call me back. You know what I think you should say?"

"I'll call you back."

"All right. Goodbye. I love you."

"I love *you*, Anita. Goodbye."

"Doctor Shepherd is on the phone," said Katharine.

Paul picked up the now moist instrument again. "What's the matter now, Shep?"

"There's an unauthorized man in Building 57! Get the guards down here."

"Is it Finnerty?"

"An unauthorized man," said Shepherd stubbornly.

"All right. Is it an unauthorized Finnerty?"

"Yes—but that's beside the point. It makes no difference what his name is. He's roaming around without an escort, and you know how Kroner feels about that."

"I gave him permission. I know he's down there."

"You're putting *me* in a sweet spot."

"I don't get you."

"I mean I'm responsible for these buildings, and now you're telling me to ignore very specific orders from Kroner. Am I supposed to be left holding the bag if word gets out?"

"Look, just forget it. It's all right. I'll take the responsibility."

"In other words, you *order* me to let Finnerty go through unescorted."

"Yes—that's it. I *order* you."

"O.K., I just wanted to make sure I had it straight. Berringer wondered about it, too, so I had him listen in."

"Berringer?" said Paul.

"Yeah!" said Berringer.

"Just keep this under your hat is all."

"You're the boss," said Berringer flatly.

"All squared away now, Shepherd?" said Paul.

"I guess. And are we to understand that you've authorized him to make drawings, too?"

"Drawings?"

"Layouts."

At this point Paul realized that his judgment had been pushed into the background by more emotional matters, but he decided it was too late to do anything about it gracefully. "Let him do what he wants. He may come up with some useful ideas. All right?"

"You're the boss," said Shepherd. "Isn't that right, Berringer?"

"He's the boss," said Berringer.

"I'm the boss," said Paul, and he let the telephone clatter into its cradle.

Bud Calhoun was still trying to patch things up with Katharine in the next office. His voice had become wheedling and penetrating. Paul could understand snatches of it.

"As far as thet goes," Bud was saying, "it wouldn't be much of a trick to replace *him* with a gadget." Paul had a good idea where Bud's stubby index finger was pointing.

Chapter IX

FINNERTY apparently found plenty to entertain himself with in the Ilium Works. He didn't appear in Paul's office until late in the afternoon. When he did arrive, Katharine Finch gave a small cry of surprise. He'd let himself in through two locked doors with keys he'd presumably failed to turn in when he left the plant for Washington years before.

Paul's door was ajar, and he heard the conversation.

"Don't go for your rod, lady. The name's Finnerty."

Katharine did have a gun somewhere in her desk, though no ammunition. That secretaries should be armed was a regulation held over from the old days, too; one Kroner thought well enough of to revive in a directive.

"You're not authorized to have those keys," she said coldly.

"Have you been crying?" said Finnerty.

"I'll see if Doctor Proteus can see you."

"What is there to cry about? See—none of the red lights are on, no buzzers going off, so all's well with the world."

"Send him in, Katharine," called Paul.

Finnerty walked in and sat on the edge of Paul's desk. "What's the matter with Miss Policy out there?"

"Broken engagement. What's on your mind?"

"Thought we'd have a couple of drinks—if you feel like listening."

"All right. Let me call Anita and tell her we'll be late for supper."

Katharine got Anita on the line, and Paul told his wife what he was up to.

"Have you thought out what you'd say to Kroner if he told you Pittsburgh was still open?"

"No—it's been a hell of a day."

"Well, I've been thinking about it, and—"

"Anita, I've got to go."

"All right. I love you."

"I love *you*, Anita. Goodbye." He looked up at Finnerty. "O.K., let's go." He felt somehow conspiratorial, and got a small lift from the feeling. Being with Finnerty had often had that effect. Finnerty had an air of mysteriousness about him, an implication that he knew of worlds unsuspected by anyone else—a man of unexplained absences and shadowy friends. Actually, Finnerty let Paul in on very little that was surprising, and only gave him the illusion of sharing in mysteries—if, indeed, there were any. The illusion was enough. It filled a need in Paul's life, and he went gladly for a drink with the odd man.

"Is there somewhere I can reach you?" said Katharine.

"No, I'm afraid not," said Paul. He planned to go to the Country Club, where he could be reached easily enough. But, on an impulse, he indulged his appetite for secretiveness.

Finnerty had come over in Paul's station wagon. They left it at the Works and took Paul's old car.

"Across the bridge," said Finnerty.

"I thought we'd go to the club."

"This is Thursday, isn't it? Do the civic managers still have their big dinner there on Thursdays?"

The civic managers were the career administrators who ran the city. They lived on the same side of the river as the managers and engineers of the Ilium Works, but the contact between the two groups was little more than perfunctory and, traditionally, suspicious. The schism, like so many things, dated back to the war, when the economy had, for efficiency's sake, become monolithic. The question had arisen: who was to run it, the bureaucrats, the heads of business and industry, or the military? Business and bureaucracy had stuck together long enough to overwhelm the military and had since then worked side by side, abusively and suspiciously, but, like Kroner and Baer, each unable to do a whole job without the other.

"Not much changes in Ilium," said Paul. "The civic managers will be there all right. But if we get over there this early, we can get a booth in the bar."

"I'd rather share a bed in a leprosarium."

"All right; over the bridge it is. Let me put on something more comfortable." Paul stopped his car just short of the bridge, and traded his coat for the jacket in the trunk.

"I wondered if you still did that. That's even the same jacket, isn't it?"

"Habit."

"What would a psychiatrist say about it?"

"He'd say it was a swat at my old man, who never went anywhere without a Homburg and a double-breasted suit."

"Think he was a bastard?"

"How do I know what my father was? The editor of *Who's Who* knows about as much as I do. The guy was hardly ever home."

They were driving through Homestead now. Paul suddenly snapped his fingers in recollection and turned down a side street. "I've got to stop by police headquarters for a minute. Mind waiting?"

"What's the trouble?"

"Almost slipped my mind. Somebody swiped the gun from the glove compartment, or it fell out, or something."

"Keep driving."

"It'll just take a minute, I hope."

"I took it."

"You? Why?"

"Had an idea I might want to shoot myself." He said it matter-of-factly. "Even had the barrel in my mouth for a while, and the hammer back—for maybe ten minutes."

"Where is it now?"

"Bottom of the Iroquois somewhere." He licked his lips. "Tasted oil and metal all through dinner. Turn left."

Paul had learned to listen with outward calm when Finnerty spoke of his morbid moments. When he was with Finnerty he liked to pretend that he shared the man's fantastic and alternately brilliant or black inner thoughts—almost as though he were discontent with his own relative tranquility. Finnerty had spoken dispassionately of suicide often; but, seemingly, he did it because he got pleasure from savoring the idea. If he'd felt driven to kill himself, he would have been dead long ago.

"You think I'm insane?" said Finnerty. Apparently he wanted more of a reaction than Paul had given him.

"You're still in touch. I guess that's the test."

"Barely—*barely*."

"A psychiatrist could help. There's a good man in Albany."

Finnerty shook his head. "He'd pull me back into the center, and I want to stay as close to the edge as I can without going over. Out on the edge you see all kinds of things you can't see from the center." He nodded, "Big, undreamed-of things—the people on the edge see them first." He laid his hand on Paul's shoulder, and Paul fought a reflex that suddenly made him want to get as far away as possible. "Here's the place we want," said Finnerty. "Park here."

They had circled several blocks and were back at the head of the bridge, by the same saloon Paul had visited for the whisky. Paul, with uncomfortable memories of the place, wanted to go somewhere else, but Finnerty was already out of the car and on his way in.

Gratefully, Paul saw that the street and saloon were almost deserted, so there was a good chance he wouldn't see any of the people who'd watched his confusion the day before. No hydrants were going, but from far away, from the direction of Edison Park, came faint band music—a clue as to where everyone might be.

"Hey, your headlamp's busted," said a man, peering through the doorway of the saloon.

Paul passed him quickly, without getting a good look at him. "Thanks."

Only when he'd overtaken Finnerty in the damp twilight of the inside did he turn for another look at the man—at his short, broad back. The man's neck was thick and red, and glinting behind his ears were the hooks of steel spectacles. It was the same man, Paul realized, the same man who had been sitting by Rudy Hertz—the man whose son had just turned eighteen. Paul remembered that he had promised this man, in the panic of the moment, to speak to Matheson, the placement director, about the son. Perhaps he hadn't recognized Paul. Paul slid into a booth with Finnerty, in the darkest corner of the room.

The man turned and smiled, his eyes lost behind the milky, thick lenses of his glasses. "You're entirely welcome, Doctor Proteus," he called. "It isn't often that anyone can do a favor for anyone in your position."

Paul pretended he hadn't heard, and turned his attention to Finnerty, who dug a spoon around and around and around in a sugar bowl. Some of the white grains spilled over, and Finnerty absently drew the mathematical symbol for infinity in them with the tip of his finger.

"Funny what I expected from this reunion, what I guess

everybody expects from affectionate reunions. I thought seeing you would somehow clear up all sorts of problems, get me thinking straight," said Finnerty. He had a candor about his few emotional attachments that Paul found disquieting. He used words to describe his feelings that Paul could never bring himself to use when speaking of a friend: love, affection, and other words generally consigned to young and inexperienced lovers. It wasn't homosexual; it was an archaic expression of friendship by an undisciplined man in an age when most men seemed in mortal fear of being mistaken for pansies for even a split second.

"I guess I looked forward to some sort of rebirth too," said Paul.

"But you find out quick enough that old friends are old friends, and nothing more—no wiser, no more help than anyone else. Well, what the hell, that doesn't mean I'm not damned pleased to see you again."

"No booth service until eight," called the bartender.

"I'll get them," said Finnerty. "What'll it be?"

"Bourbon—plain water. Make it a weak one. Anita's expecting us in an hour."

Finnerty came back with two strong highballs.

"Is there any water in it?" said Paul.

"There was enough water in it as it was." Finnerty swept the sugar from the table with his palm. "It's the loneliness," he said, as though picking up the thread of a conversation that had been interrupted. "It's the loneliness, the not belonging anywhere. I just about went crazy with loneliness here in the old days, and I figured things would be better in Washington, that I'd find a lot of people I admired and belonged with. Washington is worse, Paul—Ilium to the tenth power. Stupid, arrogant, self-congratulatory, unimaginative, humorless men. And the women, Paul—the dull wives feeding on the power and glory of their husbands."

"Oh, now listen, Ed," said Paul, smiling, "they're good-hearted people."

"Who isn't? I'm not, I guess. Their superiority is what gets me, this damn hierarchy that measures men against machines. It's a pretty unimpressive kind of man that comes out on top."

"Here come some more!" called the man with the thick

glasses from the door. From far off came the sound of marching, and the thump of a bass drum. The noise came closer, a whistle blew, and a brass band exploded with music.

Paul and Finnerty hurried to the door.

"Who are they?" shouted Finnerty at the man in thick glasses.

The man smiled. "Don't think they want anybody to know. Secret."

At the head of the procession, surrounded by four trumpeters dressed as Arabs, was a florid, serious old man in a turban and pantaloons, carefully cradling in his arms an elephant tusk inscribed with mysterious symbols. Behind him came an enormous square banner, held aloft by a staggering giant, and steadied in the wind, maypole fashion, by a dozen Arabs tugging at colored ropes. The banner, which from a distance had given promise of explaining all, was embroidered with four lines of long-forgotten—or perhaps recently invented—script, and with four green owls against a field of apricot. After it came the band, which carried out the Arabian motif. There were owl-bearing pennants hung from the brasses, and the banner's message was repeated, in case anyone had missed it, on a cart-borne bass drum perhaps twelve feet in diameter.

"Hooray," said the man in thick glasses mildly.

"Why are you cheering?" said Finnerty.

"Don't you think something's called for? Cheering Luke Lubbock mostly. He's the one with the tusk."

"Doing a swell job," said Finnerty. "What's he represent?"

"Secret. He couldn't be it any more, if he told."

"Looks like he's about the most important thing."

"Next to the tusk."

The parade turned a corner, the whistle blew again, and the music stopped. Down the street, another whistle shrilled, and the whole business began again as a company of kilted bagpipers swung into view.

"Parade competition down at the park," said the man with the glasses. "They'll be coming by for hours. Let's go in and have a drink."

"On us?" said Finnerty.

"Who else?"

"Wait," said Paul, "this should be interesting."

An automobile had just come from the north side of the river, and its driver honked irritably at the marchers, who blocked his way. The horn and the bagpipes squalled at one another until the last rank of marchers had turned down the side street. Paul recognized the driver too late to get out of sight. Shepherd looked at him with puzzlement and mild censure, waved vaguely, and drove on. Peering through the back window were the small eyes of Fred Berringer.

Paul refused to attach any importance to the incident. He sat down in the booth with the short, heavy man, while Finnerty went after more drinks.

"How's your son?" said Paul.

"Son, Doctor? Oh, oh, of course—my son. You said you were going to talk to Matheson about him, didn't you? What did the good Matheson say?"

"I haven't seen him yet. I've been meaning to, but the opportunity hasn't come up."

The man nodded. "Matheson, Matheson—beneath that cold exterior, there beats a heart of ice. Well, it's just as well. There's no need to talk to him now. My boy's all set."

"Oh, really? I'm glad to hear that."

"Yes, he hanged himself this morning in the kitchen."

"Lord!"

"Yes, I told him what you said yesterday, and it was so discouraging that he just gave up. It's the best way. There *are* too many of us. Upps! You're spilling your drink!"

"What's going on here?" said Finnerty.

"I was just telling the Doctor here that my son couldn't find any good reason for being alive, so he quit it this morning—with an ironing cord."

Paul covered his eyes. "Jesus, oh Jesus I'm sorry."

The man looked up at Finnerty with a mixture of bewilderment and exasperation. "Now, hell, why'd I have to go and do that? Have a drink, Doctor, and pull yourself together. I haven't got a son, never had one." He shook Paul's arm. "Hear me? It's a lot of crap."

"Then why don't I bust your stupid head open?" said Paul, half standing in the booth.

"Because you're wedged in too tightly," said Finnerty, pushing him back down. He set the drinks before them.

"Sorry," said the man to Paul. "I just wanted to see how one of those superbrains worked. What's your I.Q., Doctor?"

"It's a matter of record. Why don't you go look it up?" It was a matter of record. Everyone's I.Q., as measured by the National Standard General Classification Test, was on public record—in Ilium, at the police station. "Go on," he said acidly, "experiment with me some more. I love it."

"You picked a bad specimen if you're out to find out what the rest of them across the river are like," said Finnerty. "This guy's an odd one."

"You're an engineer too."

"Until I quit."

The man looked surprised. "You know, this is really very illuminating, if you're not kidding me. There are malcontents, eh?"

"Two that we know of," said Finnerty.

"Well, you know, in a way I wish I hadn't met you two. It's much more convenient to think of the opposition as a nice homogeneous, dead-wrong mass. Now I've got to muddy my thinking with exceptions."

"How have you got yourself typed," said Paul, "as an upstate Socrates?"

"The name is Lasher, the Reverend James J. Lasher, R-127 and SS-55. Chaplain, Reconstruction and Reclamation Corps."

"The first number's for Protestant minister. What's the second, that SS thing?" said Finnerty.

"Social scientist," said Lasher. "The 55 designates an anthropologist with a master's degree."

"And what does an anthropologist do these days?" said Paul.

"Same thing a supernumerary minister does—becomes a public charge, a bore, or possibly a rum-dum, or a bureaucrat." He looked back and forth between Paul and Finnerty. "You, I know, Doctor Proteus. And you?"

"Finnerty, Edward Francis Finnerty, Ph.D., one-time EC-002."

"There's a collector's item—a double-o-two number!" said Lasher. "I've known several single-o men, but never a double-o. I guess you're the highest classification I ever had friendly words with. If the Pope set up shop in this country, he'd be only one notch up—in the R-numbers of course. He'd be an

R-001. I heard somewhere that the number was being held for him, over the objections of Episcopal bishops who want R-001 themselves. Delicate business."

"They could give him a negative number," said Paul.

"That the Episcopalians would go along with. My glass is empty."

"What was this business about the people across the river being the opposition?" said Paul. "You think they do the Devil's work, do you?"

"That's pretty strong. I will say you've shown up what thin stuff clergymen were peddling, most of them. When I had a congregation before the war, I used to tell them that the life of their spirit in relation to God was the biggest thing in their lives, and that their part in the economy was nothing by comparison. Now, you people have engineered them out of their part in the economy, in the market place, and they're finding out—most of them—that what's left is just about zero. A good bit short of enough, anyway. My glass is empty."

Lasher sighed. "What do you expect?" he said. "For generations they've been built up to worship competition and the market, productivity and economic usefulness, and the envy of their fellow men—and boom! it's all yanked out from under them. They can't participate, can't be useful any more. Their whole culture's has been shot to hell. My glass is empty."

"I just had it filled again," said Finnerty.

"Oh, so you did." Lasher sipped thoughtfully. "These displaced people need something, and the clergy can't give it to them—or it's impossible for them to take what the clergy offers. The clergy says it's enough, and so does the Bible. The people say it isn't enough, and I suspect they're right."

"If they were so fond of the old system, how come they were so cantankerous about their jobs when they had them?" said Paul.

"Oh, this business we've got now—it's been going on for a long time now, not just since the last war. Maybe the actual jobs weren't being taken from the people, but the sense of participation, the sense of importance was. Go to the library sometime and take a look at magazines and newspapers clear back as far as World War II. Even then there was a lot of talk about know-how winning the war of production—*know-how*, not people, not the *mediocre* people running most of the machines. And the hell of it was that it was pretty much true. Even then, half the people or more didn't understand much about the machines they worked at or the things they were making. They were participating in the economy all right, but not in a way that was very satisfying to the ego. And then there was all this let's-not-shoot-Father-Christmas advertising."

"How's that?" said Paul.

"You know—those ads about the American system, meaning managers and engineers, that made America great. When you finished one, you'd think the managers and engineers had given America everything: forests, rivers, minerals, mountains, oil—the works.

"Strange business," said Lasher. "This crusading spirit of the managers and engineers, the idea of designing and manufacturing and distributing being sort of a holy war: all that folklore was cooked up by public relations and advertising men hired by managers and engineers to make big business popular in the old days, which it certainly wasn't in the beginning. Now, the engineers and managers believe with all their hearts the glorious things their forebears hired people to say about them. Yesterday's snow job becomes today's sermon."

"Well," said Paul, "you'll have to admit they did some pretty wonderful things during the war."

"Of course!" said Lasher. "What they did for the war effort really was something like crusading; but"—he shrugged—"so was what everybody else did for the war effort. Everybody behaved wonderfully. Even I."

"You keep giving the managers and engineers a bad time," said Paul. "What about the scientists? It seems to me that—"

"Outside the discussion," said Lasher impatiently. "They simply add to knowledge. It isn't knowledge that's making trouble, but the uses it's put to."

Finnerty shook his head admiringly. "So what's the answer right now?"

"That is a frightening question," said Lasher, "and also my favorite rationalization for drinking. This is my last drink, incidentally; I don't like being drunk. I drink because I'm scared—just a little scared, so I don't have to drink much. Things, gentlemen, are ripe for a phony Messiah, and when he comes, it's sure to be a bloody business."

"Messiah?"

"Sooner or later someone's going to catch the imagination of these people with some new magic. At the bottom of it will be a promise of regaining the feeling of participation, the feeling of being needed on earth—hell, *dignity*. The police are bright enough to look for people like that, and lock them up under the antisabotage laws. But sooner or later someone's going to keep out of their sight long enough to organize a following."

Paul had been watching his expression closely, and decided that, far from being in horror of the impending uprising, Lasher was rather taken by the idea. "And then what?" said Paul. He picked up his glass and rattled the ice cubes against his teeth. He'd finished his second drink and wanted another.

Lasher shrugged. "Oh, hell—prophecy's a thankless business, and history has a way of showing us what, in retrospect, are very logical solutions to awful messes."

"Prophesy anyway," said Finnerty.

"Well—I think it's a grave mistake to put on public record everyone's I.Q. I think the first thing the revolutionaries would want to do is knock off everybody with an I.Q. over 110, say. If I were on your side of the river, I'd have the I.Q. books closed and the bridges mined."

"Then the 100's would go after the 110's, the 90's after the 100's, and so on," said Finnerty.

"Maybe. Something like that. Things are certainly set up for a class war based on conveniently established lines of demarkation. And I must say that the basic assumption of the present setup is a grade-A incitement to violence: the smarter you are, the better you are. Used to be that the richer you were, the better you were. Either one is, you'll admit, pretty tough for the have-not's to take. The criterion of brains is better than the one of money, but"—he held his thumb and forefinger about a sixteenth of an inch apart—"about *that* much better."

"It's about as rigid a hierarchy as you can get," said Finnerty. "How's somebody going to up his I.Q.?"

"Exactly," said Lasher. "And it's built on more than just

brain power—it's built on special kinds of brain power. Not only must a person be bright, he must be bright in certain approved, useful directions: basically, management or engineering."

"Or marry someone who's bright," said Finnerty.

"Sex can still batter down all sorts of social structures—you're right," Lasher agreed.

"Big tits will get you in anywhere," said Finnerty.

"Well, it's comforting to know that something hasn't changed in centuries, isn't it?" Lasher smiled.

There was a mild commotion at the bar, and Lasher leaned out of the booth to see what was going on. "Hey," he called, "Luke Lubbock—come over here."

Luke, the serious old man who had borne the elephant tusk at the head of the parade, came over from the bar, gulping his beer as he came, and looking nervously at the clock. He was perspiring and short of breath, like a man who'd been running. He had a large parcel wrapped in brown paper under his arm.

Paul welcomed the opportunity to study Luke's magnificent costume more closely. Like a stage set, it was designed to impress at a distance. Nearness showed that the splendor was a fraud of cheap cloth, colored glass, and radiator paint. At his waist was a jeweled poniard, basically plywood, with an owl on its hilt. Counterfeit rubies as big as robin's eggs, mounted in golden sunbursts, were hung at random on the front of his lavender blouse. About the cuffs of his blouse and jade-green pantaloons were circlets of tiny bells, and—again—perched at the upturned tips of his golden slippers were a pair of miniature owls.

"Luke, you look wonderful," said Lasher.

Luke's eyes flashed agreement, but he was an important man, in too much of a hurry to respond to flattery. "It's too much, too much," he said. "Now I got to change so's I can march with the Parmesans. They're waiting up the street, and I got to change, and some damn fool's locked hisself in the can, so I got no place to change." He looked around quickly. "Would you let me do it in the booth, and kind of screen me?"

"You bet," said Finnerty.

They let Luke squirm into the shadows of the booth, and Paul found himself keeping a playful, leering lookout for women.

Muttering, Luke started to disrobe. He dropped his belt and poniard on the table, where they struck with an impressive thump. The glittering heap grew and grew, until, from a distance, it might have looked good enough to be at the end of a rainbow.

Paul relaxed his vigil for an instant to glance at Luke, and he was shocked at the transformation. The man was in his underwear now, ragged and drab, and none-too-clean. And Luke had somehow shrunk and saddened and was knobbed and scarred and scrawny. He was subdued now, talking not at all, and meeting no one's eyes. Almost desperately, hungrily, he ripped open the brown parcel and took from it a pale-blue uniform, encrusted with gold embroidery and piped in scarlet. He pulled on the trousers and black boots, and the jacket with its ponderous epaulets. Luke was growing again, getting his color back, and as he strapped on his saber he was talkative again—important and strong. He bundled up his other costume in the brown paper, left the parcel with the bartender, and rushed into the street, waving naked steel.

A whistle blew, and the Parmesans fell in behind him, to be led to glorious exploits in a dreamworld those on the sidewalk could only speculate about.

"Harmless magic: good, old-fashioned bunkum," laughed Lasher. "Talk about your hierarchies: Luke, with an I.Q. of about 80, has titles that'd make Charlemagne sound like a cook's helper. But that sort of business wears thin pretty quick for everybody but a few Luke Lubbocks. The lodge turnover is terrific." He stood. "No more for me, thanks." He rapped on the table. "But someday, gentlemen, someone is going to give them something to sink their teeth in—probably you, and maybe me."

"We'll give them something to sink their teeth in?" said Paul. He noticed he was getting somewhat thick of speech.

"You'll be what they'll get to sink their teeth in." Lasher laid his hand on Paul's shoulder. "One more thing: I want to be sure you understand that men really *do* worry about what there is for their sons to live for; and some sons *do* hang themselves."

"And this is as old as life itself," said Paul.

"Well?" said Lasher.

"Well, it's too bad. I'm certainly not overjoyed about it."

"You figure to be the new Messiah?" said Finnerty.

"Sometimes I think I'd like to be—if only in self-defense. Also, it'd be a swell way to get rich. Trouble is, I can be sold or unsold on anything too easily. I enjoy being talked into something. Pretty shaky outlook for a Messiah. Besides, who ever heard of a short, fat, middle-aged Messiah with bad eyesight? And I haven't got that common touch. Frankly, the masses give me a pain in the tail, and I guess I show it." He made clucking sounds with his tongue. "I'm going to get myself a uniform, so I'll know what I think and stand for."

"Or two—like Luke Lubbock," said Paul.

"All right, two. But that's the absolute maximum any self-respecting human being ought to permit himself." He sipped from Paul's highball. "Well, good night."

"Have another," said Finnerty.

"No—I mean it. I don't like getting tight."

"All right. I want to see you again, anyway. Where can I find you?"

"Here, most likely." He wrote an address on a paper napkin. "Or try here." He looked closely at Finnerty. "You know, wash your face, and you might do real well as a Messiah."

Finnerty looked startled, and didn't laugh.

Lasher picked up a hard-boiled egg at the bar, crackled its shell by rolling it along the keyboard of the player piano, and walked out into the evening.

"Magnificent, wasn't he?" said Finnerty raptly. His gaze returned reluctantly from the door to Paul. Paul saw his eyes take on a glaze of ennui, of letdown, and he knew that Finnerty had found a new friend who made Paul look very pale indeed.

"Your orders, gentlemen?" said a short, dark waitress, with a hard, trim figure. She looked at the television screen while waiting for them to reply. The sound never seemed to be turned on, only the video. An anxious young man in a long sports coat jiggled up and down on the screen, and blew through a saxophone.

The saloon was filling up, and many of the flamboyantly and enigmatically costumed marchers had come in for refreshment, giving the place an atmosphere of international unrest and intrigue.

One small young man in mufti, with immensely wise and large eyes, leaned back against the table in Paul's and Ed's booth and watched the television screen with what seemed to be more than routine interest. He turned casually to Paul. "What you think he's playing?"

"Beg pardon?"

"The guy on television—what's the name of the song?"

"I can't hear it."

"I know," he said impatiently, "that's the *point.* Guess from just seeing."

Paul frowned at the screen for a moment, tried to jiggle as the saxophonist jiggled, and to fit a song to the rhythm. Suddenly his mind clicked, and the tune was flowing in his imagination as surely as though the sound had been turned on. " 'Rosebud.' The song is 'Rosebud,' " said Paul.

The young man smiled quietly. " 'Rosebud,' eh? Just for laughs, want to put a little money on it? I'll say it's—um, ah, well—'Paradise Moon,' maybe."

"How much?"

The young man studied Paul's jacket, and then, with slight surprise, his expensive trousers and shoes. "Ten?"

"Ten, by God. 'Rosebud'!"

"What's he say it is, Alfy?" called the bartender.

"He says 'Rosebud,' I say 'Paradise Moon.' Turn her on."

The last notes of "Paradise Moon" blared from the loudspeaker, the saxophonist grimaced and backed off the screen. The bartender winked admiringly at Alfy and turned down the volume again.

Paul handed Alfy the ten. "Congratulations."

Alfy sat down in the booth without being invited. He looked at the screen, blew smoke through his nose, and closed his eyes reflectively. "What you figure they're playing now?"

Paul decided to buckle down and get his money back. He looked hard at the screen, and took his time. The whole orchestra was in view now, and, once he thought he'd picked up the thread of a melody, he looked from musician to musician for confirmation. "An old, old one," he said. " 'Stardust.' "

"For ten it's 'Stardust'?"

"For ten."

"What is it, Alfy?" called the bartender.

Alfy jerked a thumb at Paul. "This kid's fair. He says 'Stardust,' and I can see where he gets it. He's right about the oldy, but he picked the wrong one. 'Mood Indigo' is the name." He looked sympathetically at Paul. "It's a tough one all right." He snapped his fingers.

The bartender twisted the volume knob, and "Mood Indigo" filled the air.

"Wonderful!" said Paul, and he turned to Finnerty for confirmation. Finnerty was lost in his own thoughts, and his lips moved slightly, as though in an imaginary conversation. Despite the noise and excitement of Alfy's performances, he apparently hadn't noticed them.

"A knack," said Alfy modestly. "Like anything else: you know, keep at it long enough, and you surprise yourself. Couldn't tell you—in real detail, you know—how I did it. Gets to be another sense—you kind of *feel* it."

The bartender, the waitress, and several other bystanders had fallen silent in order to hear Alfy's words.

"Oh, there's some tricks," said Alfy. "Watch the bass drum quiver instead of what the guy's doing with the traps. Get the basic beat that way. Lot of people watch the traps, see, and the guy may be going off on a tangent. Things like that you can learn. And, you gotta know instruments—how they make a high note, how they make a low one. But that ain't enough." His voice took on a respectful, almost reverent tone. "It's kind of spooky what else it takes."

"He does classical stuff too," said the bartender eagerly. "Oughta see him with the Boston Pops on Sunday nights."

Alfy ground out his cigarette impatiently. "Yeah, yeah—classics," he said, frowning, mercilessly airing his inner doubts about himself. "Yeah, I was lucky last Sunday when you saw me. But I ain't got the repertory for that. I'm over my head, and you can't pick up in the middle of the classics. And you play hell building a repertory of that stuff, when you gotta wait sometimes a year, two years, to see the thing twice." He rubbed his eyes, as though remembering hours of concentration before a video screen. "You gotta see 'em plugged and plugged and plugged. And all the time new ones—and lots of 'em steals from oldies."

"Tough, eh?" said Paul.

Alfy raised his eyebrows. "Yeah, it's tough—like anything else. Tough to be the best."

"There's punks trying to break in, but they can't touch Alfy," said the bartender.

"They're good in their specialties—usually the quick killings," said Alfy. "You know, the minute a new number's out, they try and cash in on it before everybody's seen it. But none of 'em's making a living at it, I'll tell you that. Got no repertory, and that's what it takes to keep going day in, day out."

"This is your living?" said Paul. He hadn't succeeded in keeping the sense of whimsey out of his voice, and quick resentment was all about him.

"Yeah," said Alfy coldly, "this is my living. A buck here, ten cents there—"

"Twenty bucks here," said Paul. This seemed to soften most of the expressions.

The bartender was anxious to maintain a friendly atmosphere. "Alfy started out as a pool shark, eh, Alfy?" he said briskly.

"Yeah. But the field's crowded. Maybe room for ten, twenty guys going at it steady. There must of been a couple of hundred of us trying to make a go of it with pool. The Army and the Reeks and Wrecks were on my tail, so I started looking around for something else. Funny, without thinking much about it, I'd been doing this since I was a kid. It's what I should of gone into right from the first. Reeks and Wrecks," he said contemptuously, apparently recalling how close he came to being drafted into the R and R Corps. "Army!" He spat.

A couple of soldiers and a large number of men from the Reeks and Wrecks heard him insult their organizations, and they did nothing but nod, sharing his contempt.

Alfy looked at the screen. "'Baby, Dear Baby, Come Home With Me Now,'" he said. "A newy." He hurried to the bar to study the movements of the band more closely. The bartender rested his hand on the volume knob and watched anxiously for Alfy's signals. Alfy would raise an eyebrow, and the bartender would turn up the volume. It would be on for a few seconds, Alfy would nod, and off it would go again.

"What'll it be, boys?" said the waitress.

"Hmmm?" said Paul, still fascinated by Alfy. "Oh—bourbon

and water." He was experimenting with his eyes, and finding that they didn't work too well.

"Irish and water," said Finnerty. "Hungry?"

"Yeah—give us a couple of hard-boiled eggs, please." Paul felt wonderful, at one with the saloon, and, by extension, with all humanity and the universe. He felt witty, and on the verge of a splendid discovery. Then he remembered. "Holy God! Anita!"

"Where?"

"At home—waiting." Unsteadily, mumbling cheery greetings to all he passed, Paul got to the telephone booth, which reeked with a previous occupant's cigar smoke. He called home.

"Look, Anita—I won't be home for supper. Finnerty and I got to talking, and—"

"It's all right, dear. Shepherd told me not to wait."

"Shepherd?"

"Yes—he saw you down there, and told me you didn't look like a man on his way home."

"When did you see him?"

"He's here now. He came to apologize for last night. Everything's all ironed out, and we're having a very nice time."

"Oh? You accepted his apology?"

"Let's say we arrived at an understanding. He's worried that you'll turn in a bad report on him to Kroner, and I did everything I could to make him think you were considering it seriously."

"Oh, now listen, I'm not going to turn in any bad report on that—"

"It's the way *he* plays. Fight fire with fire. I got him to agree not to spread any more tales about you. Aren't you proud of me?"

"Yeah, sure."

"Now you've got to keep working on him, keep him worried."

"Uh-huh."

"Now, you just go ahead and have a good time. It does you good to get away now and then."

"Yes'm."

"And please try to get Finnerty to move out."

"Yes'm."

"Do you think I nag you?"

"No'm."

"Paul! Would you like it if I didn't take an interest?"

"No'm."

"All right. You just go ahead and get drunk. It'll do you good. Eat something, though. I love you."

"I love *you*." He hung up, and turned to face the world through the steamy window of the phone booth. Along with his feeling of dizziness was a feeling of newness—the feeling of fresh, strong identity growing within him. It was a generalized love—particularly for the little people, the common people, God bless them. All his life they had been hidden from him by the walls of his ivory tower. Now, this night, he had come among them, shared their hopes and disappointments, understood their yearnings, discovered the beauty of their simplicities and their earthy values. This was *real*, this side of the river, and Paul loved these common people, and wanted to help, and let them know they were loved and understood, and he wanted them to love him too.

When he got back to the booth, two young women were sitting with Finnerty, and Paul loved them instantly.

"Paul—I'd like you to meet my cousin Agnes from Detroit," said Finnerty. He rested his hand on the knee of a fat and determinedly cheerful redhead sitting next to him. "And this," he said, pointing across the table at a tall, homely brunette, "is *your* cousin Agnes."

"How do you do, Agnes and Agnes."

"Are you as crazy as he is?" said the brunette suspiciously. "If you are, I'm going home."

"Good, clean, fun-loving American type, Paul is," said Finnerty.

"Tell me about yourself," said Paul expansively.

"My name isn't Agnes, it's Barbara," said the brunette. "And she's Martha."

"What'll it be?" said the waitress.

"Double Scotch and water," said Martha.

"Same," said Barbara.

"That'll be four dollars for the ladies' drinks," said the waitress.

Paul handed her a five.

"Holy smokes!" said Barbara, staring at the identification card in Paul's billfold. "This guy's an engineer!"

"You from *across* the river?" said Martha to Finnerty.

"Deserters."

Both girls moved away, and with their backs against the wall of the booth, they looked at Paul and Finnerty with puzzlement. "I'll be go to hell," said Martha at last. "What you want to talk about? I had algebra in high school."

"We're just plain folks," said Paul.

"What'll it be?" said the waitress.

"Scotch, double," said Martha.

"Same," said Barbara.

"Come here, damn it," said Finnerty, pulling Martha to his side again.

Barbara still kept her distance from Paul and looked at him distastefully. "What are you doing over here—having a good laugh at the dumb bunnies?"

"I like it over here," said Paul earnestly.

"You're making fun of me."

"Honest, I'm not at all. Did I say anything that sounded like I was?"

"You're thinking it," she said.

"That'll be four dollars for the ladies' drinks," said the waitress.

Paul paid again. He didn't know what to say next to Barbara. He didn't want to make a pass at her. He simply wanted her to be friendly and companionable, and to see that he wasn't a stuffed shirt at all. Far from it.

"They don't castrate you when they give you an engineering degree," Finnerty was saying to Martha.

"They might as well," said Martha. "Some of the kids that come over from across the river—you'd think they were."

"After our time," said Finnerty. "I meant they didn't *use* to."

To build up more of an atmosphere of intimacy, rapport, Paul casually picked up one of the shot-glasses before Barbara and sipped at it. It then dawned on him that the shots of expensive Scotch, which had been arriving as though by bucket brigade, were no more than brown water. "Smooth," he said.

"So what am I supposed to do, have a nervous breakdown?" said Barbara. "Let me out."

"No, please, that's all right. Just talk to me is all. I understand."

"What'll it be?" said the waitress.

"Scotch, double, with water," said Paul.

"Trying to make me feel bad?"

"I want you to feel good. If you need money, I want to help." He meant it with all his heart.

"Suit yourself, plunger," said Barbara. She looked restlessly about the room.

Paul's eyelids grew heavier and heavier and heavier as he tried to think of the phrase that would break the ice with Barbara. He folded his arms on the table top and, for just an instant's rest, he laid his head on them.

When he opened his eyes again, Finnerty was shaking him, and Barbara and Martha had gone. Finnerty helped him out onto the sidewalk for air.

The out-of-doors was a nightmare of light and noise, and Paul could see that some sort of torchlight parade was under way. He burst into a cheer as he recognized Luke Lubbock, who was being borne by in a sedan chair.

When Finnerty had established him back in the booth, a speech, the nugget of the whole evening's nebulous impressions, composed itself in Paul's mind, took on form and polish inspirationally, with no conscious effort on his part. He had only to deliver it to make himself the new Messiah and Ilium the new Eden. The first line was at his lips, tearing at them to be set free.

Paul struggled to stand on the bench, and from there he managed to step to the stable. He held his hands over his head for attention.

"Friends, my friends!" he cried. "We must meet in the middle of the bridge!" The frail table suddenly lurched beneath him. He heard the splitting of wood, cheers, and again—darkness.

The next voice was the bartender's. "Come on—closing time. Gotta lock up," said the bartender gently.

Paul sat up and groaned. His mouth was dry, and his head ached. The table was gone from the booth, and there were only cracked plaster and boltheads to show where it had once been moored to the wall.

The saloon seemed deserted, but the air was filled with a painful clangor. Paul peered out of the booth and saw a man mopping the floor. Finnerty sat at the player piano, savagely improvising on the brassy, dissonant antique.

Paul shuffled over to the piano and laid his hand on Finnerty's shoulder. "Let's go home."

Finnerty continued to lash at the keys. "Staying!" he shouted above the music. "Go home!"

"Where you going to stay?"

Then Paul saw Lasher, who sat unobtrusively in the shadows, leaning against the wall in a chair. Lasher tapped his thick chest. "With me," he said with his lips.

Finnerty shook off Paul's hand and wouldn't answer.

"O.K.," said Paul fuzzily. "So long."

He stumbled into the street and found his car. He paused for a moment to listen to Finnerty's hellish music echoing from the façades of the sleeping town. The bartender stood respectfully at a distance from the frenzied pianist, afraid to interrupt.

Chapter X

AFTER THE NIGHT with Finnerty and Lasher, and with the good little people, Alfy, Luke Lubbock, the bartender, and Martha and Barbara, Doctor Paul Proteus slept until late in the afternoon. When he awoke, Anita was out of the house, and with a dry mouth, burning eyes, and a stomach that felt as though it were stuffed with cat fur, he went to his responsible post in the Ilium Works.

The eyes of Doctor Katharine Finch, his secretary, were bloodshot for another reason, a reason so all-consuming that she took little note of the condition of Paul.

"Doctor Kroner called," she said mechanically.

"Oh? He wants me to call back?"

"Doctor Shepherd took the message."

"He did, eh? Anything else?"

"The police?"

"Police? What did they want?"

"Doctor Shepherd took the message."

"All right." Everything seemed hot and bright and soporific. He sat on the edge of her desk, and rested. "Get Dog-Eat-Dog on the phone."

"That won't be necessary. He's in your office now."

Wondering bleakly what grievance or slight or infraction of rules Shepherd wanted to see him about, Paul pushed open his office door gingerly.

Shepherd sat at Paul's desk, absorbed in signing a stack of reports. He didn't look up. Briskly, his eyes still on the papers, he flicked on the intercom set. "Miss Finch—"

"Yessir."

"On this monthly security report: did Doctor Proteus tell you how he planned to handle Finnerty's admission without escort yesterday?"

"I planned to keep my big mouth shut about it," said Paul.

Shepherd looked up with seeming pleasure and surprise. "Well, speak of the Devil." He made no move to get out of Paul's chair. "Say," he said with hearty camaraderie, "I guess you were really hung over, eh, boy? Should have taken the whole day off. I know my way around well enough to fill in for you."

"Thanks."

"No trouble. There really isn't a heck of a lot to the job."

"I expected Katharine to watch over things for me, and call for help if she needed it."

"You know what Kroner would think of *that*. It doesn't take a whole lot more trouble to do things right, Paul."

"Do you mind telling me what Kroner wanted?"

"Oh, yes—he wants to see you tonight instead of Thursday. He's got to be in Washington tomorrow night, and for the rest of the week."

"Wonderful. And what's the good news from the police?"

Shepherd laughed richly. "Some foul-up. They were all excited about a pistol they found down by the river. They claimed the serial numbers were for a gun checked out to you. I told them to check again—that no man who's bright enough to be manager of the Ilium Works is dumb enough to leave a pistol around loose."

"That's a nice tribute, Shep. Mind if I use my phone?"

Shepherd pushed the phone across the desk and went back to signing: "Lawson Shepherd, in absence of P. Proteus."

"Did you tell him I had a hangover?"

"Hell no, Paul. I covered up for you all right."

"What did you say was wrong?"

"Nerves."

"Great!" Katharine was getting Kroner's office on the line for Paul.

"Doctor Proteus in Ilium would like to speak to Doctor Kroner. He's returning Doctor Kroner's call," said Katharine.

It wasn't a day for judging proportions. Paul had been able to take the disturbances of Kroner, Shepherd, and the police with something bordering on apathy. Now, however, he found himself enraged by the ceremony of official telephone etiquette—time-consuming pomp and circumstance lovingly preserved by the rank-happy champions of efficiency.

"Is Doctor Proteus on?" said Kroner's secretary. "Doctor Kroner is in."

"Just a moment," said Katharine. "Doctor Proteus, Doctor Kroner is in and will speak to you."

"All right, I'm on."

"Doctor Proteus is on the line," said Katharine.

"Doctor Kroner, Doctor Proteus is on the line."

"Tell him to go ahead," said Kroner.

"Tell Doctor Proteus to go ahead," said Kroner's secretary.

"Doctor Proteus, please go ahead," said Katharine.

"This is Paul Proteus, Doctor Kroner. I'm returning your call." A little bell went "*tink-tink-tink*," letting him know his conversation was being recorded.

"Shepherd said you'd been having trouble with your nerves, my boy."

"Not quite right. A touch of some kind of virus."

"Lot of that floating around. Well, do you feel well enough to come over to my house tonight?"

"Love it. Is there anything I should bring—anything in particular you want to discuss?"

"Like Pittsburgh?" said Shepherd in a stage whisper.

"No, no, purely social, Paul—just good talk is all. We haven't had a good, friendly talk for a long while. Mom and I would just like to see you socialwise."

Paul thought back. He hadn't been invited to Kroner's socialwise for a year, since he'd been sized up for his last raise. "Sounds like fun. What time?"

"Eight, eight-thirty."

"And Anita's invited too?" It was a mistake. It slipped out without his thinking about it.

"Of course! You never go anywhere socially without her, do you?"

"Oh, no, sir."

"I should hope not." He laughed perfunctorily. "Well, goodbye."

"What did he say?" said Shepherd.

"He said you had no damn business signing those reports for me. He said Katharine Finch was to take off your name with ink-eradicator at once."

"Say, now just hold on," said Shepherd, standing.

Paul saw that all of the desk drawers were ajar. In the bottom drawer the neck of the empty whisky bottle was in plain view. He slammed each of the drawers shut in quick succession. When he came to the bottom one, he took out the bottle and held it out to Shepherd. "Here—want this? Might be valuable sometime. It's got my fingerprints all over it."

"Are you going to get me canned—is that it?" said Shepherd eagerly. "You want to make an issue of it in front of Kroner? Let's go. I'm ready any time. Let's see if you can make it stick."

"Get down where you belong. Go on. Clear out of this office, and don't come back unless I tell you to come back. Katharine!"

"Yes?"

"If Doctor Shepherd comes in this office again without permission, you're to shoot him."

Shepherd slammed the door, railed against Paul to Katharine, and left.

"Doctor Proteus, the police are on the phone," said Katharine.

Paul stalked out of the office and went home.

It was the maid's day off, and Paul found Anita in the kitchen, the picture, minus children, of domesticity.

The kitchen was, in a manner of speaking, what Anita had given of herself to the world. In planning it, she had experienced all the anguish and hellfire of creativity—tortured by doubts, cursing her limitations, at once hungry for and fearful of the opinions of others. Now it was done and admired, and the verdict of the community was: Anita was *artistic*.

It was a large, airy room, larger than most living rooms. Rough-hewn rafters, taken from an antique barn, were held against the ceiling by concealed bolts fixed in the steel framing of the house. The walls were wainscoted in pine, aged by sandblasting, and given a soft yellow patina of linseed oil.

A huge fireplace and Dutch oven of fieldstone filled one wall. Over them hung a long muzzle-loading rifle, powder horn, and bullet pouch. On the mantel were candle molds, a coffee mill, an iron and trivet, and a rusty kettle. An iron cauldron, big enough to boil a missionary in, swung at the end of a long arm in the fireplace, and below it, like so many black offspring, were a cluster of small pots. A wooden butter churn held the door open, and clusters of Indian corn hung from the molding at aesthetic intervals. A colonial scythe stood in one corner, and two Boston rockers on a hooked rug faced the cold fireplace, where the unwatched pot never boiled.

Paul narrowed his eyes, excluding everything from his field of vision but the colonial tableau, and imagined that he and Anita had pushed this far into the upstate wilderness, with the nearest neighbor twenty-eight miles away. She was making soap, candles, and thick wool clothes for a hard winter ahead, and he, if they weren't to starve, had to mold bullets and go shoot a bear. Concentrating hard on the illusion, Paul was able to muster a feeling of positive gratitude for Anita's presence, to thank God for a woman at his side to help with the petrifying amount of work involved in merely surviving. As, in his imagination, he brought home a bear to Anita, and she cleaned it and salted it away, he felt a tremendous lift—the two of them winning by sinew and guts a mountain of strong, red meat from an inhospitable world. And he would mold more bullets, and she would make more candles and soap from the bear fat, until late at night, when Paul and Anita would tumble down together on a bundle of straw in the corner, dog-tired and sweaty, make love, and sleep hard until the brittle-cold dawn. . . .

"*Urdle-urdle-urdle*," went the automatic washing machine. "*Urdle-urdle-ur dull!*"

Reluctantly, Paul let his field of vision widen to include the other side of the room, where Anita sat on a ladder-back chair before the cherry breakfront that concealed the laundry console. The console had been rolled from the breakfront, whose façade of drawers and doors was one large piece, making the breakfront sort of a small garage for the laundry equipment. The doors of a corner cabinet were open, revealing a television screen, which Anita watched intently. A doctor was telling an old lady that her grandson would probably be paralyzed from the waist down for the rest of his life.

"*Urdle-urdle-urdle*," went the console. Anita paid no attention. "*Znick. Bazz-wap!*" Chimes sounded. Still Anita ignored it. "*Azzzzzzzzzzzzzz. Froomp!*" The top of the console popped open, and a basket of dry laundry burst from it like a great chrysanthemum, white, fragrant, and immaculate.

"Hello," said Paul.

Anita motioned for him to be silent, and wait until the program was over, which meant the commercial too. "All right," she said at last and turned down the volume. "Your blue suit is laid out on the bed."

"Oh? What for?"

"What do you mean, what for? For going over to Kroner's."

"How did you know that?"

"Lawson Shepherd called to tell me."

"Deuced nice of him."

"Nice of someone to tell me what's going on, since you won't."

"What else'd he say?"

"He supposed you and Finnerty must have had a wonderful time, judging from how terrible you looked this afternoon."

"He knows as much about it as I do."

Anita lit a cigarette, shook out the match with a flourish, and squinted through the smoke she let out through her nose. "Were there girls, Paul?"

"In a manner of speaking. Martha and Barbara. Don't ask me who had who."

"Had?"

"Sat with."

She hunched in the chair, looked out the window soberly, and kept her cigarette hot with quick, shallow puffs, and her eyes watered in the dramatic gusts from her nose. "You don't have to tell me about it, if you don't want to."

"I won't, because I can't remember." He started to laugh. "One was called Barbara, and the other was called Martha, and beyond that, as the saying goes, everything went black."

"Then you don't know what happened? I mean, anything could have happened?"

His smile withered. "I mean everything really went black, and nothing could have happened. I was clay curled up in a booth."

"And you remember nothing?"

"I remember a man named Alfy, who makes his living as a television shark, a man named Luke Lubbock, who can be whatever his clothes are, a minister who gets a kick out of seeing the world go to hell, and—"

"And Barbara and Martha."

"And Barbara and Martha. And parades—my God, parades."

"Feel better?"

"No. But you should, because I think Finnerty's found a new home and a new friend."

"Thank God for that. I want you to make it clear to Kroner tonight that he forced himself on our hospitality, that we were as upset by him as anyone was."

"That isn't quite true."

"Well then, keep it to yourself, if you like him so much."

She lifted the lid of the schoolmaster's desk, where she made out the daily menus and compared her stubs with the bank statements, and took from it three sheets of paper. "I know you think I'm silly, but it's worth a little trouble to do things right, Paul."

The papers contained some sort of an outline, with major divisions set off by Roman numerals, and with sub-sub-sub-sub-sub-divisions as small as (a). At random, and with his headache taking on new vitality, he chose item III., A., 1., a.: "Don't smoke. Kroner is trying to break the habit."

"Maybe it would help to read it aloud," said Anita.

"Maybe it'd be better if I read it alone, where there aren't any distractions."

"It took most of the afternoon."

"I expect it did. It's the most thorough job you've done yet. Thanks, darling, I appreciate it."

"I love you, Paul."

"I love *you*, Anita."

"Darling—about Martha and Barbara—"

"I promise you, I didn't touch them."

"I was going to ask, did anybody see you with them?"

"I guess they did, but nobody of any importance. Not Shepherd, certainly."

"If it ever got back to Kroner, I don't know what I'd do. He might laugh off the drinking, but the women—"

"I went to bed with Barbara," said Paul suddenly.

"I thought you did. That's your affair." She was tiring of the conversation, apparently, and she looked restively at the television screen.

"And Shepherd saw me coming downstairs with her."

"Paul!"

"Joke."

She put her hand over her heart. "Oh—thank the Lord."

" 'Summer Loves,' " said Paul, looking at the television screen judiciously.

"What's that?"

"The band—they're playing 'Summer Loves.'" He whistled a few bars.

"How can you tell, with the volume off?"

"Go ahead, turn it up."

Apathetically, she turned the knob, and "Summer Loves," as sweet and indigestible as honey cake, oozed into the air.

Humming along with the orchestra, Paul went up the steps to his bedroom, reading the outline as he went:

"IV., A., I. If Kroner asks you why you want Pittsburgh, say it is because you can be of greater service . . . a. Soft-pedal bigger house and raise and prestige."

Fuzzily, Paul was beginning to see that he had made an ass of himself in the eyes of those on both sides of the river. He remembered his cry of the night before: "We must meet in the middle of the bridge!" He decided that he would be about the only one interested in the expedition, the only one who didn't feel strongly about which bank he was on.

If his attempt to become the new Messiah had been successful, if the inhabitants of the north and south banks had met in the middle of the bridge with Paul between them, he wouldn't have had the slightest idea of what to do next. He knew with all his heart that the human situation was a frightful botch, but it was such a logical, intelligently arrived-at botch that he couldn't see how history could possibly have led anywhere else.

Paul did a complicated sum in his mind—his savings account plus his securities plus his house plus his cars—and wondered if he didn't have enough to enable him simply to quit, to stop being the instrument of any set of beliefs or any whim of history that might raise hell with somebody's life. To live in a house by the side of a road. . . .

Chapter XI

THE SHAH OF BRATPUHR, looking as tiny and elegant as a snuffbox in one end of the vast cavern, handed the *Sumklish* bottle back to Khashdrahr Miasma. He sneezed, having left the heat of summer above a moment before, and the sound chattered along the walls to die whispering in bat roosts deep in Carlsbad Caverns.

Doctor Ewing J. Halyard was making his thirty-seventh pilgrimage to the subterranean jungle of steel, wire, and glass that filled the chamber in which they stood, and thirty larger ones beyond. This wonder was a regular stop on the tours Halyard conducted for a bizarre variety of foreign potentates, whose common denominator was that their people represented untapped markets for America's stupendous industrial output.

A rubber-wheeled electric car came to a stop by the elevator, where the Shah's party stood, and an Army major, armed with a pistol, dismounted and examined their credentials slowly, thoroughly.

"Couldn't we speed this up a little, Major?" said Halyard. "We don't want to miss the ceremony."

"Perhaps," said the major. "But, as officer of the day, I'm responsible for nine billion dollars' worth of government property, and if something should happen to it somebody might be rather annoyed with me. The ceremony has been delayed, anyway, so you won't miss anything. The President hasn't showed up yet."

The major was satisfied at last, and the party boarded the open vehicle.

"*Siki?*" said the Shah.

"This is EPICAC XIV," said Halyard. "It's an electronic computing machine—a brain, if you like. This chamber alone, the smallest of the thirty-one used, contains enough wire to reach from here to the moon four times. There are more vacuum tubes in the entire instrument than there were vacuum tubes in the State of New York before World War II." He had recited these figures so often that he had no need for the descriptive pamphlet that was passed out to visitors.

Khashdrahr told the Shah.

The Shah thought it over, snickered shyly, and Khashdrahr joined him in the quiet, Oriental merriment.

"Shah said," said Khashdrahr, "people in his land sleep with smart women and make good brains cheap. Save enough wire to go to moon a thousand times."

Halyard chuckled appreciatively, as he was paid to do, wiped aside the tears engendered by his ulcer, and explained that cheap and easy brains were what was wrong with the world in the bad old days, and that EPICAC XIV could consider simultaneously hundreds or even thousands of sides of a question utterly fairly, that EPICAC XIV was wholly free of reason-muddying emotions, that EPICAC XIV never forgot anything—that, in short, EPICAC XIV was dead right about everything. And Halyard added in his mind that the procedure described by the Shah had been tried about a trillion times, and had yet to produce a brain that could be relied upon to do the right thing once out of a hundred opportunities.

They were passing the oldest section of the computer now, what had been the whole of EPICAC I, but what was now little more than an appendix or tonsil of EPICAC XIV. Yet, EPICAC I had been intelligent enough, dispassionate enough, retentive enough to convince men that he, rather than they, had better do the planning for the war that was approaching with stupifying certainty. The ancient phrase used by generals testifying before appropriation committees, "all things considered," was given some validity by the ruminations of EPICAC I, more validity by EPICAC II, and so on, through the lengthening series. EPICAC could consider the merits of high-explosive bombs as opposed to atomic weapons for tactical support, and keep in mind at the same time the availability of explosives as opposed to fissionable materials, the spacing of enemy foxholes, the labor situation in the respective processing industries, the probable mortality of planes in the face of enemy antiaircraft technology, and on and on, if it seemed at all important, to the number of cigarettes and Cocoanut Mound Bars and Silver Stars required to support a high-morale air force. Given the facts by human beings, the war-born EPICAC series had offered the highly informed guidance that the reasonable, truth-loving, brilliant, and highly trained core of American genius could have delivered had they had inspired leadership, boundless resources, and two thousand years.

Through the war, and through the postwar years to the present, EPICAC's nervous system had been extended outward through Carlsbad Caverns—intelligence bought by the foot and pound and kilowatt. With each addition, a new, unique individual had been born, and now Halyard, the Shah, and Khashdrahr were arriving at the bunting-covered platform, where the President of the United States of America, Jonathan Lynn, would dedicate to a happier, more efficient tomorrow, EPICAC XIV.

The trio sat down on folding chairs and waited quietly with the rest of the distinguished company. Whenever there was a break in the group's whispering, EPICAC's hummings and clickings could be heard—the sounds attendant to the flow of electrons, now augmenting one another, now blocking, shuttling through a maze of electromagnetic crises to a condition that was translatable from electrical qualities and quantities to a high grade of truth.

EPICAC XIV, though undedicated, was already at work, deciding how many refrigerators, how many lamps, how many turbine-generators, how many hub caps, how many dinner plates, how many door knobs, how many rubber heels, how many television sets, how many pinochle decks—how many everything America and her customers could have and how much they would cost. And it was EPICAC XIV who would decide for the coming years how many engineers and managers and research men and civil servants, and of what skills, would be needed in order to deliver the goods; and what I.Q. and aptitude levels would separate the useful men from the useless ones, and how many Reconstruction and Reclamation Corps men and how many soldiers could be supported at what pay level and where, and . . .

"Ladies and Gentlemen," said the television announcer, "the President of the United States."

The electric car pulled up to the platform, and President Jonathan Lynn, born Alfred Planck, stood and showed his white teeth and frank gray eyes, squared his broad shoulders, and ran his strong, tanned hands through his curly hair. The television cameras dollied and panned about him like curious, friendly dinosaurs, sniffing and peering. Lynn was boyish, tall, beautiful, and disarming, and, Halyard thought bitterly, he had gone directly from a three-hour television program to the White House.

"Is this man the spiritual leader of the American people?" asked Khashdrahr.

Halyard explained the separation of Church and State, and met, as he had expected to meet, with the Shah's usual disbelief and intimations that he, Halyard, hadn't understood the question at all.

The President, with an endearing, adolescent combination of brashness and shyness, and with the barest trace of a Western drawl, was now reading aloud a speech someone had written about EPICAC XIV. He made it clear that he wasn't any scientist, but just plain folks, standing here, humble before this great new wonder of the world, and that he was here because American plain folks had chosen him to represent them at occasions like this, and that, looking at this modern miracle, he was overcome with a feeling of deep reverence and humility and gratitude . . .

Halyard yawned, and was annoyed to think that Lynn, who had just read "order out of chaos" as "order out of koze," made three times as much money as he did. Lynn, or, as Halyard preferred to think of him, Planck, hadn't even finished high school, and Halyard had known smarter Irish setters. Yet, here the son-of-a-bitch was, elected to more than a hundred thousand bucks a year!

"You mean to say that this man governs without respect to the people's spiritual destinies?" whispered Khashdrahr.

"He has no religious duties, except very general ones, token ones," said Halyard, and then he started wondering just what the hell Lynn did do. EPICAC XIV and the National Industrial, Commercial, Communications, Foodstuffs, and Resources Board did all the planning, did all the heavy thinking. And the personnel machines saw to it that all governmental jobs of any consequence were filled by top-notch civil servants. The more Halyard thought about Lynn's fat pay check, the madder he got, because all the gorgeous dummy had to do was read whatever was handed to him on state occasions: to be suitably awed and reverent, as he said, for all the ordinary, stupid people who'd elected him to office, to run wisdom from somewhere else through that resonant voicebox and between those even, pearly choppers.

And Halyard suddenly realized that, just as religion and government had been split into disparate entities centuries before, now, thanks to the machines, politics and government lived side by side, but touched almost nowhere. He stared at President Jonathan Lynn and imagined with horror what the country must have been like when, as today, any damn fool little American boy might grow up to be President, but when the President had had to actually run the country!

President Lynn was explaining what EPICAC XIV would do for the millions of plain folks, and Khashdrahr was translating for the Shah. Lynn declared that EPICAC XIV was, in effect, the greatest individual in history, that the wisest man that had ever lived was to EPICAC XIV as a worm was to that wisest man.

For the first time the Shah of Bratpuhr seemed really impressed, even startled. He hadn't thought much of EPICAC XIV's physical size, but the comparison of the worm and the wise man struck home. He looked about himself apprehensively, as though the tubes and meters on all sides were watching every move.

The speech was over, and the applause was dying, and Doctor Halyard brought the Shah to meet the President, and the television cameras nuzzled about them.

"The President is now shaking hands with the Shah of Bratpuhr," said the announcer. "Perhaps the Shah will give us the fresh impressions of a visitor from another part of the world, from another way of life."

"*Allasan Khabou pillan*?" said the Shah uncertainly.

"He wonders if he might ask a question," said Khashdrahr.

"Sure, you bet," said the President engagingly. "If I don't know the the answers, I can get them for you."

Unexpectedly, the Shah turned his back to the President and walked alone, slowly, to a deserted part of the platform.

"Wha'd I do wrong?" said Lynn.

"Ssssh!" said Khashdrahr fiercely, and he placed himself, like a guard, between the puzzled crowd and the Shah.

The Shah dropped to his knees on the platform and raised

his hands over his head. The small, brown man suddenly seemed to fill the entire cavern with his mysterious, radiant dignity, alone there on the platform, communing with a presence no one else could sense.

"We seem to be witnessing some sort of religious rite," said the announcer.

"Can't you keep your big mouth shut for five seconds?" said Halyard.

"Quiet!" said Khashdrahr.

The Shah turned to a glowing bank of EPICAC's tubes and cried in a piping singsong voice:

"Allakahi baku billa,
Moumi a fella nam;
Serani assu tilla,
Touri serin a sam."

"The crazy bastard's talking to the machine," whispered Lynn.

"Ssssh!" said Halyard, strangely moved by the scene.

"*Siki?*" cried the Shah. He cocked his head, listening. "*Siki?*" The word echoed and died—lonely, lost.

"*Mmmmmm*," said EPICAC softly. "*Dit, dit. Mmmmm. Dit.*"

The Shah sighed and stood, and shook his head sadly, terribly let down. "*Nibo*," he murmured. "*Nibo.*"

"What's he say?" said the President.

"'*Nibo*'—'nothing.' He asked the machine a question, and the machine didn't answer," said Halyard. "*Nibo.*"

"Nuttiest thing I ever heard of," said the President. "You have to punch out the questions on that thingamajig, and the answers come out on tape from the whatchamacallits. You can't just talk to it." A doubt crossed his fine face. "I mean, you can't, can you?"

"No sir," said the chief engineer of the project. "As you say, not without the thingamajigs and whatchamacallits."

"What'd he say?" said Lynn, catching Khashdrahr's sleeve.

"An ancient riddle," said Khashdrahr, and it was plain that he didn't want to go on, that something sacred was involved. But he was also a polite man, and the inquiring eyes of the crowd demanded more of an explanation. "Our people believe," he said shyly, "that a great, all-wise god will come among us one day, and we shall know him, for he shall be able to answer the riddle, which EPICAC could not answer. When he comes," said Khashdrahr simply, "there will be no more suffering on earth."

"All-wise god, eh?" said Lynn. He licked his lips and patted down his unruly forelock. "How's the riddle go?"

Khashdrahr recited:

"Silver bells shall light my way,
And nine times nine maidens fill my day,
And mountain lakes will sink from sight,
And tigers' teeth will fill the night."

President Lynn squinted at the cavern roof thoughtfully. "Mmm. Silver bells, eh?" He shook his head. "That's a stinker, you know? A real stinker. I give up."

"I'm not surprised," said Khashdrahr. "I'm not surprised. I expect you do."

Halyard helped the Shah, who seemed to have been aged and exhausted by the emotional ordeal, into the electric car.

As they rode to the foot of the elevator, the Shah came back to life somewhat and curled his lip at the array of electronics about them. "*Baku!*" he said.

"That's a new one on me," said Halyard to Khashdrahr, feeling warmly toward the little interpreter, who had squared away Jonathan Lynn so beautifully. "What's *Baku?*"

"Little mud and straw figures made by the Surrasi, a small infidel tribe in the Shah's land."

"This looks like mud and straw to him?"

"He was using it in the broader sense, I think, of false god."

"Um," said Halyard. "Well, how are the Surrasi doing?"

"They all died of cholera last spring." He added after a moment, "Of course." He shrugged, as though to ask what else people like that could possibly expect. "*Baku.*"

Chapter XII

THE KRONER HOME, just outside Albany, was a Victorian mansion, perfectly restored and maintained down to the filigree along the eaves, and the iron spikes along the roof peak. The archprophet of efficiency, Kroner, preferred it to the gracile, wipe-clean-with-a-damp-cloth steel and glass machines almost all of the engineers and managers lived in. Though Kroner had never accounted for his having bought the place—beyond saying that he liked lots of room—it was so in keeping with him that no one gave the anachronism more than passing thought.

A portrait painter had sensed the rightness of the setting, with no clues other than Kroner's face. The painter had been commissioned to do portraits of all the district managers. He did them from photographs, since the managers were too busy—or prudently claimed to be—to sit. Intuitively, the painter had depicted Kroner in a red plush chair, with a massive wedding ring prominently displayed, and with a background of heavy velvet drapes.

The mansion was one more affirmation of Kroner's belief that nothing of value changed; that what was once true is always true; that truths were few and simple; and that a man needed no knowledge beyond these truths to deal wisely and justly with any problem whatsoever.

"Come in," rumbled Kroner gently, answering the door himself. He seemed to fill the whole house with his slow strength and rock-bound calm. He was as informal as he ever became, having replaced his double-breasted suit coat with a single-breasted one of a slightly lighter shade and with suede patches at the elbows. The coat, he explained to visitors, was something his wife had given him years ago, something which he'd only recently mustered nerve enough to wear.

"I love your house more every time I see it," said Anita.

"You must tell Janice that." Janice was Mrs. Kroner, who smiled sweetly from the living room. She was a fat repository of truisms, adages, and homilies, and was usually addressed by the young engineers and managers as "Mom."

Mom, Paul recalled, had never liked that Finnerty boy, who would never call her Mom nor confide in her. Once, after she'd prodded him to unburden himself and feel better, he'd rather testily told her that he'd already fled one mother. Paul she liked, because Paul, as a youngster, *had* confided in her now and then. He would never do it again, but his demeanor before her conveyed that his failure to confide recently wasn't due to revulsion, but to a lack of problems.

"Hello, Mom," said Paul.

"Hello, Mom," said Anita.

"You children take a load off your feet," said Mom. "Now just tell me all about yourselves."

"Well, we've redone the kitchen," said Anita.

Mom was thrilled, eager for details.

Kroner hung his huge head, as though listening intently to the small talk, or, more likely, Paul thought, counting away the seconds before it would be polite to separate the men and women—a custom of the house.

As Anita paused for breath, Kroner stood, beamed, and suggested that Paul come into his study to see the guns. It was the same gambit every time—the men were to see the guns. Years ago, Anita had made the mistake of saying she was interested in guns, too. Kroner had politely told her that his weren't the kind women liked.

Mom's response was always the same, too: "Oh guns—I hate them. I can't see why men want to go around shooting sweet little animals."

The fact was, Kroner never fired his guns. His pleasure seemed to be in owning and handling them. He also used them for props, to give an air of informality to his man-to-man talks. He announced raises and promotions, demotions and firings, and praised or warned, always in seemingly casual asides made while swabbing a bore.

Paul followed him into the dark-paneled study, and waited for him to choose his weapon from the gunrack that filled one wall. Kroner ran his index finger along the collection, like a stick along a picket fence. It had been a matter of speculation among Kroner's underlings as to whether there was any significance in the guns he chose for a particular discussion. For a while the rumor was current that shotguns were bad news, rifles were good news. But it hadn't withstood the test of time. Kroner finally chose a ten-gauge shotgun, broke open the breach, and squinted through the bore at a streetlight outside.

"Wouldn't dare shoot modern ammunition in this one," said Kroner. "Twist barrel—thing'd go all to pieces. But look at that inlay work, Paul."

"Beautiful. Priceless."

"Some man spent maybe two years on it. Time didn't mean anything in those days. The industrial dark ages, Paul."

"Yessir."

He selected a cleaning rod and lined up on his desk top a can of oil, a jar of grease, and several cloth patches. "Got to keep after a bore, or it'll pit on you just like that." He snapped his fingers. He oiled a patch, twisted it about the tip of the cleaning rod. "Especially in this climate."

"Yessir." Paul started to light a cigarette, and then remembered Anita's warning in the outline.

Kroner drove the cleaning rod downward. "Where's Ed Finnerty, by the way?"

"Don't know, sir."

"Police are looking for him."

"Really?"

Kroner slid the patch back and forth and didn't look at Paul. "Uh-huh. Now that he's out of a job, he's got to register with the police, and he hasn't."

"I left him downtown in Homestead last night."

"I know that. I thought maybe you knew where he went."

Kroner had a habit of saying he already knew what he'd just been told. Paul was sure the old man didn't really know anything about the night before. "I haven't any idea." He didn't want to make trouble for anyone. Let the police find out that Finnerty was with Lasher, if they could.

"Umm hmmm. See that pit right there?" He held the muzzle of the gun a few inches from Paul's face and pointed out a tiny flaw. "That's what happens if you let a bore go for even a month. They'll run right away with you."

"Yessir."

"He isn't to be trusted any more, Paul. He isn't right in his head, and it wouldn't do to take chances with him, would it?"

"Nossir."

Kroner dabbed at the pit with the corner of a patch. "I supposed you saw it that way. That's why it's a little difficult for me to understand why you let him wander around the plant unescorted."

Paul reddened. No words came.

"Or why you'd let him have your gun. He isn't authorized for firearms any more, you know. Yet they tell me they found your pistol covered with his fingerprints."

Before Paul could order his thoughts, Kroner clapped him on his knee and laughed like Santa Claus. "I'm so sure you've got a good explanation, I don't even want to hear it. Got a lot of faith in you, my boy. Don't want to see you get into any trouble. Now that your father's gone, I feel it's sort of up to me to watch out for you."

"That's nice of you, sir."

Kroner turned his back to Paul, assumed a ready stance with the shotgun, and picked off an imaginary bird flushed from behind the desk. "Kaplowie!" He ejected an imaginary shell. "These are dangerous times—more dangerous than you'd suspect from the surface. Kaplowie! But it's also the Golden Age, isn't it, Paul?"

Paul nodded.

Kroner turned to look at him. "I said, isn't this the Golden Age?"

"Yessir. I nodded."

"Pull!" said Kroner, apparently imagining clay pigeons now. "Kaboom! There have always been doubters, criers of doom, stoppers of progress."

"Yessir. About Finnerty and the pistol, I—"

"Behind us now, forgotten," said Kroner impatiently. "The slate is clean. As I was about to say, look where we are now, because men went right ahead and took forward steps with stout hearts, in spite of the people telling them not to."

"Yessir."

"Kaplowie! Some men try to make light of what we're doing, what men like your father did, by saying it's just gadgeteering, blind tinkering. It's more than that, Paul."

Paul leaned forward, eager to hear what this extra quality might be. He'd felt for some time that everyone else in the system must be seeing something he was missing. Perhaps this was it, perhaps the beginning of an overwhelming fervor like his father's.

"It's a sight more than gadgeteering, I'll tell you, Paul."

"Yessir?"

"It's strength and faith and determination. Our job is to open new doors at the head of the procession of civilization. That's what the engineer, the manager does. There is no higher calling."

Dejectedly, Paul let his spine sag back in the chair.

Kroner put a fresh patch on the cleaning rod and began swabbing the bore again. "Paul—Pittsburgh is still open. The field has been narrowed down to two men."

It was somewhat startling that he said it just that way, the way Anita had said he would. He wondered what it was she thought he should say in response. He'd never given her a chance to say, and hadn't read the outline. "It's a wonderful chance to be of real service," he said. He supposed that was pretty close to what she had in mind.

Paul felt lightheaded, having borrowed Anita's thoughts for want of enthusiasm of his own. He was being offered the Pittsburgh job, lots more money, and, since he would have risen so high with the greater portion of his life still ahead, the assurance that he would almost certainly go clear to the top. The moment of his arrival at this point of immense good fortune was curiously bland. He had known it was coming for a long time. Kroner had wanted it for him and had come close to promising it to him often—always in the name of his father. When advances had come, as now, there had been a vestigal sort of ritual of surprise and congratulation, as though Paul, like his ancestors, had arrived by cunning, tenacity, and God's will or the Devil's laxness.

"It's a tough decision, Paul, between you and Fred Garth." Garth was a much older man, nearly Kroner's age, manager of the Buffalo Works. "Frankly, Garth hasn't got your technical imagination, Paul. As a manager he's excellent, but if it wasn't for prodding, the Buffalo Works would be just as it was when he took over five years ago. But he's steady and reliable, Paul, and there's never been any question that he was one of us, that he put progress and the system ahead of his own interests."

"Garth's a fine man," said Paul. Garth was, too: four-square, desperate to please, and he seemed to have an anthropomorphic image of the corporate personality. Garth stood in relation to that image as a lover, and Paul wondered if this prevalent type of relationship had ever been given the consideration it deserved by sexologists. On second thought, he supposed that it had—the general phenomenon of a lover's devotion to the unseen—in studies of nuns' symbolic marriages to Christ. At any rate, Paul had seen Garth at various stages of his love affair, unable to eat for anxiety, on a manic crest, moved to maudlin near-crying at recollections of the affair's tender beginnings. In short, Garth suffered all the emotional hazards of a perennial game of she-loves-me, she-loves-me-not. To carry out directions from above—an irritating business for Paul—was, for Garth, a favor to please a lady. "I'd like to see him get the job."

"I'd like to see you get the job, Paul." Kroner's expression indicated that the mention of Garth had been so much window dressing. "You've got imagination and spirit and ability—"

"Thank you, sir."

"Let me finish. Imagination, spirit, and ability, and, for all I know, I may be completely wrong in calling your loyalty into question."

"Loyalty?"

Kroner laid the shotgun aside and pulled up a chair to face Paul's. He laid his big hands on Paul's knees and lowered his thick brows. The situation had the quality of a séance, with Kroner as the medium. Again, as he had felt when Kroner took his hand at the Country Club, Paul felt his strength and will dwarfed by the old man. "Paul, I want you to tell me what's on your mind."

The hands on his knees tightened. Paul struggled resentfully against the urge to pour his heart out to this merciful, wise, gentle father. But his sullenness decayed. Paul began to talk.

His formless misgivings and disquiet of a week before, he realized, had shape now. The raw material of his discontent was now cast in another man's molds. He was saying what Lasher had said the night before, talking about the spiritual disaster across the river, about the threat of revolution, about the hierarchy that was a nightmare to most. The way he phrased it, it wasn't a condemnation, it was a plea for refutation.

Kroner, his hands still on Paul's knees, hung his head lower and lower.

Paul came to the end, and Kroner stood and turned his back to stare out of the window. The spell was still in force, and Paul looked expectantly at the broad back, waiting for wisdom.

Kroner turned suddenly. "So you're against us."

"I didn't mean to say that, certainly. They're questions that deserve some sort of answer."

"Keep to your own side of the river, Paul! Your job is management and engineering. I don't know what the answers are to Lasher's questions. I do know that it's far easier to ask questions than to answer them. I know that there have always been questions, and men like Lasher ready to make trouble by asking them."

"You know about Lasher?" Paul hadn't mentioned his name.

"Yes, I've known about him for quite some time. And, as of this noon, I know what you and Lasher and Finnerty were up to last night." He looked sad. "As district industrial security officer, there isn't much I don't know, Paul. And sometimes, like now, I wish I didn't know so much."

"And Pittsburgh?"

"I still think you're the man for the job. I'm going to pretend that you didn't do last night what you did, didn't say just now what you said. I don't believe it came from your heart."

Paul was amazed. By some freakish circumstance he'd apparently clinched the job—after having arrived with the vague intention of disqualifying himself.

"This is the main stretch, Paul. Now it's all up to you."

"I could go on the wagon, I suppose."

"It's a little more complicated than that, I'm afraid. In a very short while you managed to pile up a fairly impressive police dossier: the pistol, letting Finnerty into the plant, last night's indiscretions—and, well, I've got to be able to explain it all away to the satisfaction of Headquarters. You could go to prison, you know."

Paul laughed nervously.

"I want to be able to say, Paul, that you were doing special security work for me, and I'd like to prove it."

"I see." Paul didn't.

"You'll agree that both Lasher and Finnerty are dangerous men, potential saboteurs who should be put where they can't do any harm." He took the shotgun down from the rack again and distorted his face as he cleaned around the ejector with a toothpick. "So," he said after a few moments of silence, "I'll want you to testify that they tried to get you into a plot to sabotage the Ilium Works."

The door flew open, and Baer came in, grinning. "Congratulations, my boy. Congratulations. Wonderful, wonderful, wonderful."

"Congratulations?" said Paul.

"Pittsburgh, my boy, Pittsburgh!"

"It hasn't quite been settled," said Kroner.

"But you said yesterday—"

"A little something's come up since then." Kroner winked at Paul. "Nothing very serious, though, eh, Paul? A little hurdle."

"Um, oh, I see, uh-huh; a hurdle, a hurdle. I see. Um."

Paul was shaken and confused by what had just happened to him, and he hid his lack of composure behind a vacuous smile. He wondered if Baer had come in on cue.

"Paul here had some questions," said Kroner.

"Questions? Questions, my boy?"

"He wanted to know if we weren't doing something bad in the name of progress."

Baer sat on the desk and began taking kinks out of the telephone cord. He was thinking very hard, and from the man's expression Paul could only conclude that the question had never come to Baer's attention before. Now that it had, he was giving it his earnest consideration. "Is progress bad? Uh-huh—good question." He looked up from the cord. "I don't know, don't know. Maybe progress is bad, eh?"

Kroner looked at him with surprise. "Look, you know darn good and well history's answered the question a thousand times."

"It has? Has it? You know; I wouldn't. Answered it a thousand times, has it? That's good, good. All I know is, you've got to act like it has, or you might as well throw in the towel.

Don't know, my boy. Guess I should, but I don't. Just do my job. Maybe that's wrong."

It was Kroner's turn to be dismayed. "Well, what say to a refresher?" he said briskly.

"I say yes to a refresher," said Paul gratefully.

Kroner chuckled. "There, there; it wasn't so rough, now was it?"

"Nope."

"That's my boy. Chin up."

As Baer, Paul, and Kroner filed into the living room, Mom was telling Anita sadly that it took all kinds of people to make a world.

"I just want to make sure everybody understands he invited himself," said Anita. "Mom, there wasn't a thing we could do about it."

Kroner dusted his hands. "Well, what say to a pick-me-up?"

"Wonderful, wonderful, wonderful," said Baer.

"Did you men have a good time with those awful guns?" said Mom, wrinkling her nose.

"Swell, Mom," said Paul.

Anita caught Paul's eyes, and raised her brows questioningly.

Paul nodded slightly.

She smiled and lay back in her chair, exhausted, satisfied.

Mom handed out small glasses of port, while Kroner tinkered with the phonograph. "Where is it?" he said.

"Now, now—right where it always is, on the turntable," said Mom.

"Oh yes—here it is. I thought maybe somebody else had been playing something since I used it."

"No. Nobody's been near the phonograph since last night."

Kroner held the tone arm over the spinning record. "This is for you, Paul. When I said pick-me-up I really had this in mind more than the wine. This is meat for the spirit. This can pull me out of a slump like nothing I can think of."

"I gave it to him last month, and I can't think of anything that's ever pleased him as much," said Mom.

Kroner lowered the needle into the groove and hurried to a chair and covered his eyes before the music began.

The volume was turned way up, and suddenly the loudspeaker howled:

"Ooooooooooooh, give me some men, who are stout-hearted men, who will fight for the right they adore . . ."

Paul looked around the room. Kroner was clumping his feet up and down and jerking his head from side to side. Mom was jerking her head too, and so were Baer and Anita—Anita more violently than any of them.

Paul sighed, and began to jerk his head, too.

"Shoulder to shoulder, and bolder and bolder, they grow as they go to the fore! Ooooooooooooh . . ."

Chapter XIII

LYING ABED after the stout-hearted men's evening at the Kroners', Doctor Paul Proteus, son of a successful man, himself rich with prospects of being richer, counted his material blessings. He found that he was in excellent shape to afford integrity. He was worth, without having to work another day in his life, almost three-quarters of a million dollars.

For once, his dissatisfaction with his life was specific. He was reacting to an outrage that would be regarded as such by almost any man in any period in history. He had been told to turn informer on his friend, Ed Finnerty. This was about as basic as an attack on integrity could be, and Paul received it with the same sort of relief that was felt when the first shots of the last war were fired—after decades of tension.

Now he could damn well lose his temper and quit.

Anita slept—utterly satisfied, not so much by Paul as by the social orgasm of, after years of the system's love play, being offered Pittsburgh.

She had delivered a monologue on the way home from Albany—a recitation that might have come from Shepherd. She'd reviewed Paul's career from the instant of their marriage onward, and Paul was surprised to learn that his path was strewn with bodies—men who had tried to best him, only to be chagrined and ruined.

She made the carnage so vivid that he was obliged for a moment to abandon his own thoughts, to see if there was the slightest truth in what she was saying. He went over the scalps she was counting one by one—men who had competed with him for this job or that—and found that they all had done well for themselves and were quite unbroken either financially or in spirit. But to Anita they were dead men, shot squarely between the eyes, and good riddance of bad rubbish.

Paul hadn't told Anita the conditions he would have to meet before he could have Pittsburgh. And he didn't intimate that he was going to do anything but take the job proudly, joyfully.

Now, lying beside her, he congratulated himself on his calm, on his being wily for the first time in his life, really. He wasn't going to tell Anita that he was quitting for a long time, not until she was ready. He would subtly re-educate her to a new set of values, and *then* quit. Otherwise the shock of being the wife of a nobody might do tragic things. The only grounds on which she met the world were those of her husband's rank. If he were to lose the rank it was frighteningly possible that she would lose touch with the world altogether, or, worse for Paul, leave him.

And Paul didn't want either of those things to happen. She was what fate had given him to love, and he did his best to love her. He knew her too well for her conceits to be offensive most of the time, to be anything but pathetic.

She was also more of a source of courage than he cared to admit.

She also had a sexual genius that gave Paul his one unqualified enthusiasm in life.

And Anita had also made possible, by her dogged attention to details, the luxury of his detached, variously amused or cynical outlook on life.

She was also all he had.

A vague panic welled up cold in his chest, driving away drowsiness when he would most have welcomed it. He began to see that he, too, would be in for a shock. He felt oddly disembodied, an insubstantial wisp, nothingness, a man who declined to be any more. Suddenly understanding that he, like Anita, was little more than his station in life, he threw his arms around his sleeping wife, and laid his head on the breast of his fellow wraith-to-be.

"Mmmmm?" said Anita "Mmmmmmm?"

"Anita—"

"Mmm?"

"Anita, I love you." The compulsion was upon him to tell her everything, to mingle his consciousness with hers. But as he momentarily raised his head from the drugging warmth and fragrance of her bosom, cool, fresh air from the Adirondacks bathed his face, and wisdom returned. He said nothing more to her.

"I love *you*, Paul," she murmured.

Chapter XIV

DOCTOR PAUL PROTEUS was a man with a secret. Most of the time it was an exhilarating secret, and he extracted momentary highs of joy from it while dealing with fellow members of the system in the course of his job. At the beginning and close of each item of business he thought, "To hell with you."

It was to hell with them, to hell with everything. This secret detachment gave him a delightful sense of all the world's being a stage. Waiting until the time when he and Anita would be in mental shape to quit and start a better life, Paul acted out his role as manager of the Ilium Works. Outwardly, as manager, he was unchanged; but inwardly he was burlesquing smaller, less free souls who would have taken the job seriously.

He had never been a reading man, but now he was developing an appetite for novels wherein the hero lived vigorously and out-of-doors, dealing directly with nature, dependent upon basic cunning and physical strength for survival—woodsmen, sailors, cattlemen. . . .

He read of these heroes with a half-smile on his lips. He knew his enjoyment of them was in a measure childish, and he doubted that a life could ever be as clean, hearty, and satisfying as those in the books. Still and all, there was a basic truth underlying the tales, a primitive ideal to which he could aspire. He wanted to deal, not with society, but only with Earth as God had given it to man.

"Is that a good book, Doctor Proteus?" said Doctor Katharine Finch, his secretary. She'd come into his office carrying a large gray cardboard box.

"Oh—hello, Katharine." He laid the book down with a smile. "Not great literature; I'll promise you that. Pleasant relaxation is all. All about bargemen on the old Erie Ship Canal." He tapped the broad, naked chest of the hero on the book jacket. "Don't make men like that any more. Well, what's in the box? That for me?"

"It's your shirts. They just came by mail."

"Shirts?"

"For the Meadows."

"Oh, *those* things. Open them up. What color are they?"

"Blue. You're on the Blue Team this year." She laid the shirts on the desk.

"Oh, no!" Paul stood and held one of the deep blue T-shirts at arm's length. "Dear God in heaven—no!" Across the chest of each of the shirts, in blazing gold letters, was the word "Captain." "Katharine, they can't do this to me."

"It's an honor, isn't it?"

"Honor!" He exhaled noisily and shook his head. "For fourteen days, Katharine, I, Queen of the May and captain of the Blue Team, am going to have to lead my men in group singing, marches, greased-pole climbing, volley ball, horseshoes, softball, golf-ball driving, badminton, trapshooting, capture the flag, Indian wrestling, touch football, shuffleboard, and trying to throw the other captains into the lake. Agh!"

"Doctor Shepherd was very pleased."

"He always has been fond of me."

"No—I mean he was pleased about being a captain himself."

"Oh? Shepherd is a captain?" Paul's raised eyebrows were part of an old reflex, the wary reaction of a man who has been in the system for a good many years. Being chosen to captain one of the four teams *was* an honor, if a man gave a damn about such things. It was a way the higher brass had of showing favor, and, politically, Shepherd's having been chosen a captain was a striking business. Shepherd had always been a nobody at the Meadows, whose chief fame was as a pretty fair softball pitcher. Now, suddenly, he was a captain. "Which team?"

"Green. His shirts are on my desk. Green with orange lettering. Very vivid."

"Green, eh?" Well, if one cared about such things, Green was the lowest in the unofficial hierarchy of teams. It was one of those things that was understood without anyone's saying anything about it. Having looked this far into the piddling matter, Paul congratulated himself for having been named captain of the Blue, which, again, everybody seemed to feel was the team with the most tone. Not that it made any difference at all any more. Made none. Silly. To hell with it.

"They certainly give you enough shirts," said Katharine, counting. "Nine, ten, eleven, twelve."

"Nothing like enough. For two weeks you drink and sweat, drink and sweat, drink and sweat, until you feel like a sump pump. This is a day's supply at the outside."

"Uh-huh. Well, sorry, that's all there is in the box except this book." She held up the volume, which looked like a hymnal.

"Hi ho—*The Meadows Songbook*," said Paul wearily. He leaned back and closed his eyes. "Pick a song, Katharine, any song, and read it aloud."

"Here's the song for the Green Team, Doctor Shepherd's team. To the tune of the *William Tell* overture."

"The whole overture?"

"That's what it says here."

"Well, go ahead and give it a try."

She cleared her throat, started to sing softly, thought better of it, and lapsed into plain reading:

"Green oh Green oh Green's the team!
Mightiest e'er the world has seen!
Red, Blue, White will scream,
When
They see the great Green Team!"

"That'll put hair on your chest, Katharine."

"Oh, gosh but it'll be fun! You *know* you'll love it when you get up there."

Paul opened his eyes to see that Katharine was reading another song, and her eyes shone with excitement and she rocked her head from side to side. "What's that you're reading now?"

"Oh, I wish I were a man! I was just reading your song."

"My song?"

"The Blue Team's song."

"Oh—*my* song. By all means, let's hear it."

She whistled a few bars of "Indiana," and then sang, this time heartily:

"Oh you Blue Team, you tried and true team,
There are no teams as good as you!
You will smash Green, also the Red Team,

And the White Team you'll batter, too.
They'd better scurry before your fury,
And in a hurry, without a clue;
Because the Blue Team's a tried and true team,
And there's no team as good as you!"

"Hmmm."

"And you *will* win, too. I know you will," said Katharine.

"You going to be at the Mainland?" The Mainland was a camp for wives and children, and women employees whose development wasn't yet complete, across the water from the Meadows, the island where the men went.

"That's as close as I can get to the real thing," said Katharine wistfully.

"That's close enough, believe me. Tell me, is Bud Calhoun going to be there?"

She colored, and he was instantly sorry he'd asked. "He had an invitation, I know," she said, "but that was before—" She shrugged unhappily. "And you know what the *Manual* says."

"The machines can't stand him any more," said Paul heavily. "Why don't they build in a gimmick that will give a man a free drink before he gets the ax? Do you know what he's up to now?"

"I haven't talked to him or seen him, but I did call up Matheson's office to find out what was going to be done with him. They said he was going to be a project supervisor for the—" her voice caught—"for the Reeks and Wrecks." Emotion was giving her a rough going-over now, and she left Paul's office hurriedly.

"I'm sure he'll do well," Paul called after her. "I'll bet we won't know our city a year from now, with him thinking up things for the Reeks and Wrecks to do."

Her phone rang, and she relayed the information to Paul that Doctor Edward Finnerty was at the gate, wanting in.

"Bind his hands and feet, put a bag over his head, and have four men bring him up. Fixed bayonets, of course. And be sure and get a picture of it for Shepherd."

Ten minutes later, Finnerty was escorted into Paul's office by an armed guard.

"For heaven's sake—look at you!" said Paul. Finnerty's hair

was cut and combed, his face was pink, shining, and shaved, and his seersucker suit, while worn and a poor fit, was crisp and sanitary-looking.

Finnerty looked at him blankly, as though he couldn't guess what the fuss was about. "I'd like to borrow your car."

"Promise to wipe off the fingerprints when you're through?"

"Oh—you're sore about that pistol business, I suppose. Sorry. I meant to throw it in the river."

"You know about it, then?"

"Sure—and about how Shepherd turned in a report on you, too, telling how you let me in the plant without an escort. Tough." Finnerty, after less than a week in Homestead, had taken on rough, swashbuckling mannerisms—glaringly synthetic. He also seemed to be getting a real kick out of being a liability as an associate for anyone respectable.

Paul was amazed, as he had been amazed at Kroner's, by how much others knew about his affairs. "How do you know so much?"

"You'd be surprised who knows what, and how they find out. Surprise the pants off you to know what goes on in this world. My eyes are just opening." He leaned forward earnestly. "And, Paul—I'm finding myself. At last I'm finding myself."

"What do you look like, Ed?"

"Those dumb bastards across the river—they're *my* kind of people. They're real, Paul, real!"

Paul had never doubted that they were real, and so found himself without any sort of comment or emotional response for Finnerty's important announcement. "Well, I'm glad you've found yourself after all these years," he said. Finnerty had been finding himself ever since Paul had known him. And, weeks later, he'd always deserted that self with angry cries of impostor, and discovered another. "That's swell, Ed."

"Well, anyway, how about the keys to the car?"

"Is it fair to ask what for?"

"This is a milk run. I want to pick up my clothes and stuff at your house and run them over to Lasher's."

"You're living with Lasher?"

Finnerty nodded. "Surprising how well we hit it off, right from the first." His tone implied the barest trace of contempt for Paul's shallow way of life. "Keys?"

Paul threw them to him. "How do you plan to use the rest of your life, Ed?"

"With the people. That's my place."

"You know the cops are after you for not registering?"

"Spice of life."

"You can be jailed, you know."

"You're afraid to live, Paul. That's what's the matter with you. You know about Thoreau and Emerson?"

"A little. About as much as you did before Lasher primed you, I'll bet."

"Anyway, Thoreau was in jail because he wouldn't pay a tax to support the Mexican War. He didn't believe in the war. And Emerson came to jail to see him. 'Henry,' he said, 'why are you here?' And Thoreau said, 'Ralph, why *aren't* you here?' "

"I should want to go to jail?" said Paul, trying to get some sort of message for himself out of the anecdote.

"You shouldn't let fear of jail keep you from doing what you believe in."

"Well, it doesn't." Paul reflected that the big trouble, really, was finding something to believe in.

"All right, so it doesn't." There was weary disbelief in Finnerty's voice. He was apparently getting bored with his convention-ridden former friend from the north side of the river. "Thanks for the car."

"Any time." Paul was relieved when the door closed behind the new—this week's—Finnerty.

Katharine opened the door again. "He scares me," she said.

"You needn't be scared. He wastes all his energy on games with himself. There goes your phone."

"It's Doctor Kroner," said Katharine. "Yes," she said into the telephone, "Doctor Proteus is in."

"Would you please put him on," said Kroner's secretary.

"Doctor Proteus speaking."

"Doctor Proteus is on," said Katharine.

"Just a moment. Doctor Kroner wishes to speak with him. Doctor Kroner, Doctor Proteus in Ilium is on the line."

"Hello, Paul."

"How do you do, sir."

"Paul, about this Finnerty and Lasher business—" His playfully conspiratorial tone implied that the proposed prosecution of these two was sort of a practical joke. "Just wanted to tell you that I called Washington about it, to let them in on what we're going to do, and they say we should hold off for a while. They say the whole thing ought to be well planned at the top level. It's apparently bigger stuff than I thought." His voice dropped to a whisper. "It's beginning to look like a problem nationwise, not just Iliumwise."

Paul was pleased that there was to be a delay, but the reason for it was a surprise. "How could Finnerty get to be a problem nationwise or even Iliumwise? He's only been here a few days."

"Idle hands do the Devil's work, Paul. He's probably been getting into bad company, and it's the bad company we're really after. Anyway, the top brass wants in on whatever we do, and they want to have a meeting about it at the Meadows. Let's see—sixteen days from now."

"Fine," said Paul, and added, in his mind, the imaginary seal he affixed to all official business these days—"And to hell with you." He had no intention of turning informer on anyone. He would simply stall until he and Anita were fully prepared to say, "To hell with you, to hell with everything," aloud.

"We think the world of you over here, Paul."

"Thank you, sir."

Kroner was silent for a moment. Suddenly he shouted into the phone, almost rupturing Paul's eardrum.

"Beg your pardon, sir?" The message had been so loud as to be all pain and no sense.

Kroner chuckled, and lowered his voice a little. "I said, who's going to win, Paul?"

"Win?"

"The Meadows, the Meadows! Who's going to win?"

"Oh—the Meadows," said Paul. It was a nightmarish conversation, with Kroner vehement and happy, and with Paul devoid of the vaguest notion as to what was being discussed.

"What team?" said Kroner, a shade peevishly.

"Oh. Oh! The *Blue Team* is going to win!" He filled his lungs. "Blue!" he shouted.

"You bet your life we're going to win!" Kroner shouted back. "The Blues are behind you, Cap'n!" Kroner, then, was on the Blue Team, too. He started to sing in his rumbling basso:

"Oh you Blue Team, you tried and true team,
There are no teams as good as you!
You will smash Green, also the Red Team,
And the White Team you'll batt—"

The song was interrupted by a cry: "White's going to win! Go, White!" It was Baer, yelling in the background. "So you think Blue's going to win, do you, do you, eh? Win? Think Blue's going to win, eh, eh? The White Team will trim you, trim you—aha, aha—trim the daylights out of the Blue Team."

There was the sound of laughter and banter and scuffling, and Kroner picked up the Blue Team's song where he'd left off:

"They'd better scurry before your fury,
And in a hurry, without a clue;
Because the—"

Baer's piercing voice cut through Kroner's bass with the White Team's song, to the tune of "Tramp, Tramp, Tramp":

"White, White, White's the one to watch for.
Blue, Green, Red will come to grief.
Before the fury of the White
They'll get knocked clear out of—"

The scuffling grew louder, and the songs degenerated into panting laughter. There was a clatter in Paul's receiver, a cry, a click, and then the dial tone.

Paul restored the receiver to its cradle with a limp hand. There was no quitting before the Meadows, he told himself glumly—no re-educating Anita and quitting in the few days remaining. The Meadows would have to be endured, and, worse luck, he would have to endure it as captain of the Blue Team.

His glance passed over the hairy tan chest, frank gray eyes, and keg-sized biceps of the man on the book jacket, and his thoughts slid easily, gratefully, into the fantasy of the new, good life ahead of him. Somewhere, outside of society, there was a place for a man—a man and wife—to live heartily and blamelessly, *naturally*, by hands and wits.

Paul studied his long, soft hands. Their only callus was on the large finger of his right hand. There, stained a dirty orange by cigarette tars, a tough hump had grown over the years, protecting his finger against the attrition of pen and pencil shafts. Skills—that was what the hands of the heroes in the novels had, skills. To date, Paul's hands had learned to do little save grip a pen, pencil, toothbrush, hair brush, razor, knife, fork, spoon, cup, glass, faucet, doorknob, switch, handkerchief, towel, zipper, button, snap, bar of soap, book, comb, wife, or steering wheel.

He recalled his college days, and was sure he'd learned some sort of manual skill there. He'd learned to make mechanical drawings. That was when the lump on his finger had begun to grow. What else? He'd learned to bounce a ball off several walls with skill, and to the consternation of most of his squash opponents. He'd been good enough to make the quarter-finals of the Regional Collegiate Squash Tournament two years in a row. He used to be able to do *that* with his hands.

What else?

Again uneasiness crept up on him—the fear that there was far too little of him to get along anywhere outside the system, to get along at all contentedly. He might go into some small business, such as the one he claimed to be in when he didn't want to be recognized—wholesale groceries. But he would still be caught in the mesh of the economy and its concomitant hierarchy. The machines wouldn't let him into that business, anyway, and even if they would, there'd be no less nonsense and posturing. Moreover, despite the fact that Paul was saying to hell with the whole system, he was aware that the relatively unskilled and dull business of buying and selling was beneath him. So to hell with it. The only thing worse would be complete idleness, which Paul could afford, but which, he was sure, was as amoral as what he was quitting.

Farming—now *there* was a magic word. Like so many words with a little magic from the past still clinging to them, the word "farming" was a reminder of what rugged stock the present generation had come from, of how tough a thing a human being could be if he had to. The word had little meaning in the present. There were no longer farmers, but only agricultural engineers. In the rich Iroquois Valley in Ilium County, thousands of settlers had once made their living from the soil. Now Doctor Ormand van Curler managed the farming of the whole county with a hundred men and several millions dollars' worth of machinery.

Farming. Paul's pulse quickened, and he daydreamed of living a century before—living in one of the many farmhouses now crumbling into their foundations over the valley. He chose one farmhouse in particular for his fantasy, one close to the edge of town that he'd often admired. He suddenly realized that the farm, the little patch of the past, *wasn't* a part of van Curler's farm system. He was almost sure it wasn't.

"Katharine," he called excitedly, "get me the Ilium Real Estate Manager on the phone."

"Ilium Real Estate Office. Doctor Pond speaking." Pond's speech was effeminate, lisping.

"Doctor Pond, this is Doctor Proteus at the Works."

"Well! What can I do for *you*, Doctor Proteus?"

"You know that farmhouse out on King Street, just outside the city limits?"

"Mmmm. Just a moment." Paul heard a machine shuffling through cards, and then a bell announced that the card had been found. "Yes, the Gottwald place. I have the card right here."

"What's being done with it?"

"A good question! What can be done with it? I wish I knew. It was a hobby with Gottwald, you know, keeping it just like an old-fashioned farm. When he died, the heirs wanted to get van Curler to take it over, but he said it wasn't worth bothering with. Two hundred acres is all, and he'd have to cut down the windbreaks to connect it with other fields so he could farm it efficiently. Then the heirs found out that they couldn't have sold it to the Farm System anyway. It's in the deed that the place has to be kept old-fashioned." He laughed bitterly. "So all old Gottwald left his heirs was a nice headache, a white elephant."

"How much?"

"Are you serious? The thing's a museum exhibit, Doctor. I mean, almost nothing mechanical on the place. Even if you could beat the restrictions in the deed, it'd cost you thousands to get it in shape."

"How much?" The farm was looking better and better.

"Eighteen thousand, it says on the card." Before Paul could

close the deal that instant, Pond added, "but you can get it for fifteen, I'm sure. How would twelve suit you?"

"Would five hundred hold it until I can look it over?"

"It's been holding itself for almost fourteen years. Go on out and have a look, if you really feel you have to. After you've thrown up, there are some really nice things I'd like to show you." The machine riffled through its cards again. "For instance, there's a nice Georgian house on Griffin Boulevard. Electronic door openers, thermostatically controlled windows, radar range, electrostatic dust precipitators, ultrasonic clothes washer built in, forty-inch television screens in the master bedroom, guest room, living room, kitchen, and rumpus rooms, and twenty-inch screens in the maids' rooms and the kiddies' rooms, and—"

"Where can I get the key to the farm?"

"Oh, *that* thing. Well, to give you an idea of what you're getting into, there is no lock. There's a latchstring."

"Latchstring?"

"Yes, latchstring. I had to go out myself to find out what the darn thing is. There's a latch on the inside of the door, with a string tied to it. When you want to let somebody just walk in, you stick the little string through a hole in the door, so the string dangles outside. If you don't want people walking in, you pull the string in through the hole. Ghastly?"

"I'll survive somehow. Is the latchstring out?"

"There's a caretaker there, detailed from the Reeks and Wrecks. I'll call him and tell him to put it out. Confidentially, I'm sure they'll take eight."

Chapter XV

THE LATCHSTRING at the Gottwald house was out for Doctor Paul Proteus.

He tugged at it, listened with satisfaction as the latch disengaged itself inside, and walked in. The living room was dimly lit through tiny-paned, dusty windows, and what light did get in died without reflection on dull, dark antique surfaces. The floor rose and fell like a springboard beneath Paul's feet.

"The house breathes *with* you, like good underwear," said a lisping voice from the shadows. Paul looked in the direction from which it had come. The man sucked on his cigarette, lighting his moon face with a pink glow. "Doctor Proteus?"

"Yes."

"I'm Doctor Pond. Would you like me to turn on the lights?"

"Please, Doctor."

"Well, there aren't any. Kerosene lanterns throughout. Want to wash your hands or something?"

"Well, not—"

"Because, if you do, there's a pump in the back yard, and an outhouse by the chicken coop. Would you like to see the termites, the dry rot, the hog pen, and the manure-spreader, or shall we go to see that Georgian on Griffin Boulevard?" He walked to where they could see each other. Doctor Pond was very young, fat, and earnest, and plainly distressed by his surroundings.

"You're certainly eager to sell me the place," said Paul, laughing. With each new inconvenience, the place became more irresistible. It was a completely isolated backwater, cut off from the boiling rapids of history, society, and the economy. Timeless.

"I have a certain responsibility," said Doctor Pond carefully. "An administrator without a certain awareness, above and beyond the *Manual*, is like a ship without a rudder."

"He is?" said Paul absently. He was peering through a back window into the barnyard, and beyond that, through an opened barn door, where he could see the firm buff flank of a cow.

"Yes," said Doctor Pond, "like a ship without a rudder. For example, while the *Manual* doesn't tell me to do it, I make very sure that every man gets a house suited to his station on the ladder of life. The way a man lives can destroy or increase the stature of his job—can increase or decrease the stability and prestige of the entire system."

"You say I can get this whole farm for eight?"

"Please, Doctor—you put me in an uncomfortable position. I was excited when you first called, because this place has been such a headache for so long. But then my conscience started to work on me, and, well, I simply can't let you do it."

"I'll take it. Do the animals go with it?"

"Everything goes with it. That's in Gottwald's will and in the deed. It has to be kept just as it is and it must be farmed. See how impossible it is? Now, shall we go to Griffin Boulevard, where there's just the right house for the Manager of the Ilium Works?" When he spoke the title, his voice sounded like a choir of French horns.

"I want this."

"If you try to force me to sell it, I'll quit." Doctor Pond reddened. "My classification number may be twice what yours is, but I have a certain amount of integrity."

The word, coming from Pond, struck Paul as ridiculous at first, and he started to smile about it. Then he saw how tense the man was, and realized that what Pond was talking about was, by God, integrity. This pipsqueak of a man in a pipsqueak job had pipsqueak standards he was willing to lay his pipsqueak life down for. And Paul had a vision of civilization as a vast and faulty dike, with thousands of men like Doctor Pond in a rank stretching to the horizon, each man grimly stopping a leak with his finger.

"This would be a hobby, of course—a plaything," Paul lied. "I'd go on living where I'm living now."

Doctor Pond sighed and sank into a chair. "Oh—thank the Lord! Oh! You have no idea how much better I feel." He laughed in nervous relief. "Of course, of course, of course. And you'd keep Mr. Haycox on?"

"Who is Mr. Haycox?"

"The Reek and Wreck who's assigned to keep the place going. He's under orders from the Reeks and Wrecks, but of course the Gottwald estate pays him. You'd have to do the same."

"I'd like to meet him."

"He's an antique too." He threw his hands over his head. "What a place. I think you're mad, simply mad. But he who pays the piper calls the tune."

"As long as he doesn't threaten to disgrace the system."

"Exactly! That's almost good enough to carve over your mantel, but I doubt if the deed will let you."

"How about, 'After us the deluge.'" said Paul.

"Hmm?" Doctor Pond tried to make sense of the quotation, seemingly decided that it was some archaic, pleasant sentiment for those who understood poetry, and smiled. "That's nice too." Apparently the word "deluge" stuck in his mind. "Now, about the cellar here: it has an earth floor and *is* damp." He leaned out of the back door, wrinkled his nose in the sweet, stringent odor of manure cooking in the sunlight, and shouted, "Mr. Haycox! Oh, Mr. Haycox!"

Paul had opened the back of a grandfather clock. "I'll be damned," he said under his breath. "Wooden works." He checked his own watch, the shock-proof, waterproof, antimagnetic, glow-in-the-dark, self-winding chronometer Anita had given him for Christmas, and found that the grandfather clock was off by about twelve minutes. Indulging an atavistic whim, he set his watch to correspond with the hands of the relic, which grated and creaked away the seconds, sounding like a wooden ship straining in a strong wind.

The house was certainly one of the oldest in the valley. The rough rafters were inches above Paul's head, and the fireplace was sooted black, and there wasn't a true right angle anywhere. The house seemed to have twisted and stretched on its foundations until it had found a position of comfort for all of its parts—like a sleeping dog.

More remarkable than the way the house had relieved its stresses was the way it conformed to Paul's particular, not to say peculiar, needs. Here was a place where he could work with his hands, getting life from nature without being disturbed by any human beings other than his wife. Not only that, but Anita, with her love for things colonial, would be enchanted, stunned, even, by this completely authentic microcosm of the past.

"Ah," said Doctor Pond, "Mr. Haycox at last. When you yell for him, he never yells back. Just starts coming, taking his own sweet time."

Paul watched Mr. Haycox's heavy-footed progress across the hard-packed earth of the barnyard. The caretaker was an old man, with close-cropped white hair, coarse, tanned skin, and, like Rudy Hertz, with remarkably big hands. Unlike Rudy, Mr. Haycox wasn't desiccated. His flesh was firm, hard, and well colored. The chief toll he seemed to have paid time was in teeth, of which he had few. He might have been part of a pageant recalling farm life as it had once been. He wore old-fashioned blue denim overalls, a wide-brimmed straw hat, and heavy, crusty work shoes.

As though to point up the anachronism of Mr. Haycox and the Gottwald place for Paul, one of Doctor Ormand van Curler's men, riding on a tractor, appeared on the other side of the windbreak, snappy in spotless white coveralls, a red baseball cap, cool sandals which almost never touched the ground, and white gloves which, like Paul's hands, rarely touched anything but steering wheels, levers, and switches.

"What do *you* want?" said Mr. Haycox. "What's the matter now?" His voice was strong. He had none of the sheepishness or obsequiousness Paul had seen so frequently in Reeks and Wrecks. Mr. Haycox bore himself as though he owned the place, wanted the talk to be as brief and pithy as possible, and doubted that whatever was wanted of him could possibly be more important than what he had been doing.

"Doctor Proteus—this is Mr. Haycox."

"How are you?" said Paul.

" 'Do," said Mr. Haycox. "What kind of doctor?"

"Doctor of Science," said Paul.

Mr. Haycox seemed annoyed and disappointed. "Don't call that kind a doctor at all. Three kinds of doctors: dentists, vets, and physicians. You one of those?"

"No. Sorry."

"Then you ain't a doctor."

"He *is* a doctor," said Doctor Pond earnestly. "He knows

how to keep machines healthy." He was trying to build up the importance of graduate degrees in the mind of this clod.

"Mechanic," said Mr. Haycox.

"Well," said Doctor Pond, "you can go to college and learn to be a specialist in all sorts of things besides making people or animals well. I mean, after all. The modern world would grind to a halt if there weren't men with enough advanced training to keep the complicated parts of civilization working smoothly."

"Um," said Mr. Haycox apathetically. "What do you keep working so smoothly?"

Doctor Pond smiled modestly. "I spent seven years in the Cornell Graduate School of Realty to qualify for a Doctor of Realty degree and get this job."

"Call yourself a doctor, too, do you?" said Mr. Haycox.

"I think I can say without fear of contradiction that I earned that degree," said Doctor Pond coolly. "My thesis was the third longest in any field in the country that year—eight hundred and ninety-six pages, double-spaced, with narrow margins."

"Real-estate salesman," said Mr. Haycox. He looked back and forth between Paul and Doctor Pond, waiting for them to say something worth his attention. When they'd failed to rally after twenty seconds, he turned to go. "I'm doctor of cowshit, pigshit, and chickenshit," he said. "When you doctors figure out what you want, you'll find me out in the barn shoveling *my* thesis."

"Mr. Haycox!" said Doctor Pond, furious. "You'll stay here until we're through with you!"

"Thought you was." He stopped, and stood perfectly motionless.

"Doctor Proteus is buying the farm."

"*My* farm?" Mr. Haycox turned slowly to face them, and real concern was in his eyes.

"The farm you've been taking care of," said Doctor Pond.

"*My* farm."

"The Gottwald estate's farm," said Doctor Pond.

"That a man?"

"You know it isn't."

"Well, I'm a man. As far as men go, this here is my farm more'n it's anybody else's. I'm the only man who ever cared about it, ever did anything about it." He turned earnestly to Paul. "You know the will says you got to keep it just like it is?"

"I plan to."

"And keep me on," said Mr. Haycox.

"Well, I don't know for sure," said Paul. This was a complication he hadn't foreseen. He planned to do the work himself. That was the point of the undertaking.

"That *isn't* in the will," said Doctor Pond, pleased to have found something that shocked respect into Mr. Haycox.

"All the same, you got to keep me on," said Mr. Haycox. "This is what I do." He gestured at the yard and buildings, all neat. "This is what I've done."

"Gottwald bought this place from Mr. Haycox's father," Doctor Pond explained. "There was some sort of informal agreement, I think, that Mr. Haycox could have the job of caretaker for his lifetime."

"Informal, hell!" said Mr. Haycox. "He *promised*, Gottwald did. This here's been our family's for more'n a hundred years—lots more. And I'm the last of the line, and Gottwald promised, by God, he promised it'd be the same as mine till it came time for me to go."

"Well, the time has come," said Doctor Pond.

"Dead—Gottwald meant when I was dead. I got twice as many years behind me as you do, sonny boy, and twice as many ahead of me." He moved closer to Doctor Pond, and squinted at him. "I've moved so many big piles of shit in my life, figure I could throw a little dab like you clean over the barn."

Doctor Pond's eyes widened, and he backed away. "We'll see about that," he said faintly.

"Look," said Paul hastily, "I'm sure we can work this out. Soon as I close the deal, Mr. Haycox, you'll be working for me."

"Things going to be *just* like they were?"

"My wife and I'll be coming out from time to time." Now didn't seem to be the time to tell him or anyone that he and Anita would be permanent residents.

Haycox didn't care for this much. "When?"

"We'll give you plenty of notice."

He nodded grimly. Then, unexpectedly and charmingly, Mr. Haycox smiled. "Wonder if I went and offended that there

Doctor of Realty?" Pond had fled. "Well, I'll be getting back to work. Long as this here is going to be your farm, you might's well fix the pump. Needs a new packing."

"Afraid I don't know how," said Paul.

"Maybe," said Mr. Haycox walking away, "maybe if you'd of gone to college another ten or twenty years, somebody would of gotten around to showing you how, *Doctor*."

Chapter XVI

ANITA seemingly mistook Paul's quiet excitement for daydreams of happy hours to come at the Meadows, which were less than two weeks away.

She didn't know that he was learning to be a farmer and laying the groundwork for teaching her to be a farmer's wife.

It was a hot Saturday, and on the pretext of buying himself a fielder's mitt, Paul went to his farm—to his and Mr. Haycox's farm. There Mr. Haycox condescendingly and impatiently imparted half-truths about running the place, and gave Paul a vague confidence that he could get the hang of it after a while.

That evening at suppertime, Paul, satisfyingly pooped after having trailed Mr. Haycox for hours, asked his wife if she knew what day the coming Wednesday was.

She looked up from a list of things she was to pack for her trip to the Mainland and, more important, for Paul's trip to the Meadows. "Can't imagine. Have you got nice-looking tennis shoes for the trip?"

"They'll do. For your information, next Wednesday is—"

"Shepherd is taking twelve pairs of socks—all green. He's a captain, too, you know."

"I know."

"What do you make of that? It's kind of a surprise: the first time you get to be captain, he does too."

"Maybe he sent a coupon to the Rosicrucians. How on earth do you know how many pairs of socks he's taking?"

"Well, he hasn't got a wife to help him plan, so he came over this afternoon to get my help. So I made a list of things he ought to take. Men are so helpless."

"They muddle through. Did he have anything interesting to say?"

She laid down the list and looked at him reproachfully. "Only about the police report about your pistol, and another one about the underworld people you were with that awful night in Homestead." She wadded her napkin and threw it down petulantly. "Paul—why don't you tell me these things? Why do I always have to find out from someone else?"

"Underworld!" snorted Paul. "Oh, for heaven's sake."

"Shepherd says Lasher and Finnerty are being watched as potential saboteurs."

"Everybody's being watched! Why do you listen to that old woman of a man!"

"Why don't *you* tell me what's going on?"

"Because those things were trivial. Because I was afraid you wouldn't see them that way and get all upset—the way you're getting upset. It's all fixed. Kroner fixed it."

"Shepherd said you could get ten years for the pistol business alone."

"Next time he's over, ask him if he has any idea how much time I'd get if I mashed up his long nose for him."

Paul's muscles were tight from the unaccustomed rigors of the afternoon, and animal smells had communicated to him a feel of primitive strength. The notion of pushing Shepherd's face in—a bizarre sport in a lifetime of pacifistic notions—came as an unexpected complement to the day. "Well, to hell with the captain of the Green Team, I say. Again I'll ask, what day is the coming Wednesday?"

"I'm sure I don't know."

"Our engagement anniversary."

It was an anniversary with disquieting connotations for both of them—an anniversary that neither had ever mentioned in their years of marriage. It was the date on which Anita had announced to Paul that she was with child, his child, and on which he had responded by offering her his name, etc. Now, with the event softened by years of more or less adequate marriage, Paul thought that they might sentimentally make it something that it was not. The anniversary, more to the point, fell at an ideal time for the beginning of his re-education program for Anita.

"And I have a special evening planned," he said; "not like any evening we've ever had together, darling."

"Funny, I'd forgotten the date completely. Really? Next Wednesday?" She gave him an odd, rebuking smile, as though the story of their engagement had got twisted in her mind—as though she thought *he* had brought about the event by a now insignificant deception. "Well that's sweet," she said. "Kind of cute of you to remember. But, with the Meadows so close—"

She was of such a methodical nature that, when something of importance was in the offing, other aspects of life could have no importance at all. To her it seemed almost indecent to give attention to anything but the crucial matter of the Meadows.

"To hell with the Meadows."

"You don't mean that."

"I mean we're still going out next Wednesday."

"Well, I hope you know what you're doing. You're the captain."

"I'm the captain."

Chapter XVII

EDGAR R. B. HAGSTROHM, thirty-seven, R&R–131313, Undercoater First Class, 22nd Surface Preserving Battalion, 58th Maintenance Regiment, 110th Building and Grounds Division, Reconstruction and Reclamation Corps, had been named after his father's favorite author, the creator of Tarzan—Tarzan, who, far away from the soot and biting winter of the Hagstrohms' home town, Chicago, made friends with lions and elephants and apes, and swung through trees on vines, and was built like a brick outhouse with square wheels and Venetian blinds, and took what he wanted of civilization's beautiful women in tree houses, and left the rest of civilization alone. E. R. B. Hagstrohm liked Tarzan as much as his father had, and hated being a little man and being in Chicago ten times as much.

And Edgar was reading about Tarzan in the bedroom when his fat wife, Wanda, called to him from her station before the picture window in the front room of their prefabricated home in Proteus Park, Chicago, a postwar development of three thousand dream houses for three thousand families with presumably identical dreams. "Gosh, here he comes, Edgar!"

"All right, all right, all right," said Edgar. "So he's coming! So what am I supposed to do, holler bloody murder, kiss his feet, and faint?" He took his time about getting off the bed, and he didn't smooth out the dent he'd made in the bedding. He laid his book open on the bedside table, so the visitors would see that he was a reader, and started for the living room. "What's he look like, Wan?"

"You gotta see, Ed—like a Chinese bird cage or something, all gold and fancy."

The Shah of Bratpuhr had asked his guide, Doctor Ewing J. Halyard, if he might see the home of a typical *Takaru*, freely translated, from one culture to another, as "average man." The request had been made as they were passing through Chicago from Carlsbad Caverns, and Halyard had stopped off at the local personnel office for the name of a representative American in the neighborhood.

The personnel machines had considered the problem and ejected the card of Edgar R. B. Hagstrohm, who was statistically average in every respect save for the number of his initials: his age (36), his height (5′ 7″), his weight (148 lbs.), his years of marriage (11), his I.Q. (83), the number of his children (2: 1 m., 9; 1 f., 6), the number of his bedrooms (2), his car (3 yr. old Chev. 2 dr. sed.), his education (h.s. grad, 117th in class of 233; maj. in business practice; 2nd string f'ball, b'k'tb'l; soc. comm., sen'r play; no coll.), his vocation (R&R), his avocations (spec'r sports, TV, softb'l, f'sh'g), and his war record (5 yrs., 3 ov'sea; T-4 radioman; 157th Inf. Div.; battle stars: Hjoring, Elbesan, Kabul, Kaifen, Ust Kyakhta; wounded 4 times; P'ple H't, 3 cl.; Silv. Star; Br'ze Star, 2 cl.; G'd Cond. Med.).

And the machines could have made an educated guess that, since Hagstrohm had gone that far in being average, he had probably been arrested once, had had sexual experience with five girls before marrying Wanda (only moderately satisfying), and had had two extramarital adventures since (one fleeting and foolish, the other rather long and disturbing), and that he would die at the age of 76.2 of a heart attack.

What the machines couldn't guess was that Edgar's second extramarital affair, the deep one, was with a widow named Marion Frascati, that it was still going on, and that Marion's deceased husband had been Lou Frascati, a second-coater first class, Edgar's best friend. To their own profound shock, Edgar and Marion had found themselves in each other's arms a scant month after good old Lou's death. And again, and again, and again—and they'd tried to bring it to an end, honest-to-God they had. But it was like a bright, fat cherry on the gray mush of their lives. And they thought, wistfully, weakly, that maybe it wouldn't really matter as long as no one was hurt—the kids, sweet, loyal Wanda. And that Lou wouldn't have wanted anything more, now that he had another variety of bliss, than that good old Edgar and good old Marion make the most of life while they had the use of their flesh.

But they hadn't believed it. And the kids noticed something screwy was going on, and Wanda'd cried a couple of times lately and refused to tell him why, and probably Lou, wherever he was. . . . Anyway, Edgar was going to go on seeing

Marion, but he was going to tell Wanda, God bless her and God help her—tell her, and— Who was banging on the Hagstrohm door but the goddam Shah of Bratpuhr, for Chrissakes.

"Come in, come in," said Edgar, and he added under his breath, "your majesty, your highness, emperor of the universe and all the ships at sea, you nosy son-of-a-bitch."

When Halyard had phoned him about the visit, Hagstrohm had made a point of not being impressed by the Shah's title, or by Halyard's rank. It was rarely that he got the opportunity to show what he thought of rank—that a man was a man for all that. He was going to behave perfectly naturally, just as he would if the callers had been fellow Reeks and Wrecks. Wanda had taken a different view, and had started frantically to clean the place from top to bottom, and to make lemonade and send Edgar, Jr., out for little cookies, but big Edgar had put a stop to all that. He put the kids out, and that was the only cleaning up that was to be done.

The door opened, and in came the Shah, followed by Khashdrahr, Halyard, and Doctor Ned Dodge, the manager of Proteus Park.

"Aha!" said the Shah, gingerly touching the enameled steel wall of the living room. "Mmmmm."

Edgar held out his hand, and the parade brushed past it, heedless. "Well, kiss mine," he muttered.

"Eh?" said Doctor Dodge.

"You heard me."

"You're not in a saloon now, Hagstrohm," whispered Dodge. "Watch yourself; this is international relations."

"All right if I go to a saloon?"

"What's eating you, anyway?"

"The guy walks into my house and won't even shake my hand."

"It's not the custom in his country."

"Is it in yours?"

Dodge turned his back and grinned hospitably at the Shah. "Two bedrooms, living room with dining alcove, bath, and kitchen," he said. "This is the M-17 house. Radiant heating in the floor. The furniture was designed after an exhaustive national survey of furniture likes and dislikes. The house, the furniture, and the lot are sold as a package. Simplified planning and production all the way round."

"*Lakki-ti, Takaru*?" piped the Shah, looking at Edgar closely for the first time.

"What's he say?"

"He wants to know if you like it here," said Khashdrahr.

"Sure—I guess. It's all right. I suppose. Yeah."

"It's nice," said Wanda.

"Now, if you'll follow me into the kitchen," said Doctor Dodge, leaving Wanda and Edgar behind, "you'll see the radar range. Cooks by high frequency, and cooks the inside of whatever's being cooked as fast as the outside. Cooks anything in a matter of seconds, with perfect control. Make bread without a crust, if you want to."

"What is the matter with crust on bread?" asked Khashdrahr politely.

"And this is the ultrasonic dishwasher and clotheswasher," said Dodge. "High-frequency sound passing through the water strips dirt and grease off anything in a matter of seconds. Dip in, take out, bingo!"

"And then what does the woman do?" asked Khashdrahr.

"Then she puts the clothes or dishes in this drier, which dries them out in a matter of seconds, and—here's a nifty trick, I think—gives the clothes a spanking-clean outdoors odor, like they were dried in the sun, see, with this little ozone lamp in here."

"And then what?" asked Khashdrahr.

"She feeds the clothes through this ironer, which can do what was an hour's ironing before the war in three minutes. Bing!"

"And then what does she do?" asked Khashdrahr.

"And then she's done."

"And then what?"

Doctor Dodge reddened perceptibly. "Is this a joke?"

"No," said Khashdrahr. "The Shah would like to know what it is that the woman *Takaru*—"

"What's a *Takaru*?" said Wanda suspiciously.

"Citizen," said Halyard.

"Yes," said Khashdrahr, smiling at her oddly, "citizen. The Shah would like to know why she has to do everything so quickly—this in a matter of seconds, that in a matter of seconds. What is it she is in such a hurry to get at? What is it she has to do, that she mustn't waste any time on these things?"

"Live!" said Doctor Dodge expansively. "Live! Get a little fun out of life." He laughed, and clapped Khashdrahr on the back, as though to jar him into feeling some of the jollity in this average American man's home.

The effect on Khashdrahr and the Shah was a poor one. "I see," said the interpreter coldly. He turned to Wanda. "And how is it you live and get so much fun out of life?"

Wanda blushed and looked down at the floor, and worried the carpet edge with her toe. "Oh, television," she murmured. "Watch that a lot, don't we, Ed? And I spend a lot of time with the kids, little Delores and young Edgar, Jr. You know. Things."

"Where are the children now?" asked Khashdrahr.

"Over at the neighbors' place, the Glocks, watching television, I expect."

"Would you like to see the ultrasonic washer work?" said Doctor Dodge. "Right before your eyes, bing! Takes off egg, lipstick, bloodstains—"

"The transducer's shot again," said Edgar, "so the washer's out of commission. Wanda's been doing the washing in a tub for a month now, waiting for a new transducer."

"Oh, I don't mind," said Wanda. "Really, I like doin' 'em that way. It's kind of a relief. A body needs a change. I don't mind. Gives me something to do."

Halyard ended the silence that followed her statement with a brisk suggestion that they leave these good people alone and have a look at the central recreation pavilion down the street.

"If we hurry," said Doctor Dodge, "we'll probably catch the leathercraft class still in session."

The Shah patted the radar stove, the laundry console, and peered for a moment at the television screen, which showed five persons seated around a conference table, arguing earnestly. "*Brahouna*!" he chuckled.

Khashdrahr nodded. "*Brahouna*! Live!"

As the party left, Halyard was explaining that the house and contents and car were all paid for by regular deductions from Edgar's R&RC pay check, along with premiums on his combination health, life, and old age security insurance, and that the furnishings and equipment were replaced from time to time with newer models as Edgar—or the payroll machines, rather—completed payments on the old ones. "He has a *complete* security package," said Halyard. "His standard of living is constantly rising, and he and the country at large are protected from the old economic ups and down by the orderly, predictable consumer habits the payroll machines give him. Used to be he'd buy on impulse, illogically, and industry would go nutty trying to figure out what he was going to buy next. Why, I remember when I was a little boy, we had a crazy neighbor who blew all his money on an electric organ, while he still had an old-fashioned icebox and kerosene stove in his kitchen!"

Edgar closed the door and leaned against it, against the door of his M-17 castle.

Wanda sank to the couch. "The place looked nice, I think," she said. She said it whenever a visitor—Amy Glock, Gladys Pelrine, the Shah of Bratpuhr, anybody—left.

"Yep," said Edgar. And he felt evil and damned as he looked at Wanda, good, good soul, who'd never done anything to offend him, whose love for him was as big as all outdoors. He fingered the three ten-dollar bills in his pocket, his take-home pay—cigarette money, recreation money, small luxury money the machines let him have. This tiny atom of the economy under his control he was going to spend, not on himself or Wanda or the kids, but on Marion. Edgar's troubled heart had gone out to the crazy man in Halyard's story, the guy who'd bought himself an electric organ. Expensive, impractical, strictly personal—above and beyond the goddamned package.

But deceit was another thing. "Wanda," said Edgar, "I'm no good."

She knew what he was talking about, all right. She wasn't in the least surprised. "Yes, you are, Edgar," she said lamely. "You're a fine man. I understand."

"About Marion?"

"Yes. She's very beautiful and charming. And I'm not exactly a girl any more, and I expect I'm pretty dull." She started to cry, and, good soul that she was, she tried to keep him from seeing it. She hurried into the kitchen, took four suppers from the deep freeze, and thrust them into the radar range. "Call the children, will you please, Edgar?" she said in a small, high voice. "Supper will be ready in twenty-eight seconds."

Edgar shouted the children's names into the twilight, and returned to Wanda. "Listen, Wan—it isn't you. The Lord knows it isn't your fault." He hugged her from behind, and she twisted away and pretended to adjust dials on the range, though there was no adjusting to be done. Clockwork was doing everything.

Chimes rang, the clockwork clicked, and the range's humming stopped. "Call the children before everything gets cold," she said.

"They're coming." Edgar tried to hug her again, and she let him this time. "Listen," he said passionately, "it's the world, Wan—me and the world. I'm no good to anybody, not in *this* world. Nothing but a Reek and Wreck, and that's all my kids'll be, and a guy's got to have kicks or he doesn't want to live—and the only kicks left for a dumb bastard like me are the bad ones. I'm no good, Wan, no good!"

"It's me that's no good to anybody," said Wanda wearily. "Nobody needs me. You or even little old Delores could run the house and all, it's so easy. And now I'm too fat for anybody but the kids to love me. My mother got fat, and my grandmother got fat, and guess it's in the blood; but somebody needed them, they were still some good. But you don't need me, Ed, and you can't help it if you don't love me any more. Just the way men are, and you can't help it if you're the way God made you." She looked at him lovingly, pityingly. "Poor man."

Delores and Edgar, Jr., bustled in, and Edgar and Wanda composed themselves and told their children all about the Shah.

The subject was soon exhausted, and at dinner only the children spoke and touched their food.

"Somebody sick?" said Edgar, Jr.

"Your mother isn't well. She has a headache," said Edgar.

"Yeah? That's too bad, Mom."

"Just a little thing," said Wanda. "It'll pass."

"How about you, Pop?" said Edgar, Jr. "You well enough to take in the basketball game at the pavilion tonight?"

Edgar kept his eyes on his plate. "Like to," he mumbled. "Promised Joe I'd go bowling with him tonight."

"Joe Prince?"

"Yeah, Joe Prince."

"Why, Daddy," said Delores, "we saw Mr. Prince over to the Glocks', and he said he was going to the basketball game."

"He did not!" said Edgar, Jr., fiercely. "Just be quiet. You don't know what you're talking about. He didn't say that at all."

"He did, too!" said Delores stubbornly. "He said—"

"Delores, honey," said Wanda, "I'm sure you misunderstood Mr. Prince."

"Yes," said Edgar, Jr., "I remember now he said he was going bowling with Pop. Sis got it all wrong, Mom." His hands were trembling, and, clumsily, he knocked over his milk glass. Both he and his father jumped to their feet to catch it before it toppled all the way. Young Edgar caught it, and when his eyes met old Edgar's they were full of hate. "Guess I'm too tired to go to the ball game after all," he said. "Guess I'll stay home and watch television with Mom."

"Don't miss any good times on my account," said Wanda. "I get along just fine by myself."

There was a series of sharp taps on the picture window, and the Hagstrohms looked up to see the Shah of Bratpuhr rattling his ringed fingers against the glass. He had just returned from the pavilion to the limousine, which had been left in front of the Hagstrohm's M-17 home.

"*Brahouna*!" cried the Shah cheerfully. He waved. "*Brahouna, Takaru.*"

" 'Live!' " translated Krashdrahr.

Chapter XVIII

WHEN WEDNESDAY CAME, Paul stopped by his farm early in the morning and gave Mr. Haycox his instructions. Mr. Haycox made it clear that he wasn't a parlor maid.

Reluctantly, Paul gave Mr. Haycox to understand that he could do the job or clear out, and that the job had better be well done. It was that important to Paul that everything be perfect for the delicate transformation of Anita.

"You think you can just go around buying anybody to do anything you damn please," said Mr. Haycox. "Well, you're mistaken this time, Doctor. You can take your doctor's degree, and—"

"I don't want to fire you."

"Then don't!"

"For the last time, as a favor to me—"

"Why didn't you say so in the first place?"

"Say what?"

" 'As a favor.' "

"All right; as a favor—"

"As a favor, just this once," said Mr. Haycox. "I'm no parlor maid, but I try to be a good friend."

"Thanks."

"Nothing at all. Don't mention it."

During the day, Anita called Paul to ask what she was to wear.

"Old clothes."

"A barn dance?"

"Not quite, but close. Dress as though it were."

"Paul, with the Meadows so close and all, do you think we should be going out and tearing around?"

"The Meadows isn't a funeral."

"It could be, Paul."

"Just for tonight, let's forget the Meadows. Tonight it's going to be just Paul and Anita, and to hell with everybody else."

"That's very easy to say, Paul. It's a sweet idea and everything, but—"

"But what?" he asked irritably.

"Well, I don't know; I don't want to nag, but it does seem to me that you're being awfully slap-happy about the Meadows, about the Blue Team."

"What should I be doing?"

"Shouldn't you be training or something? I mean, shouldn't you be getting lots of sleep and eating the right foods and jogging around a little after work? And cutting down on cigarettes, maybe?"

"What?"

"You've got to be in shape if the Blue Team's going to win."

Paul laughed.

"Now listen, Paul, you needn't laugh. Shepherd says he's seen careers made and broken by how men made out as team captains at the Meadows. Shepherd's given up smoking completely."

"You can tell him I've taken up hashish to speed up my reaction time. His fast ball will look like a toy balloon blowing over home plate. We *are* going out tonight."

"All right," she said gloomily. "All right."

"I love you, Anita.

"I love *you*, Paul."

And she was ready when he got home, not as Ilium's Lady of the Manor but as a trim, kittenish girl in denim trousers rolled above her knees. She wore one of Paul's shirts, with its tails knotted below her breasts, white sneakers, and a red bandana about her neck.

"Is this right?"

"Perfect."

"Paul—I don't understand what's going on. I called up the Country Club, and they don't know about any barn dance. And neither do the clubs in Albany, Troy, or Schenectady." Anita, Paul knew, hated surprises, couldn't bear not to be on top of every situation.

"This is a private one," said Paul. "Just for the two of us. You'll see when the time comes."

"I want to know now."

"Where are our anniversary martinis?" The table where the pitcher and glasses awaited him every night was bare.

"You're on the wagon until after the Meadows."

"Don't be ridiculous! Everybody is going to be drinking for two weeks up there."

"Not the captains. Shepherd says *they* can't afford to drink."

"That shows how much he knows. The drinks are on the house."

Paul mixed martinis, drank more than his usual ration, and changed into a suit of stiff, crackling denim overalls he'd bought in Homestead that afternoon. He was sorry to see that Anita was getting no pleasure from the suspense he'd built up. Instead of happy anticipation, she showed signs of suspicion.

"Ready?" he said brightly.

"Yes—I suppose."

They walked in silence to the garage. With a grand gesture, Paul held the car door open.

"Oh, Paul, *not* the old car."

"There's a reason."

"There couldn't be a reason good enough to get me in that thing."

"Please, Anita—you'll see soon enough why we've got to take this one."

She got in and sat on the edge of the seat, trying to come in contact with the car as little as possible. "Honestly! I mean really!"

They rode like strangers. On the long grade by the golf course, however, she unbent a trifle. In the beams of the headlights was a pale and hairy man in green shorts, green socks, and a green shirt with the word "Captain" written across it. The man was jogging along the shoulder of the road, now and then breaking his pace to pirouette and shadowbox, then picking up his jogging again.

Paul blasted Shepherd with his automobile horn, and was delighted to see him bound across the ditch to get out of his way.

Anita rolled down her window and cheered.

The captain of the Green Team waved, his face twisted by exertion.

Paul pressed the throttle to the floor, laying down a cloud of burned oil and carbon monoxide.

"That man's got a lot of get up and go," said Anita.

"He fills me full of lie down and die," said Paul.

They were passing the battlements of the Ilium Works now,

and one of the guards, recognizing Paul's car from his pillbox, waggled his fifty-caliber machine gun in friendly fashion.

Anita, who had been getting more and more restless, made as though to grab the wheel. "Paul! Where are you going? Are you crazy?"

He brushed her hand away, smiled, and kept on going across the bridge into Homestead.

The bridge was blocked again by Reeks and Wrecks who were painting yellow lines to mark traffic lanes. Paul looked at his watch. They had ten more minutes until time for, as the expression went, knocking off work. Paul wondered if Bud Calhoun had thought up this project. Like most of the R&R projects, it was, to Paul at least, ironic. The four-lane bridge had, before the war, been jammed with the cars of workers going to and from the Ilium Works. Four lanes had been nothing like enough, and a driver stayed within his lane or got the side of his car ground off. Now, at any time of day, a driver could swerve from one side of the bridge to the other with perhaps one chance in ten thousand of hitting another vehicle.

Paul came to a stop. Three men were painting, twelve were directing traffic, and another twelve were resting. Slowly, they opened a lane.

"Hey, Mac, your headlamp's busted."

"Thanks," said Paul.

Anita slid across the seat to get close to him, and he saw that she was scared stiff. "Paul—this is awful. Take me home."

Paul smiled patiently and drove into Homestead. The hydrant in front of the saloon by the end of the bridge was going again, and he had to park down the block. The same dirty boy was making paper boats for the amusement of the crowd. Leaning against a building and smoking nervously was a seedy old man who looked familiar to Paul. Then Paul realized that the man was Luke Lubbock, the indefatigable joiner, who was lost in the limbo of mufti, waiting for the next parade or meeting to start. With mixed emotions he looked around for Lasher and Finnerty, but saw no sign of them. Very probably they were in the saloon's dark, rearmost booth, agreeing on everything.

"Paul—is this your idea of a joke? Take me home, *please.*"

"Nobody's going to hurt you. These people are just your fellow Americans."

"Just because they were born in the same part of the world as I was, that doesn't mean I have to come down here and wallow with them."

Paul had expected this reaction, and remained patient in the face of it. Of all the people on the north side of the river, Anita was the only one whose contempt for those in Homestead was laced with active hatred. She was also the only wife on the north side who had never been to college at all. The usual attitude of the Country Club set toward Homesteaders was contempt, all right, but it had an affectionate and amused undertone, the same sort of sentiment felt by most for creatures of the woods and fields. Anita hated Homesteaders.

If Paul were ever moved to be extremely cruel to her, the cruelest thing he could do, he knew, would be to point out to her why she hated as she did: if he hadn't married her, this was where she'd be, what she'd be.

"We're not getting out," said Paul. "We'll just sit here a few minutes and watch. Then we'll move on."

"Watch what?"

"Whatever there is to see. The line painters, the man running the hydrant, the people watching him, the little boy making boats, the old men in the saloon. Just keep looking around. There's plenty to see."

She didn't look around, but slouched down in the seat and stared at her hands.

Paul had an idea what she was thinking—that for some reason she couldn't understand, he was doing this to humiliate her, to recall her humble origins. Had that been what he wanted to do, he would have been completely successful, because her virulent hate had decayed. She'd fallen silent and tried to make herself small.

"You know why I brought you here?"

Her voice was a whisper. "No. But I want to go home, Paul. Please?"

"Anita—I brought us here because I think it's high time we got a completely new perspective, not on just our relationship to ourselves, but on our relationship to society as a whole." He didn't like the sound of the words as they came out, sententious and inflated. Their impact on Anita was nothing.

He tried again: "In order to get what we've got, Anita, we have, in effect, traded these people out of what was the most important thing on earth to them—the feeling of being needed and useful, the foundation of self-respect." That wasn't much good either. He wasn't getting through to Anita yet. She still seemed certain that she was somehow being punished by him.

He tried once more: "Darling, when I see what we've got, and then see what these people have got, I feel like a horse's ass."

A glimmering of understanding crossed Anita's face. Guardedly, she cheered up a little. "Then you're not mad at me?"

"Lord, no. Why should I be mad at you?"

"I don't know. I thought maybe you thought I nagged too much—or maybe you thought something was going on between Shepherd and me."

This last—this suggestion that he would ever worry about Shepherd—threw Paul completely off the orderly course of re-educating Anita. The notion that he might be jealous of the captain of the Green Team was so ludicrous, showed so poor an understanding, that it commanded his full attention. "I'll be jealous of Shepherd when you're jealous of Katharine Finch," he laughed.

This, to his surprise, Anita chose to take seriously. "You don't mean that!"

"Mean what?"

"That I should be jealous of Katharine Finch. That dumpy little—"

"Wait a minute!" The conversation was really afield now. "I just meant there was about as much chance of there being something between Katharine and me as there was of there being something between you and Shepherd."

She was still on the defensive, and apparently hadn't grasped the negative sense of his parallel. She came back at him aggressively. "Well, Shepherd is certainly a more attractive man than Katharine is a woman."

"I'm not arguing that," said Paul desperately. "I don't want to argue that at all. There isn't anything between Katharine and me, and there isn't anything between you and Shepherd. I was simply pointing out how absurd it would be for either one of us to suspect the other."

"You don't think I'm attractive?"

"I think you're devastatingly attractive. You know that." His voice had gotten loud, and as he glanced out at the street scene he saw that he and Anita, the would-be observers, were being observed. A paper boat shot the rapids to the storm sewer unnoticed. "I didn't bring us here to accuse each other of adultery," he whispered hoarsely.

"Then why did you?"

"I told you: so we could both get the feel of the world as a whole, not just our side of the river. So we could see what our way of life has done to the lives of others."

Anita was on top of the situation now, having successfully attacked and confused Paul, and having found that she wasn't being baited or punished. "They all look perfectly well fed to me."

"But they've had the spiritual stuffing knocked out of them by people like my father, like Kroner and Baer and Shepherd, like us."

"They couldn't have been too well stuffed in the first place, or they wouldn't be here."

Paul was mad, and the delicate mechanism that kept him from hurting her stripped its gears. "Here, but for the grace of God, go you!"

"Paul!" She burst into tears. "That's not fair," she said brokenly. "Not at all fair. I don't know why you had to say that."

"It isn't fair for you to cry."

"You're cruel, that's what you are—just plain cruel. If you wanted to hurt me, congratulate yourself. You certainly did." She blew her nose. "I must have had something these people don't, or you wouldn't have married me."

"Oligomenorrhea," he said.

She blinked. "What's that?"

"Oligomenorrhea—that's what you had that these others don't. Means delayed menstrual period."

"How on earth did you ever learn a word like that?"

"I looked it up a month after we were married, and it etched itself on the inside of my skull."

"Oh." She turned crimson. "You've said enough, quite enough," she said bitterly. "If you won't drive me home, I'll walk."

Paul started the car, abused the gears with savage satisfaction, and drove back across the bridge, toward the north side of the river.

When they'd reached the mid-point of the bridge, he was still warmed and excited by the sudden fight with Anita. By the time they were under the guns of the Ilium Works, rationality and remorse were setting in.

The fight had been a complete surprise. Never had they gone at it so poisonously. More surprising, Paul had been the vicious one, and Anita had been little more than a victim. Confusedly he tried to remember the events that had led up to the fight. His memory was no help.

And how completely fruitless and destructive the fight had been! In the heat of a bad instant he had said what he knew would hurt her most, would, by extension, make her hate him most. And he hadn't wanted to do that. God knows he hadn't. And here he was with his cheery and careful plans for starting a new life with her shot to hell.

They were passing the golf course now. In minutes they'd be home.

"Anita—"

By way of an answer, she turned on the car radio and impatiently twiddled the dials, waiting for the volume to come up, presumably to drown him out. The radio hadn't worked for years.

"Anita—listen. I love you more than anybody on earth. Good God but I'm sorry about what we said to each other."

"I didn't say anything to you like what you said to me."

"I could cut my tongue out for having said those things."

"Don't use any of our good kitchen knives."

"It was a freak."

"So am I, apparently. You passed our driveway."

"I meant to. I have a surprise for you. Then you'll see how much I really love you—how insignificant that stupid fight was."

"I've had quite enough surprises tonight, thank you. Turn around, please. I'm worn out."

"This surprise cost eight thousand, Anita. Still want to turn around?"

"Think I can be bought, do you?" she said angrily, but her expression was softening, answering her own question. "What on earth could it be? Really? Eight thousand dollars?"

Paul relaxed, settling back in his seat to enjoy the ride. "You don't belong in Homestead, sweetheart."

"Oh, hell—maybe I do."

"No, no. You've got something the tests and machines will never be able to measure: you're artistic. That's one of the tragedies of our times, that no machine has ever been built that can recognize that quality, appreciate it, foster it, sympathize with it."

"It is," said Anita sadly. "It is, it is."

"I love you, Anita."

"I love *you*, Paul."

"Look! A deer!" Paul flicked on his bright lights to illuminate the animal, and recognized the captain of the Green Team, still jogging, but now in an advanced state of exhaustion. Shepherd's legs flailed about weakly and disjointedly, and his feet struck the pavement with loud, limp slaps. There was no recognition in his eyes this time, and he floundered on heedlessly.

"With every step he hammers another nail into my coffin," said Paul, lighting a fresh cigarette from the one he had just finished.

Ten minutes later he stopped the car, went around to Anita's side, and affectionately offered his arm. "The latchstring is out, darling, for a whole new and happier life for the two of us."

"What does that mean?"

"You'll see." He led her to the front door of the low little house through a dark, fragrant tunnel roofed and walled by lilacs. He took her hand and placed it on the latchstring. "Pull."

She tugged gingerly. The latch inside clattered free, and the door swung open. "Oh! Ohhhh—Paul!"

"Ours. This belongs to Paul and Anita."

She walked in slowly, her head back, her nostrils wide. "I feel like crying, it's so darling."

Hastily, Paul checked the preparations for the tricky hours ahead, and was delighted. Mr. Haycox, probably in an orgy of masochism, had scrubbed every surface. Gone were the soot and dust, leaving only the clean, soft, glowing patina of age over everything—the pewter on the mantel, the cherry case of the grandfather clock, the black ironware on the hearth, the walnut stock and silver inlays of the long rifle on the wall, the tin potbellies of the kerosene lamps, the warm, worn maple of the chairs. . . . And on a table in the center of the room, looking archaic, too, in the soft light, were two glasses, a pitcher, a bottle of gin, a bottle of vermouth, and a bucket of ice. And beside these were two glasses of whole, fresh milk from the farm, fresh hard-boiled eggs from the farm, fresh peas from the farm, and fresh fried chicken from the farm.

As Paul mixed the drinks, Anita went about the room sighing happily, touching everything lovingly. "Is it really ours?"

"As of yesterday. I signed the final papers. Do you really feel at home here?"

She dropped into a chair before the fireplace and took the glass he handed her. "Can't you tell? Don't I radiate how I feel?" She laughed quietly. "He wants to know if I like it. It's priceless, you brilliant darling, and you got it for eight thousand dollars! Aren't you smart!"

"Happy anniversary, Anita."

"I want a stronger word than happy."

"Ecstatic anniversary, Anita."

"Ecstatic anniversary to you, Paul. I love you. Lord, how I love you!"

"I love *you*." He had never loved her so much.

"Do you realize, darling, that that grandfather clock alone is worth almost a thousand dollars?"

Paul felt terribly clever. It was fantastic how well things were turning out. Anita's contentment with the place was genuine, and the process of weaning her from one house to another, from one way of life to another, seemed, in a miraculous few minutes, to have been almost completed. "This *is* your kind of surroundings, isn't it."

"You know it is."

"Did you know the clock had wooden works? Think of it? Every part whittled out of wood."

"Don't worry about it. That's easily remedied."

"Hmm?"

"We can get an electric movement put in."

"But the whole charm—"

She was in a transport of creativity now, and didn't hear him. "You see—with the pendulum gone, an electrostatic dust precipitator would fit right in the lower part of the case."

"Oh."

"And you know where I'd put it?"

He looked around the room and saw no spot for it other than where it was. "That niche there seems ideal."

"In the front hall! Can't you just see it there?"

"There is no front hall," he said in puzzlement. The front door opened right into the living room.

"*Our* front hall, silly."

"But, Anita—"

"And that spice cabinet on the wall—wouldn't it be darling with some of the drawers sticking out, and with philodendron growing from them? I know just the spot in the guest room."

"Swell."

"And these priceless rafters, Paul! This means we can have rough-hewn beams in our living room, too. Not just in the kitchen, but the living room too! And I'll eat your classification card if that dry-sink won't take our television set."

"I was looking forward to eating it myself," said Paul quietly.

"And these wide-board floors: you can imagine what they'll do for the rumpus room."

"What did the rumpus room ever do for me?" said Paul grimly.

"What did you say?"

"I said, what did the rumpus room ever do for me?"

"Oh. I see." She laughed perfunctorily and, her eyes bright, she searched for more plunder.

"Anita—"

"Yes? Oh! What a delightful Cape Cod lighter."

"Listen to me for just a minute."

"Certainly, darling."

"I bought this place for us to live in."

"You mean just the way it is?"

"Exactly. It can't be changed."

"You mean we can't take any of these things out?"

"No. But we can move ourselves in."

"This is another one of your jokes. Don't tease me, darling. I'm having such a good time."

"I'm not teasing! This is the life I want. This is where I want to live it."

"It's so dark, I can't see by your face whether you're serious or not. Turn on the lights."

"No lights."

"No electricity?"

"Only what's in your hair."

"How do they run the furnace?"

"No furnace."

"And the stove?"

"Firewood. And the refrigerator is a cold spring."

"How perfectly hideous!"

"I'm serious, Anita. I want us to live here."

"We'd die in six months."

"The Haycox family lived here for generations."

"You *are* playful tonight, aren't you? Just so straight-faced and everything, keeping your joke alive. Come here and kiss me, you sweet clown."

"We're going to spend the night here, and tomorrow I'm going to do the chores. Will you give it a try, anyway?"

"And I'll be a good old fat farm Mama, and get breakfast on the wood stove—coffee, home-grown eggs and cream, home-baked biscuits drowned in homemade butter and jam."

"Would you?"

"I'd drown in butter and jam first."

"You could learn to love this life."

"I couldn't, and you know it."

His temper was rising again, in response to bitter disappointment, as it had done an hour before in Homestead. And again he was looking for something short of a slap in her face that would shock humility into her. The sentence that came out had been ready for a long time. He spoke it now, not because now was the right time, but because it packed a punch.

"It doesn't matter what you think," he said evenly. "I've made up my mind to quit my job and live here. Do you understand? I'm going to quit."

She folded her arms across her chest, as though fighting a chill, and rocked in silence for a few moments. "I thought maybe that was coming," she said at last. "I thought maybe that was what you were up to. I'd hoped it wasn't, Paul. I'd prayed it wasn't. But—well, here we are, and you've said it." She lit a cigarette, smoked it in shallow, tasteless puffs, and blew the smoke through her nose. "Shepherd said you would."

"He said I was about to quit?"

"No. He said you were a quitter." She sighed heavily. "He knows you better than I do, apparently."

"God knows it'd be easy enough to stick with the system, and keep going right on up. It's getting out that takes nerve."

"But why quit, if it's so easy to stick with it?"

"Didn't you hear anything I said in Homestead? That's why I took you there, so you'd get the feel of things."

"That silly business about Katharine Finch and Shepherd?"

"No, no—God no. About how people like us have taken all the self-respect from all the others."

"You said you felt like a horse's ass. I remember that."

"Don't you, sometimes?"

"What an idea!"

"Your conscience, dammit—doesn't it ever bother you?"

"Why should it? I've never done anything dishonest."

"Let me put it another way: do you agree things are a mess?"

"Between us?"

"Everywhere! The world!" She could be appallingly near-sighted. Whenever possible, she liked to reduce any generalization to terms of herself and persons she knew intimately. "Homestead, for instance."

"What else could we possibly give the people that they haven't got?"

"There! You made my point for me. You said, what else could *we* give *them*, as though everything in the world were ours to give or withhold."

"Somebody's got to take responsibility, and that's just the way it is when somebody does."

"That's just it: things haven't always been that way. It's new, and it's people like us who've brought it about. Hell, everybody used to have some personal skill or willingness to work or something he could trade for what he wanted. Now that the machines have taken over, it's quite somebody who has anything to offer. All most people can do is hope to be given something."

"If someone has brains," said Anita firmly, "he can still get to the top. That's the American way, Paul, and it hasn't changed." She looked at him appraisingly. "Brains and nerve, Paul."

"And blinders." The punch was gone from his voice, and he felt drugged, a drowsiness from a little too much to drink, from scrambling over a series of emotional peaks and pits, from utter frustration.

Anita caught the strap of his overalls and pulled him down to kiss him. Paul yielded stiffly.

"Ohhhhhhh," she chided, "you're *such* a little boy sometimes." She pulled him down again, this time making sure he kissed her on the lips. "You stop worrying, now, you hear?" she whispered in his ear.

"Descent into the Maelstrom," he thought wearily, and closed his eyes, and gave himself over to the one sequence of events that had never failed to provide a beginning, a middle, and a satisfactory end.

"I love you, Paul," she murmured. "I don't want my little boy to worry. You're not going to quit, sweetheart. You're just awfully tired."

"Mmmm."

"Promise not to think any more about it?"

"Mmmm."

"And, we *are* going to Pittsburgh, aren't we?"

"Mmmm."

"And what team is going to win at the Meadows?"

"Mmmm."

"Paul—"

"Hmmm?"

"What team is going to win?"

"Blue," he whispered sleepily. "Blue, by God, Blue."

"That's my boy. Your father would be awfully proud."

"Yup."

He carried her across the wide-board floor into the pine-wainscoted bedroom and laid her down on a patchwork quilt on a bird's-eye maple bed. There, Mr. Haycox had told him, six independent people had died, and fourteen had been born.

Chapter XIX

DOCTOR PAUL PROTEUS, for want of a blow severe enough to knock him off the course dictated by the circumstances of his birth and training, arrived uneventfully at the day when it was time for men whose development was not yet complete to go to the Meadows.

The crisis was coming, he knew, when he would have to quit or turn informer, but its approach was unreal, and, lacking a decisive plan for meeting it, he forced a false tranquillity on himself—a vague notion that everything would come out all right in the end, the way it always had for him.

The big passenger plane, after an hour in the air, circled over the shore, where the pine forest met the waters at the source of the St. Lawrence. The plane dropped lower, and the landing strip in the forest could be seen, and then the cluster of log lodges and dining hall and shuffleboard courts and tennis courts and badminton courts and softball diamonds and swings and slides and bingo pavilion of the Mainland, the camp for women and children. And jutting into the river was a long dock and three white yachts, the port of embarkation for men going to the island called the Meadows.

"I guess this is just about goodbye," said Paul to Anita, as the plane came to a stop.

"You look wonderful," said Anita, straightening his blue captain's shirt for him. "And what team is going to win?"

"Blue," said Paul. "*Gott mit uns.*"

"Now, I'm going to be working on Mom here, while—"

"Ladies over here!" boomed the public address system. "Men will assemble over on the dock. Leave your luggage where it is. It will be in your cabins when you arrive."

"Goodbye, darling," said Anita.

"Goodbye, Anita."

"I love you, Paul."

"I love *you*, Anita."

"Come on," said Shepherd, who had arrived on the same plane. "Let's get going. I'm anxious to see just how hot this Blue Team is."

"Blue Team, eh?" said Baer. "Worried about the Blue Team, are you, eh? Eh? White. White's the one to look out for, boy." He stretched out his white shirt for them to admire. "See? See? That's the shirt to look out for. See? Aha, aha—"

"Where's Doctor Kroner?" said Shepherd.

"Went up yesterday," said Paul. "He's among the official greeters, so he's already on the island." He waved once more to Anita, who was going down a gravel path toward the Mainland's buildings with a dozen other women, Katharine Finch and Mom Kroner among them, and a handful of children. All day, planes would be bringing more.

Anita sidled up to Mom and took her fat arm.

Concealed loudspeakers in the virgin forest burst into song:

"To you, beautiful lady, I raise my eyes;
My heart, beautiful lady, to your heart sighs.
Come, come, beautiful lady, to Paradise . . ."

The song died in a clatter in the loudspeaker, a cough, and then a command: "Men with classification numbers from zero to one hundred will please board the *Queen of the Meadows*; those with numbers from one hundred to two hundred and fifty will board the *Meadow Lark*; those with numbers above two hundred and fifty will get on the *Spirit of the Meadows*."

Paul, Shepherd, Baer, and the rest of the contingent from the Albany-Troy-Schenectady-Ilium area walked out onto the dock where earlier arrivals were waiting. All put on dark glasses, which they would wear during the next two weeks to protect their eyes from the unrelenting glare of the summer sun on the river, and on the whitewashed buildings, white gravel paths, white beach, and white cement courts of the Meadows.

"Green's going to win!" shouted Shepherd.

"You tell 'em, Cap!"

Everyone shouted and sang, the marine engines burbled and roared, and the three yachts shot toward the island in V-formation.

Squinting through spray, Paul watched the Meadows come closer and closer, hot, bleached, and sanitary. The white serpent stretching the island's length could now be seen as a row of white cubes, the insulated cement-block structures called, in Meadows parlance dating back to more primitive facilities, tents. The amphitheater on the island's northernmost tip looked like a dinner plate, and the sports area around it was a geometric patchwork of every imaginable kind of court. Whitewashed rocks everywhere framed the paths and gar——

The air quaked with a sharp, painful crash. And another. Another. "*Blam!*"

Rockets from the island were exploding overhead. In another minute the three yachts were rumbling and fuming into their slips, and the band was playing "The Star-Spangled Banner."

"And the rockets red glare,
The bombs bursting in air . . ."

The bandmaster held up his baton, and the bandsmen paused significantly.

"*Vuuuuzzzzzzip!*" went a rocket. "*Kablooooom!*"

"Gave proof through the night,
That our flag was still there . . ."

After the anthem came a cheery kaleidoscope of "Pack Up Your Troubles," "I Want a Girl," "Take Me Out to the Ball Game," "Working on the Railroad."

The new arrivals scrambled over the decks to catch the hands extended from the wharf by a rank of older men, most of whom were fat, gray, and balding. These were the Grand Old Men—the district managers, the regional managers, the associate vice-presidents and assistant vice-presidents and vice-presidents of the Eastern and Middle-Western divisions.

"Welcome aboard!" was the greeting, and always had been. "Welcome aboard!"

Paul saw that Kroner was reserving his big hand and welcome for him, and he picked his way across the deck until he reached the hand, took it, and stepped to the wharf.

"Good to have you aboard, Paul."

"Thank you, sir. It's good to be aboard." A number of the other older men paused in their greetings to look in friendly fashion at the bright young son of their departed wartime leader.

"Report to the Ad Building for registration, then check into your tents to make sure your luggage is there," said the public address system. "Get to know your tentmate, then lunch."

With the band leading them, the new arrivals swung along the gravel walk to the Administration Building.

Across the building's entrance was a banner declaring: "The Blue Team Welcomes You to the Meadows."

There were cries of good-natured outrage, and human pyramids were built in a twinkling, with the top men clawing down the infuriating message.

A young member of the Blue Team slapped Paul on the back. "What an idea, Cap'n!" he crowed. "Boy, that really showed 'em who's got the wide-awake outfit. And we'll go on showing these guys, too."

"Yep," said Paul, "you bet. That's the spirit." Apparently this was the youngster's first visit to the Meadows. In this state of nature he didn't know that the banner was the work of a special committee whose sole mission was to stir up team rivalry. There would be more such goads at every turn.

Inside the door was a green placard: "Abandon All Hope, Ye Who Don't Wear Green Shirts!"

Shepherd whooped delightedly, brandished the placard overhead, and in the next second was thrown to the floor by a wave of Blues, Whites, and Reds.

"No rough-housing indoors!" said the loudspeaker sharply. "You know the rules. No rough-housing indoors. Save your ginger for the playing field. After registration, report to your tents, get to know your buddies, and be back for lunch in fifteen minutes."

Paul arrived at his tent ahead of his as yet unknown buddy. The two of them, according to the foreword in the *Song Book*, would develop a sort of common-law brotherhood as a result of their having shared so much beauty, excitement, and deep emotion together.

The chill of the air-conditioned room made him feel dizzy. Coming out of this flicker of vertigo, Paul's eyes focused on a dinner-plate-sized badge on the pillow of his bunk. "Dr. Paul Proteus, Wks. Mgr., Ilium, N. Y.," it said. And, below this, "Call Me Paul or Pay Me $5." The second part of the legend was on every badge. The only man who was not to be called by his first name at the Meadows was the Old Man himself, the successor of Paul's father, Doctor Francis Eldgrin Gelhorne. He, National Industrial, Commercial, Communications, Foodstuffs, and Resources Director, was damn well Doctor Gelhorne, sir, at any hour of the night or day, and anywhere he went.

And then Paul saw the badge on his buddy's pillow: "Dr. Frederick Garth, Wks. Mgr., Buffalo, N. Y. Call Me Fred or Pay Me $5."

Paul sat down on the edge of his bed and struggled against the uneasy perplexity the sight of Garth's badge had precipitated. He had known many men, Shepherd for instance, who were forever seeing omens and worrying about them—omens in a superior's handshake, in the misspelling of a name in an official document, in the seating arrangement of a banquet table, in a superior's asking for or offering a cigarette, in the tone of . . . Paul's career, until recent weeks, had been graceful and easy all the way, and he'd found omen analysis dull, profitless. For him the omens were all good—or had been until now. Now, he, too, was growing aware of possibly malevolent spooks, revealing themselves in oblique ways.

Was it chance or ignorance or some subtle plot that had put him in the same cell with Garth, the other candidate for Pittsburgh? And why had Shepherd been made a captain, when the honor was reserved for those who were going high and far indeed? And why. . . . Manfully, Paul turned his thoughts into other channels, superficially, at least, and managed to laugh like a man who didn't give a damn about the system any more.

His buddy walked in, gray at the temples, tired, pale, and kind. Fred Garth wanted desperately to be liked by everyone, and had achieved a sort of social limbo, affecting no one very much one way or the other. He had risen because of this quality rather than in spite of it. Time and time again two powerful personalities, backed by impressive factions, had aspired for the same job. And the top brass, fearing a split if they chose one faction's man over the other, had named Garth as an inoffensive compromise candidate. There was a feeling, general enough not to be branded sour grapes, that Garth was all but over his head in the big assignments compromise politics had handed him. Now, though he was only in his early fifties, he seemed terribly old—willing, good-hearted, but apologetically weak, used up.

"Doctor Proteus! I mean Paul." Garth shook his head,

laughed as though he'd done a comical thing, and offered a five-dollar bill to Paul.

"Forget it, Doctor Garth," said Paul, and handed it back to him. "I mean Fred. How are you?"

"Fine, fine. Can't complain. How's the wife and children?"

"All fine, fine, thanks."

Garth blushed. "Oh say, I'm sorry."

"About what?"

"I mean, that was silly of me, asking about your children when you haven't got any."

"Silly of me not to have any."

"Maybe, maybe. It's a trial, though, watching your kids grow up, wondering if they've got what it takes, seeing 'em just about killing themselves before the General Classification Tests, then waiting for the grades—" The sentence ended in a sigh. "I've just gone through that GCT business with my oldest, Brud, and I've got to live through the whole nightmare twice more still, with Alice and little Ewing."

"How'd Brud make out?"

"Hmmm? Oh—how'd he make out? His heart's in the right place. He wants to do well, and he boned up harder for the tests than any kid in the neighborhood. He does the best he can."

"Oh—I see."

"Well, he's going to get another crack at the tests—different ones, of course. He was under the weather when he took them the first time—tail end of some virus business. He didn't miss by much, and the Appeal Board made a special ruling. He gets his second chance tomorrow, and we'll have the grades around suppertime."

"He'll make it this time," said Paul.

Garth shook his head. "You'd think they'd give a kid something for trying, wouldn't you? God, you oughta see the little guy plugging away."

"Nice day," said Paul, changing the distressing subject.

Garth looked out of the window abstractedly. "It is, isn't it. God smiles on the Meadows."

"Probably did before we occupied it."

"I didn't make that up."

"Make what up?"

"About God smiling. That's from Doctor Gelhorne, of course. Remember? He said that last year on the closing day."

"Yep." Doctor Gelhorne said so many memorable things, it was hard for a person to stow them all away in his treasure house of souvenirs.

"Lunch!" said the loudspeakers. "Lunch! Remember the rule: get to know somebody new at each meal. Have your buddy on one side, but a stranger on the other. Lunch! Lunch!" Irrelevantly, the speakers blared "Oh How I Hate to Get Up in the Morning." Paul and Garth and five hundred other pairs walked across the parade ground to the dining hall.

As the crowd bore Paul and his buddy through the swinging screen doors, Kroner caught his arm and drew him to one side. Garth, like the good buddy he wanted to be, stepped out of line and waited.

"Tomorrow night," said Kroner. "The big meeting is tomorrow night—after the keynote play and bonfire."

"Fine."

"I told you the Old Man himself is coming. It's going to be that important. *You're* going to be that important. I don't quite know what's up, but I've a hunch it's going to be the biggest thing in your career."

"Gosh."

"Don't worry. With the blood you've got in your veins, you've got more than what it'll take to do the job—whatever it is."

"Thanks."

Paul got back in line with Garth. "He certainly likes you, doesn't he?" said Garth.

"Old friend of my father's. Said it was good to have me aboard."

"Oh." Garth looked a little embarrassed. Paul's bald lie had pointed up for the first time their competitive situation. He let the lie pass. Shepherd would have hounded Paul, and, more subtly, Kroner, until he'd learned every word that had passed between them.

Paul felt real warmth for Garth. "Come on, buddy, let's find a couple of strangers."

"It's going to be tough. We've been around a long time, Paul."

"Look for some apple-cheeked youngster fresh out of school."

"There's one."

"Berringer!" said Paul, amazed. When the machines had made a list of Ilium men eligible for the Meadows, Berringer's card had stayed in its slot. He was the last man in the whole Works who deserved an invitation. Yet, here he was.

Berringer seemed to know what was going through Paul's head, and he returned Paul's gaze with an insolent smile.

Baer stepped between them. "Forgot, forgot—supposed to tell you," he said. "Berringer, about Berringer. Kroner said to tell you, and I forgot, forgot."

"How the hell did he get up here?"

"Kroner brought him up. Last minute thing, see? Hmm? Kroner thought it'd break his father's heart if the boy wasn't asked, and after what happened to Checker Charley and all."

"There goes the merit system," said Paul.

Baer nodded. "Yep—there it goes, there it goes, all right." He shrugged and raised his eyebrows quizzically. "Zip zip, out the window."

Paul reflected that Baer was possibly the most just, reasonable, and candid person he'd ever known—remarkably machine-like in that the only problems he interested himself in were those brought to him, and in that he went to work on all problems with equal energy and interest, insensitive to quality and scale.

Paul glanced once more at Berringer, saw his luncheon companion was Shepherd and that his shirt was green, and forgot about him.

He and Garth finally found a pair of very young strangers with two empty seats between them, and sat down.

The redheaded youngster next to Paul looked at his badge. "Oh, Doctor Proteus. I've heard of you. How are you, sir?"

"Paul, not Doctor. Fine, how are you—" he studied his companion's badge—"Doctor Edmund L. Harrison, of the Ithaca Works?"

"Get to know the man next to you," said the loudspeaker. "Don't talk to anyone you know."

"Married?" said Paul.

"That's what you're here for, to get to know new people, to broaden your horizons," said the loudspeaker.

"Nossir, I'm en——"

"The more contacts you make here at the Meadows," said the loudspeaker, "the more smoothly industry will function, co-operationwise."

"I'm engaged," said Doctor Harrison.

"An Ithaca girl?"

"Two seats right over here, gentlemen—over in the corner. Right over there. Let's get our seats quickly, because there's a full program, and everybody wants to get down to knowing everybody else," said the loudspeaker.

"Nossir," said Doctor Harrison. "Atlanta." He looked at Paul's badge again. "Aren't you the son of—"

"Now that we're all seated and getting to know one another, how about a little song to pull us all together?" said the loudspeaker.

"Yes, he was my father," said Paul.

"Turn to page twenty-eight of the *Song Book*," said the loudspeaker. "Twenty-eight, twenty-eight!"

"He was quite a man," said Harrison.

"Yes," said Paul.

" 'Wait Till the Sun Shines, Nellie!' " shouted the loudspeaker. "Find it? Twenty-eight! All right, now, let's go!"

The band at the far end of the hall, amplified to the din of an elephant charge, smashed and hewed at the tune as though in a holy war against silence. It was impossible even to be cordial to oneself in the midst of the uproar. Paul's stomach knotted and his tastebuds went dead, and the delicious, expensive food went down his gullet like boiled horsemeat and hominy grits.

"Paul, Paul, Paul, oh Paul!" shouted Baer from across the table. "Paul!"

"What?"

"That's you—you they're calling for; they're calling for you!"

"Don't tell me the captain of the Blue Team is such a coward he ran out at the last minute," the loudspeaker was saying sarcastically. "Come on! Where's that Blue captain?"

Paul stood, and held up his hand. "Here," he said, in a voice inaudible even to himself.

Cheers and boos greeted him, in a proportion of one to

three. He was pelted by wadded paper napkins and maraschino cherries from the tops of salads.

"Well," said the loudspeaker tauntingly, "let's hear your song."

Hands gripped Paul and hoisted him into the air, and he was borne down the aisle toward the bandstand by a flying wedge of blue-shirted men. They dumped him on the bandstand and formed a cordon about him. The master of ceremonies, a fat, red old man with breasts like a woman's sticking through his wet T-shirt, thrust a *Song Book* into his hands. The band blasted out the fight song of the Blue Team.

"Oh you Blue Team, you tried and true team," said Paul. His voice came back at him, strange and frightening, amplified electronically to fierce defiance and determination. "There are no teams as good as you!"

At this point he was completely drowned out by the stamping of feet, whistles, catcalls, and the clank of spoons on glasses. The master of ceremonies, delighted with the high spirits he was evoking, handed Paul a blue banner to wave. No sooner were Paul's hands on the staff than he saw the ranks of his protectors split wide open. Berringer, his head lowered, his thick legs driving, charged him.

In the scuffle, Paul swung at the informality-maddened Berringer, missed, and was knocked, *hors de combat*, off the bandstand and halfway through the kitchen doors.

"Please! Please!" the loudspeaker was pleading. "There are very few rules at the Meadows, but the few that there are *must* be observed! Get back to your seat, now, you in the green shirt. There's to be no rough stuff indoors. Do you understand?"

Laughter was general.

"One more outburst like this one, and you'll be asked to leave the island!"

Kind hands picked up Paul, and he found himself looking into the grave, dull face of Luke Lubbock, the perennial joiner, who wore a busboy's uniform. One of the cooks, who had been watching with disdain, turned away quickly when Paul looked at him, and disappeared into the big meat locker.

As Paul's teammates carried him back to his seat, he realized fleetingly, as a fragment of a nightmare, that the cook had been Alfy, the master of silent television.

"Now, now," said the loudspeaker. "No more rough stuff, or we'll have to call off the rest of the fun. Now, where's the captain of the White Team?"

When the fun was over, Paul and Doctor Harrison of Ithaca walked out together.

"You have ten minutes of free time until the memorial service," said the loudspeaker. "Ten minutes to make new contacts before the memorial service."

"Nice meeting you, sir," said Doctor Harrison.

"I enj——"

"My wild Irish rose," howled the loudspeaker, "the sweetest flow'r that grows—" The refrain ended in a clatter. "Your attention, please. The Program Committee has just informed me that we're running seven minutes behind schedule, so would you please form up at the Oak right away, please. The memorial service will take place right away."

A reverent hush settled like smog over the perspiring crowd that had dispersed over the shuffleboard courts and around the ping-pong tables near the dining hall. Now they began to form about the Oak, the official symbol for the entire national organization. Its image was on every letterhead, and, stitched in a rectangle of white silk, its image snapped in the breeze, just below the American Flag on the parade-ground mast.

The youngsters imitated the oldsters' uniform stances of piety: eyes fixed on the lower branches of the magnificent old tree, hands folded before their genitals.

"White's going to win!" cried a short, thin youngster with big teeth.

The older men looked at him with sadness, with melancholy rebuke. Now was not the time for such horseplay. Now was almost the only time that was not the time. The youngster's outburst of infinite bad taste would poison his next two weeks, and probably his career. He had in an instant become "the boy who yelled at memorial service." That described him, and nobody would care to investigate him any further. Now, if he turned out to be a spectacular athlete . . . No. His flaccid physique and pale skin indicated that this avenue to forgiveness was closed to him.

Paul looked at him sympathetically, and recalled similar bad starts from the past. The man would be terribly lonely, turn to a career of surly drinking, and never be invited again.

The only sounds now were the rustling of leaves and the fluttering of the flags, and now and then the clatter of dishes and silverware from the dining hall.

A harried-looking photographer ran in front of the group, dropped to one knee, fired a flashbulb, and ran away again.

"*Vuuuuzzzzzip!*" went a rocket. "*Kabloooom!*" A parachuted American Flag was flung from the bomb to drift lazily to the river.

Kroner detached himself from the crowd and walked soberly to the thick tree trunk. He turned and looked down at his hands thoughtfully. His first words were so soft, so choked with emotion, that few heard them. He inhaled deeply, threw back his shoulders, raised his eyes, and gathered strength to say them again.

In the brief moment before Kroner spoke again, Paul looked about himself. His eyes met those of Shepherd and Berringer, and what passed between them was tender and sweet. The crowd had miraculously become a sort of homogenized pudding. It was impossible to tell where one ego left off and the next began.

"It is our custom," said Kroner; "it is the custom here at the Meadows—our custom, our Meadows—to meet here under our tree, our symbol of strong roots, trunk, and branches, our symbol of courage, integrity, perseverance, beauty. It is our custom to meet here to remember our departed friends and co-workers."

And now he forgot the crowd, and talked to the fat cumulus clouds scudding over the blue sky. "Since last we met, Doctor Ernest S. Bassett has left our world for his reward in a better one. Ernie, as you all know, was—"

The photographer ran out, flashed a bulb in Kroner's face, and disappeared again.

"Ernie was manager of the Philadelphia Works for five years, of the Pittsburgh Works for seven. He was my friend; he was *our* friend: a great American, a great engineer, a great manager, a great pioneer at the head of the procession of civilization, opening new, undreamed-of doors to better things, for better living, for more people, at less cost."

Now and then brokenly, Kroner told of Ernie Bassett as a young engineer, and he traced his career from works to works.

"He gave himself unstintingly engineeringwise, managershipwise, personalitywise, Americanwise, and—" Kroner paused to look impressively from face to face. Again he talked to the clouds—"heartwise."

A man stepped from the crowd to hand Kroner a long white box. Kroner opened it slowly and studied it thoughtfully before showing its contents to anyone else. At last he reached in and unfurled a blue and white pennant, the Armed Forces "E" that Bassett had won during the war as manager of the Philadelphia Works.

A muted bugle played taps.

Kroner knelt at the foot of the tree and placed Ernie Bassett's pennant there.

The photographer dashed up, got the picture, and dashed away.

"*Vuuuuzzzzzip! Kabloooom!*"

A male choir, concealed in the shrubbery, sang ever so softly —to the tune of "Love's Sweet Song":

> "Fellows at the Meadows,
> Lift your tankards high;
> Toast our living symbol, reaching toward the sky.
> Grown from but an acorn,
> Giant now you are;
> May you ne'er stop growing;
> Rise to the stars!
> Proud sy-him-bol a-hov
> Ourrrrrrrs."

"A minute of silence in unspoken prayer for departed friends," said the loudspeaker.

All through the minute of silence, Paul was aware of a snuffling in the background. Someone's dam of reserve had broken under the impact of the ceremony—someone who must have been awfully close to Bassett. There were tears standing in many eyes, and here and there teeth were sunk in unstable lips, but nowhere could Paul see the sobber. Suddenly he spotted him, not in the crowd, but in the dining hall. Luke Lubbock, a pile of dirty dishes in his arms, had been completely carried away. Big, honest tears for the manager of the Pittsburgh Works flooded his cheeks. Rather roughly, the headwaiter hustled him away from the screen door.

"Vuuuuzzzzzip! Kabloooom!"

The band exploded into "The Stars and Stripes Forever," and Kroner was half led from the tree by other oldsters who had known Bassett well. The crowd dispersed.

Paul looked longingly at the doors of the saloon, which was located in a separate white building. He tested the doors to make sure they were really locked, and of course they were. The saloon never opened until the cocktail hour, after the games.

"Your attention!" said the loudspeaker. "Your attention, please. The program for the rest of the day:

"In ten minutes the teams will meet at their captains' tents for assignments to various sports. Formal competition will not begin until tomorrow morning. After assignment, relax, get to know your buddy, don't hang around with the same old crowd.

"Cocktails at five-thirty. Supper at six-thirty. Now—attention to this change: the keynote play and bonfire will *not* take place tonight. Will *not.* They will take place tomorrow night, and there will be a group sing tonight in the amphitheater instead. Taps at midnight.

"Team captains, team captains—will you please report to your tents."

Without much hope, Paul rattled the saloon doors, thinking he might be able to talk a floor sweeper inside into getting him a little something.

"I've just been informed," said the loudspeaker, "I've just been informed that the captain of the Blue Team is not in his tent. Doctor Paul Proteus; Doctor Paul . . ."

Chapter XX

THE SHAH OF BRATPUHR'S golden turban hung unfurled like a roller towel in heaven from the hat rack in Miami Beach.

"*Puku pala koko, puku ebo koko, nibo aki koko,*" said the Shah.

"What's the foreign gentleman after?" asked Homer Bigley, proprietor of the barber shop.

"He wants a little off the sides, a little off the back, and leave the top alone," mumbled Khashdrahr Miasma, under a steaming towel in the barber chair next to the Shah's.

Doctor Ewing J. Halyard was giving himself a ragged manicure with his teeth in one of the waiting chairs, while his charges received their first American haircuts. He smiled and nodded at whatever was being said, but heard nothing save the soft crackle of the letter in his breast pocket as he shifted nervously in a search for comfort no chair could give him. The letter, from the personnel officer of the State Department, had pursued him from New York to Utica to Niagara Falls to Camp Drum to Indianapolis to St. Louis to Fort Riley to Houston to Hollywood to the Grand Canyon to Carlsbad Caverns to Hanford to Chicago to Miami Beach, where he roosted long enough for the letter to catch him—catch him like a javelin, quivering squarely between the shoulder-blades of his spirit. He was lobster-red from a day on the sand, but beneath this stinging veneer of fine health and spirits he was cold and dead-white with fear. "My dear Mr. Halyard," it had begun. "My dear *Mr.* . . ."

While Halyard brooded, Homer Bigley, with the reflexes born of a life of barbering, selected his scissors, clicked them in air about the sacred head, and, as though his right hand were serviced by the same nerve as his diaphragm and voicebox, he began to cut hair and talk—talked to the uncomprehending Shah after the fashion of an extroverted embalmer chatting with a corpse.

"Yessir, picked a nice time to come. They call this the off-season, but I say it's the nicest time of year. Cheapest time, too. But that isn't what I meant. It's fifteen degrees cooler right here and now than it is in New York City, and I'll bet not one person in fifty up north knows that. Just because the fact hasn't been promoted. Everything's promotion. Ever stop to think about that? Everything you think you think because somebody promoted the ideas. Education—nothing but promotion.

"Good promotion and bad promotion. Barbers, now, they get a lot of bad promotion on account of cartoons and television comedians, you know? Can't pick up a magazine or turn on the television without you see a joke about a barber cutting somebody. And sure, maybe that's good for a little snicker, maybe, and God knows the world can use a few snickers, but I don't think it's right to hurt somebody to give somebody else a snicker. I mean that it all kind of cancels out, and nobody's ahead. And I just wonder if any of those comedians or cartoon people ever stop to think about the thousands of barbers who go from one year to the next without they ever cut a customer, and still these people go around telling everybody that barbers are slashing so many arteries and veins you wonder how the sewers can handle it all. But seems like nobody ever thinks about what's maybe sacred to somebody, any more.

"Matter of fact, of course, used to be barbers did *bleed* people, of course, and got paid for it, too. One of the oldest professions on earth, if you stop to think about it, but nobody does. Used to be sort of doctors, bleeding people and setting their bones and all, and then the doctors got sore and took over all that stuff and left the barbers haircutting and shaving. Very interesting history. But my father used to say, before he died, of course, that the barbers would be here long after the last doctor's laid away, and there was a lot in what he said. He was worth listening to.

"Nowadays, by golly, it takes more time and skill to cut hair'n to do what the doctors do. If you had syphilis or the clap or scarlet fever or yellow fever or pneumonia or cancer or something, why, hell, I could cure you while I was drawing the water for a shampoo. Take a little old needle, puncho! squirto! miracle! and give you a clean bill of health along with your change. Any barber could do what a doctor does nowadays. But I'll give you fifty dollars if you can show me a doctor who can cut hair.

"Now, they say barbering isn't a profession, but you take the other professions that got so big for their breeches since the Middle Ages and look down on barbering. You take medicine, you take the law. Machinery!

"Doctor doesn't use his head and education to figure out what's the matter with you. Machines go over you—measure this, measure that. Then he picks out the right miracle stuff, and the only reason he does is on account of the machines tell him that's what to do. And the lawyers! Of course, I say it's a pretty good thing what happened to them, because it was a bad thing for them, which couldn't help to be a good thing for everybody else. I didn't say that. My father said it. Those are his words. But the law's the law now, and not a contest between a lot of men paid to grin and lie and yell and finagle for whatever somebody wanted them to grin and lie and yell and finagle about. By golly, the lie detectors know who's lying and who's telling the truth, and those old card machines know how the law runs on whatever the case is about, and they can find out a helluva sight quicker'n you can say habeas corpus what judges did about cases like that before. And that settles it. No more of this fast footwork. Hell, if I had a lie detector and card machines and all, I could run a law business here and fix you up with a divorce or a million-dollar damage suit or whatever you needed whatsoever while you were sticking your feet and a dime into that shoeshine machine.

"Used to be sort of high and mighty, sort of priests, those doctors and lawyers and all, but they're beginning to look more and more like mechanics. Dentists are holding up pretty good, though. They're the exception that proves the rule, I say. And barbering—one of the oldest professions on earth, incidentally—has held up better than all the rest. Machines separated the men from the boys, you might say.

"The men from the boys—that's what they used to say in the Army, Sergeant Elm Wheeler would. Memphis boy. 'Here we go, boys,' he'd say. 'Here's where we separate the men from the boys.' And off we'd go for the next hill, and the medics'd follow and separate the dead from the wounded. And then Wheeler'd say, 'Here we go, here's where we separate the men from the boys.' And that went on till we got separated from our battalion and Wheeler got his head separated from his shoulders.

"But you know, terrible as that mess was—not just Wheeler,

but the whole war—it brought out the greatness in the American people. There's something about war that brings out greatness. I hate to say that, but it's true. Of course, maybe that's because you can get great so quick in a war. Just one damn fool thing for a couple of seconds, and you're great. I could be the greatest barber in the world, and maybe I am, but I'd have to prove it with a lifetime of great haircutting, and then nobody'd notice. That's just the way peacetime things are, you know?

"But Elm Wheeler, you couldn't help but notice him when he went hog-wild after he got a letter from his wife saying she'd had a baby, and he hadn't seen her for two years. Why, he read that and ran up to a machine-gun nest and shot and hand-grenaded everybody in it something awful, then he ran up to another one and mashed up all the people there with his rifle butt, and then, after he'd busted that, he started after a mortar emplacement with a rock in each hand, and they got him with a shell fragment. You could of paid a surgeon a thousand dollars, and he couldn't of done a nicer job. Well, Elm Wheeler got the Congressional Medal for that, and they laid it in his coffin with him. Just laid it there. Couldn't hang it around his neck, and if they'd put it on his chest, I expect they'd of had to use solder, he was so full of lead and scrap iron.

"But *he* was great, and nobody'd argue about that, but do you think he could of been great today, in this modern day and age? Wheeler? Elm Wheeler? You know what he would be today? A Reek and Wreck, that's all. The war made him, and this life would of killed him.

"And another nice thing about war—not that anything about war is nice, I guess—is that while it's going on and you're in it, you never worry about doing the right thing. See? Up there, fighting and all, you couldn't be righter. You could of been a heller at home and made a lot of people unhappy and all, and been a dumb, mean bastard, but you're king over there—king to everybody, and especially to yourself. This above all, be true to yourself, and you can't be false to anybody else, and that's it—in a hole, being shot at and shooting back.

"These kids in the Army now, that's just a place to keep 'em off the streets and out of trouble, because there isn't anything else to do with them. And the only chance they'll ever get to be anybody is if there's a war. That's the only chance in the world they got of showing anybody they lived and died, and for something, by God.

"Used to be there was a lot of damn fool things a dumb bastard could do to be great, but the machines fixed that. You know, used to be you could go to sea on a big clipper ship or a fishing ship and be a big hero in a storm. Or maybe you could be a pioneer and go out west and lead the people and make trails and chase away Indians and all that. Or you could be a cowboy, or all kinds of dangerous things, and *still* be a dumb bastard.

"Now the machines take all the dangerous jobs, and the dumb bastards just get tucked away in big bunches of prefabs that look like the end of a game of Monopoly, or in barracks, and there's nothing for them to do but set there and kind of hope for a big fire where maybe they can run into a burning building in front of everybody and run out with a baby in their arms. Or maybe hope—though they don't say so out loud because the last one was so terrible—for another war. Course, there isn't going to be another one.

"And, oh, I guess machines have made things a lot better. I'd be a fool to say they haven't, though there's plenty who say they haven't, and I can see what they mean, all right. It does seem like the machines took all the good jobs, where a man could be true to hisself and false to nobody else, and left all the silly ones. And I guess I'm just about the end of a race, standing here on my own two feet.

"And I'm lucky barbering held out as long as it did—long enough to take care of me. And I'm glad I don't have any kids. That way it comes out even, and I don't have to think about this shop not being here for them, about nothing being for them but the Army or the Reeks and Wrecks, probably—unless an engineer or manager or research man or bureaucrat got at my wife, and the kids had their brains instead of mine. But Clara'd let one of those jerks at her just about as quick as you could stuff a pound of oleomargerine up a cat's ass with a hot awl.

"Anyway, I hope they keep those barber machines out of Miami Beach for another two years, and then I'll be ready to retire and the hell with them. They had the man who invented the damn things on television the other night, and turns out he's a barber hisself. Said he kept worrying and worrying about somebody was going to invent a haircutting machine that'd put him out of business. And he'd have nightmares about it, and when he'd wake up from them, he'd tell hisself all the reasons why they couldn't ever make a machine that'd do the job—you know, all the complicated motions a barber goes through. And then, in his next nightmare, he'd dream of a machine that did one of the jobs, like combing, and he'd see how it worked clear as a bell. And it was just a vicious circle. He'd dream. Then he'd tell hisself something the machine couldn't do. Then he'd dream of a machine, and he'd see just how a machine *could* do what he'd said it couldn't do. And on and on, until he'd dreamed up a whole machine that cut hair like nobody's business. And he sold his plans for a hundred thousand bucks and royalties, and I don't guess he has to worry about anything any more.

"Ever stop to think what a funny thing the human mind is? And there you are, sir, how's that look to you?"

"*Sumklish*," said the Shah, and he took a long drink from the flask Khashdrahr handed him. He studied himself soberly in the mirror Bigley held up for him. "*Nibo bakula ni provo*," he said at last.

"He likes it?" asked Bigley.

"He says it's nothing a turban won't cover," said Khashdrahr, whose haircut was also over. He called to Halyard. "Your turn, Doctor."

"Hmmm?" said Halyard absently, looking up from the letter. "Oh—no haircut for me. Think we ought to go back to the hotel for a rest, eh?" He glanced at the letter once more:

My dear Mr. Halyard:

We have just completed an audit of the personnel cards for our Department, checking the information coded on them against the facts.

During this audit, it was discovered that you failed to meet the physical-education requirements for a bachelor's degree from Cornell University, and that the degree was awarded you through a clerical oversight of this deficiency. I regret to inform you that you are, therefore, technically without a bachelor's degree, and, hence, technically ineligible for the M.A. and Ph.D. degrees which also appear on your record.

Since there are, as you know, severe penalties for willfully coding false information on personnel cards, we are obliged to advise you that you are officially without a college degree of any sort, and that you are transferred from staff to probationary status for a period of eight weeks, in which time you will return to Cornell and make up this deficiency.

Perhaps you can work this small chore into your itinerary, and give the Shah an opportunity to see a representative American institution of higher learning.

I have been in touch with Cornell about this mix-up, and they assure me that they will arrange for you to take the physical-education tests whenever you like. You will not have to take the course, but only the final examinations. These tests, I understand, are quite simple: swim six lengths of the swimming pool, twenty pushups, fifteen chinnings, climb a rope, stand on your . . .

Chapter XXI

THE MOON was full over the Thousand Islands, and, on one of them at least, there were a thousand eyes to see it. The cream of the East and Middle West, engineeringwise and managerwise, was met in the amphitheater of the Meadows. It was the second night, the night of the keynote play and the bonfire. The stage in the center of the circling stone seats was hidden beneath a pair of steel quarter-spheres, which would presently open like the shells of a steamed quahog.

Kroner sat down next to Paul and laid his hand on Paul's knee. "Nice night, boy."

"Yessir."

"Think we've got a good team this year, Paul."

"Yessir. They look good." After one day of competition, the Blue Team did look good, good despite the large proportion of top—hence tired and old—executives in its ranks. That afternoon the Blues had knocked the captain of the Greens, Shepherd, out of the box after three innings. Shepherd, in his determination to win and his horror of losing, had blown up completely.

Paul, by contrast, had played heads-up ball all the way, effortlessly, laughingly, wholly out of character. In analyzing the magical quality of the afternoon during the cocktail hour, Paul realized what had happened: for the first time since he'd made up his mind to quit, he really hadn't given a damn about the system, about the Meadows, about intramural politics. He'd tried not to give a damn before, but he hadn't had much luck. Now, suddenly, as of the afternoon, he was his own man.

Paul was half tight, and pleased with himself. Everything was going to be just fine.

"The Old Man wants to start the meeting shortly after his plane lands," said Kroner, "so we'll have to leave whatever's going on."

"O.K.," said Paul. "Swell." Swell night, tangy air, and a drowsy sort of harmlessness over everything. Maybe he'd give notice tonight, if he felt like it. No hurry. "Fine."

"Everybody in their seats, please," said the loudspeaker.

"Will everybody take their seats. The Program Committee has just informed me that we are eight minutes behind time, so will everybody take their seats."

Everybody did. The band, wearing summer tuxedos, struck up a medley of Meadows favorites. The music faded. The quarter-spheres opened a trifle at the top, freeing a beam of light that shot through cigarette smoke to the deep-blue heavens. The music stopped, machinery underground grumbled, and the quarter-spheres sank into the earth, revealing:

An old man, with a white beard reaching to his waist, wearing a long white robe and golden sandals and a blue conical hat speckled with golden stars, sits atop an extraordinarily tall stepladder. He looks wise, just, and tired by responsibility. In one hand he holds a large dust cloth. Beside the ladder, and of the same height, is a slender pole. Another just like it stands across the stage. Between the two poles is a loop of wire, passing, like a clothesline, over pulleys fixed to the poles. Hanging from the wire are a series of metallic stars about two feet across. They are coated with fluorescent paint, so that a beam of invisible infrared light, playing on one star, then another, makes them come alive with dazzling color.

The old man, oblivious to the audience, contemplates the stars strung out before him, unhooks the star nearest to him, studies its surface, polishes a tarnished spot on it, shakes his head sadly, and lets the star fall. He looks down at the fallen star with regret, then at those still on the wire, then at the audience. He speaks.

OLD MAN. I am the Sky Manager. It is I who keep night skies shining brightly; I who, when a star's glory is tarnished beyond restoration, must take it from the firmament. Every hundred years I climb my ladder to keep the heavens bright. And now my time has come again.

(*He pulls on the wire, bringing another star within reach. He removes the star and examines it.*)

And this is a strange star to be shining in the modern heavens. And yet, a hundred years ago, when I last kept my vigil, it was proud and new, and only a few meteors, destroying themselves in a brilliant instant, shone more brightly than this. (*He holds up the star, and the infrared light makes it glow brightly, bringing out the lettering which says, "Labor Unionism." He dusts it desultorily, shrugs, and lets it drop.*) In brave company. (*Looks down at scrap heap.*) With stars named Rugged Individualism, Socialism, Free Enterprise, Communism, Fascism, and—(*Leaves sentence unfinished, and sighs.*)

It is not an easy job, not always a pleasant one. But One far wiser than I, infinitely good, has decreed that it must be done (*sighs*), and be done dispassionately.

(*He pulls on wire, and brings in another star, the biggest of all. The infrared light hits it, and it lights up brilliantly, and on it is the image of the Oak, the symbol of the organization.*)

Alas, a young beauty. But already there are those who hate the sight of it, who clamor for it to be torn from the heavens. (*He dabs at it with his dust cloth, shrugs, and holds the star at arm's length, preparatory to dropping it.*) *Enter a clean-cut, handsome young engineer from audience.*

YOUNG ENG. (*Shakes foot of ladder.*) No! No, Sky Manager, no!

OLD MAN. (*Looks down curiously.*) What is this? A mere stripling challenges the caretaker of the heavens? *Enter unkempt young radical through trap door in stage.*

RADICAL. (*Sneeringly*) Take it down.

YOUNG ENG. There's never been a more brilliant, beautiful star!

RADICAL. There's never been a bloodier, blacker one!

OLD MAN. (*Looks perplexedly from the two men to the star and back.*) Hmmmm. Are you prepared to appeal the fate of this star with reason rather than emotion? My duties require that I be the sworn enemy of emotion.

YOUNG ENG. I am!

RADICAL. I, too. (*Smiles.*) And I promise to take very little of your time.

CLOSE QUARTER-SPHERES.

OPEN QUARTER-SPHERES.

A tall judge's rostrum now surrounds the old man's ladder. The old man wears a judge's wig and robes. The radical and the young engineer are similarly robed and wigged after the fashion of English barristers.

OFFSTAGE VOICE. Oyez, oyez, oyez! The Court of Celestial Relations is now in session!

OLD MAN. (*Bangs with gavel.*) Order in the court. The prosecution will proceed.

RADICAL. (*Offensively ingratiating.*) Your honor, ladies and gentlemen of the jury, the prosecution will show that the star in question is as tarnished—nay, black!—as any ever hung in the heavens. I will call but one witness, but that witness in effect is a million witnesses, each of whom could tell the same sordid tale, tell the unvarnished truth in the same simple words from the heart. I'd like to call John Averageman to the stand.

OFFSTAGE VOICE. John Averageman, John Averageman. Take the stand, please. *Enter John Averageman through trap door in stage floor.*

(*He is slightly pudgy, shy, middle-aged, endearing. His clothes are cheap, verging on being comical. He is in awe of the court, and has perhaps had a couple of drinks to bolster his nerve.*)

RADICAL. (*Touches John's arm.*) I'm looking out for you, John. Take your time about answering. Don't let them rattle you. Let me do the thinking, and you'll be all right.

OFFSTAGE VOICE. Do you solemnly swear to tell the truth, the whole truth, and nothing but the truth, so help you God?

JOHN. (*Looks questioningly at radical.*) Do I?

RADICAL. You do.

JOHN. Yessir, I do.

RADICAL. John, suppose you tell the court what you did before the war, before this new star arose to spoil, to besmirch the heavens.

JOHN. I was a machinist in the Averagetown Works of the Averagetown Manufacturing Company.

RADICAL. And now?

JOHN. I'm in the Reconstruction and Reclamation Corps, sir. Shovelman First Class.

RADICAL. Suppose, for the edification of the court, you tell us what you made before the star arose, and what you make now.

JOHN. (*Stares upward, remembering and computing with difficulty.*) Well, sir, when the defense work and all got going before the war, seems to me I could make better'n a hundred a week with overtime. Best week I ever had, I guess, was about a hundred and forty-five dollars. Now I get thirty a week.

RADICAL. Uh-huh. In other words, as that star went up, your

income dropped. To be exact, John, your income dropped about eighty per cent.

YOUNG ENG. (*Jumps to feet impulsively, likably.*) Your honor, I—

OLD MAN. Wait until the cross-examination.

YOUNG ENG. Yessir. Sorry, sir.

RADICAL. I think we've made it amply clear that the American standard of living has tumbled eighty per cent. (*His features assume an annoyingly pious expression.*) But enough of merely materialistic considerations. What has the ascent of this star meant to John Averageman in terms of his spirit? John, tell the court what you told me. Remember? About the engineers and managers—

JOHN. Yessir. (*Looks hesitantly at young engineer.*) No offense, sir—

RADICAL. (*Prodding.*) The truth can never be spoken without someone getting hurt, John. Go right ahead.

JOHN. Well, sir, it hurts a man a lot to be forgotten. You know—to have the fellers in charge, the engineers and managers, just sort of look right through him like they don't see him. A guy likes to know somebody thinks enough of him to look out for him.

YOUNG ENG. (*Urgently*) Your honor!

OLD MAN. (*Severely*) I will not tolerate any further interruptions from you. The issues are far graver than I thought. (*To radical*) Please proceed.

RADICAL. Go ahead, John.

JOHN. Well, sir, that's just about it. Kind of summing up, seems like these days the engineers and managers and the like are everything, and the average man is just nothing any more.

RADICAL. (*Pretends to be overcome by the tragedy of John's testimony. After seemingly searching for words and struggling with emotion for thirty seconds, he at last speaks, choked up and angry.*) Star of wonder, star of might; star of wondrous beauty bright. Take it down. (*Shakes fist.*) Take it down! (*Gestures at John.*) We've heard the voice of the people—the people, yes. "Take it down!" they say.

Who is it that says, "Leave it up?" Who? Not John, not the people. Who? (*Dramatically, he produces a pamphlet from his breast pocket.*) Your honor, ladies and gentlemen of the jury (*reads from pamphlet*), at the start of the war, the average income for engineers and managers in this great land of ours was $8,449.27.

Now, on this poisoned night, as the black star reaches its zenith, eighty per cent of John Averageman's pay check has been wrenched from him. And what is the average pay check for engineers and managers, you ask? (*Reads from the pamphlet again, with bitter emphasis on every syllable.*) Fifty-seven thousand eight hundred and ninety-six dollars and forty-one cents!

(*Explosively.*) Your witness!

(*Radical slinks over to the far post and leans against it to watch contemptuously.*)

YOUNG ENG. (*Softly, kindly*) John.

JOHN. (*Suspiciously, hostilely*) Yessir?

YOUNG ENG. John, tell me—when you had this large income, before the star arose, did you by any chance have a twenty-eight-inch television set?

JOHN. (*Puzzled*) No, sir.

YOUNG ENG. Or a laundry console or a radar stove or an electronic dust precipitator?

JOHN. No, sir, I didn't. Them things were for the rich folks.

YOUNG ENG. And tell me, John, when you had all that money, did you have a social insurance package that paid *all* of your medical bills, all of your dentist bills, and provided for food, housing, clothes, and pocket money in your old age?

JOHN. No, sir. There wasn't no such thing then, in those days.

YOUNG ENG. But you have them now, now that the (*sarcastically*) black star has risen, haven't you?

JOHN. Yessir, that's right, I do. But—

YOUNG ENG. John, you've heard of Julius Caesar? Good, you have. John, do you suppose that Caesar, with all his power and wealth, with the world at his feet, do you suppose he had what you, Mr. Averageman, have today?

JOHN. (*Surprised*) Come to think of it, he didn't. Huh! What do you know?

RADICAL. (*Furiously*) I object! What has Caesar got to do with it?

YOUNG ENG. Your honor, the point I was trying to make was that John, here, since the star in question has risen, has become far richer than the wildest dreams of Caesar or Napoleon or Henry VIII! Or *any* emperor in history! Thirty dollars, John—yes, that is how much money you make. But, not with all his gold and armies could Charlemagne have gotten one single electric lamp or vacuum tube! He would have given anything to get the security and health package you have, John. But could he get it? No!

JOHN. Well, for heaven's sakes! But—

YOUNG ENG. (*Anticipates John's objection.*) But the engineers and managers have forgotten Mr. Averageman?

JOHN. Yessir, that's what I was going to say.

YOUNG ENG. John, do you know that no manager or engineer would have a job if it weren't for you? How could we forget you for even a minute, when every minute of our lives is spent trying to give *you* what you want! Do you know who my boss is, John?

JOHN. Don't believe I ever met the gentleman.

YOUNG ENG. (*Smiling*) Oh, I think maybe you have. He's you, John! If I can't give you what you want, I'm through. We're all through, and down comes the star.

JOHN. (*Blushing*) Gosh, I never looked at it quite that way before, sir. (*Laughs modestly.*) But I guess that's right, isn't it? What do you know about that? But—

YOUNG ENG. But I make too much money? Fifty-seven thousand dollars? Is that what worries you?

JOHN. Yessir, that's a lot of money.

YOUNG ENG. John, before that star arose, the payroll for producing what I produce for you, for my boss, Mr. Averageman, ran to more than fifty-seven thousand dollars a week. Not a year, mind you, but a week! It looks to me, John, like you, the consumer, are the big winner, not me.

JOHN. (*Whistles low, under his breath.*) Is that a fact! (*Points suddenly at radical, who is very restive.*) But, he said—

YOUNG ENG. We've answered everything he's said, John. And I'd like to add one little thought. He'd like to take advantage of your good nature. He wants power, and he doesn't care about anything else. He'd like to make you swallow his half-truths, John, and get you to help him pull down the star, and put himself in power, and the whole world back in the Dark Ages!

JOHN. (*Glowering.*) Oh, he would, would he?

(*Radical looks worried, then frightened and chagrined, and suddenly makes dash for trap door in stage. John is right after him, and trap door closes. Stage lights fade, and blue feature spot comes up on young engineer, who moves directly to center of stage. Band starts "Battle Hymn of the Republic" softly, almost imperceptibly.*)

YOUNG ENG. (*Reflectively, soberly, conversationally*) Yes, there are those who've clamored so loudly against our star that some have been convinced it is tarnished. And if that star were to come down, it would be partly our fault. Yes, ours! Every minute of the day we should be pointing out how beautiful it is, and why it is beautiful. We hold our peace too much.

(*Points at star. Infrared beam hits it, making it glow beautifully.*) Under it, we've become rich beyond the wildest dreams of the past! Civilization has reached the dizziest heights of all time!

(*Music swells a little in volume.*)

Thirty-one point seven times as many television sets as all the rest of the world put together!

(*Music gets louder.*)

Ninety-three per cent of all the world's electrostatic dust precipitators! Seventy-seven per cent of all the world's automobiles! Ninety-eight per cent of its helicopters! Eighty-one point nine per cent of its refrigerators!

(*Music gets louder still.*)

Seventy-one point three per cent of the world's generating capacity!

Eighty-five per cent of its industrial control vacuum tubes!

Sixty-nine per cent of its fractional horsepower motors!

Ninety-eight point three per cent of . . .

(*Music crescendos, drowning him out.*)

(*Fade feature spot. Launch rockets from shore.*)

CLOSE QUARTER-SPHERES.

OPEN QUARTER-SPHERES.

The young engineer is gone, and so are the trappings of the court. The old man is at the top of his ladder, alone with his stars, as he was at the beginning.

He holds out the star bearing the image of the Oak, smiles, hooks it onto the wire, and sends it out, where it glows in infrared.

OLD MAN. Yes, out it goes again, brighter than all the rest. (*He reaches under his robe, and comes out with a powerful flashlight, whose beam he aims directly upward.*) And when I come back to examine the stars for stains in

another century, will it gleam as it does now? Or? (*Looks meaningfully at the foot of the ladder.*) Well, what determines whether it will be tarnished or not? (*Looks at the audience.*) It depends on— (*Suddenly brings down the flashlight, so its beam strikes face after face after face in the audience.*) You! And You! And You! etc.
(*Fire rockets. Hit "Stars and Stripes Forever" hard.*)

CLOSE QUARTER-SPHERES.
(*Turn on amphitheater floodlights.*)

Kroner's hand crashed down on Paul's knee. "Phwew! The best keynoter yet! Paul—the story, the whole story in a nutshell!"

"You'll be interested in knowing—" said the loudspeaker over the applause. "Here's an announcement of interest: In the past, the keynote plays have been written by professional writers under our supervision. This play you've just seen was written, believe it or not, by an engineer and manager within the organization! Bill Holdermann, stand up! Stand up! Stand up, Bill!"

The audience went wild.

"I knew it!" shouted Kroner. "It was real! It went right to the heart. It had to be somebody inside!"

Holdermann, a shaggy, worn-out nobody from the Indianapolis Works, stood a few rows ahead of Paul, red, smiling, and with tears in his eyes. At the sunset of life, he had arrived. Perhaps a muffled wisp of the applause reached the ears of his wife, the woman who had had faith in him when no one else had, across the water, on the Mainland.

"Bonfire in five minutes," said the loudspeaker. "Five minutes to make new contacts, then the bonfire."

Shepherd struggled through the crowd and took Kroner's attention away from Paul. "'Not with all his gold and armies,'" Shepherd quoted from the play. "'Not with all his gold and armies could Charlemagne have gotten one single electric lamp or vacuum tube!'" He shook his head wonderingly, admiringly. "Don't tell me art is dying."

"Art who?" said Paul under his breath, and he walked away from them, into the twilight at the fringe of the ring of floodlights. The rest of the crowd drifted, tightly packed, toward the shore, where Luke Lubbock, Alfy, and others of the service were pouring kerosene on a hillock of pine fagots.

The play was virtually the same play that had begun every Meadows session, even before the war, when the island had belonged to a steel company. Twenty years ago, Paul's father had brought him up here, and the play's message had been the same: that the common man wasn't nearly as grateful as he should be for what the engineers and managers had given him, and that the radicals were the cause of the ingratitude.

When Paul had first seen the allegory, as a teen-ager, he'd been moved deeply. He had been struck full force by its sublime clarity and simplicity. It *was* a story in a nutshell, and the heroic struggle against ingratitude was made so vivid for his young mind that he'd worshipped his father for a little while as a fighter, a latter-day Richard the Lionhearted.

"Well," his father had said after that first play, years ago, "what are you thinking, Paul?"

"I had no idea—no idea that's what was going on."

"That's the story," his father had said sadly. "The whole story. That's the way it is."

"Yessir." Their eyes had met, and an inexpressibly sweet sense of eternal tragedy had passed between them, between their generations—a legacy of *Weltschmerz* as old as humanity.

Now, Paul stood by himself on a dark walk, bewildered by the picture of, as Kroner put it, the men at the head of the procession of civilization, the openers of doors to undreamed-of new worlds. This silly playlet seemed to satisfy them completely as a picture of what they were doing, why they were doing it, and who was against them, and why some people were against them. It was a beautifully simple picture these procession leaders had. It was as though a navigator, in order to free his mind of worries, had erased all the reefs from his maps.

Suddenly, light flashed in Paul's eyes, but less dazzling light than the Sky Manager's. He faced his own image in a mirror framed by fluorescent lamps. Over the mirror was the legend, THE BEST MAN IN THE WORLD FOR THE BEST JOB IN THE WORLD. The island was covered with such booby traps. The lamps about this mirror were old ones, and they gave off a wavering light tinged with greens and purples. They gave his skin the quality of corroded copper, and his lips and eye rims were lavender. He discovered that there was nothing disquieting about seeing himself dead. An awakening conscience, unaccompanied by new wisdom, made his life so damned lonely, he decided he wouldn't much mind being dead. And the good offices of the cocktail hour were wearing away.

A drone in the sky to the east distracted him—probably the amphibian bearing the priceless two hundred and fifty pounds of Doctor Francis Eldgrin Gelhorne, and his know-how.

Paul took a step down the path, which turned off the lights, and headed back toward the bonfire, which was sending sparks and flames up hundreds of feet and turning the faces about it to a sweaty pink.

A professional actor, painted bronze, wearing an eagle-feather war bonnet and a beaded G-string, held up his hand and tilted his head back proudly. The crowd fell silent. "How!" He looked earnestly from face to face. "How! Many moons ago, my people made their home on this island."

The amphibian was circling the island now, coming lower.

"It's the Old Man all right," whispered Kroner to Paul. "Wouldn't look good to walk out on the ceremony, though. We'll have to stick it out."

"My people were brave people," said the Indian. "My people were proud and honest people. My people worked hard, played hard, fought hard, until it was time to go to the Happy Hunting Ground."

The same actor had been hired to play the Indian for years, ever since Paul had been coming to the Meadows. He'd been hired originally for his deep voice and beautiful muscles. Now, Paul noticed, his belly cast a shadow over his G-string, his left calf had developed a varicose vein, and war paint failed to hide the gray bags under his eyes. He had become such a regular at the Meadows, such a vital symbol—surpassed in that function only by Doctor Gelhorne and the Oak—that he was a man apart from the other hired help, on a first-name footing with the brass, and with the drinking privileges of a regular guest.

"Now our braves are gone, our strong young men—gone from this island, which belonged to my people, lo, these many moons ago," said the Indian. "Now other young men come. But the spirit of my people lives on, the Spirit of the Meadows.

It is everywhere: in the wind through the pines, in the lapping of the great blue water, in the whir of an eagle wing, in the growl of summer thunder. No man can call this island his, no man can be happy here, who does not harken to the Spirit, who does not take the Oath of the Spirit."

There was the clattering of the switch in the loudspeaker again. "Young braves at the Meadows for the first time step forward," said a pontifical voice, not that of the usual drover.

"Raise your right hands," said the Indian. "Repeat after me the Oath of the Spirit of the Meadows. I solemnly swear by the voice in the pines—"

"By the voice in the pines," said the neophytes.

"By the lapping of the great blue water, by the whir of the eagle wing—"

The Old Man's plane had skated across the water to the shore on the other side of the island and was roaring its engines as it inched up a ramp onto land.

"By the growl of the summer thunder," said the Indian.

"By the growl of the summer thunder."

"I will uphold the Spirit of the Meadows," said the Indian. "I will obey the wise commands of my chiefs, for the good of the people. I will work and fight fearlessly, tirelessly for a better world. I will never say the job is done. I will uphold the honor of my profession and what I represent at all times. I will seek out enemies of the people, enemies of a better world for all children, relentlessly."

"Relentlessly!" said someone in the crowd near Paul, passionately. He turned to see that Luke Lubbock, again swept into the mainstream of pomp and circumstance, held his hand high and swore to everything that came along. In Luke's left hand was a fire extinguisher, apparently for use in case the blaze spread.

When the oath was done, the Indian looked and saw it was good. "The Spirit of the Meadows is pleased," he said. "The Meadows belong to these stout-hearted braves, and it shall be a proud, happy place as it was, lo, these many moons ago."

A smoke bomb concealed before him screened him for a startling instant, and he was gone.

"The saloon is open," said the loudspeaker. "The saloon is open, and will be open until midnight."

Paul found himself walking beside the pleasant youngster he'd met at lunch, Doctor Edmund Harrison of the Ithaca Works. Shepherd and Berringer were right behind, flattering the life out of Kroner.

"Well, how'd you like it, Ed?" said Paul.

Harrison looked at him searchingly, started to smile, and seemed to think it inadvisable. "Very well done," he said carefully. "Very professional."

"Jesus Christ," Berringer was saying, "I mean, Christ, boy, that was a show. You know, it's entertainment, and still you learn something, too. Christ! When you do both, that's art, boy. Christ, and that wasn't cheap to put on, either, I'll bet."

Ed Harrison of Ithaca stopped and picked up a bit of stone from the side of the path. "I'll be damned," he said. "An arrowhead!"

"A nice one, too," said Paul, admiring the relic.

"So there really *were* Indians on this island," said Harrison.

"For chrissakes, you crazy bastard," said Berringer. "You deaf, dumb, and blind? Whaddya think they been trying to tell you for the past half-hour?"

Chapter XXII

THE MEETING of Doctors Paul Proteus, Anthony Kroner, Lou MacCleary, Executive Manager of National Industrial Security, and Francis Eldgrin Gelhorne, National Industrial, Commercial, Communications, Foodstuffs, and Resources Director, was to take place at the Meadows in the so-called Council House. The Council House was a frame building, away from the rest, that had been built in the old, wilder days as a lazaretto for surly drunks. Drinking at the Meadows had become more careful since the war—more mature, Kroner said—so the pesthouse fell into disuse and was finally converted into a meeting place for top-policy brass.

All save Doctor Gelhorne were now seated around a long meeting table, looking thoughtfully at the empty chair Gelhorne would be filling any minute. It was a time for silence. The mixing, the making of new contacts, the packing up of troubles in old kit bags went on noisily across the island, in the saloon. Here in the Council House there was no joy, only the summer-cottage aroma of mildew and incipient dry rot, and a grave awareness on the part of each of the three men that the world was their apple.

The shouts and songs that floated over the greensward from the saloon, Paul noted, had a piping quality. There wasn't the inimitable hoarseness of an honest-to-God drunk in the lot. It was unthinkable that there was a man in the saloon without a glass in his hand, but it was also unlikely that many men would have their glasses filled more than twice. They didn't drink at the Meadows now the way they used to in the old days when Finnerty and Shepherd and Paul had joined the organization. It used to be that they'd come up to the Meadows to relax and really tie one on as a relief from the terribly hard work of war production. Now the point seemed to be to pretend drunkenness, but to stay sober and discard only those inhibitions and motor skills one could safely do without.

Paul supposed there would be a couple of men who wouldn't realize what was going on, who would earnestly try to get as drunk as everyone else seemed. They would be frightfully alone and lost when the party broke up. And there would be one or two lonely drunks with nothing to lose anyway, men who had fallen into disfavor one way or another, who knew they had received their last invitation. And what the hell, the liquor was free. *De mortuis nil nisi bonum.*

There was a voice on the porch of the Council House. Doctor Gelhorne was on the other side of the door, pausing a moment for some last word with the world outside. "Look at those youngsters over there," Paul heard the Old Man say, "and tell me God isn't in his heaven."

As the doorknob turned, Paul continued to contemplate trivia, to atomize the fixtures and conventions of the only way of life he'd ever known, an easy, comfortable life, with simple answers for every doubt. That he was quitting that life, that now was perhaps the time he would do it—the grand idea overshadowing all the little ones—rarely occupied his consciousness. It showed itself mainly in a sensation of being disembodied, or now and then of standing in a chilling wind. Maybe the right time to quit would come now, or a few months from now. There was no need to hurry, no need at all.

The door opened.

The three waiting men stood.

In came Doctor Francis Eldgrin Gelhorne, National Industrial, Commercial, Communications, Foodstuffs, and Resources Director. His spherical bulk was enclosed in a double-breasted, dark-blue suit. His single concession to the Meadows' tradition of informality was an unbuttoned collar and the sliding of his necktie knot a fraction of an inch below where it should have been. Though he was seventy, his hair was as thick and black as a twenty-year-old Mexican's. His fatness was turned into something impressive rather than comical by his perpetual I-smell-excrement expression.

He seemed to be the end of a race, as, Paul reflected, so many leaders seemed to be. It was hard to believe that when Gelhorne was gone there would ever be another man as wonderfully old, shrewd, and unafraid as he.

He cleared his throat. "We're here because somebody wants to kill us, wreck the plants, and take over the country. That plain enough for you?"

Everyone nodded.

"The Ghost Shirt Society," said Doctor Lou MacCleary, Executive Manager of National Industrial Security.

"The Ghost Shirt Society," said Doctor Gelhorne acidly. "Give a name to something, and you think you've got it. But you haven't got it. All you've got's the name. That's why we're here. All we've got is the name."

"Yessir," said Lou. "The Ghost Shirt Society. And we think the headquarters is in Ilium."

"We think," said Doctor Gelhorne. "We don't know anything."

"Yessir," said Lou.

Gelhorne fidgeted for a moment and looked about the room. His eyes fell on Paul. "How are you, Doctor Proteus?"

"Fine, thank you, sir."

"Uh-huh. Good. That's good." He turned to Lou MacCleary. "Let's see that report of yours that tells everything we don't know about the Ghost Shirt Society."

MacCleary gave him a thick typewritten manuscript.

Gelhorne, his lips moving, leafed through it, frowning. No one spoke or smiled or looked at anyone else.

Paul considered the notion of Doctor Gelhorne's being the last of a race, and decided it was true. He had got to the top through a disorderly route that the personnel machines would never tolerate. Had machines been watching things when Gelhorne started his climb to the top, his classification card would have come flying out of the card files like an old Wheaties box top.

He had no college degree of any kind, other than bouquets of honorary doctorates that had come to him in his late fifties and sixties.

He'd had nothing to do with industry, in fact, until he was thirty. Before that, he'd pulled a mail-order taxidermy business out of bankruptcy, sold his interest in it, and bought a trailer truck. He'd built his fleet to five trucks when he received a hot market tip, sold his business, invested the proceeds, and tripled his wealth. With this bonanza, he'd bought the largest, yet failing, ice-cream plant in Indianapolis, and put the business in the black inside of a year by building ice-cream routes servicing Indianapolis manufacturing plants during the lunch hour. In another year, he had his trucks carrying sandwiches and coffee along with ice cream. In another year, he was running plant cafeterias all over town, and the ice-cream business had become a minor division of Gelhorne Enterprises.

He'd found that many of the manufacturing firms were owned by third- or fourth-generation heirs who, by some seeming law of decay, didn't have the nerve or interest the plants' founders had had. Gelhorne, half playfully at first, had offered these heirs advice, and found them amazingly eager to surrender responsibility. He'd bought in, watched and learned, and, discovering nerve was as valuable as special knowledge, he'd become manager and part owner of a dozen small plants.

When war became certain and the largest corporations were looking about for new manufacturing facilities, Gelhorne had delivered his prosperous community of plants to General Steel, and become an officer of that corporation. The rule-of-thumb familiarity he had with many different industries, as represented by the plants he'd taken over, had been broader than that of any executives General Steel had developed within its own organization, and Gelhorne was soon spending all his time at the side of the corporation's war-rattled president.

There he'd come to the attention of Paul's father in Washington, and Paul's father had made Gelhorne his general executive manager when the whole economy had been made one flesh. When Paul's father died, Gelhorne had taken over.

It could never happen again. The machines would never stand for it.

Paul remembered a week end long ago, when he had been a tall, skinny, polite, and easily embarrassed youth, and Gelhorne had paid a call. Gelhorne had suddenly reached out and caught Paul by the arm as Paul passed his chair. "Paul, boy."

"Yessir?"

"Paul, your father tells me you're real smart."

Paul had nodded uncomfortably.

"That's good, Paul, but that isn't enough."

"No, sir."

"Don't be bluffed."

"No, sir, I won't."

"Everybody's shaking in his boots, so don't be bluffed."

"No, sir."

"Nobody's so damn well educated that you can't learn ninety per cent of what he knows in six weeks. The other ten per cent is decoration."

"Yes, sir."

"Show me a specialist, and I'll show you a man who's so scared he's dug a hole for himself to hide in."

"Yes, sir."

"Almost nobody's competent, Paul. It's enough to make you cry to see how bad most people are at their jobs. If you can do a half-assed job of anything, you're a one-eyed man in the kingdom of the blind."

"Yes, sir."

"Want to be rich, Paul?"

"Yes, sir—I guess so. Yes, sir."

"All right. I got rich, and I told you ninety per cent of what I know about it. The rest is decoration. All right?"

"Yes, sir."

Now, after many years, Paul and Doctor Francis Eldgrin Gelhorne were looking at each other over the long table in the Council House at the Meadows. They weren't close friends, and there was none of Kroner's aromatic paternalism about Gelhorne. This was business.

"There's nothing new about the Society in this report," said Gelhorne.

"Only the part about Finnerty," said Lou MacCleary. "It's been slow going."

"It certainly has," said Doctor Gelhorne. "Well, Doctor Proteus and Doctor Kroner, the point is that this Ghost Shirt nonsense might turn out to be something pretty big. And Lou, here, hasn't been able to get an agent into it to find out what they're up to or who's running it."

"This bunch is smart," said Lou. "They're being pretty selective about who gets in."

"But we think we know how to get a man into it," said Gelhorne. "We think they'd be very tempted by a discontented manager and engineer. We think they've already recruited at least one."

"Finnerty," said Kroner heavily. "He finally registered with the police, incidentally."

"Oh?" said MacCleary. "What did he say he was doing with his time?"

"Says he's getting out Braille editions of pornography."

"He's being pretty cute now," said Gelhorne, "but I think we'll fix his wagon all right. But that's a side issue. The point we're getting at, Paul, is that I think they'll take you into the Ghost Shirt Society under the right conditions."

"Conditions, sir?"

"If we fire you. As of now, as far as anyone outside this room knows, you're through. The rumor's already circulating at the saloon, isn't it, Lou?"

"Yes, sir. I let it slip in front of Shepherd at dinner."

"Good boy," said Gelhorne. "He'll be taking over Ilium, by the way."

"Sir, about Pittsburgh—" said Kroner worriedly. "I promised Paul that he was slated for that job when he was finished with the investigation."

"That's right. In the meanwhile, Garth will run the works there." Gelhorne stood briskly. "All right, Paul? Everything clear? You're to get off the island tonight and back to Ilium." He smiled. "It's really a break for you, Paul. It gives you a chance to clear up your record."

"Record, sir?" Things were happening so quickly now that Paul could only seize upon a word and repeat it as a question in order to keep in the conversation.

"That business of letting Finnerty go through the plant unescorted, and the pistol affair."

"The pistol affair," said Paul. "Can I tell my wife?"

"I'm afraid not," said Lou. "The plan is that nobody outside this room is to know."

"It'll be hard, I know," said Gelhorne sympathetically. "But just now I'm remembering a young boy who told me he didn't want to be an engineer when he grew up, he wanted to be a soldier. You know who that boy was, Paul?"

"Me?" said Paul bleakly.

"You. Well, now you're in the front lines, and we're proud of you."

"Your father would be proud of you, Paul," said Kroner.

"I guess he would. He really would be, wouldn't he," said

Paul. Gratefully he was welcoming the blind, envigorating heat of anger. "Sir, Doctor Gelhorne, may I say one more thing before you leave?"

Kroner was holding the door open for the Old Man. "All right, by all means."

"I quit."

Gelhorne, Kroner, and MacCleary laughed. "Wonderful," said the Old Man. "That's the spirit. Keep that up, and you'll fool the hell out of them."

"I mean it! I'm sick of the whole childish, stupid, blind operation."

"Attaboy," said Kroner, smiling encouragingly.

"Give us two minutes to get to the saloon before you leave," said MacCleary. "Wouldn't do for us to be seen together now. And don't worry about packing. Your stuff is being packed right now, and it'll be down at the dock in time for the last boat."

He shut the door behind himself, Gelhorne, and Kroner.

Paul sank heavily back into his chair. "I quit, I quit, I quit," he said. "Do you hear me? I quit!"

"What a night," he heard Lou say on the porch.

"God smiles on the Meadows," said Doctor Gelhorne.

"Look!" said Kroner.

"The moon?" said Lou. "It *is* beautiful."

"The moon, yes—but look at the Oak."

"Oh—and the man," said Doctor Gelhorne. "What do you know about that!"

"A man, standing there alone with the Oak, with God and the Oak," said Kroner.

"Is the photographer around?" said Lou.

"Too late—he's going away now," said Kroner.

"Who was he?" said Doctor Gelhorne.

"We'll never know," said Lou.

"I don't want to know," said Kroner. "I want to remember this scene and think of him as a little bit of all of us."

"You're talking poetry," said the Old Man. "That's good, that's good."

Paul, alone inside, exhaled a puff of smoke with too much force, and coughed.

The men on the porch whispered something.

"Well, gentlemen," said Doctor Gelhorne, "shall we go?"

Chapter XXIII

IF DOCTOR PAUL PROTEUS, former manager of the Ilium Works, hadn't found reality disquieting at all points, he wouldn't have shown himself in the saloon before boarding the last boat for the Mainland. As he made his way along the gravel path toward the noise and light of the saloon, however, the field of his consciousness narrowed down to a pinprick, and filling the field was a twinkling shot-glass.

The crowd fell silent as he entered, and then exploded into even greater excesses of happy noise. Quickly as Paul glanced about the room, he didn't catch a single man looking at him, nor, in the blurred vision of excitement, did he recognize a single face among these old friends.

"Bourbon and water," he said to the bartender.

"Sorry, sir."

"Sorry about what?"

"I can't serve you."

"Why not?"

"I've been told you're no longer a guest at the Meadows, sir." There was a prim satisfaction in the bartender's voice.

A number of people observed the incident, Kroner among them, but no one made a move to change the bartender's ruling.

It was a crude moment, and in its fetid atmosphere Paul made an ultimately crude suggestion to the bartender, and turned to leave with dignity.

What he still had to learn was that without rank, without guest privileges, he lived on a primitive level of social justice. He wasn't prepared when the bartender vaulted the bar and spun him around.

"Nobody says that to me, sonny Jim," said the bartender.

"Who the hell do you think you are?" said Paul.

"I'm no goddamn saboteur," said the bartender hotly. Everyone heard it, the ugliest word in the language, one that permitted no muttering withdrawal, no shaking of hands and forgetting it. Son-of-a-bitch could be softened with a smile, but not saboteur.

Somehow the idea of a wrecker of machines had become the smallest part of the word, like the crown of an iceberg. The greatest part of its mass, the part that called forth such poisonous emotions, was undefined: an amalgam of perversions, filth, disease, a galaxy of traits, any one of which would make a man a despicable outcast. The saboteur wasn't a wrecker of machines but an image every man prided himself on being unlike. The saboteur was the man who, if dead, would no longer make the world a trying place to live in.

"You want me to say it again?" said the bartender. "Saboteur. You're a stinking saboteur."

It was an electrifying situation, an elemental situation. Here one big man had offered the ultimate insult to another big man. No one looked as though he were willing to bring the drama to an end, or as though he thought he could. It was like seeing a man caught in a threshing machine, beyond saving. As long as God had precipitated the tragedy, the onlookers might as well watch and learn what a threshing machine would do to a man once it caught him.

Paul hadn't hit anyone since his sophomore year in high school. He had none of what bayonet instructors hoped to instill in their pupils, the will to close with the enemy. It was an unpromising sort of will, he thought. Still, obedient to some system of involuntary nerves and glands, his hands tightened into fists, and his feet spaced themselves to form a solid bipod from which to swing.

Just as there is no encore for the *1812 Overture* save "The Stars and Stripes Forever," so Paul had no choice of rejoinders. "Saboteur yourself," he said evenly, and swung at the bartender's nose.

Absurdly, the bartender collapsed, snuffling and snorting. Paul walked out into the night, like Wild Bill Hickock, like Dan'l Boone, like the bargeman on the book jacket, like— He was suddenly spun around again. For a split second, he saw the bartender's red nose, white face, white apron, and white fist. A brilliant flash illuminated the inside of his skull, and then midnight.

"Doctor Proteus—Paul."

Paul opened his eyes to find himself staring up at the Big

Dipper. A cool breeze played across his aching head, and he couldn't see where the voice was coming from. Someone had stretched him out on the cement bench that ran the length of the dock, to be loaded with the band and the outgoing mail aboard the last boat for the Mainland.

"Doctor Proteus—"

Paul sat up. His lower lip was shredded and puffed, and his mouth tasted of blood.

"Paul, sir—"

The voice seemed to be coming from behind the spiraea hedge at the foot of the dock. "Who's that?"

Young Doctor Edmund Harrison emerged from the shrubbery furtively, a highball in his hand. "I thought you might want this."

"That's real Christian of you, Doctor Harrison. Guess I'm well enough to sit up and take nourishment now."

"Wish *I*'d thought of it. It was Kroner's idea."

"Oh? Any message?"

"Yes—but I don't think you'll want it. I wouldn't, if I were in your spot."

"Go ahead."

"He says to tell you it's always darkest before the dawn, and every cloud has a silver lining."

"Um."

"But you ought to see the bartender," said Harrison brightly.

"Aaaaaah. Tell me all."

"He's got a nosebleed that won't stop because he can't stop sneezing. Looks like a vicious circle that with luck could last for years."

"Wonderful." Paul felt better. "Look, you'd better beat it before your luck runs out and somebody sees you with me."

"Mind telling me what on earth you did?"

"It's a long, sordid story."

"I guess. Boy! one day you're king, the next day you're out on your tail. What're you going to do?"

Talking softly there in the dark, Paul began to appreciate what a remarkable young man he'd picked to sit down beside the first day—this Ed Harrison. Harrison had apparently taken a liking to Paul, and now, with no personal reasons for turning against Paul, he was sticking with him as a friend. This was integrity, all right, and a rare variety, because it often amounted, as it might amount now, to career suicide.

"What am I going to do? Farm, maybe. I've got a nice little farm."

"Farm, eh?" Harrison clucked his tongue reflectively. "Farm. Sounds wonderful. I've thought of that: up in the morning with the sun; working out there with your hands in the earth, just you and nature. If I had the money, sometimes I think maybe I'd throw this—"

"You want a piece of advice from a tired old man?"

"Depends on which tired old man. You?"

"Me. Don't put one foot in your job and the other in your dreams, Ed. Go ahead and quit, or resign yourself to this life. It's just too much of a temptation for fate to split you right up the middle before you've made up your mind which way to go."

"That's what happened to you?"

"Something like that." He handed Harrison the empty glass. "Thanks, better beat it. Tell Doctor Kroner it never rains but what it pours."

The cabin cruiser, *Spirit of the Meadows*, grumbled into her slip, and Paul climbed aboard. A few minutes later the band got on with their instruments, and a last call was put out over the loudspeakers. The lights in the saloon blinked off, and knots of remarkably sobered roisterers crossed the parade ground to their tents.

The rattle of the switch, the scratch of a needle, and the loudspeakers sang for the last time that night:

"Fare thee well, for I must leave you,
Please don't let this parting grieve you;
Fare thee well, the time has come for us to say goodbye.
Adieu, adieu, kind friends, adieu, yes, adieu! . . ."

And Paul waved wanly, apathetically. This was goodbye to his life so far, to the whole of his father's life. He hadn't had the satisfaction of telling someone he'd quit, of being believed; but he'd quit. Goodbye. None of this had anything to do with him any more. Better to be nothing than a blind doorman at the head of civilization's parade.

And as Paul said these things to himself, a wave of sadness

washed over them as though they'd been written in sand. He was understanding now that no man could live without roots—roots in a patch of desert, a red clay field, a mountain slope, a rocky coast, a city street. In black loam, in mud or sand or rock or asphalt or carpet, every man had his roots down deep—in *home.* A lump grew in his throat, and he couldn't do anything about it. Doctor Paul Proteus was saying goodbye forever to home.

"So long," he said. And then, in spite of himself, "So long, gang."

A laggard group, genuinely inebriated, was being coaxed out of the saloon. They were singing an effusively sentimental rendition of "Toast the Oak." They draped their arms over each other's shoulders; and made clumsily for the great tree. Their voices came clearly to Paul over the flat, green lawns:

"Grown from but an acorn,
Giant now you are;
May you ne'er stop growing;
Rise to the stars!
Proud sy-him-bol a-hov
Ourrrrrrrs."

There was a reverent pause, broken by an exclamation. "Jesus!" It was Berringer's voice, Berringer's word.

"'Smatter?"

"Look at the tree—around the bottom!"

"Holy smokes!"

"Somebody's stripped the bark off clear around," said Berringer hollowly.

"Who?"

"Who do you think?" said Berringer. "That stinking saboteur. Where is he?"

The *Spirit of the Meadows* gunned her engines and backed into open water.

"Hey," cried a lonely, frightened voice in the night. "Hey—somebody's killed the Oak."

"Killed the Oak," echoed the shore.

The loudspeakers clattered on again, and a chilling war whoop filled the air. "Beware the Ghost Shirt!" shrieked a terrible voice.

"Ghost Shirt," said the shore, and all was deathly still.

Chapter XXIV

En route by air from Miami Beach to Ithaca, New York, home of Cornell University, the Shah of Bratpuhr caught a nasty cold. When seven *prakhouls* (that quantity of fluid that can be contained in the skin of an adult male Bratpuhrian marmot) of *Sumklish* improved the Shah's spirits but did nothing for his respiratory system, it was decided that the plane should land in Harrisburg, Pennsylvania, in order that the Shah might rest and try the magic of American medicine.

With seven *prakhouls* of *Sumklish* under his belt, the Shah called cheery messages to pretty female *Takarus* on his way to the doctor's office.

"Pitty fit-fit, sibi Takaru? Niki fit-fit. Akka sahn nibo fit-fit, simi Takaru?"

Khashdrahr, who was without the benefit of *Sumklish*, was livid with embarrassment. "Shah says it is a nice day," he explained unhappily.

"*Fit-fit, pu sibi bonanza?*" called the Shah to a small blonde who had her hands in a streetcorner manicure machine.

She blushed, and jerked her hands from the machine and stalked away, leaving the machine to buff away at nothingness. A street urchin stuck his grubby hands in for the remainder of the operation, and drew them out with gleaming, red-enameled nails.

"I'm glad he likes the weather," said Halyard glumly. For many weeks now, they'd traveled without the subject's coming up once, and Halyard had hopefully told himself that the Shah really was different from his other guests in this respect, different from the French and Bolivians and Czechs and Japanese and Panamanians and Yaps and . . . But, no. The Shah, too, was now getting curious about American-type women. Halyard, at a frightful price in dignity, was once more going to have to perform the role of utterly perfect host—or pimp.

"*Fit-fit?*" called the Shah, as they pulled up to a stoplight.

"Look," said Halyard reproachfully to Khashdrahr, "tell him he just can't walk up to any American girl at all and ask her to sleep with him. I'll see what I can do, but it won't be easy."

Khashdrahr told the Shah, who waved him away. Before anyone could stop him, the Shah was out on the sidewalk, confidently confronting a startlingly beautiful, dark-skinned brunette. "*Fit-fit, sibi Takaru*?"

"Please," said Halyard to her, "please excuse my friend. He's a bit under the weather."

She took the Shah's arm, and together they climbed back into the limousine.

"I'm afraid there's been a terrible misunderstanding, young lady," said Halyard. "I hardly know how to put it. I, ah, he, that is— What I mean to say, rather, is he wasn't offering you a ride."

"He was asking for something, wasn't he?"

"Yes."

"There's been no misunderstanding."

"*Fit-fit*," said the Shah.

"Quite so," said Halyard.

Khashdrahr began looking out of the window with fresh interest, wildness, in fact, and Halyard had difficulty holding himself in check.

"Here we are," said the driver. "Here's Doctor Pepkowitz's office."

"Yes, well, you wait in the car, young lady," said Halyard, "while the Shah goes in here for a cold treatment."

The Shah was grinning, and inhaling and exhaling rapidly.

"His sniffles are gone," said Khashdrahr wonderingly.

"Drive on," said Halyard. He had seen a similar miracle cure of an Ecuadorian brigadier's hives.

The girl seemed restless and unhappy, and utterly out of character, Halyard thought. She smiled constantly, unconvincingly, and was apparently anxious to get the whole thing over with. Halyard still couldn't believe that she knew what the whole thing was.

"Where are we going now?" she said, grimly cheerful. "A hotel, I suppose."

"Yes," said Halyard unevenly.

"Good." She patted the Shah on his shoulder, and burst into tears.

The Shah was distressed and tried clumsily to comfort her. "*Oh, nibo souri, sibi Takaru. Akka sahn souri? Ohhh. Tipi Takaru. Ahhhh.*"

"There, now," said Halyard. "See here."

"I don't do this every day," she said, blowing her nose. "Please excuse me. I'll try to be better."

"Certainly. We understand," said Halyard. "The whole thing has been a terrible mistake. Where would you like us to leave you off?"

"Oh, no—I'm going through with it," she said gloomily.

"Please—" said Halyard. "Perhaps it would be better for all concerned if—"

"If I lost my husband? Better if he shot himself or starved?"

"Certainly not! But why would those terrible things happen if you refused to— That is—"

"It's a long story." She dried her eyes. "My husband, Ed, is a writer."

"What's his classification number?" said Halyard.

"That's just it. He hasn't one."

"Then how can you call him a writer?" said Halyard.

"Because he writes," she said.

"My dear girl," said Halyard paternally, "on that basis, we're all writers."

"Two days ago he had a number—W-441."

"Fiction novice," Halyard explained to Khashdrahr.

"Yes," she said, "and he was to have it until he'd completed his novel. After that, he was supposed to get either a W-440—"

"Fiction journeyman," said Halyard.

"Or a W-255."

"Public relations," said Halyard.

"Please, what are public relations?" said Khashdrahr.

"That profession," said Halyard, quoting by memory from the *Manual*, "that profession specializing in the cultivation, by applied psychology in mass communication media, of favorable public opinion with regard to controversial issues and institutions, without being offensive to anyone of importance, and with the continued stability of the economy and society its primary goal."

"Oh well, never mind," said Khashdrahr. "Please go on with your story, *sibi Takaru*."

"Two months ago he submitted his finished manuscript to the National Council of Arts and Letters for criticism and assignment to one of the book clubs."

"There are twelve of them," Halyard interrupted. "Each one selects books for a specific type of reader."

"There are twelve types of readers?" said Khashdrahr.

"There is now talk of a thirteenth and fourteenth," said Halyard. "The line has to be drawn somewhere, of course, because of the economics of the thing. In order to be self-supporting, a book club has to have at least a half-million members, or it isn't worth setting up the machinery—the electronic billers, the electronic addressers, the electronic wrappers, the electronic presses, and the electronic dividend computers."

"And the electronic writers," said the girl bitterly.

"That'll come, that'll come," said Halyard. "But Lord knows getting manuscripts isn't any trick. *That's* hardly the problem. Machinery's the thing. One of the smaller clubs, for instance, covers four city blocks. DSM."

"DSM?" said Khashdrahr.

"Excuse me. Dog Story of the Month."

Khashdrahr and the Shah shook their heads slowly and made clucking sounds. "Four city blocks," echoed Khashdrahr hollowly.

"Well, a fully automatic setup like that makes culture very cheap. Book costs less than seven packs of chewing gum. And there are picture clubs, too—pictures for your walls at amazingly cheap prices. Matter of fact, culture's so cheap, a man figured he could insulate his house cheaper with books and prints than he could with rockwool. Don't think it's true, but it's a cute story with a good point."

"And painters are well supported under this club system?" asked Khashdrahr.

"Supported—I guess!" said Halyard. "It's the Golden Age of Art, with millions of dollars a year poured into reproductions of Rembrandts, Whistlers, Goyas, Renoirs, El Grecos, Degas', da Vincis, Michelangelos . . ."

"These club members, they get just any book, any picture?" asked Khashdrahr.

"I should say not! A lot of research goes into what's run off, believe me. Surveys of public reading tastes, readability and appeal tests on books being considered. Heavens, running off an unpopular book would put a club out of business like that!" He snapped his fingers ominously. "The way they keep culture so cheap is by knowing in advance what and how much of it people want. They get it right, right down to the color of the jacket. Gutenberg would be amazed."

"Gutenberg?" said Khashdrahr.

"Sure—the man who invented movable type. First man to mass-produce Bibles."

"*Alla sutta takki*?" said the Shah.

"Eh?" said Halyard.

"Shah wants to know if he made a survey first."

"Anyway," said the girl, "my husband's book was rejected by the Council."

"Badly written," said Halyard primly. "The standards are high."

"Beautifully written," she said patiently. "But it was twenty-seven pages longer than the maximum length; its readability quotient was 26.3, and—"

"No club will touch anything with an R.Q. above 17," explained Halyard.

"And," the girl continued, "it had an antimachine theme."

Halyard's eyebrows arched high. "Well! I should hope they wouldn't print it! What on earth does he think he's doing? Good lord, you're lucky if he isn't behind bars, inciting to advocate the commission of sabotage like that. He didn't really think somebody'd print it, did he?"

"He didn't care. He had to write it, so he wrote it."

"Why doesn't he write about clipper ships, or something like that? This book about the old days on the Erie Canal—the man who wrote that is cleaning up. Big demand for that bare-chested stuff."

She shrugged helplessly. "Because he never got mad at clipper ships or the Erie Canal, I guess."

"He sounds very maladjusted," said Halyard distastefully. "If you ask me, my dear, he needs the help of a competent psychiatrist. They do wonderful things in psychiatry these days. Take perfectly hopeless cases, and turn them into grade A citizens. Doesn't he believe in psychiatry?"

"Yes, indeed. He watched his brother find peace of mind through psychiatry. That's why he won't have anything to do with it."

"I don't follow. Isn't his brother happy?"

"Utterly and always happy. And my husband says somebody's just *got* to be maladjusted; that somebody's got to be uncomfortable enough to wonder where people are, where they're going, and why they're going there. That was the trouble with his book. It raised those questions, and was rejected. So he was ordered into public-relations duty."

"So the story has a happy ending after all," said Halyard.

"Hardly. He refused."

"Lordy!"

"Yes. He was notified that, unless he reported for public-relations duty by yesterday, his subsistence, his housing permit, his health and security package, *everything*, would be revoked. So today, when you came along, I was wandering around town, wondering what on earth a girl could do these days to make a few dollars. There aren't many things."

"This husband of yours, he'd rather have his wife a— Rather, have her—" Halyard cleared his throat—"than go into public relations?"

"I'm proud to say," said the girl, "that he's one of the few men on earth with a little self-respect left."

Khashdrahr translated this last bit, and the Shah shook his head sadly. The Shah removed a ruby ring and pressed it into her hand. "*Ti, sibi Takaru. Dibo. Brahous brahouna, houna saki. Ippi goura Brahouna ta tippo a mismit.*" He opened the limousine door for her.

"What did the gentleman say?" she asked.

"He said to take the ring, pretty little citizen," said Khashdrahr tenderly. "He said goodbye and good luck, and that some of the greatest prophets were crazy as bedbugs."

"Thank you, sir," she said, climbing out and starting to cry again. "God bless you."

The limousine pulled away from her. The Shah waved wistfully. "*Dibo, sibi Takaru*," he said, and was seized by a violent sneezing fit. He blew his nose. "*Sumklish*!"

Khashdrahr handed him the sacred flask.

Chapter XXV

WHEN the *Spirit of the Meadows* churned up to the dock at the Mainland, the public address system, turned low, was murmuring "Good Night, Sweetheart," a sweet wraith of music a whisper above the voice in the pines, the lapping of the great blue water, the whir of the eagle wing.

No lights shone from the women's and children's lodges. In the Central Administration Building was a single square of light, silhouetting a sleeping clerk.

As Paul made for it, to ask the clerk where he might find Anita, lights flashed in his night-accustomed eyes. When his pupils had adjusted themselves to the glare, he found himself staring at his reflection in a mirror again, under the legend, THE BEST WIFE FOR THE BEST MAN FOR THE BEST JOB IN THE WORLD.

He hurried past the mirror, wondering how many times Anita had contemplated her reflection and the legend here, wondering how she would take the news that her Best Man had become merely a man, with no job at all.

He woke up the clerk, who called the matron in charge of the lodge where Anita slept.

"What's matter with the party over there?" said the clerk sleepily, waiting for the matron to answer. "You're about the tenth guy to come over here tonight. Usually they don't start coming until about the fourth day. Now, what's the matter with the matron, anyway? The phone's right by her bunk." He glanced at the clock. "You know what time it is? You haven't got time to make a nickel. The last boat back for the island leaves in three minutes."

"Keep ringing. I'm not going back."

"If you're going to spend the night, don't tell me about it. There're about twenty-seven rules against it."

Paul handed him a ten-dollar bill. "Keep ringing."

"For that, you can be invisible for a week. Whaddya like? Blondes, brunettes, redheads? Aha! She answered. Where the hell you been?" he asked the matron. "You got a Mrs. Paul Proteus there?" He nodded. "Uh-huh, uh-huh. O.K. Leave a note on her bunk, will you." He turned to Paul. "She's out, Doctor."

"Out?"

"Walking in the moonlight, probably. Matron says she's a great walker."

If Anita was a great walker, it was news to Paul. He'd seen her drive a car to the house across the street from theirs, and she denied all the tenets of physical culture by remaining young and graceful while eating like a farmhand and conserving her strength like a princess. Bound feet and six-inch fingernails wouldn't have restricted her activities in the least.

Paul sat down on a wicker chair in the cool blue shadows of the Administration Building's porch and rested his feet on the peeling bark of the log railing to wait.

Now the lights along the walks blinked on and off, a silent signal, warning that the last boat was about to leave for the island.

There was laughing, and quick crunching in the gravel, and a couple ran from the woods toward the dock. Their insistence on keeping their arms about each other's waists made their progress as graceless as a sack race. This annoyed Paul as a critic. It was painful to watch a clumsily conducted mating rite, knowing, from long experience with the skilled Anita, how much like a dance it could be when done properly.

There—she was making him slow down now, and their gait through the trees, against the moon, was more orderly. Paul had been sure that the farewell kiss would be an ungainly business, but, all credit to her, they stopped, and took the time and stances to do it right. Good.

Paul watched them with increasing identification with the man. Paul had always been a petty thief of others' high moments, and his hunger for this particular sort of moment was acute. With his old life gone, and his new one, whatever it was to be, not yet begun, he was voracious for love—Anita's love, vividly imagined love, vicarious love—any love, whatever was immediately available.

Now she was coming back, slowly, thoughtfully, content. Wonderful.

The lights on the booby-trap mirror flashed on. The woman

smoothed her slacks over her hips and tucked in a wisp of hair. She lingered before her image a long time, turning this way and that, seemingly pleased, as well she might be, by the shape of her breasts ingenuously hidden under tight green cotton, with the word "Captain" undulating uphill, downdale.

"Anita!"

She jumped, and quickly folded her arms across her bosom in a protective gesture. Slowly her arms went to her sides again, and she stood erect, a woman with nothing to hide, least of all Shepherd's shirt. "Hello, Paul." She walked over to the porch where he sat, stately, cold, and sat down beside him. "Well?"

When he said nothing, her poise began to fail, and she plucked nervously at the bark on the log railing, pulling off little strips and throwing them out into the summer night. "Go ahead," she said at last.

"*Me* go ahead?" said Paul.

"Don't you think an explanation is in order?"

"Decidedly."

"You *did* get fired, didn't you?"

"Yes, but not for breaking a Commandment."

"Is wearing another man's shirt adultery in your book?" Underneath, she was plainly rattled.

Paul was delighted. He was sure now that he could bluff her into coming away with him. It was inconceivable that she was using the boring, sententious, contentious Shepherd for anything but a hollow threat to him, but this semblance of wrongdoing could now be turned to advantage. "Wouldn't you say the shirt was symptomatic, coupled with fornication in the underbrush?" he said.

"If you mean do I love him, the answer is yes."

Paul laughed quietly.

"I'm glad you're taking it so well," she said primly. "I guess it proves what I thought all along."

"Which was—?"

Unexpectedly she burst into tears. "That I wasn't any damn use to you at all! Finnerty was right," she sobbed. "All you need is something stainless steel, shaped like a woman, covered with sponge rubber, and heated to body temperature."

It was Paul's turn to be startled. "Anita—darling, listen."

"And you'd lend it to anybody, if you didn't need it just then."

"Hell's bells, I—"

"I'm sick of being treated like a machine! You go around talking about what engineers and managers do to all the other poor, dumb people. Just look what an engineer and manager did to me!"

"For heaven's sakes, sweetheart, I—"

"You talk about how wrong it is for smart people to lord it over people who aren't so smart, and then go around our house showing off your great big I.Q. like it was on a sandwich sign. All right, so I'm dumb."

"No you aren't, Angel. Listen, I—"

"Saboteur!"

Paul fell back in his seat and shook his head, as though groggily trying to avoid a clubbing. "For the love of God, listen, will you?" he begged.

"Go on." She was magnificently on top of the situation again.

"Darling, what you say may be true. I don't know. But please, sweetheart, wife, I need you now like I never needed anybody in all my life."

"Ten minutes ought to take care of that. At the outside," she added scornfully.

"For richer, for poorer, in sickness as in health," said Paul. "Remember that, Anita? Do you remember?"

"You're still rich, and you're not sick." She looked at him with passing concern. "You're not sick, are you?"

"At heart."

"You'll get used to it. I did."

"I'm sorry, Anita—I didn't know it had been that bad. I see now that it probably was."

"Next time I'll marry for love."

"Shepherd?"

"He needs me, respects me, believes in the things I believe in."

"I hope you'll be very happy," said Paul, standing.

Her lips trembled, and she burst into tears again. "Paul, Paul, Paul."

"Hmmmm?"

"I like you. Don't forget that ever."

"And I like *you*, Anita."

"Doctor Proteus," called the clerk through the window.

"Yes?"

"Doctor Kroner called and said you were to be driven over to the railroad station tonight. The jeep's on the other side of the building, waiting. We've got half an hour to make the 12:52."

"Coming."

"Kiss me," said Anita.

It was a stunning kiss, and, in its wake of lackadaisicalness, Paul realized that she had had absolutely nothing to gain by the kiss, that she had done it out of, of all things, the goodness of her heart.

"Come with me, Anita," he whispered

"I'm not as dumb as you think." She pushed him away firmly. "Goodbye."

Chapter XXVI

DOCTOR PAUL PROTEUS, an unclassified human being, was put aboard the 12:52, where he shared an ancient coach, half cuspidor, half humidor, with sixty troops on furlough from Camp Drum.

"*Great Bend. The stop is Great Bend*," said a tape recording through a loudspeaker over Paul's head. The engineer pressed a button in his cab as he pulled into each station, down came the steps, and out came the voice. "*Next station, Carthage. Next station, Carthage. Click.*"

"'*Board*!" bawled another loudspeaker on the outside of the car.

An old man, kissing his wife goodbye on the rotting planks of the Great Bend platform, looked apologetically at the urgent voice, as though to ask the man to wait just a second more for him to say one last word. "'*Board*!" Machinery whirred, and the coach steps arose from the platform, nestled into one another, and disappeared into their niche.

"Coming! Coming!" cried the old man, and jogged unhappily toward the moving train as fast as his brittle legs would carry him. He caught the handrail, swung aboard, and stood panting in the vestibule. He fumbled for his ticket, dropped it into the mechanism on the door. The mechanism considered it, found everything in order, pulled back the door bolt, and let him into the frieze and cast-iron monument to tobacco.

He settled, winded, in the seat next to Paul's. "Son-of-a-bitch won't even wait a second for an old man," he said bitterly.

"It's a machine," said Paul. "All automatic."

"Don't mean he ain't a son-of-a-bitch."

Paul nodded appreciatively.

"Used to be conductor on this line."

"Oh?" The man had the florid, righteous look of a specialized bore, and Paul wasn't interested in listening to him.

"Yes, forty-one years," he said. "For-tee-wunnnn years!"

"Huh!"

"For-tee-wunnnn. Two times twenty plus one. And I'd like to see one of them machines deliver a baby."

"Huh! You delivered a baby, eh?"

"Yep. Little boy. By coincidence I done it in the men's room." He chuckled richly. "For-tee-wunnnn years!"

"Huh."

"And I never seen the machine yet that'd watch out for a little girl three years old all the way from St. Louis to Poughkeepsie."

"Nope. Guess not," said Paul. He filed this remark away for his next meeting with Bud Calhoun. He could see the device now—sort of an Iron Maiden, without the spikes, of course, and electronic, of course, that would grasp a little girl firmly at St. Louis, and eject her into the arms of relatives at Poughkeepsie.

"For-tee-wunnnn years! With machines you get *quan*-titty, but you don't get *qual*-itty. Know what I mean?"

"Yup," said Paul.

"*Carthage*," said the tape recording. "*The stop is Carthage. Next station, Deer River*."

Paul settled back against the unyielding seat with a sigh of relaxation, and closed his eyes in a pretense of sleep.

"For-tee-wunnnn years! These machines never help an old lady down the steps."

In time the old conductor ran out of examples of man's superiority over machines and took to anticipating the tape recording's station calling, casually, contemptuously, as though any fool could do it. "Deer River. The stop is Deer River. Next station, Castorland."

"*Deer River. The stop is Deer River*," said the tape recording. "*Next station, Castorland*."

"Ha! What'd I tell you?"

Paul actually did drop off to sleep fitfully, and at last, at Constableville, he saw his companion slipping his ticket into the door slot and being let off. Paul checked his ticket to make sure it wasn't bent or torn, that it would unlock the door at Ilium. He'd heard tales of addled old ladies locked aboard cars for days for having misplaced their tickets, or for having missed their stops. Hardly a newspaper was printed that didn't have a human interest story about car clean-up crews from the Reeks and Wrecks liberating somebody.

The old displaced conductor disappeared into the Constableville night, and Paul wondered at what thorough believers in mechanization most Americans were, even when their lives had been badly damaged by mechanization. The conductor's plaint, like the lament of so many, wasn't that it was unjust to take jobs from men and give them to machines, but that the machines didn't do nearly as many human things as good designers could have made them do.

"*Constableville. The stop is Constableville. Next station, Remsen.*"

A poker game was going on in the facing seats behind Paul, and a superannuated first sergeant, zebra-like under symbols for patience, individual bloodlettings, and separations from home, was telling tales of the last war—of the Last War.

"Jesus," he said, riffling through the deck absently, as though his mind were a thousand miles away, "there we was, and there they was. Imagine the men's room there's a hog-back, with the bastards dug in deep on the reverse slope." The recruits looked at the men's room through narrowed, battle-wise eyes, and the sergeant shuffled the cards some more. "The night before, lucky shot knocked out the generator."

"Holy cow!" said a recruit.

"You can say that again," said the sergeant. "Anyway—five-card stud, nothing wild—there we were with no juice, eighteen of us facing five hundred of them. The microwave sentinels, the proximity mines, the electric fence, the fire-control system, the remote-control machine gun nests—pfft! No juice, Queen, ace, ace, and dealer gets a deuce. Bet the first ace.

"Well, boys—a dime to me? Raise it a dime just to make things interesting. Well, boys, then the fun started. At seven hundred hours they tried a hundred-man patrol on us, to see what we had. And we had nothin'! And communications was cut to hell, so we couldn't call for nothin'. All our robot tanks'd been pulled out to support a push the 106th was makin', so we was really alone. Snafu. So, I sent Corporal Merganthaler back to battalion for help. —Two queens, no help, two aces, and dealer catches another lousy deuce. Bet the aces. So over they come, screamin' bloody murder, and us with nothing but our goddamn rifles and bayonets workin'. Looked like a tidal wave comin' over at us. —Aces check? Aw, hell, deuces'll try a dime. —Just then, up comes Merganthaler with a truck and generator he's moonlight-requisitioned from the 57th. We hooked her into our lines, cranked her up, and my God, I wish you could of seen it. The poor bastards fryin' on the electric fence, the proximity mines poppin' under 'em, the microwave sentinels openin' up with the remote-control machine-gun nests, and the fire-control system swiveling the guns and flamethrowers around as long as anything was quiverin' within a mile of the place. And that's how I got the Silver Star."

Paul shook his head slightly as he listened to the sergeant's absurd tale. That, then, was the war he had been so eager to get into at one time, the opportunity for basic, hot-tempered, hard-muscled heroism he regretted having missed. There had been plenty of death, plenty of pain, all right, and plenty of tooth-grinding stoicism and nerve. But men had been called upon chiefly to endure by the side of the machines, the terrible engines that fought with their own kind for the right to gorge themselves on men. Horatio on the bridge had become a radio-guided rocket with an atomic warhead and a proximity fuse. Roland and Oliver had become a pair of jet-driven computers hurtling toward each other far faster than the flight of a man's scream. The great tradition of the American rifleman survived only symbolically, in volleys fired into the skies over the dead in thousands of military cemeteries. Those in the graves, the front-line dead, were heirs to another American tradition as old as that of the rifleman, but once a peaceful tradition—that of the American tinker.

"Gosh! Sarge, how come you never went after a commission?"

"Me go back to college at my age? I'm not the school kind, sonny. Gettin' that B.S. was enough for me. Two more years and an M.A. for a pair of lousy gold bars? Naaaaaah! —And a queen, and no help, and a jack, and no help, and a five, and no help, and dealer gets a—what do you know? Three deuces. Looks like my lucky day, boys."

"*Middleville. The stop is Middleville. Next station, Herkimer.*"

"Sarge, d'ya mind talkin' about your wound stripes?"

"Hmmm? No—guess not. This 'un's for a dose of Gamma rays at Kiukiang. This 'un's—lemme see—radioactive dust in the bronchial tubes at Afyon Karahisar. And this little bastard—uh—trenchfoot at Kransystav."

"Sarge, what was the best piece you ever had?"

"A little redheaded half-Swede, half-Egyptian in Farafangana," said the Sarge without hesitation.

"Boy! I hope that's where they send me."

That much of a fine old American military tradition, Paul supposed, would always be alive—send me where the tail is.

"*Herkimer. The stop is Herkimer. Next station, Little Falls.*"

"Say, Sarge, is this train a local?"

"You might call it that. How's about a round of cold hands for the odd change?" said the sergeant.

"O.K. with me. Oops. Lousy trey. A queen for Charley. An eight for Lou. And, I'll be go to hell, the Sarge catches a bullet."

"Say, Sarge, hear Pfc. Elmo Hacketts is shipping out."

"Yep. Been asking for overseas ever since he joined the outfit. Pair of treys for Ed, nothing for Charley, jack for Lou, and dealer catches a— I'll be damned."

"Ace!"

"*Little Falls. The stop is Little Falls. Next station, Johnsonville.*"

"Here we go around again, and— What you know about that?" said the sergeant. "Ed's got three treys. Yep—hate to see Hacketts go. With a coupla years seasoning, I could see him as a helluva fine guidon bearer. But, if he wants to throw all that over, that's his business. Nothing for Charley, and Lou gets my ace. Three treys got it so far."

"Where's Hacketts going? You know?"

"And no help, and help, and no help, and no help," said the sergeant. "Yeah, his orders came through today. Last time around, boys. No help, no help, no help, and—"

"Jesus!"

"Sorry about that third ace, Ed. Guess that one's mine too. Yeah, Hacketts gets his overseas duty all right. Shipping out for Tamanrasset tomorrow morning."

"Tamanrasset?"

"The Sahara Desert, you dumb bastard. Don't you know any geography?" He grinned wolfishly. "How about a little blackjack for laughs?"

Paul sighed for Hacketts, born into a spiritual desert, now being shipped to where the earth was sterile, too.

"*Johnsonville . . . Ft. Plain . . . Fonda . . . Ft. Johnson*

. . . Amsterdam . . . Schenectady . . . Cohoes . . . Watervliet . . . Albany . . . Rensselaer . . . Ilium, the stop is Ilium."

Bleary-eyed, Paul shuffled to the door, inserted his ticket, and stepped onto the Ilium station platform.

The door on the baggage compartment clattered open, a coffin slid onto a waiting freight elevator and was taken into the refrigerated bowels of the station.

No cabs had bothered to meet the unpromising train. Paul phoned the cab company, but no one answered. He looked helplessly at the automatic ticket vendor, the automatic nylon vendor, the automatic coffee vendor, the automatic gum vendor, the automatic book vendor, the automatic newspaper vendor, the automatic toothbrush vendor, the automatic Coke vendor, the automatic shoeshine machine, the automatic photo studio, and walked out into the deserted streets on the Homestead side of the river.

It was eight miles through Homestead, across the bridge, and up the other side of the river to home. Not home, Paul thought, but the house where his bed was.

He felt dull, mushy inside, with an outer glaze of bright heat—sleepy yet sleepless, assailed by thoughts yet thoughtless.

His footsteps echoed against Homestead's gray façades, and lifeless neon tubes, proclaiming one thing and another of no importance at this hour, were empty, cold glass for want of the magic of electrons in flight through inert gas.

"Lonesome?"

"Huh?"

A young woman, with bosoms like balloon spinnakers before the wind, looked down from a second-story window. "I said, are you lonesome?"

"Yes," said Paul simply.

"Come on up."

"Well," Paul heard himself saying, "all right, I will."

"The door next to the Automagic Market."

He climbed the long, dark stairway, each riser of which proclaimed Doctor Harry Friedmann to be a painless dentist, licensed under the National Security and Health Plan. "Why," asked Friedmann rhetorically, "settle for less than a D-006?"

The door on the hallway, next to Doctor Friedmann's, was open, the woman waiting.

"What's your name, honey?"

"Proteus."

"Any relation to the big cheese across the river?"

"My half-brother."

"You the black sheep, honey?"

"Yup."

"Screw your brother."

"Please," said Paul.

He awoke once during the remainder of the night with her, awoke from a dream in which he saw his father glowering at him from the foot of the bed.

She mumbled in her sleep.

As Paul dropped off once more, he murmured an automatic reply. "And I love *you*, Anita."

Chaper XXVII

DOCTOR PAUL PROTEUS had been his own man, alone in his own house for a week. He'd been expecting some sort of communication from Anita, but nothing came. There was nothing more, he realized wonderingly, to be said. She was still at the Mainland, probably. The Meadows session had another week to run. After that would come the muddle of her separating her effects from his—and divorce. He wondered on what grounds she would divorce him. Extreme mental cruelty amused him, and he supposed it was close enough to the truth. Any variation from any norm pained her terribly. She'd have to leave New York State, of course, since the only grounds for divorce there were adultery, and incitement to conspire to advocate sabotage. A case could be made for either, he supposed, but not with dignity.

Paul had gone to his farm once, and, in the manner of a man dedicating his life to God, he'd asked Mr. Haycox to put him to work, guiding the hand of Nature. The hand he grasped so fervently, he soon discovered, was coarse and sluggish, hot and wet and smelly. And the charming little cottage he'd taken as a symbol of the good life of a farmer was as irrelevant as a statue of Venus at the gate of a sewage-disposal plant. He hadn't gone back.

He'd been to the Works once. The machinery had been shut off during the Meadows session, and only the guards were on duty. Four of them, now officious and scornful, had telephoned to Kroner at the Meadows for instructions. Then they'd escorted him to what had been his desk, where he'd picked up a few personal effects. They'd made a list of what he'd taken, and questioned his claim to each item. Then they'd marched him back into the outside world, and shut the gates against him forever and ever.

Paul was in the kitchen now, before the laundry console, seated on a stool, watching television. It was late afternoon, and, for the unadorned hell of it, he was doing his own laundry.

"*Urdle-urdle-urdle*," went the console. "*Urdle-urdle-ur dull!*

Znick. Bazz-wap!" Chimes sounded. "*Azzzzzzzzzz. Fromp!*" Up came the anticlimactic offering: three pairs of socks, three pairs of shorts, and the blue Meadows' T-shirts, which he was using for pajamas.

On the television screen, a middle-aged woman was counseling her teen-age son, whose hair and clothes were disordered and soiled.

"Fightin' don't help, Jimmy," she was saying sadly. "Lord knows nobody ever brought any more sunshine into the world by bloodyin' somebody's nose, or by havin' his own nose bloodied."

"I know—but he said my I.Q. was 59, Ma!" The boy was on the point of tears, he was so furious and hurt. "And he said Pop was a 53!"

"Now, now—that's just child's talk. Don't you pay it no mind, Jimmy."

"But it's true," said the boy brokenly. "Ma, it's true. I went down to the police station and looked it up! Fifty-nine, Ma! and poor Pop with a 53." He turned his back, and his voice was a bitter whisper: "And you with a 47, Ma. A 47."

She bit her lip and looked heartbroken, then, seeming to draw strength miraculously from somewhere above eye level, she gripped the kitchen table. "Jimmy, look at your mother."

He turned slowly.

"Jimmy, I.Q. isn't everything. Some of the unhappiest people in this world are the smartest ones."

Since the start of his week of idleness at home, Paul had learned that this, with variations, was the basic problem situation in afternoon dramas, with diseases and injuries of the optic nerve and locomotor apparatus close seconds. One program was an interminable exploration of the question: can a woman with a low I.Q. be happily married to a man with a high one? The answer seemed to be yes and no.

"Jimmy, boy, son—I.Q. won't get you happiness, and St. Peter don't give I.Q. tests before he lets you in those Pearly Gates. The wickedest people that ever lived was the smartest."

Jimmy looked suspicious, then surprised, then guardedly willing to be convinced. "You mean—a plain fellow like me, just another guy, folks like us, Ma, you mean we're as good as, as, as, well, Doctor Garson, the Works Manager?"

"Doctor Garson, with his 169 I.Q.? Doctor Garson, with his Ph.D., D.Sc., and his Ph. and D. I-don't-know-what-else? Him?"

"Yeah, Ma. Him."

"Him? Doctor Garson? Jimmy, son, boy—have you seen the bags under his eyes? Have you seen the lines in his face? He's carryin' the world around on his shoulders, Jimmy. That's what a high I.Q. got him, Doctor Garson. Do you know how old he is?"

"An awful old man, Ma."

"He's ten years younger than your Pa, Jimmy. *That's* what brains got him."

Pa came in at that moment, wearing the brassard of a Reconstruction and Reclamation Corps Asphalt Leveler, First Class. He was cheery, pink, in first-rate health. "Hi, there, folks," he said. "Everything hunky-dory in my little old home, eh?"

Jimmy exchanged glances with his mother, and smiled oddly. "Yessir, reckon it is. I mean, you're darn right it is!"

In came the organ music, the announcer, and the washless, rinseless wash powder, and Paul turned down the volume.

The door chimes were ringing, and Paul wondered how long they'd been at it. He might have turned on the televiewer, to see if the bell ringer was worth opening the door for, but he was hungry for companionship—just about any kind—and he went to the door gladly, gratefully.

A policeman looked at him coldly. "Doctor Proteus?"

"Yes?"

"I'm from the police."

"So I see."

"You haven't registered."

"Oh." Paul smiled. "Oh—I've been meaning to do that." And he had meant to do it, too.

The policeman did not smile. "Then why haven't you?"

"I haven't found the time."

"You better start looking for it, hard, Doc."

Paul was annoyed by this rude young man, and he was inclined, as he had been inclined with the bartender at the Meadows, to put him in his place. But he thought better of it this time. "All right. I'll be down to register tomorrow morning."

"You'll be down to register in an hour, today, Doc." The honorific *Doc*, Paul was learning, could be spoken in such a way as to make a man wish to God he'd never come within ten miles of a university.

"Yes—all right, whatever you say."

"And your industrial identification card—you've failed to turn that in."

"Sorry. I'll do that."

"And your firearms and ammunition permit."

"I'll bring that."

"And your club membership card."

"I'll find it."

"And your airline pass."

"All right."

"And your executive security and health policy. You'll have to get a regular one."

"Whatever you say."

"I think that's all. If anything else comes up, I'll let you know."

"I'm sure you will."

The young policeman's expression softened suddenly, and he shook his head. "Lo! How the mighty are fallen, eh, Doc?"

"Lo! indeed," said Paul.

And an hour later Paul reported politely at the police station, with a shoebox full of revoked privileges.

While he waited for someone to notice him, he interested himself in the radiophoto machine behind glass in one corner, which was fashioning a portrait of a fugitive, and noting beside it a brief biography. The portrait emerged from a slit in the top of the machine bit by bit—first the hair, then the brows, on line with the word WANTED, and then, on line with the large, fey eyes, the name: Edgar Rice Burroughs Hagstrohm, R&R-131313. Hagstrohm's sordid tale emerged along with his nose: "Hagstrohm cut up his M-17 home in Chicago with a blowtorch, went naked to the home of Mrs. Marion Frascati, the widow of an old friend, and demanded that she come to the woods with him. Mrs. Frascati refused, and he disappeared into the bird sanctuary bordering the housing development. There he eluded police, and is believed to have made his escape dropping from a tree onto a passing freight—

"You!" said the desk sergeant. "Proteus!"

Registration involved the filling out of a long, annoyingly

complicated form that started with his name and highest classification number, investigated his reasons for having fallen from grace, asked for the names of his closest friends and relatives, and ended with an oath of allegiance to the United States of America. Paul signed the document in the presence of two witnesses, and watched a coding clerk translate it, on a keyboard, into terms the machines could understand. Out came a card, freshly nicked and punched.

"That's all," said the police sergeant. He dropped the card into a slot, and the card went racing through a system of switches and sidings, until it came to rest against a thick pile of similar cards.

"What does that mean?" said Paul.

The sergeant looked at the pile without interest. "Potential saboteurs."

"Wait a minute—what's going on here? Who says I am?"

"No reflection on you," said the sergeant patiently. "Nobody's said you are. It's all automatic. The machines do it."

"What right have they got to say that about me?"

"Oh, they know, they know," said the sergeant. "They've been around. They do that with anybody who's got more'n four years of college and no job." He studied Paul through narrowed lids. "And you'd be surprised, Doc, how right they are."

A detective walked in, perspiring and discouraged.

"Any break on the Freeman case, Sid?" said the sergeant, losing interest in Paul.

"Nah. All the good suspects came off clean as a whistle on the lie detector."

"Did you check the tubes?"

"Sure. We put in a whole new set, had the circuits checked. Same thing. Innocent, every damn one of 'em. Not that every damned one of 'em wouldn't of liked to of knocked him off." He shrugged. "Well, more leg work. We've got one lead: the sister says she saw a strange man around the back of Freeman's house a half-hour before he got it."

"Got a description?"

"Partial." He turned to the coding clerk. "Ready, Mac?"

"All set. Shoot."

"Medium height. Black shoes, blue suit. No tie. Wedding

ring. Black hair, combed straight back. Clean-shaven. Warts on hands and back of neck. Slight limp."

The clerk, expressionless, punched keys as he talked.

"*Dinga-dinga-dinga-ding!*" went the machine, and out came a card.

"Herbert J. van Antwerp," said Mac. "Forty-nine fifty-six Collester Boulevard."

"Nice work," said the sergeant. He picked up a microphone. "Car 57, car 57—proceed to . . ."

As Paul walked into the bright sunlight of the street, a Black Maria, its siren silent, its tires humming the song of new rubber on hot tar, turned into the alleyway that ran behind the station house.

Paul peered curiously at it as it stopped by a barred door.

A policeman dismounted from the back of the shiny black vehicle and waved a riot gun at Paul. "All right, all right, no loitering there!"

Paul started to move on, lingering an instant longer for a glimpse of the prisoner, who sat deep in the wagon's dark interior, misty, futile, between two more men with riot guns.

"Go on, beat it!" shouted the policeman at Paul again.

Paul couldn't believe that the man would actually loose his terrible hail of buckshot on a loiterer, and so loitered a moment longer. His awe of the riot gun's yawning bore was tempered by his eagerness to see someone who had made a worse botch of getting along in society than he had.

The iron door of the station house clanged open, and three more armed policemen waited to receive the desperado. The prospect of his being at large in the alley for even a few seconds was so harrowing, seemingly, that the policeman who had been badgering Paul now gave his full attention to covering the eight or ten square feet the prisoner would cross in an instant. Paul saw his thumb release the safety catch by the trigger guard.

"All righty, no funny stuff, you hear?" said a nervous voice in the wagon. "Out you go!"

A moment later, Doctor Fred Garth, wearing a badly torn Blue Team shirt, unshaven, his eyes wide, emerged into the daylight, manacled and sneering.

Before Paul could believe in the senseless scene, his old

tent- and teammate, his buddy, the man next in line for Pittsburgh, was inside.

Paul hurried around to the front, and back into the office where he'd filled out the papers and turned in his credentials.

The sergeant looked up at him superciliously. "Yes?"

"Doctor Garth—what's he doing here?" said Paul.

"Garth? We got no Garth here."

"I saw them bring him in the back door."

"Naah." The sergeant went back to his reading.

"Look—he's one of my best friends."

"Should of stuck with your dog and your mother," said the sergeant without looking up. "Beat it."

Bewildered, Paul wandered back to the street, left his old car parked in front of the station house, and walked up the hill to the main street of Homestead, to the saloon at the foot of the bridge.

The town hall clock struck four. It might have struck midnight or seven or one, for all the difference it made to Paul. He didn't have to be anywhere at any time any more—ever, he supposed. He made up his own reasons for going somewhere, or he went without reasons. Nobody had anything for him to do anywhere. The economy was no longer interested. His card was of interest now only to the police machines, who regarded him, the instant his card was introduced, with instinctive distrust.

The hydrant was going as usual, and Paul joined the crowd. He found himself soothed by the cool spray from the water. He waited with eagerness for the small boy to finish fashioning his paper boat, and enjoyed the craft's jolting progress toward certain destruction in the dark, gurgling unknown of the storm sewer.

"Interesting, Doc?"

Paul turned to find Alfy, the television shark, at his elbow. "Well! Thought you were at the Meadows."

"Thought *you* were. How's the lip?"

"Healing. Tender."

"If it's any consolation, Doc, the bartender's still sneezing."

"Good, wonderful. Did you get fired?"

"Didn't you know? Everybody got sacked, the whole service staff, after that tree business." He laughed. "They're doing their own cooking, making their own beds, raking the horseshoe pits, and all, all by theirselves."

"Everybody?"

"Everybody below works manager."

"They're cleaning their own latrines, too?"

"The dumb bunnies, Doc, with I.Q.'s under 140."

"What a thing. Still play games, do they?"

"Yep. Last I heard, Blue was way out ahead."

"You don't mean it!"

"Yeah, they were so ashamed of you, they just about killed theirselves to win."

"And Green?"

"Cellar."

"In spite of Shepherd?"

"You mean Jim Thorpe? Yeah, he entered everything, and tried to make every point."

"So—"

"So nobody made any points. Last I heard, his team was trying to convince him he had virus pneumonia and ought to spend a couple of days in the infirmary. He's got something, that's for sure." Alfy looked at his watch. "Say, there's some chamber music on channel seven. Care to play?"

"Not with you."

"Just for the hell of it. No money. I'm just getting checked out on chamber music. A whole new field. C'mon, Doc, we'll learn together. You watch the cello and bass, and I'll watch the viola and violin. O.K.? Then we'll compare notes and pool our knowledge."

"I'll buy you a beer. How's that?"

"That's good; that's very good."

In the bar's damp twilight, Paul saw a teen-ager looking at him hopefully from a booth. Before him, on the table top, were three rows of matches: three in the first row, five in the second, seven in the third.

"Hello," said the young man uneasily, hopefully. "Very interesting game here. The object of the game is to make the other guy take the last match. You can take as many or as few as you want from any given row at each turn."

"Well—" said Paul.

"Go ahead," said Alfy.

"For two dollars?" said the youngster nervously.

"All right, for two." Paul took a match from the longest row.

The youngster frowned and looked worried, and countered. Three moves later, Paul left him looking disconsolately at the last match. "Goddammit, Alfy," he said miserably, "look at that. I lost."

"This is your first day!" said Alfy sharply. "Don't get discouraged. All right, so you lost. So you're just starting out." Alfy clapped the boy on the shoulder. "Doc, this is my kid brother, Joe. He's just starting out. The Army and the Reeks and Wrecks are hot for his body, but I'm trying to set him up in business for hisself instead. We'll see how this match business works out, and if it doesn't, we'll think of something else."

"I used to play it in college," said Paul apologetically. "I've had a lot of experience."

"College!" said Joe, awed, and he smiled and seemed to feel better. "Jesus, no wonder." He sighed and sat back, depressed again. "But I don't know, Alfy—I'm about ready to throw in the towel. Let's face it, I haven't got the brains." He lined up the matches again, and picked at them, playing a game with himself. "I work at it, and I just don't seem to get any better at it."

"Sure you work!" said Alfy. "Everybody works at something. Getting out of bed's work! Getting food off your plate and into your mouth's work! But there's two kinds of work, kid, work and *hard* work. If you want to stand out, have something to sell, you got to do *hard* work. Pick out something impossible and do it, or be a bum the rest of your life. Sure, everybody worked in George Washington's time, but George Washington worked *hard*. Everybody worked in Shakespeare's time, but Shakespeare worked *hard*. I'm who I am because I work *hard*."

"O.K., O.K., O.K.," said Joe. "Me, Alfy, I haven't got the brains, the eye, the push. Maybe I better go down to the Army."

"You can change your name before you do, kid, and don't bother me again," said Alfy tensely. "Anybody by the name of Tucci stands on his own two feet. It's always been that way, and that's the way it's always going to be."

"O.K.," said Joe, coloring. "Awri. So I give it a try for a couple more days."

"O.K.!" said Alfy. "See that you do."

As Alfy hurried to the television set, Paul stayed at his side. "Listen, do you happen to know who Fred Garth is?"

"Garth?" He laughed. "I didn't at first, but I sure as hell do now. He's the one that ringbarked the oak."

"No!"

"Yep. And they never even thought of questioning him. *He* was on the committee that was supposed to do the questioning."

"How'd they catch him?"

"Gave hisself away. When the tree surgeon got there to patch up the tree, Garth tossed his tools in the drink."

"Alfy!" said the bartender. "You missed the first number."

Alfy pulled up a bar stool.

Paul sat down next to him and engaged the bartender in conversation. Their talk was disjointed, as Alfy kept the man busy twisting the television set's volume knob.

"Ever see Finnerty around?" said Paul.

"The piano player?"

"Yeah."

"What if I have?"

"I'd just like to see him, is all. A friend of mine."

"Lot's of people'd like to see Finnerty these days."

"Uh-huh. Where's he keep himself?"

The bartender looked at him appraisingly. "Nobody sees Finnerty these days."

"Oh? He's not living with Lasher any more?"

"Full of questions today, aren't you? Nobody sees Lasher these days."

"I see." Paul didn't. "They leave town?"

"Who knows? Come on, I haven't got all day. What'll it be?"

"Bourbon and water."

The bartender mixed the drink, set it before Paul, and turned his back.

Paul drank the health of his hostile or apathetic companions in the new life he'd chosen, coughed, smiled, smacked his lips judiciously, trying to determine what wasn't quite right about the drink, and fell senseless from the barstool.

Chapter XXVIII

"FROM BLUE CAYUGA," piped the young voices in the autumn evening—

"From hill and dell,
Far rings the story of the glory of Cornell—"

Doctor Harold Roseberry, PE-002, laid two documents side by side on the naked, waxy expanse of the top of his rosewood desk. The desk, big enough for a helicopter to land on, was a gift from the Cornell alumni, and a silver plate on one corner said so. Justification of the lavish gift was inlaid in precious woods on the desk top: the football scores run up by the Big Red during the past five seasons. The why and wherefore of this object, at least, would leave no questions in the minds of future archæologists.

"From East and West the crashing echoes answering call," cried the young voices, and Doctor Roseberry found it extremely difficult to concentrate on the two documents before him: a memo from the dean of the School of Arts and Sciences, a quaint, antique man in a quaint, antique part of the university; and a five-year-old letter from a carping alumnus who objected to the deportment of the team when off the playing field. The memo from the dean said that a Mr. Ewing J. Halyard had arrived in town in order to show the university to the Shah of Bratpuhr, and, incidentally, to make up a seventeen-year-old credit deficiency in physical education. The memo asked that Doctor Roseberry assign one of his staff to the chore of giving Halyard the final physical-education tests the next morning.

"Cornell victorious!
The champions of all!"

came the voices.

Doctor Roseberry was inclined to react ironically to the last line of the song. "Certainly, victorious last year, four years afore that," he muttered in his pregnant solitude. But here was another year that might not look so hot inlaid in rosewood. "Tomorrow and tomorrow and tomorrow," he said wearily. Every coach in the Ivy League was out to knock him down to a PE-003 again, and two losses would do it. Yale and Penn were loaded. Yale had floated a bond to buy the whole Texas A&M backfield, and Penn had bought Breslaw from Wisconsin for $43,000.

Roseberry groaned. "How the hell long they think a man can play college football?" he wanted to know. Six years before, Cornell had bought him from Wabash College, and asked him to list his idea of a dream team. Then, by God they'd bought it for him.

"But what the hell they think they bought?" he asked himself. "Sumpin' made outa steel and *see*-ment? Supposed to last a lifetime, is it?" They hadn't bought him so much as a water boy since, and the average age of the Big Red was now close to thirty-one.

"Far above Cayuga's waters,
With its waves of blue,
Stands our noble Alma Mater,
Glorious to view—"

came the voices.

"Certainly it's glorious," said Doctor Roseberry. "Who the hell you figure paid for it?" In its first two years the football team had paid for itself. In the next three, it had paid for a new chemistry building, a heat and power laboratory, a new administration building for the Agricultural Engineering Department, and four new professorial chairs: the Philosophy of Creative Engineering, Creative Engineering History, Creative Public Relations for Engineers, and Creative Engineering and the Captive Consumer.

Roseberry, who wasn't expected to pay any attention to the academic side of the university, had nonetheless kept a careful accounting of all these improvements, glorious to view, that had been added since he and his football team had arrived far above Cayuga's waters. In anticipation of a poor season, he was roughing out in his mind a polemic letter to the alumni, in which the academic expenditures would figure prominently.

He had the first line of the letter, following the salutation, "Sportsmen," already perfected, and enjoyed imagining it written out in capitals:

"IS THE FOOTBALL BUSINESS AT CORNELL GOING TO BE RUN ON A BUSINESS-LIKE BASIS, OR IS THE BIG RED GOING TO BE BLED WHITE?"

And then the next sentence sprang inspirationally to mind: "IN THE PAST FIVE YEARS, NOT ONE CENT HAS BEEN REINVESTED IN THE BUSINESS, NOT ONE CENT LAID ASIDE FOR DEPRECIATION!"

He saw now that the whole thing would have to be in caps. The situation called for a letter with real punch.

The telephone rang.

"Doctor Roseberry speakin'."

"This is Buck Young, Doc. Note here says you wanted me to call." The husky voice was tinged with uneasiness, just as Roseberry had hoped it would be. He could imagine that Buck had sat by the phone with the note in his hand for several minutes before he'd dialed. Now that Buck had gone this far, Roseberry told himself, he'd go the rest of the way too.

"Yeah, yeah," said Roseberry, smiling captivatingly. "Bucky boy, how are you?"

"Fine. What's on your mind?"

"Maybe I should ask what's on yours."

"Thermodynamics. Stress analysis. Fluid flow. Differential equations."

"Aaah," said Roseberry, "why'n't you loosen up and have a beer with me down at The Dutch? You hear the news I got, I think maybe you'll get something else on your mind."

"Cheer, cheer, here we are again
To cheer with all our might—"

sang the voices, and Doctor Roseberry waited impatiently for the racket to stop. If they had to have a football rally, he wished they'd hold it somewhere where it wouldn't bother him and his team. That was another thing: Cornell was so cheap, they quartered their athletes on the campus rather than setting up a separate establishment away from all the student racket. "Wait'll they shut up, Bucky boy, and I can hear myself think."

"Cheer, cheer, here we are again,
To cheer for the Red and White!"

Either Cornell was going to get progressive, or they could find themselves another coach, Roseberry told himself. Now, Tennessee—there *was* a progressive setup. *They* kept *their* team in Miami Beach, and no wonder Milankowitz went there for $35,000, after he turned down Chicago for $40,000. "O.K., Bucky, I can hear again. What about I meet you down at The Dutch for a couple of quick ones in fifteen minutes?"

The voice was faint, reluctant. "Just for half an hour."

Doctor Roseberry climbed into his black convertible in the team parking lot, and drove over to the Delta Upsilon fraternity house, on whose lawn he'd first spotted Buck Young playing interfraternity football. There, Young had done things for Delta Upsilon for nothing that any college in the country would have considered a steal at $50,000 a year.

That had been last fall, and D.U. had eked out the interfraternity football championship with 450 points to their opponents' six. Young had scored 390 of the points, and had thrown the passes for the other 54, the remaining touchdown being accounted for by a George Ward, whose name had somehow burned itself into Roseberry's memory along with all of the other statistics.

But Young had said firmly, when Roseberry had approached him, that he played football for fun, and that he wanted to be an engineer. A year ago, with the Big Red by far the biggest thing in the East, with the Yale and Penn alumni still to mobilize their economic resources, Roseberry could afford to be amused by Young's preference for a career in engineering. Now nothing was amusing, and Roseberry saw Young as his one chance to remain a PE-002 under the fouled-up Cornell football economics. He would sell a couple of superannuated linemen to Harvard, who would buy anything that was cheap, and use the proceeds to buy himself the services of Young at far below their value on the open market.

The Dutch, its paneling antiqued by the condensation from breaths of generations of adolescent alcoholics, was packed and noisy, and in almost every hand was the drink fashionable that season, benedictine and Pluto water, with a sprig of mint.

Doctor Roseberry was cheered and toasted by the children as he entered. He grinned, and colored becomingly, and inwardly demanded of himself and history, "What the hell these baby engineers got to do'th me, for chrissakes?" He pushed his way through the crowd, which claimed him for reasons not at all clear, to a dark corner booth, where Purdy and McCloud, the linemen whom he intended to sell to Harvard, were nursing the one beer a night apiece permitted during training. They were talking quietly, but darkly, and, as Doctor Roseberry approached, they looked up, but didn't smile.

"Evenin' boys," said Doctor Roseberry, sitting down on the small ledge not occupied by McCloud's backside, and keeping his eyes on the door through which Buck Young would be coming.

They nodded, and went on with their conversation. "No reason," said McCloud, "why a man can't play college ball till he's forty, if he takes good care of hisself." McCloud was thirty-six.

"Sure," said Purdy gravely, "a older man's got a certain matoority you don't find in the young ones." Purdy was thirty-seven.

"Look at Moskowitz," said McCloud.

"Yup. Forty-three, and still goin' strong. No reason why he shou'n't keep goin' until he's fifty. No reason why most men shou'n't."

"Bet I could go to the Reeks and Wrecks now and put together a Ivy League championship team out of guys past forty who're s'posed to be through."

"Planck," said Purdy. "Poznitsky."

"McCarren," said McCloud, "Mirro, Mellon. Ain't that right, Doc?" McCloud asked Roseberry the question casually.

"Yup, guess so. Hope so. Better. Kind of outfit I've got to work with."

"Um," said McCloud. He stared down into his beer, finished it off with a flourish, and looked plaintively at Roseberry. "O.K. if I have one more short one tonight?"

"Sure—why the hell not?" said Roseberry. "I'll even buy it."

McCloud and Purdy looked distressed at this, and both, on

second thought, figured they'd better keep in good shape for the important Big Red season ahead.

Roseberry offered no reply to this clumsy gambit.

"Better not hit that stuff too hard," said a leering student, pointing to the two bottles of beer. "Not if Cornell's going to go on ruling the Ivy League, you better not, boys."

Purdy glowered at him, and the youngster retreated into the crowd. "One minute, they ask you should go out and bust both arms and legs so's they can say how tough Cornell is. Then the next minute, they want you should live like a goddam missionary," said Purdy bitterly.

"Like in the Army," said McCloud.

The subject reminded Doctor Roseberry of the letter and the memo he'd been reading in his office, and he patted his breast pocket to make sure he still had them.

"Like in the Army," said Purdy, "only no pension."

"Sure, give the best years of your life to some college, and what the hell they do when you're through? Toss you right into the Reeks and Wrecks. The hell with *you*, buddy."

"Look at Kisco," said Purdy.

"Died for dear old Rutgers, and his widow's got what?"

"Nuttin'! Nuttin' but a chenille *R* she can use as a bathmat, and a government pension."

"Shoulda saved his money!" said Doctor Roseberry impatiently. "He was makin' more'n the college president. How come he was so poor? Whose fault that?"

Purdy and McCloud looked down at their big hands and fidgeted. Both of them, in their prime, had made as much as the late Buddy Kisco, who had actually died for Rutgers. But both were likewise broke—forever broke, building flamboyant mansions in Cayuga Heights, buying new cars every six months, dressing expensively. . . .

"That's the thing," said McCloud plaintively. "A athalete has to keep up appearances. Sure, people think a athalete makes plenty, and he do on paper. But people never stop to think he's allus gotta keep up a expensive front."

Purdy leaned forward in excited agreement. "For who?" he demanded rhetorically. "For the athalete?"

"For Cornell!" said McCloud.

"Damn right!" said Purdy, leaning back, satisfied.

Buck Young, tall, massive, shy, appeared in the doorway and looked around the room. Doctor Roseberry stood and waved, and left Purdy and McCloud to join him at the door.

"Bucky boy!"

"Doc." Buck seemed somewhat ashamed to be seen with the coach, and looked hopefully at a vacant booth. He was behaving as though he were keeping an appointment with a dope peddler, and, in a way, Doctor Roseberry reflected cheerfully, he was.

"Buck, I'm not going to waste any words, because there isn't much time. This offer won't be open many more days. Maybe it'll be off tomorrow. It's all up to the alumni," he lied.

"Uh-huh," said Buck.

"I'm prepared to offer you thirty thousand, Buck, six hundred a week, all year round, startin' tomorrow. What do you say?"

Young's Adam's apple bobbed. He cleared his throat. "Every week?" he asked faintly.

"That's how much we think of you, boy. Don't sell yourself short."

"And I could study, too? You'd give me time off for classes and study?"

Roseberry frowned. "Well—there's some pretty stiff rulings about that. You can't play college football, *and* go to school. They tried that once, and you know what a silly mess that was."

Buck ran his blunt fingers through his hair. "Golly, I dunno. That's a lot of money, but my family'd be awful surprised and disappointed. I mean—"

"I'm not askin' it for me, Buck! Think of your schoolmates. You want them to lose a game this year?"

"No," he murmured.

"Thirty-five grand, Buck."

"Jesus, I—"

"I have heard every word you've said," said a young redhead thickly. He wasn't drinking benedictine and Pluto water, but sloshed instead a puddle of whisky and water on the table as he sat down by Buck, facing Doctor Roseberry, uninvited. Beneath his open-necked shirt the red of a Meadows T-shirt showed plainly. "Heard it all," he said, and he laid his hand on Buck's shoulder gravely. "Here you are at a crossroads, my boy.

You're lucky. Not many crossroads left for people. Nothing but one-way streets with cliffs on both sides."

"Who the hell are you?" said Doctor Roseberry irritably.

"Doctor, *Doctor*, mind you, Edmond L. Harrison of the Ithaca Works. Call me Ed, or pay me five dollars."

"Let's get away from this lush," said Doctor Roseberry.

Harrison banged on the table with his fist. "Hear me out!" He appealed to Buck, whose exit he blocked. "The eminent Doctor Roseberry represents one road, and I the other. I am you, if you continue on your present course, five years from now."

His eyes were half closed, and after the fashion of benign drunks he seemed on the verge of tears, so powerfully was he compelled to love and help others. "If you are good," he said, "and if you are thoughtful, a fractured pelvis on the gridiron will pain you less than a life of engineering and management. In that life, believe me, the thoughtful, the sensitive, those who can recognize the ridiculous, die a thousand deaths."

Doctor Roseberry leaned back and folded his hands across his flat, hard belly. If he'd thought of it, he would have hired a professional actor to do what Doctor Harrison was doing for nothing. "How do you mean?" he asked helpfully.

"The best man I knew at the Meadows—"

"The *Meadows*?" said Buck in awe.

"The Meadows," said Harrison, "where the men at the head of the procession of civilization demonstrate in private that they are ten-year-olds at heart, that they haven't the vaguest notion of what they're doing to the world."

"They're opening new doors at the head of the procession!" said Buck hotly, shocked by the blunt, near-sabotage talk, and now fighting it, like the good citizen he was. He'd learned the resounding phrase about opening doors in a freshman orientation program, at which a Doctor Kroner had been the impressive chief speaker.

"Slamming doors in everybody's face," said Harrison. "That's what they're doing."

"Keep your voice down," warned Doctor Roseberry.

"I don't care," said Harrison stridently, "not after what they did to the only grownup there. They gave Proteus the sack, that's what they did."

"Proteus has been dead for years," said Buck, sure Harrison was a fake.

"His son, his son, Paul," said Harrison. "So let me say, my boy, go out and make your money on the gridiron, with blood and sweat and sinew. There's honor and glory in that—a little, anyway—and you'll never hate yourself. But keep the hell away from the head of the procession, where you'll get it in the neck if you can't get a lump in your throat over the ups and downs of a bunch of factories." He attempted to rise, failed once, made it the next time. "And now, goodbye."

"Where are you going?" said Doctor Roseberry. "Stick around, stick around."

"Where? First to shut off that part of the Ithaca works for which I am responsible, and then to an island, perhaps, a cabin in the north woods, a shack in the Everglades."

"And do what?" said Buck, baffled.

"Do?" said Harrison. "*Do*? That's just it, my boy. All of the doors have been closed. There's nothing to do but to find a womb suitable for an adult, and crawl into it. One without machines would suit me particularly."

"What have you got against machines?" said Buck.

"They're slaves."

"Well, what the heck," said Buck. "I mean, they aren't people. They don't suffer. They don't mind working."

"No. But they compete with people."

"That's a pretty good thing, isn't it—considering what a sloppy job most people do of anything?"

"Anybody that competes with slaves becomes a slave," said Harrison thickly, and he left.

A dark man, dressed like a student, but much older-looking, set down his untouched benedictine and Pluto water on the bar, studied the faces of Roseberry and Young as though memorizing them, and followed Harrison out of the building.

"Let's go out in the lobby, where we can talk," said Roseberry, as a cycle of songs began.

"Cheer, cheer, here we are again," cried the young voices, and Young and Roseberry moved into the lobby.

"Well?" said Doctor Roseberry.

"I—"

"Doctor Roseberry, I believe?"

Roseberry looked up at the intruder, a sandy-mustached gentleman, in a violet shirt, matching boutonniere, and a gay waistcoat contrasting with his dark suit. "Yes?"

"My name is Halyard, E. J., of the State Department. And these gentlemen here are the Shah of Bratpuhr, and his interpreter, Khashdrahr Miasma. We were just leaving for the president's house, and I happened to spot you."

"Charmed," said Doctor Roseberry.

"*Brahous brahouna, bouna saki*," said the Shah, bowing slightly.

Halyard laughed nervously. "Guess we have a little business tomorrow morning, eh?"

"Oh," said Roseberry, "*you're* the one—the one for the phys. ed. finals."

"Yes, yes indeed. Haven't had a cigarette in two weeks. Will it take long?"

"No, I don't think so. Fifteen minutes ought to do the trick."

"Oh? That short a time, eh? Well, well." The tennis shoes and shorts he'd bought that afternoon wouldn't get much wear in that time.

"Oh, 'scuse me, gents," said Roseberry. "This here's Buck Young. Student just now."

"*Lakki-ti Takaru*?" the Shah asked Buck.

" 'Like it here?' " translated Khashdrahr.

"Yessir. Very much, sir, your highness."

"A lot different from my day," said Halyard. "By gosh, we had to get up every morning bright and early, climb the hill in all kinds of weather, and sit there and listen to some of the dullest lectures you ever heard of. And, of course, some poor fish would have to get up in front of us and talk every day of the week, and chances are he wasn't much of a speaker, and anyway no showman."

"Yes, the professional actors and the television circuits are a big improvement, sir," said Buck.

"And the exams!" said Halyard. "Pretty cute, you know, punching out the answers, and then finding out right off if you passed or flunked. Boy, believe me, we used to have to write our arms off, and then we'd have to wait weeks for a prof to grade the exams. And plenty of times they made bad mistakes on the grades."

"Yessir," said Buck politely.

"Well, I'll see one of your assistants tomorrow, eh?" said Halyard to Roseberry.

"I intend I should give you the tests personal," said Roseberry.

"Well! I guess *that's* an honor, with the season just beginning."

"Sure," said Roseberry. He reached into his breast pocket and produced the letter and the memo. He handed the letter to Halyard. "Here's something you should oughta read before you come."

"Fine, thanks." Halyard took it, supposing it was a list of the things he would have to do. He smiled warmly at Roseberry, who had given every indication that Halyard would be given an exceedingly simple and short series of tests. A mere fifteen minutes, he'd said. That would do it.

Halyard glanced at the letter, and couldn't imagine what it was all about at first. It was addressed to the president of Cornell, Doctor Albert Herpers, not to him. Moreover, the date on it indicated that it was five years old.

Dear Doctor Herpers: he read—

> I had occasion to see the wearers of the Red and White after the Penn game in Philadelphia this Thanksgiving, and I must say I was ashamed to admit to anyone that I had ever come within fifty miles of Ithaca.
>
> I was dining in the Club Cybernetics after the game, when the team, led by this new man, Doctor Roseberry, arrived en masse . . .

The letter went on to describe the bacchanal that followed, with particular emphasis on the crudities of Roseberry's behavior—

> while, mind you, all were wearing what I, perhaps in my old-fashioned way, consider sacred, the C of the Big Red. . . .
>
> In view of this, Doctor Herpers, I feel constrained to point out, as a loyal alumnus, that Doctor Roseberry, in his first year with the Big Red, is off to an extremely poor start. In the brief time of his incumbency, I have no doubt that the shockingly public moral turpitude of the team has made a worse name for what I was once proud to claim

as my Alma Mater than a lifetime of gridiron victories can possibly offset. . . .

It is my fervent hope that Roseberry will be forced to resign forthwith, or, failing that, that outraged alumni sell him to some Grade C school forthwith.

To this end, I am sending copies of this letter to the Alumni Secretary, to each of the local alumni chapters, to the Trustees, and to the Secretary of Athletics in Washington, D. C.

Very truly yours,
Doctor Ewing J. Halyard

"Oh," said Halyard, his poise gone, suddenly looking ridiculous in the clothes that had been high fashion a moment before. "Saw this, did you?"

"Doctor Herpers thought I'd be interested."

A sickly grin framed Halyard's white teeth. "Long time ago, wasn't it, Doctor? Seems like a hundred years."

"Like yesterday."

"Ha ha. Lot of water under the dam since those days, eh?"

The Shah looked questioningly at Khashdrahr for an explanation of what made Halyard so gray suddenly. Khashdrahr shrugged.

"*Over* the dam," said Buck Young, filling the grim void in the conversation. "Or under the *bridge*."

"Yes. Quite so," said Halyard hollowly. "Well, best we should go. See you in the morning."

"Wouldn't miss it for the world."

Doctor Roseberry turned back to Buck Young, as Halyard, his face somber, shepherded the Shah and Khashdrahr into the Ithaca night. The Shah was sneezing violently.

"Well, kid," said Roseberry. "What say to thirty-five grand? Yes or no?"

"I—"

"Thirty-six."

"Yes," whispered Buck. "Hell yes."

When the two went back into The Dutch to drink to the deal, Purdy and McCloud were still talking gloomily in their dark corner.

"Sure," said Purdy, "Roseberry's a tough guy to work for, but thank God you ain't workin' for Harvard."

McCloud nodded. "Yeah, work there, and 'ey won't letch wear nothin' but dark-gray flannels in the winter, and seersucker in the summer."

They both shuddered, and furtively refilled their glasses from a half-case hidden under the table.

"Wit'out shoulders," said Purdy.

Chapter XXIX

DOCTOR PAUL PROTEUS, to all practical purposes Mr. Paul Proteus, dreamed of nothing but pleasant things under the benign drug, and spoke simultaneously, without reflection but truthfully, on whatever subject was brought to his attention. The talking he did, the answering of questions, went on as though it were being done by a person hired to represent him, while Paul personally gave his attention to entertaining phantasmagoria within the privacy of his closed eyelids.

"Did you really get fired, or was it a pretense?" said the voice.

"Pretense. Supposed to get into the Ghost Shirt Society and find out what they're up to. Only I quit, and they don't know that, yet." Paul chuckled.

And in his dream, Paul danced powerfully, gracefully, to the hectic rhythms of the *Building 58 Suite.*

"*Furrazz-ow-ow-ow-ow-ow-ak! ting!*" went lathe group three, and Paul leapt and spun among the machines, while, pink amid the gray machines in the building's center, Anita lay invitingly in a rainbow-colored nest of control wires. Her part in the dance called for her only to lie there motionless, while Paul approached and fled, approached and fled in frenzied, random action.

"Why are you quitting?"

"Sick of my job."

"Because what you were doing was morally bad?" suggested the voice.

"Because it wasn't getting anybody anywhere. Because it was getting everybody nowhere."

"Because it was evil?" insisted the voice.

"Because it was pointless," said Paul's representative, as Kroner joined the ballet, ponderously, earthbound, with a methodical marching to the voices of the punch presses in the basement: "*Aw-grumph! tonka-tonka. Aw-grumph! tonka-tonka . . .*"

Kroner looked lovingly at Paul, caught him as he bounded past, and carried him in a bearlike embrace toward Anita. Paul squirmed free in the nick of time, and off he went again, leaving Kroner in tears, urging Anita to follow him into the out-of-doors.

"Then you're against the organization now?"

"I'm *not with* them now."

Shepherd, clumsily but energetically, entered the growing tableau from the basement, choosing as his theme the hoarse voices of the welders: "*Vaaaaaaa-zuzip! Vaaaaaaa-zuzip!*" Shepherd marked time with one foot, watching Paul's gyrations, another rejection of Kroner, another effort to coax the dead-panned Anita from her nest amid the machines. Shepherd watched with puzzlement and disdain, shrugged, and walked straight to Kroner and Anita. The three settled in the nest of wires, and together followed Paul's movements with baffled, censorious eyes.

Suddenly, a window by which Paul was bounding flew open, and Finnerty's face was thrust into the opening.

"Paul!"

"Yes, Ed?"

"You're on our side now!"

The *Building 58 Suite* stopped abruptly, and a black curtain fell between Paul and the rest of the cast, save Finnerty.

"Hmmm?" said Paul.

"You're on our side," said Finnerty. "If you're not with them, you're with us!"

Paul's head was aching now, and his lips were dry. He opened his eyes and saw Finnerty's face, gross, caricatured by its closeness.

"With who? Whom?"

"The Ghost Shirt Society, Paul."

"Oh, them. What do they think, Ed?" he asked drowsily. He was on a mattress, he realized, in a chamber whose air was still and damp, dense with the feel of dead mass pressing down from above. "What they think, Ed?"

"That the world should be restored to the people."

"By all means," said Paul, trying to nod. His muscles were only faintly connected to his will, and his will, in turn, was a fuzzy, ineffectual thing. "People oughta get it back."

"You're going to help."

"Yup," murmured Paul. He was in a highly tolerant mood,

full of admiration and well-wishing for anyone with convictions, and cheerfully *hors de combat* under the influence of the drug. Obviously, he couldn't be expected to do anything. And Finnerty began to fade again, and Paul danced once more in Building 58, danced God knows why, uncertain that there was an audience anywhere to appreciate his exertions.

"What do you think?" he heard Finnerty say.

"He'll do nicely," he heard another voice reply, and he recognized the voice as Lasher's.

"What's a ghost shirt?" murmured Paul between prickling lips.

"Toward the end of the nineteenth century," said Lasher, "a new religious movement swept the Indians in this country, Doctor."

"The Ghost Dance, Paul," said Finnerty.

"The white man had broken promise after promise to the Indians, killed off most of the game, taken most of the Indians' land, and handed the Indians bad beatings every time they'd offered any resistance," said Lasher.

"Poor Injuns," murmured Paul.

"This is serious," said Finnerty. "Listen to what he's telling you."

"With the game and land and ability to defend themselves gone," said Lasher, "the Indians found out that all the things they used to take pride in doing, all the things that had made them feel important, all the things that used to gain them prestige, all the ways in which they used to justify their existence—they found that all those things were going or gone. Great hunters had nothing to hunt. Great fighters did not come back from charging into repeating-arms fire. Great leaders could lead the people nowhere but into death in hopeless attack, or deeper into wastelands. Great religious leaders could no longer show that the old religious beliefs were the way to victory and plenty."

Paul, suggestible under the drug, was deeply disturbed by the plight of the redskins. "Golly."

"The world had changed radically for the Indians," said Lasher. "It had become a white man's world, and Indian ways in a white man's world were irrelevant. It was impossible to hold the old Indian values in the changed world. The only thing they could do in the changed world was to become second-rate white men or wards of the white men."

"Or they could make one last fight for the old values," said Finnerty with relish.

"And the Ghost Dance religion," said Lasher, "was that last, desperate defense of the old values. Messiahs appeared, the way they're always ready to appear, to preach magic that would restore the game, the old values, the old reasons for being. There were new rituals and new songs that were supposed to get rid of the white men by magic. And some of the more warlike tribes that still had a little physical fight left in them added a flourish of their own—the Ghost Shirt."

"Oho," said Paul.

"They were going to ride into battle one last time," said Lasher, "in magic shirts that white men's bullets couldn't go through."

"Luke! Hey, Luke!" called Finnerty. "Stop the mimeo machine a second and come on over here."

Paul heard footsteps shuffling across the damp floor. He opened his eyes to see Luke Lubbock, his features sour with the tragic stoicism of a dispossessed redskin, standing by his bed, wearing a white shirt fringed in an imitation of a buckskin shirt, and decorated with thunderbirds and stylized buffalo worked into the fabric with brightly insulated bits of wire.

"Ug," said Paul.

"Ug," said Luke, without hesitation, deep in his role.

"This isn't any joke, Paul," said Finnerty.

"Everything's a joke until the drug wears off," said Lasher.

"Does Luke think *he's* bulletproof?" said Paul.

"It's the symbolism of the thing!" said Finnerty. "Don't you get it yet?"

"I expect," said Paul amiably, dreamily. "Sure. You bet. I guess."

"What *is* the symbolism?" asked Finnerty.

"Luke Lubbock wants his buffaloes back."

"Paul—come on, snap out of it!" said Finnerty.

"Okey dokey."

"Don't you see, Doctor?" said Lasher. "The machines are to

practically everybody what the white men were to the Indians. People are finding that, because of the way the machines are changing the world, more and more of their old values don't apply any more. People have no choice but to become second-rate machines themselves, or wards of the machines."

"God help us," said Paul. "But, I dunno, this Ghost Shirt thing—it's kind of childish, isn't it? Dressing up like that, and—"

"Childish—like Hitler's Brown Shirts, like Mussolini's Black Shirts. Childish like any uniform," said Lasher. "We don't deny it's childish. At the same time, we admit that we've got to be a little childish, anyway, to get the big following we need."

"Wait until he sits in on some meetings," said Finnerty. "They're like something out of *Alice in Wonderland*, Paul."

"All meetings are," said Lasher. "But, by some magic that's beyond my comprehension, meetings get things done. I could do with a little more dignity and maturity in our operations, because those are the things we're fighting for. But first of all we've got to fight, and fighting is necessarily undignified and immature."

"Fight?" said Paul.

"Fight," said Lasher. "And there's hope of putting up a good fight. This business of one set of values being replaced by force by another set of values has come up often enough in history—"

"Among the Indians and the Jews and a lot of other people who've been tyrannized by outsiders," said Finnerty.

"Yes, it's come up often enough for us to make a good guess as to what can happen this time," said Lasher. He paused. "What we can make happen."

"Beat it, Luke," said Finnerty.

"Yessir."

"Paul, are you listening?" said Finnerty.

"Yep. Interesting."

"All right," said Lasher, his voice low. "In the past, in a situation like this, if Messiahs showed up with credible, dramatic messages of hope, they often set off powerful physical and spiritual revolutions in the face of terrific odds. If a Messiah shows up now with a good, solid, startling message, and if he keeps out of the hands of the police, he can set off a revolution—maybe one big enough to take the world away from the machines, Doctor, and give it back to the people."

"And you're just the boy to do it, too, Ed," said Paul.

"That's what I thought too," said Lasher, "at first. Then I realized we could do much better starting off with a name that was already well known."

"Sitting Bull?" said Paul.

"Proteus," said Lasher.

"You don't have to do anything but keep out of sight," said Finnerty. "Everything will be done for you."

"*Is* being done," said Lasher.

"So you just rest now," said Finnerty gently. "Build up your strength."

"I—"

"You don't matter," said Finnerty. "You belong to History now."

A heavy door thumped shut, and Paul knew that he was alone again, and that History, somewhere on the other side of the door, would let him out only when it was good and ready to.

Chapter XXX

History, personified at this point in the life of Doctor Paul Proteus by Ed Finnerty and the Reverend James J. Lasher, let Paul out of his cell in an old Ilium air-raid shelter only in order for him to eliminate the wastes accrued in the process of his continued existence as an animal. Other signs of his being alive—outcries, protests, demands, profanity—were beneath History's notice until the proper time came, when the door swung open, and Ed Finnerty ushered Paul into his first meeting of the Ghost Shirt Society.

When Paul was led into the meeting chamber, another segment of the air-raid shelter system, everyone stood: Lasher, at the head of the table, Bud Calhoun, Katharine Finch, Luke Lubbock, Paul's tenant farmer Mr. Haycox, and a score of others, whose names Paul didn't know.

It wasn't a brilliant-looking aggregation of conspirators, on the whole, but a righteous and determined one. Paul supposed that Lasher and Finnerty had gathered the group on the basis of availability and trustworthiness rather than talent, starting, seemingly, with some of the more intelligent regulars at the saloon at the foot of the bridge. While the group was predominantly composed of Iliumites, Paul learned, every region of the country was represented.

Amid the mediocrity was a scattering of men who radiated a good deal of competence and, incidentally, prosperity, who seemed, like Paul, in the act of deserting a system that had treated them very well indeed.

As Paul studied these interesting exceptions, he looked at one of the seedier members adjacent, and was surprised by another familiar face—that of Professor Ludwig von Neumann, a slight, disorderly old man, who had taught political science at Union College in Schenectady until the Social Sciences Building had been torn down to make space for the new Heat and Power Laboratory. Paul and von Neumann had known each other slightly as members of the Ilium Historical Society, before the Historical Society Building had been torn down to make room for the new Ilium Atomic Reactor.

"Here he is," said Finnerty proudly.

Paul was given a polite round of applause. The expressions of the applauders were somewhat chilly, giving Paul to understand that he could never *really* be a full partner in their enterprise, since he had not been with them from the beginning.

The only exceptions to this snobbery were Katharine Finch, formerly Paul's secretary, and Bud Calhoun, both of whom seemed as amiable and unchanged as though they were lounging in Paul's outer office at the Works in the old days. Bud, Paul reflected, moved from situation to situation in the protective atmosphere of his imagination, while Katharine was similarly insulated by her adoration for Bud.

The formality of the meeting, the purposefulness in the faces, bluffed Paul into holding his peace for the moment. The chair on Lasher's left was pulled out for him, and Finnerty took the chair on Lasher's right.

As Paul sat down, he noted that only Luke Lubbock wore a ghost shirt, and he supposed that Luke couldn't accomplish anything without a uniform of some sort.

"Meeting of the Ghost Shirt Society will come to order," said Lasher.

Paul, with a trace of drug-inspired whimsey still in his bloodstream, had expected a show of fraternal-order nonsense, full of quasi-Indian talk. Instead, save for Luke Lubbock's shirt, the meeting belonged very much to the present, a sordid, realistic present, an angry present.

The Ghost Shirt Society, then, was simply a convenient and dramatic title for a businesslike group, a title whose historical roots were of interest principally to Lasher and his disciple Finnerty, who entertained each other with elaborate commentaries on the insufferable status quo. For the rest, simple commentaries, special personal resentments, were reasons enough for joining anything that promised a change for the better. *Promised a change for the better, or*, Paul amended his thought after looking into some of the eyes, *promised some excitement for a change.*

What Bud Calhoun was doing here, Paul couldn't imagine, since Bud wasn't at all interested in political action and was without capacity for resentment. As Bud had said of himself,

"All Ah want is time an' equipmen' to faht around with, and Ah'm happy as a pig in mud."

"We'll start with you, Z-11," said Lasher, looking at Katharine.

There were circles under Katharine's gentle, wondering eyes, and she looked startled when Lasher called on her, as though Lasher, the meeting, the underground chamber, had suddenly risen about her in her clean, girlish world. "Oh," she said, and rattled the papers on the table before her. "We now have seven hundred and fifty-eight ghost shirts on hand. Our quota for now was a thousand," she said wearily, "but Mrs. Fishbein—"

"No names!" cried several of the members.

"Sorry." She blushed, and referred to her papers. "Er, X-229 came down with cataracts and had to stop the design work. She'll be all right in about six weeks, and can get back to work. Also—there's a shortage of red wire."

"A-12!" said Lasher.

"Yessir," said a swarthy man, and Paul recognized him as one of the Works security guards out of uniform. A-12 wrote down the requisition for red wire, and grinned sheepishly at Paul.

"The shirts that *are* done are packaged, ready for delivery," said Katharine.

"Very good," said Lasher. "G-17, have you anything to report?"

Bud Calhoun smiled, and leaned back and rubbed his hands. "Comin' along jes' fine. Got two models ready fo' trial out at L-56's place some dark night."

"They'll make it through a works fence all right?" asked Lasher.

"Like a dose of salts," said Bud, " 'thout trippin' the alarm, neither."

"Who cares if the alarm's tripped or not?" said Finnerty. "The whole country's going to be in an uproar anyway."

"Just th'owed thet in," said Bud. "Also got an idea for a gimmick thet'd feed powah into the telephone system so it'd knock the guards flat on theah tails when they try to call for he'p." He chuckled merrily.

"Thought we were going to cut the phone wires."

"Could do thet, I s'pose," said Bud.

"What we want from you," said Lasher, "is a design for a good practical, cheap armored car for breaking through the works fences, something our people all over the country ought to be able to knock together in a hurry, with jalopies and sheet metal."

"Hell, we got thet," said Bud. "What Ah'm thinkin' of now, is how we can *really* fox 'em. See, if we wanted to, Ah figger we could fix a li'l ol—"

"Talk to me about it *after* the meeting," said Lasher.

Bud looked momentarily unhappy, and then began sketching on a pad before him. Paul saw that he had drawn an armored car, to which he was adding antennae, a radar dome, spikes, flails, and other instruments of terrible slaughter. His eyes met Paul's, and he nodded. "Very in'er'stin' problem," he whispered.

"All right," said Lasher. "Recruiting. D-71—got something for us?"

"He's in Pittsburgh," said Finnerty.

"That's right," said Lasher. "Forgot. Seeing what he can do with the Moose there."

Luke Lubbock cleared his throat several times, and riffled papers. "Sir, he asked me to give his report, sir."

"Go ahead."

"We got a man in every chapter of the Royal Parmesans. That's fifty-seven chapters."

"Good men?" said someone.

"You can count on D-71," said Lasher. "Anybody he or his boys recruit gets exactly the same treatment you did—the Mickey, then the questioning under sodium pentathol."

"O.K.," said the questioner. "Just wanted to make sure nobody was getting sloppy at this stage of the game."

"Relax," said Finnerty, very tough, out of the corner of his mouth.

"Him too?" said the questioner, pointing at Paul.

"Him especially," said Lasher. "We know things about Proteus he'd be surprised to know about himself."

"No names," said Paul.

Everybody laughed. It seemed to be a welcome bit of humor that broke the tension of the meeting.

"What's funny?" said Paul.

"You're *the* name," said Lasher.

"Now wait, just a minute—"

"What are you worried about? You don't have to do anything," said Finnerty. "What a break, Paul. Wouldn't *we* like to be able to serve the cause just sitting down here, keeping away from the cops—no responsibilities, no chances to take."

"It's pretty soft all right," said Paul, "but not quite soft enough. I'm walking out. Sorry."

"They'll kill you, Paul," said Finnerty.

"You'd kill him, if you were told to," said Lasher.

Finnerty nodded. "That's right, Paul, I would. I'd have to."

Paul sank back into his chair. He found that he wasn't really shocked by the alternatives of life and death just presented to him. It was such a *clean-cut* proposition, unlike anything he'd ever encountered before. Here were honest-to-God black and white, not at all like the muddy pastels he'd had to choose from while in industry. Having it put like that, *Do as we say or get killed*, had the same liberating effect as the drug of a few hours ago had had. He couldn't make his own decisions for reasons anybody could understand.

So Paul leaned back in his chair and began to take a real interest in what was going on.

Luke Lubbock finished reading D-71's report on recruiting in the lodges across the country. The goal, to have at least two influential Ghost Shirt Society members in every major social organization in every major industrial city, was about sixty per cent realized.

"S-1—what have you got to say for yourself?" said Lasher.

"We're getting the word around about who the *Leader* is," said Finnerty. "Take a few days to see what sort of effect it has."

"Don't see how it could be anything but good," said Lasher.

"Recruiting should really go to town now," said Finnerty.

"What's the score on that television bug?" asked the Works security guard. "Wasn't you going after him personal?"

"Alfy Tucci?" said Finnerty.

"No names!"

"Kick that name around all you want," said Lasher glumly. "He isn't ours."

"That's right," said Finnerty. "He isn't anybody's, and never will be. He never joined anything, his father never joined anything, and his grandfather never joined anything, and if he ever has a son, *he'll* never join anything either."

"What's his reason?" asked Paul.

"Says it's all he can do to figure out what he represents without trying to represent a thousand other people besides," said Finnerty.

"Are there any conditions under which he'd join?" asked the man who'd been nervous about loose recruiting methods.

"One," said Finnerty. "When everybody looks and thinks exactly the way Alfy Tucci does."

Lasher smiled sadly. "The great American individual," he said. "Thinks he's the embodiment of liberal thought throughout the ages. Stands on his own two feet, by God, alone and motionless. He'd make a good lamp post, if he'd weather better and didn't have to eat. All right, where were we?"

"We got a date yet?" asked Mr. Haycox politely.

"We'll get a date two days before it happens, and no sooner!" said Lasher.

"Could I ask a question?" said Paul.

"Don't know why not. I haven't succeeded in heading anybody else off, yet."

"What, generally, is supposed to happen on *this date*?"

"A special meeting of every chapter of every big social organization in the country, outside of the engineers' and managers', will have been called. At the meetings, our people, big men in the organizations, will tell the members that all over the country men are marching through the streets on their way to wreck the automatic factories and give America back to the people. Then they'll put on their ghost shirts and lead whoever will follow, starting with a few more of our people planted around.

"This is the headquarters group here, but the movement is largely decentralized, with regional and local people responsible for their areas. We give them help on organization and recruiting and objectives and tactics, but, on the big day, the local people will be pretty much on their own. We'd like to have a bigger organization, a more centralized one. But that would lay us that much more open to the police. The way things stand now, the police don't know who we are and what we've got. On paper, we don't look like much. Actually, with our people placed right, we have a tremendous potential in fellow travelers."

"How many do you suppose will follow?" said Paul.

"As many people as are bored to death or sick of things the way they are," said Lasher.

"All of 'em," said Finnerty.

"And then what?" said Paul.

"And then we get back to basic values, basic virtues!" said Finnerty. "Men doing men's work, women doing women's work. People doing people's thinking."

"Which reminds me," said Lasher. "Who's going to do the job on EPICAC?"

"Last I heard D-71 say was, it's between the Moose and the Elks in Roswell who's goin' to do it," said Luke Lubbock.

"Put them both on it," said Lasher. "G-17, any bright ideas on how to knock off EPICAC?"

"Bes' idee," said Bud, " 'd be to put some kind of bomb in the coke machines. They got one in every chambah. That way, we'd git all of him, not just part." His hands were working in air, fashioning a booby trap for a coke machine. "See? Take a li'l ol' coke bottle, only fill her full of nitro. Then we run a li'l ol'—"

"All right. Make a sketch and give it to D-17, so he can get it to the right people."

"An' balooooooowie!" said Bud, bringing his fist down on the table.

"Great," said Lasher. "Anybody else got anything on his mind?"

"What about the Army?" said Paul. "What if they're called out to—"

"Both sides had better throw in the towel if somebody's crazy enough to give *them* real rifles and ammunition," said Lasher. "Fortunately, I think both sides know that."

"Where we stand now?" asked the nervous man.

"Not bad, not good," said Lasher. "We could put on a pretty good show now, if they forced our hand. But give us two more months, and we'll really have a surprise for them. All right, let's get this meeting over with, so we can all get to work. Transportation?"

On and on the reports went: transportation, communications, security, finance, procurement, tactics . . .

Paul felt as though he'd seen the surface scraped from a clean, straight rafter, and been shown the tunnels and flimsy membranes of a termite metropolis within.

"Public information?" said Lasher.

"We've mailed out warning letters to all the bureaucrats, engineers, and managers with classification numbers below one hundred," said Professor von Neumann. "Carbon copies to the news service, the radio network, and the television network."

"Damn good letter," said Finnerty.

"Rest of you like to hear it?" said von Neumann.

There were nods around the table.

"Countrymen," the professor read—

"Admittedly, we are all in this together. But—

"You, more than any of us, have spoken highly of progress recently, spoken highly of the good brought by great and continued material change.

"You, the engineers and managers and bureaucrats, almost alone among men of higher intelligence, have continued to believe that the condition of man improves in direct ratio to the energy and devices for using energy put at his disposal. You believed this through the three most horrible wars in history, a monumental demonstration of faith.

"That you continue to believe it now, in the most mortifying peacetime in history, is at least disturbing, even to the slow-witted, and downright terrifying to the thoughtful.

"Man has survived Armageddon in order to enter the Eden of eternal peace, only to discover that everything he had looked forward to enjoying there, pride, dignity, self-respect, work worth doing, has been condemned as unfit for human consumption.

"Again, let me say we are all in this together, but the rest of us, for what we perceive as good, plain reasons, have changed our minds about the divine right of machines, efficiency, and organization, just as men of another age changed their minds about the divine right of kings, and about the divine rights of many other things.

"During the past three wars, the right of technology to increase in power and scope was unquestionably, in point of national survival, almost a divine right. Americans owe their lives to superior machines, techniques, organization, and managers and engineers. For these means of surviving the wars, the Ghost Shirt Society and I thank God.

But we cannot win good lives for ourselves in peacetime by the same methods we used to win battles in wartime. The problems of peace are altogether more subtle.

"I deny that there is any natural or divine law requiring that machines, efficiency, and organization should forever increase in scope, power, and complexity, in peace as in war. I see the growth of these now, rather, as the result of a dangerous lack of law.

"The time has come to stop the lawlessness in that part of our culture which is your special responsibility.

"Without regard for the wishes of men, any machines or techniques or forms of organization that can economically replace men do replace men. Replacement is not necessarily bad, but to do it without regard for the wishes of men is lawlessness.

"Without regard for the changes in human life patterns that may result, new machines, new forms of organization, new ways of increasing efficiency, are constantly being introduced. To do this without regard for the effects on life patterns is lawlessness.

"I am dedicated, and the members of the Ghost Shirt Society are dedicated, to bringing this lawlessness to an end, to give the world back to the people. We are prepared to use force to end the lawlessness, if other means fail.

"I propose that men and women be returned to work as controllers of machines, and that the control of people by machines be curtailed. I propose, further, that the effects of changes in technology and organization on life patterns be taken into careful consideration, and that the changes be withheld or introduced on the basis of this consideration.

"These are radical proposals, extremely difficult to put into effect. But the need for their being put into effect is far greater than all of the difficulties, and infinitely greater than the need for our national holy trinity, Efficiency, Economy, and Quality.

"Men, by their nature, seemingly, cannot be happy unless engaged in enterprises that make them feel useful. They must, therefore, be returned to participation in such enterprises.

"I hold, and the members of the Ghost Shirt Society hold:

"That there must be virtue in imperfection, for Man is imperfect, and Man is a creation of God.

"That there must be virtue in frailty, for Man is frail, and Man is a creation of God.

"That there must be virtue in inefficiency, for Man is inefficient, and Man is a creation of God.

"That there must be virtue in brilliance followed by stupidity, for Man is alternately brilliant and stupid, and Man is a creation of God.

"You perhaps disagree with the antique and vain notion of Man's being a creation of God.

"But I find it a far more defensible belief than the one implicit in intemperate faith in lawless technological progress—namely, that man is on earth to create more durable and efficient images of himself, and, hence, to eliminate any justification at all for his own continued existence.

"Faithfully yours,
"Doctor Paul Proteus."

Professor von Neumann took off his glasses, rubbed his eyes, and stared at a paper clip before him, waiting for someone to say something.

"Yeah," said the transportation chairman tentatively. "Kinda long-haired, though, ain't it?"

"Sounded purty good," said the security chairman, "but shun't there be sumpin' in there 'bout— Well, I'm no good at words, but somebody else could fix it up. I don't know how to say it good, exactly."

"Go on, try," said Finnerty.

"Well, it just don't seem like nobody feels he's worth a crap to nobody no more, and it's a hell of a screwy thing, people gettin' buggered by things they made theirselves."

"That's in there," said Lasher.

Paul coughed politely. "Uh, you want me to sign it?"

Von Neumann looked surprised. "Heavens, they were signed and mailed out hours ago, while you were asleep."

"Thank you."

"You're welcome, Paul," said the professor absently.

"You don't expect that they'll really go along with us on the new controls, do you?" said the nervous man.

"Not for a minute," said Lasher. "But it will certainly get word around about us. When the big day comes, we want everybody to know that ours is a great, big bandwagon."

"*Cops*!" cried someone from far away in the network of chambers.

Gunfire boomed, echoed and crackled in the distance.

"The west exit!" commanded Lasher.

Papers were snatched from the table, stuffed into envelopes; lanterns were blown out. Paul felt himself swept along through the dark corridors by the fleeing crowd. Doors opened and shut, people stumbled and bumped into pillars and one another, but made no outcry.

Suddenly, Paul realized that the sound of the others' feet had stopped, and that he was following only the echoes of his own. Panting, stumbling in a nightmare of the policemen's echoing shouts and running footfalls, he blundered about the passages and chambers, coming again and again to barriers of dead rock. At last, as he turned away from one of these, he was dazzled by a flashlight beam.

"There's one, Joe. Get him!"

Paul charged past the flashlight, swinging both fists.

Something crashed against the side of his head, and he sprawled on the wet floor.

"Here's one that didn't get away, by God," he heard a voice say.

"Really socked him one, didn't you?"

"Don't pay to mess around with no stinking sabotoors, by God."

"Must be one of the small fry, eh?"

"Sure. Whadja expect? You think this was Proteus walking around in little circles all by hisself, like he don't know which way's up? Nossir, boy, Proteus is in the next county by now, lookin' out for his own sweet tail first, last, and always."

"Sabotagin' bastard."

"Yeah. O.K., you, on your feet and shag your tail."

"What happened?" mumbled Paul.

"Police. You just got brained for savin' Proteus' hide. Why'n't you wise up? He's nuts, guy. Hell, he's got it in his head *he's* gonna be king."

Chapter XXXI

PAUL'S CELLMATE in the basement of police Headquarters was a small, elegant young Negro named Harold, who was in jail for petty sabotage. He had smashed a traffic safety education box—a tape-recording and loudspeaker arrangement—that had been fixed to a lamppost outside his bedroom window.

"'Look out!' it say. 'Don't *you* go crossin' in the middle of the block!'" said Harold, mimicking the tape recording. "Fo' two years, ol' loudmouth and me done lived together. An' evah last time some'un come on pas', they hits 'at 'lectric eye, and ol' loudmouth, *he* just naturally *gotta* shoot off his big *ba*-zoo. 'Don' step out 'tween two parked cars,' he say. No matter who 'tis, no matter what tahm 'tis. Loudmouth, *he* don' care. Jus' gotta be sociable. 'Cayful, now! Don' you do this! Don' you do that!' Ol' mangy dog come bah at three in the mornin', and ol' loudmouth jus' gotta get his two cents wuth in. 'If you drahve,' he tells that ol' mangy dog, 'if you drahve, don' drink!' Then an' ol' drunk comes crawlin' along, and ol' gravelthroat tells *him* it's a city ohdnance ev'y bicycle jus' *gotta* have a *re*-flectah on the back."

"How long you in for?" said Paul.

"Fahve days. Judge said Ah could walk raht out. All Ah had to do was say Ah's sorry. Ah ain' goin' do that, 'cause," said Harold, "Ah *ain'* sorry."

Paul was glad that Harold was too bound up in his act of integrity to explore Paul's troubles. Not that it would have pained Paul to talk about them, but because they were extraordinarily difficult to describe. His own motivation was obscure, the cast was unwieldy, and, Paul realized, the denouement was still to come. Through all his adventures, he had been a derelict, tossed this way, then that. He had yet to lay a firm hand on the tiller.

The managers and engineers still believed he was their man; the Ghost Shirt Society was just as convinced that he belonged to them, and both had demonstrated that there was no middle ground for him.

When the police had identified Paul, they had been embarrassed by his I.Q., and his rank in the criminal hierarchy: the archcriminal, the would-be king of the saboteurs. There was no comparable rank in the Ilium police force, and the police had, out of humbleness and lifelong indoctrination, sent for inquisitors with adequate classification numbers and I.Q.'s.

Meanwhile, Paul and Harold passed the time of day.

"Ain' a *bit* sorry," said Harold. "Wha's 'at tap-tap-tappin'?"

The irregular tapping came from the other side of the sheet-metal wall that separated Paul's and Harold's barred cell from the totally enclosed tank for desperados next door.

Experimentally, Paul tapped on his side.

"Twenty-three—eight—fifteen," came the reply. Paul recognized the schoolboy's code: one for *A*, two for *B* . . . "Twenty-three—eight—fifteen" was "Who?"

Paul tapped out his name, and added his own query.

"Seven—one—eighteen—twenty—eight."

"Garth!" said Paul aloud, and he tapped out, "Chin up, boy." An exotic emotion welled up within him, and it took him a moment to understand it. For the first time in the whole of his orderly life he was sharing profound misfortune with another human being. Fate was making him feel a warmth for Garth, the colorless, the nervous, the enervated, that he had never felt for Anita, for Finnerty, for his parents, for anyone. "You fixed the tree?"

"You bet," tapped Garth.

"Why?"

"Boy flunked GCT again. He cracked up."

"Lord! Sorry," tapped Paul.

"Dead weight on world. Useless. Drag."

"Not so."

"But only God can make tree," tapped Garth.

"Blessed are fetishists. Inherited earth," tapped Paul.

"Rot, corrosion on our side."

"What next for you?" tapped Paul.

Garth tapped out the story of his being discovered as the criminal at the Meadows, of the furor, the threats, the actual tears shed over the wounded oak. He'd been locked up in the Council House, and guarded by dozens of angry, stalwart young engineers and managers. He'd been promised grimly that he would get the book thrown at him—years of prison, fines that would wipe him out.

When the police had arrived on the island to pick him up, they'd caught the hysteria of the brass and had treated Garth like one of the century's most terrible criminals.

"Only when we got back here and they booked me did they wake up," he tapped.

Paul, himself awed by Garth's crime, was puzzled by this twist. "How so?" he tapped.

"Ha!" tapped Garth. "What's my crime?"

Paul laughed wonderingly. "Treeslaughter?" he tapped.

"Attempted treeslaughter," tapped Garth. "Thing's still alive, though probably never have acorns again."

"Proteus!" called the cellblock loudspeaker. "Visitors. Stay where you are, Harold."

"Ain' going nowhere, 'cause Ah ain' sorry," said Harold. " 'Cayful, look out, now. Walk facin' the traffic.' "

The cell door buzzed and opened, and Paul walked to the green door of the visitors' room. The green door opened, whispered shut behind him, and he found himself face to face with Anita and Kroner.

Both were dressed funereally, as though not to compete for glamour with the corpse. Gravely, wordlessly, Anita handed him a carton containing a milkshake and a sheaf of funny-papers. She lifted her veil and pecked him on his cheek.

"Paul, my boy," rumbled Kroner. "It's been hard, hasn't it? How are you, my boy?"

Paul stepped back out of reach of the big, sapping, paternal hands. "Fine, thanks."

"Congratulations, Paul, darling," said Anita, her voice tiny.

"For what?"

"She knows, my boy," said Kroner. "She knows you're a secret agent."

"And I'm awfully proud of you."

"When do I get out?"

"Right away. Just as soon as we can transcribe what you found out about the Ghost Shirts, who they are, how they work," said Kroner.

"Home is all ready, Paul," said Anita. "I let the maid off, so we could have an old-fashioned American homecoming."

Paul could see her creating this old-fashioned atmosphere—putting a drop of Tabu on the filter of the electronic dust precipitator, setting the clockwork on the master control panel, which would thaw a steak dinner and load it into the radar stove at the proper moment, and turn on the television just as they crossed the threshold. Goaded by a primitive and insistent appetite, Paul gave her offer cautious consideration. He was pleased to find a higher order of human need asserting itself, a need that made him think, if not feel, that he didn't give a damn if he never slept with her again. She seemed to sense this, too, and, for want of any proclivities to interest Paul save sex, her smile of welcome and forgiveness became a thin and chilling thing indeed.

"Your bodyguards can eat later," said Kroner. He chuckled. "Say, that was quite a letter you wrote for the Ghost Shirts. Sounded wonderful, till you tried to make sense out of it."

"You couldn't?" said Paul.

Kroner shook his head. "Words."

"But it did one thing I'll bet you never expected," said Anita. "Can I tell him—about the new job?"

"Yes, Paul," said Kroner, "the Eastern Division needs a new manager of engineering."

"And *you're* the man, darling!" said Anita.

"Manager of engineering?" said Paul. "What about Baer?" Somehow Paul had expected the rest of the world to hold firm while his own life went spinning. And of that rest of the world nothing had seemed more firm than the union of Baer, the engineering genius, and Kroner, the rock of faith in technology. "He isn't dead, is he?"

"No," said Kroner sadly, "no, he's still alive—physically, that is." He placed a microphone on a table and moved up a chair, so that Paul might testify in comfort. "Well, who knows—maybe what happened is just as well. Poor Baer never was too stable, you know." He adjusted the microphone. "There. Now, you come over here, Paul, my boy."

"What about Baer?" insisted Paul.

"Oh," sighed Kroner, "he read that fool letter, cleaned out his desk drawers, and walked out. Sit right here, Paul."

The letter, then, had been *that* good, Paul thought, astonished at the upheaval it had caused in at least one man's life.

But then he wondered if the letter hadn't won Baer's support by default of the opposition rather than by its being unanswerable. If someone with quicker wits than Kroner's had been at hand to argue against the letter, perhaps Baer would still have been on the job in Albany. "What was the official reaction to the letter?" asked Paul.

"Classified as top secret," said Kroner, "so anybody trying to circulate it will come under the National Security Act. So don't worry, my boy, it isn't going any farther."

"There *is* going to be an official reply, isn't there?" said Paul.

"That'd be playing right into their hands, wouldn't it—acknowledging publicly that this Ghost Shirt nonsense is worth the notice of the system? That's exactly what they *want* to have happen! Come on, now, sit down, and let's get this over with, so you can get home and have a well-earned rest."

Absently, Paul sat down before the microphone, and Kroner switched on the recorder. The official reaction to the Ghost Shirt Society was the official response to so many things: to ignore it, as pressing and complicated matters were ignored in the annual passion plays at the Meadows. It was as though the giving or withholding of official recognition were life or death to ideas. And there was the old Meadows team spirit in the reaction, too, the spirit that was supposed to hold the system together: the notion that the opposition wanted nothing but to win and humiliate, that the object of competition was total victory, with mortifying defeat the only alternative imaginable.

"Now then," said Kroner, "who's really at the head of this monkey business, this Ghost Shirt Society?"

Here it was again, the most ancient of roadforks, one that Paul had glimpsed before, in Kroner's study, months ago. The choice of one course or the other had nothing to do with machines, hierarchies, economics, love, age. It was a purely internal matter. Every child older than six knew the fork, and knew what the good guys did here, and what the bad guys did here. The fork was a familiar one in folk tales the world over, and the good guys and the bad guys, whether in chaps, breech-clouts, serapes, leopardskins, or banker's gray pinstripes, all separated here.

Bad guys turned informer. Good guys didn't—no matter when, no matter what.

Kroner cleared his throat. "I said, 'who's their leader, Paul?' "

"I am," said Paul. "And I wish to God I were a better one."

The instant he'd said it, he knew it was true, and knew what his father had known—what it was to belong and believe.

Chapter XXXII

"DO YOU SWEAR to tell the truth, the whole truth, and nothing but the truth, so help you God?"

"I do," said Paul.

The courtroom television cameras dollied back from his face, to reveal on fifty million television screens the tableau of the Ilium Federal Courtroom's south wall. There, beside and above Doctor Paul Proteus, sat the judge—the Sky Manager, Paul thought. The accused, seated on the witness stand, resembled less a man than an old-fashioned switchboard, with wires running from temperature-, pressure-, and moisture-sensitive instruments at his wrists, armpits, chest, temples, and palms. These, in turn, ran to a gray cabinet under the witness stand, where their findings were interpreted and relayed to a dial a yard in diameter over Paul's head.

The indicator needle on the dial, now pointing straight down, was pivoted so as to swing easily between a black *T* on the right and a red *F* on the left, or to a series of arbitrarily calibrated points between them.

Paul had pleaded guilty to conspiring to advocate the commission of sabotage, but was now being tried for treason, three weeks after his arrest.

"Doctor Proteus," said the prosecutor nastily. The television cameras closed in on his sneer and panned to the beads of sweat on Paul's forehead. "You have pleaded guilty to conspiracy to advocate the commission of sabotage, isn't that so?"

"It is." The needle swung toward *T*, and back to the neutral position, proving that, to the best of Paul's knowledge, it was indeed true.

"This conspiracy, of which you are the head, has as its method, and I quote from your famous letter, 'We are prepared to use force to end the lawlessness, if other means fail.' Those are your words, Doctor?"

"They were written by someone else, but I'm in sympathy with them," said Paul.

"And the word, 'lawlessness,' refers in this case to the present mechanized economy?"

"And future."

"Your goal, as I understand it, was to destroy machines in order that people might take a more personal part in production?"

"Some of the machines."

"What machines, Doctor?"

"That would have to be worked out."

"Oho! You haven't worked *that* out yet, eh?"

"The first step would be to get Americans to agree that limitations be placed on the scope of machines."

"You would get this agreement by force, if necessary? You would force this artificial condition, this step backward, on the American people?"

"What distinguishes man from the rest of the animals is his ability to do artificial things," said Paul. "To his greater glory, I say. And a step backward, after making a wrong turn, is a step in the right direction."

The television cameras looked deep into the prosecutor's righteously angry eyes, and backed away, awed at the still unloosed mighty lightning there.

Paul looked too, and saw that the prosecutor knew a great deal more than he had yet revealed. But Paul doubted that the prosecutor knew his secretary was a member of the Ghost Shirt Society, and that Paul's answers, while registering as heartfelt on the lie detector, were a synthesis of the best thinking and phrasing of Lasher, Finnerty, and Professor von Neumann.

Paul was at ease, filled with the euphoria of well-publicized martyrdom for a cause in which he believed. There was no more question in his mind than there was in the prosecutor's that what the Ghost Shirt Society proposed to do was treason. The machines and the institutions of government were so integrated that trying to attack one without damaging the other was like trying to remove a diseased brain in order to save a patient. There would have to be a seizure of power—a benevolent seizure, but a seizure nonetheless.

The only old acquaintances in the room were Kroner, who seemed close to tears, and the fat, pig-eyed Fred Berringer, who was present, Paul supposed, to see the murder of Checker Charley avenged.

Anita hadn't come to court, nor had Shepherd. The two of

them, presumably, were too busy mapping future campaigns to give more than a brief, pious prayer for those caught on the barbed wire of the battlefield of life. There was no need for Anita's coming to court to show the world how she felt about her erring husband. She had made that clear in several interviews with the press. She had married Paul, she'd explained, when she was but a child, and she thanked God things had come to a head while she was still young enough to salvage a little real happiness for herself. "Salvage" seemed a particularly apt term to Paul, with its implications of picking over city dumps and dragging harbor bottoms, for Anita had announced in her next breath that she was going to marry Doctor Lawson Shepherd as soon as she could get a divorce from Paul.

Paul had read her public declarations with ennui, as though they were gossip about someone else, about a television starlet's accusations against a middle-aged producer, say. The thing he concentrated on now, a far more entertaining and consequential enterprise, was the saying of as many poignant, antimachine, pro–Ghost Shirt Society things as he could over a nationwide television network.

"This *use of force*—you don't regard that as a levying of war against the United States, as treason, Doctor?" wheedled the prosecutor.

"The sovereignty of the United States resides in the people, not in the machines, and it's the people's to take back, if they so wish. The machines," said Paul, "have exceeded the personal sovereignty willingly surrendered to them by the American people for good government. Machines and organization and pursuit of efficiency have robbed the American people of liberty and the pursuit of happiness."

Paul twisted his head, and saw that the needle pointed at *T.*

"The witness will keep his head to the front," said the judge sternly. "His concern is with telling the truth, the whole truth, and nothing but the truth. The indicator will take care of itself."

The prosecutor turned his back to Paul, as though finished with him, and suddenly wheeled to shake a finger at him. "You are a patriot, are you, Doctor?"

"I try to be."

"Your chief wish is to serve the American people well?"

"It is." Paul was puzzled by this new line of questioning, for which no one had prepared him.

"That is your basic reason for serving as nominal head of the Ghost Shirt Society—to do good?"

"It is," said Paul.

A ripple of whispers and a creaking of chairs under shifting bottoms told Paul that something had gone wrong with the lie detector's indicator.

The judge hammered with his gavel. "Order in the court. The court engineer will please check the tubes and circuits."

The engineer wheeled his steel cart up to the witness stand, and impersonally tested the connections to Paul. He took meter readings at various points along the circuits, slid the gray box out from under the witness stand, took out each of the tubes and tested them, and put everything back together, all in less than two minutes. "Everything in order, your honor."

"The witness will please tell what he considers to be a lie," said the judge.

"Every new piece of scientific knowledge is a good thing for humanity," said Paul.

"Object!" said the prosecutor.

"This is off the record—a test of the instrument," said the judge.

"Swung to the left, all righty," said the engineer.

"Now a truth," said the judge.

"The main business of humanity is to do a good job of being human beings," said Paul, "not to serve as appendages to machines, institutions, and systems."

"Swung to *T*, O.K.," said the engineer, tucking a metal clip just a little deeper into Paul's armpit.

"Now, a half-truth," said the judge.

"I am contented," said Paul.

The spectators chuckled appreciatively.

"Square in the middle," said the engineer.

"Proceed with the examination," said the judge.

"I will ask the good patriotic doctor the same question," said the prosecutor. "Doctor, your part in this plot to overthrow the—ah—machines: you say it was motivated solely by your desire to serve the American people?"

"I think so."

Again the telltale restlessness in the courtroom.

"You *think* so, eh?" said the prosecutor. "Do you know where the needle pointed on that one, Doctor, patriot, latter-day Patrick Henry?"

"No," said Paul uncomfortably.

"Squarely between *T* and *F*, Doctor. Apparently you're not sure. Perhaps we can dissect this half-truth and remove from it a whole one—like removing a tumor."

"Um."

"Could it be, Doctor, that this hate of what you describe as an injustice to humanity is in fact a hate of something a good bit less abstract?"

"Maybe. I don't quite follow you."

"I'm talking about your hate for some*one*, Doctor."

"I don't know who you're talking about."

"The needle says you *do* know, Doctor—that you *do* know your red-white-and-blue patriotism is really an expression of hate and resentment—hate and resentment for one of the greatest true patriots in American history, your father!"

"Nonsense!"

"The needle says you lie!" The prosecutor turned away from Paul in seeming disgust. "Ladies and gentlemen of the jury and the television audience: I submit that this man before you is little more than a spiteful boy, to whom this great land of ours, this great economy of ours, this civilization of ours, has become a symbol of his father! A father whom, subconsciously, he would have liked to destroy!

"A father, ladies and gentlemen of the jury and the television audience, to whom we are all in debt for our lives, for it was he, more than any other American, who mustered the forces of know-how, and brought civilization to victory!

"But this boy chose to resent, to hate this brilliant apparition on the pages of history, out of whose loins he had sprung. And now, as a man, he has transferred this hate to what might very well serve as a symbol for his father, your land, ladies and gentlemen of the jury and the television audience, and mine.

"Call it Oedipus complex, if you will. He's a grown man now, and I call it treason! Deny it, Doctor, deny it!

"Deny it," he said again, his voice little more than a whisper.

The cameras about-faced, and closed in on Paul like dogs closing in on a coon shot from a tree.

"Apparently I can't deny it," said Paul. He looked down helplessly, wonderingly, at the wires monitoring every reflex God had given him with which to defend himself. A moment before, he had been a glib mouthpiece for a powerful, clever organization. Now, suddenly, he was all alone, dealing with a problem singularly his own.

"If my father were a petshop proprietor," he said at last, "I suppose I would be a subconscious dog poisoner."

The cameras dollied back and forth impatiently, panned across the spectators, glanced at the judge, and returned to Paul.

"But, even if there weren't this unpleasant business between me and the memory of my father, I think I would believe in the arguments against the lawlessness of the machines. There are men who don't hate their fathers, so far as I know, who believe in the arguments. What the hate does, I think, is to make me not only believe, but want to *do* something about the system. Does the needle agree?"

A number of spectators nodded.

"Good. So far, so good. I suspect that all people are motivated by something pretty sordid, and I guess the clinical data bears me out on that. Sordid things, for the most part, are what make human beings, my father included, move. That's what it is to be human, I'm afraid.

"What the prosecutor has just done is to prove what everything about this world we've made for ourselves seems determined to prove, what the Ghost Shirt Society is determined to disprove: that I'm no good, you're no good, that we're no good because we're human."

Paul gazed into the television camera lenses and imagined the millions now watching, now listening, and he wondered if he'd made sense to any of them. He tried to think of some vivid image that would bring his point home to them all. An image came to mind; he rejected it as indelicate, could find no other, and so blurted it out anyway.

"The most beautiful peonies I ever saw," said Paul, "were grown in almost pure cat excrement. I—"

Bagpipes and drums howled from the street below.

"What's going on out there?" demanded the judge.

"Parade, sir," said a guard, leaning out of the window.

"What organization is it?" said the judge. "I'll have every last one of them hauled in for this outrage."

"Dressed like Scotchmen, sir," said the guard, "with a couple fellas up front that look kind of like Injuns."

"All right," said the judge irritably, "we'll stop the testimony until they're past."

A brickbat shattered a courtroom window, showering the American flag to the judge's right with bits of glass.

Chapter XXXIII

THE STATE DEPARTMENT limousine, bound for New York City, crossed the Iroquois River at Ilium once more. In the back seat were Mr. Ewing J. Halyard, the Shah of Bratpuhr, spiritual leader of 6,000,000 members of the Kolhouri sect, and Khashdrahr Miasma, interpreter, and nephew of the Shah. The Shah and Khashdrahr, languishing with nostalgia for the temple bells, the splash of the fountain, and the cries of the *houri selano* in the palace courtyard, were going home.

When the expedition had crossed this bridge before, at the beginning of their trip, Halyard and the Shah, each in the fashion of his own culture, had been equals in splendor, with Khashdrahr coming off a poor, self-effacing third. Now, the hierarchy of the travelers had shifted. Khashdrahr's function had been extended, so that he served not only as a language bridge between the Shah and Halyard, but as an intermediate social step between them as well.

Wondering at the mechanics of being a human being, mechanics far beyond the poor leverage of free will, *Mr.* Halyard found himself representing the fact of no rank as plainly as *Doctor* Halyard had once represented a great deal of rank. Though he had told his charges nothing of the physical-education examination that could mean life or death to his career, they had sensed the collapse of his status the instant he'd been brought back from the Cornell gymnasium and revived.

When Halyard had recovered, and changed from the ruined shorts and tennis shoes into street clothes, he had seen in the mirror, not a brilliantly fashionable cosmopolite, but an old, overdressed fool. Off had come the boutonniere, the contrasting waistcoat, the colored shirt. Accessory by accessory, garment by garment, he'd stripped away the symbols of the discredited diplomat. Now he was, spiritually and sartorially, whites, grays, and blacks.

As though there were anything of Halyard left to crush, one more crushing blow had fallen. The State Department's personnel machines, automatically, with a respect for law and order never achieved by human beings, had started fraud proceedings against him, since he had never been entitled to his Ph.D., his classification numbers, or, more to the point, to his pay check.

"I'm going to bat for you," his immediate superior had written, but it was, Halyard knew, an archaic incantation in a wilderness of metal, glass, plastic, and inert gas.

"*Khabu*?" said the Shah, without looking at Halyard.

"Where are we?" said Khashdrahr to Halyard, filling the social gap for form's sake, though the Bratpuhrian word, God knows, was familiar enough to Halyard by now.

"Ilium. Remember? We crossed here before, going the other way."

"*Nakka Takaru tooie*," said the Shah, nodding.

"Eh?"

"Where the *Takaru* spit in your face," said Khashdrahr.

"Oh—that." Halyard smiled. "I hope you don't take that home as your chief recollection of the United States. Perfectly ridiculous incident, isolated, irrational. It certainly isn't any indication of the temperament of the American people. That one neurotic *would* have to manifest his aggressions in front of you gentlemen. Believe me, you could travel this country for the next hundred years and never see another outburst like that."

Halyard let none of his bitterness show. With a melancholy spitefulness he continued, for these last days of his career, to perform his job impeccably. "Forget about him," he said, "and remember all the other things you've seen, and try to imagine how your own nation might be transformed."

The Shah made thoughtful clucking sounds.

"At no expense whatsoever to you," said Halyard, "America will send engineers and managers, skilled in all fields, to study your resources, blueprint your modernization, get it started, test and classify your people, arrange credit, set up the machinery."

The Shah shook his head wonderingly. "*Prakka-fut takki sihn*," he said at last, "*souli, sakki EPICAC, siki Kanu pu*?"

"Shah says," said Khashdrahr, "'Before we take this first step, please, would you ask EPICAC what people are for?'"

The limousine came to a stop at the head of the bridge on the Homestead side, blocked this time, not by a Reconstruction and Reclamation Corps crew, but by a phalanx of Arabs. They were led, as though the significance of the banners and costumes weren't confusing enough, by two men wearing Indian shirts and war paint.

"*Dinko?*" said the Shah.

"Army?" said Khashdrahr.

Halyard had his first good chuckle in many weeks. That anyone, even a foreigner, could look on this colorful tangle of banners, sashes, and toy weapons as an effective fighting force! "Just some people having a little fun dressing up."

"Some of them have guns," said Khashdrahr.

"Wood, cardboard, and paint," said Halyard. "All make-believe." He picked up the speaking tube and spoke to the driver: "See if you can't ease past them and down a side street, toward the courthouse. Things ought to be quieter down there."

"Yessir," said the driver uneasily. "I don't know, though, sir. I don't like the way they're looking at us, and all that traffic on the other side looked like they were running away from something. Maybe we should turn around and—"

"Nonsense. Lock the doors, lean on the horn, and go on through. Things have come to a pretty pass if this sort of monkey business has the right of way over official business."

The bulletproof windows slithered to the top, the door locks clicked, and the limousine nosed diffidently into the apricot, green, and gold ranks of the Arabs.

Jeweled dirks and scimitars stabbed and slashed at the limousine's armored sides. Above the howls of the Arabs came crashes of gunfire. Two great pimples appeared suddenly in the side of the car, inches from Halyard's head.

Halyard, the Shah, and Khashdrahr threw themselves on the floor. The limousine plunged through the raging ranks, and down a side street.

"Head for the courthouse!" cried Halyard to the driver from the floor, "then out Westinghouse Boulevard!"

"The hell with you!" said the driver. "I'm bailing out right here. The whole town's going nuts!"

"Stay at the wheel or I kill you!" said Khashdrahr savagely. He was shielding the Shah's sacred body with his own poor flesh, and he held the point of a golden dagger against the back of the driver's neck.

Khashdrahr's next words were lost in an explosion nearby,

followed by cheers and a hail of rubble on the limousine's top and hood.

"Here's the courthouse!" said the driver.

"Good. Turn left!" commanded Halyard.

"My God!" cried the driver. "Look!"

"What's the matter?" quavered Halyard, prone with Khashdrahr and the Shah. He could see only sky and building tops and passing skeins of smoke.

"The Scotchmen," said the driver hollowly. "My God, here come the Scotchmen." The limousine stopped with a shriek of rubber.

"All right, back up and—"

"You got radar down there on the floor? Take a look out the back window, *then* tell me we should back up."

Halyard raised his head cautiously above the window sill. The limousine was trapped by bagpipers ahead, and, behind, by a squad of gold-epauleted Royal Parmesans, who had sallied from an Automagic Market across the street from the courthouse.

An explosion hurled the market's conveyers and clips of canned goods through the windows. An Automagic cashier rolled into the street, still miraculously upright on its round pedestal. "Did you see our special in Brussels sprouts?" it said, tripped on its own wire, and crashed to the pavement by the limousine, spewing cash from a mortal wound.

"It isn't us they're after!" called the driver. "Look!"

The Royal Parmesans, the Scotchmen, and a handful of Indians had joined forces and were ramming the courthouse door with a felled telephone pole.

The door burst into kindling, and the attackers were carried inside by the ram's momentum.

A moment later they emerged with a man on their shoulders. In the midst of their frenzied acclamation, he was marionette-like. As though to perfect the impression, bits of wire dangled from his extremities.

"To the Works!" cried the Indians.

The host, bearing their hero aloft like another banner beside the Stars and Stripes, followed the Indians toward the bridge across the Iroquois, cheering, skirling, smashing, dynamiting, and beating drums.

The limousine stayed where it had been trapped by the Royal Parmesans and Scotchmen for an hour, while the dull thunder of explosions walked about the city like the steps of drunken giants, and afternoon turned to twilight under a curtain of smoke. Each time escape seemed possible, and Halyard raised his head to investigate a lull, fresh contingents of vandals and looters sent him to the floor again.

"All right," he said at last, "I think maybe we're all right now. Let's try to make it to the police station. We can get protection there until this thing plays itself out."

The driver leaned on the steering wheel and stretched insolently. "You think you've been watching a football game or something? You think maybe everything's going to be just the way it was before?"

"I don't know what's going on, and neither do you. Now, drive to the police station, do you understand?" said Halyard.

"You think you can order me around, just because you've got a Ph.D. and I've got nothing but a B.S.?"

"Do as he says," hissed Khashdrahr, placing the point of his knife in the back of the driver's neck again.

The limousine moved down the littered, now-deserted streets toward the headquarters of Ilium's keepers of the peace.

The street before the police station was snow-white, paved with bits of punctured pasteboard: the fifty-thousand-card deck with which the Ilium personnel and crime-prevention machines had played their tireless games—shuffling, dealing, off the bottom, off the top, out of the middle, palming, marking, reading, faster than the human eye could follow, controlling every card, and implacably protecting the interests of the house, always the house, any house.

The doors of the building had been torn from their hinges, and within were rolling dunes of dumped files.

Halyard opened his window a crack. "Hello, there," he called, and waited hopefully for a policeman to appear. "I say, hello!" He opened his door cautiously.

Before he could close it again, two Indians with pistols jerked the door wide open.

Khashdrahr lunged at them with his knife, and was knocked senseless. He fell on top of the quivering Shah.

"I say," said Halyard, and was knocked cold, too.

"To the Works!" ordered the Indians.

When Halyard regained consciousness he found himself with his aching head on the limousine floor, halfway out of the open door.

The car was parked in front of a saloon near the bridge. The front of the saloon had been sandbagged, and inside were men operating radios, moving pins on maps, oiling weapons, and watching the clock. By the head of the bridge itself were crude breastworks of sandbags and timbers, facing the pillboxes and turrets of the Ilium Works across the river. Men in every conceivable type of uniform wandered about the fortifications in a holiday spirit, coming and going as they pleased, on missions seemingly best known to themselves.

The commandeering Indians and the driver were gone, while Khashdrahr and the Shah, bewildered and frightened, were being castigated by a tall, gaunt man who wore an Indian shirt but no war paint.

"Goddammit!" said the tall man. "The Knights of Kandahar are supposed to be manning the roadblock on Griffin Boulevard. What the hell you doing here?"

"We—" said Khashdrahr.

"Haven't got time to listen to excuses. Get back to your organization on the double!"

"But—"

"Lubbock!" cried the tall man.

"Yessir."

"Give these men transportation to the Griffin Boulevard block, or put 'em under arrest for insubordination."

"Yessir. Ammo truck's leaving now, sir." Lubbock hustled the Shah and Khashdrahr into the back of a truck, atop cases of handmade grenades.

"*Brouha batouli, nibo. Nibo!*" cried the Shah piteously. "*Nibo!*"

The truck meshed its gears and disappeared into the smoke.

"I say," said Halyard thickly.

"Finnerty!" cried a short, fat man in thick glasses from the door of the saloon. "The state police are trying to break through the Griffin Boulevard roadblock! Who've we got for reinforcements?"

Finnerty's eyes widened, and he ran his hands through his

hair. "Sent back two stragglers, and that's it. The VFW and the Knights of Pythias wandered off, and the Masons never did show up. Tell them we haven't got any reserves!"

A geyser of flame and shattered masonry spouted from the Ilium Works across the river, and Halyard saw that where the Stars and Stripes had flown over the works manager's office, a white flag now snapped in the smoky wind.

"For chrissake!" said Finnerty. "Get the Moose and Elks on the radio and tell them to quit it. They're supposed to occupy the Works, not atomize it."

"Baker Dog Three," said Lasher into a microphone. "Baker Dog Three. Protect all equipment in the Works until decision can be made as to proper disposition. Can you hear me, Baker Dog Three?"

The crowd by the saloon fell silent, to hear the reply of the Moose and Elks above the shushing noise of the loudspeaker.

"Baker Dog Three—did you hear me?" shouted Lasher.

"*Zowie!*" came a faraway cry in the speaker, and another volcano erupted in the Works.

"Lubbock!" said Finnerty. "Take over. I'm going over there to teach those babies a little discipline. We'll see who's running this show!" He climbed into a car, and sped across the bridge to the Works.

"Salt Lake City is ours!" shouted another radio operator inside the saloon.

"Oakland and Salt Lake and Ilium so far!" said Lasher. "What about Pittsburgh?"

"No reply."

"Pittsburgh's the key," said Lasher. "Keep trying." He glanced to the south over his shoulder, and a look of horror crossed his face. "Who set the museum on fire?" He shouted into his microphone desperately, "All posts! All posts! Protect all property! Vandalism and looting will be punished by death. Attention all posts—can you hear me?"

Silence.

"Moose? Elks? Knights of Pythias? VFW? Eagles? Hello! Anybody—can you hear me? Hello!"

Silence.

"Proteus!" called an Arab, staggering up to the saloon door, brandishing a bottle. "Where'sh Proteus? Give us a word."

Paul, haggard and aged, appeared beside Lasher in the saloon door. "God help us, gentlemen," he said slowly. "God help us. If we've won, it means that now the hard part begins."

"Jesus—you'd think we losht," said the Arab. "Shorry now I ashked for a word."

"Lou!"

"Right here," said the drunk Arab.

"Lou, boy—we forgot the bakery. Still poopin' out bread like nobody's business.

"Can't have it doin' that," said Lou. "Le'sh go knock the crap out of it."

"Listen, wait," said Paul. "We'll need the bakery."

"Machine, ain't it?" said Lou.

"Yes, sure, but there's no sense in—"

"Then le'sh go knock the crap out of it. And, by God, here'sh ol' Al to go with us. Where you been, y'ol' horsethief?"

"Blew up the goddam sewage 'sposal plant," said Al proudly.

" 'At's the shtuff! Give the friggin' worl' back to the friggin' people."

Chapter XXXIV

"I DON'T UNDERSTAND about Pittsburgh," said Finnerty. "I knew Seattle and Minneapolis were touch-and-go, but Pittsburgh!"

"And St. Louis and Chicago," said Paul, shaking his head.

"And Birmingham and Boston and New York," said Lasher, smiling sadly. He seemed curiously at peace, inexplicably satisfied.

"Pfft!" said Finnerty.

"Ilium came off like clockwork, anyway, and Salt Lake and Oakland," said Professor von Neumann. "So I think we can say that the theory of attack was essentially valid. The execution, of course, was something else again."

"It always is," said Lasher.

"What makes you so cheery?" said Paul.

"Would a good cry make you feel better, Doctor?" said Lasher.

"Now all we have to do is close ranks with Salt Lake City and Oakland, and strangle the country into submission," said Finnerty.

"I wish now we'd sent one of our Illium people out to get EPICAC," said von Neumann. "EPICAC was worth three Pittsburghs."

"Too bad about the Roswell Moose, all right," said Lasher. "D-71 said they were crazy about the idea of getting EPICAC."

"Too crazy," said Paul.

"Nitro's tricky enough stuff, without having crazy men trying to get it into Coke bottles," said Finnerty.

The four thought-chiefs of the Ghost Shirt Society were seated about what had once been Paul's desk, the works manager's desk in the Ilium Works.

The revolution was not yet a day old. It was early in the morning, before sunrise, but here and there burning buildings made patches of Ilium as bright and hot as tropical noon.

"I wish they'd attack, and get it over with," said Paul.

"It'll take them a little while to get their nerve back, after what the Knights of Kandahar did to the state police on Griffin

Boulevard," said Finnerty. He sighed. "By God, if only we'd had a few more outfits like that in Pittsburgh—"

"And St. Louis," said Paul, "and Seattle and Minneapolis and Boston and—"

"Let's talk about something else," said Finnerty. "How's the arm, Paul?"

"Not bad," said Paul, stroking the makeshift splint. The Messiah of the Ghost Shirt Society had had his left arm broken by a rock while exercising his magnetism on a crowd interested in seeing the power station blown up. "How's the head, Professor?"

"Ringing," said von Neumann, adjusting his bandage. He had been struck by the Sacred Mace of The Order of the Aurora Borealis while giving a crowd reasons for not felling a two-hundred-foot radio tower.

"Glockenspiel or carillon?" said Lasher. "And how are your own contusions and abrasions, Ed?"

Finnerty twisted his neck and raised his arms experimentally. "Nothing, really. If the pain gets any worse, I can simply kill myself." He had been floored and trampled by stampeding Moose and Elks while explaining that the Works should be kept intact until a cool decision could be made as to which machines should be destroyed, which retained.

Fire spurted skyward from Homestead.

"Keeping the map right up to the minute, Professor?" said Lasher.

Professor von Neumann looked out at the new blaze through field glasses, and made a black *X* on the map before him. "Post office, most likely."

The map of the city had been clean and crackling at the start of the campaign, with a dozen small red circles indicating the primary objectives of the Ilium *Putsch*: the police station, the courthouse, communications centers, sites for roadblocks, the Ilium Works. After these objectives were taken, with a minimum of bloodshed and damage, the plan of operations declared, the systematic replacement of automatic control devices by human beings was to begin. The more important of these secondary objectives were circled in green.

But now the map was smudged and limp. Overlying the scattered constellation of red and green circles was a black, continuous smear of *X*'s that marked what *had* been taken, and, moreover, destroyed.

Lasher glanced at his watch. "I've got 4 A.M. That right?"

"Who knows?" said Finnerty.

"Can't you see the City Hall clock from there?"

"They got that hours ago."

"And they're likely to be after your watch any minute," said Paul. "Better put it back in your pocket."

"What gets me are the specialists," said Finnerty. "Some guys seem to have it in for just one kind of machine, and leave everything else alone. There's a little colored guy going around town with a shotgun, blasting nothing but those little traffic safety boxes."

"Lord," said Paul, "I didn't think it'd be like this."

"You mean losing?" said Lasher.

"Losing, winning—whatever this mess is."

"It has all the characteristics of a lynching," said the professor. "It's on such a big scale, though, I suppose genocide is closer. The good die with the bad—the flush toilets with the automatic lathe controls."

"I wonder if things would have been much different if it hadn't been for the liquor," said Paul.

"You can't ask men to attack pillboxes cold sober," said Finnerty.

"And you can't ask them to stop when they're drunk," said Paul.

"Nobody said it wasn't going to be messy," said Lasher.

A terrific explosion lifted the floor and dropped it.

"Boy!" said Luke Lubbock, standing guard in what had been Katharine Finch's office.

"What was it, Luke?" called Lasher.

"Gasoline storage tanks. Boy!"

" 'Ray," said Paul dismally.

"*People of Ilium!*" boomed a voice from the sky. "*People of Ilium!*"

Paul, Lasher, Finnerty, and von Neumann hurried to the opening where the floor-to-ceiling window had once been. Looking up, they saw a robot helicopter in the sky, its belly and blades reddened by the fires below.

"*People of Ilium, lay down your arms!*" said its loudspeaker.

"*Oakland and Salt Lake City have been restored to order. Your cause is lost. Overthrow your false leaders.*

"*You are completely surrounded, cut off from the rest of the world. The blockade will not be lifted until Proteus, Lasher, Finnerty, and von Neumann are turned over to the authorities beyond the Griffin Boulevard roadblock.*

"*We could bomb and strafe you, but that is not the American way. We could send in tanks, but that is not the American way.*

"*This is an ultimatum: surrender your false leaders and lay down your arms within the next six hours, or suffer in the ruins of your own making for the next six months, cut off from the rest of the world. Click.*

"*People of Ilium, lay down your arms! Oakland and Salt Lake City have been re——*"

Luke Lubbock aimed his rifle and fired.

"*Beeby dee bobble dee beezle!*" said the loudspeaker shrilly. "*Noozle ah reeble beejee boo.*"

"Put it out of its misery," said Finnerty.

Luke fired again.

The helicopter floundered off clumsily, still haranguing the town. "*Beeby dee bobble dee beezle! Noozle ah reeble beejee . . .*"

"Where are you going, Paul?" said Finnerty.

"A walk."

"Mind if I come?"

"That's a small matter these days."

And the two walked out of the building and down the broad, littered boulevard that split the plant, past numbered façades that had nothing but silence, rubble, and scrap behind them.

"Not enough of it left for this to be like old times, eh?" said Finnerty, after they had walked some distance without speaking.

"New era," said Paul.

"Drink to it?" said Finnerty, taking a pint from the pocket of his ghost shirt.

"To the new era."

They sat down together before Building 58, and wordlessly passed the bottle back and forth.

"You know," said Paul at last, "things wouldn't have been so bad if they'd stayed the way they were when we first got here. Those were passable days, weren't they?" He and Finnerty were feeling a deep, melancholy rapport now, sitting amid the smashed masterpieces, the brilliantly designed, beautifully made machines. A good part of their lives and skills had gone into making them, making what they'd helped to destroy in a few hours.

"Things don't stay the way they are," said Finnerty. "It's too entertaining to try to change them. Remember the excitement of recording Rudy Hertz's movements, then trying to run automatic controls from the tape?"

"It worked!" said Paul.

"Damn right!"

"And then putting lathe group three together," said Paul. "Those weren't our ideas, of course."

"No, but we got ideas of our own later on. Wonderful ideas," said Finnerty. "Happiest I ever was, I guess, Paul; so damn engrossed, I never looked up to notice anything else."

"Most fascinating game there is, keeping things from staying the way they are."

"If only it weren't for the people, the goddamned people," said Finnerty, "always getting tangled up in the machinery. If it weren't for them, earth would be an engineer's paradise."

"Let's drink to that."

They did.

"You were a good engineer, Paul."

"You too, Ed. And there's no shame in that."

They shook hands warmly.

When they got back to the former works manager's office, they found Lasher and von Neumann asleep.

Finnerty shook Lasher's shoulder. "Master! *Maestro*! *Maître*!"

"Hmm?" The squat, homely man fumbled for his thick glasses, found them, and sat up. "Yes?"

"Doctor Proteus here has asked me a very interesting question," said Finnerty. "I was unable to supply him with a satisfactory answer."

"You're drunk. Go away, and let an old man sleep."

"This won't take long," said Finnerty. "Go ahead, Paul."

"What became of the Indians?" said Paul.

"What Indians?" said Lasher wearily.

"The original Ghost Shirt Society—the Ghost Dance Indians," said Finnerty. "Eighteen-ninety and all that."

"They found out the shirts weren't bulletproof, and magic didn't bother the U.S. Cavalry at all."

"So—"

"So they were killed or gave up trying to be good Indians, and started being second-rate white men."

"And the Ghost Dance movement proved what?" said Paul.

"That being a good Indian was as important as being a good white man—important enough to fight and die for, no matter what the odds. They fought against the same odds we fought against: a thousand to one, maybe, or a little more."

Paul and Ed Finnerty looked at him incredulously.

"You thought we were sure to lose?" said Paul huskily.

"Certainly," said Lasher, looking at him as though Paul had said something idiotic.

"But you've been talking all along as though it were almost a sure thing," said Paul.

"Of course, Doctor," said Lasher patronizingly. "If we hadn't all talked that way, we wouldn't have had that one chance in a thousand. But I didn't let myself lose touch with reality."

Lasher, Paul realized, was the only one who hadn't lost touch with reality. He, alone of the four leaders, seemed unshocked by the course of events, undisturbed by them, even, inexplicably, at peace. Paul, perhaps, had been the one most out of touch, having had little time for reflection, having been so eager to join a large, confident organization with seeming answers to the problems that had made him sorry to be alive.

Finnerty was covering his initial surprise at Lasher's statement, so perfect an apostle was he. Most of all, apparently, he wanted to remain intellectually as one with the dynamic Lasher, and he, too, now looked at Paul as though surprised to find that Paul wasn't sure what was going on.

"If we didn't have a chance, then what on earth was the sense of—?" Paul left the sentence unfinished, and included the ruins of Ilium in a sweep of his hand.

Lasher was fully awake now, and he stood, and paced up and down the room, apparently irritated that he should have to explain something so obvious. "It doesn't matter if we win or lose, Doctor. The important thing is that we tried. For the record, we tried!" He walked behind Paul's old desk and faced Paul and Finnerty across it.

"What record?" said Paul.

Suddenly Lasher underwent a transformation. He showed a side of himself he had mentioned, but which Paul had found impossible to imagine.

And, with the transformation, the desk became a pulpit.

"Revolutions aren't my main line of business," said Lasher, his voice deep and rolling. "I'm a minister, Doctor, remember? First and last, I'm an enemy of the Devil, a man of God!"

Chapter XXXV

AS THE SUN arose over Ilium, and the embers of the town seemed gray in the light of the eternal fire ninety-three million miles away, the State Department limousine, flying a ghost shirt from its radio antenna, crept through the streets.

Bodies lay everywhere, in grotesque attitudes of violent death, but manifesting the miracle of life in a snore, a mutter, the flight of a bubble from the lips.

In the early light, the town seemed an enormous jewel box, lined with the black and gray velvet of fly-ash, and filled with millions of twinkling treasures: bits of air conditioners, amplidynes, analyzers, arc welders, batteries, belts, billers, bookkeeping machines, bottlers, canners, capacitors, circuitbreakers, clocks, coin boxes, calorimeters, colorimeters, computers, condensers, conduits, controls, converters, conveyers, cryostats, counters, cutouts, densitometers, detectors, dust precipitators, dishwashers, dispensers, dynamometers, dynamotors, electrodes, electronic tubes, exciters, fans, filers, filters, frequency changers, furnaces, fuses, gages, garbage disposers, gears, generators, heat exchangers, insulators, lamps, loudspeakers, magnets, mass spectrometers, motor generators, motors, noisemeters, oscillographs, panelboards, personnel machines, photoelectric cells, potentiometers, pushbuttons, radios, radiation detectors, reactors, recorders, rectifiers, reducers, regulators, relays, remote controls, resistors, rheostats, selsyns, servos, solenoids, sorters, spectrophotometers, spectroscopes, springs, starters, straingages, switchboards, switches, tape recorders, tachometers, telemeters, television sets, television cameras, testers, thermocouples, thermostats, timers, toasters, torquemeters, traffic controls, transistors, transducers, transformers, turbines, vacuum cleaners, vacuum gages, vacuum tubes, venders, vibration meters, viscosimeters, water heaters, wheels, X-ray spectrogoniometers, zymometers . . .

At the wheel of the limousine was Doctor Edward Francis Finnerty. Beside him was Doctor Paul Proteus. In the back seat were the Reverend James J. Lasher and Professor Ludwig von Neumann, and, asleep on the floor, lay Mr. Ewing J. Halyard of the State Department. In a world of ruins and deep sleep, Halyard's form on the floor was hardly cause for curiosity, comment, or remedial action.

The brains of the Ghost Shirt Society were touring the strongpoints on the frontiers of their Utopia. And everywhere they found the same things: abandoned weapons, abandoned posts, mounds of expended ammunition, and riddled machinery.

The four had come to an exciting decision: during the six months of blockade threatened by the authorities, they would make the ruins a laboratory, a demonstration of how well and happily men could live with virtually no machines. They saw now the common man's wisdom in wrecking practically everything. That *was* the way to do it, and the hell with moderation!

"All right, so we'll heat our water and cook our food and light and warm our homes with wood fires," said Lasher.

"And walk wherever we're going," said Finnerty.

"And read books instead of watching television," said von Neumann. "The Renaissance comes to upstate New York! We'll rediscover the two greatest wonders of the world, the human mind and hand."

"No quarter asked, no quarter given," said Paul as they contemplated the entire furnishings of an M-11 house, dragged into a vacant lot and hacked to bits.

"This is like the Indians' massacre of Custer and his men," said Lasher reflectively. "The Little Bighorn. One isolated victory against an irresistable tide. More and more whites where Custer came from; more and more machines where these came from. But we may win yet. Well! What is that noise? Somebody awake?"

A faint hubbub came from around a corner, from where the railroad station had been, where it still was after a fashion. Finnerty turned the corner for a better look at the celebrators.

In the station's waiting room, carnage was everywhere. The terrazzo floor, depicting an earlier slaughter of Iliumites by Oneida Indians, was strewn with the guts and internal secretions of the automatic ticket vendor, the automatic nylon vendor, the automatic coffee vendor, the automatic newspaper vendor, the automatic toothbrush vendor, the automatic shoeshine machine, the automatic photo studio, the automatic baggage checker, the automatic insurance salesman . . .

But around one machine a group had gathered. The people were crowding one another excitedly, as though a great wonder were in their midst.

Paul and Finnerty left the car to examine the mystery, and saw that the center of attention was an Orange-O machine. Orange-O, Paul recalled, was something of a *cause célèbre*, for no one in the whole country, apparently, could stomach the stuff—no one save Doctor Francis Eldgrin Gelhorne, National Industrial, Commercial, Communications, Foodstuffs, and Resources Director. As a monument to him, Orange-O machines stood shoulder-to-shoulder with the rest, though the coin-box collectors never found anything in the machines but stale Orange-O.

But now the excretor of the blended wood pulp, dye, water, and orange-type flavoring was as popular as a nymphomaniac at an American Legion convention.

"O.K., now let's try anotha' nickel in her an' see how she does," said a familiar voice from behind the machine—the voice of Bud Calhoun.

"*Clunkle*" went the coin, and then a whir, and a gurgle.

The crowd was overjoyed.

"Filled the cup almost to the top that time; and she's nice and cold now, too," called the man by the machine's spout.

"But the light behind the Orange-O sign didn't light up," said a woman. "Supposed to."

"We'll fix that, won't we, Bud?" said another voice from behind the machine. "You people get me about three feet of that red wire hanging out of the shoeshine machine, and somebody let me borrow their penknife a second." The speaker stood up and stretched, and smiled contentedly, and Paul recognized him: the tall, middle-aged, ruddy-faced man who'd fixed Paul's car with the sweatband of his hat long ago.

The man had been desperately unhappy then. Now he was proud and smiling because his hands were busy doing what they liked to do best, Paul supposed—replacing men like himself with machines. He hooked up the lamp behind the Orange-O sign. "There we are."

Bud Calhoun bolted on the back. "Now try her."

The people applauded and lined up, eager for their Orange-O. The first man up emptied his cup, and went immediately to the end of the line for seconds.

"Now, le's have a look at this li'l ol' ticket seller," said Bud. "Oh, oh. Got it right through the microphone."

"I knew we'd be able to use the telephone out in the street for something," said the ruddy man. "I'll go get it."

The crowd, filled with Orange-O, was drifting over to encourage them in their new enterprise.

When Paul and Finnerty returned to the limousine, they found Lasher and von Neumann looking extremely glum, engaged in conversation with a bright-looking teen-ager.

"Have you seen an eight-horsepower electric motor lying around anywhere?" said the youngster. "One that isn't busted up too bad?"

Lasher shook his head.

"Well, I just have to keep looking, I guess," said the youngster, picking up a cardboard carton jammed with gears, tubes, switches, and other odd parts. "This place is a gold mine, all right, but it's tough finding exactly what you need."

"I imagine," said Lasher.

"Yep, if I had a decent little motor to go with what I got," said the youngster excitedly, "I'll betch anything I could make a gadget that'd play drums like nothing you ever heard before. See, you take a selsyn, and—"

"Proteus! Finnerty!" said Lasher irritably. "What's been keeping you?"

"Didn't know you were in a hurry to get anywhere," said Finnerty.

"Well, I am. Let's go."

"Where to?" Finnerty started the car.

"Griffin Boulevard. The roadblock."

"What's going on out there?" asked Paul.

"The authorities are waiting for the people of Ilium to turn over their false leaders," said Lasher. "Anybody want to get out? I'll drive myself, if you like."

Finnerty stopped the car.

"Well?" said Lasher.

"I suppose now *is* the time," said von Neumann matter-of-factly.

Paul said nothing, but made no move to get out.

Finnerty waited a moment longer, then pressed down on the accelerator.

No one spoke until they reached the concertina of barbed wire, the felled telephone poles, and the sandbags of the Griffin Boulevard roadblock. Two brown men, elegantly costumed —Khashdrahr Miasma and the Shah of Bratpuhr—huddled together, asleep in a slit trench to the left of the barricade. Beyond the barbed wire, their wheels toward heaven, were two riddled, abandoned state police cars.

Professor von Neumann looked out over the countryside through his field glasses. "Aha! The authorities." He handed the glasses to Paul. "There—to the left of that barn. See?"

Paul squinted at the three armored cars by the barn, and the police with their riot guns, lounging, smoking, chatting cheerfully.

Lasher patted Paul on his shoulder as Paul handed the glasses on to him. "Smile, Doctor Proteus—you're *somebody* now, like your old man was. Who's got a bottle?"

Finnerty produced one.

Lasher took it, and toasted the others. "To all good Indians," he said, "past, present, and future. Or, more to the point—to the record."

The bottle went around the group.

"The record," said Finnerty, and he seemed satisfied with the toast. He had got what he wanted from the revolution, Paul supposed—a chance to give a savage blow to a close little society that made no comfortable place for him.

"To the record," said von Neumann. He, too, seemed at peace. To him, the revolution had been a fascinating experiment, Paul realized. He had been less interested in achieving a premeditated end than in seeing what would happen with given beginnings.

Paul took the bottle and studied Lasher for a moment over its fragrant mouth. Lasher, the chief instigator of it all, was contented. A lifelong trafficker in symbols, he had created the revolution as a symbol, and was now welcoming the opportunity to die as one.

And that left Paul. "To a better world," he started to say, but he cut the toast short, thinking of the people of Ilium, already eager to recreate the same old nightmare. He shrugged. "To the record," he said, and smashed the empty bottle on a rock.

Von Neumann considered Paul and then the broken glass. "This isn't the end, you know," he said. "Nothing ever is, nothing ever will be—not even Judgment Day."

"Hands up," said Lasher almost gaily. "Forward March."

THE SIRENS OF TITAN

For Alex Vonnegut, Special Agent, with love—

“Every passing hour brings the Solar System forty-three thousand miles closer to Globular Cluster M13 in Hercules—and still there are some misfits who insist that there is no such thing as progress.”

—RANSOM K. FERN

All persons, places, and events in this book are real. Certain speeches and thoughts are necessarily constructions by the author. No names have been changed to protect the innocent, since God Almighty protects the innocent as a matter of Heavenly routine.

CHAPTER ONE

Between Timid and Timbuktu

"I guess somebody up there likes me."

—MALACHI CONSTANT

EVERYONE now knows how to find the meaning of life within himself.

But mankind wasn't always so lucky. Less than a century ago men and women did not have easy access to the puzzle boxes within them.

They could not name even one of the fifty-three portals to the soul.

Gimcrack religions were big business.

Mankind, ignorant of the truths that lie within every human being, looked outward—pushed ever outward. What mankind hoped to learn in its outward push was who was actually in charge of all creation, and what all creation was all about.

Mankind flung its advance agents ever outward, ever outward. Eventually it flung them out into space, into the colorless, tasteless, weightless sea of outwardness without end.

It flung them like stones.

These unhappy agents found what had already been found in abundance on Earth—a nightmare of meaninglessness without end. The bounties of space, of infinite outwardness, were three: empty heroics, low comedy, and pointless death.

Outwardness lost, at last, its imagined attractions.

Only inwardness remained to be explored.

Only the human soul remained *terra incognita.*

This was the beginning of goodness and wisdom.

What were people like in olden times, with their souls as yet unexplored?

The following is a true story from the Nightmare Ages, falling roughly, give or take a few years, between the Second World War and the Third Great Depression.

•

There was a crowd.

The crowd had gathered because there was to be a materialization. A man and his dog were going to materialize, were going to appear out of thin air—wispily at first, becoming, finally, as substantial as any man and dog alive.

The crowd wasn't going to get to see the materialization. The materialization was strictly a private affair on private property, and the crowd was emphatically not invited to feast its eyes.

The materialization was going to take place, like a modern, civilized hanging, within high, blank, guarded walls. And the crowd outside the walls was very much like a crowd outside the walls at a hanging.

The crowd knew it wasn't going to see anything, yet its members found pleasure in being near, in staring at the blank walls and imagining what was happening inside. The mysteries of the materialization, like the mysteries of a hanging, were enhanced by the wall; were made pornographic by the magic lantern slides of morbid imaginations—magic lantern slides projected by the crowd on the blank stone walls.

The town was Newport, Rhode Island, U.S.A., Earth, Solar System, Milky Way. The walls were those of the Rumfoord estate.

Ten minutes before the materialization was to take place, agents of the police spread the rumor that the materialization had happened prematurely, had happened outside the walls, and that the man and his dog could be seen plain as day two blocks away. The crowd galloped away to see the miracle at the intersection.

The crowd was crazy about miracles.

At the tail end of the crowd was a woman who weighed three hundred pounds. She had a goiter, a caramel apple, and a gray little six-year-old girl. She had the little girl by the hand and was jerking her this way and that, like a ball on the end of a rubber band. "Wanda June," she said, "if you don't start acting right, I'm never going to take you to a materialization again."

The materializations had been happening for nine years, once every fifty-nine days. The most learned and trustworthy men in the world had begged heartbrokenly for the privilege of seeing a materialization. No matter how the great men worded their requests, they were turned down cold. The refusal was always the same, handwritten by Mrs. Rumfoord's social secretary.

Mrs. Winston Niles Rumfoord asks me to inform you that she is unable to extend the invitation you request. She is sure you will understand her feeling in the matter: that the phenomenon you wish to observe is a tragic family affair, hardly a fit subject for the scrutiny of outsiders, no matter how nobly motivated their curiosities.

Mrs. Rumfoord and her staff answered none of the tens of thousands of questions that were put to them about the materializations. Mrs. Rumfoord felt that she owed the world very little indeed in the way of information. She discharged that incalculably small obligation by issuing a report twenty-four hours after each materialization. Her report never exceeded one hundred words. It was posted by her butler in a glass case bolted to the wall next to the one entrance to the estate.

The one entrance to the estate was an Alice-in-Wonderland door in the west wall. The door was only four-and-a-half feet high. It was made of iron and held shut by a great Yale lock.

The wide gates of the estate were bricked in.

The reports that appeared in the glass case by the iron door were uniformly bleak and peevish. They contained information that only served to sadden anyone with a shred of curiosity. They told the exact time at which Mrs. Rumfoord's husband Winston and his dog Kazak materialized, and the exact time at which they dematerialized. The states of health of the man and his dog were invariably appraised as *good*. The reports implied that Mrs. Rumfoord's husband could see the past and the future clearly, but they neglected to give examples of sights in either direction.

Now the crowd had been decoyed away from the estate to permit the untroubled arrival of a rented limousine at the small iron door in the west wall. A slender man in the clothes of an Edwardian dandy got out of the limousine and showed a paper to the policeman guarding the door. He was disguised by dark glasses and a false beard.

The policeman nodded, and the man unlocked the door

himself with a key from his pocket. He ducked inside, and slammed the door behind himself with a clang.

The limousine drew away.

Beware of the dog! said a sign over the small iron door. The fires of the summer sunset flickered among the razors and needles of broken glass set in concrete on the top of the wall.

The man who had let himself in was the first person ever invited by Mrs. Rumfoord to a materialization. He was not a great scientist. He was not even well-educated. He had been thrown out of the University of Virginia in the middle of his freshman year. He was Malachi Constant of Hollywood, California, the richest American—and a notorious rakehell.

Beware of the dog! the sign outside the small iron door had said. But inside the wall there was only a dog's skeleton. It wore a cruelly spiked collar that was chained to the wall. It was the skeleton of a very large dog—a mastiff. Its long teeth meshed. Its skull and jaws formed a cunningly articulated, harmless working model of a flesh-ripping machine. The jaws closed so—clack. Here had been the bright eyes, there the keen ears, there the suspicious nostrils, there the carnivore's brain. Ropes of muscle had hooked here and here, had brought the teeth together in flesh so—clack.

The skeleton was symbolic—a prop, a conversation piece installed by a woman who spoke to almost no one. No dog had died at its post there by the wall. Mrs. Rumfoord had bought the bones from a veterinarian, had had them bleached and varnished and wired together. The skeleton was one of Mrs. Rumfoord's many bitter and obscure comments on the nasty tricks time and her husband had played on her.

Mrs. Winston Niles Rumfoord had seventeen million dollars. Mrs. Winston Niles Rumfoord had the highest social position attainable in the United States of America. Mrs. Winston Niles Rumfoord was healthy and handsome, and talented, too.

Her talent was as a poetess. She had published anonymously a slim volume of poems called *Between Timid and Timbuktu.* It had been reasonably well received.

The title derived from the fact that all the words between *timid* and *Timbuktu* in very small dictionaries relate to *time.*

But, well-endowed as Mrs. Rumfoord was, she still did

troubled things like chaining a dog's skeleton to the wall, like having the gates of the estate bricked up, like letting the famous formal gardens turn into New England jungle.

The moral: Money, position, health, handsomeness, and talent aren't everything.

Malachi Constant, the richest American, locked the Alice-in-Wonderland door behind him. He hung his dark glasses and false beard on the ivy of the wall. He passed the dog's skeleton briskly, looking at his solar-powered watch as he did so. In seven minutes, a live mastiff named Kazak would materialize and roam the grounds.

"Kazak bites," Mrs. Rumfoord had said in her invitation, "so please be punctual."

Constant smiled at that—the warning to be punctual. To be punctual meant to exist as a point, meant that as well as to arrive somewhere on time. Constant existed as a point—could not imagine what it would be like to exist in any other way.

That was one of the things he was going to find out—what it was like to exist in any other way. Mrs. Rumfoord's husband existed in another way.

Winston Niles Rumfoord had run his private space ship right into the heart of an uncharted chrono-synclastic infundibulum two days out of Mars. Only his dog had been along. Now Winston Niles Rumfoord and his dog Kazak existed as wave phenomena—apparently pulsing in a distorted spiral with its origin in the Sun and its terminal in Betelgeuse.

The earth was about to intercept that spiral.

Almost any brief explanation of chrono-synclastic infundibula is certain to be offensive to specialists in the field. Be that as it may, the best brief explanation is probably that of Dr. Cyril Hall, which appears in the fourteenth edition of *A Child's Cyclopedia of Wonders and Things to Do*. The article is here reproduced in full, with gracious permission from the publishers:

CHRONO-SYNCLASTIC INFUNDIBULA—*Just imagine that your Daddy is the smartest man who ever lived on Earth, and he knows everything there is to find out, and he is exactly right about everything, and he can prove he is right about everything. Now imagine another little child on some nice world a million light years away, and that little child's Daddy is the smartest man who ever lived on that nice world so far away. And he is just as smart and just as right as your Daddy is. Both Daddies are smart, and both Daddies are right.*

Only if they ever met each other they would get into a terrible argument, because they wouldn't agree on anything. Now, you can say that your Daddy is right and the other little child's Daddy is wrong, but the Universe is an awfully big place. There is room enough for an awful lot of people to be right about things and still not agree.

The reason both Daddies can be right and still get into terrible fights is because there are so many different ways of being right. There are places in the Universe, though, where each Daddy could finally catch on to what the other Daddy was talking about. These places are where all the different kinds of truths fit together as nicely as the parts in your Daddy's solar watch. We call these places chrono-synclastic infundibula.

The Solar System seems to be full of chrono-synclastic infundibula. There is one great big one we are sure of that likes to stay between Earth and Mars. We know about that one because an Earth man and his Earth dog ran right into it.

You might think it would be nice to go to a chrono-synclastic infundibulum and see all the different ways to be absolutely right, but it is a very dangerous thing to do. The poor man and his poor dog are scattered far and wide, not just through space, but through time, too.

Chrono (kroh-no) means time. Synclastic (sin-class-tick) means curved toward the same side in all directions, like the skin of an orange. Infundibulum (in-fun-dib-u-lum) is what the ancient Romans like Julius Caesar and Nero called a funnel. If you don't know what a funnel is, get Mommy to show you one.

The key to the Alice-in-Wonderland door had come with the invitation. Malachi Constant slipped the key into his fur-lined trouser pocket and followed the one path that opened before him. He walked in deep shadow, but the flat rays of the sunset filled the treetops with a Maxfield Parrish light.

Constant made small motions with his invitation as he proceeded, expecting to be challenged at every turn. The invitation's ink was violet. Mrs. Rumfoord was only thirty-four, but she wrote like an old woman—in a kinky, barbed hand. She plainly detested Constant, whom she had never met. The spirit of the invitation was reluctant, to say the least, as though written on a soiled handkerchief.

"During my husband's last materialization," she had said in the invitation, "he insisted that you be present for the next. I was unable to dissuade him from this, despite the many obvious drawbacks. He insists that he knows you well, having met you on Titan, which, I am given to understand, is a moon of the planet Saturn."

There was hardly a sentence in the invitation that did not contain the verb *insist*. Mrs. Rumfoord's husband had insisted on her doing something very much against her own judgment, and she in turn was insisting that Malachi Constant behave, as best he could, like the gentleman he was not.

Malachi Constant had never been to Titan. He had never, so far as he knew, been outside the gaseous envelope of his native planet, the Earth. Apparently he was about to learn otherwise.

The turns in the path were many, and the visibility was short. Constant was following a damp green path the width of a lawn mower—what was in fact the swath of a lawn mower. Rising on both sides of the path were the green walls of the jungle the gardens had become.

The mower's swath skirted a dry fountain. The man who ran the mower had become creative at this point, had made the path fork. Constant could choose the side of the fountain on which he preferred to pass. Constant stopped at the fork, looked up. The fountain itself was marvelously creative. It was a cone described by many stone bowls of decreasing diameters. The bowls were collars on a cylindrical shaft forty feet high.

Impulsively, Constant chose neither one fork nor the other, but climbed the fountain itself. He climbed from bowl to bowl, intending when he got to the top to see whence he had come and whither he was bound.

Standing now in the topmost, in the smallest of the baroque fountain's bowls, standing with his feet in the ruins of birds' nests, Malachi Constant looked out over the estate, and over a large part of Newport and Narragansett Bay. He held up his watch to sunlight, letting it drink in the wherewithal that was to solar watches what money was to Earth men.

The freshening sea breeze ruffled Constant's blue-black hair. He was a well-made man—a light heavyweight, dark-skinned, with poet's lips, with soft brown eyes in the shaded caves of a Cro-Magnon brow-ridge. He was thirty-one.

He was worth three billion dollars, much of it inherited.

His name meant *faithful messenger.*

He was a speculator, mostly in corporate securities.

In the depressions that always followed his taking of alcohol, narcotics, and women, Constant pined for just one thing—a single message that was sufficiently dignified and important to merit his carrying it humbly between two points.

The motto under the coat of arms that Constant had designed for himself said simply, *The Messenger Awaits.*

What Constant had in mind, presumably, was a first-class message from God to someone equally distinguished.

Constant looked at his solar watch again. He had two minutes in which to climb down and reach the house—two minutes before Kazak would materialize and look for strangers to bite. Constant laughed to himself, thinking how delighted Mrs. Rumfoord would be were the vulgar, parvenu Mr. Constant of Hollywood to spend his entire visit treed on the fountain by a thoroughbred dog. Mrs. Rumfoord might even have the fountain turned on.

It was possible that she was watching Constant. The mansion was a minute's walk from the fountain—set off from the jungle by a mowed swath three times the width of the path.

The Rumfoord mansion was marble, an extended reproduction of the banqueting hall of Whitehall Palace in London. The mansion, like most of the really grand ones in Newport, was a collateral relative of post offices and Federal court buildings throughout the land.

The Rumfoord mansion was an hilariously impressive expression of the concept: People of substance. It was surely one of the greatest essays on density since the Great Pyramid of Khufu. In a way it was a better essay on permanence than the Great Pyramid, since the Great Pyramid tapered to nothingness as it approached heaven. Nothing about the Rumfoord mansion diminished as it approached heaven. Turned upside down, it would have looked exactly the same.

The density and permanence of the mansion were, of course, at ironic variance with the fact that the quondam matter of the house, except for one hour in every fifty-nine days, was no more substantial than a moonbeam.

Constant climbed down from the fountain, stepping onto the rims of bowls of ever-increasing sizes. When he got to the bottom, he was filled with a strong wish to see the fountain go. He thought of the crowd outside, thought of how they, too, would enjoy seeing the fountain go. They would be enthralled —watching the teeny-weeny bowl at the tippy-tippy top brimming over into the next little bowl . . . and the next little bowl's brimming over into the next little bowl . . . and the next little bowl's brimming over into the next bowl . . . and on and on and on, a rhapsody of brimming, each bowl singing its own merry water song. And yawning under all those bowls was the upturned mouth of the biggest bowl of them all . . . a regular Beelzebub of a bowl, bone dry and insatiable . . . waiting, waiting, waiting for that first sweet drop.

Constant was rapt, imagining that the fountain was running. The fountain was very much like an hallucination—and hallucinations, usually drug-induced, were almost all that could surprise and entertain Constant any more.

Time passed quickly. Constant did not move.

Somewhere on the estate a mastiff bayed. The baying sounded like the blows of a maul on a great bronze gong.

Constant awoke from his contemplation of the fountain. The baying could only be that of Kazak, the hound of space. Kazak had materialized. Kazak smelled the blood of a parvenu.

Constant sprinted the remainder of the distance to the house.

An ancient butler in knee breeches opened the door for Malachi Constant of Hollywood. The butler was weeping for joy. He was pointing into a room that Constant could not see. The butler was trying to describe the thing that made him so happy and full of tears. He could not speak. His jaw was palsied, and all he could say to Constant was, "Putt putt—putt putt putt."

The floor of the foyer was a mosaic, showing the signs of the zodiac encircling a golden sun.

Winston Niles Rumfoord, who had materialized only a minute before, came into the foyer and stood on the sun. He was much taller and heavier than Malachi Constant—and he was the first person who had ever made Constant think that there might actually be a person superior to himself. Winston Niles Rumfoord extended his soft hand, greeted Constant familiarly, almost singing his greeting in a glottal Groton tenor.

"Delighted, delighted, delighted, Mr. Constant," said Rumfoord. "How nice of you to commmmmmmmme."

"My pleasure," said Constant.

"They tell me you are possibly the luckiest man who ever lived."

"That might be putting it a little too strong," said Constant.

"You won't deny you've had fantastically good luck financially," said Rumfoord.

Constant shook his head. "No. That would be hard to deny," he said.

"And to what do you attribute this wonderful luck of yours?" said Rumfoord.

Constant shrugged. "Who knows?" he said. "I guess somebody up there likes me," he said.

Rumfoord looked up at the ceiling. "What a charming concept—someone's liking you up there."

Constant, who had been shaking hands with Rumfoord during the conversation, thought of his own hand, suddenly, as small and clawlike.

Rumfoord's palm was callused, but not horny like the palm of a man doomed to a single trade for all of his days. The calluses were perfectly even, made by the thousand happy labors of an active leisure class.

For a moment, Constant forgot that the man whose hand he shook was simply one aspect, one node of a wave phenomenon extending all the way from the Sun to Betelguese. The handshake reminded Constant what it was that he was touching—for his hand tingled with a small but unmistakable electrical flow.

Constant had not been bullied into feeling inferior by the tone of Mrs. Rumfoord's invitation to the materialization. Constant was a male and Mrs. Rumfoord was a female, and Constant imagined that he had the means of demonstrating, if given the opportunity, his unquestionable superiority.

Winston Niles Rumfoord was something else again—morally, spatially, socially, sexually, and electrically. Winston Niles Rumfoord's smile and handshake dismantled Constant's high opinion of himself as efficiently as carnival roustabouts might dismantle a Ferris wheel.

Constant, who had offered his services to God as a messenger, now panicked before the very moderate greatness of Rumfoord. Constant ransacked his memory for past proofs of his own greatness. He ransacked his memory like a thief going through another man's billfold. Constant found his memory stuffed with rumpled, overexposed snapshots of all the women he had had, with preposterous credentials testifying to his ownership of even more preposterous enterprises, with testimonials that attributed to him virtues and strengths that only three billion dollars could have. There was even a silver medal with a red ribbon—awarded to Constant for placing second in the hop, skip, and jump in an intramural track meet at the University of Virginia.

Rumfoord's smile went on and on.

To follow the analogy of the thief who is going through another man's billfold: Constant ripped open the seams of his memory, hoping to find a secret compartment with something of value in it. There was no secret compartment—nothing of value. All that remained to Constant were the husks of his memory—unstitched, flaccid flaps.

The ancient butler looked adoringly at Rumfoord, went through the cringing contortions of an ugly old woman posing for a painting of the Madonna. "The mah-stuh—" he bleated. "The young mah-stuh."

"I can read your mind, you know," said Rumfoord.

"Can you?" said Constant humbly.

"Easiest thing in the world," said Rumfoord. His eyes twinkled. "You're not a bad sort, you know—" he said, "particularly when you forget who you are." He touched Constant lightly on the arm. It was a politician's gesture—a vulgar public gesture by a man who in private, among his own kind, would take wincing pains never to touch anyone.

"If it's really so important to you, at this stage of our relationship, to feel superior to me in some way," he said to Constant pleasantly, "think of this: You can reproduce and I cannot."

He now turned his broad back to Constant, led the way through a series of very grand chambers.

He paused in one, insisted that Constant admire a huge oil painting of a little girl holding the reins of a pure white pony.

The little girl wore a white bonnet, a white, starched dress, white gloves, white socks, and white shoes.

She was the cleanest, most frozen little girl that Malachi Constant had ever seen. There was a strange expression on her face, and Constant decided that she was worried about getting the least bit dirty.

"Nice picture," said Constant.

"Wouldn't it be too bad if she fell into a mud puddle?" said Rumfoord.

Constant smiled uncertainly.

"My wife as a child," said Rumfoord abruptly, and he led the way out of the room.

He led the way down a back corridor and into a tiny room hardly larger than a big broom closet. It was ten feet long, six feet wide, and had a ceiling, like the rest of the rooms in the mansion, twenty feet high. The room was like a chimney. There were two wing chairs in it.

"An architectural accident—" said Rumfoord, closing the door and looking up at the ceiling.

"Pardon me?" said Constant.

"This room," said Rumfoord. With a limp right hand, he made the magical sign for spiral staircase. "It was one of the few things in life I ever really wanted with all my heart when I was a boy—this little room."

He nodded at shelves that ran six feet up the window wall. The shelves were beautifully made. Over the shelves was a driftwood plank that had written on it in blue paint: SKIP'S MUSEUM.

Skip's Museum was a museum of mortal remains—of endoskeletons and exoskeletons—of shells, coral, bone, cartilage, and chiton—of dottles and orts and residua of souls long gone. Most of the specimens were those that a child—presumably Skip—could find easily on the beaches and in the woods of Newport. Some were obviously expensive presents to a child extraordinarily interested in the science of biology.

Chief among these presents was the complete skeleton of an adult human male.

There was also the empty suit of armor of an armadillo, a stuffed dodo, and the long spiral tusk of a narwhal, playfully labeled by Skip, *Unicorn Horn*.

"Who is Skip?" said Constant.

"I am Skip," said Rumfoord. "Was."

"I didn't know," said Constant.

"Just in the family, of course," said Rumfoord.

"Um," said Constant.

Rumfoord sat down in one of the wing chairs, motioned Constant to the other.

"Angels can't either, you know," said Rumfoord.

"Can't what?" said Constant.

"Reproduce," said Rumfoord. He offered Constant a cigarette, took one himself, and placed it in a long, bone cigarette holder. "I'm sorry my wife was too indisposed to come downstairs—to meet you," he said. "It isn't you she's avoiding —it's me."

"You?" said Constant.

"That's correct," said Rumfoord. "She hasn't seen me since my first materialization." He chuckled ruefully. "Once was enough."

"I—I'm sorry," said Constant. "I don't understand."

"She didn't like my fortunetelling," said Rumfoord. "She found it very upsetting, what little I told her about her future. She doesn't care to hear more." He sat back in his wing chair, inhaled deeply. "I tell you, Mr. Constant," he said genially, "it's a thankless job, telling people it's a hard, hard Universe they're in."

"She said you'd told her to invite me," said Constant.

"She got the message from the butler," said Rumfoord. "I dared her to invite you, or she wouldn't have done it. You might keep that in mind: the only way to get her to do anything is to tell her she hasn't got the courage to do it. Of course, it isn't an infallible technique. I could send her a message now, telling her that she doesn't have the courage to face the future, and she would send me back a message saying I was right."

"You—you really can see into the future?" said Constant. The skin of his face tightened, felt parched. His palms perspired.

"In a punctual way of speaking—yes," said Rumfoord. "When I ran my space ship into the chrono-synclastic infundibulum, it came to me in a flash that everything that ever has been always will be, and everything that ever will be always has been." He chuckled again. "Knowing that rather takes the glamour out of fortunetelling—makes it the simplest, most obvious thing imaginable."

"You told your wife everything that was going to happen to her?" said Constant. This was a glancing question. Constant had no interest in what was going to happen to Rumfoord's wife. He was ravenous for news of himself. In asking about Rumfoord's wife, he was being coy.

"Well—not everything," said Rumfoord. "She wouldn't let me tell her everything. What little I did tell her quite spoiled her appetite for more."

"I—I see," said Constant, not seeing at all.

"Yes," said Rumfoord genially, "I told her that you and she were to be married on Mars." He shrugged. "Not married exactly—" he said, "but bred by the Martians—like farm animals."

Winston Niles Rumfoord was a member of the one true American class. The class was a true one because its limits had been clearly defined for at least two centuries—clearly defined for anyone with an eye for definitions. From Rumfoord's small class had come a tenth of America's presidents, a quarter of its explorers, a third of its Eastern Seaboard governors, a half of its full-time ornithologists, three-quarters of its great yachtsmen, and virtually all of its underwriters of the deficits of grand opera. It was a class singularly free of quacks, with the notable exception of political quacks. The political quackery was a means of gaining office—and was never carried into private life. Once in office, members of the class became, almost without exception, magnificently responsible.

If Rumfoord accused the Martians of breeding people as though people were no better than farm animals, he was accusing the Martians of doing no more than his own class had done. The strength of his class depended to some extent on sound money management—but depended to a much larger extent on marriages based cynically on the sorts of children likely to be produced.

Healthy, charming, wise children were the desiderata.

The most competent, if humorless, analysis of Rumfoord's

class is, beyond question, Waltham Kittredge's *The American Philosopher Kings.* It was Kittredge who proved that the class was in fact a family, with its loose ends neatly turned back into a hard core of consanguinity through the agency of cousin marriages. Rumfoord and his wife, for instance, were third cousins, and detested each other.

And when Rumfoord's class was diagramed by Kittredge, it resembled nothing so much as the hard, ball-like knot known as a *monkey's fist.*

Waltham Kittredge often floundered in his *The American Philosopher Kings*, trying to translate the atmosphere of Rumfoord's class into words. Like the college professor he was, Kittredge groped only for big words, and, finding no apt ones, he coined a lot of untranslatable new ones.

Of all Kittredge's jargon, only one term has ever found its way into conversation. The term is *un-neurotic courage.*

It was that sort of courage, of course, that carried Winston Niles Rumfoord out into space. It was pure courage—not only pure of lusts for fame and money, but pure of any drives that smack of the misfit or screwball.

There are, incidentally, two strong, common words that would have served handsomely, one or the other, in place of all of Kittredge's jargon. The words are *style* and *gallantry.*

When Rumfoord became the first person to own a private space ship, paying fifty-eight million dollars out of his own pocket for it—that was style.

When the governments of the earth suspended all space exploration because of the chrono-synclastic infundibula, and Rumfoord announced that he was going to Mars—that was style.

When Rumfoord announced that he was taking a perfectly tremendous dog along, as though a space ship were nothing more than a sophisticated sports car, as though a trip to Mars were little more than a spin down the Connecticut Turnpike—that was style.

When it was unknown what would happen if a space ship went into a chrono-synclastic infundibulum, and Rumfoord steered a course straight for the middle of one—that was gallantry indeed.

•

To contrast Malachi Constant of Hollywood with Winston Niles Rumfoord of Newport and Eternity:

Everything Rumfoord did he did *with* style, making all mankind look good.

Everything Constant did he did *in* style—aggressively, loudly, childishly, wastefully—making himself and mankind look bad.

Constant bristled with courage—but it was anything but un-neurotic. Every courageous thing he had ever done had been motivated by spitefulness and by goads from childhood that made fear seem puny indeed.

Constant, having just heard from Rumfoord that he was to be mated to Rumfoord's wife on Mars, looked away from Rumfoord to the museum of remains along one wall. Constant's hands were clasped together, tightening on each other pulsingly.

Constant cleared his throat several times. Then he whistled thinly between his tongue and the roof of his mouth. In all, he was behaving like a man who was waiting for a terrible pain to pass. He closed his eyes and sucked in air between his teeth. "Loo dee doo, Mr. Rumfoord," he said softly. He opened his eyes. "Mars?" he said.

"Mars," said Rumfoord. "Of course, that isn't your ultimate destination—or Mercury either."

"Mercury?" said Constant. He made an unbecoming quack of that lovely name.

"Your destination is Titan," said Rumfoord, "but you visit Mars, Mercury, and Earth again before you get there."

It is crucial to understand at what point in the history of punctual space exploration it was that Malachi Constant received the news of his prospective visits to Mars, Mercury, Earth, and Titan. The state of mind on Earth with regard to space exploration was much like the state of mind in Europe with regard to exploration of the Atlantic before Christopher Columbus set out.

There were these important differences, however: the monsters between space explorers and their goals were not imaginary, but numerous, hideous, various, and uniformly cataclysmic;

the cost of even a small expedition was enough to ruin most nations; and it was a virtual certainty that no expedition could increase the wealth of its sponsors.

In short, on the basis of horse sense and the best scientific information, there was nothing good to be said for the exploration of space.

The time was long past when one nation could seem more glorious than another by hurling some heavy object into nothingness. Galactic Spacecraft, a corporation controlled by Malachi Constant, had, as a matter of fact, received the very last order for such a showpiece, a rocket three hundred feet high and thirty-six feet in diameter. It had actually been built, but the fire order had never come.

The ship was called simply *The Whale*, and was fitted with living quarters for five passengers.

What had brought everything to such an abrupt halt was the discovery of the chrono-synclastic infundibula. They had been discovered mathematically, on the basis of bizarre flight patterns of unmanned ships sent out, supposedly, in advance of men.

The discovery of the chrono-synclastic infundibula said to mankind in effect: "*What makes you think you're going anywhere?*"

It was a situation made to order for American fundamentalist preachers. They were quicker than philosophers or historians or anybody to talk sense about the truncated Age of Space. Two hours after the firing of *The Whale* was called off indefinitely, the Reverend Bobby Denton shouted at his Love Crusade in Wheeling, West Virginia:

"'And the Lord came down to see the city and the tower, which the children of men builded. And the Lord said, "Behold, the people is one, and they have all one language; and this they begin to do; and now *nothing will be restrained from them, which they have imagined to do.* Go to, let us go down, and there confound their language, that they may not understand one another's speech." So the Lord scattered them abroad from thence upon the face of all the earth; and they left off to build the city. Therefore is the name of it called Babel; because the Lord did there confound the language of all the earth: and from thence did the Lord scatter them abroad upon the face of the earth.'"

Bobby Denton spitted his audience on a bright and loving gaze, and proceeded to roast it whole over the coals of its own iniquity. "Are these not Bible times?" he said. "Have we not builded of steel and pride an abomination far taller than the Tower of Babel of old? And did we not mean, like those builders of old, to get right into Heaven with it? And haven't we heard it said many times that the language of scientists is international? They all use the same Latin and Greek words for things, and they all talk the language of numbers." This seemed a particularly damning piece of evidence to Denton, and the Love Crusaders agreed bleakly without quite understanding why.

"So why should we cry out in surprise and pain now when God says to us what He said to the people who builded the Tower of Babel: 'No! Get away from there! You aren't going to Heaven or anywhere else with that thing! Scatter, you hear? Quit talking the language of science to each other! Nothing will be restrained from you which you have imagined to do, if you all keep on talking the language of science to each other, and I don't want that! I, your Lord God on High *want* things restrained from you, so you will quit thinking about crazy towers and rockets to Heaven, and start thinking about how to be better neighbors and husbands and wives and daughters and sons! Don't look to rockets for salvation—look to your homes and churches!' "

Bobby Denton's voice grew hoarse and hushed. "You want to fly through space? God has already given you the most wonderful space ship in all creation! Yes! Speed? You want speed? The space ship God has given you goes sixty-six thousand miles an hour—and will keep on running at that speed for all eternity, if God wills it. You want a space ship that will carry men in comfort? You've got it! It won't carry just a rich man and his dog, or just five men or ten men. No! God is no piker! He's given you a space ship that will carry billions of men, women, and children! Yes! And they don't have to stay strapped in chairs or wear fishbowls over their heads. No! Not on God's space ship. The people on God's space ship can go swimming, and walk in the sunshine and play baseball and go ice skating and go for family rides in the family automobile on Sunday after church and a family chicken dinner!"

Bobby Denton nodded. "Yes!" he said. "And if anybody thinks his God is mean for putting things out in space to stop us from flying out there, just let him remember the space ship God already gave us. And we don't have to buy the fuel for it, and worry and fret over what kind of fuel to use. No! God worries about all that.

"God told us what *we* had to do on this wonderful space ship. He wrote the rules so anybody could understand them. You don't have to be a physicist or a great chemist or an Albert Einstein to understand them. No! And He didn't make a whole lot of rules, either. They tell me that if they were to fire *The Whale*, they would have to make eleven thousand separate checks before they could be sure it was ready to go: Is this valve open, is that valve closed, is that wire tight, is that tank full?—and on and on and on to eleven thousand things to check. Here on God's space ship, God only gives us ten things to check—and not for any little trip to some big, dead poisonous stones out in space, but for a trip to the Kingdom of Heaven! Think of it! Where would you rather be tomorrow—on Mars or in the Kingdom of Heaven?

"You know what the check list is on God's round, green space ship? Do I have to tell you? You want to hear God's countdown?"

The Love Crusaders shouted back that they did.

"Ten!—" said Bobby Denton. "Do you covet thy neighbor's house, or his manservant, or his maidservant, or his ox, or his ass, or anything that is thy neighbor's?"

"No!" cried the Love Crusaders.

"Nine!—" said Bobby Denton. "Do you bear false witness against thy neighbor?"

"No!" cried the Love Crusaders.

"Eight!—" said Bobby Denton. "Do you steal?"

"No!" cried the Love Crusaders.

"Seven!—" said Bobby Denton. "Do you commit adultery?"

"No!" cried the Love Crusaders.

"Six!—" said Bobby Denton. "Do you kill?"

"No!" cried the Love Crusaders.

"Five!—" said Bobby Denton. "Do you honor thy father and thy mother?"

"Yes!" cried the Love Crusaders.

"Four!—" said Bobby Denton. "Do you remember the Sabbath day, and keep it holy?"

"Yes!" cried the Love Crusaders.

"Three!—" said Bobby Denton. "Do you take the name of the Lord thy God in vain?"

"No!" cried the Love Crusaders.

"Two!—" said Bobby Denton. "Do you make any graven images?"

"No!" cried the Love Crusaders.

"One!—" cried Bobby Denton. "Do you put any gods before the one true Lord thy God?"

"No!" cried the Love Crusaders.

"Blast off!" shouted Bobby Denton joyfully. "Paradise, here we come! Blast off, children, and Amen!"

"Well—" murmured Malachi Constant, there in the chimneylike room under the staircase in Newport, "it looks like the messenger is finally going to be used."

"What was that?" said Rumfoord.

"My name—it means *faithful messenger*," said Constant. "What's the message?"

"Sorry," said Rumfoord, "I know nothing about any message." He cocked his head quizzically. "Somebody said something to you about a message?"

Constant turned his palms upward. "I mean—what am I going to go to all this trouble to get to Triton for?"

"Titan," Rumfoord corrected him.

"Titan, Triton," said Constant. "What the blast would I go there for?" Blast was a weak, prissy, Eagle-Scoutish word for Constant to use—and it took him a moment to realize why he had used it. Blast was what space cadets on television said when a meteorite carried away a control surface, or the navigator turned out to be a space pirate from the planet Zircon. He stood. "Why the hell should I go there?"

"You do—I promise you," said Rumfoord.

Constant went over to the window, some of his arrogant strength returning. "I tell you right now," he said, "I'm not going."

"Sorry to hear that," said Rumfoord.

"I'm supposed to do something for you when I get there?" said Constant.

"No," said Rumfoord.

"Then why are you sorry?" said Constant. "What's it to you?"

"Nothing," said Rumfoord. "I'm only sorry for you. You'll really be missing something."

"Like what?" said Constant.

"Well—the most pleasant climate imaginable, for one thing," said Rumfoord.

"Climate!" said Constant contemptuously. "With houses in Hollywood, the Vale of Kashmir, Acapulco, Manitoba, Tahiti, Paris, Bermuda, Rome, New York, and Capetown, I should leave Earth in search of happier climes?"

"There's more to Titan than just climate," said Rumfoord. "The women, for instance, are the most beautiful creatures between the Sun and Betelgeuse."

Constant guffawed bitterly. "Women!" he said. "You think I'm having trouble getting beautiful women? You think I'm love-starved, and the only way I'll ever get close to a beautiful woman is to climb on a rocket ship and head for one of Saturn's moons? Are you kidding? I've had women so beautiful, anybody between the Sun and Betelgeuse would sit down and cry if the women said as much as hello to 'em!"

He took out his billfold, and slipped from it a photograph of his most recent conquest. There was no question about it—the girl in the photograph was staggeringly beautiful. She was Miss Canal Zone, a runner-up in the Miss Universe Contest—and in fact far more beautiful than the winner of the contest. Her beauty had frightened the judges.

Constant handed Rumfoord the photograph. "They got anything like that on Titan?" he said.

Rumfoord studied the photograph respectfully, handed it back. "No—" he said, "nothing like that on Titan."

"O.K.," said Constant, feeling very much in control of his own destiny again, "climate, beautiful women—what else?"

"Nothing else," said Rumfoord mildly. He shrugged. "Oh—art objects, if you like art."

"I've got the biggest private art collection in the world," said Constant.

Constant had inherited this famous art collection. The collection had been made by his father—or, rather, by agents of his father. It was scattered through museums all over the world, each piece plainly marked as a part of the Constant Collection. The collection had been made and then deployed in this manner on the recommendation of the Director of Public Relations of Magnum Opus, Incorporated, the corporation whose sole purpose was to manage the Constant affairs.

The purpose of the collection had been to prove how generous and useful and sensitive billionaires could be. The collection had turned out to be a perfectly gorgeous investment, as well.

"That takes care of art," said Rumfoord.

Constant was about to return the photograph of Miss Canal Zone to his billfold, when he felt that he held not one photograph but two. There was a photograph behind that of Miss Canal Zone. He supposed that that was a photograph of Miss Canal Zone's predecessor, and he thought that he might as well show Rumfoord her, too—show Rumfoord what a celestial lulu he had given the gate to.

"There—there's another one," said Constant, holding out the second photograph to Rumfoord.

Rumfoord made no move to take the photograph. He didn't even bother to look at it. He looked instead into Constant's eyes and grinned roguishly.

Constant looked down at the photograph that had been ignored. He found that it was not a photograph of Miss Canal Zone's predecessor. It was a photograph that Rumfoord had slipped to him. It was no ordinary photograph, though its surface was glossy and its margins white.

Within the margins lay shimmering depths. The effect was much like that of a rectangular glass window in the surface of a clear, shallow, coral bay. At the bottom of that seeming coral bay were three women—one white, one gold, one brown. They looked up at Constant, begging him to come to them, to make them whole with love.

Their beauty was to the beauty of Miss Canal Zone as the glory of the Sun was to the glory of a lightning bug.

Constant sank into a wing chair again. He had to look away from all that beauty in order to keep from bursting into tears.

"You can keep that picture, if you like," said Rumfoord. "It's wallet size."

Constant could think of nothing to say.

"My wife will still be with you when you get to Titan," said Rumfoord, "but she won't interfere if you want to frolic with these three young ladies. Your son will be with you, too, but he'll be quite as broad-minded as Beatrice."

"Son?" said Constant. He had no son.

"Yes—a fine boy named Chrono," said Rumfoord.

"Chrono?" said Constant.

"A Martian name," said Rumfoord. "He's born on Mars—by you, out of Beatrice."

"Beatrice?" said Constant.

"My wife," said Rumfoord. He had become quite transparent. His voice was becoming tinny, too, as though coming from a cheap radio. "Things fly this way and that, my boy," he said, "with or without messages. It's chaos, and no mistake, for the Universe is just being born. It's the great becoming that makes the light and the heat and the motion, and bangs you from hither to yon.

"Predictions, predictions, predictions," said Rumfoord musingly. "Is there anything else I should tell you? Ohhhhh—yes, yes, yes. This child of yours, this boy named Chrono—

"Chrono will pick up a little strip of metal on Mars—" said Rumfoord, "and he will call it his 'good-luck piece.' Keep your eye on that good-luck piece, Mr. Constant. It's unbelievably important."

Winston Niles Rumfoord vanished slowly, beginning with the ends of his fingers, and ending with his grin. The grin remained some time after the rest of him had gone.

"See you on Titan," said the grin. And then it was gone.

"Is it all over, Moncrief?" Mrs. Winston Niles Rumfoord called down to the butler from the top of the spiral staircase.

"Yes, Mum—he's left," said the butler, "and the dog, too."

"And that Mr. Constant?" said Mrs. Rumfoord—said Beatrice. She was behaving like an invalid—tottering, blinking hard, making her voice like wind in the treetops. She wore a long white dressing gown whose soft folds formed a counterclockwise spiral in harmony with the white staircase. The train of the gown cascaded down the top riser, making Beatrice continuous with the architecture of the mansion.

It was her tall, straight figure that mattered most in the display. The details of her face were insignificant. A cannonball, substituted for her head, would have suited the grand composition as well.

But Beatrice did have a face—and an interesting one. It could be said that she looked like a buck-toothed Indian brave. But anyone who said that would have to add quickly that she looked marvelous. Her face, like the face of Malachi Constant, was a one-of-a-kind, a surprising variation on a familiar theme—a variation that made observers think, *Yes—that would be another very nice way for people to look.* What Beatrice had done with her face, actually, was what any plain girl could do. She had overlaid it with dignity, suffering, intelligence, and a piquant dash of bitchiness.

"Yes," said Constant from below, "that Mr. Constant is still here." He was in plain view, leaning against a column in the arch that opened onto the foyer. But he was so low in the composition, so lost in architectural details as to be almost invisible.

"Oh!" said Beatrice. "How do you do." It was a very empty greeting.

"How do *you* do," said Constant.

"I can only appeal to your gentlemanly instincts," said Beatrice, "in asking you not to spread the story of your meeting with my husband far and wide. I can well understand how tremendous the temptation to do so must be."

"Yes—" said Constant, "I could sell my story for a lot of money, pay off the mortgage on the homestead, and become an internationally famous figure. I could hob-nob with the great and near-great, and perform before the crowned heads of Europe."

"You'll pardon me," said Beatrice, "if I fail to appreciate sarcasm and all the other brilliant nuances of your no doubt famous wit, Mr. Constant. These visits of my husband's make me ill."

"You never see him any more, do you?" said Constant.

"I saw him the first time he materialized," said Beatrice, "and that was enough to make me ill for the rest of my days."

"I liked him very much," said Constant.

"The insane, on occasion, are not without their charms," said Beatrice.

"Insane?" said Constant.

"As a man of the world, Mr. Constant," said Beatrice, "wouldn't you say that any person who made complicated and highly improbable prophecies was mad?"

"Well—" said Constant, "is it really very crazy to tell a man who has access to the biggest space ship ever built that he's going out into space?"

This bit of news, about the accessibility of a space ship to Constant, startled Beatrice. It startled her so much that she took a step back from the head of the staircase, separated herself from the rising spiral. The small step backward transformed her into what she was—a frightened, lonely woman in a tremendous house.

"You have a space ship, do you?" she said.

"A company I control has custody of one," said Constant. "You've heard of *The Whale*?"

"Yes," said Beatrice.

"My company sold it to the Government," said Constant. "I think they'd be delighted if someone would buy it back at five cents on the dollar."

"Much luck to you on your expedition," said Beatrice.

Constant bowed. "Much luck to *you* on *yours*," he said.

He left without another word. In crossing the bright zodiac on the foyer floor, he sensed that the spiral staircase now swept down rather than up. Constant became the bottommost point in a whirlpool of fate. As he walked out the door, he was delightfully aware of pulling the aplomb of the Rumfoord mansion right out with him.

Since it was foreordained that he and Beatrice were to come together again, to produce a child named Chrono, Constant was under no compunction to seek and woo her, to send her so much as a get-well card. He could go about his business, he thought, and the haughty Beatrice would have to damn well come to him—like any other bimbo.

He was laughing when he put on his dark glasses and false beard and let himself out through the little iron door in the wall.

The limousine was back, and so was the crowd.

The police held open a narrow path to the limousine door. Constant scuttled down it, reached the limousine. The path closed like the Red Sea behind the Children of Israel. The cries of the crowd, taken together, were a collective cry of indignation and pain. The crowd, having been promised nothing, felt cheated, having received nothing.

Men and boys began to rock Constant's limousine.

The chauffeur put the limousine in gear, made it creep through the sea of raging flesh.

A bald man made an attempt on Constant's life with a hot dog, stabbed at the window glass with it, splayed the bun, broke the frankfurter—left a sickly sunburst of mustard and relish.

"Yah, yah, yah!" yelled a pretty young woman, and she showed Constant what she had probably never showed any other man. She showed him that her two upper front teeth were false. She let those two front teeth fall out of place. She shrieked like a witch.

A boy climbed on the hood, blocking the chauffeur's view. He ripped off the windshield wipers, threw them to the crowd. It took the limousine three-quarters of an hour to reach a fringe of the crowd. And on the fringe were not the lunatics but the nearly sane.

Only on the fringe did the shouts become coherent.

"Tell us!" shouted a man, and he was merely fed up—not enraged.

"We've got a right!" shouted a woman. She showed her two fine children to Constant.

Another woman told Constant what it was the crowd felt it had a right to. "We've got a right to know what's going on!" she cried.

The riot, then, was an exercise in science and theology—a seeking after clues by the living as to what life was all about.

The chauffeur, seeing at last a clear road before him, pressed the accelerator to the floor. The limousine zoomed away.

A huge billboard flashed by. LET'S TAKE A FRIEND TO THE CHURCH OF OUR CHOICE ON SUNDAY! it said.

CHAPTER TWO

Cheers in the Wirehouse

"Sometimes I think it is a great mistake to have matter that can think and feel. It complains so. By the same token, though, I suppose that boulders and mountains and moons could be accused of being a little too phlegmatic."

—WINSTON NILES RUMFOORD

THE LIMOUSINE zoomed north out of Newport, turned down a gravel road, kept a rendezvous with a helicopter that was waiting in a pasture.

The purpose of Malachi Constant's switch from the limousine to the helicopter was to prevent anyone's following him, to prevent anyone's discovering who the bearded and bespectacled visitor to the Rumfoord estate had been.

No one knew where Constant was.

Neither the chauffeur nor the pilot knew the true identity of their passenger. Constant was Mr. Jonah K. Rowley to both.

"Mist' Rowley, suh—?" said the chauffeur, as Constant stepped out of the limousine.

"Yes?" said Constant.

"Wasn't you scared, suh?" said the chauffeur.

"Scared?" said Constant, sincerely puzzled by the question. "Of what?"

"Of what?" said the chauffeur incredulously. "Why, of all them crazy people who liked to lynch us."

Constant smiled and shook his head. Not once in the midst of the violence had he expected to be hurt. "It hardly helps to panic, do you think?" he said. In his own words he recognized Rumfoord's phrasing—even a little of Rumfoord's aristocratic yodel.

"Man—you must have some kind of guardian angel—lets you keep cool as a cucumber, no matter what," said the chauffeur admiringly.

This comment interested Constant, for it described well his attitude in the midst of the mob. He took the comment at first as an analogy—as a poetic description of his mood. A man who had a guardian angel would certainly have felt just as Constant had—

"Yes, suh!" said the chauffeur. "Sumpin' sure must be lookin' out for *you*!"

Then it hit Constant: *This was exactly the case.*

Until that moment of truth, Constant had looked upon his Newport adventure as one more drug-induced hallucination—as one more peyotl party—vivid, novel, entertaining, and of no consequence whatsoever.

The little door had been a dreamy touch . . . the dry fountain another—and the huge painting of the all white touch-me-not little girl with the all white pony . . . and the chimneylike room under the spiral staircase . . . and the photograph of the three sirens on Titan . . . and Rumfoord's prophecies . . . and the discomfiture of Beatrice Rumfoord at the top of the stairs . . .

Malachi Constant broke into a cold sweat. His knees threatened to buckle and his eyelids came unhinged. He was finally understanding that every bit of it had been real! He had been calm in the midst of the mob because he knew he wasn't going to die on Earth.

Something was looking out for him, all right.

And whatever it was, it was saving his skin for—

Constant quaked as he counted on his fingers the points of interest on the itinerary Rumfoord had promised him.

Mars.

Then Mercury.

Then Earth again.

Then Titan.

Since the itinerary ended on Titan, presumably that was where Malachi Constant was going to die. He was going to *die* there!

What had Rumfoord been so cheerful about?

Constant shuffled over to the helicopter, rocked the great, ramshackle bird as he climbed inside.

"You Rowley?" said the pilot.

"That's right," said Constant.

"Unusual first name you got, Mr. Rowley," said the pilot.

"Beg your pardon?" said Constant nauseously. He was looking through the plastic dome of the cockpit cover—looking up into the evening sky. He was wondering if there could possibly be eyes up there, eyes that could see everything he did. And if there were eyes up there, and they wanted him to do certain things, go certain places—how could they make him?

Oh God—but it looked thin and cold up there!

"I said you've got an unusual first name," said the pilot.

"What name's that?" said Constant, who had forgotten the foolish first name he had chosen for his disguise.

"Jonah," said the pilot.

Fifty-nine days later, Winston Niles Rumfoord and his loyal dog Kazak materialized again. A lot had happened since their last visit.

For one thing, Malachi Constant had sold out all his holdings in Galactic Spacecraft, the corporation that had the custody of the great rocket ship called *The Whale*. He had done this to destroy every connection between himself and the only known means of getting to Mars. He had put the proceeds of the sale into MoonMist Tobacco.

For another thing, Beatrice Rumfoord had liquidated her diversified portfolio of securities, and had put the proceeds into shares of Galactic Spacecraft, intending thereby to get a leather-lunged voice in whatever was done with *The Whale*.

For another thing, Malachi Constant had taken to writing Beatrice Rumfoord offensive letters, in order to keep her away—in order to make himself absolutely and permanently intolerable to her. To see one of these letters was to see them all. The most recent one went like this, written on stationery of Magnum Opus, Inc., the corporation whose sole purpose was to manage the financial affairs of Malachi Constant.

Hello from sunny California, Space Baby! Gee, I am sure looking forward to jazzing a high-class dame like you under the twin moons of Mars. You're the only kind of dame I never had, and I'll bet your kind is the greatest. Love and kisses for a starter. Mal.

For another thing, Beatrice had bought a capsule of cyanide—more deadly, surely, than Cleopatra's asp. It was Beatrice's intention to swallow it if ever she had to share so much as the same time zone with Malachi Constant.

For another thing, the stock market had crashed, wiping out Beatrice Rumfoord, among others. She had bought Galactic Spacecraft shares at prices ranging from 151½ to 169. The stock had fallen to 6 in ten trading sessions, and now lay there, trembling fractional points. Since Beatrice had bought on margin as well as for cash, she had lost everything, including her Newport home. She had nothing left but her clothes, her good name, and her finishing school education.

For another thing, Malachi Constant had thrown a party two days after returning to Hollywood—and only now, fifty-six days later, was it petering out.

For another thing, a genuinely bearded young man named Martin Koradubian had identified himself as the bearded stranger who had been invited into the Rumfoord estate to see a materialization. He was a repairer of solar watches in Boston, and a charming liar.

A magazine had bought his story for three thousand dollars.

Sitting in Skip's Museum under the spiral staircase, Winston Niles Rumfoord read Koradubian's magazine story with delight and admiration. Koradubian claimed in his story that Rumfoord had told him about the year Ten Million A.D.

In the year Ten Million, according to Koradubian, there would be a tremendous house-cleaning. All records relating to the period between the death of Christ and the year One Million A.D. would be hauled to dumps and burned. This would be done, said Koradubian, because museums and archives would be crowding the living right off the earth.

The million-year period to which the burned junk related would be summed up in history books in one sentence, according to Koradubian: *Following the death of Jesus Christ, there was a period of readjustment that lasted for approximately one million years.*

Winston Niles Rumfoord laughed and laid Koradubian's article aside. Rumfoord loved nothing more than a thumping good fraud. "Ten Million A.D.—" he said out loud, "a great year for fireworks and parades and world's fairs. A merry time for cracking open cornerstones and digging up time capsules."

Rumfoord wasn't talking to himself. There was someone else in Skip's Museum with him.

The other person was his wife Beatrice.

Beatrice was sitting in the facing wing chair. She had come downstairs to ask her husband's help in a time of great need.

Rumfoord blandly changed the subject.

Beatrice, already ghostly in a white peignoir, turned the color of lead.

"What an optimistic animal man is!" said Rumfoord rosily. "Imagine expecting the species to last for ten million more years—as though people were as well-designed as turtles!" He shrugged. "Well—who knows—maybe human beings will last that long, just on the basis of pure cussedness. What's your guess?"

"What?" said Beatrice.

"Guess how long the human race will be around," said Rumfoord.

From between Beatrice's clenched teeth came a frail, keen, sustained note so high as to be almost above the range of the human ear. The sound bore the same ghastly promise as the whistle of fins on a falling bomb.

Then the explosion came. Beatrice capsized her chair, attacked the skeleton, threw it crashing into a corner. She cleaned off the shelves of Skip's Museum, bouncing specimens off the walls, trampling them on the floor.

Rumfoord was flabbergasted. "Good God—" he said, "what made you do that?"

"Don't you know everything?" said Beatrice hysterically. "Does anybody have to tell you anything? Just read my mind!"

Rumfoord put his palms to his temples, his eyes wide. "Static—all I get is static," he said.

"What else *would* there be but static!" said Beatrice. "I'm going to be thrown right out in the street, without even the price of a meal—and my husband laughs and wants me to play guessing games!"

"It wasn't any *ordinary* guessing game," said Rumfoord. "It was about how long the human race was going to last. I thought that might sort of give you more perspective about your own problems."

"The hell with the human race!" said Beatrice.

"You're a member of it, you know," said Rumfoord.

"Then I'd like to put in for a transfer to the chimpanzees!"

said Beatrice. "No chimpanzee husband would stand by while his wife lost all her coconuts. No chimpanzee husband would try to make his wife into a space whore for Malachi Constant of Hollywood, California!"

Having said this ghastly thing, Beatrice subsided some. She wagged her head tiredly. "How long *is* the human race going to be around, Master?"

"I don't know," said Rumfoord.

"I thought you knew everything," said Beatrice. "Just take a look at the future."

"I look at the future," said Rumfoord, "and I find that I shall not be in the Solar System when the human race dies out. So the end is as much a mystery to me as to you."

In Hollywood, California, the chimes of the blue telephone in the rhinestone phone booth by Malachi Constant's swimming pool were ringing.

It is always pitiful when any human being falls into a condition hardly more respectable than that of an animal. How much more pitiful it is when the person who falls has had all the advantages!

Malachi Constant lay in the wide gutter of his kidney-shaped swimming pool, sleeping the sleep of a drunkard. There was a quarter of an inch of warm water in the gutter. Constant was fully dressed in blue-green evening shorts and a dinner jacket of gold brocade. His clothes were soaked.

He was all alone.

The pool had once been covered uniformly by an undulating blanket of gardenias. But a persistent morning breeze had moved the blooms to one end of the pool, as though folding a blanket to the foot of a bed. In folding back the blanket, the breeze revealed a pool bottom paved with broken glass, cherries, twists of lemon peel, peyotl buttons, slices of orange, stuffed olives, sour onions, a television set, a hypodermic syringe, and the ruins of a white grand piano. Cigar butts and cigarette butts, some of them marijuana, littered the surface.

The swimming pool looked less like a facility for sport than like a punchbowl in hell.

One of Constant's arms dangled in the pool itself. From the

wrist underwater came the glint of his solar watch. The watch had stopped.

The telephone's chimes persisted.

Constant mumbled but did not move.

The chimes stopped. Then, after twenty seconds, the chimes began again.

Constant groaned, sat up, groaned.

From the inside of the house came a brisk, efficient sound, high heels on a tile floor. A ravishing, brassy blond woman crossed from the house to the phone booth, giving Constant a look of haughty contempt.

She was chewing gum.

"Yah?" she said into the telephone. "Oh—it's you again. Yah—he's awake. Hey!" she yelled at Constant. She had a voice like a grackle. "Hey, space cadet!" she yelled.

"Hm?" said Constant.

"The guy who's president of that company you own wants to talk to you."

"Which company?" said Constant.

"Which company *you* president of?" said the woman into the telephone. She got her answer. "Magnum Opus," she said. "Ransom K. Fern of Magnum Opus," she said.

"Tell him—tell him I'll call him back," said Constant.

The woman told Fern, got another message to relay to Constant. "He says he's quitting."

Constant stood unsteadily, rubbing his face with his hands. "Quitting?" he said dully. "Old Ransom K. Fern quitting?"

"Yah," said the woman. She smiled hatefully. "He says you can't afford to pay his salary any more. He says you better come in and talk to him before he goes home." She laughed. "He says you're broke."

Back in Newport, the racket of Beatrice Rumfoord's outburst had attracted Moncrief the butler to Skip's Museum. "You called, Mum?" he said.

"It was more of a scream, Moncrief," said Beatrice.

"She doesn't want anything, thank you," said Rumfoord. "We were simply having a spirited discussion."

"How *dare* you say whether I want something or not?" said

Beatrice hotly to Rumfoord. "I'm beginning to catch on that you're not *nearly* as omniscient as you pretend to be. It so happens I want something very much. I want *a number of things* very much."

"Mum?" said the butler.

"I'd like you to let the dog in, please," said Beatrice. "I'd like to pet him before he goes. I would like to find out if a chrono-synclastic infundibula kills love in a dog the way it kills love in a man."

The butler bowed and left.

"That was a pretty scene to play before a servant," said Rumfoord.

"By and large," said Beatrice, "my contribution to the dignity of the family has been somewhat greater than yours."

Rumfoord hung his head. "I've failed you in some way? Is that what you're saying?"

"In *some* way?" said Beatrice. "In *every* way!"

"What would you have me do?" said Rumfoord.

"You could have told me this stock-market crash was coming!" said Beatrice. "You could have spared me what I'm going through now."

Rumfoord's hands worked in air, unhappily trying on various lines of argument for size.

"Well?" said Beatrice.

"I just wish we could go out to the chrono-synclastic infundibula together," said Rumfoord. "So you could see for once what I was talking about. All I can say is that my failure to warn you about the stock-market crash is as much a part of the natural order as Halley's Comet—and it makes an equal amount of sense to rage against either one."

"You're saying you have no character, and no sense of responsibility toward me," said Beatrice. "I'm sorry to put it that way, but it's the truth."

Rumfoord rocked his head back and forth. "A truth—but, oh God, what a punctual truth," he said.

Rumfoord retreated into his magazine again. The magazine opened naturally to the center spread, which was a color ad for MoonMist Cigarettes. MoonMist Tobacco, Ltd., had been bought recently by Malachi Constant.

Pleasure in Depth! said the headline on the ad. The picture that went with it was the picture of the three sirens of Titan. There they were—the white girl, the golden girl, and the brown girl.

The fingers of the golden girl were fortuitously spread as they rested on her left breast, permitting an artist to paint in a MoonMist Cigarette between two of them. The smoke from her cigarette passed beneath the nostrils of the brown and white girls, and their space-annihilating concupiscence seemed centered on mentholated smoke alone.

Rumfoord had known that Constant would try to debase the picture by using it in commerce. Constant's father had done a similar thing when he found he could not buy Leonardo's "Mona Lisa" at any price. The old man had punished Mona Lisa by having her used in an advertising campaign for suppositories. It was the free-enterprise way of handling beauty that threatened to get the upper hand.

Rumfoord made a buzzing sound on his lips, which was a sound he made when he approached compassion. The compassion he approached was for Malachi Constant, who was having a far worse time of it than Beatrice.

"Have I heard your whole defense?" said Beatrice, coming behind Rumfoord's chair. Her arms were folded, and Rumfoord, reading her mind, knew that she thought of her sharp, projected elbows as bullfighter's swords.

"I beg your pardon?" said Rumfoord.

"This silence—this hiding in the magazine—this is the sum and total of your rebuttal?" said Beatrice.

"Rebuttal—a punctual word if there ever was one," said Rumfoord. "I say this, and then you rebut me, then I rebut you, then somebody else comes in and rebuts us both." He shuddered. "What a nightmare where everybody gets in line to rebut each other."

"Couldn't you, this very moment," said Beatrice, "give me stock-market tips that would enable me to gain back everything I lost and more? If you had one shred of concern for me, couldn't you tell me exactly how Malachi Constant of Hollywood is going to try to trick me into going to Mars, so I could outwit him?"

"Look," said Rumfoord, "life for a punctual person is like a roller coaster." He turned to shiver his hands in her face. "All kinds of things are going to happen to you! Sure," he said, "I can see the whole roller coaster you're on. And sure—I could give you a piece of paper that would tell you about every dip and turn, warn you about every bogeyman that was going to pop out at you in the tunnels. But that wouldn't help you any."

"I don't see why not," said Beatrice.

"Because you'd *still* have to take the roller-coaster ride," said Rumfoord. "I didn't design the roller coaster, I don't own it, and I don't say who rides and who doesn't. I just know what it's shaped like."

"And Malachi Constant is part of the roller coaster?" said Beatrice.

"Yes," said Rumfoord.

"And there's no avoiding him?" said Beatrice.

"No," said Rumfoord.

"Well—suppose you tell me then, just what steps bring us together," said Beatrice, "and let me do what little I can."

Rumfoord shrugged. "All right—if you wish," he said. "If it would make you feel better—

"At this very moment," he said, "the President of the United States is announcing a New Age of Space to relieve unemployment. Billions of dollars are going to be spent on unmanned space ships, just to make work. The opening episode in this New Age of Space will be the firing of *The Whale* next Tuesday. *The Whale* will be renamed *The Rumfoord* in my honor, will be loaded with organ-grinder monkeys, and will be fired in the general direction of Mars. You and Constant will both take part in the ceremonies. You will go on board for a ceremonial inspection, and a faulty switch will send you on your way with the monkeys."

It is worth stopping the narrative at this point to say that this cock-and-bull story told to Beatrice is one of the few known instances of Winston Niles Rumfoord's having told a lie.

This much of Rumfoord's story was true: *The Whale* was going to be renamed and fired on Tuesday, and the President of the United States *was* announcing a New Age of Space.

Some of the President's comments at the time bear repeating—and it should be remembered that the President gave the word "progress" a special flavor by pronouncing it *prog-erse*.

He also flavored the words "chair" and "warehouse," pronouncing them *cheer* and *wirehouse*.

"Now, some people are going around saying the American economy is old and sick," said the President, "and I frankly can't understand how they can say such a thing, because there is now more opportunity for progerse on all fronts than at any time in human history.

"And there is one frontier we can make particular progerse on and that is the great frontier of space. We have been turned back by space once, but it isn't the American way to take no for an answer where progerse is concerned.

"Now, people of faint heart come to see me every day at the White House," said the President, "and they weep and wail and say, 'Oh, Mr. President, the wirehouses are all full of automobiles and airplanes and kitchen appliances and various other products,' and they say, 'Oh, Mr. President, there is nothing more that anybody wants the factories to make because everybody already has two, three, and four of everything.'

"One man in particular, I remember, was a cheer manufacturer, and he had way overproduced, and all he could think about was all those cheers in the wirehouse. And I said to him, 'In the next twenty years, the population of the world is going to double, and all those billions of new people are going to need things to sit down on, so you just hang on to those cheers. Meanwhile, why don't you forget about those cheers in the wirehouse and think about progerse in space?'

"I said to him and I say to you and I say to everybody, 'Space can absorb the productivity of a trillion planets the size of earth. We could build and fire rockets forever, and never fill up space and never learn all there is to know about it.'

"Now, these same people who like to weep and wail so much say, 'Oh, but Mr. President, what about the chrono-synclastic infundibula and what about this and what about that?' And I say to them, 'If people listened to people like you, there wouldn't ever be any progerse. There wouldn't be the telephone or anything. And besides,' I tell them and I tell you and I tell everybody, 'we don't have to put people in the rocket ships. We will use the lower animals only.' "

There was more to the speech.

•

Malachi Constant of Hollywood, California, came out of the rhinestone phone booth cold sober. His eyes felt like cinders. His mouth tasted like horseblanket purée.

He was positive that he had never seen the beautiful blond woman before.

He asked her one of the standard questions for times of violent change. "Where is everybody?" he said.

"You threw 'em all out," said the woman.

"I did?" said Constant.

"Yah," said the woman. "You mean you drew a blank?"

Constant nodded weakly. During the fifty-six-day party he had reached a point where he could draw almost nothing else. His aim had been to make himself unworthy of any destiny—incapable of any mission—far too ill to travel. He had succeeded to a shocking degree.

"Oh, it was quite a show," said the woman. "You were having as good a time as anybody, helping shove the piano in the pool. Then, when it finally went in, you got this big crying jag."

"Crying jag," echoed Constant. That was something new.

"Yah," said the woman. "You said you had a very unhappy childhood, and made everybody listen to how unhappy it was. How your father never even threw a ball to you once—any kind of ball. Half the time nobody could understand you, but every time somebody could understand you, it was about how there never was any kind of ball.

"Then you talked about your mother," said the woman, "and you said if she was a whore, then you were proud to be a son of a whore, if that's what a whore was. Then you said you'd give an oil well to any woman who'd come up to you and shake your hand and say real loud, so everybody could hear, 'I'm a whore, just like your mother was.' "

"What happened then?" said Constant.

"You gave an oil well to every woman at the party," said the woman. "And then you started crying worse than ever, and you picked me out, and you told everybody I was the only person in the whole Solar System you could trust. You said everybody else was just waiting for you to fall asleep, so they could put you on a rocket ship and shoot you at Mars. Then you made everybody go home but me. Servants and everybody.

"Then we flew down to Mexico and got married, and then we came back here," she said. "Now I find out you haven't got a pot to piss in or a window to throw it out of. You better go down to the office and find out what the hell is going on, on account of my boyfriend is a gangster, and he'll kill you if I tell him you aren't providing for me right.

"Hell," she said, "I had an unhappier childhood than you did. My mother was a whore and my father never came home, either—but we were *poor* besides. At least you had billions of dollars."

In Newport, Beatrice Rumfoord turned her back to her husband. She stood on the threshold of Skip's Museum, facing the corridor. Down the corridor came the sound of the butler's voice. The butler was standing in the front doorway, calling to Kazak, the hound of space.

"I know a little something about roller coasters, too," Beatrice said.

"That's good," said Rumfoord emptily.

"When I was ten years old," said Beatrice, "my father got it into his head that it would be fun for me to ride a roller coaster. We were summering on Cape Cod, and we drove over to an amusement park outside of Fall River.

"He bought two tickets on the roller coaster. He was going to ride with me.

"I took one look at the roller coaster," said Beatrice, "and it looked silly and dirty and dangerous, and I simply refused to get on. My own father couldn't make me get on," said Beatrice, "even though he was Chairman of the Board of the New York Central Railroad.

"We turned around and came home," said Beatrice proudly. Her eyes glittered, and she nodded abruptly. "That's the way to treat roller coasters," she said.

She stalked out of Skip's Museum, went to the foyer to await the arrival of Kazak.

In a moment, she felt the electric presence of her husband behind her.

"Bea—" he said, "if I seem indifferent to your misfortunes, it's only because I know how well things are going to turn out in the end. If it seems crude of me not to hate the idea of your pairing off with Constant, it's only an humble admission on my part that he's going to make you a far better husband than I ever was or will be.

"Look forward to being really in love for the first time, Bea," said Rumfoord. "Look forward to behaving aristocratically without any outward proofs of your aristocracy. Look forward to having nothing but the dignity and intelligence and tenderness that God gave you—look forward to taking those materials and nothing else, and making something exquisite with them."

Rumfoord groaned tinnily. He was becoming insubstantial. "Oh, God—" he said, "you talk about roller coasters—

"Stop and think sometime about the roller coaster I'm on. Some day on Titan, it will be revealed to you just how ruthlessly I've been used, and by whom, and to what disgustingly paltry ends."

Kazak now flung himself into the house, flews flapping. He landed skidding on the polished floor.

He ran in place, trying to make a right-angle turn in Beatrice's direction. Faster and faster he ran, and still he could get no traction.

He became translucent.

He began to shrink, to fizz crazily on the foyer floor like a ping-pong ball in a frying pan.

Then he disappeared.

There was no dog any more.

Without looking behind, Beatrice knew that her husband had disappeared, too.

"Kazak?" she said faintly. She snapped her fingers, as though to attract a dog. Her fingers were too weak to make a sound.

"Nice doggy," she whispered.

CHAPTER THREE

United Hotcake Preferred

"Son—they say there isn't any royalty in this country, but do you want me to tell you how to be king of the United States of Amercia? Just fall through the hole in a privy and come out smelling like a rose."

—NOEL CONSTANT

MAGNUM OPUS, the Los Angeles Corporation that managed Malachi Constant's financial affairs, was founded by Malachi's father. It had a thirty-one-story building for its home. While Magnum Opus owned the whole building, it used only the top three floors, renting out the rest to corporations it controlled.

Some of these corporations, having been sold recently by Magnum Opus, were moving out. Others, having been bought recently by Magnum Opus, were moving in.

Among the tenants were Galactic Spacecraft, MoonMist Tobacco, Fandango Petroleum, Lennox Monorail, Fry-Kwik, Sani-Maid Pharmaceuticals, Lewis and Marvin Sulfur, Dupree Electronics, Universal Piezoelectric, Psychokinesis Unlimited, Ed Muir Associates, Max-Mor Machine Tools, Wilkinson Paint and Varnish, American Levitation, Flo-Fast, King O'Leisure Shirts, and the Emblem Supreme Casualty and Life Assurance Company of California.

The Magnum Opus Building was a slender, prismatic, twelve-sided shaft, faced on all twelve sides with blue-green glass that shaded to rose at the base. The twelve sides were said by the architect to represent the twelve great religions of the world. So far, no one had asked the architect to name them.

That was lucky, because he couldn't have done it.

There was a private heliport on top.

The shadow and flutter of Constant's helicopter settling to the heliport seemed to many of the people below to be like the shadow and flutter of the Bright Angel of Death. It seemed that way because of the stock-market crash, because money and jobs were so scarce—

And it seemed especially that way to them because the things that had crashed the hardest, that had pulled everything down with them, were the enterprises of Malachi Constant.

Constant was flying his own helicopter, since all his servants had quit the night before. Constant was flying it badly. He set it down with a crash that sent shivers through the building.

He was arriving for a conference with Ransom K. Fern, President of Magnum Opus.

Fern waited for Constant on the thirty-first floor—a single, vast room that was Constant's office.

The office was spookily furnished, since none of the furniture had legs. Everything was suspended magnetically at the proper height. The tables and the desk and the bar and the couches were floating slabs. The chairs were tilted, floating bowls. And most eerie of all, pencils and pads were scattered at random through the air, ready to be snatched by anyone who had an idea worth writing down.

The carpet was as green as grass for the simple reason that it was grass—living grass as lush as any putting green.

Malachi Constant sank from the heliport deck to his office in a private elevator. When the elevator door whispered open, Constant was startled by the legless furnishings, by the floating pencils and pads. He had not been in his office for eight weeks. Somebody had refurnished the place.

Ransom K. Fern, aging President of Magnum Opus, stood at a floor-to-ceiling window, looking out over the city. He wore his black Homburg hat and his black Chesterfield coat. He carried his whangee walking stick at port arms. He was exceedingly thin—always had been.

"A butt like two beebees," Malachi Constant's father Noel had said of Fern. "Ransom K. Fern is like a camel who has burned up both his humps, and now he's burning up everything else but his hair and eyeballs."

According to figures released by the Bureau of Internal Revenue, Fern was the highest-paid executive in the country. He had a salary of a flat million dollars a year—plus stock-option plans and cost-of-living adjustments.

He had joined Magnum Opus when he was twenty-two years old. He was sixty now.

"Some—somebody's changed all the furniture," said Constant.

"Yes," said Fern, still looking out over the city, "somebody changed it."

"You?" said Constant.

Fern sniffed, took his time about answering. "I thought we ought to demonstrate our loyalty to some of our own products."

"I—I never saw anything like it," said Constant. "No legs—just floating in air."

"Magnetism, you know," said Fern.

"Why—why I think it looks wonderful, now that I'm getting used to it," said Constant. "And some company we own makes this stuff?"

"American Levitation Company," said Fern. "You said to buy it, so we bought it."

Ransom K. Fern turned away from the window. His face was a troubling combination of youth and age. There was no sign in the face of any intermediate stages in the aging process, no hint of the man of thirty or forty or fifty who had been left behind. Only adolescence and the age of sixty were represented. It was as though a seventeen-year-old had been withered and bleached by a blast of heat.

Fern read two books a day. It has been said that Aristotle was the last man to be familiar with the whole of his own culture. Ransom K. Fern had made an impressive attempt to equal Aristotle's achievement. He had been somewhat less successful than Aristotle in perceiving patterns in what he knew.

The intellectual mountain had labored to produce a philosophical mouse—and Fern was the first to admit that it was a mouse, and a mangy mouse at that. As Fern expressed the philosophy conversationally, in its simplest terms:

"You go up to a man, and you say, 'How are things going, Joe?' And he says, 'Oh, fine, fine—couldn't be better.' And you look into his eyes, and you see things really couldn't be much worse. When you get right down to it, everybody's having a perfectly lousy time of it, and I mean everybody. And the hell of it is, nothing seems to help much."

This philosophy did not sadden him. It did not make him brood.

It made him heartlessly watchful.

It helped in business, too—for it let Fern assume automatically that the other fellow was far weaker and far more bored than he seemed.

Sometimes, too, people with strong stomachs found Fern's murmured asides funny.

His situation, working for Noel Constant and then Malachi, conspired nicely to make almost anything he might say bitterly funny—for he was superior to Constant *père* and *fils* in every respect but one, and the respect excepted was the only one that really mattered. The Constants—ignorant, vulgar, and brash—had copious quantities of dumb luck.

Or had had up to now.

Malachi Constant had still to get it through his head that his luck was gone—every bit of it. He had still to get it through his head, despite the hideous news Fern had given him on the telephone.

"Gee," said Constant ingenuously, "the more I look at this furniture, the more I like it. This stuff should sell like hotcakes." There was something pathetic and repellent about Malachi Constant's talking business. It had been the same with his father. Old Noel Constant had never known anything about business, and neither had his son—and what little charm the Constants had evaporated the instant they pretended that their successes depended on their knowing their elbows from third base.

There was something obscene about a billionaire's being optimistic and aggressive and cunning.

"If you ask me," said Constant, "that was a pretty sound investment—a company that makes furniture like this."

"United Hotcake preferred," said Fern. United Hotcake preferred was a favorite joke of his. Whenever people came to him, begging for investment advice that would double their money in six weeks, he advised them gravely to invest in this fictitious stock. Some people actually tried to follow his advice.

"Sitting on an American Levitation couch is harder than standing up in a birchbark canoe," said Fern dryly. "Throw yourself into one of these so-called chairs, and it will bounce you off the wall like a stone out of a slingshot. Sit on the edge of your desk, and it will waltz you around the room like a Wright brother at Kitty Hawk."

Constant touched his desk ever so lightly. It shuddered nervously.

"Well—they still haven't got all of the bugs out of it, that's all," said Constant.

"Truer words were never spoken," said Fern.

Constant now made a plea that he had never had to make before. "A guy is entitled to a mistake now and then," he said.

"Now and then?" said Fern, raising his eyebrows. "For three months you have made nothing but wrong decisions, and you've done what I would have said was impossible. You've succeeded in more than wiping out the results of almost forty years of inspired guessing."

Ransom K. Fern took a pencil from the air and broke it in two. "Magnum Opus is no more. You and I are the last two people in the building. Everyone else has been paid off and sent home."

He bowed and moved toward the door. "The switchboard has been arranged so that all incoming calls will come directly to your desk here. And when you leave, Mr. Constant, sir, remember to turn out the lights and lock the front door."

A history of Magnum Opus, Inc., is perhaps in order at this point.

Magnum Opus began as an idea in the head of a Yankee traveling salesman of copper-bottomed cookware. That Yankee was Noel Constant, a native of New Bedford, Massachusetts. He was the father of Malachi.

The father of Noel, in turn, was Sylvanus Constant, a loom fixer in the New Bedford Mills of the Nattaweena Division of the Grand Republic Woolen Company. He was an anarchist, though he never got into any trouble about it, except with his wife.

The family could trace its line back through an illegitimacy to Benjamin Constant, who was a tribune under Napoleon from 1799 to 1801, and a lover of Anne Louise Germaine

Necker, Baronne de Stael-Holstein, wife of the then Swedish ambassador to France.

One night in Los Angeles, at any rate, Noel Constant got it into his head to become a speculator. He was thirty-nine at the time, single, physically and morally unattractive, and a business failure. The idea of becoming a speculator came to him as he sat all alone on a narrow bed in Room 223 of the Wilburhampton Hotel.

The most valuable corporate structure ever to be owned by one man could not have had humbler headquarters in the beginning. Room 223 of the Wilburhampton was eleven feet long and eight feet wide, and had neither telephone nor desk.

What it did have was a bed, a three-drawer dresser, old newspapers lining the drawers, and, in the bottom drawer, a Gideon Bible. The newspaper page that lined the middle drawer was a page of stock-market quotations from fourteen years before.

There is a riddle about a man who is locked in a room with nothing but a bed and a calendar, and the question is: How does he survive?

The answer is: He eats dates from the calendar and drinks water from the springs of the bed.

This comes very close to describing the genesis of Magnum Opus. The materials with which Noel Constant built his fortune were hardly more nourishing in themselves than calendar dates and bedsprings.

Magnum Opus was built with a pen, a check book, some check-sized Government envelopes, a Gideon Bible, and a bank balance of eight thousand, two hundred and twelve dollars.

The bank balance was Noel Constant's share in the estate of his anarchist father. The estate had consisted principally of Government bonds.

And Noel Constant had an investment program. It was simplicity itself. The Bible would be his investment counselor.

There are those who have concluded, after studying Noel Constant's investment pattern, that he was either a genius or had a superb system of industrial spies.

He invariably picked the stock market's most brilliant performers days or hours before their performances began. In twelve months, rarely leaving Room 223 in the Wilburhampton Hotel, he increased his fortune to a million and a quarter.

Noel Constant did it without genius and without spies.

His system was so idiotically simple that some people can't understand it, no matter how often it is explained. The people who can't understand it are people who have to believe, for their own peace of mind, that tremendous wealth can be produced only by tremendous cleverness.

This was Noel Constant's system:

He took the Gideon Bible that was in his room, and he started with the first sentence in Genesis.

The first sentence in Genesis, as some people may know, is: "In the beginning God created the heaven and the earth." Noel Constant wrote the sentence in capital letters, put periods between the letters, divided the letters into pairs, rendering the sentence as follows: "I.N., T.H., E.B., E.G., I.N., N.I., N.G., G.O., D.C., R.E., A.T., E.D., T.H., E.H., E.A., V.E., N.A., N.D., T.H., E.E., A.R., T.H."

And then he looked for corporations with those initials, and bought shares in them. His rule at the beginning was that he would own shares in only one corporation at a time, would invest his whole nest-egg in it, and would sell the instant the value of his shares had doubled.

His very first investment was International Nitrate. After that came Trowbridge Helicopter, Electra Bakeries, Eternity Granite, Indiana Novelty, Norwich Iron, National Gelatin, Granada Oil, Del-Mar Creations, Richmond Electroplating, Anderson Trailer, and Eagle Duplicating.

His program for the next twelve months was this: Trowbridge Helicopter again, ELCO Hoist, Engineering Associates, Vickery Electronics, National Alum, National Dredging, Trowbridge Helicopter again.

The third time he bought Trowbridge Helicopter, he didn't buy a piece of it. He bought the whole thing—lock, stock, and barrel.

Two days after that, the company landed a long-term Government contract for intercontinental ballistic missiles, a contract that made the company worth, conservatively, fifty-nine million dollars. Noel Constant had bought the company for twenty-two million.

The only executive decision he ever made relative to the company was contained in an order written on a picture postcard of the Wilburhampton Hotel. The card was addressed to the president of the company, telling him to change the name of the company to Galactic Spacecraft, Inc., since the company had long since outgrown both Trowbridges and helicopters.

Small as this exercise of authority was, it was significant, for it showed that Constant had at last become interested in something he owned. And, though his holdings in the firm had more than doubled in value, he did not sell them all. He sold only forty-nine per cent of them.

Thereafter, he continued to take the advice of his Gideon Bible, but he kept big pieces of any firm he really liked.

During his first two years in Room 223 of the Wilburhampton, Noel Constant had only one visitor. That visitor did not know he was rich. His one visitor was a chambermaid named Florence Whitehill, who spent one night out of ten with him for a small, flat fee.

Florence, like everyone else in the Wilburhampton, believed him when he said he was a trader in stamps. Personal hygiene was not Noel Constant's strongest suit. It was easy to believe that his work brought him into regular contact with mucilage.

The only people who knew how rich he was were employees of the Bureau of Internal Revenue and of the august accounting firm of Clough and Higgins.

Then, after two years, Noel Constant received his second visitor in Room 223.

The second visitor was a thin and watchful blue-eyed man of twenty-two. He engaged Noel Constant's serious attention by announcing that he was from the United States Bureau of Internal Revenue.

Constant invited the young man into his room, motioned for him to sit on the bed. He himself remained standing.

"They sent a child, did they?" said Noel Constant.

The visitor was not offended. He turned the gibe to his own advantage, using it in an image of himself that was chilling indeed: "A child with a heart of stone and a mind as quick as a mongoose, Mr. Constant," he said. "I have also been to Harvard Business School."

"That may be so," said Constant, "but I don't think you can hurt me. I don't owe the Federal Government a dime."

The callow visitor nodded. "I know," he said. "I found everything in apple-pie order."

The young man looked around the room. He wasn't surprised by its squalor. He was worldly enough to have expected something diseased.

"I've been over your income-tax reports for the past two years," he said, "and, by my calculations, you are the luckiest man who ever lived."

"Lucky?" said Noel Constant.

"I think so," said the young visitor. "Don't *you* think so? For instance—what does ELCO Hoist Company manufacture?"

"ELCO Hoist?" said Noel Constant blankly.

"You owned fifty-three per cent of it for a period of two months," said the young visitor.

"Why—hoists—things for lifting various articles," said Noel Constant stuffily. "And various allied products."

The young visitor's smile made cat's whiskers under his nose. "For your information," he said, "ELCO Hoist Company was a name given by the Government in the last war to a top-secret laboratory that was developing underwater listening gear. After the war, it was sold to private enterprise, and the name was never changed—since the work was still top secret, and the only customer was still the Government.

"Suppose you tell me," said the young visitor, "what it was you learned about Indiana Novelty that made you think it was a shrewd investment? Did you think they made little party poppers with paper hats inside?"

"I have to answer these questions for the Bureau of Internal Revenue?" said Noel Constant. "I have to describe every company I owned in detail, or I can't keep the money?"

"I was simply asking for my own curiosity. From your reaction, I gather that you haven't the remotest idea what Indiana Novelty does. For your information, Indiana Novelty manufactures nothing, but holds certain key patents on tire-recapping machinery."

"Suppose we get down to the Bureau of Internal Revenue business," said Noel Constant curtly.

"I'm no longer with the Bureau," said the young visitor. "I resigned my one-hundred-and-fourteen-dollar-a-week job this morning in order to take a job making two thousand dollars a week."

"Working for whom?" said Noel Constant.

"Working for you," said the young man. He stood, held out his hand. "Ransom K. Fern is the name," he said.

"I had a professor in the Harvard Business School," said young Fern to Noel Constant, "who kept telling me that I was smart, but that I would have to *find my boy*, if I was going to be rich. He wouldn't explain what he meant. He said I would catch on sooner or later. I asked him how I could go looking for my boy, and he suggested that I work for the Bureau of Internal Revenue for a year or so.

"When I went over your tax returns, Mr. Constant, it suddenly came to me what it was he meant. He meant I was shrewd and thorough, but I wasn't remarkably lucky. I had to find somebody who had luck in an astonishing degree—and so I have."

"Why should I pay you two thousand dollars a week?" said Noel Constant. "You see my facilities and my staff here, and you know what I've done with them."

"Yes—" said Fern, "and I can show you where you should have made two hundred million where you made only fifty-nine. You know absolutely nothing about corporate law or tax law—or even commonsense business procedure."

Fern thereupon proved this to Noel Constant, father of Malachi—and Fern showed him an organizational plan that had the name Magnum Opus, Incorporated. It was a marvelous engine for doing violence to the spirit of thousands of laws without actually running afoul of so much as a city ordinance.

Noel Constant was so impressed by this monument to hypocrisy and sharp practice that he wanted to buy stock in it without even referring to his Bible.

"Mr. Constant, sir," said young Fern, "don't you understand? Magnum Opus is you, with you as chairman of the board, with me as president.

"Mr. Constant," he said, "right now you're as easy for the Bureau of Internal Revenue to watch as a man on a street corner selling apples and pears. But just imagine how hard you would be to watch if you had a whole office building jammed to the rafters with industrial bureaucrats—men who lose things and use the wrong forms and create new forms and demand everything in quintuplicate, and who understand perhaps a third of what is said to them; who habitually give misleading answers in order to gain time in which to think, who make decisions only when forced to, and who then cover their tracks; who make perfectly honest mistakes in addition and subtraction, who call meetings whenever they feel lonely, who write memos whenever they feel unloved; men who never throw anything away unless they think it could get them fired. A single industrial bureaucrat, if he is sufficiently vital and nervous, should be able to create a ton of meaningless papers a year for the Bureau of Internal Revenue to examine. In the Magnum Opus Building, we will have thousands of them! And you and I can have the top two stories, and you can go on keeping track of what's really going on the way you do now." He looked around the room. "How do you keep track now, by the way—writing with a burnt match on the margins of a telephone directory?"

"In my head," said Noel Constant.

"There is one more advantage I have yet to point out," said Fern. "Some day your luck is going to run out. And then you're going to need the shrewdest, most thorough manager you can hire—or you'll crash all the way back to pots and pans."

"You're hired," said Noel Constant, father of Malachi.

"Now, where should we erect the building?" said Fern.

"I own this hotel, and this hotel owns the lot across the street," said Noel Constant. "Build it on the lot across the street." He held up an index finger as crooked as a crankshaft. "There's just one thing—"

"Yes, sir?" said Fern.

"I'm not moving into it," said Noel Constant. "I'm staying right here."

Those who want more-detailed histories of Magnum Opus, Inc., can go to their public libraries and ask for either Lavina Waters' romantic *Too Wild a Dream?* or Crowther Gomburg's harsh *Primordial Scales.*

Miss Waters' volume, while fuddled as to business details, contains the better account of the chambermaid Florence Whitehill's discovery that she was pregnant by Noel Constant, and her discovery that Noel Constant was a multi-multi-millionaire.

Noel Constant married the chambermaid, gave her a mansion and a checking account with a million dollars in it. He told her to name the child Malachi if it was a boy, and Prudence if it was a girl. He asked her to please keep coming to see him once every ten days in Room 223 of the Wilburhampton Hotel, but not to bring the baby.

Gomburg's book, while first-rate on business details, suffers from Gomburg's central thesis, to the effect that Magnum Opus was a product of a complex of inabilities to love. Reading between the lines of Gomburg's book, it is increasingly clear that Gomburg is himself unloved and unable to love.

Neither Miss Waters nor Gomburg, incidentally, discovered Noel Constant's investment method. Ransom K. Fern never discovered it either, though he tried hard enough.

The only person Noel Constant ever told was his son, Malachi, on Malachi's twenty-first birthday. That birthday party of two took place in Room 223 of the Wilburhampton. It was the first time father and son had ever met.

Malachi had come to see Noel by invitation.

Human emotions being what they are, young Malachi Constant paid more attention to a detail in the room's furnishings than he did to the secret of how to make millions or even billions of dollars.

The money-making secret was so simple-minded to begin with, that it didn't require much attention. The most complicated part of it had to do with the manner in which young Malachi was to pick up the torch of Magnum Opus when Noel had, at long last, laid it down. Young Malachi was to ask Ransom K. Fern for a chronological list of the investments of Magnum Opus, and, reading down the margin, young Malachi would learn just how far old Noel had gone in the Bible, and where young Malachi should begin.

The detail in the furnishings of Room 223 that interested young Malachi so was a photograph of himself. It was a photograph of himself at the age of three—a photograph of a sweet, pleasant, game little boy on an ocean beach.

It was thumbtacked to the wall.

It was the only picture in the room.

Old Noel saw young Malachi looking at the picture, and was confused and embarrassed by the whole thing about fathers and sons. He ransacked his mind for something good to say, and found almost nothing.

"My father gave me only two pieces of advice," he said, "and only one of them has stood the test of time. They were: 'Don't touch your principal,' and 'Keep the liquor bottle out of the bedroom.'" His embarrassment and confusion were now too great to be borne. "Good-by," he said abruptly.

"Good-by?" said young Malachi, startled. He moved toward the door.

"Keep the liquor bottle out of the bedroom," said the old man, and he turned his back.

"Yes, sir, I will," said young Malachi. "Good-by, sir," he said, and he left.

That was the first and last time that Malachi Constant ever saw his father.

His father lived for five more years, and the Bible never played him false.

Noel Constant died just as he reached the end of this sentence: "And God made two great lights: the greater light to rule the day, and the lesser light to rule the night: he made the stars also."

His last investment was in Sonnyboy Oil at 17¼.

The son took over where the father had left off, though Malachi Constant did not move into Room 223 in the Wilburhampton.

And, for five years, the luck of the son was as sensational as the luck of the father had been.

And now, suddenly, Magnum Opus lay in ruins.

There in his office, with the floating furniture and the grass carpet, Malachi Constant still could not believe that his luck had run out.

"Nothing left?" he said faintly. He managed to smile at Ransom K. Fern. "Come on, guy—I mean there's got to be something left."

"I thought so, too, at ten o'clock this morning," said Fern. "I was congratulating myself on having buttressed Magnum Opus against any conceivable blow. We were weathering the depression quite nicely—yes, and your mistakes, too.

"And then, at ten-fifteen, I was visited by a lawyer who was apparently at your party last night. You, apparently, were giving away oil wells last night, and the lawyer was thoughtful enough to draw up documents which, if signed by you, would be binding. They were signed by you. You gave away five hundred and thirty-one producing oil wells last night, which wiped out Fandango Petroleum.

"At eleven," said Fern, "the President of the United States announced that Galactic Spacecraft, which we had sold, was receiving a three-billion contract for the New Age of Space.

"At eleven-thirty," said Fern, "I was given a copy of *The Journal of the American Medical Association*, which was marked by our public relations director, 'FYI.' These three letters, as you would know if you had ever spent any time in your office, mean 'for your information.' I turned to the page referred to, and learned, for my information, that MoonMist Cigarettes were not *a* cause but the *principal* cause of sterility in both sexes wherever MoonMist cigarettes were sold. This fact was discovered not by human beings but by a computing machine. Whenever data about cigarette smoking was fed into it, the machine grew tremendously excited, and no one could figure out why. The machine was obviously trying to tell its operators something. It did everything it could to express itself, and finally managed to get its operators to ask it the right questions.

"The right questions had to do with the relationship of MoonMist Cigarettes to human reproduction. The relationship was this:

"People who smoked MoonMist Cigarettes couldn't have children, even if they wanted them," said Fern.

"Doubtless," said Fern, "there are gigolos and party girls and New Yorkers who are grateful for this relief from biology. In the opinion of the Legal Department of Magnum Opus, before that department was liquidated, however, there are several million persons who can sue successfully—on the grounds that MoonMist Cigarettes did them out of something rather valuable. Pleasure in depth, indeed.

"There are approximately ten million ex-smokers of MoonMist in this country," said Fern, "all sterile. If one in ten sues you for damages beyond price, sues you for the modest sum of five thousand dollars—the bill will be five billion dollars, excluding legal fees. And you haven't got five billion dollars. Since the stock-market crash and your acquisition of such properties as American Levitation, you aren't worth even five hundred million.

"MoonMist Tobacco," said Fern, "that's you. Magnum Opus," said Fern, "that's you, too. All the things you are are going to be sued and sued successfully. And, while the litigants may not be able to get blood from turnips, they can certainly ruin the turnips in the process of trying."

Fern bowed again. "I now perform my last official duty, which is to inform you that your father wrote you a letter which was to be given to you only if your luck turned for the worse. My instructions were to place that letter under the pillow in Room 223 in the Wilburhampton, if your luck ever really turned sour. I placed the letter under the pillow an hour ago.

"And I will now, as an humble and loyal corporate servant, ask you for one small favor," said Fern. "If the letter seems to cast the vaguest light on what life might be about, I would appreciate your telephoning me at home."

Ransom K. Fern saluted by touching the shaft of his cane to his Homburg hat. "Good-by, Mr. Magnum Opus, Jr. Good-by."

The Wilburhampton Hotel was a frumpish, three-story Tudor structure across the street from the Magnum Opus Building, standing in relation to that building like an unmade bed at the feet of the Archangel Gabriel. Pine slats were tacked to the stucco exterior of the hotel, simulating half-timbered construction. The backbone of the roof had been broken intentionally, simulating great age. The eaves were plump and low, tucked under, simulated thatch. The windows were tiny, with diamond-shaped panes.

The hotel's small cocktail lounge was known as the Hear Ye Room.

In the Hear Ye Room were three people—a bartender and two customers. The two customers were a thin woman and a fat man—both seemingly old. Nobody in the Wilburhampton had ever seen them before, but it already seemed as though they had been sitting in the Hear Ye Room for years. Their protective coloration was perfect, for they looked half-timbered and broken-backed and thatched and little-windowed, too.

They claimed to be pensioned-off teachers from the same high school in the Middle West. The fat man introduced himself as George M. Helmholtz, a former bandmaster. The thin woman introduced herself as Roberta Wiley, a former teacher of algebra.

They had obviously discovered the consolations of alcohol and cynicism late in life. They never ordered the same drink twice, were avid to know what was in this bottle and what was in that one—to know what a golden dawn punch was, and a Helen Twelvetrees, and a *pluie d'or*, and a merry widow fizz.

The bartender knew they weren't alcoholics. He was familiar with the type, and loved the type: they were simply two *Saturday Evening Post* characters at the end of the road.

When they weren't asking questions about the different things to drink, they were indistinguishable from millions of other American barflies on the first day of the New Age of Space. They sat solidly on their barstools, staring straight ahead at the ranks of bottles. Their lips moved constantly—experimenting dismayingly with irrelevant grins and grimaces and sneers.

Evangelist Bobby Denton's image of Earth as God's space ship was an apt one—particularly with reference to barflies. Helmholtz and Miss Wiley were behaving like pilot and co-pilot of an enormously pointless voyage through space that was expected to take forever. It was easy to believe that they had begun the voyage nattily, flushed with youth and technical training, and that the bottles before them were the instruments they had been watching for years and years and years.

It was easy to believe that each day had found the space boy and the space girl microscopically more slovenly than the day before, until now, when they were the shame of the Pan-Galactic Space Service.

Two buttons on Helmholtz's fly were open. There was shaving cream in his left ear. His socks did not match.

Miss Wiley was a crazy-looking little old lady with a lantern jaw. She wore a frizzy black wig that looked as though it had been nailed to a farmer's barn door for years.

"I see where the President has ordered a whole brand-new Age of Space to begin, to see if that won't help the unemployment picture some," said the bartender.

"Uh, huh," said Helmholtz and Miss Wiley simultaneously.

Only an observant and suspicious person would have noticed a false note in the behavior of the two: Helmholtz and Miss Wiley were *too interested in time.* For people who had nothing much to do and nowhere much to go, they were extraordinarily interested in their watches—Miss Wiley in her mannish wrist watch, Mr. Helmholtz in his gold pocket watch.

The truth of the matter was that Helmholtz and Miss Wiley weren't retired school teachers at all. They were both males, both masters of disguise. They were crack agents for the Army of Mars, the eyes and ears for a Martian press gang that hovered in a flying saucer two hundred miles overhead.

Malachi Constant didn't know it, but they were waiting for him.

Helmholtz and Wiley did not accost Malachi Constant when he crossed the street to the Wilburhampton. They gave no sign that he mattered to them. They let him cross the lobby and board the elevator without giving him a glance.

They did, however, glance at their watches again—and an observant and suspicious person would have noticed that Miss Wiley pressed a button on her watch, starting a stopwatch hand on its twitching rounds.

Helmholtz and Miss Wiley were not about to use violence on Malachi Constant. They had never used violence on anyone, and had still recruited fourteen thousand persons for Mars.

Their usual technique was to dress like civil engineers and offer not-quite-bright men and women nine dollars an hour, tax free, plus food and shelter and transportation, to work on a secret Government project in a remote part of the world for three years. It was a joke between Helmholtz and Miss Wiley that they had never specified *what* government was organizing the project, and that no recruit had ever thought to ask.

Ninety-nine per cent of the recruits were given amnesia upon arriving on Mars. Their memories were cleaned out by mental-health experts, and Martian surgeons installed radio antennas in their skulls in order that the recruits might be radio-controlled.

And then the recruits were given new names in the most

haphazard fashion, and were assigned to the factories, the construction gangs, the administrative staff, or to the Army of Mars.

The few recruits who were not treated in this way were those who demonstrated ardently that they would serve Mars heroically without being doctored at all. Those lucky few were welcomed into the secret circle of those in command.

Secret agents Helmholtz and Wiley belonged to this circle. They were in full possession of their memories, and they were not radio-controlled. They adored their work, just as they were.

"What's that there Slivovitz like?" Helmholtz asked the bartender, squinting at a dusty bottle on the bottom row. He had just finished a sloe gin rickey.

"I didn't even know we had it," said the bartender. He put the bottle on the bar, tilting it away from himself so he could read the label. "Prune brandy," he said.

"Believe I'll try that next," said Helmholtz.

Ever since the death of Noel Constant, Room 223 in the Wilburhampton had been left empty—as a memorial.

Malachi Constant now let himself into Room 223. He had not been in the room since the death of his father. He closed the door behind him, and found the letter under the pillow.

Nothing in the room had been changed but the linen. The picture of Malachi as a little boy on the beach was still the only picture on the wall.

The letter said:

Dear Son: Something big and bad has happened to you or you wouldn't be reading this letter. I am writing this letter to tell you to calm down about the bad things and kind of look around and see if something good or something important anyway happened on account of we got so rich and then lost the boodle again. What I want you to try and find out is, is there anything special going on or is it all just as crazy as it looked to me?

If I wasn't a very good father or a very good anything that was because I was as good as dead for a long time before I died. Nobody loved me and I wasn't very good at anything and I couldn't find any hobbies I liked and I was sick and tired of selling pots and pans and watching television so I was as good as dead and I was too far gone to ever come back.

That is when I started the business with the Bible and you know what happened after that. It looked as though somebody or something wanted me to own the whole planet even though I was as good as dead. I kept my eyes open for some kind of signal that would tell me what it was all about but there wasn't any signal. I just went on getting richer and richer.

And then your mother sent me that picture of you on the beach and the way you looked at me out of that picture made me think maybe you were what all the big money buildup was for. I decided I would die without ever seeing any sense to it and maybe you would be the one who would all of a sudden see everything clear as a bell. I tell you even a half-dead man hates to be alive and not be able to see any sense to it.

The reason I told Ransom K. Fern to give you this letter only if your luck turned bad is that nobody thinks or notices anything as long as his luck is good. Why should he?

So have a look around for me, boy. And if you go broke and somebody comes along with a crazy proposition my advice is to take it. You might just learn something when you're in a mood to learn something. The only thing I ever learned was that some people are lucky and other people aren't and not even a graduate of the Harvard Business School can say why.

Yours truly—your Pa

There was a knock on the door of Room 223.

The door opened before Constant could reply to the knock.

Helmholtz and Miss Wiley let themselves in. They entered at precisely the right instant, having been advised by their superiors as to when, to the second, Malachi Constant would finish the letter. They had been told, too, precisely what to say to him.

Miss Wiley removed her wig, revealing herself to be a scrawny man, and Helmholtz composed his features to reveal that he was fearless and used to command.

"Mr. Constant," said Helmholtz, "I am here to inform you that the planet Mars is not only populated, but populated by a large and efficient and military and industrial society. It has been recruited from Earth, with the recruits being transferred to Mars by flying saucer. We are now prepared to offer you a direct lieutenant-colonelcy in the Army of Mars.

"Your situation on Earth is hopeless. Your wife is a beast. Moreover, our intelligence informs us that here on Earth you will not only be made penniless by civil suits, but that you will be imprisoned for criminal negligence as well.

"In addition to a pay scale and privileges well above those

accorded lieutenant-colonels in Earthling armies, we can offer you immunity from all Earthling legal harassment, and an opportunity to see a new and interesting planet, and an opportunity to think about your native planet from a fresh and beautifully detached viewpoint."

"If you accept the commission," said Miss Wiley, "raise your left hand and repeat after me—"

On the following day, Malachi Constant's helicopter was found empty in the middle of the Mojave Desert. The footprints of a man led away from it for a distance of forty feet, then stopped.

It was as though Malachi Constant had walked forty feet, and had then dissolved into thin air.

On the following Tuesday, the space ship known as *The Whale* was rechristened *The Rumfoord* and was readied for firing.

Beatrice Rumfoord smugly watched the ceremonies on a television set two thousand miles away. She was still in Newport. *The Rumfoord* was going to be fired in exactly one minute. If destiny was going to get Beatrice Rumfoord on board, it was going to have to do it in one hell of a hurry.

Beatrice was feeling marvelous. She had proved so many good things. She had proved that she was mistress of her own fate, could say *no* whenever she pleased—and make it stick. She had proved that her husband's omniscient bullying was all a bluff—that he wasn't much better at forecasts than the United States Weather Bureau.

She had, moreover, worked out a plan that would enable her to live in modest comfort for the rest of her days, and would, at the same time, give her husband the treatment he deserved. The next time he materialized, he would find the estate teeming with gawkers. Beatrice was going to charge them five dollars a head to come in through the Alice-in-Wonderland door.

This was no pipe dream. She had discussed it with two supposed representatives of the mortgage-holders on the estate—and they were enthusiastic.

They were with her now, watching the preparations for the firing of *The Rumfoord* on television. The television set was in the same room with the huge painting of Beatrice as an immaculate little girl in white, with a white pony all her own. Beatrice smiled up at the painting. The little girl had yet to get the least bit soiled.

The television announcer now began the last minute's countdown for the firing of *The Rumfoord*.

During the countdown, Beatrice's mood was birdlike. She could not sit still and she could not keep quiet. Her restlessness was a result of happiness, not of suspense. It was a matter of indifference to her whether *The Rumfoord* was a fizzle or not.

Her two visitors, on the other hand, seemed to take the firing very seriously—seemed to be praying for the success of the shot. They were a man and a woman, a Mr. George M. Helmholtz and his secretary, a Miss Roberta Wiley. Miss Wiley was a funny-looking little old thing, but very alert and witty.

The rocket went up with a roar.

It was a flawless shot.

Helmholtz sat back and heaved a manly sigh of relief. Then he smiled and beat his thick thighs exuberantly. "By glory—" he said, "I'm proud to be an American—and proud to be living in the time I do."

"Would you like something to drink?" said Beatrice.

"Thank you very much—" said Helmholtz, "but I daren't mix business with pleasure."

"Isn't the business all over?" said Beatrice. "Haven't we discussed everything?"

"Well—Miss Wiley and I had hoped to take an inventory of the larger buildings on the grounds," said Helmholtz, "but I'm afraid it's gotten quite dark. Are there floodlights?"

Beatrice shook her head. "Sorry," she said.

"Perhaps you have a powerful flashlight?" said Helmholtz.

"I can probably get you a flashlight," said Beatrice, "but I don't think it's really necessary for you to go out there. I can tell you what all the buildings are." She rang for the butler, told him to bring a flashlight. "There's the tennis house, the greenhouse, the gardener's cottage, what used to be the gate house, the carriage house, the guest house, the tool shed, the bath house, the kennel, and the old water tower."

"Which one is the new one?" said Helmholtz.

"The *new* one?" said Beatrice.

The butler returned with a flashlight, which Beatrice gave to Helmholtz.

"The metal one," said Miss Wiley.

"Metal?" said Beatrice puzzled. "There aren't any *metal* buildings. Maybe some of the weathered shingles have kind of a silvery look." She frowned. "Did somebody tell you there was a metal building here?"

"We saw it when we came in," said Helmholtz.

"Right by the path—in the undergrowth near the fountain," said Miss Wiley.

"I can't imagine," said Beatrice.

"Could we go out and have a look?" said Helmholtz.

"Yes—of course," said Beatrice, rising.

The party of three crossed the zodiac on the foyer floor, moved into the balmy dark.

The flashlight beam danced before them.

"Really—" said Beatrice, "I'm as curious to find out what it is as you are."

"It looks like kind of a prefabricated thing made out of aluminum," said Miss Wiley.

"It looks like a mushroom-shaped water tank or something," said Helmholtz, "only it is squatting right on the ground."

"Really?" said Beatrice.

"You know what I said it was, don't you?" said Miss Wiley.

"No—" said Beatrice, "what *did* you say it was?"

"I have to whisper," said Miss Wiley playfully, "or somebody will want to lock me up in the crazy house." She put her hand to her mouth, directing her loud whisper to Beatrice. "Flying saucer," she said.

CHAPTER FOUR

Tent Rentals

Rented a tent, a tent, a tent;
Rented a tent, a tent, a tent.
Rented a tent!
Rented a tent!
Rented a, rented a tent.

—SNARE DRUM ON MARS

THE MEN had marched to the parade ground to the sound of a snare drum. The snare drum had this to say to them:

Rented a tent, a tent, a tent;
Rented a tent, a tent, a tent.
Rented a tent!
Rented a tent!
Rented a, rented a tent.

They were an infantry division of ten thousand men, formed in a hollow square on a natural parade ground of solid iron one mile thick. The soldiers stood at attention on orange rust. They shivered rigidly, being as much like iron as they could be —both officers and men. Their uniforms were a rough-textured, frosty green—the color of lichens.

The army had come to attention in utter silence. No audible or visible signal had been given. They had come to attention as a man, as though through a stupendous coincidence.

The third man in the second squad of the first platoon of the second company of the third battalion of the second regiment of the First Martian Assault Infantry Division was a private who had been broken from lieutenant-colonel three years before. He had been on Mars for eight years.

When a man in a modern army is broken from field grade to private, it is likely that he will be old for a private, and that his comrades in arms, once they get used to the fact that he isn't an officer any more, will, out of respect for his failing legs, eyes, and wind, call him something like *Pops*, or *Gramps*, or *Unk*.

The third man in the second squad of the first platoon of the second company in the third battalion of the second regiment of the First Martian Assault Infantry Division was called *Unk.* Unk was forty years old. Unk was a well-made man—a light heavyweight, dark-skinned, with poet's lips, with soft brown eyes in the shaded caves of a Cro-Magnon brow ridge. Incipient baldness had isolated a dramatic scalplock.

An illustrative anecdote about Unk:

One time, when Unk's platoon was taking a shower, Henry Brackman, Unk's platoon sergeant, asked a sergeant from another regiment to pick out the best soldier in the platoon. The visiting sergeant, without any hesitation, picked Unk, because Unk was a compact, nicely muscled, intelligent man among boys.

Brackman rolled his eyes. "Jesus—you'd think so, wouldn't you?" he said. "That's the platoon f–kup."

"You kidding me?" said the visiting sergeant.

"Hell no, I ain't kidding you," said Brackman. "Look at him —been standing there for ten minutes, and hasn't touched a piece of soap yet. Unk! Wake up, Unk!"

Unk shuddered, stopped dreaming under the tepid drizzle of the shower head. He looked questioningly at Brackman, bleakly co-operative.

"Use some soap, Unk!" said Brackman. "For Chrissakes, use some soap!"

Now, on the iron parade ground, Unk stood at attention in the hollow square like all the rest.

In the middle of the hollow square was a stone post with iron rings fixed to it. Chains had been drawn rattling through the rings—had been drawn tight around a red-haired soldier standing against a post. The soldier was a clean soldier—but he was not a neat soldier, for all the badges and decorations had been stripped off his uniform, and he had no belt, no necktie, no snow-white puttees.

Everybody else, including Unk, was all spiffed up. Everybody else looked very nice indeed.

Something painful was going to happen to the man at the stake—something from which the man would want to escape very much, something from which he was not going to escape, because of the chains.

And all the soldiers were going to watch.

The event was being given great importance.

Even the man at the stake was standing at attention, being the best soldier he knew how to be, under the circumstances.

Again—no audible or visible order was given, but the ten thousand soldiers executed the movement of *parade rest* as a man.

So did the man at the stake.

Then the soldiers relaxed in ranks, as though given the order *at ease.* Their obligations under this order were to relax, but to keep their feet in place, and to keep silent. The soldiers were free to think a little now, and to look around and to send messages with their eyes, if they had messages and could find receivers.

The man at the stake tugged against his chains, craned his neck to judge the height of the stake to which he was chained. It was as though he thought he might escape by use of the scientific method, if only he could find out how high the stake was and what it was made of.

The stake was nineteen feet, six and five thirty-seconds inches high, not counting the twelve feet, two and one-eighth inches of it embedded in the iron. The stake had a mean diameter of two feet, five and eleven thirty-seconds inches, varying from this mean, however, by as much as seven and one thirty-second inches. The stake was composed of quartz, alkali, feldspar, mica, and traces of tourmaline and hornblende. For the information of the man at the stake: He was one hundred and forty-two million, three hundred and forty-six thousand, nine hundred and eleven miles from the Sun, and help was not on its way.

The red-haired man at the stake made no sound, because soldiers at ease were not permitted to make sounds. He sent a message with his eyes, however, to the effect that he would like to scream. He sent the message to anyone whose eyes would meet his. He was hoping to get the message to one person in particular, to his best friend—to Unk. He was looking for Unk.

He couldn't find Unk's face.

If he had found Unk's face, there wouldn't have been any blooming of recognition and pity on Unk's face. Unk had just come out of the base hospital, where he had been treated for mental illness, and Unk's mind was almost a blank. Unk didn't recognize his best friend at the stake. Unk didn't recognize anybody. Unk wouldn't have even known his own name was Unk, wouldn't even have known he was a soldier, if they hadn't told him so when they discharged him from the hospital.

He had gone straight from the hospital to the formation he was in now.

At the hospital they told him again and again and again that he was the best soldier in the best squad in the best platoon in the best company in the best battalion in the best regiment in the best division in the best army.

Unk guessed that was something to be proud of.

At the hospital they told him he had been a pretty sick boy, but he was fully recovered now.

That seemed like good news.

At the hospital they told him what his sergeant's name was, and what a sergeant was, and what all the symbols of ranks and grades and specialties were.

They had blanked out so much of Unk's memory that they even had to teach him the foot movements and the manual of arms all over again.

At the hospital they even had to explain to Unk what Combat Respiratory Rations or CRR's or goofballs were—had to tell him to take one every six hours or suffocate. These were oxygen pills that made up for the fact that there wasn't any oxygen in the Martian atmosphere.

At the hospital they even had to explain to Unk that there was a radio antenna under the crown of his skull, and that it would hurt him whenever he did something a good soldier wouldn't ever do. The antenna also would give him orders and furnish drum music to march to. They said that not just Unk but everybody had an antenna like that—doctors and nurses and four-star generals included. It was a very democratic army, they said.

Unk guessed that was a good way for an army to be.

At the hospital they gave Unk a small sample of the pain his antenna would stick him with if he ever did anything wrong.

The pain was horrible.

Unk was bound to admit that a soldier would be crazy not to do his duty at all times.

At the hospital they had said the most important rule of all was this one: Always obey a direct order without a moment's hesitation.

Standing there in formation on the iron parade ground, Unk realized that he had a lot to relearn. At the hospital they hadn't taught him everything there was to know about living.

The antenna in his head brought him to attention again and his mind went blank. Then the antenna put Unk at parade rest again, then at attention again, then made him give a rifle salute, then put him at ease again.

His thinking began again. He caught another glimpse of the world around him.

Life was like that, Unk told himself tentatively—blanks and glimpses, and now and then maybe that awful flash of pain for doing something wrong.

A small, low-flying, fast-flying moon sailed in the violet sky overhead. Unk didn't know why he thought so, but he thought the moon was moving too fast. It didn't seem right. And the sky, he thought, should be blue instead of violet.

Unk felt cold, too, and he longed for more warmth. The unending cold seemed as wrong, as unfair, somehow, as the fast moon and the violet sky.

Unk's divisional commander was now talking to Unk's regimental commander. Unk's regimental commander spoke to Unk's battalion commander. Unk's battalion commander spoke to Unk's company commander. Unk's company commander spoke to Unk's platoon leader, who was Sergeant Brackman.

Brackman came up to Unk and ordered him to march up to the man at the stake in a military manner and strangle him until he was dead.

Brackman told Unk it was a direct order.

So Unk did it.

He marched up to the man at the stake. He marched in time to the dry, tinny music of one snare drum. The sound of the snare drum was really just in his head, coming from his antenna:

Rented a tent, a tent, a tent;
Rented a tent, a tent, a tent.
Rented a tent!
Rented a tent!
Rented a, rented a tent.

When Unk got to the man at the stake, Unk hesitated for just a second—because the red-haired man at the stake looked so unhappy. Then there was a tiny warning pain in Unk's head, like the first deep nip of a dentist's drill.

Unk put his thumbs on the red-haired man's windpipe, and the pain stopped right away. Unk didn't press with his thumbs, because the man was trying to tell him something. Unk was puzzled by the man's silence—and then realized that the man's antenna must be keeping him silent, just as antennas were keeping all of the soldiers silent.

Heroically, the man at the stake now overcame the will of his antenna, spoke rapidly, writhingly. "Unk . . . Unk . . . Unk . . ." he said, and the spasms of the fight between his own will and the will of the antenna made him repeat the name idiotically. "*Blue stone, Unk*," he said. "*Barrack twelve . . . letter*."

The warning pain nagged in Unk's head again. Dutifully, Unk strangled the man at the stake—choked him until the man's face was purple and his tongue stuck out.

Unk stepped back, came to attention, did a smart about-face and returned to his place in ranks—again accompanied by the snare drum in his head:

Rented a tent, a tent, a tent;
Rented a tent, a tent, a tent.
Rented a tent!
Rented a tent!
Rented a, rented a tent.

Sergeant Brackman nodded at Unk, winked affectionately.

Again the ten thousand came to attention.

Horribly, the dead man at the stake struggled to come to attention, too, rattling his chains. He failed—failed to be a perfect soldier—not because he didn't want to be one but because he was dead.

Now the great formation broke up into rectangular components. These marched mindlessly away, each man hearing a snare drum in his head. An observer would have heard nothing but the tread of boots.

An observer would have been at a loss as to who was really

in charge, since even the generals moved like marionettes, keeping time to the idiotic words:

Rented a tent, a tent, a tent;
Rented a tent, a tent, a tent.
Rented a tent!
Rented a tent!
Rented a, rented a tent.

CHAPTER FIVE

Letter from an Unknown Hero

"We can make the center of a man's memory virtually as sterile as a scalpel fresh from the autoclave. But grains of new experience begin to accumulate on it at once. These grains in turn form themselves into patterns not necessarily favorable to military thinking. Unfortunately, this problem of recontamination seems insoluble."

—DR. MORRIS N. CASTLE,
Director of Mental Health, Mars

UNK'S FORMATION halted before a granite barrack, before a barrack in a perspective of thousands, a perspective that ran to seeming infinity on the iron plain. Before every tenth barrack was a flagpole with a banner snapping in the keen wind.

The banners were all different.

The banner that fluttered like a guardian angel over Unk's company area was very gay—red and white stripes, and many white stars on a field of blue. It was Old Glory, the flag of the United States of America on Earth.

Down the line was the red banner of the Union of Soviet Socialist Republics.

Past that was a wonderful green, orange, yellow, and purple banner, showing a lion holding a sword. It was the flag of Ceylon.

And past that was a red ball on a white field, the flag of Japan.

The banners signified the countries that the various Martian units would attack and paralyze when the war between Mars and Earth began.

Unk saw no banners until his antenna let his shoulders sag, let his joints loosen—let him fall out. He gawked at the long perspective of barracks and flagpoles. The barrack before which he stood had a large number painted over the door. The number was 576.

Some part of Unk found the number fascinating, made Unk

study it. Then he remembered the execution—remembered that the red-headed man he had killed had told him something about a blue stone and barrack twelve.

Inside barrack 576, Unk cleaned his rifle, found it an extremely pleasant thing to do. He found, moreover, that he still knew how to take the weapon apart. That much of his memory, at any rate, had not been wiped out at the hospital. It made him furtively happy to suspect that there were probably other parts of his memory that had been missed as well. Why this suspicion should make him furtively happy he didn't know.

He swabbed away at his rifle's bore. His weapon was an 11-millimeter German Mauser, single shot, a type of rifle that made its reputation when used by the Spaniards in the Earthling Spanish-American War. All of the Martian Army's rifles were of about the same vintage. Martian agents, working quietly on Earth, had been able to buy huge quantities of Mausers and British Enfields and American Springfields for next to nothing.

Unk's squadmates were swabbing their bores, too. The oil smelled good, and the oily patches, twisting through the rifling, resisted the thrust of the cleaning rod just enough to be interesting. There was hardly any talk.

No one seemed to have taken particular notice of the execution. If there had been a lesson in the execution for Unk's squadmates, they were finding the lesson as digestible as Pablum.

There had been only one comment on Unk's participation in the execution, and that had come from Sergeant Brackman. "You done all right, Unk," said Brackman.

"Thanks," said Unk.

"This man done all right, didn't he?" Brackman asked Unk's squadmates.

There had been some nods, but Unk had the impression that his squadmates would have nodded in response to any positive question, would have shaken their heads in response to any negative one.

Unk withdrew the rod and patch, slipped his thumb under the open breech, caught the sunlight on his oily thumbnail. The thumbnail sent the sunlight up the bore. Unk put his eye to the muzzle and was thrilled by perfect beauty. He could have stared happily at the immaculate spiral of the rifling for hours, dreaming of the happy land whose round gate he saw at the other end of the bore. The pink under his oily thumbnail at the far end of the barrel made that far end seem a rosy paradise indeed. Some day he was going to crawl down the barrel to that paradise.

It would be warm there—and there would be only one moon, Unk thought, and the moon would be fat, stately, and slow. Something else about the pink paradise at the end of the barrel came to Unk, and Unk was puzzled by the clarity of the vision. There were three beautiful women in that paradise, and Unk knew exactly what they looked like! One was white, one was gold, and one was brown. The golden girl was smoking a cigarette in Unk's vision. Unk was further surprised to find that he even knew what kind of cigarette the golden girl was smoking.

It was a MoonMist Cigarette.

"Sell MoonMist," Unk said out loud. It felt good to say that —felt authoritative, shrewd.

"Huh?" said a young colored soldier, cleaning his rifle next to Unk. "What's that you say, Unk?" he said. He was twenty-three years old. His name was stitched in yellow on a black patch over his left breast pocket.

Boaz was his name.

If suspicions had been permitted in the Army of Mars, Boaz would have been a person to suspect. His rank was only Private, First Class, but his uniform, though regulation lichen green, was made of far finer stuff, and was much better tailored than the uniform of anyone around him—including the uniform of Sergeant Brackman.

Everyone else's uniform was coarse, scratchy—held together by clumsy stitches of thick thread. And everyone else's uniform looked good only when the wearer stood at attention. In any other position, an ordinary soldier found that his uniform tended to bunch and crackle, as though made of paper.

Boaz's uniform followed his every movement with silken grace. The stitches were numerous and tiny. And most puzzling of all: Boaz's shoes had a deep, rich, ruby luster—a luster that other soldiers could not achieve no matter how much they might polish their shoes. Unlike the shoes of anyone else in the company area, the shoes of Boaz were genuine leather from Earth.

"You say sell something, Unk?" said Boaz.

"Dump MoonMist. Get rid of it," murmured Unk. The words made no sense to him. He had let them out simply because they had wanted out so badly. "Sell," he said.

Boaz smiled—ruefully amused. "Sell it, eh?" he said. "O.K., Unk—we sell it." He raised an eyebrow. "What we gonna sell, Unk?" There was something particularly bright and piercing about the pupils of his eyes.

Unk found this yellow brightness, this sharpness of Boaz's eyes disquieting—increasingly so, as Boaz continued to stare. Unk looked away, looked by chance into the eyes of some of his other squadmates—found their eyes to be uniformly dull. Even the eyes of Sergeant Brackman were dull.

Boaz's eyes continued to bite into Unk. Unk felt compelled to meet their gaze again. The pupils were seeming diamonds.

"You don't remember me, Unk?" said Boaz.

The question alarmed Unk. For some reason, it was important that he not remember Boaz. He was grateful that he really didn't remember him.

"Boaz, Unk," said the colored man. "I'm Boaz."

Unk nodded. "How do you do?" he said.

"Oh—I don't do what you'd call real bad," said Boaz. He shook his head. "You don't remember nothing about me, Unk?"

"No," said Unk. His memory was nagging him a little now—telling him that he might remember something about Boaz, if he tried as hard as he could. He shushed his memory. "Sorry—" said Unk. "My mind's a blank."

"You and me—we're buddies," said Boaz. "Boaz and Unk."

"Um," said Unk.

"You remember what the buddy system is, Unk?" said Boaz.

"No," said Unk.

"Ever' man in ever' squad," said Boaz, "he got a buddy. Buddies share the same foxhole, stick right close to each other in attacks, cover each other. One buddy get in trouble in hand-to-hand, other buddy come up and help, slip a knife in."

"Um," said Unk.

"Funny," said Boaz, "what a man'll forget in the hospital

and what he'll still remember, no matter what they do. You and me—we trained as buddies for a whole year, and you done forgot that. And then you say that thing 'bout cigarettes. What kind cigarettes, Unk?"

"I—I forget," said Unk.

"Try and remember now," said Boaz. "You had it once." He frowned and squinted, as though trying to help Unk remember. "I think it's *so* interesting what a man can remember after he's been to the hospital. Try and remember everything you can."

There was a certain effeminacy about Boaz—in the nature of a cunning bully's chucking a sissy under the chin, talking baby-talk to him.

But Boaz liked Unk—that was in his manner, too.

Unk had the eerie feeling that he and Boaz were the only real people in the stone building—that the rest were glass-eyed robots, and not very well-made robots at that. Sergeant Brackman, supposedly in command, seemed no more alert, no more responsible, no more in command than a bag of wet feathers.

"Let's hear all you can remember, Unk," wheedled Boaz. "Old buddy—" he said, "just remember all you can."

Before Unk could remember anything, the head pain that had made him get on with the execution hurt him again. The pain did not stop, however, with the warning nip. While Boaz watched expressionlessly, the pain in Unk's head became a whanging, flashing thing.

Unk stood, dropped his rifle, clawed at his head, reeled, screamed, fainted.

When Unk came to on the barrack floor, his buddy Boaz was daubing Unk's temples with a cold washrag.

Unk's squadmates stood in a circle around Unk and Boaz. The faces of the squadmates were unsurprised, unsympathetic. Their attitude was that Unk had done something stupid and unsoldierly, and so deserved what he got.

They looked as though Unk had done something as militarily stupid as silhouetting himself against the sky or cleaning a loaded weapon, as sneezing on patrol or contracting and not reporting a venereal disease, as refusing a direct order or sleeping through reveille, as being drunk on guard or drawing to an inside straight, as keeping a book or a live hand grenade in his footlocker, as asking who had started the Army anyway and why . . .

Boaz was the only one who looked sorry about what had happened to Unk. "It was all my fault, Unk," he said.

Sergeant Brackman now pushed through the circle, stood over Unk and Boaz. "Wha'd he do, Boaz?" said Brackman.

"I was kidding him, Sergeant," said Boaz earnestly. "I told him to try an' remember back as far as he could. I never dreamed he'd go and do it."

"Oughta have more sense than to kid a man just back from the hospital," said Brackman gruffly.

"Oh, I know it—I know it," said Boaz, full of remorse. "My buddy—" he said. "God *damn* me!"

"Unk," said Brackman, "didn't they tell you about remembering at the hospital?"

Unk shook his head vaguely. "Maybe," he said. "They told me a lot."

"That's the worst thing you can *do*, Unk—remembering back," said Brackman. "That's what they put you in the hospital for in the first place—on account of you remembered too much." He made cups of his stubby hands, held in them the heart-breaking problem Unk had been. "Holy smokes," he said, "you were remembering so much, Unk, you weren't worth a nickel as a soldier."

Unk sat up, laid his hand on his breast, found that the front of his blouse was wet with tears. He thought of explaining to Brackman that he hadn't really tried to remember back, that he'd known instinctively that that was a bad thing to do—but that the pain had hit him *anyway*. He didn't tell Brackman that for fear that the pain would come again.

Unk groaned and blinked away the last of the tears. He wasn't going to do anything he wasn't ordered to do.

"As for you, Boaz—" said Brackman. "I don't know but what a week's latrine duty would maybe teach you something about horseplay with people just out of the hospital."

Something formless in Unk's memory told Unk to watch the by-play between Brackman and Boaz closely. It was somehow important.

"A week, Sergeant?" said Boaz.

"Yes, by God—" said Brackman, and then he shuddered and closed his eyes. Plainly, his antenna had just given him a little stab of pain.

"A whole week, Sarge?" asked Boaz innocently.

"A day," said Brackman, and it was less a threat than a question. Again Brackman reacted to pain in his head.

"Starting when, Sarge?" asked Boaz.

Brackman fluttered his stubby hands. "Never mind," he said. He looked rattled, betrayed—haunted. He lowered his head, as though better to fight the pain if it came again. "No more horseplay, damn it," he said, his voice deep in his throat. And he hurried away, hurried into his room at the end of the barrack, slammed the door.

The company commander, a Captain Arnold Burch, came into the barrack for a surprise inspection.

Boaz was the first to see him. Boaz did what a soldier was supposed to do under such circumstances. Boaz shouted, "*A-tennnn-hut!*" Boaz did this, though he had no rank at all. It is a freak of military custom that the lowliest private can command his equals and noncommissioned superiors to attention, if he is the first to detect the presence of a commissioned officer in any roofed-over structure not in a combat area.

The antennas of the enlisted men responded instantly, straightened the men's backs, locked their joints, hauled in their guts, tucked in their butts—made their minds go blank. Unk sprang up from the floor, stood stiff and shivering.

Only one man was slow about coming to attention. That man was Boaz. And when he did come to attention, there was something insolent and loose and leering about the way he did it.

Captain Burch, finding Boaz's attitude profoundly offensive, was about to speak to Boaz about it. But the Captain no sooner got his mouth open than pain hit him between the eyes.

The captain closed his mouth without having made a sound.

Under the baleful gaze of Boaz, he came smartly to attention, did an about-face, heard a snare drum in his head, and marched out of the barrack in step with the drum.

When the captain was gone, Boaz did not put his squadmates at ease again, though it was in his power to do so. He had a small control box in his right front trouser pocket that could make his squadmates do just about anything. The box was the size of a one-pint hip flask. Like a hip flask, the box was curved to fit a body curve. Boaz chose to carry it on the hard, curved face of his thigh.

The control box had six buttons and four knobs on it. By manipulating these, Boaz could control anybody who had an antenna in his skull. Boaz could administer pain in any amount to that anybody—could bring him to attention, could make him hear a snare drum, could make him march, halt, fall in, fall out, salute, attack, retreat, hop, skip, jump. . . .

Boaz had no antenna in his own skull.

As free as it wanted to be—that's how free the free will of Boaz was.

Boaz was one of the real commanders of the Army of Mars. He was in command of one-tenth of the force that was to attack the United States of America when the attack on Earth was mounted. Down the line were units training to attack Russia, Switzerland, Japan, Australia, Mexico, China, Nepal, Uruguay. . . .

To the best of Boaz's knowledge, there were eight hundred real commanders of the Army of Mars—not one of them with an apparent rank above buck sergeant. The nominal commander of the entire Army, General of the Armies Borders M. Pulsifer, was in fact controlled at all times by his orderly, Corporal Bert Wright. Corporal Wright, the perfect orderly, carried aspirin for the General's almost chronic headaches.

The advantages of a system of secret commanders are obvious. Any rebellion within the Army of Mars would be directed against the wrong people. And, in time of war, the enemy could exterminate the entire Martian officer class without disturbing the Army of Mars in the least.

"Seven hundred and ninety-nine," said Boaz out loud, correcting his own understanding of the number of real commanders. One of the real commanders was dead, having been strangled at the stake by Unk. The strangled man had been Private Stony Stevenson, former real commander of a British attack unit. Stony had become so fascinated by Unk's struggles to understand what was going on that he had begun, unconsciously, to help Unk think.

Stevenson had suffered the ultimate humiliation for this. An antenna had been installed in his skull, and he had been forced by it to march to the stake like a good soldier—there to await murder by his protégé.

Boaz let his squadmates go on standing at attention—let them go on quivering, thinking nothing, seeing nothing. Boaz went to Unk's cot, lay down on it with his big, lustrous shoes on the brown blanket. He folded his hands behind his head—arched his body like a bow.

"Awwwww—" said Boaz, somewhere between a yawn and a groan. "Awwwww—now, men, men, men," he said, letting his mind idle. "God damn, now, men," he said. It was lazy, nonsense talk. Boaz was a little bored with his toys. It occurred to him to have them fight each other—but the penalty for doing that, if he got caught, was the same penalty Stony Stevenson had paid.

"Awwwww—now, men. Really now, men," said Boaz languidly.

"God damn it now, men," he said. "I got it *made.* You men got to admit that. Old Boaz is doing how you might say real fine."

He rolled off the bed, landed on all fours, sprang to his feet with pantherlike grace. He smiled dazzlingly. He was doing everything he could to enjoy the fortunate position in life that was his. "You boys ain't got it so bad," he said to his rigid squadmates. "You oughta see how we treat the generals, if you think you's bad off." He chuckled and cooed. "Two nights ago us real commanders got ourselves in a argument about which general could run the fastest. Next thing you know, we got all twenty-three generals out of bed, all bare-ass naked, and we lined 'em up like they was race horses, and then we put our money down and laid the odds, and then we sent them generals off like the devil was after 'em. General Stover, he done placed first, with General Harrison right behind him, and with General Mosher behind *him.* Next morning, ever' general in the Army was stiff as a board. Not one of 'em could remember a thing about the night before."

Boaz chuckled and cooed again, and then he decided that

his fortunate position in life would look a lot better if he treated it seriously—showed what a load it was, showed how honored he felt to have a load like that. He reared back judiciously, hooked his thumbs under his belt and scowled. "Oh," he said, "it ain't all play by any means." He sauntered over to Unk, stood inches away from him, looked him up and down. "Unk, boy—" he said, "I'd hate to tell you how much time I've spent thinking about you—worrying about you, Unk."

Boaz rocked on his feet. "You *will* try an' puzzle things out, won't you! You know how many times they had you in the hospital, trying to clean out that memory of yours? Seven times, Unk! You know how many times they usually have to send a man to have his memory cleaned out? Once, Unk. One time!" Boaz snapped his finger under Unk's nose. "And that does it, Unk. One time, and the man never bothers hisself about anything ever after." He shook his head wonderingly. "Not *you*, though, Unk."

Unk shuddered.

"I keeping you at attention too long, Unk?" said Boaz. He gritted his teeth. He couldn't forbear torturing Unk from time to time.

For one thing, Unk had had everything back on Earth, and Boaz had had nothing.

For another thing, Boaz was wretchedly dependent on Unk —or would be when they hit Earth. Boaz was an orphan who had been recruited when he was only fourteen—and he didn't have the haziest notion as to how to have a good time on Earth.

He was counting on Unk to show him how.

"You want to know who you are—where you come from—what you were?" said Boaz to Unk. Unk was still at attention, thinking nothing, unable to profit from whatever Boaz might tell him. Boaz wasn't talking for Unk's benefit anyway. Boaz was reassuring himself about the buddy who was going to be by his side when they hit Earth.

"Man—" said Boaz, scowling at Unk, "you are one of the luckiest men ever lived. Back there on Earth, man, you were King!"

Like most pieces of information on Mars, Boaz's pieces of

information about Unk were underdeveloped. He could not say from where, exactly, the pieces had come. He had picked them out of the general background noises of army life.

And he was too good a soldier to go around asking questions, trying to round out his knowledge.

A soldier's knowledge wasn't supposed to be round.

So that Boaz didn't really know anything about Unk except that he had been very lucky once. He embroidered on this.

"I mean—" said Boaz, "there wasn't anything you couldn't have, wasn't anything you couldn't do, wasn't no place you couldn't go!"

And while Boaz stressed the marvel of Unk's good luck on Earth, he was expressing a deep concern for another marvel—his superstitious conviction that his own luck on Earth was sure to be rotten.

Boaz now used three magical words that seemed to describe the maximum happiness a person could achieve on Earth: *Hollywood night clubs.* He had never seen Hollywood, had never seen a night club. "Man," he said, "you were in and out of Hollywood night clubs all day and all night long.

"Man," said Boaz to uncomprehending Unk, "you had everything a man needs to really lead hisself a life on Earth, and you knowed how to *do* it, too.

"Man," said Boaz to Unk, trying to conceal the pathetic formlessness of his aspirations. "We're going to go into some fine places and order us up some fine things, and circulate and carry on with some fine people, and just generally have us a good whoop-dee-doo." He seized Unk's arm, rocked him. "Buddies—that's us, buddy. Boy—we're going to be a famous pair—going everwhere, doing everthing.

" 'Here comes lucky old Unk and his buddy Boaz!' " said Boaz, saying what he hoped Earthlings would be saying after the conquest. " 'And there they go, happy as two birds!' " He chuckled and cooed about the happy, birdlike pair.

His smile withered.

His smiles never lasted very long. Somewhere deep inside Boaz was worried sick. He was worried sick about losing his job. It had never been clear to him how he had landed the job—the great privilege. He didn't even know who had given him the swell job.

Boaz didn't even know who was in command of the real commanders.

He had never received an order—not from anyone who was superior to the real commanders. Boaz based his actions, as did all the real commanders, on what could be best described as conversational tidbits—tidbits circulated on the real-commander level.

Whenever the real commanders got together late at night, the tidbits were passed around with the beer and the crackers and cheese.

There would be a tidbit, for instance, about waste in the supply rooms, and another about the desirability of soldiers' actually getting hurt and mad during ju-jitsu training, another about soldiers' shabby tendency to skip loops in lacing up their puttees. Boaz himself would pass these on, without any idea as to their point of origin—and he would base his actions on them.

The execution of Stony Stevenson by Unk had also been announced in this way. Suddenly, it had been the topic of conversation.

Suddenly, the real commanders had placed Stony under arrest.

Boaz now fingered the control box in his pocket, without actually touching a control. He took his place among the men he controlled, came to attention voluntarily, pressed a button, and relaxed as his squadmates relaxed.

He wanted a drink of hard liquor very much. And he was entitled to liquor, too, whenever he wanted it. Unlimited supplies of all kinds of liquor were flown in from Earth regularly for the real commanders. And the officers could have all the liquor they wanted, too, though they couldn't get the good stuff. What the officers drank was a lethal green liquor made locally out of fermented lichens.

But Boaz never drank. One reason he didn't drink was that he was afraid that alcohol would impair his efficiency as a soldier. Another reason he didn't drink was that he was afraid that he would forget himself and offer an enlisted man a drink.

The penalty for a real commander who offered an enlisted man an alcoholic beverage was death.

"Yes, Lord," said Boaz, adding his voice to the hubbub of the relaxing men.

•

Ten minutes later, Sergeant Brackman declared a recreation period, during which everyone was supposed to go out and play German batball, the chief sport of the Army of Mars.

Unk stole away.

Unk stole away to barrack 12 to look for the letter under the blue rock—the letter that his red-headed victim had told him about.

The barracks in the area were empty.

The banner at the head of the mast before them was thin air.

The empty barracks had been the home of a battalion of Martian Imperial Commandos. The Commandos had disappeared quietly in the dead of night a month before. They had taken off in their space ships, their faces blackened, their dog tags taped so as not to clink—their destination secret.

The Martian Imperial Commandos were experts at killing sentries with loops of piano wire.

Their secret destination was the Earthling moon. They were going to start the war there.

Unk found a big blue stone outside the furnace room of barrack twelve. The stone was a turquoise. Turquoises are very common on Mars. The turquoise Unk found was a flagstone a foot across.

Unk looked under it. He found an aluminum cylinder with a screw cap. Inside the cylinder was a very long letter written in pencil.

Unk did not know who had written it. He was in poor shape for guessing, since he knew the names of only three people—Sergeant Brackman, Boaz, and Unk.

Unk went into the furnace room and closed the door.

He was excited, though he didn't know why. He began to read by the light from the dusty window.

Dear Unk:—the letter began.

Dear Unk:—the letter began: *They aren't much, God knows—but here are the things I know for sure, and at the end you will find a list of questions you should do your best to find answers to. The questions are important. I have thought harder about them than I have about the answers I already have. That is the first thing I know for sure: (1.) If the questions don't make sense, neither will the answers.*

All the things that the writer knew for sure were numbered, as though to emphasize the painful, step-by-step nature of the game of finding things out for sure. There were one hundred and fifty-eight things the writer knew for sure. There had once been one hundred and eighty-five, but seventeen had been crossed off.

The second item was, *(2.) I am a thing called alive.*

The third was, *(3.) I am in a place called Mars.*

The fourth was, *(4.) I am in a part of a thing called an army.*

The fifth was, *(5.) The army plans to kill other things called alive in a place called Earth.*

Of the first eighty-one items, not one was crossed out. And, in the first eighty-one items, the writer progressed to subtler and subtler matters, and mistakes grew more numerous.

Boaz was explained and dismissed by the writer very early in the game.

(46.) Watch out for Boaz, Unk. He is not what he seems.

(47.) Boaz has something in his right-hand pocket that hurts people in the head when they do something Boaz doesn't like.

(48.) Some other people have things that can hurt you in the head, too. You can't tell by looking who has one, so be sweet to everybody.

(71.) Unk, old friend—almost everything I know for sure has come from fighting the pain from my antenna, said the letter to Unk. *Whenever I start to turn my head and look at something, and the pain comes, I keep turning my head anyway, because I know I am going to see something I'm not supposed to see. Whenever I ask a question, and the pain comes, I know I have asked a really good question. Then I break the question into little pieces, and I ask the pieces of the questions. Then I get answers to the pieces, and then I put the answers all together and get an answer to the big question.*

(72.) The more pain I train myself to stand, the more I learn. You are afraid of the pain now, Unk, but you won't learn anything if you don't invite the pain. And the more you learn, the gladder you will be to stand the pain.

There in the furnace room of the empty barrack, Unk laid the letter aside for a moment. He felt like crying, for the heroic writer's faith in Unk was misplaced. Unk knew he couldn't stand a fraction of the pain the writer had stood—couldn't possibly love knowledge that much.

Even the little sample twinge they had given him in the hospital had been excruciating. He gulped air now, like a fish dying on a riverbank, remembering the big pain Boaz had slammed him with in the barrack. He would rather die than risk another pain like that.

His eyes watered.

If he had tried to speak, he would have sobbed.

Poor Unk didn't want any trouble from anybody ever again. Whatever information he gained from the letter—information gained by another man's heroism—he would use to avoid any more pain.

Unk wondered if there were people who could stand more pain than others. He supposed this was the case. He supposed tearfully that he was especially sensitive in this regard. Without wishing the writer any harm, Unk wished the writer could feel, just once, the pains as Unk felt them.

Then maybe the writer would address his letters to someone else.

Unk had no way of judging the quality of the information contained in the letter. He accepted it all hungrily, uncritically. And, in accepting it, Unk gained an understanding of life that was identical with the writer's understanding of life. Unk wolfed down a philosophy.

And mixed in with the philosophy were gossip, history, astronomy, biology, theology, geography, psychology, medicine —and even a short story.

Some random examples:

Gossip: *(22.) General Borders is drunk all the time. He is so drunk he can't even tie his shoelaces so they will stay tied. Officers are as mixed up and unhappy as anybody. You used to be one, Unk, with a battalion all your own.*

History: *(26.) Everybody on Mars came from Earth. They thought they would be better off on Mars. Nobody can remember what was so bad about Earth.*

Astronomy: *(11.) Everything in the whole sky revolves around Mars once a day.*

Biology: *(58.) New people come out of women when men and women sleep together. New people hardly ever come out of women on Mars because the men and the women sleep in different places.*

Theology: *(15.) Somebody made everything for some reason.*

Geography: *(16.) Mars is round. The only city on it is called Phoebe. Nobody knows why it is called Phoebe.*

Psychology: *(103.) Unk, the big trouble with dumb bastards is that they are too dumb to believe there is such a thing as being smart.*

Medicine: *(73.) When they clean out a man's memory on this place called Mars, they don't really clean it completely. They just clean out the middle of it, sort of. They always leave a lot of stuff in the corners. There is a story around about how they tried cleaning out a few memories completely. The poor people who had that done to them couldn't walk, couldn't talk, couldn't do anything. The only thing anybody could think of to do with them was to housebreak them, teach them a basic vocabulary of a thousand words, and give them jobs in military or industrial public relations.*

The short story: *(89.) Unk, your best friend is Stony Stevenson. Stony is a big, happy, strong man, and he drinks a quart of whisky a day. Stony doesn't have an antenna in his head, and he can remember everything that ever happened to him. He pretends to be an intelligence scout, but he is one of the real commanders. He radio-controls a company of assault infantrymen who are going to attack a place on Earth called England. Stony is from England. Stony likes the Army of Mars because there is so much to laugh about. Stony laughs all the time. He heard what an eightball you were, Unk, so he came over to your barrack to have a look at you. He pretended he was a friend of yours, so he could hear you talk. After a while, you got to trust him, Unk, and you told him some of your secret theories about what life on Mars was all about. Stony tried to laugh, but then he realized that you had turned up some things that he didn't know anything about. He couldn't get over it, because he was supposed to know everything, and you weren't supposed to know anything. And then you told Stony a lot of the big questions you wanted answered, and Stony knew the answers to only about half of them. And Stony went back to his barrack, and the questions he didn't know the answers to kept going around and around in his head. He couldn't sleep that night, even though he drank and drank and drank. He was catching on that somebody was using him, and he didn't have any idea who it was. He didn't even know why there had to be an Army of Mars in the first place. He didn't even know why Mars was going to attack Earth. And the more he remembered about Earth, the more he realized that the Army of Mars didn't have the chance of a snowball in hell. The big attack on Earth would be suicide for sure. Stony wondered who he could talk to about this, and there just wasn't anybody but you, Unk. So Stony staggered out of bed about an hour before sunrise, and he sneaked in your barrack, Unk, and he woke you up. He told you everything about Mars he knew. And he said that from now on he would tell you every bloody thing he found out, and you were supposed to tell him every bloody thing you found out. And every so often you two would get off somewhere and try to fit things together. And he gave you a bottle of whisky. And you both drank from it, and Stony said you were his best bloody friend. He said you were the only bloody friend he had ever had on Mars, even though he laughed all the time, and he cried, and almost woke up people around your bunk. He told you to watch out for Boaz, and then he went back to his barrack and slept like a baby.*

The letter, from the point of the short story on, was proof of the effectiveness of the secret observation team of Stony Stevenson and Unk. From that point on, the things known for sure in the letter were almost all introduced by phrases like: *Stony says*—and *You found out*—and *Stony told you*—and *You told Stony*—and *You and Stony got roaring drunk out on the rifle range one night, and you two crazy bums decided*—

The most important thing that the two crazy bums decided was that the man who was in actual command of everything on Mars was a big, genial, smiling, yodeling man who always had a big dog with him. This man and his dog, according to the letter to Unk, appeared at secret meetings of the real commanders of the Army of Mars about once every hundred days.

The letter said nothing about it, because the writer knew nothing about it, but this man and his dog were Winston Niles

Rumfoord and Kazak, the hound of space. And their appearances on Mars were not irregular. Being chrono-synclastic infundibulated, Rumfoord and Kazak appeared as predictably as Halley's Comet. They appeared on Mars once every one hundred and eleven days.

As the letter to Unk said, *(155.) According to Stony, this big guy and his dog show up at the meetings, and just snow everybody under. He is a big charm boy, and by the time a meeting is over everybody is trying to think just exactly the way he thinks. Every idea anybody has comes from him. He just smiles and smiles and yodels and yodels in that fancy voice of his, and fills everybody up with new ideas. And then all the people at the meeting pass around the ideas as though they had thought them up themselves. He is crazy about the game of German batball. Nobody knows what his name is. He just laughs, if anybody asks him. He usually wears the uniform of the Parachute Ski Marines, but the real commanders of the Parachute Ski Marines swear they've never seen him anywhere but at the secret meetings.*

(156.) Unk, old pal, said the letter to Unk, *every time you and Stony find out something new, add it on to this letter. Keep this letter well hidden. And every time you change its hiding place, be sure to tell Stony where you put it. That way, even if you go to the hospital to have your memory cleaned out, Stony can tell you where to go to have your memory filled up again.*

(157.) Unk—you know why you keep on going? You keep on going because you have a mate and a child. Almost nobody on Mars has either one. Your mate's name is Bee. She is an instructress at the Schliemann Breathing School in Phoebe. Your son's name is Chrono. He lives in the grade school in Phoebe. According to Stony Stevenson, Chrono is the best German batball player in the school. Like everybody else on Mars, Bee and Chrono have learned to get along all alone. They don't miss you. They never think of you. But you have to prove to them that they need you in the biggest way possible.

(158.) Unk, you crazy son-of-a-bitch, I love you. I think you are the cat's pajamas. When you get this little family of yours together, swipe a space ship and go flying away to somewhere peaceful and beautiful, some place where you don't have to take goofballs all the

time to stay alive. Take Stony with you. And when you get settled down, all of you spend a lot of time trying to figure out why whoever made everything went and made it.

All that remained for Unk to read of the letter was the signature.

The signature was on a separate page.

Before turning to the signature, Unk tried to imagine the character and appearance of the writer. The writer was fearless. The writer was such a lover of truth that he would expose himself to any amount of pain in order to add to his store of truth. He was superior to Unk and Stony. He watched and recorded their subversive activities with love, amusement, and detachment.

Unk imagined the writer as being a marvelous old man with a white beard and the build of a blacksmith.

Unk turned the page and read the signature.

I remain faithfully yours—was the sentiment expressed above the signature.

The signature itself filled almost the whole page. It was three block letters, six inches high and two inches wide. The letters were executed clumsily, with a smeary black kindergarten exuberance.

This was the signature:

The signature was Unk's.

Unk was the hero who had written the letter.

Unk had written the letter to himself before having his memory cleaned out. It was literature in its finest sense, since it made Unk courageous, watchful, and secretly free. It made him his own hero in very trying times.

Unk did not know that the man he had murdered at the stake was his best friend, was Stony Stevenson. Had he known that, he might have killed himself. But Fate spared him that awful knowledge for many years.

When Unk got back to his barrack, jungle knives and bayonets were being honed with harsh *scree-scraws.* Everyone was sharpening a blade.

And everywhere were sheepish smiles of a peculiar sort. The smiles spoke of sheep who, under proper conditions, could commit murder gladly.

Orders had just been received that the regiment was to proceed with all possible haste to its space ships.

The war with Earth had begun.

Advance units of the Martian Imperial Commandos had already obliterated Earthling installations on the Earthling moon. The Commando rocket batteries, firing from the moon, were now giving every major city a taste of hell.

And, as dinner music for those tasting hell, Martian radios were beaming this message to Earth in a maddening singsong:

Brown man, white man, yellow man—surrender or die.
Brown man, white man, yellow man—surrender or die.

CHAPTER SIX

A Deserter in Time of War

"I am at a loss to understand why German batball is not an event, possibly a key event, in the Olympic Games."

—WINSTON NILES RUMFOORD

IT WAS a six-mile march from the army camp to the plain where the invasion fleet lay. And the route of the march cut across the northwest corner of Phoebe, the only city on Mars.

The population of Phoebe at its height, according to Winston Niles Rumfoord's *Pocket History of Mars*, was eighty-seven thousand. Every soul and every structure in Phoebe was directly related to the war effort. The mass of Phoebe's workers were controlled just as the soldiers were controlled, by antennas under their skulls.

Unk's company was now marching though the northwest corner of Phoebe, on its way in the midst of its regiment to the fleet. It was thought unnecessary now to keep the soldiers moving and in ranks by means of twinges from their antennas. War fever had them now.

They chanted as they marched, and set their iron-heeled boots down hard on the iron street. Their chant was bloody:

Terror, grief, and desolation—
Hut, tup, thrup, fo!—
Come to every Earthling nation!
Hut, tup, thrup, fo!—
Earth eat fire! Earth wear chains!
Hut, tup, thrup, fo!
Break Earth's Spirit, spill Earth's brains!
Hut, tup, thrup, fo!
Scream! Tup, thrup, fo!
Bleed! Tup, thrup, fo!
Die! Tup, thrup, fo!
Doooooooooommmmmmmmmm.

The factories of Phoebe were still going full blast. No one was idling in the streets to watch the chanting heroes pass. Windows winked as dazzling torches inside went off and on. A doorway vomited spattering, smoking yellow light as metal was poured. The screams of grinding wheels cut through the soldiers' chant.

Three flying saucers, blue scout ships, skimmed low over the city, making sweet cooing sounds like singing tops. "Toodle-oo," they seemed to sing, and they skimmed away in a flat course while the surface of Mars curved away beneath them. In two shakes of a lamb's tail, they were twinkling in space eternal.

"*Terror, grief and desolation—*" chanted the troops.

But one soldier was moving his lips without making a sound. The soldier was Unk.

Unk was in the first file of the next to the last rank of his company.

Boaz was right behind him, his eyes making the back of Unk's neck itch. Boaz and Unk, moreover, were made Siamese twins by the long tube of a six-inch siege mortar which they were carrying between them.

"*Bleed! Tup, thrup, fo!*" chanted the troops. "*Die! Tup, thrup, fo! Doooooooooommmmmmmmmmm.*"

"Unk, old buddy—" said Boaz.

"Yes, old buddy?" said Unk absently. He was holding, amid the confusion of his soldier's harness, a live hand grenade. The pin had been pulled. To make it go off in three seconds, Unk had only to let go of it.

"I done fixed us up with a good assignment, old buddy," said Boaz. "Old Boaz—he takes care of his buddy, don't he, buddy?"

"That's right, buddy," said Unk.

Boaz had arranged things so that he and Unk would be on board the company mother ship for the invasion. The company mother ship, though it would, through a logistical fluke, be carrying the tube of the siege mortar, was essentially a non-combat ship. It was meant to carry only two men, the rest of the space being taken up by candy, sporting goods, recorded music, canned hamburgers, board games, goofballs, soft drinks, Bibles, note paper, barber kits, ironing boards, and other morale-builders.

"That's a lucky start, ain't it, old buddy—getting on the mother ship?"

"Lucky us, old buddy," said Unk. He had just chucked the grenade into a sewer as he passed.

There was a spout and roar from the throat of the sewer.

The soldiers hurled themselves to the street.

Boaz, as the real commander of the company, was the first to raise his head. He saw the smoke coming from the sewer, supposed that it was sewer gas that had exploded.

Boaz slipped his hand into his pocket, pressed a button, fed to his company the signal that would make them stand up again.

As they stood, Boaz stood, too. "God damn, buddy," he said, "I guess we done had a baptism of fire."

He picked up his end of the siege mortar's tube.

There was nobody to pick up the other end.

Unk had gone in search of his wife and son and his best friend.

Unk had gone over the hill on flat, flat, flat, flat Mars.

The son that Unk was looking for was named Chrono.

Chrono was, by Earthling reckoning, eight years old.

He was named after the month in which he had been born. The Martian year was divided into twenty-one months, twelve with thirty days, and nine with thirty-one. These months were named January, February, March, April, May, June, July, August, September, October, November, December, Winston, Niles, Rumfoord, Kazak, Newport, Chrono, Synclastic, Infundibulum, and Salo.

Mnemonically:

Thirty days have Salo, Niles, June, and September,
Winston, Chrono, Kazak, and November,
April, Rumfoord, Newport, and Infundibulum.
All the rest, baby mine, have thirty-one.

The month of Salo was named after a creature Winston Niles Rumfoord knew on Titan. Titan, of course, is an extremely pleasant moon of Saturn.

Salo, Rumfoord's crony on Titan, was a messenger from another galaxy who was forced down on Titan by the failure of a part in his space ship's power plant. He was waiting for a replacement part.

He had been waiting patiently for two hundred thousand years.

His ship was powered, and the Martian war effort was powered, by a phenomenon known as UWTB, or the Universal Will to Become. UWTB is what makes universes out of nothingness—that makes nothingness insist on becoming somethingness.

Many Earthlings are glad that Earth does not have UWTB.

As the popular doggerel has it:

Willy found some Universal Will to Become,
Mixed it with his bubble gum.
Cosmic piddling seldom pays:
Poor Willy's six new Milky Ways.

Unk's son Chrono was, at eight years old, a wonderful player of a game called German batball. German batball was all that he cared about. German batball was the major sport on Mars—in the grammar school, in the Army, and in the factory workers' recreation areas.

Since there were only fifty-two children on Mars, Mars got along with just one grammar school, right in the middle of Phoebe. None of the fifty-two children there had been conceived on Mars. All had been conceived either on Earth or, as in Chrono's case, on a space ship bringing new recruits to Mars.

The children in the school studied very little, since the society of Mars had no particular use for them. They spent most of their time playing German batball.

The game of German batball is played with a flabby ball the size of a big honeydew melon. The ball is no more lively than a ten-gallon hat filled with rain water. The game is something like baseball, with a batter striking the ball into a field of opposing players and running around bases; and with the fielders attempting to catch the ball and frustrate the runner. There are, however, only three bases in German batball—first, second, and home. And the batter is not pitched to. He places the ball on one fist and strikes the ball with his other fist. And if a fielder succeeds in striking the runner with the ball when the runner is between bases, the runner is deemed *out*, and must leave the playing field at once.

The person responsible for the heavy emphasis on German batball on Mars was, of course, Winston Niles Rumfoord, who was responsible for everything on Mars.

Howard W. Sams proves in his *Winston Niles Rumfoord, Benjamin Franklin, and Leonardo da Vinci* that German batball was the only team sport with which Rumfoord was at all familiar as a child. Sams shows that Rumfoord was taught the game, when a child, by his governess, a Miss Joyce MacKenzie.

Back in Rumfoord's childhood in Newport, a team composed of Rumfoord, Miss MacKenzie, and Earl Moncrief the butler, used to play German batball regularly against a team composed of Watanabe Wataru the Japanese gardener, Beverly June Wataru the gardener's daughter, and Edward Seward Darlington the half-wit stable boy. Rumfoord's team invariably won.

Unk, the only deserter in the history of the Army of Mars, now crouched panting behind a turquoise boulder and watched the school children playing German batball on the iron playground. Behind the boulder with Unk was a bicycle he had stolen from a gas-mask factory's bicycle rack. Unk did not know which child was his son, which child was Chrono.

Unk's plans were nebulous. His dream was to gather together his wife, his son, and his best friend, to steal a space ship, and to fly away to some place where they could all live happily ever after.

"Hey, Chrono!" cried a child on the playground. "You're up to bat!"

Unk peered around the boulder at home plate. The child who came up to bat there would be Chrono, would be his son.

Chrono, Unk's son, came up to bat.

He was small for his age, but surprisingly manly through the shoulders. The child's hair was jet black, bristly—and the black bristles grew in a violently counter-clockwise swirl.

The child was left-handed. The ball rested on his right fist, and he prepared to hit it with his left.

His eyes were deep-set, like his father's eyes. And his eyes were luminous under their black-thatched eaves. They glowed with an unshared rage.

Those rage-filled eyes flicked this way, then that. Their movements rattled the fielders, drawing them away from their positions, convincing them that the slow, stupid ball was going to come at them with terrible speed, was going to tear them to pieces if they dared to get in the way.

The alarm inspired by the boy at bat was felt by the teacher, too. She was in the traditional position for an umpire in German batball, between first and second base, and she was terrified. She was a frail old lady named Isabel Fenstermaker. She was seventy-three, and had been a Jehovah's Witness before having her memory cleaned out. She had been shanghaied while trying to sell a copy of *The Watchtower* to a Martian agent in Duluth.

"Now, Chrono—" she said simperingly, "it's only a game, you know."

The sky was suddenly blackened by a formation of a hundred flying saucers, the blood-red ships of the Martian Parachute Ski Marines. The combined cooing of the ships was a melodious thunder that rattled the schoolhouse windowpanes.

But, as a measure of the importance young Chrono gave to German batball when he came to bat, not a single child looked up at the sky.

Young Chrono, having brought the fielders and Miss Fenstermaker to the brink of nervous collapse, now put the ball down by his feet, took from his pocket a short strip of metal that was his good-luck piece. He kissed the strip for luck, returned the strip to his pocket.

Then he suddenly picked up the ball again, hit it a mighty *bloop*, and went scrambling around the bases.

The fielders and Miss Fenstermaker dodged the ball as though it were a red-hot cannonball. When the ball came to a stop of its own accord, the fielders went after it with a sort of ritual clumsiness. Clearly, the point of their efforts was not to hit Chrono with the ball, was not to put him out. The fielders were all conspiring to increase the glory of Chrono by making a show of helpless opposition.

Clearly, Chrono was the most glorious thing that the

children had ever seen on Mars, and any glory they themselves had came from their association with him. They would do anything to make his glory grow.

Young Chrono slid into home in a cloud of rust.

A fielder hurled the ball at him—too late, too late, much too late. The fielder ritually cursed his luck.

Young Chrono stood, dusted himself off, and again kissed his good-luck piece, thanked it for another home run. He believed firmly that all his powers came from the good-luck piece, and so did his schoolmates, and so, secretly, did Miss Fenstermaker.

The history of the good-luck piece was this:

One day the school children were taken by Miss Fenstermaker on an educational tour of a flame-thrower factory. The factory manager explained to the children all the steps in the manufacture of flame-throwers, and hoped that some of the children, when they grew up, would want to come to work for him. At the end of the tour, in the packaging department, the manager's ankle became snarled in a spiral of steel strapping, a type of strapping that was used for binding shut the packaged flame-throwers.

The spiral was a piece of jagged-ended scrap that had been cast into the factory aisle by a careless workman. The manager scratched his ankle and tore his pants before he got free of the spiral. He thereupon put on the first really comprehensible demonstration that the children had seen that day. Comprehensibly, he blew up at the spiral.

He stamped on it.

Then, when it nipped him again, he snatched it up and chopped it into four-inch lengths with great shears.

The children were edified, thrilled, and satisfied. And, as they were leaving the packaging department, young Chrono picked up one of the four-inch pieces and slipped it into his pocket. The piece he picked up differed from all the rest in having two holes drilled in it.

This was Chrono's good-luck piece. It became as much a part of him as his right hand. His nervous system, so to speak, extended itself into the metal strap. Touch it and you touched Chrono.

•

Unk, the deserter, stood up behind his turquoise boulder, walked vigorously and officiously into the school yard. He had stripped his uniform of all insignia. This gave him a rather official, warlike look, without binding him to any particular enterprise. Of all the equipment he had been carrying before he deserted, he retained only a jungle knife, his single-shot Mauser, and one grenade. These three weapons he left cached behind the boulder, along with the stolen bicycle.

Unk marched up to Miss Fenstermaker. He told her that he wished to interview young Chrono on official business at once —privately. He did not tell her that he was the boy's father. Being the boy's father entitled him to nothing. Being an official investigator entitled him to anything he might care to ask for.

Poor Miss Fenstermaker was easily fooled. She agreed to let Unk interview the boy in her own office.

Her office was crammed with ungraded school papers, some of them dating back five years. She was far behind in her work—so far behind that she had declared a moratorium on school work until she could catch up on her grading. Some of the stacks of papers had tumbled, forming glaciers that sent fingers under her desk, into the hallway, and into her private lavatory.

There was an open, two-drawer filing cabinet filled with her rock collection.

Nobody ever checked up on Miss Fenstermaker. Nobody cared. She had a teaching certificate from the State of Minnesota, U.S.A., Earth, Solar System, Milky Way, and that was all that mattered.

For his interview with his son, Unk sat behind her desk while his son Chrono stood before him. It was Chrono's wish to remain standing.

Unk, in planning the things he would say, idly opened Miss Fenstermaker's desk drawers, found that they were filled with rocks, too.

Young Chrono was shrewd and hostile, and he thought of something to say before Unk did. "Baloney," he said.

"What?" said Unk.

"Whatever you say—it's baloney," said the eight-year-old.

"What makes you think so?" said Unk.

"Everything anybody says is baloney," said Chrono. "What

you care what I think anyway? When I'm fourteen, you put a thing in my head and I do whatever you want anyway."

He was referring to the fact that antennas were not installed in the skulls of children until their fourteenth year. This was a matter of skull size. When a child reached his fourteenth birthday, he was sent to the hospital for the operation. His hair was shaved off, and the doctors and nurses joshed him about having entered adulthood. Before the child was wheeled into the operating room he was asked to name his favorite kind of ice cream. When the child awoke after the operation, a big dish of that kind of ice cream was waiting for him—maple walnut, buttercrunch, chocolate chip, anything.

"Is your mother full of baloney?" said Unk.

"She is since she came back from the hospital this last time," said Chrono.

"What about your father?" said Unk.

"I don't know anything about him," said Chrono. "I don't care. He's full of baloney like everybody else."

"Who isn't full of baloney?" said Unk.

"I'm not full of baloney," said Chrono. "I'm the only one."

"Come closer," said Unk.

"Why should I?" said Chrono.

"Because I'm going to whisper something very important."

"I doubt it," said Chrono.

Unk got up from the desk, went around to Chrono, and whispered in his ear, "I'm your father, boy!" When Unk said those words, his heart went off like a burglar alarm.

Chrono was unmoved. "So what?" he said stonily. He had never received any instructions, had never seen an example in life, that would make him think a father was of any importance. On Mars, the word was emotionally meaningless.

"I've come to get you," said Unk. "Somehow we're going to get away from here." He shook the boy gently, trying to make him bubble a little.

Chrono peeled his father's hand from his arm as though the hand were a leech. "And do what?" he said.

"Live!" said Unk.

The boy looked over his father dispassionately, seeking one good reason why he should throw in his lot with this stranger.

Chrono took his good-luck piece from his pocket, and rubbed it between his palms.

The imagined strength he got from the good-luck piece made him strong enough to trust nobody, to go on as he had for so long, angry and alone. "I'm living," he said. "I'm all right," he said. "Go to hell."

Unk took a step backward. The corners of his mouth pulled down. "Go to hell?" he whispered.

"I tell everybody to go to hell," said the boy. He was trying to be kind, but he wearied of the effort at once. "Can I go out and play batball now?"

"You'd tell your own father to go to hell?" murmured Unk. The question echoed back through Unk's emptied memory to an untouched corner where bits of his own strange childhood still lived. His own strange childhood had been spent in day-dreams of at last seeing and loving a father who did not want to see him, who did not want to be loved by him.

"I—I deserted from the army to come here—to find you," said Unk.

Interest flickered in the boy's eyes, then died. "They'll get you," he said. "They get everybody."

"I'll steal a space ship," said Unk. "And you and your mother and I will get on it, and we'll fly away!"

"To where?" said the boy.

"Some place good!" said Unk.

"Tell me about some place good," said Chrono.

"I don't know. We'll have to look!" said Unk.

Chrono shook his head pityingly. "I'm sorry," he said. "I don't think you know what you're talking about. You'd just get a lot of people killed."

"You want to stay here?" said Unk.

"I'm all right here," said Chrono. "Can I go out and play batball now?"

Unk wept.

His weeping appalled the boy. He had never seen a man weep before. He never wept himself. "I'm going out to play!" he cried wildly, and he ran out of the office.

Unk went to the window of the office. He looked out at the iron playground. Young Chrono's team was in the field now.

Young Chrono joined his teammates, faced a batter whose back was to Unk.

Chrono kissed his good-luck piece, put it in his pocket. "Easy out, you guys," he yelled hoarsely. "Come on, you guys —let's *kill* him!"

Unk's mate, the mother of young Chrono, was an instructress in the Schliemann Breathing School for Recruits. Schliemann breathing, of course, is a technique that enables human beings to survive in a vacuum or in an inhospitable atmosphere without the use of helmets or other cumbersome respiratory gear.

It consists, essentially, of taking a pill rich in oxygen. The bloodstream takes on this oxygen though the wall of the small intestine rather than through the lungs. On Mars, the pills were known officially as Combat Respiratory Rations, in popular parlance as *goofballs.*

Schliemann Breathing is at its simplest in a benign but useless atmosphere like that of Mars. The breather goes on breathing and talking in a normal manner, though there is no oxygen for his lungs to take in from the atmosphere. All he has to remember is to take his goofballs regularly.

The school in which Unk's mate was an instructress taught recruits the more difficult techniques necessary in a vacuum or in a harmful atmosphere. This involves not only pill-taking, but plugging one's ears and nostrils, and keeping one's mouth shut as well. Any effort to speak or to breathe would result in hemorrhages and probably death.

Unk's mate was one of six instructresses at the Schliemann Breathing School for Recruits. Her classroom was a bare, windowless, whitewashed room, thirty feet square. Ranged around the walls were benches.

On a table in the middle was a bowl of goofballs, a bowl of nose and ear plugs, a roll of adhesive plaster, scissors, and a small tape recorder. The purpose of the tape recorder was to play music during the long periods in which there was nothing to do but sit and wait patiently for nature to take its course.

Such a period had been reached now. The class had just been dosed with goofballs. Now the students had to sit quietly on the benches and listen to music and wait for the goofballs to reach their small intestines.

The tune being played had been pirated recently from an Earthling broadcast. It was a big hit on Earth—a trio composed for a boy, a girl, and cathedral bells. It was called "God Is Our Interior Decorator." The boy and girl sang alternate lines of the verses, and joined in close harmony on the choruses.

The cathedral bells whanged and clanged whenever anything of a religious nature was mentioned.

There were seventeen recruits. They were all in their newly issued lichen-green undershorts. The purpose of having them strip was to permit the instructress to see at a glance their external bodily reactions to Schliemann breathing.

The recruits were fresh from amnesia treatments and antenna installations at the Reception Center Hospital. Their hair had been shaved off, and each recruit had a strip of adhesive plaster running from the crown of his head to the nape of his neck.

The adhesive plaster showed where the antenna had been put in.

The recruits' eyes were as empty as the windows of abandoned textile mills.

So were the eyes of the instructress, since she, too, had recently had her memory cleaned out.

When they released her from the hospital, they told her what her name was, and where she lived, and how to teach Schliemann breathing—and that was about all the factual information they gave her. There was one other item: they told her she had an eight-year-old son named Chrono, and that she could visit him at his school on Tuesday evenings, if she liked.

The name of the instructress, of Chrono's mother, of Unk's mate, was Bee. She wore a lichen-green sweatsuit, white gym shoes, and, around her neck, a whistle on a chain and a stethoscope.

There was a rebus of her name on her sweatshirt.

She looked at the clock on the wall. Enough time had passed for the slowest digestive system to carry a goofball to the small intestine. She stood, turned off the tape recorder, and blew her whistle.

"Fall in!" she said.

The recruits had not yet had basic military training, so they were incapable of falling in with precision. Painted on the floor were squares within which the recruits were to stand in order to form ranks and files pleasing to the eye. A game resembling musical chairs was now played, with several empty-eyed recruits scuffling for the same square. In time, each found a square of his own.

"All right," said Bee, "take your plugs and plug up your noses and ears, please."

The recruits had been carrying the plugs in their clammy fists. They plugged their noses and ears.

Bee now went from recruit to recruit, making certain that all ears and nostrils were sealed.

"All right," she said, when her inspection was done. "Very good," she said. She took from the table the roll of adhesive plaster. "Now I am going to prove to you that you don't need to use your lungs at all, as long as you have Combat Respiratory Rations—or, as you'll soon be calling them in the Army, goofballs." She moved through the ranks, snipping off lengths of adhesive, sealing mouths with them. No one objected. When she got through, no one had a suitable aperture through which to issue an objection.

She noted the time, and again turned on the music. For the next twenty minutes there would be nothing to do but watch the bare bodies for color changes, for the dying spasms in the sealed and useless lungs. Ideally, the bodies would turn blue, then red, then natural again within the twenty minutes—and the rib cages would quake violently, give up, be still.

When the twenty-minute ordeal was over, every recruit would know how unnecessary lung-breathing was. Ideally, every recruit would be so confident in himself and goofballs, when his course of instruction was over, that he would be ready to spring out of a space ship on the Earthling moon or on the bottom of an Earthling ocean or anywhere, without wondering for a split second what he might be springing into.

Bee sat on a bench.

There were dark circles around her fine eyes. The circles had come after she left the hospital, and they had grown more somber with each passing day. At the hospital, they had promised her that she would become more serene and efficient with each passing day. And they had told her that, if through some fluke she should not find this to be the case, she was to report back to the hospital for more help.

"We all need help from time to time," Dr. Morris N. Castle had said. "It's nothing to be ashamed of. Some day I may need *your* help, Bee, and I won't hesitate to ask for it."

She had been sent to the hospital after showing her supervisor this sonnet, which she had written about Schliemann breathing:

Break every link with air and mist,
Seal every open vent;
Make throat as tight as miser's fist,
Keep life within you pent.
Breathe out, breathe in, no more, no more,
For breathing's for the meek;
And when in deathly space we soar,
Be careful not to speak.
If you with grief or joy are rapt,
Just signal with a tear;
To soul and heart within you trapped
Add speech and atmosphere.
Every man's an island as in lifeless space we roam.
Yes, every man's an island: island fortress, island home.

Bee, who had been sent to the hospital for writing this poem, had a strong face—high cheek-boned and haughty. She looked strikingly like an Indian brave. But whoever said so was under an obligation to add quickly that she was, all the same, quite beautiful.

Now there was a sharp knock on Bee's door. Bee went to the door and opened it. "Yes?" she said.

In the deserted corridor stood a red and sweating man in uniform. The uniform had no insignia. Slung on the man's back was a rifle. His eyes were deep-set and furtive. "Messenger," he said gruffly. "Message for Bee."

"I'm Bee," said Bee uneasily.

The messenger looked her up and down, made her feel naked. His body threw off heat, and the heat enveloped her suffocatingly.

"Do you recognize me?" he whispered.

"No," she said. His question relieved her a little. Apparently she had done business with him before. He and his visit, then, were routine—and, in the hospital, she had simply forgotten the man and his routine.

"I don't remember you, either," he whispered.

"I've been in the hospital," she said. "I had to have my memory cleaned."

"Whisper!" he said sharply.

"What?" said Bee.

"Whisper!" he said.

"Sorry," she whispered. Apparently whispering was part of the routine for dealing with this particular functionary. "I've forgotten so much."

"We *all* have!" he whispered angrily. He again looked up and down the corridor. "You are the mother of Chrono, aren't you?" he whispered.

"Yes," she whispered.

Now the strange messenger concentrated his gaze on her face. He breathed deeply, sighed, frowned—blinked frequently.

"What—what's the message?" whispered Bee.

"The message is this," whispered the messenger. "I am the father of Chrono. I have just deserted from the Army. My name is Unk. I am going to find some way for you, me, the boy, and my best friend to escape from here. I don't know how yet, but you've got to be ready to go at a moment's notice!" He gave her a hand grenade. "Hide this somewhere," he whispered. "When the time comes, you may need it."

Excited shouts came from the reception room at the far end of the corridor.

"*He said he was a confidential messenger!*" shouted a man.

"*In a pig's eye he's a messenger!*" shouted another. "*He's a deserter in time of war! Who'd he come to see?*"

"*He didn't say. He said it was top secret!*"

A whistle shrilled.

"*Six of you come with me!*" shouted a man. "*We'll search this place room by room. The rest of you surround the outside!*"

Unk shoved Bee and her hand grenade into the room, shut the door. He unslung his rifle, leveled it at the plugged and taped recruits. "One peep, one funny move out of any of you guys," he said, "and you'll all be dead."

The recruits, standing rigidly on their assigned squares on the floor, did not respond in any way.

They were pale blue.

Their rib cages were quaking.

The whole awareness of each man was concentrated in the region of a small, white, life-giving pill dissolving in the duodenum.

"Where can I hide?" said Unk. "How can I get out?"

It was unnecessary for Bee to reply. There was no place to hide. There was no way out save through the door to the corridor.

There was only one thing to do, and Unk did it. He stripped to his lichen-green undershorts, hid his rifle under a bench, put plugs in his ears and nostrils, taped his mouth, and stood among the recruits.

His head was shaved, just like the heads of the recruits. And, like the recruits, Unk had a strip of adhesive plaster running from the crown of his head to the nape of his neck. He had been such a terrible soldier that the doctors had opened his head up at the hospital to see if he might not be suffering from a malfunctioning antenna.

Bee surveyed the room with enchanted calm. She held the grenade that Unk had given her as though it were a vase with one perfect rose in it. Then she went to the place where Unk had hidden his rifle, and she put the grenade beside it—put it there neatly, with a decent respect for another's property.

Then she went back to her post at the table.

She neither stared at Unk nor avoided looking at him. As they told her at the hospital: she had been very, very sick, and she would be very, very sick again if she didn't keep her mind strictly on her work and let other people do the thinking and the worrying. At all costs, she was to keep calm.

The blustering false alarms of the men making the room-to-room search were approaching slowly.

Bee refused to worry about anything. Unk, by taking his place among the recruits, had reduced himself to a cipher. Considering him professionally, Bee saw that Unk's body was turning blue-green rather than pure blue. This might mean that he had not taken a goofball for several hours—in which case he would soon keel over.

To have him keel over would certainly be the most peaceful solution to the problem he presented, and Bee wanted peace above all else.

She didn't doubt that Unk was the father of her child. Life was like that. She didn't remember him, and she didn't bother now to study him in order to recognize him the next time—if there was going to be a next time. She had no use for him.

She noted that Unk's body was now predominantly green. Her diagnosis had been correct, then. He would keel over at any minute.

Bee daydreamed. She daydreamed of a little girl in a starched white dress and white gloves and white shoes, and with a white pony all her own. Bee envied that little girl who had kept so clean.

Bee wondered who the little girl was.

Unk fell noiselessly, as limp as a bag of eels.

Unk awoke, found himself on his back in a bunk in a space ship. The cabin lights were dazzling. Unk started to yell, but a sick headache shushed him.

He struggled to his feet, clung drunkenly to the pipe supports of the bunk. He was all alone. Someone had put his uniform back on him.

He thought at first that he had been launched into space eternal.

But then he saw that the airlock was open to the outside, and that outside was solid ground.

Unk lurched out through the airlock and threw up.

He raised his watering eyes, and saw that he was seemingly still on Mars, or on something a lot like Mars.

It was night time.

The iron plain was studded with ranks and files of space ships.

As Unk watched, a file of ships five miles long arose from the formation, sailed melodiously off into space.

A dog barked, barked with a voice like a great bronze gong.

And out of the night loped the dog—as big and terrible as a tiger.

"Kazak!" cried a man in the dark.

The dog stopped at the command, but he held Unk at bay, kept Unk flattened against the space ship with the threat of his long, wet fangs.

The dog's master appeared, the beam of a flashlight dancing before him. When he got within a few yards of Unk, he placed the flashlight under his chin. The contrasting beam and shadows made his face look like the face of a demon.

"Hello, Unk," he said. He turned the flashlight off, stepped to one side so that he was illuminated by the light spilling from the space ship. He was big, vaguely soft, marvelously self-assured. He wore the blood-red uniform and square-toed boots of a Parachute Ski Marine. He was unarmed save for a black and gold swaggerstick one foot long.

"Long time no see," he said. He gave a very small, v-shaped smile. His voice was a glottal tenor, a yodel.

Unk had no recollection of the man, but the man obviously knew Unk well—knew him warmly.

"Who am I, Unk?" said the man gayly.

Unk gasped. This had to be Stony Stevenson, had to be Unk's fearless best friend. "Stony?" he whispered.

"Stony?" said the man. He laughed. "Oh, God—" he said, "many's the time I've wished I was Stony, and many's the time I'll wish it again."

The ground shook. There was a whirlwind rush in the air. Neighboring space ships on all sides had leaped into the air, were gone.

Unk's ship now had its sector of the iron plain all to itself. The nearest ships on the ground were perhaps half a mile away.

"There goes your regiment, Unk," said the man, "and you not with them. Aren't you ashamed?"

"Who are you?" said Unk.

"What do names matter in wartime?" said the man. He put his big hand on Unk's shoulder. "Oh, Unk, Unk, Unk," he said, "what a time you've had."

"Who brought me here?" said Unk.

"The military police, bless them," said the man.

Unk shook his head. Tears ran down his cheeks. He was defeated. There was no reason for secrecy any more, even in the presence of someone who might have the power of life and death over him. As to life and death, poor Unk was indifferent. "I—I tried to bring my family together," he said. "That's all."

"Mars is a very bad place for love, a very bad place for a family man, Unk," said the man.

The man was, of course, Winston Niles Rumfoord. He was commander-in-chief of everything Martian. He was not actually a practicing Parachute Ski Marine. But he was free to wear any uniform that caught his fancy, regardless of how much hell anybody else had to go through for the privilege.

"Unk," said Rumfoord, "the very saddest love story I ever hope to hear took place on Mars. Would you like to hear it?"

"Once upon a time," said Rumfoord, "there was a man being carried from Earth to Mars in a flying saucer. He had volunteered for the Army of Mars, and already wore the dashing uniform of a lieutenant-colonel in the Assault Infantry of that service. He felt elegant, indeed, having been rather underprivileged spiritually on Earth, and assumed, as spiritually underprivileged persons will, that the uniform said lovely things about him.

"His memory hadn't been cleaned out yet, and his antenna had yet to be installed—but he was so patently a loyal Martian that he was given the run of the space ship. The recruiters have a saying about a male recruit like that—that he has named his balls Deimos and Phobus," said Rumfoord, "Deimos and Phobus being the two moons of Mars.

"This lieutenant-colonel, with no military training whatsoever, was having the experience known on Earth as *finding himself*. Ignorant as he was of the enterprise in which he was ensnarled, he was issuing orders to the other recruits, and having them obeyed."

Rumfoord held up a finger, and Unk was startled to see that it was quite translucent. "There was one locked stateroom that the man was not permitted to enter," said Rumfoord. "The crew carefully explained to him that the stateroom contained the most beautiful woman ever taken to Mars, and that any man who saw her was certain to fall in love with her. Love, they said, would destroy the value of any but the most professional soldier.

"The new lieutenant-colonel was offended by the suggestion

that he was not a professional soldier, and he regaled the crew with stories of his amatory exploits with gorgeous women—all of which had left his heart absolutely untouched. The crew remained skeptical, pretending to the opinion that the lieutenant-colonel had never, for all his lascivious questing, exposed himself to an intelligent, haughty beauty such as the one in the locked stateroom.

"The crew's seeming respect for the lieutenant-colonel was now subtly withdrawn. The other recruits sensed this withdrawal, and withdrew their own. The lieutenant-colonel in his gaudy uniform was made to feel like what he really was, after all—a strutting clown. The manner in which he could win back his dignity was never stated, but was obvious to one and all. He could win it back by making a conquest of the beauty locked in the stateroom. He was fully prepared to do this—was desperately prepared—

"But the crew," said Rumfoord, "continued to protect him from supposed amatory failure and a broken heart. His ego fizzed, it sizzled, it snapped, it crackled, it popped.

"There was a drinking party in the officers' mess," said Rumfoord, "and the lieutenant-colonel became quite drunk and loud. He bragged again of his heartless lewdnesses on Earth. And then he saw that someone had placed in the bottom of his glass a stateroom key.

"The lieutenant-colonel sneaked away to the locked stateroom forthwith, let himself in, and closed the door behind him," said Rumfoord. "The stateroom was dark, but the inside of the lieutenant-colonel's head was illuminated by liquor and by the triumphant words of the announcement he would make at breakfast the next morning.

"He took the woman in the dark easily, for she was weak with terror and sedatives," said Rumfoord. "It was a joyless union, satisfactory to no one but Mother Nature at her most callous.

"The lieutenant-colonel did not feel marvelous. He felt wretched. Foolishly, he turned on the light, hoping to find in the woman's appearance some cause for pride in his brutishness," said Rumfoord sadly. "Huddled on the bunk was a rather plain woman past thirty. Her eyes were red and her face was puffy with weeping, despair.

"The lieutenant-colonel, moreover, knew her. She was a woman that a fortune teller had promised him would one day bear his child," said Rumfoord. "She had been so high and proud the last time he saw her, and was now so crushed, that even the heartless lieutenant-colonel was moved.

"The lieutenant-colonel realized for the first time what most people never realize about themselves—that he was not only a victim of outrageous fortune, but one of outrageous fortune's cruelest agents as well. The woman had regarded him as a pig when they met before. He had now proved beyond question that he was a pig.

"As the crew had predicted," said Rumfoord, "the lieutenant-colonel was spoiled forever as a soldier. He became hopelessly engrossed in the intricate tactics of causing less rather than more pain. Proof of his success would be his winning of the woman's forgiveness and understanding.

"When the space ship reached Mars, he learned from loose talk in the Reception Center Hospital that he was about to have his memory taken away. He thereupon wrote himself the first of a series of letters that listed the things he did not want to forget. The first letter was all about the woman he had wronged.

"He looked for her after his amnesia treatment, and found that she had no recollection of him. Not only that, she was pregnant, carrying his child. His problem, thereupon, became to win her love, and through her, to win the love of her child.

"This he attempted to do, Unk," said Rumfoord, "not once, but many times. He was consistently defeated. But it remained the central problem of his life—probably because he himself had come from a shattered family.

"What defeated him, Unk," said Rumfoord, "was a congenital coldness on the part of the woman, and a system of psychiatry that took the ideals of Martian society as noble common sense. Each time the man wobbled his mate, utterly humorless psychiatry straightened her out—made her an efficient citizen again.

"Both the man and his mate were frequent visitors to the psychiatric wards of their respective hospitals. And it is perhaps food for thought," said Rumfoord, "that this supremely frustrated man was the only Martian to write a philosophy, and that this supremely self-frustrating woman was the only Martian to write a poem."

Boaz arrived at the company mother ship from the town of Phoebe, where he had gone to look for Unk. "God damn—" he said to Rumfoord, "everybody go and leave without us?" He was on a bicycle.

He saw Unk. "God damn, buddy," he said to Unk, "boy—you ever put your buddy through hell. I mean! How you get here?"

"Military police," said Unk.

"The way everybody gets everywhere," said Rumfoord lightly.

"We got to catch up, buddy," said Boaz. "Them boys ain't going to attack, if they don't have a mother ship along. What they going to fight for?"

"For the privilege of being the first army that ever died in a good cause," said Rumfoord.

"How's that?" said Boaz.

"Never mind," said Rumfoord. "You boys just get on board, close the airlock, push the *on* button. You'll catch up before you know it. Everything's all fully automatic."

Unk and Boaz got on board.

Rumfoord held open the outer door of the airlock. "Boaz—" he said, "that red button on the center shaft there—that's the *on* button."

"I know," said Boaz.

"Unk—" said Rumfoord.

"Yes?" said Unk emptily.

"That story I told you—the love story? I left out one thing."

"That so?" said Unk.

"The woman in the love story—the woman who had that man's baby?" said Rumfoord. "The woman who was the only poet on Mars?"

"What about her?" said Unk. He didn't care much about her. He hadn't caught on that the woman in Rumfoord's story was Bee, was his own mate.

"She'd been married for several years before she got to Mars," said Rumfoord. "But when the hot-shot lieutenant-colonel got to her there in the space ship bound for Mars, she was still a virgin."

Winston Niles Rumfoord winked at Unk before shutting the outside door of the airlock. "Pretty good joke on her husband, eh, Unk?" he said.

CHAPTER SEVEN

Victory

"There is no reason why good cannot triumph as often as evil. The triumph of anything is a matter of organization. If there are such things as angels, I hope that they are organized along the lines of the Mafia."

—WINSTON NILES RUMFOORD

IT HAS BEEN SAID that Earthling civilization, so far, has created ten thousand wars, but only three intelligent commentaries on war—the commentaries of Thucydides, of Julius Caesar and of Winston Niles Rumfoord.

Winston Niles Rumfoord chose 75,000 words so well for his *Pocket History of Mars* that nothing remains to be said, or to be said better, about the war between Earth and Mars. Anyone who finds himself obliged, in the course of a history, to describe the war between Earth and Mars is humbled by the realization that the tale has already been told to glorious perfection by Rumfoord.

The usual course for such a discomfited historian is to describe the war in the barest, flattest, most telegraphic terms, and to recommend that the reader go at once to Rumfoord's masterpiece.

Such a course is followed here.

The war between Mars and Earth lasted 67 Earthling days.

Every nation on Earth was attacked.

Earth's casualties were 461 killed, 223 wounded, none captured, and 216 missing.

Mars' casualties were 149,315 killed, 446 wounded, 11 captured, and 46,634 missing.

At the end of the war, every Martian had been killed, wounded, captured, or been found missing.

Not a soul was left on Mars. Not a building was left standing on Mars.

The last waves of Martians to attack Earth were, to the

horror of the Earthlings who pot-shotted them, old men, women, and a few little children.

The Martians arrived in the most brilliantly-conceived space vehicles ever known in the Solar System. And, as long as the Martian troops had their real commanders to radio-control them, they fought with a steadfastness, selflessness, and a will to close with the enemy that won the grudging admiration of everyone who fought them.

It was frequently the case, however, that the troops lost their real commanders, either in the air or on the ground. When that happened, the troops became sluggish at once.

Their biggest trouble, however, was that they were scarcely better armed than a big-city police department. They fought with firearms, grenades, knives, mortars, and small rocket-launchers. They had no nuclear weapons, no tanks, no medium or heavy artillery, no air cover, and no transport once they hit the ground.

The Martian troops, moreover, had no control over where their ships were to land. Their ships were controlled by fully automatic pilot-navigators, and these electronic devices were set by technicians on Mars so as to make the ships land at particular points on Earth, regardless of how awful the military situation might be down there.

The only controls available to those on board were two push-buttons on the center post of the cabin—one labeled *on* and one labeled *off*. The *on* button simply started a flight from Mars. The *off* button was connected to nothing. It was installed at the insistence of Martian mental-health experts, who said that human beings were always happier with machinery they thought they could turn off.

The war between Earth and Mars began when 500 Martian Imperial Commandos took possession of the Earthling moon on April 23. They were unopposed. The only Earthlings on the moon at the time were 18 Americans in the Jefferson Observatory, 53 Russians in the Lenin Observatory, and four Danish geologists at large in the Mare Imbrium.

The Martians announced their presence by radio to Earth, demanded Earth's surrender. And they gave Earth what they described as "a taste of hell."

This taste, to Earth's considerable amusement, turned out to be a very light shower of rockets carrying twelve pounds apiece of TNT.

After giving Earth this taste of hell, the Martians told Earth that Earth's situation was hopeless.

Earth thought otherwise.

In the next twenty-four hours, Earth fired 617 thermo-nuclear devices at the Martian bridgehead on the moon. Of these 276 were hits. These hits not only vaporized the bridge-head—they rendered the moon unfit for human occupation for at least ten million years.

And, in a freak of war, one wild shot missed the moon and hit an incoming formation of space ships that carried 15,671 Martian Imperial Commandos. That took care of all the Martian Imperial Commandos there were.

They wore knee spikes, and glossy black uniforms, and carried 14-inch, saw-toothed knives in their boots. Their insignia was a skull and crossbones.

Their motto was *Per aspera ad astra*, the same as the motto of Kansas, U.S.A., Earth, Solar System, Milky Way.

There was then a lull of thirty-two days, the length of time it took for the main Martian striking force to cross the void between the two planets. This hammer blow consisted of 81,932 troops in 2,311 ships. Every military unit, save for the Martian Imperial Commandos, was represented. Earth was spared suspense as to when this terrible armada might arrive. The Martian broadcasters on the moon, before being vaporized, had promised the arrival of this irresistible force in thirty-two days.

In thirty-two days, four hours, and fifteen minutes, the Martian Armada flew into a radar-directed thermo-nuclear barrage. The official estimate of the number of thermo-nuclear anti-aircraft rockets fired at the Martian armada is 2,542,670. The actual number of rockets fired is of little interest when one can express the power of that barrage in another way, in a way that happens to be both poetry and truth. The barrage turned the skies of Earth from heavenly blue to a hellish burnt orange. The skies remained burnt orange for a year and a half.

Of the mighty Martian Armada, only 761 ships carrying 26,635 troops survived the barrage and landed on Earth.

Had all these ships landed at one point, the survivors might have made a stand. But the electronic pilot-navigators of the ships had other ideas. The pilot-navigators scattered the remnants of the armada far and wide over the surface of the Earth. Squads, platoons, and companies emerged from the ships everywhere, demanding that nations of millions give in.

A single, badly scorched man named Krishna Garu attacked all of India with a double-barreled shotgun. Though there was no one to radio-control him, he did not surrender until his gun blew up.

The only Martian military success was the capture of a meat market in Basel, Switzerland, by seventeen Parachute Ski Marines.

Everywhere else the Martians were butchered promptly, before they could even dig in.

As much butchering was done by amateurs as by professionals. At the Battle of Boca Raton, in Florida, U.S.A., for instance, Mrs. Lyman R. Peterson shot four members of the Martian Assault Infantry with her son's .22 caliber rifle. She picked them off as they came out of their space ship, which had landed in her back yard.

She was awarded the Congressional Medal of Honor posthumously.

The Martians who attacked Boca Raton, incidentally, were the remains of Unk's and Boaz's company. Without Boaz, their real commander, to radio-control them, they fought listlessly, to say the least.

When American troops arrived at Boca Raton to fight the Martians, there was nothing left to fight. The civilians, flushed and proud, had taken care of everything nicely. Twenty-three Martians had been hanged from lamp posts in the business district, eleven had been shot dead, and one, Sergeant Brackman, was a grievously wounded prisoner in the jail.

The total attacking force had been thirty-five.

"Send us more Martians," said Ross L. McSwann, the Mayor of Boca Raton.

He later became a United States Senator.

And everywhere the Martians were killed and killed and killed, until the only Martians left free and standing on the face of the Earth were the Parachute Ski Marines carousing in the meat market in Basel, Switzerland. They were told by loudspeaker that their situation was hopeless, that bombers were overhead, that all streets were blocked by tanks and crack infantry, and that fifty artillery pieces were trained on the meat market. They were told to come out with their hands up, or the meat market would be blown to bits.

"Nuts!" yelled the real commander of the Parachute Ski Marines.

There was another lull.

A single Martian scout ship far out in space broadcast to Earth that another attack was on its way, an attack more terrible than anything ever known in the annals of war.

Earth laughed and got ready. All around the globe there was the cheerful popping away of amateurs familiarizing themselves with small arms.

Fresh stocks of thermo-nuclear devices were delivered to the launching pads, and nine tremendous rockets were fired at Mars itself. One hit Mars, wiped the town of Phoebe and the army camp off the face of the planet. Two others disappeared in a chrono-synclastic infundibulum. The rest became space derelicts.

It did not matter that Mars was hit.

There was no one there any more—not a soul.

The last of the Martians were on their way to Earth.

The last of the Martians were coming in three waves.

In the first wave came the army reserves, the last of the trained troops—26,119 men in 721 ships.

A half an Earthling day behind them came 86,912 recently-armed male civilians in 1,738 ships. They had no uniforms, had fired their riles only once, and had no training at all in the use of any other weapons.

A half an Earthling day behind these wretched irregulars came 1,391 unarmed women and 52 children in 46 ships.

That was all the people and all the ships that Mars had left.

The mastermind behind the Martian suicide was Winston Niles Rumfoord.

The elaborate suicide of Mars was financed by capital gains

on investments in land, securities, Broadway shows, and inventions. Since Rumfoord could see into the future, it was easy as pie for him to make money grow.

The Martian treasury was kept in Swiss banks, in accounts identified only by code numbers.

The man who managed the Martian investments, headed the Martian Procurement Program and the Martian Secret Service on Earth, the man who took orders directly from Rumfoord, was Earl Moncrief, the ancient Rumfoord butler. Moncrief, given the opportunity at the very close of his servile life, became Rumfoord's ruthless, effective, and even brilliant Prime Minister of Earthling Affairs.

Moncrief's façade remained unchanged.

Moncrief died of old age in his bed in the servants' wing of the Rumfoord mansion two weeks after the war ended.

The person chiefly responsible for the technological triumphs of the Martian suicide was Salo, Rumfoord's friend on Titan. Salo was a messenger from the planet Tralfamadore in the Small Magellanic Cloud. Salo had technological know-how from a civilization that was millions of Earthling years old. Salo had a space ship that was crippled—but, even in its crippled condition, it was by far the most marvelous space ship that the Solar System had ever seen. His crippled ship, stripped of luxury features, was the prototype of all the ships of Mars. While Salo himself was not a very good engineer, he was none the less able to measure every part of his ship, and to draw up the plans for its Martian descendants.

Most important of all—Salo had in his possession a quantity of the most powerful conceivable source of energy, UWTB, or the Universal Will to Become. Salo generously donated half of his supply of UWTB to the suicide of Mars.

Earl Moncrief, the butler, built his financial, procurement, and secret service organizations with the brute power of cash and a profound understanding of clever, malicious, discontented people who lived behind servile façades.

It was such people who took the Martian money and the Martian orders gladly. They asked no questions. They were grateful for the opportunity to work like termites on the sills of the established order.

They came from all walks of life.

The modified plans of Salo's space ship were broken down into plans for components. The plans for the components were taken by Moncrief's agents to manufacturers all over the world.

The manufacturers had no idea what the components were for. They knew only that the profits on making them were fine.

The first one hundred Martian ships were assembled by Moncrief's agents in secret depots right on Earth.

These ships were charged with UWTB given to Moncrief by Rumfoord at Newport. They were put into service at once, shuttling the first machines and the first recruits to the iron plain on Mars where the city of Phoebe would rise.

When Phoebe did rise, every wheel was turned by Salo's UWTB.

It was Rumfoord's intention that Mars should lose the war—that Mars should lose it foolishly and horribly. As a seer of the future, Rumfoord knew for certain that this would be the case—and he was content.

He wished to change the World for the better by means of the great and unforgettable suicide of Mars.

As he says in his *Pocket History of Mars*: "Any man who would change the World in a significant way must have showmanship, a genial willingness to shed other people's blood, and a plausible new religion to introduce during the brief period of repentance and horror that usually follows bloodshed.

"Every failure of Earthling leadership has been traceable to a lack on the part of the leader," says Rumfoord, "of at least one of these three things.

"Enough of these fizzles of leadership, in which millions die for nothing or less!" says Rumfoord. "Let us have, for a change, a magnificently-led few who die for a great deal."

Rumfoord had that magnificently-led few on Mars—and he was their leader.

He had showmanship.

He was genially willing to shed the blood of others.

He had a plausible new religion to introduce at the war's end.

And he had methods for prolonging the period of repentance and horror that would follow the war. These methods were variations on one theme: That Earth's glorious victory over Mars had been a tawdry butchery of virtually unarmed saints, saints who had waged feeble war on Earth in order to weld the peoples of that planet into a monolithic Brotherhood of Man.

The woman called Bee and her son, Chrono, were in the very last wave of Martian ships to approach Earth. Theirs was a wavelet, really, composed, as it was, of only forty-six ships.

The rest of the fleet had already gone down to destruction.

This last incoming wave, or wavelet, was detected by Earth. But thermo-nuclear devices were not fired at it. There were no more thermo-nuclear devices to fire.

They had all been used up.

And the wavelet came in unscathed. It was scattered over the face of the Earth.

The few people who were lucky enough to have Martians to shoot at in this last wave fired away happily—fired away happily until they discovered that their targets were unarmed women and children.

The glorious war was over.

Shame, as Rumfoord had planned it, began to set in.

The ship carrying Bee and Chrono and twenty-two other women was not fired upon when it landed. It did not land in a civilized area.

It crashed into the Amazon Rain Forest in Brazil.

Only Bee and Chrono survived.

Chrono emerged, kissed his good-luck piece.

Unk and Boaz weren't fired upon either.

A very peculiar thing happened to them after they pressed the *on* button and took off from Mars. They expected to overtake their company, but they never did.

They never even saw another space ship.

The explanation was simple, though there was no one around to make it: Unk and Boaz weren't supposed to go to Earth—not right away.

Rumfoord had had their automatic pilot-navigator set so that the ship would carry Unk and Boaz to the planet Mercury first—and then from Mercury to Earth.

Rumfoord didn't want Unk killed in the war.

Rumfoord wanted Unk to stay in some safe place for about two years.

And then Rumfoord wanted Unk to appear on Earth, as though by a miracle.

Rumfoord was preserving Unk for a major part in a pageant Rumfoord wanted to stage for his new religion.

Unk and Boaz were very lonely and mystified out there in space. There wasn't much to see or do.

"God damn, Unk—" said Boaz. "I wonder where the gang got to."

Most of the gang was hanging, at that moment, from lamp posts in the business district of Boca Raton.

Unk's and Boaz's automatic pilot-navigator, controlling the cabin lights, among other things, created an artificial cycle of Earthling nights and days, nights and days, nights and days.

The only things to read on board were two comic books left behind by the shipfitters. They were *Tweety and Sylvester*, which was about a canary that drove a cat crazy, and *The Miserable Ones*, which was about a man who stole some gold candlesticks from a priest who had been nice to him.

"What he take those candlesticks for, Unk?" said Boaz.

"Damn if I know," said Unk. "Damn if I care."

The pilot-navigator had just turned out the cabin lights, had just decreed that it be night inside.

"You don't give a damn for nothing, do you?" said Boaz in the dark.

"That's right," said Unk. "I don't even give a damn for that thing you've got in your pocket."

"What I got in my pocket?" said Boaz.

"A thing to hurt people with," said Unk. "A thing to make people do whatever you want 'em to do."

Unk heard Boaz grunt, then groan softly, there in the dark. And he knew that Boaz had just pressed a button on the thing in his pocket, a button that was supposed to knock Unk cold.

Unk didn't make a sound.

"Unk—?" said Boaz.

"Yeah?" said Unk.

"You *there*, buddy?" said Boaz, amazed.

"Where would I go?" said Unk. "You think you vaporized me?"

"You O.K., buddy?" said Boaz.

"Why wouldn't I be, buddy?" said Unk. "Last night, while you were asleep, old buddy, I took that fool thing out of your pocket, old buddy, and I opened it up, old buddy, and I tore the insides out of it, old buddy, and I stuffed it with toilet paper. And now I'm sitting on my bunk, old buddy, and I've got my rifle loaded, old buddy, and it's aimed in your direction, old buddy, and just what the hell do you think you're going to do about anything?"

Rumfoord materialized on Earth, in Newport, twice during the war between Mars and Earth—once just after the war started, and again on the day it ended. He and his dog had, at that time, no particular religious significance. They were merely tourist attractions.

The Rumfoord estate had been leased by the mortgage holders to a showman named Marlin T. Lapp. Lapp sold tickets to materializations for a dollar apiece.

Save for the appearance and then the disappearance of Rumfoord and his dog, it wasn't much of a show. Rumfoord wouldn't say a word to anyone but Moncrief, the butler, and he whispered to him. He would slouch broodingly in a wing chair in the room under the staircase, in Skip's Museum. And he would cover his eyes with one hand and twine the fingers of his other hand around Kazak's choke chain.

Rumfoord and Kazak were billed as ghosts.

There was a scaffolding outside the window of the little room, and the door to the corridor had been removed. Two lines of sightseers could file past for a peek at the chrono-synclastic infundibulated man and dog.

"I guess he don't feel much like talking today, folks," Marlin T. Lapp would say. "You got to realize he's got a lot to think about. He isn't just here, folks. Him and his dog are spread all the way from the Sun to Betelgeuse."

Until the last day of the war, all the action and all the noise was provided by Marlin T. Lapp. "I think it's wonderful of all you people, on this great day in the history of the world, to come and see this great cultural and educational and scientific exhibit," Lapp said on the last day of the war.

"If this ghost ever speaks," said Lapp, "he is going to tell us of wonders in the past and the future, and of things in the Universe as yet undreamed of. I just hope some of you are lucky enough to be here when he decides the time is ripe to tell us all he can."

"The time is ripe," said Rumfoord hollowly.

"The time is rotten-ripe," said Winston Niles Rumfoord.

"The war that ends so gloriously today was glorious only for the saints who lost it. Those saints were Earthlings like yourselves. They went to Mars, mounted their hopeless attacks, and died gladly, in order that Earthlings might at last become one people—joyful, fraternal, and proud.

"Their wish, when they died," said Rumfoord, "was not for paradise for themselves, but that the brotherhood of mankind on Earth might be enduring.

"To that end, devoutly to be wished," said Rumfoord, "I bring you word of a new religion that can be received enthusiastically in every corner of every Earthling heart.

"National borders," said Rumfoord, "will disappear.

"The lust for war," said Rumfoord, "will die.

"All envy, all fear, all hate will die," said Rumfoord.

"The name of the new religion," said Rumfoord, "is The Church of God the Utterly Indifferent.

"The flag of that church will be blue and gold," said Rumfoord. "These words will be written on that flag in gold letters on a blue field: *Take Care of the People, and God Almighty Will Take Care of Himself.*

"The two chief teachings of this religion are these," said Rumfoord: "Puny man can do nothing at all to help or please God Almighty, and Luck is not the hand of God.

"Why should you believe in this religion, rather than any other?" said Rumfoord. "You should believe in it because I, as head of this religion, can work miracles, and the head of no other religion can. What miracles can I work? I can work the miracle of predicting, with absolute accuracy, the things that the future will bring."

Rumfoord thereupon predicted fifty future events in great detail.

These predictions were carefully recorded by those present.

Needless to say, they all came true eventually—came true in great detail.

"The teachings of this religion will seem subtle and confusing at first," said Rumfoord. "But they will become beautiful and crystal clear as time goes by.

"As a presently confusing beginning," said Rumfoord, "I shall tell you a parable:

"Once upon a time, luck arranged things so that a baby named Malachi Constant was born the richest child on Earth. On the same day, luck arranged things so that a blind grandmother stepped on a rollerskate at the head of a flight of cement stairs, a policeman's horse stepped on an organ-grinder's monkey, and a paroled bank robber found a postage stamp worth nine hundred dollars in the bottom of a trunk in his attic. I ask you—is luck the hand of God?"

Rumfoord held up an index finger that was as translucent as a Limoges teacup. "During my next visit with you, fellow-believers," he said. "I shall tell you a parable about people who do things that they think God Almighty wants done. In the meanwhile, you would do well, for background on this parable, to read everything that you can lay your hands on about the Spanish Inquisition.

"The next time I come to you," said Rumfoord, "I shall bring you a Bible, revised so as to be meaningful in modern times. And I shall bring you a short history of Mars, a true history of the saints who died in order that the world might be united as the Brotherhood of Man. This history will break the heart of every human being who has a heart that can be broken."

Rumfoord and his dog dematerialized abruptly.

On the space ship out of Mars and bound for Mercury, on the space ship carrying Unk and Boaz, the automatic pilot-navigator decreed that it be day in the cabin again.

It was the dawn following the night in which Unk had told Boaz that the thing in Boaz's pocket couldn't hurt anybody any more.

Unk was asleep on his bunk in a sitting position. His Mauser rifle, loaded and cocked, lay across his knees.

Boaz was not asleep. He was lying on his bunk across the cabin from Unk. Boaz had not slept a wink. He could now, if he wanted to, disarm and kill Unk easily.

But Boaz had decided that he needed a buddy far more than he needed a means of making people do exactly what he wanted them to. During the night, he had become very unsure of what he wanted people to do, anyway.

Not to be lonely, not to be scared—Boaz had decided that those were the important things in life. A real buddy could help more than anything.

The cabin was filled with a strange, rustling, coughing sound. It was laughter. It was Boaz's laughter. What made it so strange was that Boaz had never laughed in that particular way before—had never laughed before at the things he was laughing at now.

He was laughing at the ferocious mess he was in—at the way he had pretended all his army life that he had understood everything that was going on, and that everything that was going on was just fine.

He was laughing at the dumb way he had let himself be used—by God knows who for God knows what.

"Holy smokes, buddy," he said out loud, "what we doing way out here in space? What we doing in these here clothes? Who's steering this fool thing? How come we climbed into this tin can? How come we got to shoot somebody when we get to where we're going? How come he got to try and shoot us? How come?" said Boaz. "Buddy," he said, "you tell me how come?"

Unk woke up, swung the muzzle of his Mauser around to Boaz.

Boaz went right on laughing. He took the control box out of his pocket, and he threw it on the floor. "I don't want it, buddy," he said. "That's O.K. you went and tore its insides out. I don't want it."

And then he yelled, "I don't want *none* of this crap!"

CHAPTER EIGHT

In a Hollywood Night Club

HARMONIUM—The only known form of life on the planet Mercury. The harmonium is a cave-dweller. A more gracious creature would be hard to imagine.

—*A Child's Cyclopedia of Wonders and Things to Do*

THE PLANET MERCURY sings like a crystal goblet.

It sings all the time.

One side of Mercury faces the Sun. That side has always faced the Sun. That side is a sea of white-hot dust.

The other side faces the nothingness of space eternal. That side has always faced the nothingness of space eternal. That side is a forest of giant blue-white crystals, aching cold.

It is the tension between the hot hemisphere of day-without-end and the cold hemisphere of night-without-end that makes Mercury sing.

Mercury has no atmosphere, so the song it sings is for the sense of touch.

The song is a slow one. Mercury will hold a single note in the song for as long as an Earthling millennium. There are those who think that the song was quick, wild, and brilliant once—excruciatingly various. Possibly so.

There are creatures in the deep caves of Mercury.

The song their planet sings is important to them, for the creatures are nourished by vibrations. They feed on mechanical energy.

The creatures cling to the singing walls of their caves.

In that way, they eat the song of Mercury.

The caves of Mercury are cozily warm in their depths.

The walls of the caves in their depths are phosphorescent. They give off a jonquil-yellow light.

The creatures in the caves are translucent. When they cling to the walls, light from the phosphorescent walls comes right through them. The yellow light from the walls, however, is turned, when passed through the bodies of the creatures, to a vivid aquamarine.

Nature is a wonderful thing.

The creatures in the caves look very much like small and spineless kites. They are diamond-shaped, a foot high and eight inches wide when fully mature.

They have no more thickness than the skin of a toy balloon.

Each creature has four feeble suction cups—one at each of its corners. These cups enable it to creep, something like a measuring worm, and to cling, and to feel out the places where the song of Mercury is best.

Having found a place that promises a good meal, the creatures lay themselves against the wall like wet wallpaper.

There is no need for a circulatory system in the creatures. They are so thin that life-giving vibrations can make all their cells tingle without intermediaries.

The creatures do not excrete.

The creatures reproduce by flaking. The young, when shed by a parent, are indistinguishable from dandruff.

There is only one sex.

Every creature simply sheds flakes of his own kind, and his own kind is like everybody else's kind.

There is no childhood as such. Flakes begin flaking three Earthling hours after they themselves have been shed.

They do not reach maturity, then deteriorate and die. They reach maturity and stay in full bloom, so to speak, for as long as Mercury cares to sing.

There is no way in which one creature can harm another, and no motive for one's harming another.

Hunger, envy, ambition, fear, indignation, religion, and sexual lust are irrelevant and unknown.

The creatures have only one sense: touch.

They have weak powers of telepathy. The messages they are capable of transmitting and receiving are almost as monotonous as the song of Mercury. They have only two possible messages. The first is an automatic response to the second, and the second is an automatic reponse to the first.

The first is, "*Here I am, here I am, here I am.*"

The second is, "*So glad you are, so glad you are, so glad you are.*"

There is one last characteristic of the creatures that has not been explained on utilitarian grounds: the creatures seem to like to arrange themselves in striking patterns on the phosphorescent walls.

Though blind and indifferent to anyone's watching, they often arrange themselves so as to present a regular and dazzling pattern of jonquil-yellow and vivid aquamarine diamonds. The yellow comes from the bare cave walls. The aquamarine is the light of the walls filtered through the bodies of the creatures.

Because of their love for music and their willingness to deploy themselves in the service of beauty, the creatures are given a lovely name by Earthlings.

They are called *harmoniums.*

Unk and Boaz came in for a landing on the dark side of Mercury, seventy-nine Earthling days out of Mars. They did not know that the planet on which they were landing was Mercury.

They thought the Sun was terrifyingly large—

But that didn't keep them from thinking that they were landing on Earth.

They blacked out during the period of sharp deceleration. Now they were regaining consciousness—were being treated to a cruel and lovely illusion.

It seemed to Unk and Boaz that their ship was settling slowly among skyscrapers over which searchlights played.

"They aren't shooting," said Boaz. "Either the war's over, or it ain't begun."

The merry beams of light they saw were not from searchlights. The beams came from tall crystals on the borderline between the light and dark hemispheres of Mercury. Those crystals were catching beams from the sun, were bending them prismatically, playing them over the dark side. Other crystals on the dark side caught the beams and passed them on.

It was easy to believe that the searchlights were playing over a sophisticated civilization indeed. It was easy to mistake the dense forest of giant blue-white crystals for skyscrapers, stupendous and beautiful.

Unk, standing at a porthole, wept quietly. He was weeping for love, for family, for friendship, for truth, for civilization. The things he wept for were all abstractions, since his memory could furnish few faces or artifacts with which his imagination might fashion a passion play. Names rattled in his head like dry bones. *Stony Stevenson, a friend . . . Bee, a wife . . . Chrono, a son . . . Unk, a father . . .*

The name *Malachi Constant* came to him, and he didn't know what to do with it.

Unk lapsed into a blank reverie, a blank respect for the splendid people and the splendid lives that had produced the majestic buildings that the searchlights swept. Here, surely, faceless families and faceless friends and nameless hopes could flourish like—

An apt image for flourishing eluded Unk.

He imagined a remarkable fountain, a cone described by descending bowls of increasing diameters. It wouldn't do. The fountain was bone dry, filled with the ruins of birds' nests. Unk's fingertips tingled, as though abraded by a climb up the dry bowls.

The image wouldn't do.

Unk imagined again the three beautiful girls who had beckoned him to come down the oily bore of his Mauser rifle.

"Man!" said Boaz, "everbody asleep—but not for long!" He cooed, and his eyes flashed. "When old Boaz and old Unk hits town," he said, "everbody going to wake up and stay woke up for weeks on end!"

The ship was being controlled skillfully by its pilot-navigator. The equipment was talking nervously to itself—cycling, whirring, clicking, buzzing. It was sensing and avoiding hazards to the sides, seeking an ideal landing place below.

The designers of the pilot-navigator had purposely obsessed the equipment with one idea—and that idea was to seek shelter for the precious troops and matériel it was supposed to be carrying. The pilot-navigator was to set the precious troops and matériel down in the deepest hole it could find. The assumption was that the landing would be in the face of hostile fire.

Twenty Earthling minutes later, the pilot-navigator was still talking to itself—finding as much to talk about as ever.

And the ship was still falling, and falling fast.

The seeming searchlights and skyscrapers outside were no longer to be seen. There was only inky blackness.

Inside the ship, there was silence of a hardly lighter shade. Unk and Boaz sensed what was happening to them—found what was happening unspeakable.

They sensed correctly that they were being buried alive.

The ship lurched suddenly, throwing Boaz and Unk to the floor.

The violence brought violent relief.

"Home at last," yelled Boaz. "Welcome home!"

Then the ghastly feeling of the leaf-like fall began again.

Twenty Earthling minutes later, the ship was still falling gently.

Its lurches were more frequent.

To protect themselves against the lurches, Boaz and Unk had gone to bed. They lay face down, their hands gripping the steel pipe supports of their bunks.

To make their misery complete, the pilot-navigator decreed that night should fall in the cabin.

A grinding noise passed over the dome of the ship, forced Unk and Boaz to turn their eyes from their pillows to the portholes. There was a pale yellow light outside now.

Unk and Boaz shouted for joy, ran to the portholes. They reached them just in time to be thrown to the floor again as the ship freed itself from an obstruction, began its fall again.

One Earthling minute later, the fall stopped.

There was a modest click from the pilot-navigator. Having delivered its cargo safely from Mars to Mercury, as instructed, it had shut itself off.

It had delivered its cargo to the floor of a cave one hundred and sixteen miles below the surface of Mercury. It had threaded its way down through a tortuous system of chimneys until it could go no deeper.

Boaz was the first to reach a porthole, to look out and see the gay welcome of yellow and aquamarine diamonds the harmoniums had made on the walls.

"Unk!" said Boaz. "God damn if it didn't go and set us down right in the middle of a Hollywood night club!"

A recapitulation of Schliemann breathing techniques is in

order at this point, in order that what happened next can be fully understood. Unk and Boaz, in their pressurized cabin, had been getting their oxygen from goofballs in their small intestines. But, living in an atmosphere under pressure, there was no need for them to plug their ears and nostrils, and keep their mouths shut tight. This sealing off was necessary only in a vacuum or in a poisonous atmosphere.

Boaz was under the impression that outside the space ship was the wholesome atmosphere of his native Earth.

Actually, there was nothing out there but a vacuum.

Boaz threw open both the inner and outer doors of the air-lock with a grand carelessness predicated on a friendly atmosphere outside.

He was rewarded with the explosion of the small atmosphere of the cabin into the vacuum outside.

He slammed shut the inner door, but not before he and Unk had hemorrhaged in the act of shouting for joy.

They collapsed, their respiratory systems bleeding profusely.

All that saved them from death was a fully automatic emergency system that answered the explosion with another, bringing the pressure of the cabin up to normal again.

"Mama," said Boaz, as he came to. "God damn, Mama—this sure as hell ain't Earth."

Unk and Boaz did not panic.

They restored their strength with food, rest, drink, and goofballs.

And they then plugged their ears and nostrils, shut their mouths, and explored the neighborhood of the ship. They determined that their tomb was deep, tortuous, endless—airless, uninhabited by anything remotely human, and uninhabitable by anything remotely human.

They noted the presence of the harmoniums, but could find nothing encouraging in the presence of the creatures there. The creatures seemed ghastly.

Unk and Boaz didn't really believe they were in such a place. Not believing it was the thing that saved them from panic.

They returned to their ship.

"O.K.," said Boaz calmly, "there has been some mistake. We have wound up too deep in the ground. We got to fly back on up to where them buildings are. I tell you frankly Unk, it don't seem like to me this is even Earth we're in. There's been some mistake, like I say, and we got to ask the folks in the buildings where we are."

"O.K.," said Unk. He licked his lips.

"Just push that old *on* button," said Boaz, "and up we fly like a bird."

"O.K.," said Unk.

"I mean," said Boaz, "up there, the folks in the buildings may not even *know* about all this down here. Maybe we discovered something they'll be just *amazed* about."

"Sure," said Unk. His soul felt the pressure of the miles of rock above. And his soul felt the true nature of their predicament. On all sides and overhead were passages that branched and branched and branched. And the branches forked to twigs, and the twigs forked to passages no larger than a human pore.

Unk's soul was right in feeling that not one branch in ten thousand led all the way to the surface.

The space ship, thanks to the brilliantly-conceived sensing gear on its bottom, had sensed its way easily down and down and down, through one of the very few ways in—down and down and down one of the very few ways out.

What Unk's soul hadn't suspected yet was the congenital stupidity of the pilot-navigator when it came to going up. It had never occurred to the designers that the ship might encounter problems in going up. All Martian ships, after all, were meant to take off from an unobstructed field on Mars, and to be abandoned after landing on Earth. Consequently, there was virtually no sensing equipment on the ship for hazards overhead.

"So long, old cave," said Boaz.

Casually, Unk pressed the *on* button.

The pilot-navigator hummed.

In ten Earthling seconds, the pilot-navigator was warm.

The ship left the cave floor with whispering ease, touched a wall, dragged its rim up the wall with a grinding, tearing scream, bashed its dome on an overhead projection, backed off, bashed its dome again, backed off, grazed the projection, climbed whisperingly again. Then came the grinding scream again—this time from all sides.

All upward motion had stopped.

The ship was wedged in solid rock.

The pilot-navigator whimpered.

It sent a wisp of mustard-colored smoke up through the floor-boards of the cabin.

The pilot-navigator stopped whimpering.

It had overheated, and overheating was a signal for the pilot-navigator to extricate the ship from a hopeless mess. This it proceeded to do—grindingly. Steel members groaned. Rivets snapped like rifle shots.

At last the ship was free.

The pilot-navigator knew when it was licked. It flew the ship back down to the cave floor, landing with a kiss.

The pilot-navigator shut itself off.

Unk pushed the *on* button again.

Again the ship blundered up into a blind passage, again retreated, again settled to the floor and shut itself off.

The cycle was repeated a dozen times, until it was plain that the ship would only bash itself to pieces. Already its frame was badly sprung.

When the ship settled to the cave floor for the twelfth time, Unk and Boaz went to pieces. They cried.

"We're dead, Unk—we're dead!" said Boaz.

"I've never been alive that I can remember," said Unk brokenly. "I thought I was finally going to get some living done."

Unk went to a porthole, looked out with streaming eyes.

He saw that the creatures nearest the porthole had outlined in aquamarine a perfect, pale yellow letter T.

The making of a T was well within the limits of probability for brainless creatures distributing themselves at random. But then Unk saw that the T was preceded by a perfect S. And the S was preceded by a perfect E.

Unk moved his head to one side, looked through the porthole obliquely. The movement gave him a perspective down a hundred yards of harmonium-infested wall.

Unk was flabbergasted to see that the harmoniums were forming a message in dazzling letters.

The message was this, in pale yellow, outlined in aquamarine:

IT'S AN INTELLIGENCE TEST!

CHAPTER NINE

A Puzzle Solved

In the beginning, God became the Heaven and the Earth. . . . And God said, 'Let Me be light,' and He was light.

—*The Winston Niles Rumfoord Authorized Revised Bible*

For a delicious tea snack, try young harmoniums rolled into tubes and filled with Venusian cottage cheese.

—*The Beatrice Rumfoord Galactic Cookbook*

In terms of their souls, the martyrs of Mars died not when they attacked Earth but when they were recruited for the Martian war machine.

—*The Winston Niles Rumfoord Pocket History of Mars*

I found me a place where I can do good without doing any harm.

—BOAZ IN SARAH HORNE CANBY'S *Unk and Boaz in the Caves of Mercury*

THE BEST-SELLING BOOK in recent times has been *The Winston Niles Rumfoord Authorized Revised Bible.* Next in popularity is that delightful forgery, *The Beatrice Rumfoord Galactic Cookbook.* The third most popular is *The Winston Niles Rumfoord Pocket History of Mars.* The fourth most popular is a children's book, *Unk and Boaz in the Caves of Mercury*, by Sarah Horne Canby.

The publisher's bland analysis of Mrs. Canby's book's success appears on the dust jacket: "What child wouldn't like to be shipwrecked on a space ship with a cargo of hamburgers, hot dogs, catsup, sporting goods, and soda pop?"

Dr. Frank Minot, in his *Are Adults Harmoniums?*, sees something more sinister in the love children have for the book. "Dare we consider," he asks, "how close Unk and Boaz are to the everyday experience of children when Unk and Boaz deal solemnly and respectfully with creatures that are in fact obscenely unmotivated, insensitive, and dull?" Minot, in drawing a parallel between human parents and harmoniums, refers to the dealings of Unk and Boaz with harmoniums. The harmoniums spelled out for Unk and Boaz a new message of hope or veiled derision every fourteen Earthling days—for three years.

The messages were written, of course, by Winston Niles Rumfoord, who materialized briefly on Mercury at fourteen-day intervals. He peeled off harmoniums here, slapped others up there, making the block letters.

In Mrs. Canby's tale, the first intimation given that Rumfoord is around the caves from time to time is given in a scene very close to the end—a scene wherein Unk finds the tracks of a big dog in the dust.

At this point in the story it is mandatory, if an adult is reading the story aloud to a child, for the adult to ask the child with delicious hoarseness, "Who wuzza dog?"

Dog wuzza Kazak. Dog wuzza Winston Niles Rumfoord's dreat big mean chrono-synclastic infundibulated dog.

Unk and Boaz had been on Mercury for three Earthling years when Unk found Kazak's footprints in the dust on the floor of a cave corridor. Mercury had carried Unk and Boaz twelve and a half times around the Sun.

Unk found the prints on a floor six miles above the chamber in which the dented, scarred, and rock-bound space ship lay. Unk didn't live in the space ship any more, and neither did Boaz. The space ship served merely as a common supply base to which Unk and Boaz returned for provisions once every Earthling month or so.

Unk and Boaz rarely met. They moved in very different circles.

The circles in which Boaz moved were small. His abode was fixed and richly furnished. It was on the same level as the space ship, only a quarter of a mile away from it.

The circles in which Unk moved were vast and restless. He had no home. He traveled light and he traveled far, climbing ever higher until he was stopped by cold. Where the cold stopped Unk, the cold stopped the harmoniums, too. On the upper levels where Unk wandered, the harmoniums were stunted and few.

On the cozy lower level where Boaz lived, the harmoniums were plentiful and fast-growing.

Boaz and Unk had separated after one Earthling year together in the space ship. In that first year together, it had become clear to both of them that they weren't going to get out unless something or somebody came and got them out.

That had been clear, even though the creatures on the walls continued to spell out new messages emphasizing the *fairness* of the test to which Unk and Boaz were being subjected, the ease with which they might escape, if only they would think a little harder, if they would only think a little more intricately.

"THINK!" the creatures would say.

Unk and Boaz separated after Unk went temporarily insane. Unk had tried to murder Boaz. Boaz had come into the space ship with a harmonium, which was exactly like all the other harmoniums, and he'd said, "Ain't he a cute little feller, Unk?"

Unk had gone for Boaz's throat.

Unk was naked when he found the dog tracks. The lichen green uniform and black fiber boots of the Martian Assault Infantry had been scoured to threads and dust by the touch of stone.

The dog tracks did not excite Unk. Unk's soul wasn't filled with the music of sociability or the light of hope when he saw a warm-blooded creature's tracks, saw the tracks of man's best friend. And he still had very little to say to himself when the tracks of a well-shod man joined those of the dog.

Unk was at war with his environment. He had come to regard his environment as being either malevolent or cruelly mismanaged. His response was to fight it with the only weapons at hand—passive resistance and open displays of contempt.

The footprints seemed to Unk to be the opening moves in one more fat-headed game his environment wanted to play. He would follow the tracks, but lazily, without excitement. He would follow them simply because he had nothing else scheduled for the time.

He would follow them.

He would see where they went.

His progress was knobby and ramshackle. Poor Unk had lost a lot of weight, and a lot of hair, too. He was aging fast. His eyes felt hot and his skeleton felt rickety.

Unk never shaved on Mercury. When his hair and beard got so long as to be a bother, he would hack away wads of thatch with a butcherknife.

Boaz shaved every day. Boaz gave himself a haircut twice an Earthling week with a barber kit from the space ship.

Boaz, twelve years younger than Unk, had never felt better in his life. He had gained weight in the caves of Mercury—and serenity, too.

Boaz's home vault was furnished with a cot, a table, two chairs, a punching bag, a mirror, dumbbells, a tape recorder, and a library of recorded music on tape consisting of eleven hundred compositions.

Boaz's home vault had a door on it, a round boulder with which he could plug the vault's mouth. The door was necessary, since Boaz was God Almighty to the harmoniums. They could locate him by his heartbeat.

Had he slept with his door open, he would have awakened to find himself pinned down by hundreds of thousands of his admirers. They would have let him up only when his heart stopped beating.

Boaz, like Unk, was naked. But he still had shoes. His genuine leather shoes had held up gorgeously. True—Unk had walked fifty miles to every mile walked by Boaz, but Boaz's shoes had not merely held up. They looked as good as new.

Boaz wiped, waxed, and shined them regularly.

He was shining them now.

The door of his vault was blocked by the boulder. Only four favored harmoniums were inside with him. Two were wrapped about his upper arms. One was stuck to his thigh. The fourth, an immature harmonium only three inches long, clung to the inside of his left wrist, feeding on Boaz's pulse.

When Boaz found a harmonium he loved more than all the rest, that was what he did—let the creature feed on his pulse.

"You like that?" he said in his thoughts to the lucky harmonium. "Ain't that nice?"

He had never felt better physically, had never felt better

mentally, had never felt better spiritually. He was glad he and Unk had separated, because Unk liked to twist things around to where it seemed that anybody who was happy was dumb or crazy.

"What makes a man *be* like that?" Boaz asked the little harmonium in his thoughts. "What's he think he's gaining compared to what he's throwing away? No wonder he looks sick."

Boaz shook his head. "I kept trying to interest him in you fellers, and he just got madder. Never helps to get mad.

"I don't know what's going on," said Boaz in his thoughts, "and I'm probably not smart enough to understand if somebody was to explain it to me. All I know is we're being tested somehow, by somebody or some thing a whole lot smarter than us, and all I can do is be friendly and keep calm and try and have a nice time till it's over."

Boaz nodded. "That's my philosophy, friends," he said to the harmoniums stuck to him. "And if I'm not mistaken, that's yours, too. I reckon that's how come we hit it off so good."

The genuine leather toe of the shoe that Boaz was shining glowed like a ruby.

"Men—awww now, men, men, men," said Boaz to himself, staring into the ruby. When he shined his shoes, he imagined that he could see many things in the rubies of the toes.

Right now, Boaz was looking into a ruby and seeing Unk strangling poor old Stony Stevenson at the stone stake on the iron parade ground back on Mars. The horrible image wasn't a random recollection. It was dead center in Boaz's relationship with Unk.

"Don't *truth* me," said Boaz in his thoughts, "and I won't *truth* you." It was a plea he had made several times to Unk.

Boaz had invented the plea, and its meaning was this: Unk was to stop telling Boaz truths about the harmoniums, because Boaz loved the harmoniums, and because Boaz was nice enough not to bring up truths that would make Unk unhappy.

Unk didn't know that he had strangled his friend Stony Stevenson. Unk thought Stony was still marvelously alive somewhere in the Universe. Unk was living on dreams of a reunion with Stony.

Boaz was nice enough to withhold the truth from Unk, no

matter how great the provocation had been to club Unk between the eyes with it.

The horrible image in the ruby dissolved.

"Yes, Lord," said Boaz in his thoughts.

The adult harmonium on Boaz's upper left arm stirred.

"You asking old Boaz for a concert?" Boaz asked the creature in his thoughts. "That what you trying to say? You trying to say, 'Ol' Boaz, I don't want to sound ungrateful, on account of I know it's a great honor to get to be right here close to your heart. Only I keep thinking about all my friends outside, and I keep wishing they could have something good, too.' That what you trying to say?" said Boaz in his thoughts. "You trying to say, 'Please, Papa Boaz—put on a concert for all the poor friends outside'? That what you trying to say?"

Boaz smiled. "You don't have to flatter me," he said to the harmonium.

The small harmonium on his wrist doubled up, extended itself again. "What *you* trying to tell me?" he asked it. "You trying to say 'Uncle Boaz—your pulse is just too rich for a little tad like me. Uncle Boaz—please just play some nice, sweet, easy music to eat'? That what you trying to say?"

Boaz turned his attention to the harmonium on his right arm. The creature had not moved. "Ain't *you* the quiet one, though?" Boaz asked the creature in his thoughts. "Don't say much, but thinking all the time. I guess you're thinking old Boaz is pretty mean not just letting the music play all the time, huh?"

The harmonium on his left arm stirred again. "What's that you say?" said Boaz in his thoughts. He cocked his head, pretended to listen, though no sounds could travel through the vacuum in which he lived. "You say, 'Please, King Boaz, play us the *1812 Overture*'?" Boaz looked shocked, then stern. "Just because something feels better than anything else," he said in his thoughts, "that don't mean it's good for you."

Scholars whose field is the Martian War often exclaim over the queer unevenness of Rumfoord's war preparations. In some areas, his plans were horribly flimsy. The shoes he issued his ordinary troops, for instance, were almost a satire on the temporariness of the Jerry-built society of Mars—on a society whose whole purpose was to destroy itself in uniting the peoples of Earth.

In the music libraries Rumfoord personally selected for the company mother ships, however, one sees a great cultural nest egg—a nest egg prepared as though for a monumental civilization that was going to endure for a thousand Earthling years. It is said that Rumfoord spent more time on the useless music libraries than he did on artillery and field sanitation combined.

As an anonymous wit has it: "The Army of Mars arrived with three hundred hours of continuous music, and didn't last long enough to hear *The Minute Waltz* to the end."

The explanation of the bizarre emphasis on the music carried by the Martian mother ships is simple: Rumfoord was crazy about good music—a craze, incidentally, that struck him only after he had been spread through time and space by the chrono-synclastic infundibulum.

The harmoniums in the caves of Mercury were crazy about good music, too. They had been feeding on one sustained note in the song of Mercury for centuries. When Boaz gave them their first taste of music, which happened to be *Le Sacre du Printemps,* some of the creatures actually died in ecstasy.

A dead harmonium is shriveled and orange in the yellow light of the Mercurial caves. A dead harmonium looks like a dried apricot.

On that first occasion, which hadn't been planned as a concert for the harmoniums, the tape recorder had been on the floor of the space ship. The creatures who had actually died in ecstasy had been in direct contact with the metal hull of the ship.

Now, two and a half years later, Boaz demonstrated the proper way to stage a concert for the creatures so as not to kill them.

Boaz left his home vault, carrying the tape recorder and the musical selections for the concert with him. In the corridor outside were two aluminum ironing boards. These had fiber pads on their feet. The ironing boards were six feet apart, and spanning them was a stretcher made of aluminum poles and lichen-fiber canvas.

Boaz placed the tape recorder in the middle of the stretcher.

The purpose of the engine resulting was to dilute and dilute and dilute the vibrations from the tape recorder. The vibrations, before they reached the stone floor, had to struggle through the dead canvas of the stretcher, down the stretcher handles, through the ironing boards, and finally through the fiber pads on the feet of the ironing boards.

The dilution was a safety measure. It guaranteed that no harmonium would get a lethal overdose of music.

Boaz now put the tape in the recorder and turned the recorder on. Throughout the concert, he would stand guard by the apparatus. His duty was to see that no creature crept too close to the apparatus. His duty, when a creature crept too close, was to peel the creature from the wall or floor, scold it, and paste it up again a hundred yards or more away.

"If you ain't got no more sense than that," he would say in his thoughts to the foolhardy harmonium, "you're going to wind up out here in left field ever' time. Think it over."

Actually, a creature placed a hundred yards from the tape recorder still got plenty of music to eat.

The walls of the caves were so extraordinarily conductive, in fact, that harmoniums on cave walls miles away got whiffs of Boaz's concerts through the stone.

Unk, who had been following the tracks deeper and deeper into the caves, could tell from the way the harmoniums were behaving that Boaz was staging a concert. He had reached a warm level where the harmoniums were thick. Their regular pattern of alternating yellow and aquamarine diamonds was breaking up—was degenerating into jagged clumps, pinwheels, and lightning bolts. The music was making them do it.

Unk laid his pack down, then laid himself down to rest.

Unk dreamed about colors other than yellow and aquamarine.

Then he dreamed that his good friend Stony Stevenson was waiting for him around the next bend. His mind became lively with the things he and Stony would say when they met. Unk's mind still had no face to go with the name of Stony Stevenson, but that didn't matter much.

"What a pair," Unk said to himself. By that he meant that he and Stony, working together, would be invincible.

"I tell you," Unk said to himself with satisfaction, "that is one pair they want to keep apart at all costs. If old Stony and old Unk ever get together again, they better watch out. When old Stony and old Unk get together, anything can happen, and it usually does."

Old Unk chuckled.

The people who were supposedly afraid of Unk's and Stony's getting together were the people in the big, beautiful buildings up above. Unk's imagination had done a lot in three years with the glimpses he'd had of the supposed buildings—of what were in fact solid, dead, dumb-cold crystals. Unk's imagination was now certain that the masters of all creation lived in those buildings. They were Unk's and Boaz's and maybe Stony's jailers. They were experimenting with Unk and Boaz in the caves. They wrote the messages in harmoniums. The harmoniums didn't have anything to do with the messages.

Unk knew all those things for sure.

Unk knew a lot of other things for sure. He even knew how the buildings up above were furnished. The furniture didn't have any legs on it. It just floated in air, suspended by magnetism.

And the people never worked at all, and they never worried about a thing.

Unk hated them.

He hated the harmoniums, too. He peeled a harmonium from the wall and tore it in two. It shriveled at once—turned orange.

Unk flipped the two-piece corpse at the ceiling. And, looking up at the ceiling, he saw a new message written there. The message was disintegrating, because of the music. But it was still legible.

The message told Unk in five words how to escape surely, easily, and swiftly from the caves. He was bound to admit, when given the solution to the puzzle that he had failed to solve in three years, that the puzzle was simple and fair.

Unk scuttled down through the caves until he came upon Boaz's concert for the harmoniums. Unk was wild and bug-eyed with big news. He could not speak in a vacuum, so he hauled Boaz to the space ship.

There, in the inert atmosphere of the cabin, Unk told Boaz of the message that meant escape from the caves.

It was now Boaz's turn to react numbly. Boaz had thrilled to the slightest illusion of intelligence on the part of the harmoniums—but now, having heard the news that he was about to be freed from his prison, Boaz was strangely reserved.

"That—that explains that other message," said Boaz softly.

"What other message?" asked Unk.

Boaz held up his hands to represent a message that had appeared on the wall outside his home four Earthling days before. "Said, 'BOAZ, DON'T GO!'" said Boaz. He looked down self-consciously. "'WE LOVE YOU, BOAZ.' That's what it said."

Boaz dropped his hands to his side, turned away as though turning away from unbearable beauty. "I saw that," he said, "and I had to smile. I looked at them sweet, gentle fellers on the wall there, and I says to myself, 'Boys—how's old Boaz ever going to go anywhere? Old Boaz, he going to be stuck here for quite some time yet!'"

"It's a trap!" said Unk.

"It's a what?" said Boaz.

"A trap!" said Unk. "A trick to keep us here!"

The comic book called *Tweety and Sylvester* was open on the table before Boaz. Boaz didn't answer Unk right away. He leafed through the ragged book instead. "I expect," he said at last.

Unk thought about the crazy appeal in the name of love. He did something he hadn't done for a long time. He laughed. He thought it was an hysterical ending for the nightmare—that the brainless membranes on the walls should speak of love.

Boaz suddenly grabbed Unk, rattled poor Unk's dry bones. "I'd appreciate it, Unk," said Boaz tautly, "if you'd just let me think whatever I'm going to think about that message about how they love me. I mean—" he said, "you know—" he said, "it don't necessarily have to make sense to you. I mean—" he said, "you know—" he said, "there ain't really any call for you to say anything about it, one way or the other. I mean," he said, "you know—" he said, "these animals ain't necessarily your dish. You don't necessarily have to like 'em, or understand 'em, or say anything about 'em. I mean—" said Boaz, "you know—" said Boaz, "the message wasn't addressed to you. It's me they said they loved. That lets you out."

He let Unk go, turned attention to the comic book again. His broad, brown, slab-muscled back amazed Unk. Living apart from Boaz, Unk had flattered himself into thinking he was a physical match for Boaz. He saw now what a pathetic delusion this had been.

The muscles in Boaz's back slid over one another in slow patterns that were counterpoint to the quick movements of his page-turning fingers. "You know so much about traps and things," said Boaz. "How you know there ain't some worse trap waiting for us if we go flying out of here?"

Before Unk could answer him, Boaz remembered that he had left the tape recorder playing and unguarded.

"Ain't nobody watching out for 'em at all!" he cried. He left Unk, ran to rescue the harmoniums.

While Boaz was gone, Unk made plans for turning the space ship upside down. That was the solution to the puzzle of how to get out. That was what the harmoniums on the ceiling had said:

UNK, TURN SHIP UPSIDE DOWN.

The theory of turning the space ship over was sound, of course. The ship's sensing equipment was on its bottom. When turned over, the ship would be able to apply the same easy grace and intelligence to getting out of the caves that it had used in getting into them.

Thanks to a power winch and the feeble tug of gravity in the caves of Mercury, Unk had the ship turned over by the time Boaz got back. All that remained to be done for the trip out was to press the *on* button. The upside-down ship would then blunder against the cave floor, give up, retreat from the floor under the impression that the floor was a ceiling.

It would go up the system of chimneys under the impression that it was going down. And it would inevitably find the way out, under the impression that it was seeking the deepest possible hole.

The hole it would eventually find itself in would be the bottomless, sideless pit of space eternal.

Boaz came into the upside-down ship, his arms loaded with dead harmoniums. He was carrying four quarts or more of the seeming dried apricots. Inevitably he dropped some. And, in stooping to pick them up reverently, he dropped more.

Tears were streaming down his face.

"You see?" said Boaz. He was raging heartbrokenly against himself. "You see, Unk?" he said. "See what happens when somebody just runs off and forgets?"

Boaz shook his head. "This ain't all of 'em," he said. "This ain't *near* all of 'em." He found an empty carton that had once contained candy bars. He put the harmonium corpses into that.

He straightened up, his hands on his hips. Just as Unk had been amazed by Boaz's physical condition, so was Unk now amazed by Boaz's dignity.

Boaz, when he straightened up, was a wise, decent, weeping, brown Hercules.

Unk, by comparison, felt scrawny, rootless, and sore-headed.

"You want to do the dividing, Unk?" said Boaz.

"Dividing?" said Unk.

"Goofballs, food, soda pop, candy," said Boaz.

"Divide it all?" said Unk. "My God—there's enough of everything for five hundred years." There had never been any talk of dividing things before. There had been no shortage, and no threat of a shortage of anything.

"Half for you to take with you, and half to leave here with me," said Boaz.

"*Leave* with you?" said Unk incredulously. "You're—you're coming with me, aren't you?"

Boaz held up his big right hand, and it was a tender gesture for silence, a gesture made by a thoroughly great human being. "Don't truth me, Unk," said Boaz, "and I won't truth you." He brushed away his tears with a fist.

Unk had never been able to brush aside the plea about truthing. It frightened him. Some part of his mind warned him that Boaz was not bluffing, that Boaz really knew a truth about Unk that could tear him to pieces.

Unk opened his mouth and closed it again.

"You come and tell me the big news," said Boaz. " 'Boaz—' you say, 'we're going to be free!' And I get all excited, and I drop everthing I'm doin', and I get set to be free.

"And I keep saying it over to myself about how I'm going to be free," said Boaz, "and then I try to think what that's going to be like, and all I can see is people. They push me this way, then they push me that—and nothing pleases 'em, and they get madder and madder, on account of nothing makes 'em happy. And they holler at me on account of I ain't made 'em happy, and we all push and pull some more.

"And then, all of a sudden," said Boaz, "I remember all the crazy little animals I been making so happy so easy with music. And I go find thousands of 'em lying around dead, on account of Boaz forgot all about 'em, he was so excited about being free. And ever' one of them lost lives I could have saved, if I'd have just kept my mind on what I was doing.

"And then I say to myself," said Boaz, " 'I ain't never been nothing good to people, and people never been nothing good to me. So what I want to be free in crowds of people for?'

"And then I knew what I was going to say to you, Unk, when I got back here," said Boaz.

Boaz now said it:

"I found me a place where I can do good without doing any harm, and I can see I'm doing good, and them I'm doing good for know I'm doing it, and they love me, Unk, as best they can. I found me a home.

"And when I die down here some day," said Boaz, "I'm going to be able to say to myself, 'Boaz—you made millions of lives worth living. Ain't nobody ever spread more joy. You ain't got an enemy in the Universe.' " Boaz became for himself the affectionate Mama and Papa he'd never had. " 'You go to sleep now,' " he said to himself, imagining himself on a stone deathbed in the caves. " 'You're a good boy, Boaz,' " he said. " 'Good night.' "

CHAPTER TEN

An Age of Miracles

"O Lord Most High, Creator of the Cosmos, Spinner of Galaxies, Soul of Electromagnetic Waves, Inhaler and Exhaler of Inconceivable Volumes of Vacuum, Spitter of Fire and Rock, Trifler with Millennia—what could we do for Thee that Thou couldst not do for Thyself one octillion times better? Nothing. What could we do or say that could possibly interest Thee? Nothing. Oh, Mankind, rejoice in the apathy of our Creator, for it makes us free and truthful and dignified at last. No longer can a fool like Malachi Constant point to a ridiculous accident of good luck and say, 'Somebody up there likes me.' And no longer can a tyrant say, 'God wants this or that to happen, and anybody who doesn't help this or that to happen is against God.' O Lord Most High, what a glorious weapon is Thy Apathy, for we have unsheathed it, have thrust and slashed mightily with it, and the claptrap that has so often enslaved us or driven us into the madhouse lies slain!"

—THE REVEREND C. HORNER REDWINE

IT WAS a Tuesday afternoon. It was springtime in the northern hemisphere of Earth.

Earth was green and watery. The air of earth was good to breathe, as fattening as cream.

The purity of the rains that fell on Earth could be tasted. The taste of purity was daintily tart.

Earth was warm.

The surface of Earth heaved and seethed in fecund restlessness. Earth was most fertile where the most death was.

The daintily tart rain fell on a green place where there was a great deal of death. It fell on a New World country churchyard. The churchyard was in West Barnstable, Cape Cod, Massachusetts, U.S.A. The churchyard was full, the spaces between its naturally dead chinked tight by the bodies of the honored war dead. Martians and Earthlings lay side by side.

There was not a country in the world that did not have

graveyards with Earthlings and Martians buried side by side. There was not a country in the world that had not fought a battle in the war of all Earth against the invaders from Mars.

All was forgiven.

All living things were brothers, and all dead things were even more so.

The church, which squatted among the headstones like a wet mother dodo, had been at various times Presbyterian, Congregationalist, Unitarian, and Universal Apocalyptic. It was now the Church of God the Utterly Indifferent.

A seeming wild man stood in the churchyard, wondering at the creamery air, at the green, at the wet. He was almost naked, and his blue-black beard and his hair were tangled and long and shot with gray. The only garment he wore was a clinking breechclout made of wrenches and copper wire.

The garment covered his shame.

The rain ran down his coarse cheeks. He tipped back his head to drink it. He rested his hand on a headstone, more for the feel than the support of it. He was used to the feel of stones—was deathly used to the feel of rough, dry stones. But stones that were wet, stones that were mossy, stones that were squared and written on by men—he hadn't felt stones like that for a long, long time.

Pro patria said the stone he touched.

The man was Unk.

He was home from Mars and Mercury. His space ship had landed itself in a wood next to the churchyard. He was filled with the heedless, tender violence of a man who has had his lifetime cruelly wasted.

Unk was forty-three years old.

He had every reason to wither and die.

All that kept him going was a wish that was more mechanical than emotional. *He wished to be reunited with Bee, his mate, with Chrono, his son, and with Stony Stevenson, his best and only friend.*

The Reverend C. Horner Redwine stood in the pulpit of his church that rainy Tuesday afternoon. There was no one else in the church. Redwine had climbed up to the pulpit in order simply to be as happy as possible. He was not being as happy as possible under adverse circumstances. He was being as happy as possible under extraordinarily happy circumstances—for he was a much loved minister of a religion that not only promised but delivered miracles.

His church, the Barnstable First Church of God the Utterly Indifferent, had a subtitle: *The Church of the Weary Space Wanderer.* The subtitle was justified by this prophecy: That a lone straggler from the Army of Mars would arrive at Redwine's church some day.

The church was ready for the miracle. There was a hand-forged iron spike driven into the rugged oak post behind the pulpit. The post carried the mighty beam that was the rooftree. And on the nail was hung a coathanger encrusted with semi-precious stones. And on the coathanger hung a suit of clothes in a transparent plastic bag.

The prophecy was that the weary Space Wanderer would be naked, that the suit of clothes would fit him like a glove. The suit was of such a design as to fit no one but the right man well. It was one piece, lemon-yellow, rubberized, closed by a zipper, and ideally skin-tight.

The garment was not in the mode of the day. It was a special creation to add glamour to the miracle.

Stitched into the back and front of the garment were orange question marks a foot high. These signified that the Space Wanderer would not know who he was.

No one would know who he was until Winston Niles Rumfoord, the head of all churches of God the Utterly Indifferent, gave the world the Space Wanderer's name.

The signal, should the Space Wanderer arrive, was for Redwine to ring the church bell madly.

When the bell was rung madly, the parishioners were to feel ecstasy, to drop whatever they were doing, to laugh, to weep, to come.

The West Barnstable Volunteer Fire Department was so dominated by members of Redwine's church that the fire engine itself was going to arrive as the only vehicle remotely glorious enough for the Space Wanderer.

The screams of the fire alarm on top of the firehouse were to be added to the bedlam joy of the bell. One scream from the alarm meant a grass or woods fire. Two screams meant a house fire. Three screams meant a rescue. Ten screams would mean that the Space Wanderer had arrived.

Water seeped in around an ill-fitting window sash. Water crept under a loose shingle in the roof, dropped through a crack and hung in glittering beads from a rafter over Redwine's head. The good rain wet the old Paul Revere bell in the steeple, trickled down the bell rope, soaked the wooden doll tied to the end of the bell rope, dripped from the feet of the doll, made a puddle on the steeple's flagstone floor.

The doll had a religious significance. It represented a repellent way of life that was no more. It was called a *Malachi*. No home or place of business of a member of Redwine's faith was without a Malachi hanging somewhere.

There was only one proper way to hang a Malachi. That was by the neck. There was only one proper knot to use, and that was a hangman's knot.

And the rain dripped from the feet of Redwine's Malachi at the end of the bell rope—

The cold goblin spring of the crocuses was past.

The frail and chilly fairy spring of the daffodils was past.

The springtime for mankind had arrived, and the blooms of the lilac bowers outside Redwine's church hung fatly, heavy as Concord grapes.

Redwine listened to the rain, and imagined that it spoke Chaucerian English. He spoke aloud the words he imagined the rain to be speaking, spoke harmoniously, at just the noise level of the rain.

Whan that Aprille with his shoures sote
The droughte of Marche hath perced to the rote
And bathed every veyne in swich licour,
Of which vertu engendered is the flour—

A droplet fell twinkling from the rafter overhead, wet the left lens of Redwine's spectacles and his apple cheek.

Time had been kind to Redwine. Standing there in the pulpit, he looked like a ruddy, bespectacled country newsboy, though he was forty-nine. He raised his hand to brush away the wetness on his cheek, and rattled the blue canvas bag of lead shot that was strapped around his wrist.

There were similar bags of shot around his ankles and his other wrist, and two heavy slabs of iron hung on shoulder straps—one slab on his chest and one on his back.

These weights were his handicaps in the race of life.

He carried forty-eight pounds—carried them gladly. A stronger person would have carried more, a weaker person would have carried less. Every strong member of Redwine's faith accepted handicaps gladly, wore them proudly everywhere.

The weakest and meekest were bound to admit, at last, that the race of life was fair.

The liquid melodies of the rain made such lovely backgrounds for any sort of recitation in the empty church that Redwine recited some more. This time he recited something that Winston Niles Rumfoord, the Master of Newport, had written.

The thing that Redwine was about to recite with the rain chorus was a thing that the Master of Newport had written to define the position of himself with respect to his ministers, the position of his ministers with respect to their flocks, and the position of everybody with respect to God. Redwine read it to his flock on the first Sunday of every month.

"'I am not your father,'" said Redwine. "'Rather call me brother. But I am not your brother. Rather call me son. But I am not your son. Rather call me a dog. But I am not your dog. Rather call me a flea on your dog. But I am not a flea. Rather call me a germ on a flea on your dog. As a germ on a flea on your dog, I am eager to serve you in any way I can, just as you are willing to serve God Almighty, Creator of the Universe.'"

Redwine slapped his hands together, killing the imaginary germ-infested flea. On Sundays, the entire congregation slapped the flea in unison.

Another droplet fell shivering from the rafter, wet Redwine's cheek again. Redwine nodded his sweet thanks for the droplet, for the church, for peace, for the Master of Newport, for Earth, for a God Who didn't care, for everything.

He stepped down from the pulpit, making the lead balls in his handicap bags shift back and forth with a stately swish.

He went down the aisle and through the arch under the steeple. He paused by the puddle under the bell rope, looked up to divine the course the water had taken down. It was a lovely way, he decided, for spring rain to come in. If ever he were in charge of remodeling the church, he would make sure that enterprising drops of rain could still come in that way.

Just beyond the arch under the steeple was another arch, a leafy arch of lilacs.

Redwine now stepped under that second arch, saw the space ship like a great blister in the woods, saw the naked, bearded Space Wanderer in his churchyard.

Redwine cried out for joy. He ran back into his church and jerked and swung on the bell rope like a drunken chimpanzee. In the clanging bedlam of the bells, Redwine heard the words that the Master of Newport said all bells spoke.

"NO HELL!" whang-clanged the bell—

"NO HELL,

"NO HELL,

"NO HELL!"

Unk was terrified by the bell. It sounded like an angry, frightened bell to Unk, and he ran back to his ship, gashing his shin badly as he scrambled over a stone wall. As he was closing the airlock, he heard a siren wailing answers to the bell.

Unk thought Earth was still at war with Mars, and that the siren and the bell were calling sudden death down on him. He pressed the *on* button.

The automatic navigator did not respond instantly, but engaged in a fuzzy, ineffectual argument with itself. The argument ended with the navigator's shutting itself off.

Unk pressed the *on* button again. This time he kept it down by jamming his heel against it.

Again the navigator argued stupidly with itself, tried to shut itself off. When it found that it could not shut itself off, it made dirty yellow smoke.

The smoke became so dense and poisonous that Unk was obliged to swallow a goofball and practice Schliemann breathing again.

Then the pilot-navigator gave out a deep, throbbing organ note and died forever.

There was no taking off now. When the pilot-navigator died, the whole space ship died.

Unk went through the smoke to a porthole—looked out.

He saw a fire engine. The fire engine was breaking through the brush to the space ship. Men, women, and children were clinging to the engine—drenched by rain and expressing ecstasy.

Going in advance of the fire engine was the Reverend C. Horner Redwine. In one hand he carried a lemon-yellow suit in a transparent plastic bag. In the other hand he held a spray of fresh-cut lilacs.

The women threw kisses to Unk through the portholes, held their children up to see the adorable man inside. The men stayed with the fire engine, cheered Unk, cheered each other, cheered everything. The driver made the mighty motor backfire, blew the siren, rang the bell.

Everyone wore handicaps of some sort. Most handicaps were of an obvious sort—sashweights, bags of shot, old furnace grates—meant to hamper physical advantages. But there were, among Redwine's parishioners, several true believers who had chosen handicaps of a subtler and more telling kind.

There were women who had received by dint of dumb luck the terrific advantage of beauty. They had annihilated that unfair advantage with frumpish clothes, bad posture, chewing gum, and a ghoulish use of cosmetics.

One old man, whose only advantage was excellent eyesight, had spoiled that eyesight by wearing his wife's spectacles.

A dark young man, whose lithe, predaceous sex appeal could not be spoiled by bad clothes and bad manners, had handicapped himself with a wife who was nauseated by sex.

The dark young man's wife, who had reason to be vain about her Phi Beta Kappa key, had handicapped herself with a husband who read nothing but comic books.

Redwine's congregation was not unique. It wasn't especially fanatical. There were literally billions of happily self-handicapped people on Earth.

And what made them all so happy was that nobody took advantage of anybody any more.

Now the firemen thought of another way to express joy. There was a nozzle mounted amidships on the fire engine. It could be swiveled around like a machine gun. They aimed it straight up and turned it on. A shivering, unsure fountain climbed into the sky, was torn to shreds by the winds when it could climb no more. The shreds fell all around, now falling on the space ship with splattering thumps; now soaking the firemen themselves; now soaking women and children, startling them, then making them more full of joy than ever.

That water should have played such an important part in the welcoming of Unk was an enchanting accident. No one had planned it. But it was perfect that everyone should forget himself in a festival of universal wetness.

The Reverend C. Horner Redwine, feeling as naked as a pagan wood sprite in the clinging wetness of his clothes, swished a spray of lilacs over the glass of a porthole, then pressed his adoring face against the glass.

The expression of the face that looked back at Redwine was strikingly like the expression on the face of an intelligent ape in a zoo. Unk's forehead was deeply wrinkled, and his eyes were liquid with a hopeless wish to understand.

Unk had decided not to be afraid.

Neither was he in any hurry to let Redwine in.

At last he went to the airlock, unlatched both the inner and outer doors. He stepped back, waiting for someone else to push the doors open.

"First let me go in and have him put on the suit!" said Redwine to his congregation. "Then you can have him!"

There in the space ship, the lemon-yellow suit fit Unk like a coat of paint. The orange question marks on his chest and back clung without a wrinkle.

Unk did not yet know that no one else in the world was dressed like him. He assumed that many people had suits like his—question marks and all.

"This—this is Earth?" said Unk to Redwine.

"Yes," said Redwine. "Cape Cod, Massachusetts, United States of America, Brotherhood of Man."

"Thank God!" said Unk.

Redwine raised his eyebrows quizzically. "Why?" he said.

"Pardon me?" said Unk.

"Why thank God?" said Redwine. "He doesn't care what happens to you. He didn't go to any trouble to get you here safe and sound, any more than He would go to the trouble to kill you." He raised his arms, demonstrating the muscularity of his faith. The balls of shot in the handicap bags on his wrists shifted swishingly, drawing Unk's attention. From the handicap bags, Unk's attention made an easy jump to the heavy slab of iron on Redwine's chest. Redwine followed the trend of Unk's gaze, hefted the iron slab on his chest. "Heavy," he said.

"Um," said Unk.

"You should carry about fifty pounds, I would guess—after we build you up," said Redwine.

"Fifty pounds?" said Unk.

"You should be glad, not sorry, to carry such a handicap," said Redwine. "No one could then reproach you for taking advantage of the random ways of luck." There crept into his voice a beatifically threatening tone that he had not used much since the earliest days of the Church of God the Utterly Indifferent, since the thrilling mass conversions that had followed the war with Mars. In those days, Redwine and all the other young proselytizers had threatened unbelievers with the righteous displeasure of crowds—righteously displeased crowds that did not then exist.

The righteously displeased crowds existed now in every part of the world. The total membership of Churches of God the Utterly Indifferent was a good, round three billion. The young lions who had first taught the creed could now afford to be lambs, to contemplate such oriental mysteries as water trickling down a bell rope. The disciplinary arm of the Church was in crowds everywhere.

"I must warn you," Redwine said to Unk, "that when you go out among all those people you mustn't say anything that would indicate that God took a special interest in you, or that you could somehow be of help to God. The worst thing you could say, for instance, would be something like, 'Thank God for delivering me from all my troubles. For some reason He singled me out, and now my only wish is to serve Him.'

"The friendly crowd out there," continued Redwine, "could turn quite ugly quite fast, despite the high auspices under which you come."

Unk had been planning to say almost exactly what Redwine had warned him against saying. It had seemed the only proper speech to make. "What—what should I say?" said Unk.

"It has been prophesied what you will say," said Redwine, "word for word. I have thought long and hard about the words you are going to say, and I am convinced they cannot be improved upon."

"But I can't think of any words—except hello—thank you—" said Unk. "What do you *want* me to say?"

"What you do say," said Redwine. "Those good people out there have been rehearsing this moment for a long time. They will ask you two questions, and you will answer them to the best of your ability."

He led Unk through the airlock to the outside. The fire engine's fountain had been turned off. The shouting and dancing had stopped.

Redwine's congregation now formed a semicircle around Unk and Redwine. The members of the congregation had their lips pressed tightly together and their lungs filled.

Redwine gave a saintly signal.

The congregation spoke as one. "Who are you?" they said.

"I—I don't know my real name," said Unk. "They called me Unk."

"What happened to you?" said the congregation.

Unk shook his head vaguely. He could think of no apt condensation of his adventures for the obviously ritual mood. Something great was plainly expected of him. He was not up to greatness. He exhaled noisily, letting the congregation know that he was sorry to fail them with his colorlessness. "I was a victim of a series of accidents," he said. He shrugged. "As are we all," he said.

The cheering and dancing began again.

Unk was hustled aboard the fire engine, and driven on it to the door of the church.

Redwine pointed amiably to an unfurled wooden scroll over the door. Incised in the scroll and gilded were these words:

I WAS A VICTIM OF A SERIES OF ACCIDENTS,
AS ARE WE ALL.

Unk was driven on the fire engine straight from the church to Newport, Rhode Island, where a materialization was due to take place.

According to a plan that had been set up years before, other fire apparatus on Cape Cod was shifted so as to protect West Barnstable, which would be without its pumper for a little while.

Word of the Space Wanderer's coming spread over the Earth like wildfire. In every village, town, and city through which the fire engine passed, Unk was pelted with flowers.

Unk sat high on the fire engine, on a two-by-six fir timber laid across the cockpit amidships. In the cockpit itself was the Reverend C. Horner Redwine.

Redwine had control of the fire engine's bell, which he rang assiduously. Attached to the clapper of the bell was a Malachi made of high-impact plastic. The doll was of a special sort that could be bought only in Newport. To display such a Malachi was to proclaim that one had made a pilgrimage to Newport.

The entire Volunteer Fire Department of West Barnstable, with the exception of two non-conformists, had made such a pilgrimage to Newport. The fire engine's Malachi had been bought with Fire Department funds.

In the parlance of the souvenir hawkers in Newport, the Fire Department's high-impact plastic Malachi was a "genuwine, authorized, official Malachi."

Unk was happy, because it was so good to be among people again, and to be breathing air again. And everybody seemed to adore him so.

There was so much good noise. There was so much good everything. Unk hoped the good everything would go on forever.

"What happened to you?" the people all yelled to him, and they laughed.

For the purposes of mass communications, Unk shortened the answer that had pleased the little crowd so much at the Church of the Space Wanderer. "Accidents!" he yelled.

He laughed.

Oh boy.

What the hell. He laughed.

•

In Newport, the Rumfoord estate had been packed to the walls for eight hours. Guards turned thousands away from the little door in the wall. The guards were hardly necessary, since the crowd inside was monolithic.

A greased eel couldn't have squeezed in.

The thousands of pilgrims outside the walls now jostled one another piously for positions close to the loudspeakers mounted at the corners of the walls.

From the speakers would come Rumfoord's voice.

The crowd was the largest yet and the most excited yet, for the day was the long-promised Great Day of the Space Wanderer.

Handicaps of the most imaginative and effective sort were displayed everywhere. The crowd was wonderfully drab and hampered.

Bee, who had been Unk's mate on Mars, was in Newport, too. So was Bee's and Unk's son, Chrono.

"Hey!—getcher genuwine, authorized, official Malachis here," said Bee hoarsely. "Hey!—getcher Malachis here. Gotta have a Malachi to wave at the Space Wanderer," said Bee. "Get a Malachi, so the Space Wanderer can bless it when he comes by."

She was in a booth facing the little iron door in the wall of the Rumfoord estate in Newport. Bee's booth was the first in the line of twenty booths that faced the door. The twenty booths were under one continuous shed roof, and were separated from one another by waist-high partitions.

The Malachis she was hawking were plastic dolls with movable joints and rhinestone eyes. Bee bought them from a religious supply house for twenty-seven cents apiece and sold them for three dollars. She was an excellent businesswoman.

And while Bee showed the world an efficient and flashy exterior, it was the grandeur within her that sold more merchandise than anything. The carnival flash of Bee caught the pilgrims' eyes. But what brought the pilgrims to her booth and made them buy was her aura. The aura said unmistakably that Bee was meant for a far nobler station in life, that she was being an awfully good sport about being stuck where she was.

"Hey!—getcher Malachi while there's still time," said Bee. "Can't get a Malachi while a materialization's going on!"

That was true. The rule was that the concessionaires had to close their shutters five minutes before Winston Niles Rumfoord and his dog materialized. And they had to keep their shutters closed until ten minutes after the last trace of Rumfoord and Kazak had disappeared.

Bee turned to her son, Chrono, who was opening a fresh case of Malachis. "How long before the whistle?" she said. The whistle was a great steam whistle inside the estate. It was blown five minutes in advance of materializations.

Materializations themselves were announced by the firing of a three-inch cannon.

Dematerializations were announced by the release of a thousand toy balloons.

"Eight minutes," said Chrono, looking at his watch. He was eleven Earthling years old now. He was dark and smoldering. He was an expert short-changer, and was clever with cards. He was foul-mouthed, and carried a switch-knife with a six-inch blade. Chrono would not socialize well with other children, and his reputation for dealing with life courageously and directly was so bad that only a few very foolish and very pretty little girls were attracted to him.

Chrono was classified by the Newport Police Department and by the Rhode Island State Police as a juvenile delinquent. He knew at least fifty law-enforcement officers by their first names, and was a veteran of fourteen lie-detector tests.

All that prevented Chrono's being placed in an institution was the finest legal staff on Earth, the legal staff of the Church of God the Utterly Indifferent. Under the direction of Rumfoord, the staff defended Chrono against all charges.

The commonest charges brought against Chrono were larceny by sleight of hand, carrying concealed weapons, possessing unregistered pistols, discharging firearms within the city limits, selling obscene prints and articles, and being a wayward child.

The authorities complained bitterly that the boy's big trouble was his mother. His mother loved him just the way he was.

"Only eight more minutes to get your Malachi, folks," said Bee. "Hurry, hurry, hurry."

Bee's upper front teeth were gold, and her skin, like the skin of her son, was the color of golden oak.

Bee had lost her upper front teeth when the space ship in which she and Chrono had ridden from Mars crash-landed in the Gumbo region of the Amazon Rain Forest. She and Chrono had been the only survivors of the crash, and had wandered through the jungles for a year.

The color of Bee's and Chrono's skins was permanent, since it stemmed from a modification of their livers. Their livers had been modified by a three-month diet consisting of water and the roots of the salpa-salpa or Amazonian blue poplar. The diet had been a part of Bee's and Chrono's initiation into the Gumbo tribe.

During the initiation, mother and son had been staked at the ends of tethers in the middle of the village, with Chrono representing the Sun and Bee representing the Moon, as the Sun and the Moon were understood by the Gumbo people.

As a result of their experiences, Bee and Chrono were closer than most mothers and sons.

They had been rescued at last by a helicopter. Winston Niles Rumfoord had sent the helicopter to just the right place at just the right time.

Winston Niles Rumfoord had given Bee and Chrono the lucrative Malachi concession outside the Alice-in-Wonderland door. He had also paid Bee's dental bill, and had suggested that her false front teeth be gold.

The man who had the booth next to Bee's was Harry Brackman. He had been Unk's platoon sergeant back on Mars. Brackman was portly and balding now. He had a cork leg and a stainless steel right hand. He had lost the leg and hand in the Battle of Boca Raton. He was the only survivor of the battle—and, if he hadn't been so horribly wounded, he would certainly have been lynched along with the other survivors of his platoon.

Brackman sold plastic models of the fountain inside the wall. The models were a foot high. The models had spring-driven pumps in their bases. The pumps pumped water from the big bowl at the bottom to the tiny bowls at the top. Then the tiny bowls spilled into the slightly larger bowls below and . . .

Brackman had three of them going at once on the counter before him. "Just like the one inside, folks," he said. "And you can take one of these home with you. Put it in the picture window, so all your neighbors'll know you've been to Newport. Put it in the middle of the kitchen table for the kids' parties, and fill it with pink lemonade."

"How much?" said a rube.

"Seventeen dollars," said Brackman.

"Wow!" said the rube.

"It's a sacred shrine, cousin," said Brackman, looking at the rube levelly. "Isn't a toy." He reached under the counter, brought out a model of a Martian space ship. "You want a toy? Here's a toy. Forty-nine cents. I only make two cents on it."

The rube made a show of being a judicious shopper. He compared the toy with the real article it was supposed to represent. The real article was a Martian space ship on top of a column ninety-eight feet tall. The column and space ship were inside the walls of the Rumfoord estate—in the corner of the estate where the tennis courts had once been.

Rumfoord had yet to explain the purpose of the space ship, whose supporting column had been built with the pennies of school children from all over the world. The ship was kept in constant readiness. What was reputedly the longest freestanding ladder in history leaned against the column, led giddily to the door of the ship.

In the fuel cartridge of the space ship was the very last trace of the Martian war effort's supply of the Universal Will to Become.

"Uh huh," said the rube. He put the model back on the counter. "If you don't mind, I'll shop around a little more." So far, the only thing he had bought was a Robin Hood hat with a picture of Rumfoord on one side and a picture of a sailboat on the other, and with his own name stitched on the feather. His name, according to the feather, was *Delbert.* "Thanks just the same," said Delbert. "I'll probably be back."

"Sure you will, Delbert," said Brackman.

"How did you know my name was Delbert?" said Delbert, pleased and suspicious.

"You think Winston Niles Rumfoord is the only man around here with supernatural powers?" said Brackman.

A jet of steam went up inside the walls. An instant later, the voice of the great steam whistle rolled over the booths—mighty, mournful, and triumphant. It was the signal that Rumfoord and his dog would materialize in five minutes.

It was the signal for the concessionaires to stop their irreverent bawling of brummagem wares, to close their shutters.

The shutters were banged shut at once.

The effect of the closing inside the booths was to turn the line of concessions into a twilit tunnel.

The isolation of the concessionaires in the tunnel had an extra dimension of spookiness, since the tunnel contained only survivors from Mars. Rumfoord had insisted on that—that Martians were to have first choice of the concessions at Newport. It was his way of saying, "Thanks."

There weren't many survivors—only fifty-eight in the United States, only three hundred and sixteen in the entire World.

Of the fifty-eight in the United States, twenty-one were concessionaires in Newport.

"Here we go again, kiddies," somebody said, far, far, far down the line. It was the voice of the blind man who sold the Robin Hood hats with a picture of Rumfoord on one side and a picture of a sailboat on the other.

Sergeant Brackman laid his folded arms on the half-partition between his booth and Bee's. He winked at young Chrono, who was lying on an unopened case of Malachis.

"Go to hell, eh, kid?" said Brackman to Chrono.

"Go to hell," Chrono agreed. He was cleaning his nails with the strangely bent, drilled and nicked piece of metal that had been his good-luck piece on Mars. It was still his good-luck piece on Earth.

The good-luck piece had probably saved Chrono's and Bee's lives in the jungle. The Gumbo tribesmen had recognized the piece of metal as an object of tremendous power. Their respect for it had led them to initiate rather than eat its owners.

Brackman laughed affectionately. "Yessir—there's a Martian for you," he said. "Won't even get off his case of Malachis for a look at the Space Wanderer."

Chrono was not alone in his apathy about the Space Wanderer. It was the proud and impudent custom of all the concessionaires to stay away from ceremonies—to stay in the twilit tunnel of their booths until Rumfoord and his dog had come and gone.

It wasn't that the concessionaires had real contempt for Rumfoord's religion. Actually, most of them thought the new religion was probably a pretty good thing. What they were dramatizing when they stayed in their shuttered booths was that they, as Martian veterans, had already done more than enough to put the Church of God the Utterly Indifferent on its feet.

They were dramatizing the fact of their having been all used up.

Rumfoord encouraged them in this pose—spoke of them fondly as his ". . . soldier saints outside the little door. Their apathy," Rumfoord once said, "is a great wound they suffered that we might be more lively, more sensitive, and more free."

The temptation of the Martian concessionaires to take a peek at the Space Wanderer was great. There were loudspeakers on the walls of the Rumfoord estate, and every word spoken by Rumfoord inside blatted in the ears of anyone within a quarter of a mile. The words had spoken again and again of the glorious moment of truth that would come when the Space Wanderer came.

It was a big moment true believers titillated themselves about—the big moment wherein true believers were going to find their beliefs amplified, clarified, and vivified by a factor of ten.

Now the moment had arrived.

The fire engine that had carried the Space Wanderer down from the Church of the Space Wanderer on Cape Cod was clanging and shrieking outside the booths.

The trolls in the twilight of the booths refused to peek.

The cannon roared within the walls.

Rumfoord and his dog, then, had materialized—and the Space Wanderer was passing in through the Alice-in-Wonderland door.

"Probably some broken-down actor he hired from New York," said Brackman.

This got no response from anyone, not even from Chrono, who fancied himself the chief cynic of the booths. Brackman didn't take his own suggestion seriously—that the Space

Wanderer was a fraud. The concessionaires knew all too well about Rumfoord's penchant for realism. When Rumfoord staged a passion play, he used nothing but real people in real hells.

Let it be emphasized here that, passionately fond as Rumfoord was of great spectacles, he never gave in to the temptation to declare himself God or something a whole lot like God.

His worst enemies admit that. Dr. Maurice Rosenau, in his *Pan-Galactic Humbug or Three Billion Dupes* says:

Winston Niles Rumfoord, the interstellar Pharisee, Tartufe, and Cagliostro, has taken pains to declare that he is not God Almighty, that he is not a close relative of God Almighty, and that he has received no plain instructions from God Almighty. To these words of the Master of Newport we can say Amen! And may we add that Rumfoord is so far from being a relative or agent of God Almighty as to make all communication with God Almighty Himself impossible so long as Rumfoord is around!

Ordinarily, talk by the Martian veterans in the shuttered booths was sprightly—bristling with entertaining irreverence and tips on selling trashy religious articles to boobs.

Now, with Rumfoord and the Space Wanderer about to meet, the concessionaires found it very hard not to be interested.

Sergeant Brackman's good hand went up to the crown of his head. It was the characteristic gesture of a Martian veteran. He was touching the area over his antenna, over the antenna that had once done all his important thinking for him. He missed the signals.

"*Bring the Space Wanderer here!*" blatted Rumfoord's voice from the Gabriel horns on the walls.

"Maybe—maybe we should go," said Brackman to Bee.

"What?" murmured Bee. She was standing with her back to the closed shutters. Her eyes were shut. Her head was down. She looked cold.

She always shivered when a materialization was taking place.

Chrono was rubbing his good-luck piece slowly with the ball of his thumb, watching a halo of mist on the cold metal, a halo around the thumb.

"The hell with 'em—eh, Chrono?" said Brackman.

The man who sold twittering mechanical birds swung his wares overhead listlessly. A farm wife had stabbed him with a pitchfork in the Battle of Toddington, England, had left him for dead.

The International Committee for the Identification and Rehabilitation of Martians had, with the help of fingerprints, identified the bird man as Bernard K. Winslow, an itinerant chicken sexer, who had disappeared from the alcoholic ward of a London hospital.

"Thanks very much for the information," Winslow had told the committee. "Now I don't have that lost feeling any more."

Sergeant Brackman had been identified by the Committee as Private Francis J. Thompson, who had disappeared in the dead of night while walking a lonely guard post around a motor pool in Fort Bragg, North Carolina, U.S.A.

The committee had been baffled by Bee. She had no fingerprints on record. The Committee believed her to be either Florence White, a plain and friendless girl who had disappeared from a steam laundry in Cohoes, New York, or Darlene Simpkins, a plain and friendless girl who had last been seen accepting a ride with a swarthy stranger in Brownsville, Texas.

And down the line of booths from Brackman and Chrono and Bee were Martian husks who had been identified as Myron S. Watson, an alcoholic, who had disappeared from his post as a wash room attendant at Newark Airport . . . as Charlene Heller, assistant dietitian of the cafeteria of Stivers High School in Dayton, Ohio . . . as Krishna Garu, a typesetter still wanted, technically, on charges of bigamy, pandering, and nonsupport in Calcutta, India . . . as Kurt Schneider, also an alcoholic, manager of a failing travel agency in Bremen, Germany.

"The mighty Rumfoord—" said Bee.

"Pardon me?" said Brackman.

"He snatched us out of our lives," said Bee. "He put us to sleep. He cleaned out our minds the way you clean the seeds out of a jack-o'-lantern. He wired us like robots, trained us, aimed us—burned us out in a good cause." She shrugged.

"Could we have done any better if he'd left us in charge of our own lives?" said Bee. "Would we have become any more—or any less? I guess I'm glad he used me. I guess he had a lot better ideas about what to do with me than Florence White or Darlene Simpkins or whoever I was.

"But I hate him all the same," said Bee.

"That's your privilege," said Brackman. "He said that was the privilege of every Martian."

"There's one consolation," said Bee. "We're all used up. We'll never be of any use to him again."

"Welcome, Space Wanderer," blatted Rumfoord's oleomargarine tenor from the Gabriel horns on the wall. "How meet it is that you should come to us on the bright red pumper of a volunteer fire department. I can think of no more stirring symbol of man's humanity to man than a fire engine. Tell me, Space Wanderer, do you see anything here—anything that makes you think you may have been here before?"

The Space Wanderer murmured something unintelligible.

"Louder, please," said Rumfoord.

"The fountain—I remember that fountain," said the Space Wanderer gropingly. "Only—only—"

"Only?" said Rumfoord.

"It was dry then—whenever that was. It's so wet now," said the Space Wanderer.

A microphone near the fountain was now tuned into the public address system, so that the actual babble, spatter and potch of the fountain could underline the Space Wanderer's words.

"Anything else familiar, oh, Space Wanderer?" said Rumfoord.

"Yes," said the Space Wanderer shyly. "You."

"I am familiar?" said Rumfoord archly. "You mean there's a possibility that I played some small part in your life before?"

"I remember you on Mars," said the Space Wanderer. "You were the man with the dog—just before we took off."

"What happened after you took off?" said Rumfoord.

"Something went wrong," said the Space Wanderer. He sounded apologetic, as though the series of misfortunes were somehow his own fault. "A lot of things went wrong."

"Have you ever considered the possibility," said Rumfoord, "that everything went absolutely right?"

"No," said the Space Wanderer simply. The idea did not

startle him, could not startle him—since the idea proposed was so far beyond the range of his jerry-built philosophy.

"Would you recognize your mate and child?" said Rumfoord.

"I—I don't know," said the Space Wanderer.

"Bring me the woman and the boy who sell Malachis outside the little iron door," said Rumfoord. "Bring Bee and Chrono."

The Space Wanderer and Winston Niles Rumfoord and Kazak were on a scaffold before the mansion. The scaffold was at eye-level for the standing crowd. The scaffold before the mansion was a portion of a continuous system of catwalks, ramps, ladders, pulpits, steps, and stages that reached into every corner of the estate.

The system made possible the free and showy circulation of Rumfoord around the grounds, unimpeded by crowds. It meant, too, that Rumfoord could offer a glimpse of himself to every person on the grounds.

The system was not suspended magnetically, though it looked like a miracle of levitation. The seeming miracle was achieved by means of a cunning use of paint. The underpinnings were painted a flat black, while the superstructures were painted flashing gold.

Television cameras and microphones on booms could follow the system anywhere.

For night materializations, the superstructures of the system were outlined in flesh-colored electric lamps.

The Space Wanderer was only the thirty-first person to be invited to join Rumfoord on the elevated system.

An assistant had now been dispatched to the Malachi booth outside to bring in the thirty-second and thirty-third persons to share the eminence.

Rumfoord did not look well. His color was bad. And, although he smiled as always, his teeth seemed to be gnashing behind the smile. His complacent glee had become a caricature, betraying the fact that all was not well by any means.

But on and on the famous smile went. The magnificently snobbish crowd-pleaser held his big dog Kazak by a choke chain. The chain was twisted so as to nip warningly into the dog's throat. The warning was necessary, since the dog plainly did not like the Space Wanderer.

The smile faltered for an instant, reminding the crowd of what a load Rumfoord carried for them—warning the crowd that he might not be able to carry it forever.

Rumfoord carried in his palm a microphone and transmitter the size of a penny. When he did not want his voice carried to the crowd, he simply smothered the penny in his fist.

The penny was smothered in his fist now—and he was addressing bits of irony to the Space Wanderer that would have bewildered the crowd, had the crowd been able to hear them.

"This is certainly your day, isn't it?" said Rumfoord. "A perfect love feast from the instant you arrived. The crowd simply adores you. Do you adore crowds?"

The joyful shocks of the day had reduced the Space Wanderer to a childish condition—a condition wherein irony and even sarcasm were lost on him. He had been the captive of many things in his troubled times. He was now a captive of a crowd that thought he was a marvel. "They've certainly been wonderful," he said, in reply to Rumfoord's last question. "They've been grand."

"Oh—they're a grand bunch," said Rumfoord. "No mistake about that. I've been racking my brains for the right word to describe them, and you've brought it to me from outer space. *Grand* is what they are." Rumfoord's mind was plainly elsewhere. He wasn't much interested in the Space Wanderer as a person—hardly looked at him. Neither did he seem very excited about the approach of the Space Wanderer's wife and child.

"Where are they, where are they?" said Rumfoord to an assistant below. "Let's get on with it. Let's get it over with."

The Space Wanderer was finding his adventures so satisfying and stimulating, so splendidly staged, that he was shy about asking questions—was afraid that asking questions might make him seem ungrateful.

He realized that he had a terrific ceremonial responsibility and that the best thing to do was to keep his mouth shut, to speak only when spoken to, and to make his answers to all questions short and artless.

The Space Wanderer's mind did not teem with questions.

The fundamental structure of his ceremonial situation was obvious—was as clean and functional as a three-legged milking stool. He had suffered mightily, and now he was being rewarded mightily.

The sudden change in fortunes made a bang-up show. He smiled, understanding the crowd's delight—pretending to be in the crowd himself, sharing the crowd's delight.

Rumfoord read the Space Wanderer's mind. "They'd like it just as much the other way around, you know," he said.

"The other way around?" said the Space Wanderer.

"If the big reward came first, and then the great suffering," said Rumfoord. "It's the *contrast* they like. The order of events doesn't make any difference to them. It's the thrill of the *fast reverse*—"

Rumfoord opened his fist, exposed the microphone. With his other hand he beckoned pontifically. He was beckoning to Bee and Chrono, who had been hoisted onto a tributary of the gilded system of catwalks, ramps, ladders, pulpits, steps and stages. "This way, please. We haven't got all day, you know," said Rumfoord schoolmarmishly.

During the lull, the Space Wanderer felt the first real tickle of plans for a good future on Earth. With everyone so kind and enthusiastic and peaceful, not only a good life but a perfect life could be lived on Earth.

The Space Wanderer had already been given a fine new suit and a glamorous station in life, and his mate and son were to be restored to him in a matter of minutes.

All that was lacking was a good friend, and the Space Wanderer began to tremble. He trembled, for he knew in his heart that his best friend, Stony Stevenson, was hidden somewhere on the grounds, awaiting a cue to appear.

The Space Wanderer smiled, for he was imagining Stony's entrance. Stony would come running down a ramp, laughing and a little drunk. "Unk, you bloody bastard—" Stony would roar right into the public address system, "by God, I've looked in every flaming pub on bloody Earth for you—and here you've been hung up on Mercury the whole bloody time!"

As Bee and Chrono reached Rumfoord and the Space Wanderer, Rumfoord walked away. Had he separated himself from Bee, Chrono, and the Space Wanderer by a mere arm's length, his separateness might have been understood. But the gilded system enabled him to put a really respectable distance between himself and the three, and not only a distance, but a distance made tortuous by rococo and variously symbolic hazards.

It was undeniably great theater, notwithstanding Dr. Maurice Rosenau's carping comment *(op. cit.)*: "The people who watch reverently as Winston Niles Rumfoord goes dancing over his golden jungle gym in Newport are the same idiots one finds in toy stores, gaping reverently at toy trains as the trains go *chuffa-chuffa-chuffa* in and out of papier-mâché tunnels, over toothpick trestles, through cardboard cities, and into papier-mâché tunnels again. Will the little trains or will Winston Niles Rumfoord *chuffa-chuffa-chuffa* into view again? Oh, *mirabile dictu!* . . . they will!"

From the scaffold in front of the mansion Rumfoord went to a stile that arched over the crest of a boxwood hedge. On the other side of the stile was a catwalk that ran for ten feet to the trunk of a copper beech. The trunk was four feet through. Gilded rungs were fixed to the trunk by lag screws.

Rumfoord tied Kazak to the bottom rung, then climbed out of sight like Jack on the beanstalk.

From somewhere up in the tree he spoke.

His voice came not from the tree but from the Gabriel horns on the walls.

The crowd weaned its eyes from the leafy treetop, turned its eyes to the nearest loudspeakers.

Only Bee, Chrono, and the Space Wanderer continued to look up, to look up at where Rumfoord really was. This wasn't so much a result of realism as it was a result of embarrassment. By looking up, the members of the little family avoided looking at each other.

None of the three had any reason to be pleased with the reunion.

Bee was not drawn to the scrawny, bearded, happy boob in lemon-yellow long underwear. She had dreamed of a big, angry, arrogant free-thinker.

Young Chrono hated the bearded intruder on his sublime relationship with his mother. Chrono kissed his good-luck piece and wished that his father, if this really was his father, would drop dead.

And the Space Wanderer himself, sincerely as he tried, could see nothing he would have chosen of his own free will in the dark, malevolent mother and son.

By accident, the Space Wanderer's eyes met the one good eye of Bee. Something had to be said.

"How do you do?" said the Space Wanderer.

"How do *you* do?" said Bee.

They both looked up into the tree again.

"Oh, my happy, handicapped brethren," said Rumfoord's voice, "let us thank God—God, who appreciates our thanks as much as the mighty Mississippi appreciates a raindrop—that we are not like Malachi Constant."

The back of the Space Wanderer's neck ached some. He lowered his gaze. His eyes were caught by a long, straight golden runway in the middle distance. His eyes followed it.

The runway ended at Earth's longest free-standing ladder. The ladder was painted gold, too.

The Space Wanderer's gaze climbed the ladder to the tiny door of the space ship on top of the column. He wondered who would have nerve enough or reason enough to climb such a frightening ladder to such a tiny door.

The Space Wanderer looked at the crowd again. Maybe Stony Stevenson was in the crowd somewhere. Maybe he would wait for the whole show to end before he presented himself to his best and only friend from Mars.

CHAPTER ELEVEN

We Hate Malachi Constant Because . . .

"Tell me one good thing you ever did in your life."

—WINSTON NILES RUMFOORD

AND THIS is how the sermon went:

"We are *disgusted* by Malachi Constant," said Winston Niles Rumfoord up in his treetop, "because he used the fantastic fruits of his fantastic good luck to finance an unending demonstration that man is a pig. He wallowed in sycophants. He wallowed in worthless women. He wallowed in lascivious entertainments and alcohol and drugs. He wallowed in every known form of voluptuous turpitude.

"At the height of his good luck, Malachi Constant was worth more than the states of Utah and North Dakota combined. Yet, I daresay, his moral worth was not that of the most corrupt little fieldmouse in either state.

"We are *angered* by Malachi Constant," said Rumfoord up in his treetop, "because he did nothing to deserve his billions, and because he did nothing unselfish or imaginative with his billions. He was as benevolent as Marie Antoinette, as creative as a professor of cosmetology in an embalming college.

"We *hate* Malachi Constant," said Rumfoord up in his treetop, "because he accepted the fantastic fruits of his fantastic good luck without a qualm, as though luck were the hand of God. To us of the Church of God the Utterly Indifferent, there is nothing more cruel, more dangerous, more blasphemous that a man can do than to believe that—that luck, good or bad, is the hand of God!

"Luck, good or bad," said Rumfoord up in his treetop, "is *not* the hand of God.

"Luck," said Rumfoord up in his treetop, "is the way the wind swirls and the dust settles eons after God has passed by.

"Space Wanderer!" called Rumfoord from up in his treetop.

The Space Wanderer was not paying strict attention. His powers of concentration were feeble—possibly because he had been in the caves too long, or on goofballs too long, or in the Army of Mars too long.

He was watching clouds. They were lovely things, and the sky they drifted in was, to the color-starved Space Wanderer, a thrilling blue.

"Space Wanderer!" called Rumfoord again.

"You in the yellow suit," said Bee. She nudged him. "Wake up."

"Pardon me?" said the Space Wanderer.

"Space Wanderer!" called Rumfoord.

The Space Wanderer snapped to attention. "Yes, sir?" he called up into the leafy bower. The greeting was ingenuous, cheerful, and winsome. A microphone on the end of a boom was swung to dangle before him.

"Space Wanderer!" called Rumfoord, and he was peeved now, for the ceremonial flow was being impeded.

"Right here, sir!" cried the Space Wanderer. His reply boomed earsplittingly from the loudspeaker.

"Who are you?" said Rumford. "What is your real name?"

"I don't know my real name," said the Space Wanderer. "They called me Unk."

"What happened to you before you arrived back on Earth, Unk?" said Rumfoord.

The Space Wanderer beamed. He had been led to a repetition of the simple statement that had caused so much laughing and dancing and singing on Cape Cod. "I was a victim of a series of accidents, as are we all," he said.

There was no laughing and dancing and singing this time, but the crowd was definitely in favor of what the Space Wanderer had said. Chins were raised, and eyes were widened, and nostrils were flared. There was no outcry, for the crowd wanted to hear absolutely everything that Rumfoord and the Space Wanderer might have to say.

"A victim of a series of accidents, were you?" said Rumfoord up in his treetop. "Of all the accidents," he said, "which would you consider the most significant?"

The Space Wanderer cocked his head. "I'd have to think—" he said.

"I'll spare you the trouble," said Rumfoord. "The most significant accident that happened to you was your being born.

Would you like me to tell you what you were named when you were born?"

The Space Wanderer hesitated only a moment, and all that made him hesitate was a fear that he was going to spoil a very gratifying ceremonial career by saying the wrong thing. "Please do," he said.

"They called you Malachi Constant," said Rumfoord up in his treetop.

To the extent that crowds can be good things, the crowds that Winston Niles Rumfoord attracted to Newport were good crowds. They were not crowd-minded. The members remained in possession of their own consciences, and Rumfoord never invited them to participate as one in any action—least of all in applause or catcalls.

When the fact had sunk in that the Space Wanderer was the disgusting, irking, and hateful Malachi Constant, the members of the crowd reacted in quiet, sighing, personal ways—ways that were by and large compassionate. It was on their generally decent consciences, after all, that they had hanged Constant in effigy in their homes and places of work. And, while they had been cheerful enough about hanging the effigies, very few felt that Constant, in the flesh, actually deserved hanging. Hanging Malachi Constant in effigy was an act of violence on the order of trimming a Christmas tree or hiding Easter eggs.

And Rumfoord up in his treetop said nothing to discourage their compassion. "You have had the singular accident, Mr. Constant," he said sympathetically, "of becoming a central symbol of wrong-headedness for a perfectly enormous religious sect.

"You would not be attractive to us as a symbol, Mr. Constant," he said, "if our hearts did not go out to you to a certain extent. Our hearts *have* to go out to you, since all your flamboyant errors are errors that human beings have made since the beginning of time.

"In a few minutes, Mr. Constant," said Rumfoord up in his treetop, "you are going to walk down the catwalks and ramps to that long golden ladder, and you you are going to climb that ladder, and you are going to get into that space ship, and you are going to fly away to Titan, a warm and fecund moon of Saturn. You will live there in safety and comfort, but in exile from your native Earth.

"You are going to do this voluntarily, Mr. Constant, so that the Church of God the Utterly Indifferent can have a drama of dignified self-sacrifice to remember and ponder through all time.

"We will imagine, to our spiritual satisfaction," said Rumfoord up in his treetop, "that you are taking all mistaken ideas about the meaning of luck, all misused wealth and power, and all disgusting pastimes with you."

The man who had been Malachi Constant, who had been Unk, who had been the Space Wanderer, the man who was Malachi Constant again—that man felt very little upon being declared Malachi Constant again. He might, possibly, have felt some interesting things, had Rumfoord's timing been different. But Rumfoord told him what his ordeal was to be only seconds after telling him he was Malachi Constant—and the ordeal was sufficiently ghastly to command Constant's full attention.

The ordeal had been promised not in years or months or days—but in minutes. And, like any condemned criminal, Malachi Constant became a student, to the exclusion of all else, of the apparatus on which he was about to perform.

Curiously, his first worry was that he would stumble, that he would think too hard about the simple matter of walking, and that his feet would cease to work naturally, and that he would stumble on those wooden feet.

"You won't stumble, Mr. Constant," said Rumfoord up in his treetop, reading Constant's mind. "There is nowhere else for you to go, nothing else for you to do. By putting one foot in front of the other, while we watch in silence, you will make of yourself the most memorable, magnificent, and meaningful human being of modern times."

Constant turned to look at his dusky mate and child. Their gazes were direct. Constant learned from their gazes that Rumfoord had spoken the truth, that no course save the course to the space ship was open to him. Beatrice and young Chrono were supremely cynical about the festivities—but not about courageous behavior in the midst of them.

They dared Malachi Constant to behave well.

Constant rubbed his left thumb and index finger together in a careful rotary motion. He watched this pointless enterprise for perhaps ten seconds.

And then he dropped his hands to his sides, raised his eyes, and stepped off firmly toward the space ship.

As his left foot struck the ramp, his head was filled with a sound he had not heard for three Earthling years. The sound was coming from the antenna under the crown of his skull. Rumfoord, up in his treetop, was sending signals to Constant's antenna by means of a small box in his pocket.

He was making Constant's long and lonely walk more bearable by filling Constant's head with the sound of a snare drum.

The snare drum had this to say to him:

Rented a tent, a tent, a tent;
Rented a tent, a tent.
Rented a tent!
Rented a tent!
Rented a, rented a tent!

The snare drum fell silent as Malachi Constant's hand closed for the first time on a gilded rung of the world's tallest freestanding ladder. He looked up, and perspective made the ladder's summit seem as tiny as a needle. Constant rested his brow for a moment against the rung to which his hand clung.

"You have something you would like to say, Mr. Constant, before you go up the ladder?" said Rumfoord up in his treetop.

A microphone on the end of a boom was again dangled before Constant. Constant licked his lips.

"You're about to say something, Mr. Constant?" said Rumfoord.

"If you're going to talk," the technician in charge of the microphone said to Constant, "speak in a perfectly normal tone, and keep your lips about six inches away from the microphone."

"You're going to speak to us, Mr. Constant?" said Rumfoord.

"It—it's probably not worth saying," said Constant quietly, "but I'd still like to say that I haven't understood a single thing that's happened to me since I reached Earth."

"You haven't got that feeling of participation?" said Rumfoord up in his treetop. "Is that it?"

"It doesn't matter," said Constant. "I'm still going up the ladder."

"Well," said Rumfoord up in his treetop, "if you feel we are doing you some sort of injustice here, suppose you tell us something really good you've done at some point in your life, and let us decide whether that piece of goodness might excuse you from this thing we have planned for you."

"Goodness?" said Constant.

"Yes," said Rumfoord expansively. "Tell me one good thing you ever did in your life—what you can remember of it."

Constant thought hard. His principal memories were of scuttling through endless corridors in the caves. There had been a few opportunities for what might pass for goodness with Boaz and the harmoniums. But Constant could not say honestly that he had availed himself of these opportunities to be good.

So he thought about Mars, about all the things that had been contained in his letter to himself. Surely, among all those items, there was something about his own goodness.

And then he remembered Stony Stevenson—his friend. He had had a friend, which was certainly a good thing. "I had a friend," said Malachi Constant into the microphone.

"What was his name?" said Rumfoord.

"Stony Stevenson," said Constant.

"Just one friend?" said Rumfoord up in his treetop.

"Just one," said Constant. His poor soul was flooded with pleasure as he realized that one friend was all that a man needed in order to be well-supplied with friendship.

"So your claim of goodness would stand or fall, really," said Rumfoord up in his treetop, "depending on how good a friend you really were of this Stony Stevenson."

"Yes," said Constant.

"Do you recall an execution on Mars, Mr. Constant," said Rumfoord up in his treetop, "wherein you were the executioner? You strangled a man at the stake before three regiments of the Army of Mars."

This was one memory that Constant had done his best to eradicate. He had been successful to a large extent—and the rummaging he did through his mind now was sincere. He couldn't be sure that the execution had taken place. "I—I think I remember," said Constant.

"Well—that man you strangled was your great and good friend Stony Stevenson," said Winston Niles Rumfoord.

Malachi Constant wept as he climbed the gilded ladder. He paused halfway up, and Rumfoord called to him again through the loudspeakers.

"Feel more like a vitally-interested participant now, Mr. Constant?" called Rumfoord.

Mr. Constant did. He had a thorough understanding now of his own worthlessness, and a bitter sympathy for anyone who might find it good to handle him roughly.

And when he got to the top, he was told by Rumfoord not to close the airlock yet, because his mate and child would be up shortly.

Constant sat on the threshold of his space ship at the top of the ladder, and listened to Rumfoord's brief sermon about Constant's dark mate, about the one-eyed, gold-toothed woman called Bee. Constant did not listen closely to the sermon. His eyes saw a larger, more comforting sermon in the panorama of town, bay, and islands so far below.

The sermon of the panorama was that even a man without a friend in the Universe could still find his home planet mysteriously, heartbreakingly beautiful.

"I shall tell you now," said Winston Niles Rumfoord in his treetop so far below Malachi Constant, "about Bee, the woman who sells Malachis outside the gate, the dark woman who, with her son, now glowers at us all.

"While she was en route to Mars so many years ago, Malachi Constant forced his attention on her, and she bore him this son. Before then, she was my wife and the mistress of this estate. Her true name is Beatrice Rumfoord."

A groan went up from the crowd. Was it any wonder that the dusty puppets of other religions had been put away for want of audiences, that all eyes were turned to Newport? Not only was the head of the Church of God the Utterly Indifferent capable of telling the future and fighting the cruelest inequalities of all, inequalities in luck—but his supply of dumfounding new sensations was inexhaustible.

He was so well supplied with great material that he could actually let his voice trail off as he announced that the one-eyed, gold-toothed woman was his wife, and that he had been cuckolded by Malachi Constant.

"I now invite you to despise the example of her life as you have so long despised the example of the life of Malachi Constant," he said up in his treetop mildly. "Hang her alongside Malachi Constant from your window blinds and light fixtures, if you will.

"The excesses of Beatrice were excesses of reluctance," said Rumfoord. "As a younger woman, she felt so exquisitely bred as to do nothing and to allow nothing to be done to her, for fear of contamination. Life, for Beatrice as a younger woman, was too full of germs and vulgarity to be anything but intolerable.

"We of the Church of God the Utterly Indifferent damn her as roundly for refusing to risk her imagined purity in living as we damn Malachi Constant for wallowing in filth.

"It was implicit in Beatrice's every attitude that she was intellectually, morally, and physically what God intended human beings to be when perfected, and that the rest of humanity needed another ten thousand years in which to catch up. Again we have a case of an ordinary and uncreative person's tickling God Almighty pink. The proposition that God Almighty admired Beatrice for her touch-me-not breeding is at least as questionable as the proposition that God Almighty wanted Malachi Constant to be rich.

"Mrs. Rumfoord," said Winston Niles Rumfoord up in his treetop, "I now invite you and your son to follow Malachi Constant into the space ship bound for Titan. Is there something you would like to say before you leave?"

There was a long silence in which mother and son drew closer together and looked, shoulder to shoulder, at a world much changed by the news of the day.

"Are you planning to address us, Mrs. Rumfoord?" said Rumfoord up in his treetop.

"Yes," said Beatrice. "But it won't take me long. I believe everything you say about me is true, since you so seldom lie. But when my son and I walk together to that ladder and climb it, we will not be doing it for you, or for your silly crowd. We will be doing it for ourselves—and we will be proving to ourselves and to anybody who wants to watch that we aren't afraid of anything. Our hearts won't be breaking when we leave this planet. It disgusts us at least as much as we, under your guidance, disgust it.

"I do not recall the old days," said Beatrice, "when I was mistress of this estate, when I could not stand to do anything or to have anything done to me. But I loved myself the instant you told me I'd been that way. The human race is a scummy thing, and so is Earth, and so are you."

Beatrice and Chrono walked quickly over the catwalks and ramps to the ladder, climbed the ladder. They brushed past Malachi Constant in the doorway of the space ship without any sort of greeting. They disappeared inside.

Constant followed them into the space ship, and joined them as they considered the accommodations.

The condition of the accommodations was a surprise—and would have been a surprise to the custodians of the estate in particular. The space ship, seemingly inviolable at the top of a shaft in sacred precincts patrolled by watchmen, had plainly been the scene of one or perhaps several wild parties.

The bunks were all unmade. The bedding was rumpled, twisted, and wadded. The sheets were stained with lipstick and shoe polish.

Fried clams crunched greasily underfoot.

Two quart bottles of Mountain Moonlight, one pint of Southern Comfort, and a dozen cans of Narragansett Lager Beer, all empty, were scattered through the ship.

Two names were written in lipstick on the white wall by the door: *Bud and Sylvia.* And from a flange on the central shaft in the cabin hung a black brassière.

Beatrice gathered up the bottles and beer cans. She dropped them out the door. She took the brassière down, and fluttered it out the doorway, awaiting a favorable wind.

Malachi Constant, sighing and shaking his head and mourning Stony Stevenson, used his feet for push brooms. He scuffed the fried clams toward the door.

Young Chrono sat on a bunk, rubbing his good-luck piece. "Let's go, Mom," he said tautly. "For crying out loud, let's go."

Beatrice let go of the brassière. A gust caught it, carried it over the crowd, hung it in a tree next to the tree in which Rumfoord sat.

"Good-by, all you clean and wise and lovely people," said Beatrice.

CHAPTER TWELVE

The Gentleman from Tralfamadore

"In a punctual way of speaking, good-by."

—WINSTON NILES RUMFOORD

SATURN has nine moons, the greatest of which is Titan.

Titan is only slightly smaller than Mars.

Titan is the only moon in the Solar System that has an atmosphere. There is plenty of oxygen to breathe.

The atmosphere of Titan is like the atmosphere outside the back door of an Earthling bakery on a spring morning.

Titan has a natural chemical furnace at its core that maintains a uniform air temperature of sixty-seven degrees Fahrenheit.

There are three seas on Titan, each the size of Earthling Lake Michigan. The waters of all three are fresh and emerald clear. The names of the three are the Winston Sea, the Niles Sea, and the Rumfoord Sea.

There is a cluster of ninety-three ponds and lakes, incipiently a fourth sea. The cluster is known as the Kazak Pools.

Connecting the Winston Sea, the Niles Sea, the Rumfoord Sea and the Kazak Pools are three great rivers. These rivers, with their tributaries, are moody—variously roaring, listless, and torn. Their moods are determined by the wildly fluctuating tugs of eight fellow moons, and by the prodigious influence of Saturn, which has ninety-five times the mass of Earth. The three rivers are known as the Winston River, the Niles River, and the Rumfoord River.

There are woods and meadows and mountains.

The tallest mountain is Mount Rumfoord, which is nine thousand, five hundred and seventy-one feet high.

Titan affords an incomparable view of the most appallingly beautiful things in the Solar System, the rings of Saturn. These dazzling bands are forty thousand miles across and scarcely thicker than a razor blade.

On Titan the rings are called Rumfoord's Rainbow.

Saturn describes a circle around the Sun.

It does it once every twenty-nine and a half Earthling years.

Titan describes a circle around Saturn.

Titan describes, as a consequence, a spiral around the Sun.

Winston Niles Rumfoord and his dog Kazak were wave phenomena—pulsing in distorted spirals, with their origins in the Sun and their terminals in Betelgeuse. Whenever a heavenly body intercepted their spirals, Rumfoord and his dog materialized on that body.

For reasons as yet mysterious, the spirals of Rumfoord, Kazak, and Titan coincided exactly.

So Rumfoord and his dog were permanently materialized on Titan.

Rumfoord and Kazak lived there on an island one mile from shore in the Winston Sea. Their home was a flawless reproduction of the Taj Mahal in Earthling India.

It was built by Martian labor.

It was Rumfoord's wry fancy to call his Titan home *Dun Roamin.*

Before the arrival of Malachi Constant, Beatrice, Rumfoord, and Chrono, there was only one other person on Titan. That other person was named *Salo.* He was old. Salo was eleven million Earthling years old.

Salo was from another galaxy, from the Small Magellanic Cloud. He was four and a half feet tall.

Salo had a skin with the texture and color of the skin of an Earthling tangerine.

Salo had three light deer-like legs. His feet were of an extraordinarily interesting design, each being an inflatable sphere. By inflating these spheres to the size of German batballs, Salo could walk on water. By reducing them to the size of golf balls, Salo could bound over hard surfaces at high speeds. When he deflated the spheres entirely, his feet became suction cups. Salo could walk up walls.

Salo had no arms. Salo had three eyes, and his eyes could perceive not only the so-called visible spectrum, but infrared and ultraviolet and X-rays as well. Salo was punctual—that is, he lived one moment at a time—and he liked to tell Rumfoord that he would rather see the wonderful colors at the far ends of the spectrum than either the past or the future.

This was something of a weasel, since Salo had seen, living a moment at a time, far more of the past and far more of the Universe than Rumfoord had. He remembered more of what he had seen, too.

Salo's head was round and hung on gimbals.

His voice was an electric noise-maker that sounded like a bicycle horn. He spoke five thousand languages, fifty of them Earthling languages, thirty-one of them *dead* Earthling languages.

Salo didn't live in a palace, though Rumfoord had offered to have one built for him. Salo lived in the open, near the space ship that had brought him to Titan two hundred thousand years before. His space ship was a flying saucer, the prototype for the Martian invasion fleet.

Salo had an interesting history.

In the Earthling year 483,441 B.C., he was chosen by popular telepathic enthusiasm as the most handsome, healthy, clean-minded specimen of his people. The occasion was the hundred-millionth anniversary of the government of his home planet in the Small Magellanic Cloud. The name of his home planet was Tralfamadore, which old Salo once translated for Rumfoord as meaning both *all of us* and the *number 541*.

The length of a year on his home planet, according to his own calculations, was 3.6162 times the length of an Earthling year—so the celebration in which he participated was actually in honor of a government 361,620,000 Earthling years old. Salo once described this durable form of government to Rumfoord as hypnotic anarchy, but declined to explain its workings. "Either you understand at once what it is," he told Rumfoord, "or there is no sense in trying to explain it to you, Skip."

His duty, when he was elected to represent Tralfamadore, was to carry a sealed message from "One Rim of the Universe to the Other." The planners of the ceremonies were not so deluded as to believe that Salo's projected route spanned the Universe. The image was poetic, as was Salo's expedition. Salo would simply take the message and go as fast and as far as the technology of Tralfamadore could send him.

The message itself was unknown to Salo. It had been prepared by what Salo described to Rumfoord as, "A kind of university—only nobody goes to it. There aren't any buildings, isn't any faculty. Everybody's in it and nobody's in it. It's like a cloud that everybody has given a little puff of mist to, and then the cloud does all the heavy thinking for everybody. I don't mean there's *really* a cloud. I just mean it's something *like* that. If you don't understand what I'm talking about, Skip, there's no sense in trying to explain it to you. All I can say is, there aren't any meetings."

The message was contained in a sealed lead wafer that was two inches square and three-eighths of an inch thick. The wafer itself was contained in a gold mesh reticule which was hung on a stainless steel band clamped to the shaft that might be called Salo's neck.

Salo had orders not to open the reticule and wafer until he arrived at his destination. His destination was not Titan. His destination was in a galaxy that began eighteen million light-years beyond Titan. The planners of the ceremonies in which Salo had participated did not know what Salo was going to find in the galaxy. His instructions were to find creatures in it somewhere, to master their language, to open the message, and to translate it for them.

Salo did not question the good sense of his errand, since he was, like all Tralfamadorians, a machine. As a machine, he had to do what he was supposed to do.

Of all the orders Salo received before taking off from Tralfamadore, the one that was given the most importance was that *he was not, under any circumstances, to open the message along the way.*

This order was so emphasized that it became the very core of the little Tralfamadorian messenger's being.

In the Earthling year 203,117 B.C., Salo was forced down in the Solar System by mechanical difficulties. He was forced down by a complete disintegration of a small part in his ship's power plant, a part about the size of an Earthling beer-can opener. Salo was not mechanically inclined, and so had only a hazy idea as to what the missing part looked like or was supposed to do. Since Salo's ship was powered by UWTB, the Universal Will to Become, its power plant was nothing for a mechanical dilettante to tinker with.

Salo's ship wasn't entirely out of commission. It would still run—but limpingly, at only about sixty-eight thousand miles an hour. It was adequate for short hops around the Solar System, even in its crippled condition, and copies of the crippled ship did yeoman service for the Martian war effort. But the crippled ship was impossibly slow for the purposes of Salo's intergalactic errand.

So old Salo holed up on Titan and he sent home to Tralfamadore word of his plight. He sent the message home with the speed of light, which meant that it would take one hundred and fifty thousand Earthling years to get to Tralfamadore.

He developed several hobbies that helped him to pass the time. Chief among these were sculpture, the breeding of Titanic daisies, and watching the various activities on Earth. He could watch the activities on Earth by means of a viewer on the dash panel of his ship. The viewer was sufficiently powerful to let Salo follow the activities of Earthling ants, if he so wished.

It was through this viewer that he got his first reply from Tralfamadore. The reply was written on Earth in huge stones on a plain in what is now England. The ruins of the reply still stand, and are known as Stonehenge. The meaning of Stonehenge in Tralfamadorian, when viewed from above, is: "*Replacement part being rushed with all possible speed.*"

Stonehenge wasn't the only message old Salo had received.

There had been four others, all of them written on Earth.

The Great Wall of China means in Tralfamadorian, when viewed from above: "*Be patient. We haven't forgotten about you.*"

The Golden House of the Roman Emperor Nero meant: "*We are doing the best we can.*"

The meaning of the Moscow Kremlin when it was first walled was: "*You will be on your way before you know it.*"

The meaning of the Palace of the League of Nations in Geneva, Switzerland, is: "*Pack up your things and be ready to leave on short notice.*"

Simple arithmetic will reveal that these messages all arrived with speeds considerably in excess of the speed of light. Salo had sent his message of distress home with the speed of light, and it had taken one hundred and fifty thousand years to reach Tralfamadore. He had received a reply from Tralfamadore in less than fifty thousand years.

It is grotesque for anyone as primitive as an Earthling to

explain how these swift communications were effected. Suffice it to say, in such primitive company, that the Tralfamadorians were able to make certain impulses from the Universal Will to Become echo through the vaulted architecture of the Universe with about three times the speed of light. And they were able to focus and modulate these impulses so as to influence creatures far, far away, and inspire them to serve Tralfamadorian ends.

It was a marvelous way to get things done in places far, far away from Tralfamadore. It was easily the fastest way.

But it wasn't cheap.

Old Salo was not equipped himself to communicate and get things done in this way, even over short distances. The apparatus and the quantities of Universal Will to Become used in the process were colossal, and they demanded the services of thousands of technicians.

And even the heavily-powered, heavily-manned, heavily-built apparatus of Tralfamadore was not particularly accurate. Old Salo had watched many communications failures on Earth. Civilizations would start to bloom on Earth, and the participants would start to build tremendous structures that were obviously to be messages in Tralfamadorian—and then the civilizations would poop out without having finished the messages.

Old Salo had seen this happen hundreds of times.

Old Salo had told his friend Rumfoord a lot of interesting things about the civilization of Tralfamadore, but he had never told Rumfoord about the messages and the techniques of their delivery.

All that he had told Rumfoord was that he had sent home a distress message, and that he expected a replacement part to come any day now. Old Salo's mind was so different from Rumfoord's that Rumfoord couldn't read Salo's mind.

Salo was grateful for that barrier between their thoughts, because he was mortally afraid of what Rumfoord might say if he found out that Salo's people had so much to do with gumming up the history of Earth. Even though Rumfoord was chrono-synclastic infundibulated, and might be expected to take a larger view of things, Salo had found Rumfoord to be, still, a surprisingly parochial Earthling at heart.

Old Salo didn't want Rumfoord to find out what the Tralfamadorians were doing to Earth, because he was sure that Rumfoord would be offended—that Rumfoord would turn against Salo and all Tralfamadorians. Salo didn't think he could stand that, because he loved Winston Niles Rumfoord.

There was nothing offensive in this love. That is to say, it wasn't homosexual. It couldn't be, since Salo had no sex.

He was a machine, like all Tralfamadorians.

He was held together by cotter pins, hose clamps, nuts, bolts, and magnets. Salo's tangerine-colored skin, which was so expressive when he was emotionally disturbed, could be put on or taken off like an Earthling wind-breaker. A magnetic zipper held it shut.

The Tralfamadorians, according to Salo, manufactured each other. No one knew for certain how the first machine had come into being.

The legend was this:

Once upon a time on Tralfamadore there were creatures who weren't anything like machines. They weren't dependable. They weren't efficient. They weren't predictable. They weren't durable. And these poor creatures were obsessed by the idea that everything that existed had to have a purpose, and that some purposes were higher than others.

These creatures spent most of their time trying to find out what their purpose was. And every time they found out what seemed to be a purpose of themselves, the purpose seemed so low that the creatures were filled with disgust and shame.

And, rather than serve such a low purpose, the creatures would make a machine to serve it. This left the creatures free to serve higher purposes. But whenever they found a higher purpose, the purpose still wasn't high enough.

So machines were made to serve higher purposes, too.

And the machines did everything so expertly that they were finally given the job of finding out what the highest purpose of the creatures could be.

The machines reported in all honesty that the creatures couldn't really be said to have any purpose at all.

The creatures thereupon began slaying each other, because they hated purposeless things above all else.

And they discovered that they weren't even very good at slaying. So they turned that job over to the machines, too. And the machines finished up the job in less time than it takes to say, "Tralfamadore."

Using the viewer on the dash panel of his space ship, Old Salo now watched the approach to Titan of the space ship carrying Malachi Constant, Beatrice Rumfoord, and their son Chrono. Their ship was set to land automatically on the shore of the Winston Sea.

It was set to land amid two million life-sized statues of human beings. Salo had made the statues at the rate of about ten an Earthling year.

The statues were concentrated in the region of the Winston Sea because the statues were made of Titanic peat. Titanic peat abounds by the Winston Sea, only two feet under the surface soil.

Titanic peat is a curious substance—and, for the facile and sincere sculptor, an attractive one.

When first dug, Titanic peat has the consistency of Earthling putty.

After one hour's exposure to Titan's light and air, the peat has the strength and hardness of plaster of Paris.

After two hours' exposure, it is as durable as granite, and must be worked with a cold chisel.

After three hours' exposure, nothing but a diamond will scratch Titanic peat.

Salo was inspired to make so many statues by the showy ways in which Earthlings behaved. It wasn't so much what the Earthlings did as the way they did it that inspired Salo.

The Earthlings behaved at all times as though there were a big eye in the sky—as though that big eye were ravenous for entertainment.

The big eye was a glutton for great theater. The big eye was indifferent as to whether the Earthling shows were comedy, tragedy, farce, satire, athletics, or vaudeville. Its demand, which Earthlings apparently found as irresistible as gravity, was that the shows be great.

The demand was so powerful that Earthlings did almost nothing but perform for it, night and day—and even in their dreams.

The big eye was the only audience that Earthlings really cared about. The fanciest performances that Salo had seen had been put on by Earthlings who were terribly alone. The imagined big eye was their only audience.

Salo, with his diamond-hard statues, had tried to preserve

some of the mental states of those Earthlings who had put on the most interesting shows for the imagined big eye.

Hardly less surprising than the statues were the Titanic daisies that abounded by the Winston Sea. When Salo arrived on Titan in 203,117 B.C., the blooms of Titanic daisies were tiny, star-like, yellow flowers barely a quarter of an inch across.

Then Salo began to breed them selectively.

When Malachi Constant, Beatrice Rumfoord, and their son Chrono arrived on Titan, the typical Titanic daisy had a stalk four feet in diameter, and a lavender bloom shot with pink and having a mass in excess of a ton.

Salo, having watched the approaching space ship of Malachi Constant, Beatrice Rumfoord, and their son Chrono, inflated his feet to the size of German batballs. He stepped onto the emerald clear waters of the Winston Sea, crossed the waters to Winston Niles Rumfoord's Taj Mahal.

He entered the walled yard of the palace, let the air out of his feet. The air hissed. The hiss echoed from the walls.

Winston Niles Rumfoord's lavender contour chair by the pool was empty.

"Skip?" called Salo. He used this most intimate of all possible names for Rumfoord, Rumfoord's childhood name, in spite of Rumfoord's resentment of his use of it. He didn't use the name in order to tease Rumfoord. He used it in order to assert the friendship he felt for Rumfoord—to test the friendship a little, and to watch it endure the test handsomely.

There was a reason for Salo's putting friendship to such a sophomoric test. He had never seen, never even heard of friendship before he hit the Solar System. It was a fascinating novelty to him. He had to play with it.

"Skip?" Salo called again.

There was an unusual tang in the air. Salo identified it tentatively as ozone. He was unable to account for it.

A cigarette still burned in the ash tray by Rumfoord's contour chair, so Rumfoord hadn't been out of his chair long.

"Skip? Kazak?" called Salo. It was unusual for Rumfoord not to be snoozing in his chair, for Kazak not to be snoozing beside it. Man and dog spent most of their time by the pool, monitoring signals from their other selves through space and time. Rumfoord was usually motionless in his chair, the fingers of one languid, dangling hand buried in Kazak's coat. Kazak was usually whimpering and twitching dreamingly.

Salo looked down into the water of the rectangular pool. In the bottom of the pool, in eight feet of water, were the three sirens of Titan, the three beautiful human females who had been offered to the lecherous Malachi Constant so long ago.

They were statues made by Salo of Titanic peat. Of the millions of statues made by Salo, only these three were painted with lifelike colors. It had been necessary to paint them in order to give them importance in the sumptuous, oriental scheme of things in Rumfoord's palace.

"Skip?" Salo called again.

Kazak, the hound of space, answered the call. Kazak came from the domed and minareted building that was reflected in the pool. Kazak came stiffly from the lacy shadows of the great octagonal chamber within.

Kazak looked poisoned.

Kazak shivered, and stared fixedly at a point to one side of Salo. There was nothing there.

Kazak stopped, and seemed to be preparing himself for a terrible pain that another step would cost him.

And then Kazak blazed and crackled with Saint Elmo's fire.

Saint Elmo's fire is a luminous electrical discharge, and any creature afflicted by it is subject to discomfort no worse than the discomfort of being tickled by a feather. All the same, the creature appears to be on fire, and can be forgiven for being dismayed.

The luminous discharge from Kazak was horrifying to watch. And it renewed the stench of ozone.

Kazak did not move. His capacity for surprise at the amazing display had long since been exhausted. He tolerated the blaze with tired rue.

The blaze died.

Rumfoord appeared in the archway. He, too, looked frowzy and palsied. A band of dematerialization, a band of nothingness about a foot wide, passed over Rumfoord from foot to head. This was followed by two narrow bands an inch apart.

Rumfoord held his hands high, and his fingers were spread. Streaks of pink, violet, and pale green Saint Elmo's fire streamed from his fingertips. Short streaks of pale gold fizzed in his hair, conspiring to give him a tinsel halo.

"Peace," said Rumfoord wanly.

Rumfoord's Saint Elmo's fire died.

Salo was aghast. "Skip—" he said. "What's—what's the matter, Skip?"

"Sunspots," said Rumfoord. He shuffled to his lavender contour chair, lay his great frame on it, covered his eyes with a hand as limp and white as a damp handkerchief.

Kazak lay down beside him. Kazak was shivering.

"I—I've never seen you like this before," said Salo.

"There's never been a storm on the Sun like this before," said Rumfoord.

Salo was not surprised to learn that sunspots affected his chrono-synclastic infundibulated friends. He had seen Rumfoord and Kazak sick with sunspots many times before—but the most severe symptom had been fleeting nausea. The sparks and the bands of dematerialization were new.

As Salo watched Rumfoord and Kazak now, they became momentarily two-dimensional, like figures painted on rippling banners.

They steadied, became rounded again.

"Is there anything I can do, Skip?" said Salo.

Rumfoord groaned. "Will people never stop asking that dreadful question?" he said.

"Sorry," said Salo. His feet were so completely deflated now that they were concave, were suction cups. His feet made sucking sounds on the polished pavement.

"Do you *have* to make those noises?" said Rumfoord peevishly.

Old Salo wanted to die. It was the first time his friend Winston Niles Rumfoord had spoken a harsh word to him. Salo couldn't stand it.

Old Salo closed two of his three eyes. The third scanned the sky. The eye was caught by two streaking blue dots in the sky. The dots were soaring Titanic bluebirds.

The pair had found an updraft.

Neither great bird flapped a wing.

No movement of so much as a pinfeather was inharmonious. Life was but a soaring dream.

"*Graw*," said one Titanic bluebird sociably.

"*Graw*," the other agreed.

The birds closed their wings simultaneously, fell from the heights like stones.

They seemed to plummet to certain death outside Rumfoord's walls. But up they soared again, to begin another long and easy climb.

This time they climbed a sky that was streaked by the vapor trail of the space ship carrying Malachi Constant, Beatrice Rumfoord, and their son Chrono. The ship was about to land.

"Skip—?" said Salo.

"Do you *have* to call me that?" said Rumfoord.

"No," said Salo.

"Then don't," said Rumfoord. "I'm not fond of the name—unless somebody I've grown up with happens to use it."

"I thought—as a friend of yours—" said Salo, "I might be entitled—"

"Shall we just drop this guise of friendship?" said Rumfoord curtly.

Salo closed his third eye. The skin of his torso tightened. "Guise?" he said.

"Your feet are making that noise again!" said Rumfoord.

"Skip!" cried Salo. He corrected this insufferable familiarity. "*Winston*—it's like a nightmare, your talking to me this way. I thought we were friends."

"Let's say we've managed to be of some *use* to each other, and let it go at that," said Rumfoord.

Salo's head rocked gently in its gimbals. "I thought there'd been a little more to it than that," he said at last.

"Let's say," said Rumfoord acidly, "that we discovered in each other a means to our separate ends."

"I—I was glad to help you—and I hope I really *was* a help to you," said Salo. He opened his eyes. He had to see Rumfoord's reaction. Surely Rumfoord would become friendly again, for Salo really had helped him unselfishly.

"Didn't I give you half my UWTB?" said Salo. "Didn't I let you copy my ship for Mars? Didn't I fly the first few recruiting missions? Didn't I help you figure out how to control the Martians, so they wouldn't make trouble? Didn't I spend day after day helping you to design the new religion?"

"Yes," said Rumfoord. "But what have you done for me lately?"

"What?" said Salo.

"Never mind," said Rumfoord curtly. "It's the tagline on an old Earthling joke, and not a very funny one, under the circumstances."

"Oh," said Salo. He knew a lot of Earthling jokes, but he didn't know that one.

"Your feet!" cried Rumfoord.

"I'm sorry!" cried Salo. "If I could weep like an Earthling, I would!" His grieving feet were out of his control. They went on making the sounds Rumfoord suddenly hated so. "I'm sorry for everything! All I know is, I've tried every way I know how to be a true friend, and I never asked for *anything* in return."

"You didn't have to!" said Rumfoord. "You didn't have to ask for a thing. All you had to do was sit back and wait for it to be dropped in your lap."

"What was it I wanted dropped in my lap?" said Salo incredulously.

"The replacement part for your space ship," said Rumfoord. "It's almost here. It's arriving, sire. Constant's boy has it—calls it his good-luck piece—as though you didn't know."

Rumfoord sat up, turned green, motioned for silence. "Excuse me," he said. "I'm going to be sick again."

Winston Niles Rumfoord and his dog Kazak *were* sick again —more violently sick than before. It seemed to poor old Salo that this time they would surely sizzle to nothing or explode.

Kazak howled in a ball of Saint Elmo's fire.

Rumfoord stood bolt upright, his eyes popping, a fiery column.

This attack passed, too.

"Excuse me," said Rumfoord with scathing decency. "You were saying—?"

"What?" said Salo bleakly.

"You were saying something—or about to say something," said Rumfoord. Only the sweat at his temples betrayed the fact that he had just been through something harrowing. He put a cigarette in a long, bone cigarette holder, lighted it. He thrust out his jaw. The cigarette holder pointed straight up. "We won't be interrupted again for three minutes," he said. "You were saying?"

Salo recalled the subject of conversation only with effort. When he did recall it, it upset him more than ever. The worst possible thing had happened. Not only had Rumfoord found out, seemingly, about the influence of Tralfamadore on Earthling affairs, which would have offended him quite enough—but Rumfoord also regarded himself, seemingly, as one of the principal victims of that influence.

Salo had had an uneasy suspicion from time to time that Rumfoord was under the influence of Tralfamadore, but he'd pushed the thought out of his mind, since there was nothing he could do about it. He hadn't even discussed it, because to discuss it with Rumfoord would surely have ruined their beautiful friendship at once. Very lamely, Salo explored the possibility that Rumfoord did not know as much as he seemed to know. "Skip—" he said.

"Please!" said Rumfoord.

"Mr. Rumfoord—" said Salo, "you think I somehow used you?"

"Not you," said Rumfoord. "Your fellow machines back on your precious Tralfamadore."

"Um," said Salo. "You—you think you—you've been used, Skip?"

"Tralfamadore," said Rumfoord bitterly, "reached into the Solar System, picked me up, and used me like a handy-dandy potato peeler!"

"If you could see this in the future," said Salo miserably, "why didn't you mention it before?"

"Nobody likes to think he's being used," said Rumfoord. "He'll put off admitting it to himself until the last possible instant." He smiled crookedly. "It may surprise you to learn that I take a certain pride, no matter how foolishly mistaken that pride may be, in making my own decisions for my own reasons."

"I'm not surprised," said Salo.

"Oh?" said Rumfoord unpleasantly. "I should have thought it was too subtle an attitude for a *machine* to grasp."

This, surely, was the low point in their relationship. Salo *was* a machine, since he had been designed and manufactured. He didn't conceal the fact. But Rumfoord had never used the fact as an insult before. He had definitely used the fact as an insult now. Through a thin veil of noblesse oblige, Rumfoord let Salo know that to be a machine was to be insensitive, was to be unimaginative, was to be vulgar, was to be purposeful without a shred of conscience—

Salo was pathetically vulnerable to this accusation. It was a tribute to the spiritual intimacy he and Rumfoord had once shared that Rumfoord knew so well how to hurt him.

Salo closed two of his three eyes again, watched the soaring Titanic bluebirds again. The birds were as big as Earthling eagles.

Salo wished he were a Titanic bluebird.

The space ship carrying Malachi Constant, Beatrice Rumfoord, and their son Chrono sailed low over the palace, landed on the shore of the Winston Sea.

"I give you my word of honor," said Salo, "I didn't know you were being used, and I haven't the slightest idea what you—"

"Machine," said Rumfoord nastily.

"Tell me what you've been used for—please?" said Salo. "My word of honor—I don't have the foggiest—"

"Machine!" said Rumfoord.

"If you think so badly of me, Skip—Winston—Mr. Rumfoord—" said Salo, "after all I've done and tried to do in the name of friendship alone, there's certainly nothing I can say or do now to change your mind."

"Precisely what a machine *would* say," said Rumfoord.

"It's what a machine *did* say," said Salo humbly. He inflated his feet to the size of German batballs, preparing to walk out of Rumfoord's palace and onto the waters of the Winston Sea—never to return. Only when his feet were fully inflated did he catch the challenge in what Rumfoord had said. There was a clear implication that there was something Old Salo could still do to make things right again.

Even if he was a machine, Salo was sensitive enough to know that to ask what that something was would be to grovel. He steeled himself. In the name of friendship, he was going to grovel.

"Skip—" he said, "tell me what to do. Anything—anything at all."

"In a very short time," said Rumfoord, "an explosion is

going to blow the terminal of my spiral clear off the Sun, clear out of the Solar System."

"No!" cried Salo. "Skip! Skip!"

"No, no—no pity, *please*," said Rumfoord, stepping back, afraid of being touched. "It's a very good thing, really. I'll be seeing a lot of new things, a lot of new creatures." He tried to smile. "One gets tired, you know, being caught up in the monotonous clockwork of the Solar System." He laughed harshly. "After all," he said, "it isn't as though I were dying or something. Everything that ever was always will be, and everything that ever will be always was." He shook his head quickly, and cast away a tear he hadn't known was on his eyelid.

"Comforting as that chrono-synclastic infundibulated thought is," he said, "I should still like to know just what the main point of this Solar System episode has been."

"You—you've summed it up far better than anyone else could—in your *Pocket History of Mars*," said Salo.

"*The Pocket History of Mars*," said Rumfoord, "makes no mention of the fact that I have been powerfully influenced by forces emanating from the planet Tralfamadore." He gritted his teeth.

"Before my dog and I go crackling off through space like buggywhips in the hands of a lunatic," said Rumfoord, "I should very much like to know what the message you are carrying is."

"I—I don't know," said Salo. "It's sealed. I have orders—"

"Against all orders from Tralfamadore," said Winston Niles Rumfoord, "against all your instincts as a machine, but in the name of our friendship, Salo, I want you to open the message and read it to me now."

Malachi Constant, Beatrice Rumfoord, and young Chrono, their savage son, picnicked sulkily in the shade of a Titanic daisy by the Winston Sea. Each member of the family had a statue against which to lean.

Bearded Malachi Constant, playboy of the Solar System, still wore his bright yellow suit with the orange question marks. It was the only suit he had.

Constant leaned against a statue of St. Francis of Assisi. St. Francis was trying to befriend two hostile and terrifyingly huge birds, apparently bald eagles. Constant was unable to identify the birds properly as Titanic bluebirds, since he hadn't seen a Titanic bluebird yet. He had arrived on Titan only an hour before.

Beatrice, looking like a gypsy queen, smoldered at the foot of a statue of a young physical student. At first glance, the laboratory-gowned scientist seemed to be a perfect servant of nothing but truth. At first glance, one was convinced that nothing but truth could please him as he beamed at his test tube. At first glance, one thought that he was as much above the beastly concerns of mankind as the harmoniums in the caves of Mercury. There, at first glance, was a young man without vanity, without lust—and one accepted at its face value the title Salo had engraved on the statue, *Discovery of Atomic Power.*

And then one perceived that the young truth-seeker had a shocking erection.

Beatrice hadn't perceived this yet.

Young Chrono, dark and dangerous like his mother, was already committing his first act of vandalism—or was trying to. Chrono was trying to inscribe a dirty Earthling word on the base of the statue against which he had been leaning. He was attempting the job with a sharp corner of his good-luck piece.

The seasoned Titanic peat, almost as hard as diamonds, did the cutting instead, rounding off the corner's point.

The statue on which Chrono was working was of a family group—a Neanderthal man, his mate, and their baby. It was a deeply-moving piece. The squat, shaggy, hopeful creatures were so ugly they were beautiful.

Their importance and universality was not spoiled by the satiric title Salo had given the piece. He gave frightful titles to all his statues, as though to proclaim desperately that he did not take himself seriously as an artist, not for an instant. The title he gave to the Neanderthal family derived from the fact that the baby was being shown a human foot roasting on a crude spit.

The title was *This Little Piggy.*

"No matter what happens, no matter what beautiful or sad or happy or frightening thing happens," Malachi Constant told his family there on Titan, "I'm damned if I'll respond. The minute it looks like something or somebody wants me to act in some special way, I will freeze." He glanced up at the rings of Saturn, curled his lip. "Isn't that just too beautiful for words?" He spat on the ground.

"If anybody ever expects to use me again in some tremendous scheme of his," said Constant, "he is in for one big disappointment. He will be a lot better off trying to get a rise out of one of these statues."

He spat again.

"As far as I'm concerned," said Constant, "the Universe is a junk yard, with everything in it overpriced. I am through poking around in the junk heaps, looking for bargains. Every so-called bargain," said Constant, "has been connected by fine wires to a dynamite bouquet." He spat again.

"I resign," said Constant.

"I withdraw," said Constant.

"I quit," said Constant.

Constant's little family agreed without enthusiasm. Constant's brave speech was stale stuff. He had delivered it many times during the seventeen-month voyage from Earth to Titan —and it was, after all, a routine philosophy for all Martian veterans.

Constant wasn't really speaking to his family anyway. He was speaking loudly, so his voice would carry some distance into the forest of statuary and over the Winston Sea. He was making a policy statement for the benefit of Rumfoord or anybody else who might be lurking near by.

"We have taken part for the last time," said Constant loudly, "in experiments and fights and festivals we don't like or understand!"

" '*Understand—*' " came an echo from the wall of a palace on an island two-hundred yards offshore. The palace was, of course, Dun Roamin, Rumfoord's Taj Mahal. Constant wasn't surprised to see the palace out there. He had seen it when he disembarked from his space ship, had seen it shining out there like St. Augustine's City of God.

"What happens next?" Constant asked the echo. "All the statues come to life?"

" '*Life?*' " said the echo.

"It's an echo," said Beatrice.

"I know it's an echo," said Constant.

"I didn't know if you knew it was an echo or not," said Beatrice. She was distant and polite. She had been extremely decent to Constant, blaming him for nothing, expecting nothing from him. A less aristocratic woman might have put him through hell, blaming him for everything and demanding miracles.

There had been no love-making during the voyage. Neither Constant nor Beatrice had been interested. Martian veterans never were.

Inevitably, the long voyage had drawn Constant closer to his mate and child—closer than they had been on the gilded system of catwalks, ramps, ladders, pulpits, steps and stages in Newport. But the only love in the family unit was still the love between young Chrono and Beatrice. Other than the love between mother and son there was only politeness, glum compassion, and suppressed indignation at having been forced to be a family at all.

"Oh, my—" said Constant, "life is funny when you stop to think of it."

Young Chrono did not smile when his father said life was funny.

Young Chrono was the member of the family least in a position to think life was funny. Beatrice and Constant, after all, could laugh bitterly at the wild incidents they had survived. But young Chrono couldn't laugh with them, because he himself was a wild incident.

Small wonder that young Chrono's chief treasures were a good-luck piece and a switchblade knife.

Young Chrono now drew his switchblade knife, flicked open the blade nonchalantly. His eyes narrowed. He was preparing to kill, if killing should become necessary. He was looking in the direction of a gilded rowboat that had put out from the palace on the island.

It was being rowed by a tangerine-colored creature. The oarsman was, of course, Salo. He was bringing the boat in order to transport the family back to the palace. Salo was a bad oarsman, never having rowed before. He grasped the oars with his suction-cup feet.

He had one advantage over human oarsmen, in that he had an eye in the back of his head.

Young Chrono flashed light into Old Salo's eye, flashed it with his bright knife blade.

Salo's back eye blinked.

Flashing the light into the eye was not a piece of skylarking on Chrono's part. It was a piece of jungle cunning, a piece of cunning calculated to make almost any sort of sighted creature uneasy. It was one of a thousand pieces of jungle cunning that young Chrono and his mother had learned in their year together in the Amazon Rain Forest.

Beatrice's brown hand closed on a rock. "Worry him again," she said softly to Chrono.

Young Chrono again flashed the light in Old Salo's eye.

"His body looks like the only soft part," said Beatrice, without moving her lips. "If you can't get his body, try for an eye."

Chrono nodded.

Constant was chilled, seeing what an efficient unit of self-defense his mate and son made together. Constant was not included in their plans. They had no need of him.

"What should I do?" whispered Constant.

"Sh!" said Beatrice sharply.

Salo beached his gilded craft. He made it fast with a clumsy landlubber's knot to the wrist of a statue by the water. The statue was of a nude woman playing a slide trombone. It was entitled, enigmatically, *Evelyn and Her Magic Violin.*

Salo was too jangled by sorrow to care for his own safety—to understand, even, that he might be frightening to someone. He stood for a moment on a block of seasoned Titanic peat near his landing. His grieving feet sucked at the damp stone. He pried loose his feet with a tremendous effort.

On he came, the flashes from Chrono's knife dazzling him.

"Please—" he said.

A rock flew out of the knife's dazzle.

Salo ducked.

A hand siezed his bony throat, threw him down.

Young Chrono now stood astride Old Salo, his knife point pricking Salo's chest. Beatrice knelt by Salo's head, a rock poised to smash his head to bits.

"Go on—kill me," said Salo raspingly. "You'd be doing me a favor. I wish I were dead. I wish to God I'd never been assembled and started up in the first place. Kill me, put me out of my misery, and then go see him. He's asking for you."

"Who is?" said Beatrice.

"Your poor husband—my former friend, Winston Niles Rumfoord," said Salo.

"Where is he?" said Beatrice.

"In that palace on the island," said Salo. "He's dying—all alone, except for his faithful dog. He's asking for you—" said Salo, "asking for all of you. And he says he never wants to lay his eyes on me again."

Malachi Constant watched the lead-colored lips kiss thin air soundlessly. The tongue behind the lips clicked infinitesimally. The lips suddenly drew back, baring the perfect teeth of Winston Niles Rumfoord.

Constant was himself showing his teeth, preparing to gnash them appropriately at the sight of this man who had done him so much harm. He did not gnash them. For one thing, no one was looking—no one would see him do it and understand. For another thing, Constant found himself destitute of hate.

His preparations for gnashing his teeth decayed into a yokel gape—the gape of a yokel in the presence of a spectacularly mortal disease.

Winston Niles Rumfoord was lying, fully materialized, on his back on his lavender contour chair by the pool. His eyes were directed at the sky, unblinkingly and seemingly sightless. One fine hand dangled over the side of the chair, its limp fingers laced in the choke chain of Kazak, the hound of space.

The chain was empty.

An explosion on the Sun had separated man and dog. A Universe schemed in mercy would have kept man and dog together.

The Universe inhabited by Winston Niles Rumfoord and his dog was not schemed in mercy. Kazak had been sent ahead of his master on the great mission to nowhere and nothing.

Kazak had left howling in a puff of ozone and sick light, in a hum like swarming bees.

Rumfoord let the empty choke chain slip from his fingers. The chain expressed deadness, made a formless sound and a formless heap, was a soulless slave of gravity, born with a broken spine.

Rumfoord's lead-colored lips moved. "Hello, Beatrice—wife," he said sepulchrally.

"Hello, Space Wanderer," he said. He made his voice affectionate this time. "Gallant of you to come, Space Wanderer—to take one more chance with me.

"Hello, illustrious young bearer of the illustrious name of Chrono," said Rumfoord. "Hail, oh German batball star—hail, him of the good-luck piece."

The three to whom he spoke stood just inside the wall. The pool was between them and Rumfoord.

Old Salo, who had not been granted his wish to die, grieved in the stern of the gilded rowboat that was beached outside the wall.

"I am not dying," said Rumfoord. "I am merely taking my leave of the Solar System. And I am not even doing that. In the grand, in the timeless, in the chrono-synclastic infundibulated way of looking at things, I shall always be here. I shall always be wherever I've been.

"I'm honeymooning with you still, Beatrice," he said. "I'm talking to you still in a little room under the stairway in Newport, Mr. Constant. Yes—and playing peek-a-boo in the caves of Mercury with you and Boaz. And Chrono—" he said, "I'm watching you still as you play German batball so well on the iron playground of Mars."

He groaned. It was a tiny groan—and so sad.

The sweet, mild air of Titan carried the tiny groan away.

"Whatever we've said, friends, we're saying still—such as it was, such as it is, such as it will be," said Rumfoord.

The tiny groan came again.

Rumfoord watched it leave as though it were a smoke ring.

"There is something you should know about life in the Solar System," he said. "Being chrono-synclastic infundibulated, I've known about it all along. It is, none the less, such a sickening thing that I've thought about it as little as possible.

"The sickening thing is this:

"*Everything that every Earthling has ever done has been warped by creatures on a planet one-hundred-and-fifty thousand light years away.* The name of the planet is Tralfamadore.

"How the Tralfamadorians controlled us, I don't know. But I know to what end they controlled us. *They controlled us in such a way as to make us deliver a replacement part to a Tralfamadorian messenger who was grounded right here on Titan.*"

Rumfoord pointed a finger at young Chrono. "You, young man—" he said. "You have it in your pocket. In your pocket is the culmination of all Earthling history. In your pocket is the mysterious something that every Earthling was trying so desperately, so earnestly, so gropingly, so exhaustingly to produce and deliver."

A fizzing twig of electricity grew from the tip of Rumfoord's accusing finger.

"The thing you call your good-luck piece," said Rumfoord, "is the replacement part for which the Tralfamadorian messenger has been waiting so long!

"The messenger," said Rumfoord, "is the tangerine-colored creature who now cowers outside the walls. His name is Salo. I had hoped that the messenger would give mankind a glimpse of the message he was carrying, since mankind was giving him such a nice boost on his way. Unfortunately, he is under orders to show the message to no one. He is a machine, and, as a machine, he has no choice but to regard orders as orders.

"I asked him politely to show me the message," said Rumfoord. "He desperately refused."

The fizzing twig of electricity on Rumfoord's finger grew, forming a spiral around Rumfoord. Rumfoord considered the spiral with sad contempt. "I think perhaps this is it," he said of the spiral.

It was indeed. The spiral telescoped slightly, making a curtsey. And then it began to revolve around Rumfoord, spinning a continuous cocoon of green light.

It barely whispered as it spun.

"All I can say," said Rumfoord from the cocoon, "is that I have tried my best to do good for my native Earth while serving the irresistible wishes of Tralfamadore.

"Perhaps, now that the part has been delivered to the Tralfamadorian messenger, Tralfamadore will leave the Solar System alone. Perhaps Earthlings will now be free to develop and follow their own inclinations, as they have not been free to do for thousands of years." He sneezed. "The wonder is that Earthlings have been able to make as much sense as they have," he said.

The green cocoon left the ground, hovered over the dome. "Remember me as a gentleman of Newport, Earth, and the Solar System," said Rumfoord. He sounded serene again, at peace with himself, and at least equal to any creature that he might encounter anywhere.

"In a punctual way of speaking," came Rumfoord's glottal tenor from the cocoon, "good-by."

The cocoon and Rumfoord disappeared with a *pft*.

Rumfoord and his dog were never seen again.

Old Salo came bounding into the courtyard just as Rumfoord and his cocoon disappeared.

The little Tralfamadorian was wild. He had torn the message from its band around his throat with a suction-cup foot. One foot was still a suction cup, and in it was the message.

He looked up at the place where the cocoon had hovered. "Skip!" he cried into the sky. "Skip! The message! I'll tell you the message! *The message! Skiiiiiiiiiiiiiiiiiiip!*"

His head did a somersault in its gimbals. "Gone," he said emptily. He whispered, "Gone.

"Machine?" said Salo. He was speaking haltingly, as much to himself as to Constant, Beatrice and Chrono. "A machine I am, and so are my people," he said. "I was designed and manufactured, and no expense, no skill, was spared in making me dependable, efficient, predictable, and durable. I was the best machine my people could make.

"How good a machine have I proved to be?" asked Salo.

"*Dependable?*" he said. "I was depended upon to keep my message sealed until I reached my destination, and now I've torn it open.

"*Efficient?*" he said. "Having lost my best friend in the Universe, it now costs me more energy to step over a dead leaf than it once cost me to bound over Mount Rumfoord.

"*Predictable?*" he said. "After watching human beings for two hundred thousand Earthling years, I have become as skittish and sentimental as the silliest Earthling schoolgirl.

"*Durable?*" he said darkly. "We shall see what we shall see."

He laid the message he had been carrying so long on Rumfoord's empty, lavender contour chair.

"There it is—friend," he said to his memory of Rumfoord, "and much consolation may it give you, Skip. Much pain it cost your old, friend Salo. In order to give it to you—even too late—your old friend Salo had to make war against the core of his being, against the very nature of being a machine.

"You asked the impossible of a machine," said Salo, "and the machine complied.

"The machine is no longer a machine," said Salo. "The machine's contacts are corroded, his bearings fouled, his circuits shorted, and his gears stripped. His mind buzzes and pops like the mind of an Earthling—fizzes and overheats with thoughts of love, honor, dignity, rights, accomplishment, integrity, independence—"

Old Salo picked up the message again from Rumfoord's contour chair. It was written on a thin square of aluminum. The message was a single dot.

"Would you like to know how I have been used, how my life has been wasted?" he said. "Would you like to know what the message is that I have been carrying for almost half a million Earthling years—the message I am supposed to carry for eighteen million more years?"

He held out the square of aluminum in a cupped foot.

"A dot," he said.

"A single dot," he said.

"The meaning of a dot in Tralfamadorian," said Old Salo, "is—

"*Greetings.*"

The little machine from Tralfamadore, having delivered this message to himself, to Constant, to Beatrice, and to Chrono over a distance of one hundred and fifty thousand light years, bounded abruptly out of the courtyard and onto the beach outside.

He killed himself out there. He took himself apart and threw his parts in all directions.

Chrono went out on the beach alone, wandered thoughtfully among Salo's parts. Chrono had always known that his good-luck piece had extraordinary powers and extraordinary meanings.

And he had always suspected that some superior creature would eventually come to claim the good-luck piece as his own. It was in the nature of truly effective good-luck pieces that human beings never really owned them.

They simply took care of them, had the benefit of them, until the real owners, the superior owners, came along.

Chrono did not have a sense of futility and disorder.

Everything seemed in apple-pie order to him.

And the boy himself participated fitly in that perfect order.

He took his good-luck piece from his pocket, dropped it without regret to the sand, dropped it among Salo's scattered parts.

Sooner or later, Chrono believed, the magical forces of the Universe would put everything back together again.

They always did.

EPILOGUE

Reunion with Stony

"You are tired, so very tired, Space Wanderer, Malachi, Unk. Stare at the faintest star, Earthling, and think how heavy your limbs are growing."

—SALO

THERE ISN'T much more to tell.

Malachi Constant grew to be an old man on Titan.

Beatrice Rumfoord grew to be an old woman on Titan.

They died peacefully, died within twenty-four hours of each other. They died in their seventy-fourth years.

Only the Titanic bluebirds know for sure what happened, finally, to Chrono, their son.

When Malachi Constant turned seventy-four years old, he was crusty, sweet, and bandy-legged. He was totally bald, and went naked most of the time, wearing nothing but a neatly-trimmed, white vandyke beard.

He lived in Salo's grounded space ship, had been living there for thirty years.

Constant had not tried to fly the space ship. He hadn't dared to touch a single control. The controls of Salo's ship were far more complex than those of a Martian ship. Salo's dash panel offered Constant two hundred and seventy-three knobs, switches, and buttons, each with a Tralfamadorian inscription or calibration. The controls were anything but a hunch-player's delight in a Universe composed of one-trillionth part matter to one decillion parts black velvet futility.

Constant had tinkered with the ship only to the extent of finding out gingerly if, as Rumfoord had said, Chrono's good-luck piece really would serve as a part of the power plant.

Superficially, at any rate, the good-luck piece would. There was an access door to the ship's power plant that had plainly leaked smoke at one time. Constant opened it, found a sooty compartment within. And under the soot were smudged bearings and cams that related to nothing.

Constant was able to slip the holes in Chrono's good-luck piece onto those bearings and between the cams. The good-luck piece conformed to close tolerances and surrounding clearances in a way that would have pleased a Swiss machinist.

Constant had many hobbies that helped him to pass the balmy time in the salubrious clime of Titan.

His most interesting hobby was puttering around with Salo, the dismantled Tralfamadorian messenger. Constant spent thousands of hours trying to get Salo back together and going again.

So far, he had had no luck.

When Constant first undertook the reconstruction of the little Tralfamadorian, it had been with the express hope that Salo would then agree to fly young Chrono back to Earth.

Constant wasn't eager to fly back to Earth, and neither was his mate Beatrice. But Constant and Beatrice had agreed that their son, with most of his life ahead of him, should live that life with busy and jolly contemporaries on Earth.

By the time Constant was seventy-four, however, getting young Chrono back to Earth was no longer a pressing problem. Young Chrono was no longer particularly young. He was forty-two. And he had made such a thorough and specialized adjustment on Titan that it would have been cruel in the extreme to send him anywhere else.

At the age of seventeen, young Chrono had run away from his palatial home to join the Titanic bluebirds, the most admirable creatures on Titan. Chrono now lived among their nests by the Kazak pools. He wore their feathers and sat on their eggs and shared their food and spoke their language.

Constant never saw Chrono. Sometimes, late at night, he would hear Chrono's cries. Constant did not answer the cries. The cries were for nothing and nobody on Titan.

They were for Phoebe, a passing moon.

Sometimes, when Constant was out gathering Titanic strawberries or the speckled, two-pound eggs of the Titanic plover, he would come upon a little shrine made of sticks and stones in a clearing. Chrono made hundreds of these shrines.

The elements in the shrines were always the same. One large stone was at the center, representing Saturn. A wooden hoop made of a green twig was placed around it—to represent Saturn's rings. And beyond the rings were small stones to represent the nine moons. The largest of these satellite stones was Titan. And there was always the feather of a Titanic bluebird under it.

The marks on the ground made it clear that young Chrono, no longer so young, spent hours moving the elements of the system about.

When old Malachi Constant found one of his strange son's shrines in a state of neglect, he would tidy it up as best he could. Constant would weed it and rake it, and make a new twig ring for the stone that was Saturn. He would put a fresh bluebird feather under the stone that was Titan.

Tidying up the shrines was as close, spiritually, as Constant could get to his son.

He respected what his son was trying to do with religion.

And sometimes, when Constant gazed at a refurbished shrine, he moved the elements of his own life about experimentally—but he did it in his head. At such times he was likely to reflect in melancholy on two things in particular—his murder of Stony Stevenson, his best and only friend, and his winning, so late in life, the love of Beatrice Rumfoord.

Constant never found out whether Chrono knew who tidied up the shrines. Chrono may have thought his god or gods were doing it.

It was all so sad. But it was all so beautiful, too.

Beatrice Rumfoord lived alone in Rumfoord's Taj Mahal. Her contacts with Chrono were far more harrowing than Constant's. At unpredictable intervals, Chrono would swim out to the palace, dress himself from Rumfoord's wardrobe, announce that it was his mother's birthday, and spend the day in indolent, sullen, reasonably civilized discourse.

At the end of such a day, Chrono would rage at the clothes and his mother and civilization. He would tear off the clothes, scream like a bluebird, and dive into the Winston Sea.

When Beatrice had suffered through one of these birthday parties, she would thrust an oar into the sand of the beach that faced the nearest shore, and she would fly a white sheet from it.

It was a signal for Malachi Constant, begging him please to come at once, to help her calm down.

And when Constant arrived in response to the signal of distress, Beatrice always comforted herself with the same words.

"At least," she would say, "he isn't a mama's boy. And at least he had the greatness of soul to join the noblest, most beautiful creatures in sight."

The white sheet, the signal of distress, was flying now.

Malachi Constant put out from shore in a dugout canoe. The gilded rowboat that had come with the palace had long since been sunk by dry rot.

Constant was wearing an old blue wool bathrobe that had once belonged to Rumfoord. He had found it in the palace, had taken it when his Space Wanderer's suit wore out. It was his only garment, and he wore it only when he went calling on Beatrice.

Constant had in the dugout canoe with him six plovers' eggs, two quarts of wild Titanic strawberries, a three-gallon peat crock of fermented daisy milk, a bushel of daisy seeds, eight books he had borrowed from the forty-thousand-volume library in the palace, and a home-made broom and a home-made shovel.

Constant was self-sufficient. He raised or gathered or made everything he needed. This satisfied him enormously.

Beatrice was not dependent on Constant. Rumfoord had stocked the Taj Mahal lavishly with Earthling food and Earthling liquor. Beatrice had plenty to eat and drink, and always would have.

Constant was bringing native foods to Beatrice because he was so proud of his skills as a woodsman and husbandman. He liked to show off his skills as a provider.

It was a compulsion.

Constant had his broom and shovel along in the dugout canoe because Beatrice's palace was always a broom-and-shovel mess. Beatrice did no cleaning, so Constant got rid of the worst of the refuse whenever he paid her a visit.

•

Beatrice Rumfoord was a springy, one-eyed, gold-toothed, brown old lady—as lean and tough as a chair slat. But the class of the damaged and roughly-used old lady showed through.

To anyone with a sense of poetry, mortality, and wonder, Malachi Constant's proud, high-cheekboned mate was as handsome as a human being could be.

She was probably a little crazy. On a moon with only two other people on it, she was writing a book called *The True Purpose of Life in the Solar System.* It was a refutation of Rumfoord's notion that the purpose of human life in the Solar System was to get a grounded messenger from Tralfamadore on his way again.

Beatrice began the book after her son left her to join the bluebirds. The manuscript so far, written in longhand, occupied thirty-eight cubic feet inside the Taj Mahal.

Every time Constant visited her, she read aloud her latest additions to the manuscript.

She was reading out loud now, sitting in Rumfoord's old contour chair while Constant puttered about the courtyard. She was wearing a pink and white chenille bedspread that had come with the palace. Worked into the tufts of the bedspread was the message, *God does not care.*

It had been Rumfoord's own personal bedspread.

On and on Beatrice read, spinning arguments against the importance of the forces of Tralfamadore.

Constant did not listen attentively. He simply enjoyed Beatrice's voice, which was strong and triumphant. He was down in a manhole by the pool, turning a valve that would drain the water out. The water of the pool had been turned into something like cream of pea soup by Titanic algae. Every time Constant visited Beatrice he fought a losing battle against the prolific green murk.

" 'I would be the last to deny,' " said Beatrice, reading her own work out loud, " 'that the forces of Tralfamadore have had something to do with the affairs of Earth. However, those persons who have served the interests of Tralfamadore have served them in such highly personalized ways that Tralfamadore can be said to have had practically nothing to do with the case.' "

Constant, down in the manhole, put his ear to the valve he had opened. From the sound of it, the water was draining slowly.

Constant swore. One of the vital pieces of information that had disappeared with Rumfoord and died with Salo was how they had managed, in their time, to keep the pool so crystal clean. Ever since Constant had taken over maintenance of the pool, the algae had been building up. The pool's bottoms and sides were lined with a blanket of viscid slime, and the three statues in the middle, the three Sirens of Titan, were under a mucilaginous hump.

Constant knew of the significance of the three sirens in his life. He had read about it—both in the *Pocket History of Mars* and *The Winston Niles Rumfoord Authorized Revised Bible.* The three great beauties didn't mean so much to him now, really, except to remind him that sex had once bothered him.

Constant climbed out of the manhole. "Drains slower every time," he said to Beatrice. "I don't guess I can put off digging up the pipes much longer."

"That so?" said Beatrice, looking up from her writing.

"That's so," said Constant.

"Well—you do whatever needs to be done," said Beatrice.

"That's the story of my life," said Constant.

"I just had an idea that ought to go in the book," said Beatrice, "if I can just keep it from getting away."

"I'll hit it with a shovel, if it comes this way," said Constant.

"Don't say anything for a minute," said Beatrice. "Just let me get it straight in my head." She stood, and went into the entry of the palace to escape the distractions of Constant and the rings of Saturn.

She looked long at a large oil painting hanging on the entry wall. It was the only painting in the palace. Constant had had it brought all the way from Newport.

It was a painting of an immaculate little girl in white, holding the reins of a white pony all her own.

Beatrice knew who the little girl was. The painting was labeled with a brass plate that said, *Beatrice Rumfoord as a Young Girl.*

It was quite a contrast—between the little girl in white and the old lady looking at her.

Beatrice suddenly turned her back on the painting, walked out into the courtyard again. The idea she wanted to add to her book was straight in her mind now.

"The worst thing that could possibly happen to anybody," she said, "would be to not be used for anything by anybody."

The thought relaxed her. She lay down on Rumfoord's old contour chair, looked up at the appallingly beautiful rings of Saturn—at Rumfoord's Rainbow.

"Thank you for using me," she said to Constant, "even though I didn't want to be used by anybody."

"You're welcome," said Constant.

He began to sweep the courtyard. The litter he was sweeping was a mixture of sand, which had blown in from the outside, daisy-seed hulls, Earthling peanut hulls, empty cans of boned chicken, and discarded wads of manuscript paper. Beatrice subsisted mostly on daisy seeds, peanuts, and boned chicken because she didn't have to cook them, because she didn't even have to interrupt her writing in order to eat them.

She could eat with one hand and write with the other—and, more than anything else in life, she wanted to get everything written down.

With his sweeping half done, Constant paused to see how the pool was draining.

It was draining slowly. The slimy green hump that covered the three Sirens of Titan was just breaking the descending surface.

Constant leaned over the open manhole, listened to the water sounds.

He heard the music of the pipes. And he heard something else, too.

He heard the absence of a familiar and a beloved sound.

His mate Beatrice wasn't breathing any more.

Malachi Constant buried his mate in Titanic peat on the shore of the Winston Sea. She was buried where there were no statues.

Malachi Constant said good-by to her when the sky was filled with Titanic bluebirds. There must have been ten thousand, at least, of the great and noble birds.

They made night of day, made the air quake with their beating wings.

Not one bird cried out.

And in that night in the midst of day, Chrono, the son of Beatrice and Malachi, appeared on a knoll overlooking the new grave. He wore a feather cape which he flapped like wings.

He was gorgeous and strong.

"Thank you, Mother and Father," he shouted, "for the gift of life. Good-by!"

He was gone, and the birds went with him.

Old Malachi Constant went back to the palace with a heart as heavy as a cannonball. What drew him back to that sad place was a wish to leave it in good order.

Sooner or later, someone else would come.

The palace should be neat and clean and ready for them. The palace should speak well of the former tenant.

Around Rumfoord's worn contour chair were the plovers' eggs and wild Titanic strawberries, and the crock of fermented daisy milk and the basket of daisy seeds that Constant had given to Beatrice. They were perishables. They would not last until the next tenant came.

These Constant put back in his dugout canoe.

He didn't need them. Nobody needed them.

As he straightened up his old back from the canoe, he saw Salo, the little messenger from Tralfamadore, walking across the water toward him.

"How do you do," said Constant.

"How do you do," said Salo. "Thank you for putting me back together again."

"I didn't think I did it right," said Constant. "I couldn't get a peep out of you."

"You did it right," said Salo. "I just couldn't make up my mind whether or not I wanted to peep." He let the air out of his feet with a hiss. "I guess I'll be moseying along," he said.

"You're going to deliver your message after all?" said Constant.

"Anybody who has traveled this far on a fool's errand," said Salo, "has no choice but to uphold the honor of fools by completing the errand."

"My mate died today," said Constant.

"Sorry," said Salo. "I would say, 'Is there anything I can do?'—but Skip once told me that that was the most hateful and stupid expression in the English language."

Constant rubbed his hands together. The only company he had left on Titan was whatever company his right hand could be for his left. "I miss her," he said.

"You finally fell in love, I see," said Salo.

"Only an Earthling year ago," said Constant. "It took us that long to realize that a purpose of human life, no matter who is controlling it, is to love whoever is around to be loved."

"If you or your son would like a ride back to Earth," said Salo, "it wouldn't be much out of my way."

"My boy joined the bluebirds," said Constant.

"Good for him!" said Salo. "I'd join them, if they'd have me."

"Earth," said Constant wonderingly.

"We could be there in a matter of hours," said Salo, "now that the ship's running right again."

"It's lonely here," said Constant, "now that—" He shook his head.

On the trip back to Earth, Salo suspected that he had made a tragic mistake in suggesting to Constant that he return to Earth. He had begun to suspect this when Constant insisted on being taken to Indianapolis, Indiana, U.S.A.

This insistence of Constant's was a dismaying development, since Indianapolis was far from an ideal place for a homeless old man.

Salo wanted to let him off by a shuffleboard court in St. Petersburg, Florida, U.S.A., but Constant, after the fashion of old men, could not be shaken from his first decision. He wanted to go to Indianapolis, and that was that.

Salo assumed that Constant had relatives or possibly old business connections in Indianapolis, but this turned out not to be the case.

"I don't know anybody in Indianapolis, and I don't know anything about Indianapolis except for one thing," said Constant, "a thing I read in a book."

"What did you read in a book?" said Salo uneasily.

"Indianapolis, Indiana," said Constant, "is the first place in the United States of America where a white man was hanged for the murder of an Indian. The kind of people who'll hang a white man for murdering an Indian—" said Constant, "that's the kind of people for me."

Salo's head did a somersault in its gimbals. His feet made grieved sucking sounds on the iron floor. His passenger, obviously, knew almost nothing about the planet toward which he was being carried with a speed approaching that of light.

At least Constant had money.

There was hope in that. He had close to three thousand dollars in various Earthling currencies, taken from the pockets of Rumfoord's suits in the Taj Mahal.

And at least he had clothes.

He had on a terribly baggy but good tweed suit of Rumfoord's, complete with a Phi Beta Kappa key that hung from the watch chain that spanned the front of the vest.

Salo had made Constant take the key along with the suit.

Constant had a good overcoat, a hat, and overshoes, too.

With Earth only an hour away, Salo wondered what else he could do to make the remainder of Constant's life supportable, even in Indianapolis.

And he decided to hypnotize Constant, in order that the last few seconds of Constant's life, at least, would please the old man tremendously. Constant's life would end well.

Constant was already in a nearly hypnotic state, staring out at the Cosmos through a porthole.

Salo came up behind him and spoke to him soothingly.

"You are tired, so very tired, Space Wanderer, Malachi, Unk," said Salo. "Stare at the faintest star, Earthling, and think how heavy your limbs are growing."

"Heavy," said Constant.

"You are going to die some day, Unk," said Salo. "Sorry, but it's true."

"True," said Constant. "Don't be sorry."

"When you know you are dying, Space Wanderer," said Salo hypnotically, "a wonderful thing will happen to you." He then described to Constant the happy things that Constant would imagine before his life flickered out.

It would be a post-hypnotic illusion.

"Awake!" said Salo.

Constant shuddered, turned away from the porthole. "Where am I?" he said.

"On a Tralfamadorian space ship out of Titan, bound for Earth," said Salo.

"Oh," said Constant. "Of course," he said a moment later. "I must have been asleep."

"Take a nap," said Salo.

"Yes—I—I think I will," said Constant. He lay down on a bunk. He dropped off to sleep.

Salo strapped the sleeping Space Wanderer to his bunk. Then he strapped himself to his seat at the controls. He set three dials, double-checked the reading on each. He pressed a bright red button.

He sat back. There was nothing more to do now. From now on everything was automatic. In thirty-six minutes, the ship would land itself near the end of a bus line on the outskirts of Indianapolis, Indiana, U.S.A., Earth, Solar System, Milky Way.

It would be three in the morning there.

It would also be winter.

The space ship landed in four inches of fresh snow in a vacant lot on the south side of Indianapolis. No one was awake to see it land.

Malachi Constant got out of the space ship.

"That's your bus stop over there, old soldier," whispered Salo. It was necessary to whisper, for a two-story frame house with an open bedroom window was only thirty feet away. Salo pointed to a snowy bench by the street. "You'll have to wait about ten minutes," he whispered. "The bus will take you right into the center of town. Ask the driver to let you off near a good hotel."

Constant nodded. "I'll be all right," he whispered.

"How do you feel?" whispered Salo.

"Warm as toast," whispered Constant.

The complaint of a vaguely disturbed sleeper came from the open bedroom window near by. "Aw, somebody," the sleeper complained, "*afo wa, de-yah, ummmmmmmmmmmm.*"

"You really all right?" whispered Salo.

"Yes. Fine," whispered Constant. "Warm as toast."

"Good luck," whispered Salo.

"We don't say that down here," whispered Constant.

Salo winked. "I'm not *from* down here," he whispered. He looked around at the perfectly white world, felt the wet kisses of the snowflakes, pondered hidden meanings in the pale yellow streetlights that shone in a world so whitely asleep. "Beautiful," he whispered.

"Isn't it?" whispered Constant.

"*Sim-faw!*" cried the sleeper menacingly, to anyone who might menace his sleep. "*Soo! A-so! What's a mabba? Nf.*"

"You better go," whispered Constant.

"Yes," whispered Salo.

"Good-by," whispered Constant, "and thanks."

"You're entirely welcome," whispered Salo. He backed into the ship, closed the airlock. The ship arose with the sound of a man blowing over the mouth of a bottle. It disappeared into the swirling snow and was gone.

"Toodle-oo," it said.

Malachi Constant's feet squeaked in the snow as he walked to the bench. He brushed aside the snow on the bench and sat down.

"*Fraugh!*" cried the sleeper, as though he suddenly understood all.

"*Braugh!*" he cried, not liking at all what he suddenly understood.

"*Sup-foe!*" he said, saying in no uncertain terms what he was going to do about it.

"*Floof!*" he cried.

The conspirators presumably fled.

More snow fell.

The bus Malachi Constant was waiting for ran two hours late that morning—on account of the snow. When the bus did come it was too late. Malachi Constant was dead.

Salo had hypnotized him so that he would imagine, as he died, that he saw his best and only friend, Stony Stevenson.

As the snow drifted over Constant, he imagined that the clouds opened up, letting through a sunbeam, a sunbeam all for him.

A golden space ship encrusted with diamonds came skimming

down the sunbeam, landed in the untouched snow of the street.

Out stepped a stocky, red-headed man with a big cigar. He was young. He wore the uniform of the Martian Assault Infantry, Unk's old outfit.

"Hello, Unk," he said. "Get in."

"Get in?" said Constant. "Who are you?"

"Stony Stevenson, Unk. You don't recognize me?"

"Stony?" said Constant. "That's you, Stony?"

"Who else could stand the bloody pace?" said Stony. He laughed. "Get in," he said.

"And go where?" said Constant.

"Paradise," said Stony.

"What's Paradise like?" said Constant.

"Everybody's happy there forever," said Stony, "or as long as the bloody Universe holds together. Get in, Unk. Beatrice is already there, waiting for you."

"Beatrice?" said Unk, getting into the space ship.

Stony closed the airlocks, pressed the *on* button.

"We're—we're going to Paradise now?" said Constant. "I—I'm going to get into Paradise?"

"Don't ask me why, old sport," said Stony, "but somebody up there likes you."

MOTHER NIGHT

Introduction

THIS IS the only story of mine whose moral I know. I don't think it's a marvelous moral; I simply happen to know what it is: We are what we pretend to be, so we must be careful about what we pretend to be.

My personal experience with Nazi monkey business was limited. There were some vile and lively native American Fascists in my home town of Indianapolis during the thirties, and somebody slipped me a copy of *The Protocols of the Elders of Zion*, I remember, which was supposed to be the Jews' secret plan for taking over the world. And I remember some laughs about my aunt, too, who married a *German* German, and who had to write to Indianapolis for proofs that she had no Jewish blood. The Indianapolis mayor knew her from high school and dancing school, so he had fun putting ribbons and official seals all over the documents the Germans required, which made them look like eighteenth-century peace treaties.

After a while the war came, and I was in it, and I was captured, so I got to see a little of Germany from the inside while the war was still going on. I was a private, a battalion scout, and, under the terms of the Geneva Convention, I had to work for my keep, which was good, not bad. I didn't have to stay in prison all the time, somewhere out in the countryside. I got to go to a city, which was Dresden, and to see the people and the things they did.

There were about a hundred of us in our particular work group, and we were put out as contract labor to a factory that was making a vitamin-enriched malt syrup for pregnant women. It tasted like thin honey laced with hickory smoke. It was good. I wish I had some right now. And the city was lovely, highly ornamented, like Paris, and untouched by war. It was supposedly an "open" city, not to be attacked since there were no troop concentrations or war industries there.

But high explosives were dropped on Dresden by American and British planes on the night of February 13, 1945, just about twenty-one years ago, as I now write. There were no particular targets for the bombs. The hope was that they would create a lot of kindling and drive firemen underground.

And then hundreds of thousands of tiny incendiaries were scattered over the kindling, like seeds on freshly turned loam. More bombs were dropped to keep firemen in their holes, and all the little fires grew, joined one another, became one apocalyptic flame. Hey presto: fire storm. It was the largest massacre in European history, by the way. And so what?

We didn't get to see the fire storm. We were in a cool meatlocker under a slaughterhouse with our six guards and ranks and ranks of dressed cadavers of cattle, pigs, horses, and sheep. We heard the bombs walking around up there. Now and then there would be a gentle shower of calcimine. If we had gone above to take a look, we would have been turned into artifacts characteristic of fire storms: seeming pieces of charred firewood two or three feet long—ridiculously small human beings, or jumbo fried grasshoppers, if you will.

The malt syrup factory was gone. Everything was gone but the cellars where 135,000 Hansels and Gretels had been baked like gingerbread men. So we were put to work as corpse miners, breaking into shelters, bringing bodies out. And I got to see many German types of all ages as death had found them, usually with valuables in their laps. Sometimes relatives would come to watch us dig. They were interesting, too.

So much for Nazis and me.

If I'd been born in Germany, I suppose I would have *been* a Nazi, bopping Jews and gypsies and Poles around, leaving boots sticking out of snowbanks, warming myself with my secretly virtuous insides. So it goes.

There's another clear moral to this tale, now that I think about it: When you're dead you're dead.

And yet another moral occurs to me now: Make love when you can. It's good for you.

Iowa City, 1966

THE
Confessions
OF
Howard W.
Campbell, Jr.

To Mata Hari

Breathes there the man, with soul so dead,
Who never to himself hath said,
"This is my own, my native land!"
Whose heart hath ne'er within him burn'd
As home his footsteps he hath turn'd
From wandering on a foreign strand?

—SIR WALTER SCOTT

Editor's Note

In preparing this, the American edition of the confessions of Howard W. Campbell, Jr., I have had to deal with writings concerned with more than mere informing or deceiving, as the case may be. Campbell was a writer as well as a person accused of extremely serious crimes, a one-time playwright of moderate reputation. To say that he was a writer is to say that the demands of art alone were enough to make him lie, and to lie without seeing any harm in it. To say that he was a playwright is to offer an even harsher warning to the reader, for no one is a better liar than a man who has warped lives and passions onto something as grotesquely artificial as a stage.

And, now that I've said that about lying, I will risk the opinion that lies told for the sake of artistic effect—in the theater, for instance, and in Campbell's confessions, perhaps—can be, in a higher sense, the most beguiling forms of truth.

I don't care to argue the point. My duties as an editor are in no sense polemic. They are simply to pass on, in the most satisfactory style, the confessions of Campbell.

As for my own tinkerings with the text, they are few. I have corrected some spelling, removed some exclamation points, and all the italics are mine.

I have in several instances changed names, in order to spare embarrassment or worse to innocent persons still living. The names Bernard B. O'Hare, Harold J. Sparrow, and Dr. Abraham Epstein, for instance, are fictitious, insofar as this account goes. Also fictitious are Sparrow's Army serial number and the title I have given to an American Legion post in the text; there is no Francis X. Donovan Post of the American Legion in Brookline.

There is one point at which my accuracy rather than the accuracy of Howard W. Campbell, Jr., can be questioned. That point is in Chapter Twenty-two, in which Campbell quotes three of his poems in both English and German. In his manuscript, the English versions are perfectly clear. The German versions, however, recalled from memory by Campbell, are so hacked up and smeary with revisions as to be illegible, as often as not. Campbell was proud of himself as a writer in German, indifferent to his skill in English. In trying to justify his pride in his German, he worked over the German versions of the poems again and again and again, and was apparently never satisfied with them.

So, in order to offer some idea in this edition as to what the poems were like in German, I have had to commission a delicate job of restoration. The person who did this job, who made vases out of shards, so to speak, was Mrs. Theodore Rowley, of Cotuit, Massachusetts, a fine linguist, and a respectable poetess in her own right.

I have made significant cuts in only two places. In Chapter Thirty-nine, I have made a cut that was insisted upon by my publisher's lawyer. In the original of that chapter, Campbell has one of the Iron Guardsmen of the White Sons of the American Constitution shouting at a G-man, "I'm a better American than you are! My father invented 'I-Am-An-American Day'!" Witnesses agree that such a claim was made, but made without any apparent basis in fact. The lawyer's feeling is that to reproduce the claim in the body of the text would be to slander those persons who really did invent "I-Am-An-American Day."

In the same chapter, incidentally, Campbell is, according to witnesses, at his most accurate in reporting exactly what was said. The actual death speech of Resi Noth, all agree, is reproduced by Campbell, word for word.

The only other cutting I have done is in Chapter Twenty-three, which is pornographic in the original. I would have considered myself honor-bound to present that chapter unbowdlerized, were it not for Campbell's request, right in the body of the text, that some editor perform the emasculation.

The title of the book is Campbell's. It is taken from a speech by Mephistopheles in Goethe's *Faust*. As translated by Carlyle F. MacIntyre (New Directions, 1941), the speech is this:

I am a part of the part that at first was all, part of the darkness that gave birth to light, that supercilious light which now disputes with Mother Night her ancient rank and space, and yet can not succeed; no matter how it struggles, it sticks to matter and can't get free. Light flows from substance, makes it beautiful; solids can check its path, so I hope it won't be long till light and the world's stuff are destroyed together.

The dedication of the book is Campbell's too. Of the dedication, Campbell wrote this in a chapter he later discarded:

Before seeing what sort of a book I was going to have here, I wrote the dedication—"To Mata Hari." She whored in the interest of espionage, and so did I.

Now that I've seen some of the book, I would prefer to dedicate it to someone less exotic, less fantastic, more contemporary—less of a creature of silent film.

I would prefer to dedicate it to one familiar person, male or female, widely known to have done evil while saying to himself, "A very good me, the real me, a me made in heaven, is hidden deep inside."

I can think of many examples, could rattle them off after the fashion of a Gilbert and Sullivan patter song. But there is no single name to which I might aptly dedicate this book—unless it would be my own.

Let me honor myself in that fashion, then:

This book is rededicated to Howard W. Campbell, Jr., a man who served evil too openly and good too secretly, the crime of his times.

KURT VONNEGUT, JR.

THE CONFESSIONS OF HOWARD W. CAMPBELL, JR.

CHAPTER ONE

Tiglath-pileser the Third . . .

MY NAME is Howard W. Campbell, Jr.

I am an American by birth, a Nazi by reputation, and a nationless person by inclination.

The year in which I write this book is 1961.

I address this book of mine to Mr. Tuvia Friedmann, Director of the Haifa Institute for the Documentation of War Criminals, and to whomever else this may concern.

Why should this book interest Mr. Friedmann?

Because it is written by a man suspected of being a war criminal. Mr. Friedmann is a specialist in such persons. He had expressed an eagerness to have any writings I might care to add to his archives of Nazi villainy. He is so eager as to give me a typewriter, free stenographic service, and the use of research assistants, who will run down any facts I may need in order to make my account complete and accurate.

I am behind bars.

I am behind bars in a nice new jail in old Jerusalem.

I am awaiting a fair trial for my war crimes by the Republic of Israel.

It is a curious typewriter Mr. Friedmann has given to me—and an appropriate typewriter, too. It is a typewriter that was obviously made in Germany during the Second World War. How can I tell? Quite simply, for it puts at finger tips a symbol that was never used on a typewriter before the Third German Reich, a symbol that will never be used on a typewriter again.

The symbol is the twin lightning strokes used for the dreaded *S.S.*, the *Schutzstaffel*, the most fanatical wing of Nazism.

I used such a typewriter in Germany all through the war. Whenever I had occasion to write of the Schutzstaffel, which I did often and with enthusiasm, I never abbreviated it as "S.S.," but always struck the typewriter key for the far more frightening and magical twin lightning strokes.

Ancient history.

I am surrounded by ancient history. Though the jail in which

I rot is new, some of the stones in it, I'm told, were cut in the time of King Solomon.

And sometimes, when I look out through my cell window at the gay and brassy youth of the infant Republic of Israel, I feel that I and my war crimes are as ancient as Solomon's old gray stones.

How long ago that war, that Second World War, was! How long ago the crimes in it!

How nearly forgotten it is, even by the Jews—the young Jews, that is.

One of the Jews who guards me here knows nothing about that war. He is not interested. His name is Arnold Marx. He has very red hair. He is only eighteen, which means Arnold was three when Hitler died, and nonexistent when my career as a war criminal began.

He guards me from six in the morning until noon.

Arnold was born in Israel. He has never been outside of Israel.

His mother and father left Germany in the early thirties. His grandfather, he told me, won an Iron Cross in the First World War.

Arnold is studying to be a lawyer. The avocation of Arnold and of his father, a gunsmith, is archaeology. Father and son spend most all their spare time excavating the ruins of Hazor. They do so under the direction of Yigael Yadin, who was Chief of Staff of the Israeli Army during the war with the Arab States.

So be it.

Hazor, Arnold tells me, was a Canaanite city in northern Palestine that existed at least nineteen hundred years before Christ. About fourteen hundred years before Christ, Arnold tells me, an Israelite army captured Hazor, killed all forty thousand inhabitants, and burned it down.

"Solomon rebuilt the city," said Arnold, "but in 732 B.C. Tiglath-pileser the Third burned it down again."

"Who?" I said.

"Tiglath-pileser the Third," said Arnold. "The Assyrian," he said, giving my memory a nudge.

"Oh," I said. "*That* Tiglath-pileser."

"You act as though you never heard of him," said Arnold.

"I never have," I said. I shrugged humbly. "I guess that's pretty terrible."

"Well—" said Arnold, giving me a schoolmaster's frown, "it seems to me he really *is* somebody everybody ought to know about. He was probably the most remarkable man the Assyrians ever produced."

"Oh," I said.

"I'll bring you a book about him, if you like," said Arnold.

"That's nice of you," I said. "Maybe I'll get around to thinking about remarkable Assyrians later on. Right now my mind is pretty well occupied with remarkable Germans."

"Like who?" he said.

"Oh, I've been thinking a lot lately about my old boss, Paul Joseph Goebbels," I said.

Arnold looked at me blankly. "Who?" he said.

And I felt the dust of the Holy Land creeping in to bury me, sensed how thick a dust-and-rubble blanket I would one day wear. I felt thirty or forty feet of ruined cities above me; beneath me some primitive kitchen middens, a temple or two—and then—

Tiglath-pileser the Third.

CHAPTER TWO

Special Detail . . .

THE GUARD who relieves Arnold Marx at noon each day is a man nearly my own age, which is forty-eight. He remembers the war, all right, though he doesn't like to.

His name is Andor Gutman. Andor is a sleepy, not very bright Estonian Jew. He spent two years in the extermination camp at Auschwitz. According to his own reluctant account, he came this close to going up a smokestack of a crematorium there:

"I had just been assigned to the *Sonderkommando*," he said to me, "when the order came from Himmler to close the ovens down."

Sonderkommando means special detail. At Auschwitz it meant a very special detail indeed—one composed of prisoners whose duties were to shepherd condemned persons into gas chambers, and then to lug their bodies out. When the job was done, the members of the Sonderkommando were themselves killed. The first duty of their successors was to dispose of their remains.

Gutman told me that many men actually volunteered for the Sonderkommando.

"Why?" I asked him.

"If you would write a book about that," he said, "and give the answer to that question, that 'Why?'—you would have a very great book."

"Do you know the answer?" I said.

"No," he said. "That is why I would pay a great deal of money for a book with the answer in it."

"Any guesses?" I said.

"No," he said, looking me straight in the eye, "even though I was one of the ones who volunteered."

He went away for a little while, after having confessed that. And he thought about Auschwitz, the thing he liked least to think about. And he came back, and he said to me:

"There were loudspeakers all over the camp," he said, "and

they were never silent for long. There was much music played through them. Those who were musical told me it was often good music—sometimes the best."

"That's interesting," I said.

"There was no music by Jews," he said. "That was forbidden."

"Naturally," I said.

"And the music was always stopping in the middle," he said, "and then there was an announcement. All day long, music and announcements."

"Very modern," I said.

He closed his eyes, remembered gropingly. "There was one announcement that was always crooned, like a nursery rhyme. Many times a day it came. It was the call for the Sonderkommando."

"Oh?" I said.

"*Leichenträger zu Wache*," he crooned, his eyes still closed.

Translation: "Corpse-carriers to the guardhouse." In an institution in which the purpose was to kill human beings by the millions, it was an understandably common cry.

"After two years of hearing that call over the loudspeakers, between the music," Gutman said to me, "the position of corpse-carrier suddenly sounded like a very good job."

"I can understand that," I said.

"You can?" he said. He shook his head. "I can't," he said. "I will always be ashamed. Volunteering for the Sonderkommando—it was a very shameful thing to do."

"I don't think so," I said.

"I do," he said. "Shameful," he said. "I never want to talk about it again."

CHAPTER THREE

Briquets . . .

THE GUARD who relieves Andor Gutman at six each night is Arpad Kovacs. Arpad is a Roman candle of a man, loud and gay.

When Arpad came on duty at six last night, he demanded to see what I'd written so far. I gave him the very few pages, and Arpad walked up and down the corridor, waving and praising the pages extravagantly.

He didn't read them. He praised them for what he imagined to be in them.

"Give it to the complacent bastards!" he said last night. "Tell those smug briquets!"

By briquets he meant people who did nothing to save their own lives or anybody else's life when the Nazis took over, who were willing to go meekly all the way to the gas chambers, if that was where the Nazis wanted them to go. A briquet, of course, is a molded block of coal dust, the soul of convenience where transportation, storage and combustion are concerned.

Arpad, faced with the problem of being a Jew in Nazi Hungary, did not become a briquet. On the contrary, Arpad got himself false papers and joined the Hungarian S.S.

That fact is the basis for his sympathy with me. "Tell them the things a man does to stay alive! What's so noble about being a briquet?" he said last night.

"Did you ever hear any of my broadcasts?" I asked him. The medium of my war crimes was radio broadcasting. I was a Nazi radio propagandist, a shrewd and loathsome anti-Semite.

"No," he said.

So I showed him a transcript of a broadcast, a transcript furnished to me by the Haifa Institute. "Read it," I said.

"I don't have to," he said. "Everybody was saying the same things over and over and over in those days."

"Read it anyway—as a favor," I said.

So he read it, his face becoming sourer and sourer. He handed it back to me. "You disappoint me," he said.

"Oh?" I said.

"It's so weak!" he said. "It has no body, no paprika, no zest! I thought you were a master of racial invective!"

"I'm not?" I said.

"If any member of my S.S. platoon had spoken in such a friendly way about the Jews," said Arpad, "I would have had him shot for treason! Goebbels should have fired you and hired me as the radio scourge of the Jews. I would have raised blisters around the world!"

"You were already doing your part with your S.S. platoon," I said.

Arpad beamed, remembering his S.S. days. "What an Aryan I made!" he said.

"Nobody ever suspected you?" I said.

"How would they dare?" he said. "I was such a pure and terrifying Aryan that they even put me in a special detachment. Its mission was to find out how the Jews always knew what the S.S. was going to do next. There was a leak somewhere, and we were out to stop it." He looked bitter and affronted, remembering it, even though he had been that leak.

"Was the detachment successful in its mission?" I said.

"I'm happy to say," said Arpad, "that fourteen S.S. men were shot on our recommendation. Adolf Eichmann himself congratulated us."

"You met him, did you?" I said.

"Yes—" said Arpad, "and I'm sorry I didn't know at the time how important he was."

"Why?" I said.

"I would have killed him," said Arpad.

CHAPTER FOUR

Leather Straps . . .

BERNARD MENGEL, a Polish Jew who guards me from midnight until six in the morning, is also a man my age. He once saved his own life in the Second World War by playing so dead that a German soldier pulled out three of his teeth without suspecting that Mengel was not a corpse.

The soldier wanted Mengel's three gold inlays.

He got them.

Mengel tells me that I sleep very noisily here in jail, tossing and talking all night.

"You are the only man I ever heard of," Mengel said to me this morning, "who has a bad conscience about what he did in the war. Everybody else, no matter what side he was on, no matter what he did, is sure a good man could not have acted in any other way."

"What makes you think I have a bad conscience?" I said.

"The way you sleep—the way you dream," he said. "Even Hoess did not sleep like that. He slept like a saint, right up to the end."

Mengel was speaking of Rudolf Franz Hoess, the commandant of the extermination camp at Auschwitz. In his tender care, literally millions of Jews were gassed. Mengel knew a little about Hoess. Before emigrating to Israel in 1947, Mengel helped to hang Hoess.

And he didn't do it with testimony, either. He did it with his two big hands. "When Hoess was hanged," he told me, "the strap around his ankles—I put that on and made it tight."

"Did that give you a lot of satisfaction?" I said.

"No," he said. "I was like almost everybody who came through that war."

"What do you mean?" I said.

"I got so I couldn't feel anthing," said Mengel. "Every job was a job to do, and no job was any better or any worse than any other.

"After we finished hanging Hoess," Mengel said to me, "I packed up my clothes to go home. The catch on my suitcase was broken, so I buckled it shut with a big leather strap. Twice within an hour I did the very same job—once to Hoess and once to my suitcase. Both jobs felt about the same."

CHAPTER FIVE

"Last Full Measure . . ."

I TOO, knew Rudolf Hoess, Commandant of Auschwitz. I, met him at a New Year's Eve party in Warsaw during the war—the start of 1944.

Hoess heard that I was a writer, and he got me to one side at the party, and he said he wished he could write.

"How I envy you creative people—" he said to me. "Creativity is a gift from the gods."

Hoess said he had some marvelous stories to tell. He said they were all true, but that people wouldn't be able to believe them.

Hoess could not tell me the stories, he said, until the war was won. After the war, he said, we might collaborate.

"I can talk it," he said, "but I can't write it." He looked to me for pity. "When I sit down to write," he said, "I freeze."

What was I doing in Warsaw?

I had been ordered there by my boss, *Reichsleiter* Dr. Paul Joseph Goebbels, Head of the German Ministry of Popular Enlightenment and Propaganda. I had a certain amount of skill as a dramatist, and Dr. Goebbels wanted me to use it. Dr. Goebbels wanted me to write a pageant honoring the German soldiers who had given their last full measure of devotion—who had died, that is—in putting down the uprising of the Jews in the Warsaw Ghetto.

Dr. Goebbels had a dream of producing the pageant annually in Warsaw after the war, of letting the ruins of the ghetto stand forever as a setting for it.

"There would be Jews in the pageant?" I asked him.

"Certainly—" he said, "thousands of them."

"May I ask, sir," I said, "where you expect to find any Jews after the war?"

He saw the humor in this. "A very good question," he said, chuckling. "We'll have to take that up with Hoess," he said.

"With whom?" I said. I hadn't yet been to Warsaw, hadn't yet met with brother Hoess.

"He's running a little health resort for Jews in Poland," said Goebbels. "We must be sure to ask him to save us some."

Can the writing of this ghastly pageant be added to the list of my war crimes? No, thank God. It never got much beyond having a working title, which was: "Last Full Measure."

I am willing to admit, however, that I probably would have written it if there had been enough time, if my superiors had put enough pressure on me.

Actually, I am willing to admit most anything.

About this pageant: it had one peculiar result. It brought the Gettysburg Address of Abraham Lincoln to the attention of Goebbels, and then to the attention of Hitler himself.

Goebbels asked me where I'd gotten the working title, so I made a translation for him of the entire Gettysburg Address.

He read it, his lips moving all the time. "You know," he said to me, "this is a very fine piece of propaganda. We are never as modern, as far ahead of the past as we like to think we are."

"It's a very famous speech in my native land," I said. "Every schoolchild has to learn it by heart."

"Do you miss America?" he said.

"I miss the mountains, the rivers, the broad plains, the forests," I said. "But I could never be happy there with the Jews in charge of everything."

"They will be taken care of in due time," he said.

"I live for that day—my wife and I live for that day," I said.

"How is your wife?" he said.

"Blooming, thank you," I said.

"A beautiful woman," he said.

"I'll tell her you said so," I said. "It will please her immensely."

"About the speech by Abraham Lincoln—" he said.

"Sir—?" I said.

"There are phrases in here that might be used most impressively in dedications of German military cemeteries," he said. "I haven't been happy at all, frankly, with most of our funeral oratory. This seems to have the extra dimension I've been looking for. I'd like very much to send this to Hitler."

"Whatever you say, sir," I said.

"Lincoln wasn't a Jew, was he?" he said.

"I'm sure not," I said.

"It would be very embarrassing to me if he turned out to be one," he said.

"I've never heard anyone suggest that he was," I said.

"The name Abraham is very suspicious, to say the least," said Goebbels.

"I'm sure his parents didn't realize that it was a Jewish name," I said. "They must have just liked the sound of it. They were simple frontier people. If they'd known the name was Jewish, I'm sure they would have called him something more American, like George or Stanley or Fred."

Two weeks later, the Gettysburg Address came back from Hitler. There was a note from *der Fuehrer* himself stapled to the top of it. "Some parts of this," he wrote, "almost made me weep. All northern peoples are one in their deep feelings for soldiers. It is perhaps our greatest bond."

Strange—I never dream of Hitler or Goebbels or Hoess or Goering or any of the other nightmare people of the world war numbered "two." I dream of women, instead.

I asked Bernard Mengel, the guard who watches over me while I sleep here in Jerusalem, if he had any clues as to what I dreamed about.

"Last night?" he said.

"Any night," I said.

"Last night it was women," he said. "Two names you said over and over."

"What were they?" I said.

"Helga was one," he said.

"My wife," I said.

"The other was Resi," he said.

"My wife's younger sister," I said. "Just their names—that's all."

"You said 'Goodbye,'" he said.

"Goodbye," I echoed. That certainly made sense, whether I dreamed or not. Helga and Resi were both gone forever.

"And you talked about New York," said Mengel. "You mumbled, and then you said 'New York,' and then you mumbled some more."

That made sense, too, as do most of the things I dream. I lived in New York for a long time before coming to Israel.

"New York City must be Heaven," said Mengel.

"It might well be for you," I said. "It was hell for me—or not Hell, something worse than Hell."

"What could be worse than Hell?" he said.

"Purgatory," I said.

CHAPTER SIX

Purgatory . . .

ABOUT THAT PURGATORY of mine in New York City: I was in it for fifteen years.

I disappeared from Germany at the end of the Second World War. I reappeared, unrecognized, in Greenwich Village. There I rented a depressing attic apartment with rats squeaking and scrabbling in the walls. I continued to inhabit that attic until a month ago, when I was brought to Israel for trial.

There was one pleasant thing about my ratty attic: the back window of it overlooked a little private park, a little Eden formed by joined back yards. That park, that Eden, was walled off from the streets by houses on all sides.

It was big enough for children to play hide-and-seek in.

I often heard a cry from that little Eden, a child's cry that never failed to make me stop and listen. It was the sweetly mournful cry that meant a game of hide-and-seek was over, that those still hiding were to come out of hiding, that it was time to go home.

The cry was this: "Olly-olly-ox-in-free."

And I, hiding from many people who might want to hurt or kill me, often longed for someone to give that cry for me, to end my endless game of hide-and-seek with a sweet and mournful—

"Olly-olly-ox-in-free."

CHAPTER SEVEN

Autobiography . . .

I, Howard W. Campbell, Jr., was born in Schenectady, New York, on February 16, 1912. My father, who was raised in Tennessee, the son of a Baptist minister, was an engineer in the Service Engineering Department of the General Electric Company.

The mission of the Service Engineering Department was to install, maintain and repair General Electric heavy equipment sold anywhere in the world. My father, whose assignments were at first only in the United States, was rarely home. And his job demanded such varied forms of technical cleverness of him that he had scant time and imagination left over for anything else. The man was the job and the job was the man.

The only nontechnical book I ever saw him look at was a picture history of the First World War. It was a big book, with pictures a foot high and a foot-and-a-half wide. My father never seemed to tire of looking at the book, though he hadn't been in the war.

He never told me what the book meant to him, and I never asked him. All he ever said to me about it was that it wasn't for children, that I wasn't to look at it.

So, of course, I looked at it every time I was left alone. There were pictures of men hung on barbed-wire, mutilated women, bodies stacked like cordwood—all the usual furniture of world wars.

My mother was the former Virginia Crocker, the daughter of a portrait photographer from Indianapolis. She was a housewife and an amateur cellist. She played cello with the Schenectady Symphony Orchestra, and she once had dreams of my playing the cello, too.

I failed as a cellist because I, like my father, am tone-deaf.

I had no brothers and sisters, and my father was seldom home. So I was for many years the principal companion of my mother. She was a beautiful, talented, morbid person. I think she was drunk most of the time. I remember a time when she filled a saucer with a mixture of rubbing alcohol and table salt. She put the saucer on the kitchen table, turned out all the lights, and had me sit facing her across the table.

And then she touched off the mixture with a match. The flame was almost pure yellow, a sodium flame, and it made her look like a corpse to me, made me look like a corpse to her.

"There—" she said, "that's what we'll look like when we're dead."

This queer demonstration not only scared me; it scared her, too. My mother scared herself with her own queerness, and from that moment on I ceased to be her companion. From that moment on she hardly spoke to me—cut me dead, I'm sure, out of fear of doing or saying something even crazier.

All that happened in Schenectady, before I was ten.

In 1923, when I was eleven, my father was assigned to the General Electric Office in Berlin, Germany. From then on, my education, my friends, and my principal language were German.

I eventually became a playwright in the German language, and I took a German wife, the actress Helga Noth. Helga Noth was the elder of the two daughters of Werner Noth, the Chief of Police of Berlin.

My father and mother left Germany in 1939, when war came.

My wife and I stayed on.

I earned my keep until the war ended in 1945 as a writer and broadcaster of Nazi propaganda to the English-speaking world. I was the leading expert on American problems in the Ministry of Popular Enlightenment and Propaganda.

When the war was ending, I was high on the list of war criminals, largely because my offenses were so obscenely public.

I was captured by one Lieutenant Bernard B. O'Hare of the American Third Army near Hersfeld on April 12, 1945. I was on a motorcycle, unarmed. While entitled to a uniform, a blue and gold one, I was not wearing it. I was in mufti, in a blue serge suit and a moth-eaten coat with a fur collar.

As it happened, the Third Army had overrun Ohrdruf, the first Nazi death camp the Americans were to see, two days before. I was taken there, was forced to look at it all—the lime pits, the gallows, the whipping posts—at the gutted and scabby, bug-eyed, spavined dead in heaps.

The idea was to show me the consequences of what I had done.

The Ohrdruf gallows were capable of hanging six at a time. When I saw them, there was a dead camp guard at the end of each rope.

And it was expected that I would hang soon, too.

I expected it myself, and I took an interest in the peace of the six guards at the ends of their ropes.

They had died fast.

My photograph was taken while I looked up at the gallows. Lieutenant O'Hare was standing behind me, lean as a young wolf, as full of hatred as a rattlesnake.

The picture was on the cover of *Life*, and came close to winning a Pulitzer Prize.

CHAPTER EIGHT

Auf Wiedersehen . . .

I DID NOT HANG.

I committed high treason, crimes against humanity, and crimes against my own conscience, and I got away with them until now.

I got away with them because I was an American agent all through the war. My broadcasts carried coded information out of Germany.

The code was a matter of mannerisms, pauses, emphases, coughs, seeming stumbles in certain key sentences. Persons I never saw gave me my instructions, told me in which sentences of a broadcast the mannerisms were to appear. I do not know to this day what information went out through me. From the simplicity of most of my instructions, I gather that I was usually giving yes or no answers to questions that had been put to the spy apparatus. Occasionally, as during the build-up for the Normandy invasion, my instructions were more complicated, and my phrasing and diction sounded like the last stages of double pneumonia.

That was the extent of my usefulness to the Allied cause.

And that usefulness was what saved my neck.

I was provided with cover. I was never acknowledged as an American agent, but the treason case against me was sabotaged. I was freed on nonexistent technicalities about my citizenship, and I was helped to disappear.

I came to New York under an assumed name. I started a new life, in a manner of speaking, in my ratty attic overlooking the secret park.

I was left alone—so much alone that I was able to take back my own name, and almost nobody wondered if I was *the* Howard W. Campbell, Jr.

I would occasionally find my name in a newspaper or magazine—never as an important person, but as one name in a long list of names of war criminals who had disappeared. There were rumors of me in Iran, Argentina, Ireland. . . . Israeli agents were said to be looking high and low for me.

Be that as it may, no agent ever knocked on my door. Nobody knocked on my door, even though the name on my mailbox was plain for anybody to see: Howard W. Campbell, Jr.

Until the very end of my purgatory in Greenwich Village, the closest I came to being detected in my infamy was when I went to a Jewish doctor in the same building as my attic. I had an infected thumb.

The doctor's name was Abraham Epstein. He lived with his mother on the second floor. They had just moved in.

When I gave him my name, it meant nothing to him, but it did mean something to his mother. Epstein was young, fresh out of medical school. His mother was old—heavy, slow, deeply lined, sadly, bitterly watchful.

"That is a very famous name," she said. "You must know that."

"Pardon me?" I said.

"You do not know about anybody else named Howard W. Campbell, Jr.?" she said.

"I suppose there are some others," I said.

"How old are you?" she said.

I told her.

"Then you are old enough to remember the war," she said.

"Forget the war," her son said to her, affectionately but sharply. He was bandaging my thumb.

"And you never heard Howard W. Campbell, Jr., broadcasting from Berlin?" she said to me.

"I do remember now—yes," I said. "I'd forgotten. That was a long time ago. I never listened to him, but I remember he was in the news. Those things fade."

"They should fade," said young Dr. Epstein. "They belong to a period of insanity that should be forgotten as quickly as possible."

"Auschwitz," said his mother.

"Forget Auschwitz," said Dr. Epstein.

"Do you know what Auschwitz was?" his mother asked me.

"Yes," I said.

"That was where I spent my young womanhood," she said.

"And that was where my son the doctor here spent his childhood."

"I never think about it," said Dr. Epstein abruptly. "There—that thumb should be all right in a couple of days. Keep it warm, keep it dry." And he hustled me toward the door.

"*Sprechen-Sie Deutsch*?" his mother called after me as I was leaving.

"Pardon me?" I said.

"I asked if you spoke German," she said.

"Oh," I said. "No—I'm afraid not," I said. I experimented shyly with the language. "*Nein*?" I said. "That's no, isn't it?"

"Very good," she said.

"*Auf wiedersehen*," I said. "That's goodbye, isn't it?"

"Until we meet again," she said.

"Oh," I said. "Well—*auf wiedersehen*."

"*Auf wiedersehen*," she said.

CHAPTER NINE

Enter My Blue Fairy Godmother . . .

I WAS RECRUITED as an American agent in 1938, three years before America got into the war. I was recruited one spring day in the Tiergarten in Berlin.

I had been married to Helga Noth a month.

I was twenty-six.

I was a fairly successful playwright, writing in the language in which I write best, German. I had one play, "The Goblet," running in both Dresden and Berlin. Another play of mine, "The Snow Rose," was then in production in Berlin. I had just finished a third one, "Seventy Times Seven." All three plays were medieval romances, about as political as chocolate *éclairs.*

I was sitting alone on a park bench in the sunshine that day, thinking of a fourth play that was beginning to write itself in my head. It gave itself a title, which was "*Das Reich der Zwei*" —"Nation of Two."

It was going to be about the love my wife and I had for each other. It was going to show how a pair of lovers in a world gone mad could survive by being loyal only to a nation composed of themselves—a nation of two.

On a bench across the path from me a middle-aged American now sat down. He looked like a fool and a gasbag. He untied his shoelaces to relieve his feet, and he began to read a month-old copy of the Chicago *Sunday Tribune.*

Three handsome young officers of the S.S. stalked down the walk between us.

When they were gone, the man put his paper down and spoke to me in twanging Chicago English. "Nice-looking men," he said.

"I suppose," I said.

"You understand English?" he said.

"Yes," I said.

"Thank God for somebody who can understand English," he said. "I've been going crazy trying to find somebody to talk to."

"That so?" I said.

"What do you think of all this—" he said, "or aren't people supposed to go around asking questions like that?"

"All what?" I said.

"The things going on in Germany," he said. "Hitler and the Jews and all that."

"It isn't anything I can control," I said, "so I don't think about it."

He nodded. "None of your beeswax, eh?" he said.

"Pardon me?" I said.

"None of your business," he said.

"That's right," I said.

"You didn't understand that—when I said 'beeswax' instead of 'business'?" he said.

"It's a common expression, is it?" I said.

"In America it is," he said. "You mind if I come over there, so we don't have to holler?"

"As you please," I said.

"As you please," he echoed, coming over to my bench. "That sounds like something an Englishman would say."

"American," I said.

He raised his eyebrows. "Is that a fact? I was trying to guess what maybe you were, but I wouldn't have guessed that."

"Thank you," I said.

"You figure that's a compliment?" he said. "That's why you said, 'Thank you'?"

"Not a compliment—or an insult, either," I said. "Nationalities just don't interest me as much as they probably should."

This seemed to puzzle him. "Any of my beeswax what you do for a living?" he said.

"Writer," I said.

"Is that a fact?" he said. "That's a great coincidence. I was sitting over there wishing I could write, on account of I've thought up what I think's a pretty good spy story."

"That so?" I said.

"I might as well give it to you," he said. "I'll never write it."

"I've got all the projects I can handle now," I said.

"Well—some time you may run dry," he said, "and then you can use this thing of mine. There's this young American, see, who's been in Germany so long he's practically a German himself. He writes plays in German, and he's married to a beautiful German actress, and he knows a lot of big-shot Nazis who like to hang around theater people." He rattled off the names of Nazis, great and small—all of whom Helga and I knew pretty well.

It wasn't that Helga and I were crazy about Nazis. I can't say, on the other hand, that we hated them. They were a big enthusiastic part of our audience, important people in the society in which we lived.

They were people.

Only in retrospect can I think of them as trailing slime behind.

To be frank—I can't think of them as doing that even now. I knew them too well as people, worked too hard in my time for their trust and applause.

Too hard.

Amen.

Too hard.

"Who are you?" I said to the man in the park.

"Let me finish my story first," he said. "So this young man knows there's a war coming, figures America's gonna be on one side and Germany's gonna be on the other. So this American, who hasn't been anything but polite to the Nazis up to then, decided to pretend he's a Nazi himself, and he stays on in Germany when war comes along, and he gets to be a very useful American spy."

"You know who I am?" I said.

"Sure," he said. He took out his billfold, showed me a United States War Department identification card that said he was Major Frank Wirtanen, unit unspecified. "And that's who I am. I'm asking you to be an American intelligence agent, Mr. Campbell."

"Oh Christ," I said. I said it with anger and fatalism. I slumped down. When I straightened up again, I said, "Ridiculous. No—hell, no."

"Well—" he said, "I'm not too let-down, actually, because today isn't when you give me your final answer anyway."

"If you imagine that I'm going home to think it over," I said, "you're mistaken. When I go home, it will be to have a fine meal with my beautiful wife, to listen to music, to make love to my wife, and to sleep like a log. I'm not a soldier, not a political man. I'm an artist. If war comes, I won't do anything to help it along. If war comes, it'll find me still working at my peaceful trade."

He shook his head. "I wish you all the luck in the world, Mr. Campbell," he said, "but this war isn't going to let anybody stay in a peaceful trade. And I'm sorry to say it," he said, "but the worse this Nazi thing gets, the less you're gonna sleep like a log at night."

"We'll see," I said tautly.

"That's right—we'll see," he said. "That's why I said you wouldn't give me your final answer today. You'll live your final answer. If you decide to go ahead with it, you'll go ahead with it strictly on your own, working your way up with the Nazis as high as you can go."

"Charming," I said.

"Well—it has this much charm to it—" he said, "you'd be an authentic hero, about a hundred times braver than any ordinary man."

A ramrod Wehrmacht general and a fat, briefcase-carrying German civilian passed in front of us, talking with suppressed excitement.

"Howdy do," Major Wirtanen said to them amiably.

They snorted in contempt, walked on.

"You'll be volunteering right at the start of a war to be a dead man. Even if you live through the war without being caught, you'll find your reputation gone—and probably very little to live for," he said.

"You make it sound very attractive," I said.

"I think there's a chance I've made it attractive to *you*," he said. "I saw the play you've got running now, and I've read the one you're going to open."

"Oh?" I said. "And what did you learn from those?"

He smiled. "That you admire pure hearts and heroes," he said. "That you love good and hate evil," he said, "and that you believe in romance."

He didn't mention the best reason for expecting me to go on and be a spy. The best reason was that I was a ham. As a spy of the sort he described, I would have an opportunity for some pretty grand acting. I would fool everyone with my brilliant interpretation of a Nazi, inside and out.

And I *did* fool everybody. I began to strut like Hitler's right-hand man, and nobody saw the honest me I hid so deep inside.

Can I prove I was an American spy? My unbroken, lily-white neck is Exhibit A, and it's the only exhibit I have. Those whose duty it is to find me guilty or innocent of crimes against humanity are welcome to examine it in detail.

The Government of the United States neither confirms nor denies that I was an agent of theirs. That's a little something, anyway, that they don't deny the possibility.

They twitch away that tid-bit, however, by denying that a Frank Wirtanen ever served that Government in any branch. Nobody believes in him but me. So I will hereinafter speak of him often as "My Blue Fairy Godmother."

One of the many things my Blue Fairy Godmother told me was the sign and countersign that would identify me to my contact and my contact to me, if war should come.

The sign was: "Make new friends."

The countersign was: "But keep the old."

My lawyer here, the learned counsel for the defense, is a Mr. Alvin Dobrowitz. He grew up in America, something I never did, and Mr. Dobrowitz tells me that the sign and countersign are part of a song often sung by an idealistic American girls' organization called "The Brownies."

The full lyric, according to Mr. Dobrowitz is:

> Make new friends,
> But keep the old.
> One is si-il-ver,
> The o-ther's gold.

CHAPTER TEN

Romance . . .

MY WIFE never knew I was a spy.

I would have lost nothing by telling her. My telling her wouldn't have made her love me less. My telling her wouldn't have put me in any danger. It would simply have made my heavenly Helga's world, which was already something to make The Book of Revelation seem pedestrian.

The war was enough without that.

My Helga believed that I meant the nutty things I said on the radio, said at parties. We were always going to parties.

We were a very popular couple, gay and patriotic. People used to tell us that we cheered them up, made them want to go on. And Helga didn't go through the war simply looking decorative, either. She entertained the troops, often within the sound of enemy guns.

Enemy guns? Somebody's guns, anyway.

That was how I lost her. She was entertaining troops in the Crimea, and the Russians took the Crimea back. My Helga was presumed dead.

After the war, I paid a good deal of my money to a private detective agency in West Berlin to trace the wispiest word of her. Results: zero. My standing offer to the agency, unclaimed, was a prize of ten thousand dollars for clear proof that my Helga was either alive or dead.

Hi ho.

My Helga believed I meant the things I said about the races of man and the machines of history—and I was grateful. No matter what I was really, no matter what I really meant, uncritical love was what I needed—and my Helga was the angel who gave it to me.

Copiously.

No young person on earth is so excellent in all respects as to need no uncritical love. Good Lord—as youngsters play their parts in political tragedies with casts of billions, uncritical love is the only real treasure they can look for.

Das Reich der Zwei, the nation of two my Helga and I had—its territory, the territory we defended so jealously, didn't go much beyond the bounds of our great double bed.

Flat, tufted, springy little country, with my Helga and me for mountains.

And, with nothing in my life making sense but love, what a student of geography I was! What a map I could draw for a tourist a micron high, a submicroscopic *Wandervögel* bicycling between a mole and a curly golden hair on either side of my Helga's belly button. If this image is in bad taste, God help me. Everybody is supposed to play games for mental health. I have simply described the game, an adult interpretation of "This-Little-Piggy," that was ours.

Oh, how we clung, my Helga and I—how *mindlessly* we clung!

We didn't listen to each other's words. We heard only the melodies in our voices. The things we listened for carried no more intelligence than the purrs and growls of big cats.

If we had listened for more, had thought about what we heard, what a nauseated couple we would have been! Away from the sovereign territory of our nation of two, we talked like the patriotic lunatics all around us.

But it did not count.

Only one thing counted—

The nation of two.

And when that nation ceased to be, I became what I am today and what I always will be, a stateless person.

I can't say I wasn't warned. The man who recruited me that spring day in the Tiergarten so long ago now—that man told my fortune pretty well.

"To do your job right," my Blue Fairy Godmother told me, "you'll have to commit high treason, have to serve the enemy well. You won't ever be forgiven for that, because there isn't any legal device by which you can be forgiven."

"The most that will be done for you," he said, "is that your neck will be saved. But there will be no magic time when you will be cleared, when America will call you out of hiding with a cheerful: Olly-olly-ox-in-free."

CHAPTER ELEVEN

War Surplus . . .

MY MOTHER AND FATHER died. Some say they died of broken hearts. They died in their middle sixties, at any rate, when hearts break easily.

They did not live to see the end of the war, nor did they ever see their beamish boy again. They did not disinherit me, though they must have been bitterly tempted to do so. They bequeathed to Howard W. Campbell, Jr., the notorious anti-Semite, turncoat and radio star, stocks, real estate, cash and personal property which were, in 1945, at the time of probate, worth forty-eight thousand dollars.

That boodle, through growth and inflation, has come to be worth four times that much now, giving me an unearned income of seven thousand dollars a year.

Say what you like about me, I have never touched my principal.

During my postwar years as an odd duck and recluse in Greenwich Village, I lived on about four dollars a day, rent included, and I even had a television set.

My new furnishings were all war surplus, like myself—a narrow steel cot, olive-drab blankets with "U.S.A." on them, folding canvas chairs, mess kits to cook in and eat out of. Even my library was largely war surplus, coming as it did from recreation kits intended for troops overseas.

And, since phonograph records came in these unused kits, too, I got myself a war-surplus, weatherproofed, portable phonograph, guaranteed to play in any climate from the Bering Straits to the Arafura Sea. By buying the recreation kits, each one a sealed pig-in-a-poke, I came into possession of twenty-six recordings of Bing Crosby's "White Christmas."

My overcoat, my raincoat, my jacket, my socks and my underwear were war surplus, too.

By buying a war-surplus first-aid kit for a dollar, I also came into possession of a quantity of morphine. The buzzards in the war-surplus business were so glutted with carrion as to have overlooked it.

I was tempted to take the morphine, reflecting that, if it made me feel happy, I would, after all, have enough money to support the habit. But then I understood that I was already drugged.

I was feeling no pain.

My narcotic was what had got me through the war; it was an ability to let my emotions be stirred by only one thing—my love for Helga. This concentration of my emotions on so small an area had begun as a young lover's happy illusion, had developed into a device to keep me from going insane during the war, and had finally become the permanent axis about which my thoughts revolved.

And so, with my Helga presumed dead, I became a death-worshipper, as content as any narrow-minded religious nut anywhere. Always alone, I drank toasts to her, said good morning to her, said good night to her, played music for her, and didn't give a damn for one thing else.

And then one day in 1958, after thirteen years of living like that, I bought a war-surplus wood-carving set. It was surplus not from the Second World War but from the Korean war. It cost me three dollars.

When I got it home, I started to carve up my broom handle to no particular purpose. And it suddenly occurred to me to make a chess set.

I speak of suddenness here, because I was startled to find myself with an enthusiasm. I was so enthusiastic that I carved for twelve hours straight, sank sharp tools into the palm of my left hand a dozen times, and still would not stop. I was an elated, gory mess when I was finished. I had a handsome set of chessmen to show for my labors.

And yet another strange impulse came upon me.

I felt compelled to show somebody, somebody still among the living, the marvelous thing I had made.

So, made boisterous by both creativity and drink, I went downstairs and banged on the door of my neighbor, not even knowing who my neighbor was.

My neighbor was a foxy old man named George Kraft. That

was only one of his names. The real name of this old man was Colonel Iona Potapov. This antique sonofabitch was a Russian agent, had been operating continuously in America since 1935.

I didn't know that.

And he didn't know at first who I was, either.

It was dumb luck that brought us together. No conspiracy was involved at first. It was I who knocked on his door, invaded his privacy. If I hadn't carved that chess set, we never would have met.

Kraft—and I'll call him that from now on, because that's how I think of him—had three or four locks on his front door.

I induced him to unlock them all by asking him if he played chess. There was dumb luck again. Nothing else would have made him open up.

People helping me with my research later, incidentally, tell me that the name of Iona Potapov was a familiar one in European chess tournaments in the early thirties. He actually beat the Grand Master Tartakover in Rotterdam in 1931.

When he opened up, I saw that he was a painter. There was an easel in the middle of his living room with a fresh canvas on it, and there were stunning paintings by him on every wall.

When I talk about Kraft, alias Potapov, I'm a lot more comfortable than when I talk about Wirtanen, alias God-knows-what. Wirtanen has left no more of a trail than an inchworm crossing a billiard table. Evidences of Kraft are everywhere. At this very moment, I'm told, Kraft's paintings are bringing as much as ten thousand dollars apiece in New York.

I have at hand a clipping from the New York *Herald Tribune* of March third, about two weeks ago, in which a critic says of Kraft as a painter:

> Here at last is a capable and grateful heir to the fantastic inventiveness and experimentation in painting during the past hundred years. Aristotle is said to have been the last man to understand the whole of his culture. George Kraft is surely the first man to understand the whole of modern art—to understand it in his sinews and bones.
>
> With incredible grace and firmness he combines the visions of a score of warring schools of painting, past and present. He thrills and humbles us with harmony, seems to say to us, "If you want another Renaissance, this is what the paintings expressing its spirit will look like."

George Kraft, alias Iona Potapov, is being permitted to continue his remarkable art career in the Federal Penitentiary at Fort Leavenworth. We all might well reflect, along, no doubt, with Kraft-Potapov himself, on how summarily his career would have been crushed in a prison in his native Russia.

Well—when Kraft opened his door for me, I knew his paintings were good. I didn't know they were that good. I suspect that the review above was written by a pansy full of brandy Alexanders.

"I didn't know I had a painter living underneath me," I said to Kraft.

"Maybe you don't have one," he said.

"Marvelous paintings!" I said. "Where do you exhibit?"

"I never have," he said.

"You'd make a fortune if you did," I said.

"You're nice to say so," he said, "but I started painting too late." He then told me what was supposed to be the story of his life, none of it true.

He said he was a widower from Indianapolis. As a young man, he said, he'd wanted to be an artist, but he'd gone into business instead—the paint and wallpaper business.

"My wife died two years ago," he said, and he managed to look a little moist around the eyes. He had a wife, all right, but not underground in Indianapolis. He had a very live wife named Tanya in Borisoglebsk. He hadn't seen her for twenty-five years.

"When she died," he said to me, "I found my spirit wanted to choose between only two things—suicide, or the dreams I'd had in my youth. I am an old fool who borrowed the dreams of a young fool. I bought myself some canvas and paint, and I came to Greenwich Village."

"No children?" I said.

"None," he said sadly. He actually had three children and nine grandchildren. His oldest son, Ilya, is a famous rocket expert.

"The only relative I've got in this world is art—" he said, "and I'm the poorest relative art ever had." He didn't mean he was impoverished. He meant he was a bad painter. He had plenty of money, he told me. He'd sold his business in Indianapolis, he said, for a very good price.

"Chess—" he said, "you said something about chess?"

I had the chessmen I'd whittled, in a shoebox. I showed

them to him. "I just made these," I said, "and now I've got a terrific yen to play with them."

"Pride yourself on your game, do you?" he said.

"I haven't played for a good while," I said.

Almost all the chess I'd played had been with Werner Noth, my father-in-law, the Chief of Police of Berlin. I used to beat Noth pretty consistently—on Sunday afternoons when my Helga and I went calling on him. The only tournament I ever played in was an intramural thing in the German Ministry for Popular Enlightenment and Propaganda. I finished eleventh in a field of sixty-five.

In ping-pong I did a good deal better. I was ping-pong champion of the Ministry for four years running, singles and doubles. My doubles partner was Heinz Schildknecht, an expert at propagandizing Australians and New Zealanders. One time Heinz and I took on a doubles team composed of *Reichsleiter* Goebbels and *Oberdienstleiter* Karl Hederich. We sat them down 21–2, 21–1, 21–0.

History often goes hand-in-hand with sports.

Kraft had a chessboard. We set up my men on it, and we began to play.

And the thick, bristly, olive-drab cocoon I had built for myself was frayed a little, was weakened enough to let some pale light in.

I enjoyed the game, was able to come up with enough intuitively interesting moves to give my new friend entertainment while he beat me.

After that, Kraft and I played at least three games a day, every day for a year. And we built up between ourselves a pathetic sort of domesticity that we both felt need of. We began tasting our food again, making little discoveries in grocery stores, bringing them home to share. When strawberries came in season, I remember, Kraft and I whooped it up as though Jesus had returned.

One particularly touching thing between us was the matter of wines. Kraft knew a lot more than I did about wines, and he often brought home cobwebby treasures to go with a meal. But, even though Kraft always had a filled glass before him when we sat down to eat, the wine was all for me. Kraft was an alcoholic. He could not take so much as a sip of wine without starting on a bender that could last a month.

That much of what he told me about himself was true. He was a member of Alcoholics Anonymous, had been for sixteen years. While he used A.A. meetings as spy drops, his appetite for what the meetings offered spiritually was real. He once told me, in all sincerity, that the greatest contribution America had made to the world, a contribution that would be remembered for thousands of years, was the invention of A.A.

It was typical of his schizophrenia as a spy that he would use an institution he so admired for purposes of espionage.

It was typical of his schizophrenia as a spy that he should also be a true friend of mine, and that he should eventually think of a way to use me cruelly in advancing the Russian cause.

CHAPTER TWELVE

Strange Things in My Mailbox . . .

FOR A LITTLE WHILE I lied to Kraft about who I was and what I'd done. But the friendship deepened so much, so fast, that I soon told him everything.

"It's so unjust!" he said. "It makes me ashamed to be an American! Why can't the Government step forward and say, 'Here! This man you've been spitting on is a hero!'" He was indignant, and, for all I know, he was sincere in his indignation.

"Nobody spits on me," I said. "Nobody even knows I'm alive any more."

He was eager to see my plays. When I told him I didn't have copies of any of them, he made me tell him about them, scene by scene—had me performing them for him.

He said he thought they were marvelous. Maybe he was sincere. I don't know. My plays seemed vapid to me, but it's possible he liked them.

What excited him, I think, was the idea of art, and not what I'd done with it.

"The arts, the arts, the arts—" he said to me one night. "I don't know why it took me so long to realize how important they are. As a young man, I actually held them in supreme contempt. Now, whenever I think about them, I want to fall on my knees and weep."

It was late autumn. Oysters had come back in season, and we were feasting on a dozen apiece. I'd known Kraft about a year then.

"Howard—" he said to me, "future civilizations—better civilizations than this one—are going to judge all men by the extent to which they've been artists. You and I, if some future archaeologist finds our works miraculously preserved in some city dump, will be judged by the quality of our creations. Nothing else about us matter."

"Um," I said.

"You've got to write again," he said. "Just as daisies bloom as daisies and roses bloom as roses—you must bloom as a writer and I must bloom as a painter. Everything else about us is uninteresting."

"Dead men don't usually write very well," I said.

"You're not dead!" he said. "You're full of ideas. You can talk for hours on end."

"Blather," I said.

"Not blather!" he said hotly. "All you need in this world to get writing again, writing better than ever before, is a woman."

"A what?" I said.

"A woman," he said.

"Where did you get this peculiar idea—" I said, "from eating oysters? If you'll get one, I'll get one," I said. "How's that?"

"I'm too old for one to do me any good," he said, "but you're not." Again, trying to separate the real from the fake, I have to declare this conviction of the real. He was really earnest about wanting me to write again, was convinced that a woman could do the trick. "I would almost go through the humiliation of trying to be a man to a woman," he said, "if you would take a woman, too."

"I've got one," I said.

"You had one once," he said. "There's a world of difference."

"I don't want to talk about it," I said.

"I'm going to talk about it all the same," he said.

"Then talk away," I said, getting up from the table. "Be a matchmaker to your heart's content. I'm going down to see what goodies came in the mail today."

He'd annoyed me, and I went down the stairs to my mailbox, simply to walk off my annoyance. I wasn't eager to see the mail. I often went a week or more without seeing if I had any. The only things that were ever in my mailbox were dividend checks, notices of stockholders' meetings, trash mail addressed to "Boxholder," and advertising flyers for books and apparatus said to be useful in the field of education.

How did I happen to receive advertisements for educational materials? One time I applied for a job as a teacher of German in a private school in New York. That was in 1950 or so.

I didn't get the job, and I didn't want it, either. I applied, I think, simply to demonstrate to myself that there really was such a person as me.

The application form I filled out was necessarily full of lies, was such a fabric of mendacity that the school did not even bother to tell me that I was unacceptable. Be that as it may, my name somehow found its way onto a list of those supposedly in teaching. Thereafter, flyers without end flew in.

I opened my mailbox on an accumulation of three or four days.

There was a check from Coca-Cola, a notice of a General Motors stockholders' meeting, a request from Standard Oil of New Jersey that I approve a new stock-option plan for my executives, and an ad for an eight-pound weight disguised to look like a schoolbook.

Object of the weight was to give schoolchildren something to exercise with, in between classes. The ad pointed out that the physical fitness of American children was below that of the children of almost every land on earth.

But the ad for that queer weight wasn't the queerest thing in my mailbox. There were some things a lot queerer than that.

One was from the Francis X. Donovan Post of the American Legion in Brookline, Massachusetts, a letter in a legal-size envelope.

Another was a tiny newspaper rolled tight and mailed from Grand Central Station.

I opened the newspaper first, found it to be *The White Christian Minuteman*, a scabrous, illiterate, anti-Semitic, anti-Negro, anti-Catholic hate sheet published by the Reverend Doctor Lionel J. D. Jones, D.D.S. "Supreme Court," said the biggest headline, "Demands U.S. Be Mongrel!"

The second biggest headline said: "Red Cross Gives Whites Negro Blood!"

These headlines could hardly startle me. They were, after all, the sort of thing I had said for a living in Germany. Even closer to the spirit of the old Howard W. Campbell, Jr., actually, was the headline of a small story in one corner of the front page, a story titled: "International Jewry Only Winners of World War II."

I now opened the letter from the American Legion Post. It said:

Dear Howard:

I was very surprised and disappointed to hear you weren't dead yet. When I think of all the good people who died in World War Two, and then think that you're still alive and living in the country you betrayed, it makes me want to throw up. You will be happy to know that our Post resolved unanimously last night to demand that you either get hanged by the neck until dead or get deported back to Germany, which is the country you love so much.

Now that I know where you are, I will be paying you a call real soon. It will be nice to talk over old times.

When you go to sleep tonight, you smelly rat, I hope you dream of the concentration camp at Ohrdruf. I should have pushed you into a lime pit when I had the chance.

Very, very truly yours,
Bernard B. O'Hare
Post Americanism Chairman

Carbon copies to:

J. Edgar Hoover, F.B.I., Washington, D.C.
Director, Central Intelligence Agency, Washington, D.C.
Editor, *Time*, New York City
Editor, *Newsweek*, New York City
Editor, *Infantry Journal*, Washington, D.C.
Editor, *The Legion Magazine*, Indianapolis, Indiana
Chief Investigator, House Un-American Activities Committee, Washington, D.C.
Editor, *The White Christian Minuteman*, 395 Bleecker St., New York City

Bernard B. O'Hare, of course, was the young man who had captured me at the end of the war, who had frog-walked me through the death camp at Ohrdruf, who had joined me in a memorable photograph on the cover of *Life*.

When I found the letter from him in my mailbox in Greenwich Village, I was puzzled as to how he'd found out where I was.

I leafed through *The White Christian Minuteman*, found out O'Hare wasn't the only person who had rediscovered Howard W. Campbell, Jr. On page three of the *Minuteman*, under a headline that said simply, "American Tragedy!," was this brief tale:

Howard W. Campbell, Jr., a great writer and one of the most fearless patriots in American history, now lives in poverty and loneliness in the attic of 27 Bethune Street. Such is the fate of thinking men brave enough to tell the truth about the conspiracy of international Jewish bankers and international Jewish Communists who will not rest until the bloodstream of every American is hopelessly polluted with Negro and/or Oriental blood.

CHAPTER THIRTEEN

The Reverend Doctor Lionel Jason David Jones, D.D.S., D.D. . . .

I AM INDEBTED to the Haifa Institute for the Documentation of War Criminals for the source material that makes it possible for me to include in this account a biography of Dr. Jones, publisher of *The White Christian Minuteman.*

Jones, though subject to no prosecution as a war criminal, has a very fat dossier. Leafing through that treasure house of souvenirs, I find these things to be true:

The Reverend Doctor Lionel Jason David Jones, D.D.S., D.D., was born in Haverhill, Massachusetts, in 1889, was raised as a Methodist.

He was the youngest son of a dentist, the grandson of two dentists, brother of two dentists, and the brother-in-law of three dentists. He himself set out to be a dentist, but was expelled from the Dental School of the University of Pittsburgh in 1910, for what would now be diagnosed, most likely, as paranoia. In 1910, he was dismissed for simple scholastic failure.

The syndrome of his failure was anything but simple. His examination papers were quite probably the longest such papers ever written in the history of dental education, and probably the most irrelevant as well. They began, sanely enough, with whatever subject the examination required Jones to discuss. But, regardless of that subject, Jones managed to go from it to a theory that was all his own—that the teeth of Jews and Negroes proved beyond question that both groups were degenerate.

His dental work was of a high order, so the faculty hoped to see him outgrow his political interpretations of teeth. But his case grew worse, until his examinations became frantic pamphlets, warning all Protestant Anglo-Saxons to unite against Jewish-Negro domination.

When Jones began to detect proof of degeneracy in the teeth of Catholics and Unitarians, and when five loaded pistols and a bayonet were found under his mattress, Jones was finally given the old heave-ho.

Jones' parents disowned him, which is something my parents never quite did to me.

Penniless, Jones found work as an apprentice embalmer in the Scharff Brothers Funeral Home in Pittsburgh. He became manager of the home within two years. A year after that, he married the widowed owner, Hattie Scharff. Hattie was fifty-eight at the time, and Jones was twenty-four. The many investigators into Jones' life, unfriendly investigators almost to a man, have been bound to conclude that Jones really loved his Hattie. The marriage, which endured until the death of Hattie in 1928, was a happy one.

In fact, it was so happy, so whole, so self-sufficient a nation of two that Jones did almost nothing during that time by way of alerting the Anglo-Saxons. He seems to have been content to confine his remarks on racial matters to workroom jests about certain cadavers, jests that would have seemed workaday in the most liberal of embalming establishments. And the years were golden, not only emotionally and financially, but creatively as well. Working with a chemist named Dr. Lomar Horthy, Jones developed Viverine, an embalming fluid, and Gingiva-Tru, a wonderfully life-like, gum-simulating substance for false teeth.

When Jones' wife died, Jones felt the need to be reborn. He was reborn a thing he had been latently all along. Jones became the sort of racial agitator who is spoken of as having crawled out from under a rock. Jones crawled out from under his rock in 1928. He sold his funeral home for eighty-four thousand dollars, and he founded *The White Christian Minuteman*.

Jones was wiped out by the stock market crash in 1929. His paper suspended publication after fourteen issues. The fourteen issues had been mailed free to every person in *Who's Who*. The only illustrations were photographs and diagrams of teeth, and every article was an explanation of some current events in terms of Jones' theories about dentition and race.

In the next-to-the-last issue, Jones billed himself on the masthead as, "Dr. Lionel J. D. Jones, D.D.S."

Penniless again, now forty years of age, Jones answered an ad in a funeral-home trade journal. An embalming school in

Little Rock, Arkansas, needed a president. The ad was signed by the widow of the former president and owner.

Jones got the job, and the widow, too. The widow's name was Mary Alice Shoup. She was sixty-eight when Jones married her.

And Jones again became a devoted husband, a happy, whole, and quiet man.

The school he headed was named, straightforwardly enough, The Little Rock School of Embalming. It was losing eight thousand dollars a year. Jones took it out of the high-overhead field of embalming education, sold its real estate, and had it rechartered as The Western Hemisphere University of the Bible. The university held no classes, taught nothing, did all its business by mail. Its business was the awarding of doctorates in the field of divinity, framed and under glass, for eighty dollars a throw.

And Jones helped himself to a W.H.U.B. degree, out of open stock, so to speak. When his second wife died, when he brought out *The White Christian Minuteman* again, he appeared on the masthead as, "The Reverend Doctor Lionel J. D. Jones, D.D.S., D.D."

And he wrote and published at his own expense a book that combined not only dentistry and theology, but the fine arts as well. The name of the book was *Christ Was Not a Jew*. He proved his point by reproducing in the book fifty famous paintings of Jesus. According to Jones, not one painting showed Jewish jaws or teeth.

The first issues in the new series of *The White Christian Minuteman* were as unreadable as those of the old series. But then a miracle happened. The *Minuteman* jumped from four pages to eight. The make-up, the typography and the paper became snappy and handsome. Dental diagrams were replaced by newsy photographs, and the pages crackled with datelines and bylines from all over the world.

The explanation was simple—and obvious. Jones had been recruited and financed as a propaganda agent for Hitler's then-rising Third German Reich. Jones' news, photographs, cartoons and editorials were coming straight from the Nazi propaganda mills in Erfurt, Germany.

It is quite possible, incidentally, that much of his more scurrilous material was written by me.

Jones continued as a German propaganda agent even after the United States of America entered the Second World War. He wasn't arrested until July in 1942, when he was indicted with twenty-seven others for:

> Conspiring to destroy the morale and faith and confidence of the members of the military and naval forces of the United States and the people of the United States in their public officials and republican form of government; conspiring to seize upon and use and misuse the right of freedom of speech and of the press to spread their disloyal doctrines, intending and believing that any nation allowing its people the right of freedom of speech is powerless to defend itself against enemies masquerading as patriotic; and seeking to obstruct, impede, break down and destroy the proper functioning of its republican form of government under the guise of honest criticism; conspiring to render the Government of the United States bereft of the faith and confidence of the members of the military and naval forces and of the people, and thereby render that government powerless to defend the nation or the people against armed attack from without or treachery from within.

Jones was convicted. He was sentenced to fourteen years, served eight. When he was freed from Atlanta in 1950, he was a wealthy man. Viverine, his embalming fluid, and Gingiva-Tru, his counterfeit gum substance for false teeth, had both come to dominate their respective markets.

In 1955, he resumed publication of *The White Christian Minuteman*.

Five years after that, a lively elder statesman of seventy-one, an alert old man with no regrets, the Reverend Doctor Lionel J. D. Jones, D.D.S., D.D., paid me a call.

Why should I have honored him with such a full-dress biography?

In order to contrast with myself a race-baiter who is ignorant and insane. I am neither ignorant nor insane.

Those whose orders I carried out in Germany were as ignorant and insane as Dr. Jones. I knew it.

God help me, I carried out their instructions anyway.

CHAPTER FOURTEEN

View Down a Stairwell . . .

JONES paid me a call a week after I found out how upsetting the contents of my mailbox had become. I tried to call on him first. He published his vile newspaper only a few blocks away from my attic, and I went there to beg him to retract the story.

He was not in.

When I got home, there was plenty of new mail in my mailbox, almost all of it from subscribers to *The White Christian Minuteman.* The common theme was that I was not alone, was not friendless. A woman in Mount Vernon, New York, told me there was a throne in Heaven for me. A man in Norfolk said I was the new Patrick Henry. A woman in St. Paul sent me two dollars to continue my good work. She apologized. She said that was all the money she had. A man in Bartlesville, Oklahoma, asked me why I didn't get out of Jew York and come live in God's country.

I didn't have any idea how Jones had found out about me.

Kraft claimed to be mystified, too. He wasn't really mystified. He had written to Jones as an anonymous fellow-patriot, telling the glad news that I was alive. He had also asked that Jones send a complimentary copy of his great paper to Bernard B. O'Hare of the Francis X. Donovan Post of the American Legion.

Kraft had plans for me.

And he was, at the very same time, doing a portrait of me that surely showed more sympathetic insight into me, more intuitive affection than could ever have been produced by a wish to fool a boob.

I was sitting for the portrait when Jones came calling. Kraft had spilled a quart of turpentine. I opened the door to get rid of the fumes.

And a very strange chant came floating up the stairwell and through the open door.

I went out onto the landing outside the door, looked down

the oak and plaster snail of the stairwell. All I could see was the hands of four persons—hands moving up the bannister.

The group was composed of Jones and three friends.

The curious chant went with the advance of the hands. The hands would move about four feet up the bannister, stop, and then the chant would come.

The chant was a panted count to twenty. Two of Jones' party, his bodyguard and his male secretary, had very bad hearts. To keep their poor old hearts from bursting, they were pausing every few steps, timing their rests by counting to twenty.

Jones' bodyguard was August Krapptauer, former *Vice-Bundesfuehrer* of the German-American *Bund*. Krapptauer was sixty-three, had done eleven years in Atlanta, was about to drop dead. But he still looked garishly boyish, as though he went to a mortuary cosmetologist regularly. The greatest achievement of his life was the arrangement of a joint meeting of the Bund and the Ku Klux Klan in New Jersey in 1940. At that meeting, Krapptauer declared that the Pope was a Jew and that the Jews held a fifteen-million-dollar mortgage on the Vatican. A change of Popes and eleven years in a prison laundry had not changed his mind.

Jones' secretary was an unfrocked Paulist Father named Patrick Keeley. "Father Keeley," as his employer still called him, was seventy-three. He was a drunk. He had, before the Second World War, been chaplain of a Detroit club which, as later came out, had been organized by agents of Nazi Germany. The dream of the club, apparently, was to shoot the Jews. One of Father Keeley's prayers at a club meeting was taken down by a newspaper reporter, was printed in full the next morning. The prayer appealed to so vicious and bigoted a God that it attracted the astonished attention of Pope Pius XI.

Keeley was unfrocked, and Pope Pius sent a long letter to the American Hierarchy in which he said, among other things: "No true Catholic will take part in the persecution of his Jewish compatriots. A blow against the Jews is a blow against our common humanity."

Keeley never went to prison, though many of his close friends did. While his friends enjoyed steam heat, clean beds and regular meals at government expense, Keely shivered and itched and starved and drank himself blind on skid rows across the land. He would have been on a skid row still, or in a pauper's grave, if Jones and Krapptauer hadn't found and rescued him.

Keeley's famous prayer, incidentally, was a paraphrase of a satiric poem I had composed and delivered on short wave before. And, while I am setting the record straight as to my contributions to literature, may I point out that Vice-Bundesfuehrer Krapptauer's claims about the Pope and the mortgage on the Vatican were my inventions, too.

So up the stairs these people came to see me, chanting, "One, two, three, four. . . ."

And, slow as their progress was, the fourth member of the party lagged far behind.

The fourth member was a woman. All I could see of her was her pale and ringless hand.

The hand of Jones was in the lead. It glittered with rings like the hand of a Byzantine prince. An inventory of the jewelry on that hand would have revealed two wedding rings, a star-sapphire presented to him by the Mothers' Auxiliary of the Paul Revere Association of Militant Gentiles in 1940, a diamond swastika on an onyx field presented to him in 1939 by Baron Manfred Freiherr von Killinger, then German Consul General of San Francisco, and an American eagle carved in jade and mounted in silver, a piece of Japanese craftsmanship, a present from Robert Sterling Wilson. Wilson was "The Black Fuehrer of Harlem" a colored man who went to prison in 1942 as a Japanese spy.

The jewelled hand of Jones left the bannister. Jones cantered back down the stairs to the woman, said things to her I couldn't understand. And then up he came again, a remarkably sound-winded septuagenarian.

He came face to face with me, and he smiled showing me snow-white teeth set in Gingiva-Tru. "Campbell?" he said, only a little out of breath.

"Yes," I said.

"My name is Dr. Jones. I have a surprise for you," he said.

"I've already seen your paper," I said.

"No—not the paper," he said. "A bigger surprise than that."

Father Keeley and Vice-Bundesfuehrer Krapptauer now came into view, wheezing, counting to twenty in shattered whispers.

"An even bigger surprise?" I said, preparing to square him

away so savagely that he would never think of me as one of his own kind again.

"The woman I've brought with me—" he said.

"What about her?" I said.

"She's your wife," he said.

"I got in touch with her—" said Jones, "and she begged me not to tell you about her. She insisted it had to be like this, with her just walking in without any warning."

"So I could see for myself if there was still room for me in your life," said Helga. "If there is no room, I will simply say goodbye again, disappear, and never bother you again."

CHAPTER FIFTEEN

The Time Machine . . .

IF THE PALE, ringless hand on the railing below was the hand of my Helga, it was the hand of a woman forty-five years old. It was the hand of a middle-aged woman who had been a prisoner of the Russians for sixteen years, if the hand was Helga's.

It was inconceivable that my Helga could still be lovely and gay.

If Helga had survived the Russian attack on the Crimea, had eluded all the crawling, booming, whistling, buzzing, creeping, clanking, bounding, chattering toys of war that killed quickly, a slower doom, a doom that killed like leprosy, had surely awaited her. There was no need for me to guess at the doom. It was well-known, uniformly applied to all women prisoners on the Russian front—was part of the ghastly routine of any thoroughly modern, thoroughly scientific, thoroughly asexual nation at thoroughly modern war.

If my Helga had survived the battle, her captors had surely prodded her with gun muzzles into a labor gang. They had surely shepherded her into one of Mother Russia's countless huddles of squinting, lumpy, hopeless, grubbing ragbags—had surely made of my Helga a digger of root crops in frosty fields, a lead-footed, splay-fingered clearer of rubble, a nameless, sexless dragger of noisy carts.

"My wife?" I said to Jones. "I don't believe you."

"It's easy enough to prove I'm a liar, if I am a liar," he said pleasantly. "Have a look for yourself."

My pace down the stairs was firm and regular.

Now I saw the woman.

She smiled up at me, raising her chin so as to show her features frankly, clearly.

Her hair was snow-white.

Aside from that, she was my Helga untouched by time.

Aside from that, she was as lithe and blooming as my Helga had been on our wedding night.

CHAPTER SIXTEEN

A Well-preserved Woman . . .

WE CRIED, like babies, wrestled each other up the stairs to my attic.

As we passed Father Keeley and Vice-Bundesfuehrer Krapptauer, I saw that Keeley was crying. Krapptauer stood at attention, honoring the idea of an Anglo-Saxon family. Jones, further up the stairs, was radiant with pleasure in the miracle he had worked. He rubbed and rubbed his jewelled hands.

"My—my wife," I said to my old friend Kraft, as Helga and I entered my attic.

And Kraft, trying to keep from crying, chewed the bit of his cold corncob pipe in two. He never did quite cry, but he was close to doing it—genuinely close to doing it, I think.

Jones, Krapptauer and Keeley followed us in. "How is it," I said to Jones, "that it's you who gives me back my wife?"

"A fantastic coincidence—" said Jones. "One day I learned that you were still alive. A month later I learned that your wife was still alive. What can I call a coincidence like that but the Hand of God?"

"I don't know," I said.

"My paper has a small circulation in West Germany," said Jones. "One of my subscribers read about you, and he sent me a cable. He asked me if I knew your wife had just turned up as a refugee in West Berlin."

"Why didn't he cable *me*?" I said. I turned to Helga.

"Sweetheart—" I said in German, "why didn't *you* cable me?"

"We'd been apart so long—I'd been dead so long," she said in English. "I thought surely you'd built a new life, with no room in it for me. I'd hoped that."

"My life is nothing but room for you," I said. "It could never be filled by anyone but you."

"So much to say, so much to tell—," she said, melting against me. I looked down on her wonderingly. Her skin was soft and clear. She was amazingly well-preserved for a woman of forty-five.

What made her state of preservation even more remarkable was the story she now told of how she had spent the past fifteen years.

She was captured and raped in the Crimea, she said. She was shipped to the Ukraine by boxcar, was put to work in a labor gang.

"We were stumbling sluts," she said, "married to mud. When the war was over, nobody bothered to tell us. Our tragedy was permanent. No records were kept of us anywhere. We shuffled through ruined villages aimlessly. Anyone who had a menial, pointless job to do had only to wave us down and we would do it."

She separated herself from me in order to tell her yarn with larger gestures. I wandered over to my front window to listen—listen while looking through dusty panes into the twigs of a birdless, leafless tree.

Drawn crudely in the dust of three window-panes were a swastika, a hammer and sickle, and the Star and Stripes. I had drawn the three symbols weeks before, at the conclusion of an argument about patriotism with Kraft. I had given a hearty cheer for each symbol, demonstrating to Kraft the meaning of patriotism to, respectively, a Nazi, a Communist, and an American.

"Hooray, hooray, hooray," I'd said.

On and on Helga spun her yarn, weaving a biography on the crazy loom of modern history. She escaped from the labor gang after two years, she said, was caught a day later by Asiatic half-wits with submachine guns and police dogs.

She spent three years in the prison, she said, and then she was sent to Siberia as an interpreter and file clerk in a huge prisoner-of-war camp. Eight thousand S.S. men were still held captive there, though the war had been over for years.

"I was there for eight years," she said, "mercifully hypnotized by simple routines. We kept beautiful records of all those prisoners, of all those meaningless lives behind barbed-wire. Those S.S. men, once so young and lean and vicious, were growing gray and soft and self-pitying—" she said, "husbands without wives, fathers without children, shopkeepers without shops, tradesmen without trades."

Thinking about the subdued S.S. men, Helga asked herself

the riddle of the Sphinx. "What creature walks in the morning on four feet, at noon on two, at evening on three?"

"Man," said Helga, huskily.

She told of being repatriated—repatriated after a fashion. She was returned not to Berlin but to Dresden, in East Germany. She was put to work in a cigarette factory, which she described in oppressive detail.

One day she ran away to East Berlin, then crossed to West Berlin. Days after that she was winging to me.

"Who paid your way?" I said.

"Admirers of yours," said Jones warmly. "Don't feel you have to thank them. They feel they owe you a debt of gratitude they'll never be able to repay."

"For what?" I said.

"For having the courage to tell the truth during the war," said Jones, "when everybody else was telling lies."

CHAPTER SEVENTEEN

August Krapptauer Goes to Valhalla . . .

VICE-BUNDESFUEHRER KRAPPTAUER, on his own initiative, went down all those stairs to get my Helga's luggage from Jones' limousine. The reunion of Helga and me had made him feel young and courtly again.

Nobody knew what he was up to until he reappeared in my doorway with a suitcase in either hand. Jones and Keeley were filled with consternation, because of Krapptauer's syncopated, leaky old heart.

The Vice-Bundesfuehrer was the color of tomato juice.

"You fool." said Jones.

"No, no—I'm perfectly fine," said Krapptauer, smiling.

"Why didn't you let Robert do it?" said Jones. Robert was his chauffeur, sitting in the limousine below. Robert was a colored man, seventy-three years old. Robert was Robert Sterling Wilson, erstwhile jailbird, Japanese agent, and "Black Fuehrer of Harlem."

"You should have let Robert bring those things up," said Jones. "My gosh—you mustn't risk your life like that."

"It is an honor to risk my life," said Krapptauer, "for the wife of a man who served Adolf Hitler as well as Howard Campbell did."

And he dropped dead.

We tried to revive him, but he was stone dead, slack-mouthed, obscenely gaga.

I ran down to the second floor, where Dr. Abraham Epstein lived with his mother. The doctor was home. Dr. Epstein treated poor old Krapptauer pretty roughly, forced him to demonstrate for us all how really dead he was.

Epstein was Jewish, and I thought Jones or Keeley might say something to him about the ways he was punching and poking Krapptauer. But the two antique Fascists were childishly respectful and dependent.

About the only thing Jones said to Epstein, after Epstein

had pronounced Krapptauer very dead, was, "I happen to be a dentist, Doctor."

"That so?" said Epstein. He wasn't much interested. He went back to his own apartment to call an ambulance.

Jones covered Krapptauer with one of my war-surplus blankets. "Just when things were finally beginning to look up for him again," he said of the death.

"In what way?" I said.

"He was beginning to get a little organization going again," said Jones. "Not a big thing—but loyal, dependable, devoted."

"What was it called?" I said.

"The Iron Guard of the White Sons of the American Constitution," said Jones. "He had a real talent for welding perfectly ordinary youths into disciplined, determined force." Jones shook his head sadly. "He was getting such a fine response from the young people."

"He loved young people, and young people loved him," said Father Keeley. He was still weeping.

"That's the epitaph that should be carved on his tombstone," said Jones. "He used to work with youngsters in my cellar. You should see how he fixed it up for them—just ordinary kids from all walks of life."

"Kids who would ordinarily be at loose ends and getting into trouble," said Father Keeley.

"He was one of the greatest admirers you ever had," Jones said to me.

"He was?" I said.

"Back when you were broadcasting, he never missed listening to you. When he went to prison, the first thing he did was build a short-wave receiver, just so he could go on listening to you. Every day he was bubbling over with the things you'd said the night before."

"Um," I said.

"You were a beacon, Mr. Campbell," said Jones passionately. "Do you realize what a beacon you were through all those black years?"

"Nope," I said.

"Krapptauer had hoped you'd be the Idealism Officer for the Iron Guard," said Jones.

"I'm the Chaplain," said Keeley.

"Oh, who, who, who will lead the Iron Guard now?" said Jones. "Who will step forward and pick up the fallen torch?"

There was a sharp, strong knock on the door. I opened the door, and outside stood Jones' chauffeur, a wrinkled old colored man with malevolent yellow eyes. He wore a black uniform with white piping, a Sam Browne belt, a nickel-plated whistle, a *Luftwaffe* hat without insignia, and black leather puttees.

There was no Uncle Tom in this cotton-haired old colored man. He walked in arthritically, but his thumbs were hooked into his Sam Browne belt, his chin was thrust out at us, and he kept his hat on.

"Everything all right up here?" he said to Jones. "You was up here so long."

"Not quite," said Jones. "August Krapptauer died."

The Black Fuehrer of Harlem took the news in stride. "All dying, all dying," he said. "Who's gonna pick up the torch when everybody's dead?"

"I just asked the same question myself," said Jones. He introduced me to Robert.

Robert didn't shake hands. "I heard about you," he said, "but I ain't never listened to you."

"Well—" I said, "you can't please all the people all of the time."

"We was on opposite sides," said Robert.

"I see," I said. I didn't know anything about him, was agreeable to his belonging to any side that suited him.

"I was on the colored folks' side," he said. "I was with the Japanese."

"Uh-huh," I said.

"We needed you, and you needed us—" he said, speaking of the alliance between Germany and Japan in the Second World War. "Only there was a lot of things we couldn't what you'd call agree about."

"I guess that's so," I said.

"I mean I heard you say you don't think the colored people was so good," said Robert.

"Now, now," said Jones soothingly. "What useful purpose does it serve for us to squabble among ourselves? The thing to do is to pull together."

"I just want to tell him what I tell you," said Robert. "I tell this Reverend gentleman here the same thing every morning, the same thing I tell you now. I give him his hot cereal for breakfast, and then I tell him: 'The colored people are gonna rise up in righteous wrath, and they're gonna take over the world. White folks gonna finally lose!' "

"All right, Robert," said Jones patiently.

"The colored people gonna have hydrogen bombs all their own," he said. "They working on it right now. Pretty soon gonna be Japan's turn to drop one. The rest of the colored folks gonna give them the honor of dropping the first one."

"Where they going to drop it?" I said.

"China, most likely," he said.

"On other colored people?" I said.

He looked at me pityingly. "Who ever told you a Chinaman was a colored man?" he said.

CHAPTER EIGHTEEN

Werner Noth's Beautiful Blue Vase . . .

HELGA AND I were finally left alone.

We were shy.

Being a man of fairly advanced years, so many of the years having been spent in celibacy, I was more than shy. I was afraid to test my strength as a lover. And the fear was amplified by the remarkable number of youthful characteristics my Helga had miraculously retained.

"This—this is what's known as getting to know each other again," I said. Our conversation was in German.

"Yes," she said. She had gone to the front window now, was looking at the patriotic devices I'd drawn on the dusty window-panes. "Which one of these is you now, Howard?" she said.

"Pardon me?" I said.

"The hammer and sickle, the swastika, or the Stars and Stripes—" she said, "which one do you like the most?"

"Ask me about music," I said.

"What?" she said.

"Ask me what kinds of music I like these days," I said. "I have some opinions on music. I have no political opinions at all."

"I see," she said. "All right—what music do you like these days?"

" 'White Christmas'—" I said, "Bing Crosby's 'White Christmas.' "

"Excuse me?" she said.

"My favorite piece of music," I said. "I love it so much, I have twenty-six copies of it."

She looked at me blankly. "You do?" she said.

"It—it's a private joke," I said lamely.

"Oh," she said.

"Private—" I said. "I've been living alone so long, everything about me's private. I'm surprised anyone's able to understand a word I say."

"I will," she said tenderly. "Give me a little time—not much, but some—and I'll understand everything you say—again." She shrugged. "I have private jokes, too—"

"From now on—" I said, "we'll make the privacy for two again."

"That will be nice," she said.

"Nation of two again," I said.

"Yes," she said. "Tell me—"

"Anything at all," I said.

"I know how Father died, but I haven't been able to find out a thing about Mother and Resi," she said. "Have you heard a word?"

"Nothing," I said.

"When did you see them last?" she said.

I thought back, was able to give the exact date on which I'd last seen Helga's father, mother, and her pretty, imaginative little sister, Resi Noth.

"February 12, 1945," I said, and I told her about that day.

That day was a day so cold that it made my bones ache. I stole a motorcycle, and I went calling on my in-laws, on the family of Werner Noth, the Chief of Police of Berlin.

Werner Noth lived on the outskirts of Berlin, well outside the target area. He lived with his wife and daughter in a walled white house that had the monolithic, earthbound grandeur of a Roman nobleman's tomb. In five years of total war, that house had not suffered so much as a cracked window-pane. Its tall, deep-set windows on the south framed an orchard within the walls. On the north they framed the jagged monuments in the ruins of Berlin.

I was wearing a uniform. At my belt was a tiny pistol and a big, fancy, ceremonial dagger. I didn't usually wear a uniform, but I was entitled to wear one—the blue and gold uniform of a Major in the Free American Corps.

The Free American Corps was a Nazi daydream—a daydream of a fighting unit composed mainly of American prisoners of war. It was to be a volunteer organization. It was to fight only on the Russian front. It was to be a high-morale fighting machine, motivated by a love of western civilization and a dread of the Mongol hordes.

When I call this unit a Nazi daydream, incidentally, I am

suffering an attack of schizophrenia—because the idea of the Free American Corps began with me. I suggested its creation, designed its uniforms and insignia, wrote its creed.

That creed began, "I, like my honored American forefathers, believe in true freedom—"

The Free American Corps was not a howling success. Only three American P.W.'s joined. God only knows what became of them. I presume that they were all dead when I went calling on my in-laws, that I was the sole survivor of the Corps.

When I went calling, the Russians were only twenty miles from Berlin. I had decided that the war was almost over, that it was time for my career as a spy to end. I put on the uniform in order to dazzle any Germans who might try to keep me from getting out of Berlin. Tied to the back fender of my stolen motorcycle was a parcel of civilian clothes.

My call on the Noths had nothing to do with cunning. I really wanted to say goodbye to them, to have them say goodbye to me. I cared about them, pitied them—loved them in a way.

The iron gates of the great white house were open. Werner Noth himself was standing beside them, his hands on his hips. He was watching a work gang of Polish and Russian slave women. The women were lugging trunks and furniture from the house to three waiting horse-drawn wagons.

The wagon drivers were small, gold Mongols of some sort, early prizes of the Russian campaign.

The supervisor of the women was a fat, middle-aged Dutchman in a shabby business suit.

Guarding the women was a tall and ancient man with a single-shot rifle from the Franco-Prussian War.

On the old guard's ruined breast dangled the Iron Cross.

A woman slave shuffled out of the house carrying a luminously beautiful blue vase. She was shod in wooden clogs hinged with canvas. She was a nameless, ageless, sexless ragbag. Her eyes were like oysters. Her nose was frostbitten, mottled white and cherry-red.

She seemed in danger of dropping the vase, of withdrawing so deeply into herself as simply to let the vase slip away.

My father-in-law saw the vase about to drop, and he went

off like a burglar alarm. He shrieked at God to have pity on him just once, to make sense just once, to show him just one other energetic and intelligent human being.

He snatched the vase from the dazed woman. Close to unashamed tears, he asked us all to adore the blue vase that laziness and stupidity had almost let slip from the world.

The shabby Dutchman, the straw boss, now went up to the woman and repeated to her, word for word and shriek for shriek, what my father-in-law had said. The antique soldier came along with him, to represent the force that would be used on the woman, if necessary.

What was finally done with her was curious. She wasn't hurt.

She was deprived of the honor of carrying any more of Noth's things.

She was made to stand to one side while others continued to be trusted with treasures. Her punishment was to be made to feel like a fool. She had been given her opportunity to participate in civilization, and she had muffed it.

"I've come to say goodbye," I said to Noth.

"Goodbye," he said.

"I'm going to the front," I said.

"Right over that way," he said, pointing to the East. "An easy walk from here. You can make it in a day, picking buttercups as you go."

"It isn't very likely we'll see each other again, I guess," I said.

"So?" he said.

I shrugged. "So nothing," I said.

"Exactly," he said. "Nothing and nothing and nothing."

"May I ask where you're moving to?" I said.

"I am staying here," he said. "My wife and daughter are going to my brother's home outside of Cologne."

"Is there anything I can do to help?" I said.

"Yes," he said. "You can shoot Resi's dog. It can't make the trip. I have no interest in it, will not be able to give it the care and companionship Resi has led it to expect. So shoot it, please."

"Where is it?" I said.

"I think you'll find it in the music room with Resi," he said. "She knows it's to be shot. You will have no trouble with her."

"All right," I said.

"That's quite a uniform," he said.

"Thank you," I said.

"Would it be rude of me to ask what it represents?" he said. I had never worn it in his presence.

I explained it to him, showed him the device on the hilt of my dagger. The device, silver on walnut, was an American eagle that clasped a swastika in its right claw and devoured a snake in its left claw. The snake was meant to represent international Jewish communism. There were thirteen stars around the head of the eagle, representing the thirteen original American colonies. I had made the original sketch of the device, and, since I don't draw very well, I had drawn six-pointed stars of David rather than five-pointed stars of the U.S.A. The silversmith, while lavishly improving on my eagle, had reproduced my six-pointed stars exactly.

It was the stars that caught my father-in-law's fancy. "These represent the thirteen Jews in Franklin Roosevelt's cabinet," he said.

"That's a very funny idea," I said.

"Everyone thinks the Germans have no sense of humor," he said.

"Germany is the most misunderstood country in the world," I said.

"You are one of the few outsiders who really understands us," he said.

"I hope that's a compliment I deserve," I said.

"It's a compliment you didn't come by very easily," he said. "You broke my heart when you married my daughter. I wanted a German soldier for a son-in-law."

"Sorry," I said.

"You made her happy," he said.

"I hope so," I said.

"That made me hate you more," he said. "Happiness has no place in war."

"Sorry," I said.

"Because I hated you so much," he said, "I studied you. I listened to everything you said. I never missed a broadcast."

"I didn't know that," I said.

"No one knows everything," he said. "Did you know," he said, "that until almost this very moment nothing would have delighted me more than to prove that you were a spy, to see you shot?"

"No," I said.

"And do you know why I don't care now if you were a spy or not?" he said. "You could tell me now that you were a spy, and we would go on talking calmly, just as we're talking now. I would let you wander off to wherever spies go when a war is over. You know why?" he said.

"No," I said.

"Because you could never have served the enemy as well as you served us," he said. "I realized that almost all the ideas that I hold now, that make me unashamed of anything I may have felt or done as a Nazi, came not from Hitler, not from Goebbels, not from Himmler—but from you." He took my hand. "You alone kept me from concluding that Germany had gone insane."

He turned away from me abruptly. He went to the oyster-eyed woman who had almost dropped the blue vase. She was standing against a wall where she had been ordered to stand, was numbly playing the punished dunce.

Werner Noth shook her a little, trying to arouse an atom of intelligence in her. He pointed to another woman who was carrying a hideous Chinese, carved-oak dog, carrying it as carefully as though it were a baby.

"You see?" Noth said to the dunce. He wasn't intentionally tormenting the dunce. He was trying to make her, in spite of her stupidity, a better-rounded, more useful human being.

"You see?" he said again, earnestly, helpfully, pleadingly. "That's the way to handle precious things."

CHAPTER NINETEEN

Little Resi Noth . . .

I WENT into the music room of Werner Noth's emptying house and found little Resi and her dog.

Little Resi was ten years old then. She was curled in a wing-chair by a window. Her view was not of the ruins of Berlin but of the walled orchard, of the snowy lace that the treetops made.

There was no heat in the house. Resi was bundled up in a coat and scarf and thick wool stockings. A small suitcase was beside her. When the wagon train outside was ready to move, she would be ready to board it.

She had taken off her mittens, laid them neatly on the arm of the chair. She had bared her hands in order to pet the dog in her lap. The dog was a dachshund that had, on a wartime diet, lost all its hair and been all but immobilized by dropsical fat.

The dog looked like some early amphibian meant to waddle in ooze. While Resi caressed it, its brown eyes bugged with the blindness of ecstasy. Every bit of its awareness followed like thimbles the fingertips that stroked its hide.

I did not know Resi well. She had chilled me once, fairly early in the war, by lispingly calling me an American spy. Since then, I had spent as little time as possible before her childish gaze. When I came into the music room I was startled to see how much she was coming to resemble my Helga.

"Resi—?" I said.

She didn't look at me. "I know," she said. "It's time to kill the dog."

"It isn't anything I want to do very much," I said.

"Are you going to do it," she said, "or are you going to give it to somebody to do?"

"Your father asked me to do it," I said.

She turned to look at me. "You're a soldier now," she said.

"Yes," I said.

"Did you put on your uniform just for killing the dog?" she said.

"I'm going to the front," I said. "I stopped by to say goodbye."

"Which front?" she said.

"The Russians," I said.

"You'll die," she said.

"So I hear," I said. "Maybe not."

"Everybody who isn't dead is going to be dead very soon now," she said. She didn't seem to care much.

"Not everybody," I said.

"I will be," she said.

"I hope not," I said. "I'm sure you'll be fine," I said.

"It won't hurt when I get killed," she said. "Just all of a sudden I won't be any more," she said. She pushed the dog off her lap. It fell to the floor as passive as a *Knackwurst*.

"Take it," she said. "I never liked it anyway. I just felt sorry for it."

I picked up the dog.

"It will be much better off dead," she said.

"I think you're right," I said.

"I'll be better off dead, too," she said.

"That I can't believe," I said.

"Do you want me to tell you something?" she said.

"All right," I said.

"Since nobody's going to go on living much longer," she said, "I might as well tell you I love you."

"That's very sweet," I said.

"I mean really love you," she said. "When Helga was alive and you two would come here, I used to envy Helga. When Helga was dead, I started dreaming about how I would grow up and marry you and be a famous actress, and you would write plays for me."

"I am honored," I said.

"It doesn't mean anything," she said. "Nothing means anything. You go shoot the dog now."

I bowed out, taking the dog with me. I took the dog out into the orchard, put it down in the snow, drew my tiny pistol.

Three people were watching me. One was Resi, who now stood at the music-room window. Another was the ancient soldier who was supposed to be guarding the Polish and Russian women.

The third was my mother-in-law, Eva Noth. Eva Noth stood at a second-story window. Like Resi's dog, Eva Noth had fattened dropsically on wartime food. The poor woman, made into sausage by unkind time, stood at attention, seemed to think that the execution of the dog was a ceremony of some nobility.

I shot the dog in the back of the neck. The report of my pistol was small, cheap, like the tinny spit of a B.B. gun.

The dog died without a shudder.

The old soldier came over, expressing a professional's interest in the sort of wound such a small pistol might make. He turned the dog over with his boot, found the bullet in the snow, murmured judiciously, as though I had done an interesting, instructive thing. He now began to talk of all sorts of wounds he had seen or heard of, all sorts of holes in once-living things.

"You're going to bury it?" he said.

"I suppose I'd better," I said.

"If you don't," he said, "somebody will eat it."

CHAPTER TWENTY

"Hangwomen for the Hangman of Berlin . . ."

I FOUND OUT only recently, in 1958 or 1959, how my father-in-law died. I knew he was dead. The detective agency I had hired to find word of Helga had told me that much—that Werner Noth was dead.

The details of his death came to hand by chance—in a Greenwich Village barber shop. I was leafing through a girly magazine, admiring the way women were made, and awaiting my turn for a haircut. The story advertised on the magazine cover was "Hangwomen for the Hangman of Berlin." There was no reason for me to suppose that the article was about my father-in-law. Hanging hadn't been his business. I turned to the article.

And I looked for quite a while at a murky photograph of Werner Noth being hanged from an apple tree without suspecting who the hanged man was. I looked at the faces of the people at the hanging. They were mostly women, nameless, shapeless ragbags.

And I played a game, counting the ways in which the magazine cover had lied. For one thing, the women weren't doing the hanging. Three scrawny men in rags were doing it. For another thing, the women in the photograph weren't beautiful, and the hangwomen on the cover were. The hangwomen on the cover had breasts like cantaloupes, hips like horse collars, and their rags were the pathetic remains of nightgowns by Schiaparelli. The women in the photograph were as pretty as catfish wrapped in mattress-ticking.

And then, just before I began to read the story of the hanging, I began, tentatively and queasily, to recognize the shattered building in the background. Behind the hangman, looking like a mouthful of broken teeth, was all that was left of the home of Werner Noth, of the home where my Helga had been raised as a good German citizen, of the home where I had said farewell to a ten-year-old nihilist named Resi.

I read the text.

The text was by a man named Ian Westlake, and it was very well done. Westlake, an Englishman, a liberated prisoner of war, had seen the hanging shortly after his liberation by the Russians. The photographs were his.

Noth, he said, had been hanged from his own apple tree by slave laborers, mostly Poles and Russians, quartered nearby. Westlake did not call my father-in-law "The Hangman of Berlin."

Westlake went to some trouble to find out what crimes Noth had committed, and he concluded that Noth had been no better and no worse than any other big city chief of police.

"Terror and torture were the provinces of other branches of the German police," said Westlake. "Werner Noth's own province was what is regarded in every big city as ordinary law and order. The force he directed was the sworn enemy of drunks, thieves, murderers, rapists, looters, confidence men, prostitutes, and other disturbers of the peace, and it did its best to keep the city traffic moving.

"Noth's principal offense," said Westlake, "was that he introduced persons suspected of misdemeanors and crimes into a system of courts and penal institutions that was insane. Noth did his best to distinguish between the guilty and the innocent, using the most modern police methods; but those to whom he handed over his prisoners found the distinction of no importance. Merely to be in custody, with or without trial, was a crime. Prisoners of every sort were all to be humiliated, exhausted and killed."

Westlake went on to say that the slave laborers who hanged Noth had no clear idea who he was, beyond the fact that he was somebody important. They hanged him for the satisfaction of hanging somebody important.

Noth's house, said Westlake, had been demolished by Russian artillery, but Noth had continued to live in one undamaged room in the back. Westlake took an inventory of the room, found it to contain a bed, a table, and a candlestick. On the table were framed photographs of Helga, Resi, and Noth's wife.

There was a book. It was a German translation of *The Meditations of Marcus Aurelius.*

Why such a miserable magazine had bought such a fine piece of reporting was not explained. What the magazine was sure its readers would like was the description of the hanging itself.

My father-in-law was stood on a footstool four inches high. The rope was put around his neck and drawn tight over the limb of a budding apple tree. The footstool was then kicked out from under him. He could dance on the ground while he strangled.

Good?

He was revived eight times, and hanged nine.

Only after the eighth hanging were his last bits of courage and dignity gone. Only after the eighth hanging did he act like a child being tortured.

"For that performance," said Westlake, "he was rewarded with what he wanted most in all this world. He was rewarded with death. He died with an erection and his feet were bare."

I turned the page of the magazine to see if there was more. There was more, but not more of the same. There was a full-page photograph of a pretty woman with her thighs spread wide and her tongue stuck out.

The barber called out to me. He shook another man's hair out of the cloth he was going to put around my neck.

"Next," he said.

CHAPTER TWENTY-ONE

My Best Friend . . .

I'VE SAID that I'd stolen the motorcyle I rode when I called on Werner Noth for the last time. I should explain.

I didn't really steal it. I just borrowed it for all eternity from Heinz Schildknecht, my ping-pong doubles partner, my closest friend in Germany.

We used to drink together, used to talk long into the night, especially after we both lost our wives.

"I feel I can tell you anything—absolutely anything," he said to me one night, late in the war.

"I feel the same way about you, Heinz," I said.

"Anything I have is yours," he said.

"Anything I have is yours, Heinz," I said.

The amount of property between us was negligible. Neither one of us had a home. Our real estate and our furniture were blown to smithereens. I had a watch, a typewriter, and a bicycle, and that was about it. Heinz had long since traded his watch and his typewriter and even his wedding ring for black-market cigarettes. All he had left in this vale of tears, excepting my friendship and the clothes on his back, was a motorcycle.

"If anything ever happens to the motorcycle," he said to me, "I am a pauper." He looked around for eavesdroppers. "I will tell you something terrible," he said.

"Don't if you don't want to," I said.

"I want to," he said. "You are the person I can tell terrible things to. I am going to tell you something simply awful."

The place where we were drinking and talking was a pillbox near the dormitory where we both slept. It had been built very recently for the defense of Berlin, had been built by slaves. It wasn't armed, wasn't manned. The Russians weren't that close yet.

Heinz and I sat there with a bottle and a candle between us, and he told me the terrible thing. He was drunk.

"Howard—" he said, "I love my motorcycle more than I loved my wife."

"I want to be a friend of yours, and I want to believe everything you say, Heinz," I said to him, "but I refuse to believe that. Let's just forget you said it, because it isn't true."

"No," he said, "this is one of those moments when somebody really speaks the truth, one of those rare moments. People hardly ever speak the truth, but now I am speaking the truth. If you are the friend I think you are, you'll do me the honor of believing the friend I think I am when I speak the truth."

"All right," I said.

There were tears streaming down his cheeks. "I sold her jewelry, her favorite furniture, even her meat ration one time—all for cigarettes for me," he said.

"We've all done things we're ashamed of," I said.

"I would not quit smoking for her sake," said Heinz.

"We all have bad habits," I said.

"When the bomb hit the apartment, killed her and left me with nothing but a motorcycle," he said, "the black-market man offered me four thousand cigarettes for the motorcycle."

"I know," I said. He told me the same story every time he got drunk.

"And I gave up smoking at once," he said, "because I loved the motorcycle so."

"We all cling to something," I said.

"To the wrong things—" he said, "and we start clinging too late. I will tell you the one thing I really believe out of all the things there are to believe."

"All right," I said.

"All people are insane," he said. "They will do anything at any time, and God help anybody who looks for reasons."

As for the kind of woman Heinz's wife had been: I knew her only slightly, though I saw her fairly often. She was a nonstop talker, which made her hard to know, and her theme was always the same: successful people, people who saw opportunities and grasped them firmly, people who, unlike her husband, were important and rich.

"Young Kurt Ehrens—" she would say, "only twenty-six, and a full colonel in the S.S.! And his brother Heinrich—he can't be more than thirty-four, but he has eighteen thousand foreign workers under him, all building tank traps. Heinrich knows more about tank traps than any man alive, they say, and I used to dance with him."

On and on she would talk this way, with poor Heinz in the background, smoking his brains out. And one thing she did to me was make me deaf to all success stories. The people she saw as succeeding in a brave new world were, after all, being rewarded as specialists in slavery, destruction, and death. I don't consider people who work in those fields successful.

As the war drew to a close, Heinz and I couldn't drink in our pillbox any more. An eighty-eight was set up in it, and the gun was manned by boys about fifteen or sixteen years old. There was a success story for Heinz's late wife—boys that young, and yet with men's uniforms and a fully-armed death trap all their own.

So Heinz and I did our drinking and talking in our dormitory, a riding hall jammed with bombed-out government workers sleeping on straw mattresses. We kept our bottle hidden, since we did not care to share it.

"Heinz—" I said to him one night, "I wonder how good a friend you really are."

He was stung. "Why should you ask me that?" he said.

"I want to ask a favor of you—a very big one—and I don't know if I should," I said.

"I demand that you ask it!" he said.

"Lend me your motorcycle, so I can visit my in-laws tomorrow," I said.

He did not hesitate, did not quail. "Take it!" he said.

So the next morning I did.

We started out the next morning side by side, Heinz on my bicycle, me on his motorcycle.

I kicked the starter, put the motorcycle in gear, and off I went, leaving my best friend smiling in a cloud of blue exhaust.

Off I went—vroooom, ka-pow, kapow—vaaaaaaa-roooooom!

And he never saw his motorcycle or his best friend again.

I have asked the Haifa Institute for the Documentation of War Criminals if they have any news of Heinz, though he wasn't much of a war criminal. The Institute delights me with the news that Heinz is now in Ireland, is chief grounds-keeper for Baron Ulrich Werther von Schwefelbad. Von Schwefelbad bought a big estate in Ireland after the war.

The Institute tells me that Heinz is an expert on the death of Hitler, having stumbled into Hitler's bunker while Hitler's gasoline-soaked body was burning but still recognizable.

Hello, out there, Heinz, in case you read this.

I was really very fond of you, to the extent that I am capable of being fond of anybody.

Give the Blarney Stone a kiss for me.

What were you doing in Hitler's bunker—looking for your motorcycle and your best friend?

CHAPTER TWENTY-TWO

The Contents of an Old Trunk . . .

"Look," I said to my Helga in Greenwich Village, after I had told her what little I knew about her mother, father, and sister, "this attic will never do for a love nest, not even for one night. We'll get a taxi. We'll go to some hotel. And tomorrow we'll throw out all this furniture, get everything brand new. And then we'll look for a really nice place to live."

"I'm very happy here," she said.

"Tomorrow," I said, "we'll find a bed like our old bed—two miles long and three miles wide, with a headboard like an Italian sunset. Remember—oh Lord, remember?"

"Yes," she said.

"Tonight in a hotel," I said. "Tomorrow night in a bed like that."

"We leave right now?" she said.

"Whatever you say," I said.

"Can I show you my presents first?" she said.

"Presents?" I said.

"For you," she said.

"You're my present," I said. "What more would I want?"

"You might want these, too," she said, freeing the catches on a suitcase. "I hope you do." She opened the suitcase, showed me that it was full of manuscripts. Her present to me was my collected works, my collected serious works, almost every heartfelt word ever written by me, the late Howard W. Campbell, Jr. There were poems, stories, plays, letters, one unpublished book—the collected works of myself as a buoyant, free, and young, young man.

"How queer this makes me feel," I said.

"I shouldn't have brought them?" she said.

"I hardly know," I said. "These pieces of paper were me at one time." I picked up the book manuscript, a bizarre experiment called *Memoirs of a Monogamous Casanova*. "This you should have burned," I said.

"I would just as gladly burn my own right arm," she said.

I put the book aside, took up a sheaf of poems. "What does this young stranger have to say about life?" I said, and I read a poem, a poem in German, aloud:

Kühl und hell der Sonnenaufgang,
leis und süss der Glocke Klang.
Ein Magdlein hold, Krug in der Hand,
sitzt an des tiefen Brunnens Rand.

In English? Roughly:

Cool, bright sunrise—
Faint, sweet bell.
Maiden with a pitcher
By a cool, deep well.

I read that poem out loud, and then I read another. I was and am a very bad poet. I do not set down these poems to be admired. The second poem I read was, I think, the next-to-the-last poem I ever wrote. It was dated 1937, and it had this title: "*Gedanken über unseren Abstand vom Zietgeschehen*," or roughly, "Reflections on Not Participating in Current Events."

It went like this:

Eine mächtige Dampfwalze naht
und schwärtz der Sonne Pfad,
rollt über geduckte Menschen dahin,
will keiner ihr entfliehn.
Mein Lieb und ich schaun starren Blickes
das Rätsel dieses Blutgeschickes.
"Kommt mit herab," die Menschheit schreit,
"Die Walze ist die Geschichte der Zeit!"
Mein Lieb und ich gehn auf die Flucht,
wo keine Dampfwalze uns sucht,
und leben auf den Bergeshöhen,
getrennt vom schwarzen Zeitgeschehen.
Sollen wir bleiben mit den andern zu sterben?
Doch nein, wir zwei wollen nicht verderben!
Nun ist's vorbei!—Wir sehn mit Erbleichen
die Opfer der Walze, verfaulte Leichen.

In English?

I saw a huge steam roller,
It blotted out the sun.
The people all lay down, lay down;
They did not try to run.
My love and I, we looked amazed
Upon the gory mystery.
"Lie down, lie down!" the people cried,
"The great machine is history!"
My love and I, we ran away,
The engine did not find us.
We ran up to a mountain top,
Left history far behind us.
Perhaps we should have stayed and died,
But somehow we don't think so.
We went to see where history'd been,
And my, the dead did stink so.

"How is it," I said to Helga, "that you have all these things?"

"When I went to West Berlin," she said, "I went to the theater to see if there was a theater left—if there was anyone I knew left—if anyone had any news of you." She didn't have to explain which theater she meant. She meant the little theater where my plays had been produced in Berlin, where Helga had been the star so often.

"It got through most of the war, I know," I said. "It still exists?"

"Yes," she said. "And when I asked about you, they knew nothing. And when I told them what you had once meant to that theater, someone remembered that there was a trunk in the loft with your name on it."

I passed my hand over the manuscripts. "And in it were these," I said. I remembered the trunk now, remembered when I'd closed it up at the start of the war, remembered when I'd thought of the trunk as a coffin for the young man I would never be again.

"You already have copies of these things?" she said.

"No," I said. "Not a scrap."

"You don't write any more?" she said.

"There hasn't been anything I've wanted to say," I said.

"After all you've seen, all you've been through, darling?" she said.

"It's all I've seen, all I've been through," I said, "that makes it damn nearly impossible for me to say anything. I've lost the knack of making sense. I speak gibberish to the civilized world, and it replies in kind."

"There was another poem, your last poem, it must have been—" she said, "written in eyebrow pencil on the inside of the trunk lid."

"Oh?" I said.

She recited it for me:

Heir liegt Howard Campbells Geist geborgen,
frei von des Körpers quälenden Sorgen.
Sein leerer Leib durchstreift die Welt,
und kargen Lohn dafür erhält.
Triffst du die beiden getrennt allerwärts
verbrenn den Leib, doch schone dies, sein Herz.

In English?

Here lies Howard Campbell's essence,
Freed from his body's noisome nuisance.
His body, empty, prowls the earth,
Earning what a body's worth.
If his body and his essence remain apart,
Burn his body, but spare this, his heart.

There was a knock on the door.

It was George Kraft knocking on my door, and I let him in.

He was very jangled because his corn-cob pipe had disappeared. It was the first time I'd seen him without the pipe, the first time he showed me how dependent he was on the pipe for peace. He was so full of anxiety that he whined.

"Somebody took it or somebody knocked it down behind something or—I just can't imagine why anybody would have done anything with it," he whined. He expected Helga and me to share his anxiety, to think that the disappearance of the pipe was the most important event of the day.

He was insufferable.

"Why would anybody touch the pipe?" he said. "What good

would it do anybody?" He was opening and shutting his hands, blinking often, sniffling, acting like a dope addict with withdrawal symptoms, though he had never smoked anything in the missing pipe. "Just tell me—" he said, "why would anybody take the pipe?"

"I don't know, George," I said testily. "If we find it, we'll let you know."

"Could I look around for myself?" he said.

"Go ahead," I said.

And he turned the place upside down, rattling pots and pans, banging cupboard doors, fishing back of the radiators with a poker, clangingly.

The effect of this performance on Helga and me was to wed us—to urge us into an easy relationship that might otherwise have been a long while coming.

We stood side by side, resenting the invasion of our nation of two.

"It wasn't a very valuable pipe, was it?" I said.

"Yes it was—to me," he said.

"Buy another one," I said.

"I want *that* one," he said. "I'm used to it. That's the pipe I want." He opened the breadbox, looked inside.

"Maybe the ambulance attendants took it," I said.

"Why would they do that?" he said.

"Maybe they thought it belonged to the dead man," I said. "Maybe they put it in the dead man's pocket."

"That's it!" cried Kraft, and he scuttled out the door.

CHAPTER TWENTY-THREE

Chapter Six Hundred and Forty-three . . .

ONE OF THE THINGS Helga had in her suitcase, as I've already said, was a book by me. It was a manuscript. I had never intended that it be published. I regarded it as unpublishable—except by pornographers.

It was called *Memoirs of a Monogamous Casanova*. In it I told of my conquests of all the hundreds of women my wife, my Helga, had been. It was clinical, obsessed—some say, insane. It was a diary, recording day by day for the first two years of the war, our erotic life—to the exclusion of all else. There is not one word in it to indicate even the century or the continent of its origin.

There is a man of many moods, a woman of many moods. In some of the early entries, settings are referred to sketchily. But from there on, there are no settings at all.

Helga knew I kept the peculiar diary. I kept it as one of many devices for keeping our sexual pleasure keen. The book is not only a report of an experiment, but a part of the experiment it reports—a self-conscious experiment by a man and a woman to be endlessly fascinating to each other sexually—

To be more than that.

To be to each other, body and soul, sufficient reasons for living, though there might not be a single other satisfaction to be had.

The epigraph of the book is to the point, I think.

It is a poem by William Blake called "The Question Answered":

> What is it men in women do require?
> The lineaments of Gratified Desire.
> What is it women do in men require?
> The lineaments of Gratified Desire.

I might aptly add here one last chapter to the *Memoirs*, chapter 643, describing the night I spent in a New York hotel with Helga, after having been without her for so many years.

I leave it to an editor of taste and delicacy to abridge with innocent polka dots whatever might offend.

MEMOIRS OF A MONOGAMOUS CASANOVA, CHAPTER 643

We had been apart for sixteen years. My first lust that night was in my finger tips. Other parts of me . . . that were contented later were contented in a ritual way, thoroughly, to . . . clinical perfection. No part of me could complain, and no part of my wife could complain, I trust, of being victimized by busy-work, time-serving . . . or jerry-building. But my finger tips had the best of it that night. . . .

Which is not to say that I found myself to be an . . . old man, dependent, if I was to please a woman, on . . . foreplay and nothing more. On the contrary, I was as . . . ready a lover as a seventeen-year-old . . . with his . . . girl . . .

And as full of wonder.

And it was in my fingers that the wonder lived. Calm, resourceful, thoughtful, these . . . explorers, these . . . strategists, these . . . scouts, these . . . skirmishers, deployed themselves over the . . . terrain.

And all the news they gathered was good. . . .

My wife was a . . . slave girl bedded with an . . . emperor that night, seemingly struck dumb, seemingly not even able to speak a word of my language. And yet, how eloquent she was, letting her eyes, her breathing . . . express what they must, unable to keep them from expressing what they must. . . .

And how simple, how sublimely familiar was the tale her . . . body told! . . . It was like the breeze's tale of what a breeze is, like the rose's tale of what the rose is. . . .

After my subtle, thoughtful and grateful fingers came greedier things, instruments of pleasure without memories, without manners, without patience. These my slave girl met in greedy kind . . . until Mother Nature herself, who had made the most extravagant demands upon us, could ask no more. Mother Nature herself . . . called an end to the game. . . .

We rolled apart. . . .

We spoke coherently to each other for the first time since bedding down.

"Hello," she said.

"Hello," I said.

"Welcome home," she said.

End of chapter 643.

The city sky was clean and hard and bright the next morning, looking like an enchanted dome that would shatter at a tap or ring like a great glass bell.

My Helga and I stepped from our hotel to the sidewalk snappily. I was lavish in my courtliness, and my Helga was no less grand in her respect and gratitude. We had had a marvelous night.

I was not wearing war-surplus clothing. I was wearing the clothes I had put on after fleeing Berlin, after shucking off the uniform of the Free American Corps. I was wearing the clothes —fur-collared impresario's cloak and blue serge suit—I had been captured in. I was also carrying, for whimsy, a cane. I did marvelous things with the cane: rococo manuals of arms, Charlie Chaplin twirls, polo strokes at orts in the gutter.

And all the while my Helga's small hand rested on my good left arm, creeping in an endless and erotic exploration of the tingling area between the inside of my elbow and the crest of my stringy biceps.

We were on our way to buy a bed, a bed like our bed in Berlin.

But all the stores were closed. The day wasn't Sunday, and it wasn't any holiday I could think of. When we got to Fifth Avenue, there were American flags flying as far as the eye could see. "Good God Almighty," I said wonderingly.

"What does it mean?" said Helga.

"Maybe they declared war last night," I said.

She tightened her fingers on my arm convulsively. "You don't really think so, do you?" she said. She thought it was possible.

"A joke," I said. "Some kind of holiday, obviously."

"What holiday?" she said.

I was still drawing blanks. "As your host in this wonderful land of ours," I said, "I should explain to you the deep significance of this great day in our national lives, but nothing comes to me."

"Nothing?" she said.

"I'm as baffled as you are," I said. "I might as well be the Prince of Cambodia."

A uniformed colored man was sweeping the walk in front of an apartment. His blue and gold uniform bore a striking resemblance to the uniform of the Free American Corps, even to the final touch of a pale lavender stripe down his trouser legs. The name of the apartment house was stitched over his breast pocket. "Sylvan House" was the name of the place, though the only tree near it was a sapling, bandaged, armored and guy-wired.

I asked the man what day it was.

He told me it was Veterans' Day.

"What date is it?" I said.

"November eleventh, sir," he said.

"November eleventh is Armistice Day, not Veterans' Day," I said.

"Where you been?" he said. "They changed all that years ago."

"Veterans' Day," I said to Helga as we walked on. "Used to be Armistice Day. Now it's Veterans' Day."

"That upsets you?" she said.

"Oh, it's just so damn cheap, so damn typical," I said. "This used to be a day in honor of the dead of World War One, but the living couldn't keep their grubby hands off of it, wanted the glory of the dead for themselves. So typical, so typical. Any time anything of real dignity appears in this country, it's torn to shreds and thrown to the mob."

"You hate America, don't you?" she said.

"That would be as silly as loving it," I said. "It's impossible for me to get emotional about it, because real estate doesn't interest me. It's no doubt a great flaw in my personality, but I can't think in terms of boundaries. Those imaginary lines are as unreal to me as elves and pixies. I can't believe that they mark the end or the beginning of anything of real concern to a human soul. Virtues and vices, pleasures and pains cross boundaries at will."

"You've changed so," she said.

"People should be changed by world wars," I said, "else what are world wars for?"

"Maybe you've changed so much you don't really love me any more," she said. "Maybe I've changed so much—"

"After a night like last night," I said, "how could you say such a thing?"

"We really haven't talked anything over—" she said.

"What is there to talk about?" I said. "Nothing you could say would make me love you more or less. Our love is too deep for words ever to touch it. It's soul love."

She sighed. "How lovely that is—if it's true." She put her hands close together, but not touching. "Our souls in love."

"A love that can weather anything," I said.

"Your soul feels love now for my soul?" she said.

"Obviously," I said.

"And you couldn't be deceived by that feeling?" she said. "You couldn't be mistaken?"

"Not a chance," I said.

"And nothing I could say could spoil it?" she said.

"Nothing," I said.

"All right," she said, "I have something to say that I was afraid to say before. I'm not afraid to say it now."

"Say away!" I said lightly.

"I'm not Helga," she said. "I'm her little sister Resi."

CHAPTER TWENTY-FOUR

A Polygamous Casanova . . .

AFTER SHE GAVE ME the news, I took her into a nearby cafeteria so we could sit down. The ceiling was high. The lights were merciless. The clatter was hell.

"Why did you do this to me?" I said.

"Because I love you," she said.

"How could you love me?" I said.

"I've always loved you—since I was a very little girl," she said.

I put my head in my hands. "This is terrible," I said.

"I—I thought it was beautiful," she said.

"What now?" I said.

"It can't go on?" she said.

"Oh, Jesus—how bewildering," I said.

"I found the words to kill the love, didn't I—" she said, "the love that couldn't be killed?"

"I don't know," I said. I shook my head "What is this strange crime I've committed?"

"I'm the one who's committed the crime," she said. "I must have been crazy. When I escaped into West Berlin, when they gave me a form to fill out, asked me who I was, what I was—who I knew—"

"That long, long story you told—" I said, "about Russia, about Dresden—was any of it true?"

"The cigarette factory in Dresden—that was true," she said. "My running away to Berlin was true. Not much else. The cigarette factory—" she said, "that was the truest thing—ten hours a day, six days a week, ten years."

"Sorry," I said.

"I'm the one who's sorry," she said. "Life's been too hard for me ever to afford much guilt. A really bad conscience is as much out of my reach as a mink coat. Daydreams were what kept me going at that machine, day after day, and I had no right to them."

"Why not?" I said.

"They were all daydreams of being somebody I wasn't."

"No harm in that," I said.

"Look at the harm," she said. "Look at you. Look at me. Look at our love affair. I daydreamed of being my sister Helga. Helga, Helga, Helga—that's who I was. The lovely actress with the handsome playwright husband, that's who I was. Resi, the cigarette machine operator—she simply disappeared."

"You could have picked a worse person to be," I said.

She became very brave now. "It's who I am," she said. "It's who I am. I'm Helga, Helga, Helga. You believed it. What better test could I be put to? Have I been Helga to you?"

"That's a hell of a question to put to a gentleman," I said.

"Am I entitled to an answer?" she said.

"You're entitled to the answer yes," I said. "I have to answer yes, but I have to say I'm not a well man, either. My judgment, my senses, my intuition obviously aren't all they could be."

"Or maybe they are all they should be," she said. "Maybe you haven't been deceived."

"Tell me what you know about Helga," I said.

"Dead," she said.

"You're sure?" I said.

"Isn't she?" she said.

"I don't know," I said.

"I haven't heard a word," she said. "Have you?"

"No," I said.

"Living people make words, don't they?" she said. "Especially if they love someone as much as Helga loved you."

"You'd think so," I said.

"I love you as much as Helga did," she said.

"Thank you," I said.

"And you did hear from me," she said. "It took some doing, but you did hear from me."

"Indeed," I said.

"When I got to West Berlin," she said, "and they gave me the forms to fill out—name, occupation, nearest living relative—I had my choice. I could be Resi Noth, cigarette-machine operator, with no relatives anywhere. Or I could be Helga Noth, actress, wife of a handsome, adorable, brilliant playwright in the U.S.A." She leaned forward. "You tell me—" she said, "which one should I have been?"

God forgive me, I accepted Resi as my Helga again.

Once she got that second acceptance, though, she began to show in little ways that her identification with Helga wasn't as complete as she'd said. She felt free, bit by bit, to accustom me to a personality that wasn't Helga's but her own.

This gradual revelation, this weaning of me from memories of Helga, began as we left the cafeteria. She asked me a jarringly practical question:

"Do you want me to keep on bleaching my hair white," she said, "or can I let it come back the way it really is?"

"What is it really?" I said.

"Honey," she said.

"A lovely color for hair," I said. "Helga's color."

"Mine has more red in it," she said.

"I'd be interested to see it," I said.

We walked up Fifth Avenue, and a little later she said to me, "Will you write a play for me some time?"

"I don't know if I can write any more," I said.

"Didn't Helga inspire you to write?" she said.

"Not to write, but to write the way I wrote," I said.

"You wrote a special way—so she could play the part," she said.

"That's right," I said. "I wrote parts for Helga that let her be the quintessence of Helga onstage."

"I want you to do that for me some time," she said.

"Maybe I'll try," I said.

"The quintessence of Resi," she said. "Resi Noth."

We saw a Veterans' Day parade down Fifth Avenue, and I heard Resi's laugh for the first time. It was nothing like Helga's laugh, which was a rustling thing. Resi's laugh was bright, melodious. What struck her so funny was the drum majorettes, kicking at the moon, twitching their behinds, and twirling chromium dildos.

"I've never seen such a thing before," she said to me. "War must be a very sexy thing to Americans." She went on laughing, and she thrust out her bosom to see if she might not make a good drum majorette, too.

She was growing younger by the second, gayer, more raucously irreverent. Her white hair, which had made me think so recently of premature aging, now updated itself, spoke of peroxide and girls who ran away to Hollywood.

When we turned away from the parade, we looked into a store window that showed a great gilded bed, one very much like the one Helga and I once had.

And not only did the window show that Wagnerian bed, it showed a reflection of Resi and me, too, ghostlike, and with a ghostly parade behind us. The pale wraiths and the substantial bed formed an unsettling composition. It seemed to be an allegory in the Victorian manner, a pretty good barroom painting, actually, with the passing banners and the golden bed and the male and female ghosts.

What the allegory was, I cannot say. But I can offer a few more clues. The male ghost looked God-awful old and starved and moth-eaten. The female ghost looked young enough to be his daughter, sleek, bouncy, and full of hell.

CHAPTER TWENTY-FIVE

The Answer to Communism . . .

RESI AND I dawdled on our way back to my ratty attic, looked at furniture, drank here and there.

Resi went to the ladies' room in one bar, leaving me alone. A barfly started talking to me.

"You know what the answer to communism is?" he asked me.

"Nope," I said.

"Moral Rearmament," he said.

"What the hell is that?" I said.

"It's a movement," he said.

"In what direction?" I said.

"That Moral Rearmament movement," he said, "believes in absolute honesty, absolute purity, absolute unselfishness, and absolute love."

"I certainly wish them all the luck in the world," I said.

In another bar, Resi and I met a man who claimed he could satisfy, thoroughly satisfy, seven women in a night, provided they were all different.

"I mean really different," he said.

Oh, God—the lives people try to lead.

Oh, God—what a world they try to lead them in!

CHAPTER TWENTY-SIX

In Which Private Irving Buchanon and Some Others Are Memorialized . . .

RESI AND I didn't get home until after supper, after dark. Our plan was to spend another night at a hotel. We came home because Resi wanted to have a waking dream of how we would refurnish the attic, wanted to play house.

"At last I have a house," she said.

"It takes a heap of living," I said, "to make a house a home." I saw that my mailbox was stuffed again. I left the mail where it was.

"Who did that?" said Resi.

"Who did what?" I said.

"That," she said, pointing to my namecard on the mailbox. Somebody had drawn a swastika after my name in blue ink.

"It's something quite new," I said uneasily. "Maybe we'd better not go upstairs. Maybe whoever did it is up there."

"I don't understand," she said.

"You picked a miserable time to come to me, Resi," I said. "I had a cozy little burrow, where you and I might have been quite content—"

"Burrow?" she said.

"A hole in the ground, made secret and snug," I said. "But, God!—" I said in anguish, "just when you were coming to me, something laid my den wide open!" I told her how my notoriety had been renewed. "Now the carnivores," I said, "scenting a freshly opened den, are closing in."

"Go to another country," she said.

"What other country?" I said.

"Any country you like," she said. "You have the money to go anywhere you want."

"Anywhere I want—" I said.

And then a bald, bristly fat man carrying a shopping bag came in. He shouldered Resi and me away from the mailboxes with a hoarse, unapologetic bully's apology.

"'Scuse me," he said. He read the names on the mailboxes like a first-grader, putting a finger under each name, studying each name for a long, long time.

"Campbell!" he said at last, with massive satisfaction. "Howard W. Campbell." He turned to me accusingly. "You know him?" he said.

"No," I said.

"No," he said, becoming radiant with malevolence. "You look just like him." He took a copy of the *Daily News* from the shopping bag, opened it to an inside page, handed it to Resi. "Now, don't that look a lot like the gentleman you're with?" he said to her.

"Let me see," I said. I took the paper from Resi's slack fingers, saw the picture of myself and Lieutenant O'Hare, standing before the gallows at Ohrdruf so long ago.

The story underneath the picture said that the government of Israel had located me after a fifteen-year search. That government was now requesting that the United States release me to Israel for trial. What did they want to try me for? Complicity in the murder of six million Jews.

The man hit me right through the newspaper before I could comment.

Down I went, banging my head on an ash can.

The man stood over me. "Before the Jews put you in a cage in a zoo or whatever they're gonna do to you," he said, "I'd just like to play a little with you myself."

I shook my head, trying to clear it.

"Felt that one, did you?" he said.

"Yes," I said.

"That one was for Private Irving Buchanon," he said.

"Is that who you are?" I said.

"Buchanon is dead," he said. "He was the best friend I ever had. Five miles in from Omaha Beach, the Germans cut his nuts off and hung him from a telephone pole."

He kicked me in the ribs, holding Resi off with one hand. "That's for Ansel Brewer," he said, "run over by a Tiger tank at Aachen."

He kicked me again. "That's for Eddie McCarty, cut in two by a burp gun in the Ardennes," he said. "Eddie was gonna be a doctor."

He drew back his big foot to kick me in the head. "And this one—" he said, and that's the last I heard. The kick was for somebody else who'd been killed in war. It knocked me cold.

Resi told me later what the last things the man said were, and what the present for me was in the shopping bag.

"I'm one guy who hasn't forgot that war," he said to me, though I could not hear him. "Everybody else has forgot it, as near as I can tell—but not me."

And then he took from the shopping bag a hangman's knot tied in a length of lank, pale, slick new hemp. He threw it on the floor beside me.

"I brought you this," he said, "so you could save everybody a lot of trouble."

And he left.

Resi put the noose in the ash can, where it was found the next morning by a garbage-man named Lazlo Szombathy. Szombathy actually hanged himself with it—but that is another story.

As for my own story:

I regained consciousness on a ruptured studio couch in a damp, overheated room that was hung with mildewed Nazi banners. There was a cardboard fireplace, a dime-store's idea of how to have a merry Christmas. In it were cardboard birch logs, a red electric light and cellophane tongues of eternal fire.

Over this fireplace was a chromo of Adolf Hitler. It was swathed in black silk.

I myself was stripped to my olive-drab underwear, covered with a bedspread of simulated leopard skin. I groaned and sat up, skyrockets going off in my skull. I looked down at the leopard skin and mumbled something.

"What did you say, darling?" said Resi. She was sitting right beside the cot, though I hadn't seen her until she spoke.

"Don't tell me—" I said, drawing the leopard skin closer about me, "I've joined the Hottentots."

CHAPTER TWENTY-SEVEN

Finders Keepers . . .

MY RESEARCH ASSISTANTS here, lively, keen young people, have provided me with a photostat of a story in the New York *Times*, telling of the death of Lazlo Szombathy, the man who killed himself with the rope intended for me.

So I didn't dream that, either.

Szombathy did the big trick the night after I was beaten up.

He had come to this country after being a Freedom Fighter against the Russians in Hungry, according to the *Times.* He was a fratricide, according to the *Times*, having shot his brother Miklos, Second Minister of Education in Hungary.

Before he gave himself the big sleep, Szombathy wrote a note and pinned it to his trouser leg. There was nothing in the note about his having killed his brother.

His complaint was that he had been a respected veterinarian in Hungary, but that he was not permitted to practice in America. He had bitter things to say about freedom in America. He thought it was illusory.

In a final fandango of paranoia and masochism, Szombathy closed his note with a hint that he knew how to cure cancer. American doctors laughed at him, he said, whenever he tried to tell them how.

So much for Szombathy.

As for the room where I awakened after my beating: it was the cellar that had been furnished for the Iron Guard of the White Sons of the American Constitution by the late August Krapptauer, the cellar of Dr. Lionel J. D. Jones, D.D.S., D.D. Somewhere upstairs a printing press was running, turning out copies of *The White Christian Minuteman*.

From some other chamber in the cellar, partly soundproofed, came the idiotically monotonous banging of target practice.

After my beating, I had been given first aid by young Dr. Abraham Epstein, the doctor in my building who had pronounced Krapptauer dead. From Epstein's apartment, Resi had called Dr. Jones for help and advice.

"Why Jones?" I said.

He was the only person in this country I knew I could trust," said Resi. "He was the only person I knew for sure was on your side."

"What is life without friends?" I said.

I have no recollection of it, but Resi tells me that I regained consciousness in Epstein's apartment. Jones picked Resi and me up in his limousine, took me to a hospital, where I was X-rayed. I had three broken ribs taped up. After that I was taken to Jones' cellar and bedded down.

"Why here?" I said.

"It's safe," said Resi.

"From what?" I said.

"The Jews," she said.

The Black Fuehrer of Harlem, Jones' chauffeur, now came in with a tray of eggs, toast, and scalding coffee. He set it down on a table for me.

"Headache?" he asked me.

"Yes," I said.

"Take a aspirin," he said.

"Thank you for the advice," I said.

"Most things in this world don't work—" he said, "but aspirin do."

"The—the Republic of Israel really wants me—" I said to Resi in groping disbelief, "to—to try me for—for what the paper said?"

"Dr. Jones says the American Government won't let you go—" said Resi, "but that the Jews will send men to kidnap you, the way they did Adolf Eichmann."

"Such a piffling prisoner—" I murmured.

"Ain't like just having a Jew here and a Jew there after you," said the Black Fuehrer.

"What?" I said.

"I mean," he said, "they got a country now. I mean, they got Jewish battleships, they got Jewish airplanes, they got Jewish tanks. They got Jewish everything out after you but a Jewish hydrogen bomb."

"Who in God's name is doing that shooting?" I said. "Can't he stop until my head feels a little better?"

"That's your friend," said Resi.

"Dr. Jones?" I said.

"George Kraft," she said.

"Kraft?" I said. "What's he doing here?"

"He's coming with us," said Resi.

"To where?" I said.

"It's all been decided," said Resi. "Everybody agrees, darling—the best thing is for us to get out of the country. Dr. Jones has made arrangements."

"What sort of arrangements?" I said.

"He has a friend with an airplane. As soon as you're well enough, darling, we get on the plane, fly to some divine place where you aren't known—and we'll start life all over again."

CHAPTER TWENTY-EIGHT

Target . . .

I WENT TO SEE George Kraft, there in Jones' basement. I found him standing at the head of a long corridor, the far end of which was packed with sandbags. Pinned to the sandbags was a target in the shape of a man.

The target was a caricature of a cigar-smoking Jew. The Jew was standing on broken crosses and little naked women. In one hand the Jew held a bag of money labeled "International Banking." In the other hand he held a Russian flag. From the pockets of his suit, little fathers, mothers, and children in scale with the naked women under his feet, cried out for mercy.

All these details were not evident from the far end of the shooting gallery, but it wasn't necessary for me to approach the target in order to know about them.

I had drawn the target in about 1941.

Millions of copies of the target were run off in Germany. It had so delighted my superiors that I was given a bonus of a ten-pound ham, thirty gallons of gasoline, and a week's all-expenses-paid vacation for my wife and myself at the *Schreiberhau* in Riesengebirge.

I must admit that this target represents an excess of zeal, since I was not working as a graphic artist for the Nazis. I offer it in evidence against myself. I presume my authorship of it is news even to the Haifa Institute for the Documentation of War Criminals. I submit, however, that I drew the monster in order to establish myself even more solidly as a Nazi. I overdrew it, with an effect that would have been ludicrous anywhere but in Germany or Jones' basement, and I drew it far more amateurishly than I can really draw.

It succeeded, nonetheless.

I was flabbergasted by its success. The Hitler Youth and S.S. recruits fired at almost nothing else, and I even got a letter of thanks for the target from Heinrich Himmler.

"It has improved my marksmanship a hundred per cent," he

wrote. "What pure Aryan can look at that wonderful target," he said, "and not shoot to kill?"

Watching Kraft pop away at that target, I understood its popularity for the first time. The amateurishness of it made it look like something drawn on the wall of a public lavatory; it recalled the stink, diseased twilight, humid resonance, and vile privacy of a stall in a public lavatory—echoed exactly the soul's condition in a man at war.

I had drawn better than I knew.

Kraft, oblivious to me in my leopard skin, fired again. He was using a Luger as big as a siege howitzer. It was chambered and bored for mere twenty-two's however, making anti-climactic, peewee *bangs.* Kraft fired again, and a sandbag two feet to the left of the target's head bled sand.

"Try opening your eyes the next time you fire," I said.

"Oh—" he said, putting the pistol down, "you're up and around."

"Yes," I said.

"Too bad what happened," he said.

"I thought so," I said.

"Maybe it's for the best, though," he said. "Maybe we'll all wind up thanking God it happened."

"How so?" I said.

"It's jarred us out of our ruts," he said.

"That's for certain," I said.

"When you get out of this country with your girl, get yourself new surroundings, a new identity—you'll start writing again," he said, "and you'll write ten times better than you ever did before. Think of the maturity you'll be bringing to your writing!"

"My head aches too much just now—" I said.

"It'll stop aching soon," he said. "It isn't broken and it's filled with a heartbreakingly clear understanding of the self and the world."

"Um," I said.

"And I'm going to be a better painter for the change, too," he said "I've never seen the tropics before—that brutal glut of color, that visible, audible heat—"

"What's this about the tropics?" I said.

"I thought that's where we'd go," he said. "That's where Resi wants to go, too."

"You're coming, too?" I said.

"Do you mind?" he said.

"People have certainly been active while I slept," I said.

"Was that wrong of us?" said Kraft. "Did we plan anything that would be bad for you?"

"George—" I said, "why should you throw in your lot with us? Why should you come down into this cellar with the black beetles, too? You have no enemies. Stay with us, George, and you'll deserve every enemy I have."

He put his hand on my shoulder, looked deep into my eyes. "Howard—" he said, "when my wife died, I had no allegiance to anything on earth. I, too, was a meaningless fragment of a nation of two.

"And then I discovered something I had never known before—what a true friend was," he said. "I throw my lot in with you gladly, friend. Nothing else interests me. Nothing else attracts me in the least. With your permission, my paints and I would like nothing better than to go with you wherever Fate takes you next."

"This—this is friendship indeed," I said.

"I hope so," he said.

CHAPTER TWENTY-NINE

Adolf Eichmann and Me . . .

I SPENT two days in that queer basement—as a meditative invalid.

My clothes had been ruined in the beating I'd taken. So, from the resources of Jones' household, I was given other clothes. I was given a pair of shiny black trousers by Father Keeley, a silver-colored shirt by Dr. Jones, a shirt that had once been part of the uniform of a defunct American Fascist movement called, straightforwardly enough, "The Silver Shirts." And the Black Fuehrer gave me a tiny orange sports coat that made me look like an organ-grinder's monkey.

And Resi Noth and George Kraft kept me company tenderly—not only nursed me, but did my dreaming and planning for me as well. The big dream was to get out of America as soon as possible. Conversations, in which I took very little part, were a sort of roulette played with the names of warm places purported to be Edens: Acapulco . . . Minorca . . . Rhodes . . . even the Vale of Kashmir, Zanzibar, and the Andaman Islands.

The news from the outside world was not such as to make my remaining in America attractive—or even conceivable. Father Keeley went out and bought newspapers several times a day, and, for supplementary enlightenment, we had the blatting of the radio.

The Republic of Israel stepped up its demands for me, encouraged by rumors that I wasn't an American citizen, that I was, in fact, a citizen of nowhere. And the Republic's demands were framed so as to be educational, too—teaching that a propagandist of my sort was as much a murderer as Heydrich, Eichmann, Himmler, or any of the gruesome rest.

That may be so. I had hoped, as a broadcaster, to be merely ludicrous, but this is a hard world to be ludicrous in, with so many human beings so reluctant to laugh, so incapable of thought, so eager to believe and snarl and hate. So many people *wanted* to believe me!

Say what you will about the sweet miracle of unquestioning faith, I consider a capacity for it terrifying and absolutely vile.

West Germany asked the Government of the United States politely if I might be a citizen of theirs. They had no proof one way or another, since all records pertaining to me had burned during the war. If I was a citizen of theirs, they said, they would be as pleased as Israel to have me for trial.

If I was a German, they said in effect, they were certainly ashamed of a German like me.

Soviet Russia, in short words that sounded like ball bearings being dropped into wet gravel, said that no trial was necessary. A Fascist like me, they said, should be squashed underfoot like a cockroach.

But it was the anger of my neighbors that really stank of sudden death. The more barbaric newspapers printed without comment letters from people who wanted me displayed from coast to coast in an iron cage; from heroes who volunteered to serve in a firing squad for me, as though the use of small arms were a skill known to few; from people who planned to do nothing themselves, but were confident enough in American civilization to know that there were other, stronger, younger people who would know what to do.

And these last-named patriots were right in having confidence. I doubt if there has ever been a society that has been without strong and young people eager to experiment with homicide, provided no very awful penalties are attached to it.

According to the newspapers and radio, justifiably angry people had already done what they could about me, breaking into my ratty attic, smashing my windows, tearing up or carting off my worldly goods. The hated attic was now under police guard around the clock.

The New York *Post* pointed out editorially that the police could scarcely give me the protection I needed, since my enemies were so numerous and so understandably murderous. What was called for, said the *Post* helplessly, was a battalion of Marines to surround me for the rest of my days.

The New York *Daily News* suggested that my biggest war crime was not killing myself like a gentleman. Presumably Hitler was a gentleman.

The *News*, incidentally, also printed a letter from Bernard B.

O'Hare, the man who had captured me in Germany, the man who had recently written me a letter with copious carbons.

"I want this guy all for myself," O'Hare wrote of me. "I deserve this guy all for myself. I was the guy who caught him in Germany. If I'd known then he was going to get away, I would have blown his head off right then and there. If anybody sees Campbell before I do, tell him Bernie O'Hare is on his way from Boston by nonstop plane."

The New York *Times* said that tolerating and even protecting vermin like me was one of the maddening necessities in the life of a truly free society.

The United States Government, as Resi had told me, was not going to turn me over to the Republic of Israel. There was no legal machinery for that.

The United States Government did promise, however, to make a full and open review of my puzzling case, to find out exactly what my citizenship status was, to find out why I had never even been brought to trial.

That Government expressed queasy surprise that I was even within its borders.

The New York *Times* published a portrait of me as a much younger man, my official portrait as a Nazi and idol of the international airwaves. I can only guess at the year in which the picture was taken—1941, I think.

Arndt Klopfer, the photographer who took the picture of me, did his best to make me look like a Maxfield Parrish Jesus covered with cold cream. He even gave me a halo, a judiciously placed spot of nebulous light in the background. The halo was no special effect for me alone. Everybody who went to Klopfer got a halo, including Adolf Eichmann.

I can say that for certain about Eichmann, without asking for confirmation from the Haifa Institute, because Eichmann had his picture taken just ahead of mine at Klopfer's studio. It was the only time I ever met Eichmann—the only time in Germany. I met him again here in Israel—only two weeks ago, when I was incarcerated briefly in Tel Aviv.

About that reunion: I was locked up in Tel Aviv for twenty-four hours. On my way to my cell there, the guards stopped me outside Eichmann's cell to hear what we had to say to each other, if anything.

We didn't recognize each other, and the guards had to introduce us.

Eichmann was writing the story of his life, just as I am now writing the story of my life. That chinless old plucked buzzard, with six million murders to explain away, gave me a saintly smile. He was sweetly interested in his work, in me, in the guards in the prison, in everybody.

He beamed at me, and he said, "I'm not mad at anybody."

"That's certainly the way to be," I said.

"I've got some advice for you," he said.

"I'd be glad to have it," I said.

"Relax," he said, beaming, beaming, beaming. "Just relax."

"That's how I got here," I said.

"Life is divided up into phases," he said. "Each one is very different from the others, and you have to be able to recognize what is expected of you in each phase. That's the secret of successful living."

"It's good of you to share the secret with me," I said.

"I'm a writer now," he said. "I never thought I'd be a writer."

"May I ask a personal question?" I said.

"Certainly," he said benignly. "That's the phase I'm in now. This is the time for thinking and answering. Ask whatever you like."

"Do you feel that you're guilty of murdering six million Jews?" I said.

"Absolutely not," said the architect of Auschwitz, the introducer of conveyor belts into crematoria, the greatest customer in the world for the gas called Cyklon-B.

Not knowing the man for sure, I tried some intramural satire on him—what seemed to me to be intramural satire. "You were simply a soldier, were you—" I said, "taking orders from higher-ups, like soldiers around the world?"

Eichmann turned to a guard, and talked to him in rapid-fire Yiddish, indignant Yiddish. If he'd spoken it slowly, I would have understood it, but he spoke too fast.

"What did he say?" I asked the guard.

"He wondered if we'd showed you his statement," said the guard. "He made us promise not to show it to anybody until it was done."

"I haven't seen it," I said to Eichmann.

"Then how do you know what my defense is going to be?" he said.

This man actually believed that he had invented his own trite defense, though a whole nation of ninety some-odd million had made the same defense before him. Such was his paltry understanding of the God-like human act of invention.

The more I think about Eichmann and me, the more I think that he should be sent to the hospital, and that I am the sort of person for whom punishments by fair, just men were devised.

As a friend of the court that will try Eichmann, I offer my opinion that Eichmann cannot distinguish between right and wrong—that not only right and wrong, but truth and falsehood, hope and despair, beauty and ugliness, kindness and cruelty, comedy and tragedy, are all processed by Eichmann's mind indiscriminately, like birdshot through a bugle.

My case is different. I always know when I tell a lie, am capable of imagining the cruel consequences of anybody's believing my lies, know cruelty is wrong. I could no more lie without noticing it than I could unknowingly pass a kidney stone.

If there is another life after this one, I would like very much, in the next one, to be the sort of person of whom it could truly be said, "Forgive him—he knows not what he does."

This cannot be said of me now.

The only advantage to me of knowing the difference between right and wrong, as nearly as I can tell, is that I can sometimes laugh when the Eichmanns can see nothing funny.

"You still write?" Eichmann asked me, there in Tel Aviv.

"One last project—" I said, "a command performance for the archives."

"You are a professional writer?" he said.

"Some say so," I said.

"Tell me—" he said, "do you set a certain time of day aside for writing, whether you feel like it or not—or do you wait for inspiration to strike, night or day?"

"A schedule," I said, remembering back so many years.

I got some of his respect back. "Yes, yes—" he said, nodding, "a schedule. That's what I've found, too. Sometimes I simply stare at a blank sheet of paper, but I still sit here and stare at it for the whole period I've set aside for work. Does alcohol help?"

"I think it only seems to—and only seems to for about half an hour," I said. This, too, was an opinion from my youth.

Eichmann made a joke. "Listen—" he said, "about those six million—"

"Yes?" I said.

"I could spare you a few for your book," he said. "I don't think I really need them all."

I offer this joke to history, on the assumption that no tape recorder was around. This was one of the memorable quips of the bureaucratic Genghis Khan.

It's possible that Eichmann wanted me to recognize that I had killed a lot of people, too, by the exercise of my fat mouth. But I doubt that he was that subtle a man, man of as many parts as he was. I think, if we ever got right down to it, that, out of the six million murders generally regarded as his, he wouldn't lend me so much as one. If he were to start farming out all those murders, after all, Eichmann as Eichmann's idea of Eichmann would disappear.

The guards took me away, and the only other encounter I had with the Man of the Century was in the form of a note, smuggled mysteriously from his prison in Tel Aviv to mine in Jerusalem. The note was dropped at my feet by a person unknown in the exercise yard here. I picked it up, read it, and this is what it said:

"Do you think a literary agent is absolutely necessary?" The note was signed by Eichmann.

My reply was this: "For book club and movie sales in the United States of America, absolutely."

CHAPTER THIRTY

Don Quixote . . .

WE WOULD FLY to Mexico City—Kraft, Resi, and I. That became the plan. Dr. Jones would not only provide us with transportation, he would provide us with a reception committee in Mexico City as well.

From Mexico City we would go exploring by automobile, would seek some secret village in which to spend the rest of our days.

The plan was surely as charming a daydream as I had had in many a day. And it seemed not only possible but certain that I would write again.

Shyly, I told Resi so.

She wept for joy. For real joy? Who knows. I can only guarantee that the tears were wet and salty.

"Did I have anything to do with this lovely, this heavenly miracle?" she said.

"Everything," I said, holding her close.

"No, no—very little—" she said, "but some—thank God, some. The big miracle is the talent you were born with."

"The big miracle," I said, "is your power to raise the dead."

"Love does that," she said. "And it raised me, too. How alive do you think I was—before?"

"Shall I write about it?" I said. "In our village there in Mexico, on the rim of the Pacific—is that what I should write first?"

"Yes—yes, oh yes—darling, darling," she said. "I'll take such good care of you while you do it. Will—will you have any time for me?"

"The afternoons and the evenings and the nights," I said. "That's all the time I'll be able to give you."

"Have you decided on a name yet?" she said.

"Name?" I said.

"Your new name—the name of the new writer whose beautiful works come mysteriously out of Mexico," she said. "I will be Mrs.—"

"*Señora—*" I said.

"Señora who?" she said. "Señor and Señora who?"

"Christen us," I said.

"It's too important for me to decide right away," she said.

Kraft came in at this point.

Resi asked him to suggest a pseudonym for me.

"What about Don Quixote?" he said. "That," he said to Resi, "would make you Dulcinea del Toboso, and I would sign my paintings Sancho Panza."

Dr. Jones now came in with Father Keeley. "The plane will be ready tomorrow morning," he said. "You're sure you'll be well enough to travel?"

"I'm well enough right now," I said.

"The man who'll meet you in Mexico City is Arndt Klopfer," said Jones. "Can you rememeber that?"

"The photographer?" I said.

"You know him?" said Jones.

"He took my official photograph in Berlin," I said.

"He's the biggest brewer in Mexico now," said Jones.

"For God's sake," I said. "The last I heard, his studio got hit with a five-hundred-pound bomb."

"You can't keep a good man down," said Jones. "Now then—Father Keeley and I have a special request to make of you."

"Oh?" I said.

"Tonight is the weekly meeting of the Iron Guard of the White Sons of the Constitution," said Jones. "Father Keeley and I want to stage some sort of memorial service for August Krapptauer."

"I see," I said.

"Father Keeley and I don't think we could deliver the eulogy without breaking down," said Jones. "It would be a terrible emotional ordeal for either one of us. We wonder if you, a very famous speaker, a man with a golden tongue, if I may say so—we were wondering if you would accept the honor of saying a few words."

I could hardly refuse. "Thank you, gentlemen," I said. "A eulogy?"

"Father Keeley thought up a general theme, if that would help," said Jones.

"It would help a lot, a general theme would," I said. "I could certainly use one."

Father Keeley cleared his throat. "I think the theme should be," that addled old cleric said, "His Truth Goes Marching On."

CHAPTER THIRTY-ONE

"His Truth Goes Marching On . . ."

THE IRON GUARD of the White Sons of the American Constitution assembled on ranks of folding chairs in the furnace room of Dr. Jones' basement. The guardsmen were twenty in number, ranging in age from sixteen to twenty. They were all blond. They were all over six feet tall.

They were neatly dressed, wore suits and white shirts and neck-ties. All that identified them as guardsmen was a little piece of gold ribbon run though the buttonhole of the right lapel of each.

I would not have noticed this odd detail of buttonholes on the right lapels, lapels that conventionally have no buttonholes, if Dr. Jones hadn't pointed it out to me.

"It's a way they have of identifying each other, even though the ribbon isn't worn," he said. "They can see their ranks growing," he said, "without anybody else noticing it."

"They all have to take their coats to tailors and insist on buttonholes in the right lapel?" I said.

"The mothers do it," said Father Keeley.

Keeley, Jones, Resi, and I were sitting on a raised platform facing the guardsmen, our backs to the furnace. Resi was on the platform because she had agreed to say a few words to the boys about her firsthand experiences with communism behind the Iron Curtain.

"Most tailors are Jews," said Dr. Jones. "We don't want to tip our hand."

"Besides—" said Father Keeley, "it's good for the mothers to participate."

Jones' chauffeur, The Black Fuehrer of Harlem, was now on the platform with us, hanging a big canvas sign behind us, tying its grommeted ends to steam pipes.

This is what it said:

"Get plenty of education. Lead your class in all things. Keep your body clean and strong. Keep your opinions to yourself."

"These are neighborhood kids?" I asked Jones.

"Oh, no," said Jones. "Only eight of them are even from New York City. Nine are from New Jersey, two are from Peekskill—the twins—and one comes all the way from Philadelphia."

"Every week he comes from Philadelphia?" I said.

"Where else can he get what August Krapptauer was offering here?" said Jones.

"How were they recruited?" I said.

"Through my paper," said Jones, "but they really recruited themselves. Worried, conscientious parents were writing to *The White Christian Minuteman* all the time, asking me if there wasn't some youth movement that wanted to keep the American bloodstream pure. One of the most heartbreaking letters I ever saw was from a woman in Bernardsville, New Jersey. She'd let her boy go into the Boy Scouts of America, not knowing that the true name of the B.S.A. ought to be 'the Boogies and Semites of America.' And the boy got to be an Eagle Scout, and then he went into the Army, went over to Japan, and came home with a Japanese wife."

"When August Krapptauer read that letter he cried," said Father Keeley. "That's when he knew, tired as he was, he had to get back to working with youth again."

Father Keeley called the meeting to order, had us all pray. His prayer was a conventional one, asking for courage in the face of hostile hosts.

There was one unconventional touch, however, a touch I had never heard of before, even in Germany. The Black Fuehrer stood over a kettledrum in the back of the room. The drum was muffled—muffled, as it happened, by the simulated leopard skin I had worn earlier for a bathrobe. At the end of each sentence in the prayer, the Black Fuehrer gave the muffled drum a thump.

Resi's talk on the horrors of life behind the Iron Curtain was brief and dull, and so unsatisfactory from an educational standpoint that Jones had to prompt her.

"Most devoted Communists are of Jewish or Oriental blood, aren't they?" he asked her.

"What?" she said.

"Of course they are," said Jones. "It goes without saying," he said, and he dismissed her rather curtly.

Where was George Kraft? He was sitting in the audience, in the very last row, next to the muffled kettledrum.

Jones introduced me next, introduced me as a man who needed no introduction. He said I wasn't to start talking yet, because he had a surprise for me.

He certainly did.

The Black Fuehrer left his drum, went to a rheostat by the light switch, and dimmed the lights gradually as Jones talked.

Jones told, in the gathering darkness, of the intellectual and moral climate in America during the Second World War. He told of how patriotic, thoughtful white men were persecuted for their ideals, how, finally, almost all the American patriots were rotting in federal dungeons.

"Nowhere could an American find the truth," he said.

The room was pitch dark now.

"Almost nowhere," said Jones in the dark. "If a man was fortunate enough to have a short-wave radio," he said, "there was still one fountainhead of truth—just one."

And then, in the darkness, there was the crackle and susurrus of short-wave static, a fragment of French, a fragment of German, a fragment of Brahms' First Symphony, as though played on kazoos—and then, loud and clear—

This is Howard W. Campbell, Jr., one of the few remaining free Americans, speaking to you from free Berlin. I wish to welcome my countrymen, which is to say the native white gentiles, of the 106th Division, taking up positions before St. Vith tonight. To the parents of the boys in this green division, may I say that the area is presently a quiet one. The 442nd and 444th Regiments are one line—the 423rd in reserve.

There is a fine article in the current *Reader's Digest* with the title, "There are No Atheists in Foxholes." I should like to expand this theme a little and tell you that, even though this is a war inspired by the Jews, a war that only the Jews can win, there are no Jews in foxholes, either. The riflemen in the 106th can tell you that. The Jews are all too busy counting merchandise in the Quartermaster Corps or money in the Finance Corps or selling black-market cigarettes and nylons in Paris to ever come closer to the front than a hundred miles.

You folks at home, you parents and relatives of boys at the front—I want you to think of all the Jews you know. I want you to think hard about them.

Now then—let me ask you, is the war making them richer or

poorer? Do they eat better or worse than you under supposed rationing? Do they dress better or worse than you do? Do they seem to have more or less gasoline than you do?

I already know what the answers to all those questions are, and so will you, if you'll open your eyes and think hard for a minute.

Now let me ask you this:

Do you know of a single Jewish family that has received a telegram from Washington, once the capital of a free people—do you know of a single Jewish family that has received a telegram from Washington that begins, "The Secretary of War desires me to express his deep regret that your son . . ."

And so on.

There were fifteen minutes of Howard W. Campbell, Jr., the free American, there in basement darkness. I do not mean to suppress my infamy with a casual "and so on."

The Haifa Institute for the Documentation of War Criminals has recordings of every broadcast Howard W. Campbell, Jr., ever made. If someone wants to go over those broadcasts, wants to cull from them the very worst things I said, I have no objection to those culls being attached to this account as an appendix.

I can hardly deny that I said them. All I can say is that I didn't believe them, that I knew full well what ignorant, destructive, obscenely jocular things I was saying.

The experience of sitting there in the dark, hearing the things I'd said, didn't shock me. It might be helpful in my defense to say that I broke into a cold sweat, or some such nonsense. But I've always known what I did. I've always been able to live with what I did. How? Through that simple and widespread boon to modern mankind—schizophrenia.

There was one adventure in the dark worth reporting, though. Somebody put a note in my pocket, did it with intentional clumsiness, so that I would know the note was there.

When the light came on again, I could not guess who had given me the note.

I delivered my eulogy of August Krapptauer, saying, incidentally, what I pretty much believe, that Krapptauer's sort of truth would probably be with mankind forever, as long as there were men and women around who listened to their hearts instead of their minds.

I got a nice round of applause from the audience, and a drumroll from the Black Fuehrer.

I went into the lavatory to read the note.

The note was printed on lined paper torn from a small spiral notebook. This is what it said:

"Coal-bin door unlocked. Leave at once. I am waiting for you in vacant store directly across street. Urgent. Your life in danger. Eat this."

It was signed by my Blue Fairy Godmother, by Colonel Frank Wirtanen.

CHAPTER THIRTY-TWO

Rosenfeld . . .

MY LAWYER here in Jerusalem, Mr. Alvin Dobrowitz, has told me that I would surely win my case if I could produce one witness who had seen me in the company of the man known to me as Colonel Frank Wirtanen.

I met Wirtanen three times: before the war, immediately after the war, and finally, in the back of a vacant store across the street from the residence of The Reverend Doctor Lionel J. D. Jones, D.D.S., D.D. Only at the first meeting, the meeting on the park bench, did anyone see us together. And those who saw us were no more likely to fix us in their memories than were the squirrels and birds.

The second time I met him was in Wiesbaden, Germany, in the dining hall of what had once been an officers' candidate school of the Engineers Corps of the *Wehrmacht.* There was a great mural on the wall of that dining hall, a tank coming down a lovely, winding country lane. The sun was shining in the mural. The sky was clear. This bucolic scene was about to be shattered.

In a thicket, in the foreground of the mural, was a merry little band of steel-helmeted Robin Hoods, engineers whose latest prank was to mine the lane and to implement the impending merriment with an anti-tank gun and a light machine gun.

They were so happy.

How did I get to Wiesbaden?

I was taken from a Third Army prisoner-of-war pen near Ohrdruf on April 15, three days after my capture by Lieutenant Bernard B. O'Hare.

I was driven to Wiesbaden in a jeep, was guarded by a first lieutenant whose name is unknown to me. We didn't talk much. I did not interest him. He spent the entire trip in a slow-smoldering rage about something that had nothing to do with me. Had he been slighted, insulted, cheated, maligned, grievously misunderstood? I don't know.

At any rate, I don't think he would be much help as a witness. He was carrying out orders that bored him. He asked his way to the camp, and then to the dining hall. He left me at the door of the dining hall, told me to go inside and wait. And then he drove off, leaving me unguarded.

I went inside, though I might easily have wandered into the countryside again.

Inside that melancholy barn, all alone, seated on a table under the mural, was my Blue Fairy Godmother.

Wirtanen was wearing the uniform of an American soldier—zippered jacket; olive-drab trousers and shirt, the shirt open at the neck; combat boots. He had no weapon. Neither did he wear any symbol of rank or unit.

He was a short-legged man. When I saw him sitting there on the table, he was swinging his feet, and his feet were far off the floor. He must have been at least fifty-five then, seven years older than when last I'd seen him. He was bald, had put on weight.

Colonel Frank Wirtanen had the impudent, pink-baby look that victory and an American combat uniform seemed to produce in so many older men.

He beamed at me and he shook my hand warmly, and he said, "Well—what did you think of *that* war, Campbell?"

"I would just as soon have stayed out of it," I said.

"Congratulations," he said. "You lived through it, anyway. A lot of people didn't, you know."

"I know," I said. "My wife, for instance."

"Sorry about that," he said.

"You knew about it?" I said.

"I found out she was missing the same day you did," he said.

"How?" I said.

"From you," he said. "That was one of the pieces of information you broadcast that night."

This news, that I had broadcast the coded announcement of my Helga's disappearance, broadcast it without even knowing what I was doing, somehow upset me more than anything in the whole adventure. It upsets me even now. Why, I don't know.

It represented, I suppose, a wider separation of my several selves than even I can bear to think about.

At that climactic moment in my life, when I had to suppose that my Helga was dead, I would have liked to mourn as an agonized soul, indivisible. But no. One part of me told the world of the tragedy in code. The rest of me did not even know that the announcement was being made.

"That was vital military information? That had to be got out of Germany at the risk of my neck?" I said to Wirtanen.

"Certainly," he said. "The instant we got it, we began to act."

"To act?" I said, mystified. "To act how?"

"To find a replacement for you," said Wirtanen. "We thought you'd kill yourself before the sun came up again."

"I should have," I said.

"I'm damn glad you didn't," he said.

"I'm damn sorry I didn't," I said. "You would think that a man who's spent as much time in the theater as I have would know when the proper time came for the hero to die—if he was to be a hero." I snapped my fingers softly. "There goes the whole play about Helga and me, 'Nation of Two,'" I said, "because I missed my cue for the great suicide scene."

"I don't admire suicide," said Wirtanen.

"I admire form," I said. "I admire things with a beginning, a middle, an end—and, whenever possible, a moral, too."

"There's a chance she's still alive, I guess," said Wirtanen.

"A loose end," I said. "An irrelevancy. The play is over."

"You said something about a moral?" he said.

"If I'd killed myself when you expected me to kill myself," I said, "maybe a moral would have occurred to you."

"I'll have to think—" he said.

"Take your time," I said.

"I'm not used to things having form—or morals, either," he said. "If you'd died, I probably would have said something like, 'Goddamn, now what'll we do?' A moral? It's a big enough job just burying the dead, without trying to draw a moral from each death," he said. "Half the dead don't even have names. I might have said you were a good soldier."

"Was I?" I said.

"Of all the agents who were my dream children, so to speak, you were the only one who got clear through the war both reliable and alive," he said. "I did a little morbid arithmetic last night, Campbell—calculated that you, by being neither incompetent nor dead, were one in 'forty-two."

"What about the people who fed me information?" I said.

"Dead, all dead," he said. "Every one of them a woman, by the way. Seven of them, in all—each one of them, before she was caught, living only to transmit information to you. Think of it Campbell—seven women you satisfied again and again and again—and they finally died for the satisfaction that was yours to give them. And not one of them betrayed you, either, when she was caught. Think of that, too."

"I can't say you've relieved any shortage of things to think about," I said to Wirtanen. "I don't mean to diminish your stature as a teacher and philosopher, but I had things to think about even before this happy reunion. So what happens to me next?"

"You've already disappeared again," he said. "Third Army's been relieved of you, and there'll be no records here to show that you ever arrived." He spread his hands. "Where would you like to go from here, and who would you like to be?"

"I don't suppose there's a hero's welcome awaiting me anywhere," I said.

"Hardly," he said.

"Any news of my parents?" I said.

"I'm sorry to tell you—" he said, "they died four months ago."

"Both?" I said.

"Your father first—your mother twenty-four hours later. Heart both times," he said.

I cried a little about that, shook my head. "Nobody told them what I was really doing?" I said.

"Our radio station in the heart of Berlin was worth more than the peace of mind of two old people," he said.

"I wonder," I said.

"You're entitled to wonder," he said. "I'm not."

"How many people knew what I was doing?" I said.

"The good things or the bad things?" he said.

"The good," I said.

"Three of us," he said.

"That's all?" I said.

"That's a lot," he said. "Too many, really. There was me, there was General Donovan, and one other."

"Three people in all the world knew me for what I was—" I said. "And all the rest—" I shrugged.

"They knew you for what you were, too," he said abruptly.

"That wasn't me," I said, startled by his sharpness.

"Whoever it was—" said Wirtanen, "he was one of the most vicious sons of bitches who ever lived."

I was amazed. Wirtanen was sincerely bitter.

"You give me hell for that—knowing what you do?" I said. "How else could I have survived?"

"That was your problem," he said. "Very few men could have solved it as thoroughly as you did."

"You think I was a Nazi?" I said.

"Certainly you were," he said. "How else could a responsible historian classify you? Let me ask you a question—"

"Ask away," I said.

"If Germany had won, had conquered the world—" he stopped, cocked his head. "You must be way ahead of me. You must know what the question is."

"How would I have lived?" I said. "What would I have felt? What would I have done?"

"Exactly," he said. "You must have thought about it, with an imagination like yours."

"My imagination isn't what it used to be," I said. "One of the first things I discovered when I became an agent was that I couldn't afford an imagination any more."

"No answer to my question?" he said.

"Now is as good a time as any to see if I've got any imagination left," I said. "Give me a minute or two—"

"Take all the time you want," he said.

So I projected myself into the situation he described, and what was left of my imagination gave me a corrosively cynical answer. "There is every chance," I said, "that I would have become a sort of Nazi Edgar Guest, writing a daily column of optimistic doggerel for daily papers around the world. And, as senility set in—the sunset of life, as they say—I might even come to believe what my couplets said: that everything was probably all for the best."

I shrugged. "Would I have shot anybody? I doubt it. Would I have organized a bomb plot? That's more of a possibility; but I've heard a lot of bombs go off in my time, and they never impressed me much as a way to get things done. Only one thing can I guarantee you: I would never have written a play again. That skill, such as it was, is lost.

"The only chance of my doing something really violent in favor of truth or justice or what have you," I said to my Blue Fairy Godmother, "would lie in my going homicidally insane. That could happen. In the situation you suggest, I might suddenly run amok with a deadly weapon down a peaceful street on an ordinary day. But whether the killing I did would improve the world much would be a matter of dumb luck, pure and simple.

"Have I answered your question honestly enough for you?" I asked him.

"Yes, thank you," he said.

"Classify me as a Nazi," I said tiredly. "Classify away. Hang me, if you think it would tend to raise the general level of morality. This life is no great treasure. I have no postwar plans."

"I only want you to understand how little we can do for you," he said. "I see you do understand."

"How little?" I said.

"A false identity, a few red herrings, transportation to wherever you might conceivably start a new life—" he said. "Some cash. Not much, but some."

"Cash?" I said. "How was the cash value of my services arrived at?"

"A matter of custom," he said, "a custom going back to at least the Civil War."

"Oh?" I said.

"Private's pay," he said. "On my say-so, you're entitled to it for the period from when we met in the Tiergarten to the present."

"That's very generous," I said.

"Generosity doesn't amount to much in this business," he said. "The really good agents aren't interested in money at all. Would it make any difference to you if we gave you the back pay of a brigadier general?"

"No," I said.

"Or if we paid you nothing at all?"

"No difference," I said.

"It's almost never money," he said. "Or patriotism, either."

"What is it, then?" I said.

"Each person has to answer that question for himself—" said Wirtanen. "Generally spealing, espionage offers each spy an opportunity to go crazy in a way he finds irresistible."

"Interesting," I said emptily.

He clapped his hands to break the mood. "Now then—" he said, "about transportation: where to?"

"Tahiti?" I said.

"If you say so," he said. "I suggest New York. You can lose yourself there without any trouble, and there's plenty of work, if you want it."

"All right—New York," I said.

"Let's get your passport picture taken. You'll be on a plane out of here inside of three hours," he said.

We crossed the deserted parade ground together, dust devils spinning here and there. It was my fancy to think of the dust devils as the spooks of former cadets at the school, killed in war, returning now to whirl and dance on the parade ground alone, to dance in as unmilitary a fashion as they damn well pleased.

"When I told you there were only three people who knew about your coded broadcasts—" said Wirtanen.

"What about it?" I said.

"You didn't ask who the third one was," he said.

"Would it be anybody I'd ever heard of?" I said.

"Yes," he said. "He's dead now, I'm sorry to say. You used to attack him regularly in your broadcasts."

"Oh?" I said.

"The man you called Frank Delano Rosenfeld," said Wirtanen. "He used to listen to you gleefully every night."

CHAPTER THIRTY-THREE

Communism Rears Its Head . . .

THE THIRD TIME I met my Blue Fairy Godmother, and the last time, from all indications, was, as I have said, in a vacant shop across the street from the house of Jones, across the street from where Resi, George Kraft and I were hiding.

I took my time about going into that dark place, expecting, with reason, to find anything from an American Legion color guard to a platoon of Israeli paratroopers waiting to capture me inside.

I had a pistol with me, one of the Iron Guard's Lugers, chambered for twenty-two's. I had it not in my pocket but in the open, loaded and cocked, ready to go. I scouted the front of the shop without showing myself. The front was dark. And then I approached the back in short rushes, from cluster to cluster of garbage cans.

Anybody trying to jump me, to jump Howard W. Campbell, Jr., would have been filled with little holes, as though by a sewing machine. And I must say that I came to love the infantry, anybody's infantry, in that series of rushes and taking cover.

Man, I think, is an infantry animal.

There was a light in the back of the shop. I looked through a window and saw a scene of great serenity. Colonel Frank Wirtanen, my Blue Fairy Godmother, was sitting on a table again, waiting for me again.

He was an old, old man now, as sleek and hairless as Buddha.

I went in.

"I thought surely you would have retired by now," I said.

"I did—" he said, "eight years ago. Built a house on a lake in Maine with an axe and an adze and my own two hands. I was called out of retirement as a specialist."

"In what?" I said.

"In you," he said.

"Why the sudden interest in me?" I said.

"That's what I'm supposed to find out," he said.

"No mystery why the Israelis would want me," I said.

"I agree," he said. "But there's a lot of mystery about why the Russians should think you were such a fat prize."

"Russians?" I said. "What Russians?"

"The girl, Resi Noth—and the old man, the painter, the one called George Kraft," said Wirtanen. "They're both communist agents. We've been watching the one who calls himself Kraft now since 1941. We made it easy for the girl to get into the country just to find out what she hoped to do."

CHAPTER THIRTY-FOUR

Alles Kaput . . .

I SAT wretchedly on a packing case. "With a few well-chosen words," I said, "you've wiped me out. How much poorer I am in this minute than I was in the minute before!

"Friend, dream, and mistress—" I said, "*alles kaput.*"

"You've still got the friend," said Wirtanen.

"What do you mean by that?" I said.

"He's like you," said Wirtanen. "He can be many things at once—all sincerely." He smiled. "It's a gift."

"What was he planning for me?" I said.

"He wanted to uproot you from this country, get you to another one, where you could be kidnaped with fewer international complications. He tipped off Jones as to where and who you were, got O'Hare and other patriots all stirred up about you again—all as part of a scheme to pull up your roots."

"Mexico—that was the dream he gave me," I said.

"I know," said Wirtanen. "There's a plane waiting for you in Mexico City right now. If you were to fly down there, you wouldn't spend more than two minutes on the ground. Off you'd go again, bound for Moscow in the latest jet, all expenses paid."

"Dr. Jones is in on this, too?" I said.

"No," said Wirtanen. "He's got your best interests at heart. He's one of the few men you can trust."

"Why should they want me in Moscow?" I said. "What do the Russians want with me—with such a moldy old piece of surplus from World War Two?"

"They want to exhibit you to the world as a prime example of the sort of Fascist war criminal this country shelters," said Wirtanen. "They also hope that you will confess to all sorts of collusion between Americans and Nazis at the start of the Nazi regime."

"Why would I confess such a thing?" I said. "What did they plan to threaten me with?"

"That's simple," said Wirtanen. "That's obvious."

"Torture?" I said.

"Probably not," said Wirtanen. "Just death."

"I don't fear it," I said.

"Oh, it wouldn't be for you," said Wirtanen.

"For whom, then?" I said.

"For the girl you love, for the girl who loves you—" said Wirtanen. "The death, in case you were uncooperative, would be for little Resi Noth."

CHAPTER THIRTY-FIVE

Forty Rubles Extra . . .

"HER MISSION was to make me love her?" I said.

"Yes," said Wirtanen.

"She did it very well—" I said sadly, "not that it was hard to do."

"Sorry to have such news for you," said Wirtanen.

"It clears up some mysteries—not that I wanted them cleared up," I said. "Do you know what she had in her suitcase?"

"Your collected works?" he said.

"You knew about that, too? To think they would go to such pains—to give her props like those! How did they know where to look for those manuscripts?"

"They weren't in Berlin. They were neatly stored in Moscow," said Wirtanen.

"How did they get there?" I said.

"They were the main evidence in the trial of Stepan Bodovskov," he said.

"Who?" I said.

"Stepan Bodovskov was a corporal, an interpreter, with the first Russian troops to enter Berlin," said Wirtanen. "He found the trunk containing your writings in a theater loft. He took the trunk for booty."

"Some booty," I said.

"It turned out to be remarkably fine booty," said Wirtanen. "Bodovskov was fluent in German. He went through the contents of the trunk, and he decided that he had a trunkful of instant career.

"He started modestly, translating a few of your poems into Russian, and sending them off to a literary magazine. They were published and praised.

"Bodovskov next tried a play," said Wirtanen.

"Which one?" I said.

"'The Goblet,'" said Wirtanen. "Bodovskov translated that into Russian, and he had himself a villa on the Black Sea practically before they'd taken the sandbags down from the windows of the Kremlin."

"It was produced?" I said.

"Not only was it produced," said Wirtanen, "it continues to be produced all over Russia by both amateurs and professionals. 'The Goblet' is the 'Charley's Aunt' of contemporary Russian theater. You're more alive than you thought, Campbell."

"My truth goes marching on," I murmured.

"What?" said Wirtanen.

"I can't even tell you what the plot of 'The Goblet' is," I said.

So Wirtanen told it to me. "A blindingly pure young maiden," he said, "guards the Holy Grail. She will surrender it only to a knight who is as pure as herself. Such a knight comes along, and is pure enough to win the Grail.

"By winning it, he causes the girl to fall in love with him, and he falls in love with her," said Wirtanen. "Do I really have to tell you, the author, the rest?"

"It—it's as though Bodovskov really did write it—" I said, "as though I'm hearing it for the first time."

"The knight and the girl—" said Wirtanen, continuing the tale, "they begin to have impure thoughts about each other, tending, involuntarily, to disqualify themselves from any association with the Grail. The heroine urges the hero to flee with the Grail, before he becomes unworthy of it. The hero vows to flee without the Grail, leaving the heroine worthy of continuing to guard it.

"The hero makes their decision for them," said Wirtanen, "since they have both become impure in thought. The Holy Grail disappears. And, stunned by this unanswerable proof of their depravity, the two lovers confirm what they firmly believe to be their damnation with a tender night of love.

"The next morning, confident of hell-fire, they promise to give each other so much joy in life that hell-fire will be a very cheap price to pay. The Holy Grail thereupon appears to them, signifying that Heaven does not despise love like theirs. And then the Grail goes away again, forever, leaving the hero and the heroine to live happily ever after."

"My God—I *did* write that, didn't I?" I said.

"Stalin was crazy about it," said Wirtanen.

"And the other plays—?" I said.

"All produced, all well-received," said Wirtanen.

"But 'The Goblet' was Bodovskov's big hit?" I said.

"The book was the biggest hit of all," said Wirtanen.

"Bodovskov wrote a book?" I said.

"You wrote a book," said Wirtanen.

"I never did," I said.

"*Memoirs of a Monogamous Casanova*?" said Wirtanen.

"It was unprintable!" I said.

"A publishing house in Budapest will be amazed to hear that," said Wirtanen. "I'd guess they've printed something like a half-million copies."

"The communists let a book like that be published openly?" I said.

"*Memoirs of a Monogamous Casanova* is a curious little chapter in Russian history," said Wirtanen. "It could hardly be published with official approval in Russia—and yet, it was such an attractive, strangely moral piece of pornography, so ideal for a nation suffering from shortages of everything but men and women, that presses in Budapest were somehow encouraged to start printing it—and those presses have, somehow, never been ordered to stop." Wirtanen winked at me. "One of the few sly, playful, harmless crimes a Russian can commit at no risk to himself is smuggling home a copy of *Memoirs of a Monogamous Casanova*. And for whom does he smuggle it? To whom is he going to show this hot stuff? To that salty old crony, his wife.

"For years," said Wirtanen, "there was only a Russian edition. But now, it is available in Hungarian, Rumanian, Latvian, Estonian, and, most marvelous of all, German again."

"Bodovskov gets credit as the author?" I said.

"It's common knowledge that Bodovskov wrote it, though the book carries no credits—publisher, author, and illustrator supposedly unknown."

"Illustrator?" I said, harrowed by the idea of pictures of Helga and me cavorting in the nude.

"Fourteen plates in lifelike color—" said Wirtanen, "forty rubles extra."

CHAPTER THIRTY-SIX

Everything But the Squeals . . .

"IF ONLY it weren't illustrated!" I said to Wirtanen angrily.

"That makes a difference?" he said.

"It's a mutilation!" I said. "The pictures are bound to mutilate the words. Those words weren't meant to have pictures with them! With pictures, they aren't the same words!"

He shrugged. "It's pretty much out of your control, I'm afraid," he said, "unless you want to declare war on Russia."

I closed my eyes wincingly. "What is it they say in the Chicago Stockyards about what they do to a pig?"

"I don't know," said Wirtanen.

"They boast that they find a use for everything about a pig but his squeal," I said.

"So?" said Wirtanen.

"That's how I feel right now—" I said, "like a pig that's been taken apart, who's had experts find a use for every part. By God—I think they even found a use for my squeal! The part of me that wanted to tell the truth got turned into an expert liar! The lover in me got turned into a pornographer! The artist in me got turned into ugliness such as the world has rarely seen before.

"Even my most cherished memories have now been converted into catfood, glue and liverwurst!" I said.

"Which memories are those?" said Wirtanen.

"Of Helga—my Helga," I said, and I wept. "Resi killed those, in the interests of the Soviet Union. She made me faithless to those memories, and they can never be the same again."

I opened my eyes. "F—— all," I said quietly. "I suppose the pigs and I should feel honored by those who proved our usefulness. I'm glad about one thing—"

"Oh?" said Wirtanen.

"I'm glad about Bodovskov," I said. "I'm glad somebody got to live like an artist with what I once had. You said he was arrested and tried?"

"And shot," said Wirtanen.

"For plagiarism?" I said.

"For originality," said Wirtanen. "Plagiarism is the silliest of misdemeanors. What harm is there in writing what's already been written? Real originality is a capital crime, often calling for cruel and unusual punishment in advance of the *coup de grâce*."

"I don't understand," I said.

"Your friend, Kraft-Potapov, realized that you were the author of a lot of things Bodovskov claimed to have written," said Wirtanen. "He reported the facts to Moscow. Bodovskov's villa was raided. The magic trunk containing your writings was discovered under straw in the loft in his stable."

"So—?" I said.

"Every word by you in that trunk had been published," said Wirtanen.

"And—?" I said.

"Bodovskov had begun to replenish the trunk with magic of his own," said Wirtanen. "The police found a two-thousand-page satire on the Red Army, written in a style distinctly un-Bodovskovian. For that un-Bodovskovian behavior, Bodovskov was shot.

"But enough of the past!" said Wirtanen. "Listen to what I've got to tell you about the future. In about half an hour," he said, looking at his watch, "Jones' house is going to be raided. The place is surrounded now. I wanted you out of there, since it's going to be a complicated enough mess as it is."

"Where do you suggest I go?" I said.

"Don't go back to your flat," he said. "Patriots have taken the place apart. They'd probably take you apart, too, if they caught you there."

"What's going to happen to Resi?" I said.

"Deportation is all," said Wirtanen. "She hasn't committed any crimes."

"And Kraft?" I said.

"A good long stretch in prison," he said. "That's no shame. I think he'd rather go to prison than home anyway.

"The Reverend Lionel J. D. Jones, D.D.S., D.D.," said Wirtanen, "will go back to prison for illegal possession of firearms and whatever else of a straightforward criminal nature we can pin on him. Nothing is planned for Father Keeley, so I imagine he'll drift back to Skid Row again. The Black Fuehrer will be set adrift again, too."

"And the Iron Guardsmen?" I said.

"The Iron Guardsmen of the White Sons of the American Constitution," said Wirtanen, "are going to get an impressive lecture on the illegality in this country of private armies, murder, mayhem, riots, treason, and violent overthrow of the government. They'll be sent home to educate their parents, if such a thing is possible."

He looked at his watch again. "You'd better go now—get clear out of the neighborhood."

"Can I ask who your agent in Jones' house is?" I said. "Who was it that slipped the note into my pocket, telling me to come here?"

"You can ask," said Wirtanen, "but you must surely know I won't tell you."

"You don't trust me to that extent?" I said.

"How could I ever trust a man who's been as good a spy as you have?" said Wirtanen. "Hmm?"

CHAPTER THIRTY-SEVEN

Dat Old Golden Rule . . .

I LEFT WIRTANEN.

But I hadn't taken many steps before I understood that the only place I wanted to be was back in Jones' cellar with my mistress and my best friend.

I knew them for what they were, but the fact remained that they were all I had.

I returned by the same route over which I had fled, went in through Jones' coalbin door.

Resi, Father Keeley, and the Black Fuehrer were playing cards when I got back.

Nobody had missed me.

The Iron Guard of the White Sons of the American Constitution was having a class in flag courtesy in the furnace room, a class conducted by one of its own members.

Jones had gone upstairs to write, to create.

Kraft, the Russian Master Spy, was reading a copy of *Life* that had a portrait of Werner von Braun on the cover. Kraft had the magazine open to the center spread, a panorama of a swamp in the Age of Reptiles.

A small radio was playing. It announced a song. The title of the song fixed itself in my mind. This is no miracle of total recall, my remembering the title. The title was apt for the moment—for almost any moment, actually. The title was "Dat Old Golden Rule."

At my request, the Haifa Institute for the Documentation of War Criminals has run down the lyric of that song for me. The lyric is as follows:

> Oh, baby, baby, baby,
> Why do you break my heart this way?
> You say you want to go steady,
> But then all you do is stray.
> I'm so confused,

I'm not amused,
You make me feel like such a fool.
You smile and lie,
You make me cry.
Why don't you learn dat old Golden Rule?

"What's the game?" I said to the card players.

"Old Maid," said Father Keeley. He was taking the game seriously. He wanted to win, and I saw that he had the queen of spades, the Old Maid, in his hand.

It might make me seem more human at this point, which is to say more sympathetic, if I were to declare that I itched and blinked and nearly swooned with a feeling of unreality.

Sorry.

Not so.

I confess to a ghastly lack in myself. Anything I see or hear or feel or taste or smell is real to me. I am so much a credulous plaything of my senses that nothing is unreal to me. This armor-plated credulity has been continent even in times when I was struck on the head or drunk or, in one freakish adventure that need not concern this accounting, even under the influence of cocaine.

There in Jones' basement, Kraft showed me the picture of von Braun on the cover of *Life*, asked me if I knew him.

"Von Braun?" I said. "The Thomas Jefferson of the Space Age? Sure. The Baron danced with my wife once at a birthday party in Hamburg for General Walter Dornberger."

"Good dancer?" said Kraft.

"Sort of Mickey Mouse dancing—" I said, "the way all the big Nazis danced, if they had to dance."

"You think he'd recognize you now?" said Kraft.

"I know he would," I said. "I ran into him on Fifty-second Street about a month ago, and he called me by name. He was very shocked to see me in such reduced circumstances. He said he knew a lot of people in the public relations business, and he offered to talk to them about giving me a job."

"You'd be good at public relations," said Kraft.

"I certainly don't have any powerful convictions to get in the way of a client's message," I said.

The game of Old Maid broke up, with Father Keeley the loser, with that pathetic old virgin still stuck with the queen of spades.

"Well," said Keeley, as though he'd won much in the past, as though a rich future were still his, "you can't win them all."

He and the Black Fuehrer went upstairs, pausing each few steps to count to twenty.

And then Resi, Kraft-Potapov and I were alone.

Resi came over to me, put her arm around my waist, laid her cheek against my chest. "Just think, darling—" she said.

"Hmm?" I said.

"Tomorrow we'll be in Mexico," she said.

"Um," I said.

"You seem worried," she said.

"Me worry?" I said.

"Preoccupied," she said.

"Do I look preoccupied to you?" I said to Kraft. He was studying the picture of the swamp again.

"No," he said.

"My good old normal self," I said.

Kraft pointed to a pterodactyl that was winging over the swamp. "Who would think a thing like that could fly?" he said.

"Who would ever think that a ramshackle old fart like me would win the heart of such a beautiful girl, and have such a talented, loyal friend besides?" I said.

"I find it very easy to love you," said Resi. "I always have."

"I was just thinking—" I said.

"Tell me your thoughts," said Resi.

"Maybe Mexico isn't exactly what we want," I said.

"We can always move on," said Kraft.

"Maybe—there at the Mexico City airport—" I said, "maybe we could just get right on a jet—"

Kraft put his magazine down. "And go where?" he said.

"I don't know," I said. "Just go somewhere very fast. I suppose it's the idea of movement that excites me; I've been sitting still so long."

"Um," said Kraft.

"Moscow, maybe," I said.

"What?" said Kraft incredulously.

"Moscow," I said. "I'd like very much to see Moscow."

"That's a novel idea," said Kraft.

"You don't like it?" I said.

"I—I'll have to think about it," he said.

Resi started to move away from me, but I held her tight. "You think about it, too," I said to her.

"If you want me to," she said faintly.

"Heaven!" I said, and I jiggled her to make her bubble. "The more I think about it, the more attractive it becomes," I said. "If we only stayed in Mexico City for two minutes between planes, that would be long enough for me."

Kraft stood up, exercising his fingers elaborately. "This is a joke?" he said.

"Is it?" I said. "An old friend like you should be able to tell if I'm joking or not."

"You must be joking," he said. "What is there in Moscow that could interest you?"

"I'd try to locate an old friend of mine," I said.

"I didn't know you had a friend in Moscow," he said.

"I don't know that he's in Moscow—just somewhere in Russia," I said. "I'd have to make inquiries."

"What's his name?" said Kraft.

"Stepan Bodovskov—" I said, "the writer."

"Oh," said Kraft. He sat down again, picked up the magazine again.

"You've heard of him?" I said.

"No," he said.

"What about Colonel Iona Potapov?" I said.

Resi twisted away from me, stood with her back to the farthest wall.

"You know Potapov?" I asked her.

"No," she said.

"You?" I asked Kraft.

"No," he said. "Why don't you tell me about him?"

"He's a communist agent," I said. "He's trying to get me to Mexico City so I can be kidnaped and flown to Moscow for trial."

"No!" said Resi.

"Shut up!" Kraft said to her. He stood, threw the magazine aside. He went for a small pistol he had in his pocket, but I got the drop on him with the Luger.

I made him throw the pistol on the floor.

"Look at us—" he said wonderingly, as though he were an innocent bystander, "cowboys and Indians."

"Howard—" said Resi.

"Don't say a word," Kraft warned her.

"Darling—" said Resi tearfully, "the dream about Mexico—I thought it was really coming true! We were *all* going to escape!" She opened her arms. "Tomorrow—" she said weakly.

"Tomorrow—" she whispered again.

And then she went to Kraft, as though she wanted to claw him. But there was no strength in her hands. The hold they took on Kraft was feeble.

"We were all going to be born anew," she said to him brokenly. "You, too—you, too. Didn't—didn't you want that for yourself? How could you speak so warmly about the new lives we would have, and still not want them?"

Kraft did not reply.

Resi turned to me. "I am a communist agent—yes. And so is he. He *is* Colonel Iona Potapov. And our mission *was* to get you to Moscow. But I wasn't going to go through with it—because I love you, because the love you gave me was the only love I've ever had, the only love I ever will have.

"I told you I wasn't going through with it, didn't I?" she said to Kraft.

"She told me," said Kraft.

"And he agreed with me," said Resi. "And he came up with this dream of Mexico, where we would *all* get out of the trap—live happily ever after."

"How did you find out?" Kraft asked me.

"American agents followed the scheme all the way," I said. "This place is surrounded now. You're cooked."

CHAPTER THIRTY-EIGHT

Ah, Sweet Mystery of Life . . .

ABOUT THE RAID—

About Resi Noth—

About how she died—

About how she died in my arms, there in the basement of the Reverend Lionel J. D. Jones, D.D.S., D.D.—

It was wholly unexpected.

Resi seemed so in favor of life, so right for life, that the possibility of her preferring death did not occur to me.

I was sufficiently a man of the world, or sufficiently unimaginative—take your choice—to think that a girl that young and pretty and clever would have an entertaining time of it, no matter where fate and politics shoved her next. And, as I pointed out to her, nothing worse than deportation was in store for her.

"Nothing worse than that?" she said.

"That's all," I said. "I doubt that you'll even have to pay for your passage back."

"You're not sorry to see me go?" she said.

"Certainly, I'm sorry," I said. "But there's nothing I can do to keep you with me. Any minute now people are going to come in here and arrest you. You don't expect me to fight them, do you?"

"You won't fight them?" she said.

"Of course not," I said. "What chance would I have?"

"That matters?" she said.

"You mean—" I said, "why don't I die for love, like a knight in a Howard W. Campbell, Jr., play?"

"That's exactly what I mean," she said. "Why don't we die together, right here and now?"

I laughed. "Resi, darling—" I said, "you have a full life ahead of you."

"I have a full life behind me—" she said, "all in those few sweet hours with you."

"That sounds like a line I might have written as a young man," I said.

"It is a line you wrote as a young man," she said.

"Foolish young man," I said.

"I adore that young man," she said.

"When was it you fell in love with him?" I said. "As a child?"

"As a child—and then as a woman," she said. "When they gave me all the things you'd written, told me to study them, that's when I fell in love as a woman."

"I'm sorry—I can't congratulate you on your literary tastes," I said.

"You no longer believe that love is the only thing to live for?" she said.

"No," I said.

"Then tell me what to live for—anything at all," she said beseechingly. "It doesn't have to be love. Anything at all!" She gestured at objects around the shabby room, dramatizing exquisitely my own sense of the world's being a junk shop. "I'll live for that chair, that picture, that furnace pipe, that couch, that crack in the wall! Tell me to live for it, and I will!" she cried.

It was now me that her strengthless hands laid hold of. She closed her eyes, wept. "It doesn't have to be love," she whispered. "Just tell me what it should be."

"Resi—" I said gently.

"*Tell me*!" she said, and strength came into her hands, did tender violence to my clothes.

"I'm an old man—" I said helplessly. It was a coward's lie. I am not an old man.

"All right, old man—tell me what to live for," she said. "Tell me what you live for, so I can live for it, too—here or ten thousand kilometers from here! Tell me why you want to go on being alive, so I can go on wanting to be alive, too!"

And then the raiders broke in.

The forces of law and order plunged in through every door, waving guns, blowing whistles, shining dazzling lights where there was plenty of light already.

There was a small army of them, and they exclaimed over all the melodramatically evil goodies in the cellar. They exclaimed like children around a Christmas tree.

A dozen of them, all young, apple-cheeked and virtuous,

surrounded Resi, Kraft-Potapov and me, took my Luger away from me, turned us into rag dolls as they ransacked us for other weapons.

More raiders came down the stairs prodding the Reverend Dr. Lionel J. D. Jones, the Black Fuehrer, and Father Keeley before them.

Dr. Jones stopped halfway down the stairs, confronted his tormentors. "All I've done," he said majestically, "is do what you people should be doing."

"What should we be doing?" said a G-man. He was obviously in command of the raid.

"Protecting the Republic," said Jones. "Why bother us? Everything we do is to make the country stronger! Join with us, and let's go after the people who are trying to make it weaker!"

"Who's that?" said the G-man.

"I have to tell you?" said Jones. "Haven't you even found that out in the course of your work? The Jews! The Catholics! The Negroes! The Orientals! The Unitarians! The foreign-born, who don't have any understanding of democracy, who play right into the hands of the socialists, the communists, the anarchists, the anti-Christs and the Jews!"

"For your information," said the G-man in cool triumph, "I am a Jew."

"That proves what I've just been saying!" said Jones.

"How's that?" said the G-man.

"The Jews have infiltrated everything!" said Jones, smiling the smile of a logician who could never be topped.

"You talk about the Catholics and the Negroes—" said the G-man, "and yet, here your two best friends are a Catholic and a Negro."

"What's so mysterious about that?" said Jones.

"Don't you hate them?" said the G-man.

"Certainly not," said Jones. "We all believe the same basic thing."

"What's that?" said the G-man.

"This once-proud country of ours is falling into the hands of the wrong people," said Jones. He nodded, and so did Father Keeley and the Black Fuehrer. "And, before it gets back on the right track," said Jones, "some heads are going to roll."

I have never seen a more sublime demonstration of the

totalitarian mind, a mind which might be likened unto a system of gears whose teeth have been filed off at random. Such a snaggle-toothed thought machine, driven by a standard or even by a substandard libido, whirls with the jerky, noisy, gaudy pointlessness of a cuckoo clock in Hell.

The boss G-man concluded wrongly that there were no teeth on the gears in the mind of Jones. "You're completely crazy," he said.

Jones wasn't completely crazy. The dismaying thing about the classic totalitarian mind is that any given gear, though mutilated, will have at its circumference unbroken sequences of teeth that are immaculately maintained, that are exquisitely machined.

Hence the cuckoo clock in Hell—keeping perfect time for eight minutes and twenty-three seconds, jumping ahead fourteen minutes, keeping perfect time for six seconds, jumping ahead two seconds, keeping perfect time for two hours and one second, then jumping ahead a year.

The missing teeth, of course, are simple, obvious truths, truths available and comprehensible even to ten-year-olds, in most cases.

The willful filing off of gear teeth, the willful doing without certain obvious pieces of information—

That was how a household as contradictory as one composed of Jones, Father Keeley, Vice-Bundesfuehrer Krapptauer, and the Black Fuehrer could exist in relative harmony—

That was how my father-in-law could contain in one mind an indifference toward slave women and love for a blue vase—

That was how Rudolf Hoess, Commandant of Auschwitz, could alternate over the loudspeakers of Auschwitz great music and calls for corpse-carriers—

That was how Nazi Germany could sense no important differences between civilization and hydrophobia—

That is the closest I can come to explaining the legions, the nations of lunatics I've seen in my time. And for me to attempt such a mechanical explanation is perhaps a reflection of the father whose son I was. *Am.* When I pause to think about it, which is rarely, I am, after all, the son of an engineer.

Since there is no one else to praise me, I will praise myself—will say that I have never tampered with a single tooth in my thought machine, such as it is. There are teeth missing, God knows—some I was born without, teeth that will never grow. And other teeth have been stripped by the clutchless shifts of history—

But never have I willfully destroyed a tooth on a gear of my thinking machine. Never have I said to myself, “This fact I can do without.”

Howard W. Campbell, Jr., praises himself! There’s life in the old boy yet!

And, where there’s life—

There is life.

CHAPTER THIRTY-NINE

Resi Noth Bows Out . . .

"MY ONLY REGRET," Dr. Jones said to the boss G-man there on the cellar stairs, "is that I have but one life to give to my country."

"We'll see if we can't dig up some other regrets for you, too," said the boss.

Now the Iron Guard of the White Sons of the American Constitution crowded in from the furnace room. Some of the guardsmen were hysterical. The paranoia their parents had been inculcating for years had suddenly paid off. Here was persecution!

One youth clutched the staff on an American flag. He waved it back and forth, banging the eagle on the tip of the staff against overhead pipes.

"This is your country's flag!" he cried.

"We already know that," said the boss G-man. "Take it away from him!"

"This day will go down in history!" said Jones.

"Every day goes down in history," said the boss. "All right—" he said, "where's the man who calls himself George Kraft?"

Kraft raised his hand. He did it almost cheerfully.

"Is that *your* country's flag, too?" said the boss wryly.

"I'd have to look at it more closely," said Kraft.

"How does it feel to have such a long and distinguished career come to an end?" the boss asked Kraft.

"All careers do end," said Kraft. "That's something I've known for a long time."

"Maybe they'll make a movie of your life," said the boss.

Kraft smiled. "Maybe," he said. "I would want a lot of money for the rights."

"There's only one actor who could really play the part, though," said the boss. "He might be hard to get."

"Oh?" said Kraft. "Who is that?"

"Charlie Chaplin," said the boss. "Who else could play a spy who was steadily drunk from 1941 until 1948? Who else could play a Russian spy who built an apparatus composed almost entirely of American agents?"

Kraft's urbanity dropped away, revealing him as a pale and puckered old man. "That's not true!" he said.

"Ask your superiors, if you don't believe me," said the boss.

"They know?" said Kraft.

"They finally caught on," said the boss. "You were on your way home to a bullet in the back of your neck."

"Why did you save me?" said Kraft.

"Call it sentimentality," said the boss.

Kraft thought his situation over, and schizophrenia rescued him neatly. "None of this really concerns me," he said, and his urbanity returned.

"Why not?" said the boss.

"Because I'm a painter," said Kraft. "That's the main thing I am."

"Be sure to bring your paintbox to prison," said the boss. He switched his attention to Resi. "You, of course, are Resi Noth," he said.

"Yes," she said.

"Have you enjoyed your little stay in our country?" said the boss.

"What am I supposed to say?" said Resi.

"Anything you like," said the boss. "If you have any complaints, I'll pass them on to the proper authorities. We're trying to increase the tourist trade from Europe, you know."

"You say very funny things," she said unsmilingly. "I am sorry I can't say funny things back. This is not a funny time for me."

"I'm sorry to hear that," said the boss lightly.

"You aren't sorry," said Resi. "I am the only person who is sorry.

"I am sorry I have nothing to live for," said Resi. "All I have is love for one man, but that man does not love me. He is so used up that he can't love any more. There is nothing left of him but curiosity and a pair of eyes.

"I can't say anything funny," said Resi. "But I can show you something interesting."

Resi seemed to dab her lip with a finger. What she really did was put a little capsule of cyanide in her mouth.

"I will show you a woman who dies for love," she said.

Right then and there, Resi Noth pitched into my arms, stone dead.

CHAPTER FORTY

Freedom Again . . .

I WAS ARRESTED along with everyone else in the house. I was released within an hour, thanks, I suppose, to the intercession of my Blue Fairy Godmother. The place where I was held so briefly was an unmarked office in the Empire State Building.

An agent took me down on an elevator and out onto the sidewalk, restoring me to the mainstream of life. I took perhaps fifty steps down the sidewalk, and then I stopped.

I froze.

It was not guilt that froze me. I had taught myself never to feel guilt.

It was not a ghastly sense of loss that froze me. I had taught myself to covet nothing.

It was not a loathing of death that froze me. I had taught myself to think of death as a friend.

It was not heartbroken rage against injustice that froze me. I had taught myself that a human being might as well look for diamond tiaras in the gutter as for rewards and punishments that were fair.

It was not the thought that I was so unloved that froze me. I had taught myself to do without love.

It was not the thought that God was cruel that froze me. I had taught myself never to expect anything from Him.

What froze me was the fact that I had absolutely no reason to move in any direction. What had made me move through so many dead and pointless years was curiosity.

Now even that had flickered out.

How long I stood frozen there, I cannot say. If I was ever going to move again, someone else was going to have to furnish the reason for moving.

Somebody did.

A policeman watched me for a while, and then he came over to me, and he said, "You all right?"

"Yes," I said.

"You've been standing here a long time," he said.

"I know," I said.

"You waiting for somebody?" he said.

"No," I said.

"Better move on, don't you think?" he said.

"Yes, sir," I said.

And I moved on.

CHAPTER FORTY-ONE

Chemicals . . .

FROM THE Empire State Building I walked downtown. I walked all the way to my old home in Greenwich Village, to Resi's and my and Kraft's old home.

I smoked cigarettes all the way, began to think of myself as a lightning bug.

I encountered many fellow lightning bugs. Sometimes I gave the cheery red signal first, sometimes they. And I left the seashell roar and the aurora borealis of the city's heart farther and farther behind me.

The hour was late. I began to catch signals of fellow lightning bugs trapped in upper stories.

Somewhere a siren, a tax-supported mourner, wailed.

When I got at last to my building, my home, all windows were dark save one on the second floor, one window in the apartment of young Dr. Abraham Epstein.

He, too, was a lightning bug.

He glowed; I glowed back.

Somewhere a motorcycle started up, sounded like a string of firecrackers.

A black cat crossed between me and the door of the building. "Ralph?" it said.

The entrance hall of the building was dark, too. The ceiling light did not respond to the switch. I struck a match, saw that the mailboxes had all been broken into.

In the wavering light of the match and the formless surroundings, the bent and gaping doors of the mailboxes might have been the doors of cells in a jail in a burning city somewhere.

My match attracted a patrolman. He was young and lonesome.

"What are you doing here?" he said.

"I live here," I said. "This is my home."

"Any identification?" he said.

So I gave him some identification, told him the attic was mine.

"You're the reason for all this trouble," he said. He wasn't scolding me. He was simply interested.

"If you say so," I said.

"I'm surprised you came back," he said.

"I'll go away again," I said.

"I can't order you to go away," he said. "I'm just surprised you came back."

"It's all right for me to go upstairs?" I said.

"It's your home," he said. "Nobody can keep you out of it."

"Thank you," I said.

"Don't thank me," he said. "It's a free country, and everybody gets protected exactly alike." He said this pleasantly. He was giving me a lesson in civics.

"That's certainly the way to run a country," I said.

"I don't know if you're kidding me or not," he said, "but that's right."

"I'm not kidding you," I said. "I swear I'm not." This simple oath of allegiance satisfied him.

"My father was killed on Iwo Jima," he said.

"I'm sorry," I said.

"I guess there were good people killed on both sides," he said.

"I think that's true," I said.

"You think there'll be another one?" he said.

"Another what?" I said.

"Another war," he said.

"Yes," I said.

"Me too," he said. "Isn't that hell?"

"You chose the right word," I said.

"What can any one person do?" he said.

"Each person does a little something," I said, "and there you are."

He sighed heavily. "It all adds up," he said. "People don't realize." He shook his head. "What should people do?"

"Obey the laws," I said.

"They don't even want to do that, half of 'em," he said. "The things I see—the things people say to me. Sometimes I get very discouraged."

"Everybody does that from time to time," I said.

"I guess it's partly chemistry," he said.

"What is?" I said.

"Getting down in the dumps," he said. "Isn't that what they're finding out—that a lot of that's chemicals?"

"I don't know," I said.

"That's what I read," he said. "That's one of the things they're finding out."

"Very interesting," I said.

"They can give a man certain chemicals, and he goes crazy," he said. "That's one of the things they're working with. Maybe it's all chemicals."

"Very possible," I said.

"Maybe it's different chemicals that different countries eat that makes people act in different ways at different times," he said.

"I'd never thought of that before," I said.

"Why else would people change so much?" he said. "My brother was over in Japan, and he said the Japanese were the nicest people he ever met, and it was the Japanese who'd killed our father! Think about that for a minute."

"All right," I said.

"It *has* to be chemicals, doesn't it?" he said.

"I see what you mean," I said.

"Sure," he said. "You think about it some more."

"All right," I said.

"I think about chemicals all the time," he said. "Sometimes I think I should go back to school and find out all the things they've found out so far about chemicals."

"I think you should," I said.

"Maybe, when they find out more about chemicals," he said, "there won't have to be policemen or wars or crazy houses or divorces or drunks or juvenile delinquents or women gone bad or anything any more."

"That would sure be nice," I said.

"It's possible," he said.

"I believe you," I said.

"The way they're going, everything's possible now, if they just work at it—get the money and get the smartest people and get to work. Have a crash program," he said.

"I'm for it," I said.

"Look how some women go half off their nut once a month," he said. "Certain chemicals get loose, and the woman can't help but act that way. Sometimes a certain chemical will get loose after a woman's had a baby, and she'll kill the baby. That happened four doors down from here just last week."

"How awful," I said. "I hadn't heard—"

"Most unnatural thing a woman can do is kill her own baby, but she did it," he said. "Certain chemicals in the blood made her do it, even though she knew better, didn't want to do it at all."

"Um," I said.

"You wonder what's wrong with the world—" he said, "well, there's an important clue right there."

CHAPTER FORTY-TWO

No Dove, No Covenant . . .

I WENT UPSTAIRS to my ratty attic, went up the oak and plaster snail of the stairwell.

While the column of air enclosed by the stairs had carried in the past a melancholy freight of coal dust and cooking smells and the sweat of plumbing, that air was cold and sharp now. Every window in my attic had been broken. All warm gases had been whisked up the stairwell and out my windows, as though up a whistling flue.

The air was clean.

The feeling of a stale old building suddenly laid open, an infected atmosphere lanced, made clean, was familiar to me. I had felt it often enough in Berlin. Helga and I were bombed out twice. Both times there was a staircase left to climb.

One time we climbed the stairs to a roofless and windowless home, a home otherwise magically undisturbed. Another time, we climbed the stairs to cold thin air, two floors below where home had been.

Both moments at those splintered stairheads under the open sky were exquisite.

The exquisiteness went on for only a short time, naturally, for, like any human family, we loved our nests and needed them. But, for a minute or two, anyway, Helga and I felt like Noah and his wife on Mount Ararat.

There is no better feeling than that.

And then the air-raid sirens blew again, and we realized that we were ordinary people, without dove or covenant, and that the flood, far from being over, had scarcely begun.

I remember one time, when Helga and I went from the head of a splintered staircase in the sky down into a shelter deep in the ground, and the big bombs walked all around above. And they walked and they walked and they walked, and it seemed that they never would go away.

And the shelter was long and narrow, like a railroad car, and it was full.

And there was a man, a woman, and their three children on the bench facing Helga and me. And the woman started speaking to the ceiling, the bombs, the airplanes, the sky, and to God Almighty above all that.

She started softly, but she wasn't talking to anybody in the shelter itself.

"All right—" she said, "here we are. We're right down here. We hear you up there. We hear how angry you are." The loudness of her voice jumped sharply.

"Dear God, how angry you are!" she cried.

Her husband—a haggard civilian with a patch over one eye, with the recognition button of the Nazi teachers' union on his lapel—spoke to her warningly.

She did not hear him.

"What is it you want us to do?" she said to the ceiling and all that lay above. "Whatever it is you want us to do," she said, "tell us, and we'll do it!"

A bomb crashed down close by, shook loose from the ceiling a snowfall of calcimine, brought the woman to her feet shrieking, and her husband with her.

"We surrender! We give up!" she yelled, and great relief and happiness spread over her face. "You can stop now," she yelled. She laughed. "We quit! It's over!" She turned to tell the good news to her children.

Her husband knocked her cold.

That one-eyed teacher set her down on the bench, propped her against the wall. And then he went to the highest-ranking person present, a vice-admiral, as it happened. "She's a woman . . . hysterical . . . they get hysterical . . . she doesn't mean it . . . she has the Golden Order of Parenthood . . ." he said to the vice-admiral.

The vice-admiral wasn't baffled or annoyed. He didn't feel miscast. With fine dignity, he gave the man absolution. "It's all right," he said. "It's understandable. Don't worry."

The teacher marveled at a system that could forgive weakness. "*Heil Hitler*," he said, bowing as he backed away.

"*Heil Hitler*," said the vice-admiral.

The teacher now began to revive his wife. He had good news for her—that she was forgiven, that everyone understood.

And all the time the bombs walked and walked overhead, and the schoolteacher's three children did not bat an eye.

Nor, I thought, would they ever.

Nor, I thought, would I.

Ever again.

CHAPTER FORTY-THREE

St. George and the Dragon . . .

THE DOOR of my ratty attic had been torn off its hinges, had disappeared entirely. In its place the janitor had tacked a pup-tent of mine, and over the pup-tent a zigzag of boards. He had written on the zigzag boards, in gold radiator paint that reflected the light of my match:

"Nobody and nothing inside."

Be that as it may, somebody had since ripped a bottom corner of the canvas free of its tacks, giving my ratty attic a small, triangular flap-door, like a tepee.

I crawled in.

The light switch in my attic did not respond, either. What light there was came through the few unbroken window panes. The broken panes had been replaced with wads of paper, rags, clothes and bedding. Night winds whistled around these wads. What light there was was blue.

I looked out through the back windows by the stove, looked down into the foreshortened enchantment of the little private park below, the little Eden formed of joined back yards. No one was playing in it now.

There was no one in it to cry, as I should have liked someone to cry:

"*Olly-olly-ox-in-freeeeeee.*"

There was a stir, a rustle in the shadows of my attic. I imagined it to be the rustle of a rat.

I was wrong.

It was the rustle of Bernard B. O'Hare, the man who had captured me so long ago. It was the stir of my own personal Fury, the man who perceived his noblest aspect in his loathing and hounding of me.

I do not mean to slander him by associating the sound he made with the sound of a rat. I do not think of O'Hare as a rat, though his actions with regard to me had the same nagging irrelevance as the rats' scrabbling passions in my attic walls. I didn't really know O'Hare, and I didn't want to know him.

The fact of his having put me under arrest in Germany was a fact of submicroscopic interest to me. He wasn't my nemesis. My game was up long before O'Hare took me into custody. To me, O'Hare was simply one more gatherer of wind-blown trash in the tracks of war.

O'Hare had a far more exciting view of what we were to each other. When drunk, at any rate, he thought of himself as St. George and of me as the dragon.

When I first saw him in the shadows of my attic, he was seated on a galvanized bucket turned upside down. He was in the uniform of the American Legion. He had a quart of whisky with him. He had apparently been waiting for me a long time, drinking and smoking the while. He was drunk, but he had kept his uniform neat. His tie was straight. His cap was on and set at the proper angle. The uniform was important to him, was supposed to be important to me, too.

"Know who I am?" he said.

"Yes," I said.

"I'm not as young as I was once," he said. "Haven't changed much, have I?"

"No," I said. I've described him earlier in this account as having looked like a lean young wolf. When I saw him in my attic, he looked unhealthy—pale and stringy and hot-eyed. He had become less wolf than coyote, I thought. His post-war years had not been years of merry blooming.

"Expecting me?" he said.

"You told me I could," I said. I had to be polite and careful with him. I supposed correctly that he meant to hurt me. The fact that he was in a very neat uniform, and that he was smaller and much lighter than me, suggested that he had a weapon on him somewhere—most likely a gun.

He now got off the bucket, showing me, in his ramshackle rising, how drunk he was. He knocked the bucket over in the process.

He grinned. "Ever have nightmares about me, Campbell?" he said.

"Often," I said. It was a lie, of course.

"Surprised I didn't bring anybody with me?" he said.

"Yes," I said.

"Plenty of people wanted to come along," he said. "There

was a whole bunch wanted to come down with me from Boston. And after I got to New York this afternoon, I went into a bar and got talking to some strangers, and they asked if they could come along, too."

"Um," I said.

"And you know what I said to them?" he asked me.

"Nope," I said.

"I said to them, 'Sorry, boys—but this is a party just for Campbell and me. That's the way it's got to be—just the two of us, face to face,'" he said.

"Um," I said.

"'This thing's been a-building over the years,' I told 'em," said O'Hare. "'It's in the stars—' I told 'em, 'in the stars that Howard Campbell and me meet again after all these years.' Don't you feel that way?" he asked me.

"What way?" I said.

"It's in the stars," he said. "We had to meet like this, right here in this very room, and neither one of us could have avoided it if we'd tried."

"Possibly," I said.

"Just when you think there isn't any point to life—" he said, "then, all of a sudden, you realize you are being aimed right straight at something."

"I know what you mean," I said.

He swayed, steadied himself. "You know what I do for a living?" he said.

"No," I said.

"Dispatcher for frozen-custard trucks," he said.

"Pardon me?" I said.

"Fleet of trucks goes around to factories, beaches, ballgames—anywhere there's people—" O'Hare seemed to forget all about me for a few seconds, to reflect murkily on the mission of the trucks he dispatched. "Custard machine's right there on the truck," he murmured. "Two flavors is all—chocolate and vanilla." His mood was exactly what poor Resi's mood had been when she told me about the ghastly pointlessness of her job at a cigarette-making machine in Dresden.

"When the war ended," O'Hare said to me, "I expected to be a lot more in fifteen years than a dispatcher of frozen-custard trucks."

"I guess we've all had disappointments," I said.

He didn't respond to this feeble try at brotherhood. His concern was for himself alone. "I was going to be a doctor, I was going to be a lawyer, a writer, an architect, an engineer, a newspaper reporter—" he said. "There wasn't anything I couldn't be," he said.

"And then I got married—" he said, "and the wife started having kids right away, and I opened a damn diaper service with a buddy, and the buddy ran off with the money, and the wife kept having kids. After the diaper service it was Venetian blinds, and after the Venetian-blind business went bust, it was frozen custard. And all the time the wife was having more kids, and the damn car breaking down, and bill-collectors coming around, and termites boiling out of the baseboards every spring and fall."

"Sorry," I said.

"And I asked myself," said O'Hare, "what does it mean? Where do I fit in? What's the point of any of it?"

"Good questions," I said softly, and I put myself close to a pair of heavy fire-tongs.

"And then somebody sent me a copy of that newspaper with the story of how you were still alive," said O'Hare, and he relived for me the cruel excitement the story had given him. "And then it hit me—" he said, "why I was alive, and what the main thing was I was supposed to do."

He took a step toward me, his eyes wide. "Here I come, Campbell, out of the past!"

"How do you do?" I said.

"You know what you are to me, Campbell?" he said.

"No," I said.

"You're pure evil," he said. "You're absolutely pure evil."

"Thank you," I said.

"You're right—it *is* a kind of compliment," he said. "Usually a bad man's got some good in him—almost as much good as evil. But you—" he said, "you're the pure thing. For all the good there is in you, you might as well be the Devil."

"Maybe I am the Devil," I said.

"Don't think I haven't thought of that," he said.

"What do you plan to do to me?" I asked him.

"Take you apart," he said, rocking back and forth on the

balls of his feet, rolling his shoulders, loosening them. "When I heard you were alive, I knew it was something I had to do. There wasn't any way out," he said. "It had to end like this."

"I don't see why," I said.

"Then, by God, I'll show you why," he said. "I'll show you, by God, I was born just to take you apart, right here and now." He called me a yellow-belly. He called me a Nazi. And then he called me the most offensive compound word in the English language.

So I broke his good right arm with the fire-tongs.

That is the only violent act I ever committed in what has now been a long, long life. I met O'Hare in single combat, and I beat him. Beating him was easy. O'Hare was so drugged by booze and fantasies of good triumphing over evil that he hadn't expected me to defend myself.

When he realized that he'd been hit, that the dragon meant to give St. George a real tussle, he looked very surprised.

"So that's the way you want to play—" he said.

And then the agony of a multiple fracture suffused his nervous system, and tears came to his eyes.

"Get out," I said. "Or do you want me to break your other arm, and your head, too?" I put the tip of the fire-tongs by his right temple, and I said, "And I'll take the gun or the knife or whatever it is before you go."

He shook his head. The pain was so awful that he could not speak.

"You're not armed?" I said.

He shook his head again. "Fair fight," he said thickly. "Fair."

I patted his pockets, and there weren't any weapons on him. St. George had expected to take the dragon apart with his bare hands!

"You poor, silly, drunk, one-armed sonofabitch!" I said. I tore down the tent in my doorway, kicked out the zigzag of boards. I shoved O'Hare through the opening, onto the landing outside.

The railing stopped O'Hare, and he gazed down the stairwell, down a beckoning helix to the patch of sure death below.

"I'm not your destiny, or the Devil, either!" I said. "Look at you! Came to kill evil with your bare hands, and now away you go with no more glory than a man sideswiped by a Greyhound bus! And that's all the glory you deserve!" I said. "That's all that any man at war with pure evil deserves.

"There are plenty of good reasons for fighting," I said, "but no good reason ever to hate without reservation, to imagine that God Almighty Himself hates with you, too. Where's evil? It's that large part of every man that wants to hate without limit, that wants to hate with God on its side. It's that part of every man that finds all kinds of ugliness so attractive.

"It's that part of an imbecile," I said, "that punishes and vilifies and makes war gladly."

Whether it was my words or humiliation or booze or surgical shock that made O'Hare throw up, I do not know. Throw up he did. He flashed the hash down the stairwell from four stories up.

"Clean it up," I said.

He faced me, his eyes still filled with undiluted hatred. "I'll get you yet, brother," he said.

"That may be," I said. "But it won't change your destiny of bankruptcies, frozen-custard, too many children, termites, and no cash. If you want to be a soldier in the Legions of God so much," I told him, "try the Salvation Army."

And O'Hare went away.

CHAPTER FORTY-FOUR

"Kahm-boo . . ."

IT IS a common experience among jailbirds to wake up and wonder why they are in jail. A theory I propose to myself on such occasions is that I am in jail because I could not bring myself to walk through or leap over another man's vomit. I am referring to the vomit of Bernard B. O'Hare on the foyer floor at the foot of the stairwell.

I left my attic shortly after O'Hare did. There was nothing to keep me there. I took a memento with me, quite by accident. As I left my attic, I kicked something over the threshold and onto the landing. I picked it up. It was a pawn from the chess set I had carved from a broom handle.

I put it in my pocket. I have it still. As I slipped it into my pocket, the stench of the public nuisance O'Hare had created reached me.

As I descended the stairs, the stench grew worse.

When I reached the landing outside the door of young Dr. Abraham Epstein, a man who had spent his childhood in Auschwitz, the stench stopped me.

The next thing I knew, I was knocking on Dr. Epstein's door. The Doctor came to the door in bathrobe and pajamas. His feet were bare. He was startled to see me.

"Yes?" he said.

"Could I come in?" I said.

"This is a medical matter?" he said. There was a chain across the door.

"No," I said. "Personal—political."

"It can't wait?" he said.

"I'd rather it didn't," I said.

"Give me an idea of what this is all about," he said.

"I want to go to Israel to stand trial," I said.

"You what?" he said.

"I want to be tried for my crimes against humanity," I said. "I'm willing to go."

"Why come to me?" he said.

"I thought you might know somebody—somebody who'd like to be notified," I said.

"I'm not a representative of Israel," he said. "I'm an American. Tomorrow you can find all the Israelis you want."

"I'd like to surrender to an Auschwitzer," I said.

This made him mad. "Then find one who thinks about Auschwitz all the time!" he said. "There are plenty who think about nothing else. I *never* think about it!"

And he slammed the door.

I froze again, frustrated in the one purpose I'd been able to imagine for myself. What Epstein had said about Israelis being available in the morning was surely true—

But there was still the night to get through, and I could not move.

Epstein talked to his mother inside. They talked in German.

I heard only bits of what they said. Epstein was telling his mother what had just happened.

One thing I did hear that impressed me was their use of my name, the sound of my last name.

"Kahm-boo," they said again and again. That was Campbell to them.

That was the undiluted evil in me, the evil that had had its effect on millions, the disgusting creature good people wanted dead and underground—

"Kahm-boo."

Epstein's mother got so excited about Kahm-boo and what he was up to now, that she came to the door. I'm sure that she did not expect to see Kahm-boo himself. She wanted only to loathe and wonder at the air he had lately displaced.

She opened the door, her son right behind her, telling her not to do it. She almost fainted at the sight of Kahm-boo himself, Kahm-boo in a state of catalepsis.

Epstein pushed her aside, came out as though to attack me.

"What do you think you're doing?" he said. "Get the hell away from here!"

When I did not move, did not reply, did not even blink, did not even seem to breathe, he began to understand that I was a medical problem after all.

"Oh, for Christ's sake!" he lamented.

Like a friendly robot, I let him lead me inside. He took me

back into the kitchen area of his flat, sat me down at a white table there.

"Can you hear me?" he said.

"Yes," I said.

"Do you know who I am—where you are?" he said.

"Yes," I said.

"Have you ever been like this before?" he said.

"No," I said.

"You need a psychiatrist," he said. "I'm no psychiatrist."

"I told you what I need," I said. "Call up somebody—not a psychiatrist. Call up somebody who wants to give me a trial."

Epstein and his mother, a very old woman, argued back and forth about what to do with me. His mother understood my illness immediately, that it was my world rather than myself that was diseased.

"This is not the first time you've seen eyes like that," she said to her son in German, "not the first man you've seen who could not move unless someone told him where to move, who longed for someone to tell him what to do next, who would do anything anyone told him to do next. You saw thousands of them at Auschwitz."

"I don't remember," said Epstein tautly.

"All right—" said his mother, "then let *me* remember. I can remember. Every minute I can remember.

"And, as one who remembers," said his mother, "let me say that what he asks for he should have. Call someone."

"Who will I call?" said Epstein. "I'm not a Zionist. I'm an anti-Zionist. I'm not even that. I never think about it. I'm a physician. I don't know anybody who's still looking for revenge. I have nothing but contempt for them. Go away. You've come to the wrong place."

"Call somebody," said his mother.

"You still want revenge?" he asked her.

"Yes," she said.

He put his face close to mine. "And you really want to be punished?" he said.

"I want to be tried," I said.

"It's all play-acting," he said, exasperated with both of us. "It proves nothing!"

"Call somebody," said his mother.

Epstein threw up his hands. "All right! All right! I will call Sam. I will tell him he can be a great Zionist hero. He always wanted to be a great Zionist hero."

What Sam's last name was I never found out. Dr. Epstein called him from the front room of the flat while I remained in the kitchen with Epstein's old mother.

His mother sat down at the table, faced me, rested her arms on the table, studied my face with melancholy curiosity and satisfaction.

"They took all the light bulbs," she said to me in German.

"What?" I said.

"The people who broke into your apartment—they took all the light bulbs from the stairway," she said.

"Um," I said.

"In Germany, too," she said.

"Pardon me?" I said.

"That was one of the things—when the S.S. or the Gestapo came and took somebody away—" she said.

"I don't understand," I said.

"Other people would come into the building, wanting to do something patriotic," she said. "And that was one of the things they always did. Somebody always took the light bulbs." She shook her head. "Such a strange thing for somebody always to do."

Dr. Epstein came back into the kitchen dusting his hands. "All right—" he said, "three heroes will be here shortly—a tailor, a watchmaker, and a pediatrician—all delighted to play the part of Israeli parachutists."

"Thank you," I said.

The three came for me in about twenty minutes. They had no weapons, and no status as agents of Israel or as agents of anything but themselves. The only status they had was what my infamy and my anxiousness to surrender to somebody, to almost anybody, gave them.

What my arrest amounted to was a bed for the rest of the night—in the tailor's apartment, as it happened. The next morning, the three surrendered me, with my permission, to Israeli officials.

When the three came for me at Dr. Epstein's apartment, they banged on the front door loudly.

The instant they did that, I felt enormously relieved. I felt happy.

"You're all right now?" said Epstein, before he let them in.

"Yes, thank you, Doctor," I said.

"You still want to go?" he said.

"Yes," I said.

"He *has* to go," said his mother. And then she leaned closer to me, across the kitchen table. She crooned something in German, made it sound like a fragment of a ditty remembered from a happy childhood.

What she crooned was this, a command she had heard over the loudspeakers of Auschwitz—had heard many times a day for years.

"*Leichenträger zu Wache*," she crooned.

A beautiful language, isn't it?

Translation?

"Corpse-carriers to the guardhouse."

That's what that old woman crooned to me.

CHAPTER FORTY-FIVE

The Tortoise and the Hare . . .

SO HERE I AM in Israel, of my own free will, though my cell is locked and my guards have guns.

My story is told, and none too soon—for tomorrow my trial begins. The hare of history once more overtakes the tortoise of art. There will be no more time for writing. Adventuring I must go again.

There are many to testify against me. None to testify for me.

The prosecution intends to begin, I'm told, by playing recordings of the worst of my broadcasts, so the most pitiless witness against me will be myself.

Bernard B. O'Hare is in town at his own expense, annoying the prosecution with the feverish irrevelance of all he has to say.

So, too, is Heinz Schildknecht, my erstwhile best friend and doubles partner, the man whose motorcycle I stole. My lawyer says that Heinz is full of venom for me, and that Heinz, surprisingly, will make a credible witness. Whence this respectability for Heinz, who, after all, worked at a desk next to mine in the Ministry of Propaganda and Popular Enlightenment?

Surprise: Heinz is a Jew, a member of the anti-Nazi underground during the war, an Israeli agent after the war and up to the present time.

And he can prove it.

Good for Heinz!

Dr. Lionel J. D. Jones, D.D.S., D.D., and Iona Potapov *alias* George Kraft, can't come to my trial, both serving in a United States Federal Prison, as they are. They have both sent affidavits, however.

The affidavits of Dr. Jones and Kraft-Potapov aren't much help, to say the least.

Dr. Jones declares under oath that I am a saint and a martyr in the holy Nazi cause. He says, too, that I have the most perfect set of Aryan teeth he's ever seen outside of photographs of Hitler.

Kraft-Potapov declares under oath that Russian intelligence

was never able to turn up any proof that I had been an American agent. He offers the opinion that I was an ardent Nazi, but that I shouldn't be held responsible for my acts, since I was a political idiot, an artist who could not distinguish between reality and dreams.

The three men who took me into custody in Dr. Epstein's apartment are on hand for the trial—the tailor, the watchmaker, and the pediatrician—on an even more bootless junket than Bernard B. O'Hare's.

Howard W. Campbell, Jr.—this is your life!

My Israeli lawyer, Mr. Alvin Dobrowitz, has had all my New York mail forwarded here, hoping unreasonably to find in that mail some proof of my innocence.

Hi ho.

Three letters came today.

I shall open them now, reporting their contents one by one.

Hope springs eternal, they say, in the human breast. It springs eternal, at any rate, in the breast of Dobrowitz, which is, I suppose, why he costs so much.

All that I need to be a free man, says Dobrowitz, is the barest proof that there was such a person as Frank Wirtanen, and that Wirtanen made me an American spy.

Well now—about the letters for today:

The first starts off warmly enough. "Dear Friend" it calls me, in spite of all the evil things I am said to have done. It assumes that I am a teacher. I explained in an earlier chapter, I believe, how my name happened to find its way onto a list of supposed educators, how I became recipient of mail promoting materials useful to those in charge of training the young.

The letter at hand is from "Creative Playthings, Inc."

Dear Friend: [Creative Playthings says to me, here in a Jerusalem jail] Would you like to foster a creative environment for your students in their own homes? What happens to them after they leave school certainly is important. You may have a child under your direction an average of 25 waking hours per week, but the parents guide him for 45 hours. What a parent does with these hours can complicate or facilitate your program.

We believe the kind of toys Creative Playthings sponsors will genuinely stimulate—in the home—the creative environment you, as an early childhood leader, are trying to foster.

How can Creative Playthings' toys in the home do this?

Such toys can provide for the physical needs of growing children. Such toys help a child discover and experiment with life in the home and community. Such toys promote opportunities for individual expression which may be lacking in the group life of the school.

Such toys help the child work off aggressions. . . .

To which I reply:

Dear Friends: As one who has experienced extensively with life in the home and community, using real people in true-to-life situations, I doubt that any playthings could prepare a child for one millionth of what is going to hit him in the teeth, ready or not.

My own feeling is that a child should start experimenting with real people and real communities from the moment of birth, if possible. If, for some reason, these materials are not available, then playthings must be used.

But not bland, pleasing, smooth, easily manipulated playthings like those in your brochure, friends! Let there be nothing harmonious about our children's playthings, lest they grow up expecting peace and order, and be eaten alive.

As for children's working off aggressions, I'm against it. They are going to need all the aggressions they can contain for ultimate release in the adult world. Name one great man in history who did not go boiling and bubbling through childhood with a lashed-down safety valve.

Let me tell you that the children in my charge for an average of twenty-five hours a week are not likely to lose their keen edge during the forty-five hours they spend with their parents. They aren't moving hand-carved animals on and off a Noah's Ark, believe me. They are spying on real grownups all the time, learning what they fight about, what they're greedy for, how they satisfy their greed, why and how they lie, what makes them go crazy, the different ways they go crazy, and so on.

I cannot predict the fields in which these children of mine will succeed, but I guarantee success for them without exception, anywhere in the civilized world.

Yours for realistic pedagogy,
Howard W. Campbell, Jr.

The second letter?

It, too, addresses Howard W. Campbell, Jr., as "Dear Friend," proving that at least two out of three letter writers today aren't sore at Howard W. Campbell, Jr., at all. The letter is from a stockbroker in Toronto, Canada. It is addressed to the capitalistic aspect of me.

It wants me to buy stock in a tungsten mine in Manitoba. Before I did that, I would have to know more about the company. I would have to know in particular whether it had a capable and reputable management.

I wasn't born yesterday.

The third letter? It is addressed direct to me in prison here.

And—it's a curious letter, indeed. Let it here be seen whole:

Dear Howard:

The discipline of a lifetime now collapses like the fabled walls of Jericho. Who is Joshua, and what is the tune his trumpets play? I wish I knew. The music that has worked such havoc against such old walls is not loud. It is faint, diffuse, and peculiar.

Could it be the music of my conscience: That I doubt. I have done no wrong to you.

I think the music must be an old soldier's itch for just a little treason. And treason this letter is.

I here violate direct and explicit orders that were given to me, were given to me in the best interests of the United States of America. I here give you my true name, and I identify myself as the man you knew as "Frank Wirtanen."

My name is Harold J. Sparrow.

My rank at time of retirement from the United States Army was Colonel.

My serial number is 0-61134.

I exist. I can be seen, heard, and touched almost any day, in or around the only dwelling on Coggin's Pond, six miles due west of Hinkleyville, Maine.

I affirm, and will affirm under oath, that I recruited you as an American agent, and that you, at personal sacrifices that proved total, became one of the most effective agents of the Second World War.

If there must be a trial of Howard W. Campbell, Jr., by the forces of self-righteous nationalism, let it be one hell of a contest!

Yours truly,
"Frank"

So I am about to be a free man again, to wander where I please.

I find the prospect nauseating.

I think that tonight is the night I will hang Howard W. Campbell, Jr., for crimes against himself.

I *know* that tonight is the night.

They say that a hanging man hears gorgeous music. Too bad that I, like my father, unlike my musical mother, am tone-deaf. All the same, I hope that the tune I am about to hear is not Bing Crosby's "White Chrismas."

Goodbye, cruel world!

Auf wiedersehen?

STORIES

Report on the Barnhouse Effect

LET ME BEGIN by saying that I don't know any more about where Professor Arthur Barnhouse is hiding than anyone else does. Save for one short, enigmatic message left in my mailbox on Christmas Eve, I have not heard from him since his disappearance a year and a half ago.

What's more, readers of this article will be disappointed if they expect to learn how *they* can bring about the so-called "Barnhouse Effect." If I were able and willing to give away that secret, I would certainly be something more important than a psychology instructor.

I have been urged to write this report because I did research under the professor's direction and because I was the first to learn of his astonishing discovery. But while I was his student I was never entrusted with knowledge of how the mental forces could be released and directed. He was unwilling to trust anyone with that information.

I would like to point out that the term "Barnhouse Effect" is a creation of the popular press, and was never used by Professor Barnhouse. The name he chose for the phenomenon was "*dynamopsychism*," or *force of the mind*.

I cannot believe that there is a civilized person yet to be convinced that such a force exists, what with its destructive effects on display in every national capital. I think humanity has always had an inkling that this sort of force does exist. It has been common knowledge that some people are luckier than others with inanimate objects like dice. What Professor Barnhouse did was to show that such "luck" was a measurable force, which in his case could be enormous.

By my calculations, the professor was about fifty-five times more powerful than a Nagasaki-type atomic bomb at the time he went into hiding. He was not bluffing when, on the eve of "Operation Brainstorm," he told General Honus Barker: "Sitting here at the dinner table, I'm pretty sure I can flatten anything on earth—from Joe Louis to the Great Wall of China."

There is an understandable tendency to look upon Professor Barnhouse as a supernatural visitation. The First Church of

Barnhouse in Los Angeles has a congregation numbering in the thousands. He is godlike in neither appearance nor intellect. The man who disarms the world is single, shorter than the average American male, stout, and averse to exercise. His I.Q. is 143, which is good but certainly not sensational. He is quite mortal, about to celebrate his fortieth birthday, and in good health. If he is alone now, the isolation won't bother him too much. He was quiet and shy when I knew him, and seemed to find more companionship in books and music than in his associations at the college.

Neither he nor his powers fall outside the sphere of Nature. His dynamopsychic radiations are subject to many known physical laws that apply in the field of radio. Hardly a person has not now heard the snarl of "Barnhouse static" on his home receiver. The radiations are affected by sunspots and variations in the ionosphere.

However, they differ from ordinary broadcast waves in several important ways. Their total energy can be brought to bear on any single point the professor chooses, and that energy is undiminished by distance. As a weapon, then, dynamopsychism has an impressive advantage over bacteria and atomic bombs, beyond the fact that it costs nothing to use: it enables the professor to single out critical individuals and objects instead of slaughtering whole populations in the process of maintaining international equilibrium.

As General Honus Barker told the House Military Affairs Committee: "Until someone finds Barnhouse, there is no defense against the Barnhouse Effect." Efforts to "jam" or block the radiations have failed. Premier Slezak could have saved himself the fantastic expense of his "Barnhouseproof" shelter. Despite the shelter's twelve-foot-thick lead armor, the premier has been floored twice while in it.

There is talk of screening the population for men potentially as powerful dynamopsychically as the professor. Senator Warren Foust demanded funds for this purpose last month, with the passionate declaration: "He who rules the Barnhouse Effect rules the world!" Commissar Kropotnik said much the same thing, so another costly armaments race, with a new twist, has begun.

This race at least has its comical aspects. The world's best gamblers are being coddled by governments like so many nuclear physicists. There may be several hundred persons with dynamopsychic talent on earth, myself included. But, without knowledge of the professor's technique, they can never be anything but dice-table despots. With the secret, it would probably take them ten years to become dangerous weapons. It took the professor that long. He who rules the Barnhouse Effect is Barnhouse and will be for some time.

Popularly, the "Age of Barnhouse" is said to have begun a year and a half ago, on the day of Operation Brainstorm. That was when dynamopsychism became significant politically. Actually, the phenomenon was discovered in May, 1942, shortly after the professor turned down a direct commission in the Army and enlisted as an artillery private. Like X-rays and vulcanized rubber, dynamopsychism was discovered by accident.

From time to time Private Barnhouse was invited to take part in games of chance by his barrack mates. He knew nothing about the games, and usually begged off. But one evening, out of social grace, he agreed to shoot craps. It was either terrible or wonderful that he played, depending upon whether or not you like the world as it now is.

"Shoot sevens, Pop," someone said.

So "Pop" shot sevens—ten in a row to bankrupt the barracks. He retired to his bunk and, as a mathematical exercise, calculated the odds against his feat on the back of a laundry slip. His chances of doing it, he found, were one in almost ten million! Bewildered, he borrowed a pair of dice from the man in the bunk next to his. He tried to roll sevens again, but got only the usual assortment of numbers. He lay back for a moment, then resumed his toying with the dice. He rolled ten more sevens in a row.

He might have dismissed the phenomenon with a low whistle. But the professor instead mulled over the circumstances surrounding his two lucky streaks. There was one single factor in common: on both occasions, *the same thought train had flashed through his mind just before he threw the dice.* It was that thought train which aligned the professor's brain cells into what has since become the most powerful weapon on earth.

The soldier in the next bunk gave dynamopsychism its first token of respect. In an understatement certain to bring wry smiles to the faces of the world's dejected demagogues, the soldier said, "You're hotter'n a two-dollar pistol, Pop." Professor Barnhouse was all of that. The dice that did his bidding weighed but a few grams, so the forces involved were minute; but the unmistakable fact that there were such forces was earth-shaking.

Professional caution kept him from revealing his discovery immediately. He wanted more facts and a body of theory to go with them. Later, when the atomic bomb was dropped on Hiroshima, it was fear that made him hold his peace. At no time were his experiments, as Premier Slezak called them, "a bourgeois plot to shackle the true democracies of the world." The professor didn't know where they were leading.

In time, he came to recognize another startling feature of dynamopsychism: *its strength increased with use.* Within six months, he was able to govern dice thrown by men the length of a barracks distant. By the time of his discharge in 1945, he could knock bricks loose from chimneys three miles away.

Charges that Professor Barnhouse could have won the last war in a minute, but did not care to do so, are perfectly senseless. When the war ended, he had the range and power of a 37-millimeter cannon, perhaps—certainly no more. His dynamopsychic powers graduated from the small-arms class only after his discharge and return to Wyandotte College.

I enrolled in the Wyandotte Graduate School two years after the professor had rejoined the faculty. By chance, he was assigned as my thesis adviser. I was unhappy about the assignment, for the professor was, in the eyes of both colleagues and students, a somewhat ridiculous figure. He missed classes or had lapses of memory during lectures. When I arrived, in fact, his shortcomings had passed from the ridiculous to the intolerable.

"We're assigning you to Barnhouse as a sort of temporary thing," the dean of social studies told me. He looked apologetic and perplexed. "Brilliant man, Barnhouse, I guess. Difficult to know since his return, perhaps, but his work before the war brought a great deal of credit to our little school."

When I reported to the professor's laboratory for the first

time, what I saw was more distressing than the gossip. Every surface in the room was covered with dust; books and apparatus had not been disturbed for months. The professor sat napping at his desk when I entered. The only signs of recent activity were three overflowing ashtrays, a pair of scissors, and a morning paper with several items clipped from its front page.

As he raised his head to look at me, I saw that his eyes were clouded with fatigue. "Hi," he said, "just can't seem to get my sleeping done at night." He lighted a cigarette, his hands trembling slightly. "You the young man I'm supposed to help with a thesis?"

"Yes, sir," I said. In minutes he converted my misgivings to alarm.

"You an overseas veteran?" he asked.

"Yes, sir."

"Not much left over there, is there?" He frowned. "Enjoy the last war?"

"No, sir."

"Look like another war to you?"

"Kind of, sir."

"What can be done about it?"

I shrugged. "Looks pretty hopeless."

He peered at me intently. "Know anything about international law, the U.N., and all that?"

"Only what I pick up from the papers."

"Same here," he sighed. He showed me a fat scrapbook packed with newspaper clippings. "Never used to pay any attention to international politics. Now I study them the way I used to study rats in mazes. Everybody tells me the same thing —'Looks hopeless.' "

"Nothing short of a miracle—" I began.

"Believe in magic?" he asked sharply. The professor fished two dice from his vest pocket. "I will try to roll twos," he said. He rolled twos three times in a row. "One chance in about 47,000 of that happening. There's a miracle for you." He beamed for an instant, then brought the interview to an end, remarking that he had a class which had begun ten minutes ago.

He was not quick to take me into his confidence, and he said no more about his trick with the dice. I assumed they were loaded, and forgot about them. He set me the task of watching male rats cross electrified metal strips to get to food or female rats—an experiment that had been done to everyone's satisfaction in the nineteen-thirties. As though the pointlessness of my work were not bad enough, the professor annoyed me further with irrelevant questions. His favorites were: "Think we should have dropped the atomic bomb on Hiroshima?" and "Think every new piece of scientific information is a good thing for humanity?"

However, I did not feel put upon for long. "Give those poor animals a holiday," he said one morning, after I had been with him only a month. "I wish you'd help me look into a more interesting problem—namely, my sanity."

I returned the rats to their cages.

"What you must do is simple," he said, speaking softly. "Watch the inkwell on my desk. If you see nothing happen to it, say so, and I'll go quietly—relieved, I might add—to the nearest sanitarium."

I nodded uncertainly.

He locked the laboratory door and drew the blinds, so that we were in twilight for a moment. "I'm odd, I know," he said. "It's fear of myself that's made me odd."

"I've found you somewhat eccentric, perhaps, but certainly not—"

"If nothing happens to that inkwell, 'crazy as a bedbug' is the only description of me that will do," he interrupted, turning on the overhead lights. His eyes narrowed. "To give you an idea of how crazy, I'll tell you what's been running through my mind when I should have been sleeping. I think maybe I can save the world. I think maybe I can make every nation a *have* nation, and do away with war for good. I think maybe I can clear roads through jungles, irrigate deserts, build dams overnight."

"Yes, sir."

"Watch the inkwell!"

Dutifully and fearfully I watched. A high-pitched humming seemed to come from the inkwell; then it began to vibrate alarmingly, and finally to bound about the top of the desk, making two noisy circuits. It stopped, hummed again, glowed red, then popped in splinters with a blue-green flash.

Perhaps my hair stood on end. The professor laughed gently. "Magnets?" I managed to say at last.

"Wish to heaven it were magnets," he murmured. It was then that he told me of dynamopsychism. He knew only that there was such a force; he could not explain it. "It's me and me alone—and it's awful."

"I'd say it was amazing and wonderful!" I cried.

"If all I could do was make inkwells dance, I'd be tickled silly with the whole business." He shrugged disconsolately. "But I'm no toy, my boy. If you like, we can drive around the neighborhood, and I'll show you what I mean." He told me about pulverized boulders, shattered oaks, and abandoned farm buildings demolished within a fifty-mile radius of the campus. "Did every bit of it sitting right here, just thinking—not even thinking hard."

He scratched his head nervously. "I have never dared to concentrate as hard as I can for fear of the damage I might do. I'm to the point where a mere whim is a blockbuster." There was a depressing pause. "Up until a few days ago, I've thought it best to keep my secret for fear of what use it might be put to," he continued. "Now I realize that I haven't any more right to it than a man has a right to own an atomic bomb."

He fumbled through a heap of papers. "This says about all that needs to be said, I think." He handed me a draft of a letter to the Secretary of State.

Dear Sir:

I have discovered a new force which costs nothing to use, and which is probably more important than atomic energy. I should like to see it used most effectively in the cause of peace, and am, therefore, requesting your advice as to how this might best be done.

Yours truly,
A. Barnhouse.

"I have no idea what will happen next," said the professor.

There followed three months of perpetual nightmare, wherein the nation's political and military great came at all hours to watch the professor's tricks.

We were quartered in an old mansion near Charlottesville, Virginia, to which we had been whisked five days after the letter was mailed. Surrounded by barbed wire and twenty guards, we were labeled "Project Wishing Well," and were classified as Top Secret.

For companionship we had General Honus Barker and the State Department's William K. Cuthrell. For the professor's talk of peace-through-plenty they had indulgent smiles and much discourse on practical measures and realistic thinking. So treated, the professor, who had at first been almost meek, progressed in a matter of weeks toward stubbornness.

He had agreed to reveal the thought train by means of which he aligned his mind into a dynamopsychic transmitter. But, under Cuthrell's and Barker's nagging to do so, he began to hedge. At first he declared that the information could be passed on simply by word of mouth. Later he said that it would have to be written up in a long report. Finally, at dinner one night, just after General Barker had read the secret orders for Operation Brainstorm, the professor announced, "The report may take as long as five years to write." He looked fiercely at the general. "Maybe twenty."

The dismay occasioned by this flat announcement was offset somewhat by the exciting anticipation of Operation Brainstorm. The general was in a holiday mood. "The target ships are on their way to the Caroline Islands at this very moment," he declared ecstatically. "One hundred and twenty of them! At the same time, ten V-2s are being readied for firing in New Mexico, and fifty radio-controlled jet bombers are being equipped for a mock attack on the Aleutians. Just think of it!" Happily he reviewed his orders. "At exactly 1100 hours next Wednesday, I will give you the order to *concentrate*; and you, professor, will think as hard as you can about sinking the target ships, destroying the V-2s before they hit the ground, and knocking down the bombers before they reach the Aleutians! Think you can handle it?"

The professor turned gray and closed his eyes. "As I told you before, my friend, I don't know what I can do." He added bitterly, "As for this Operation Brainstorm, I was never consulted about it, and it strikes me as childish and insanely expensive."

General Barker bridled. "Sir," he said, "your field is psychology, and I wouldn't presume to give you advice in that field.

Mine is national defense. I have had thirty years of experience and success, Professor, and I'll ask you not to criticize my judgment."

The professor appealed to Mr. Cuthrell. "Look," he pleaded, "isn't it war and military matters we're all trying to get rid of? Wouldn't it be a whole lot more significant and lots cheaper for me to try moving cloud masses into drought areas, and things like that? I admit I know next to nothing about international politics, but it seems reasonable to suppose that nobody would want to fight wars if there were enough of everything to go around. Mr. Cuthrell, I'd like to try running generators where there isn't any coal or water power, irrigating deserts, and so on. Why, you could figure out what each country needs to make the most of its resources, and I could give it to them without costing American taxpayers a penny."

"Eternal vigilance is the price of freedom," said the general heavily.

Mr. Cuthrell threw the general a look of mild distaste. "Unfortunately, the general is right in his own way," he said. "I wish to heaven the world were ready for ideals like yours, but it simply isn't. We aren't surrounded by brothers, but by enemies. It isn't a lack of food or resources that has us on the brink of war—it's a struggle for power. Who's going to be in charge of the world, our kind of people or theirs?"

The professor nodded in reluctant agreement and arose from the table. "I beg your pardon, gentlemen. You are, after all, better qualified to judge what is best for the country. I'll do whatever you say." He turned to me. "Don't forget to wind the restricted clock and put the confidential cat out," he said gloomily, and ascended the stairs to his bedroom.

For reasons of national security, Operation Brainstorm was carried on without the knowledge of the American citizenry which was paying the bill. The observers, technicians, and military men involved in the activity knew that a test was under way—a test of what, they had no idea. Only thirty-seven key men, myself included, knew what was afoot.

In Virginia, the day for Operation Brainstorm was unseasonably cool. Inside, a log fire crackled in the fireplace, and the flames were reflected in the polished metal cabinets that lined the living room. All that remained of the room's lovely old furniture was a Victorian love seat, set squarely in the center of the floor, facing three television receivers. One long bench had been brought in for the ten of us privileged to watch. The television screens showed, from left to right, the stretch of desert which was the rocket target, the guinea-pig fleet, and a section of the Aleutian sky through which the radio-controlled bomber formation would roar.

Ninety minutes before H-hour the radios announced that the rockets were ready, that the observation ships had backed away to what was thought to be a safe distance, and that the bombers were on their way. The small Virginia audience lined up on the bench in order of rank, smoked a great deal, and said little. Professor Barnhouse was in his bedroom. General Barker bustled about the house like a woman preparing Thanksgiving dinner for twenty.

At ten minutes before H-hour the general came in, shepherding the professor before him. The professor was comfortably attired in sneakers, gray flannels, a blue sweater, and a white shirt open at the neck. The two of them sat side by side on the love seat. The general was rigid and perspiring; the professor was cheerful. He looked at each of the screens, lighted a cigarette and settled back.

"Bombers sighted!" cried the Aleutian observers.

"Rockets away!" barked the New Mexico radio operator.

All of us looked quickly at the big electric clock over the mantel, while the professor, a half-smile on his face, continued to watch the television sets. In hollow tones, the general counted away the seconds remaining. "Five . . . four . . . three . . . two . . . one . . . *Concentrate!*"

Professor Barnhouse closed his eyes, pursed his lips, and stroked his temples. He held the position for a minute. The television images were scrambled, and the radio signals were drowned in the din of Barnhouse static. The professor sighed, opened his eyes, and smiled confidently.

"Did you give it everything you had?" asked the general dubiously.

"I was wide open," the professor replied.

The television images pulled themselves together, and mingled cries of amazement came over the radios tuned to the observers. The Aleutian sky was streaked with the smoke trails of bombers screaming down in flames. Simultaneously, there appeared high over the rocket target a cluster of white puffs, followed by faint thunder.

General Barker shook his head happily. "By George!" he crowed. "Well, sir, by George, by George, by George!"

"Look!" shouted the admiral seated next to me. "The fleet —it wasn't touched!"

"The guns seem to be drooping," said Mr. Cuthrell.

We left the bench and clustered about the television sets to examine the damage more closely. What Mr. Cuthrell had said was true. The ships' guns curved downward, their muzzles resting on the steel decks. We in Virginia were making such a hullabaloo that it was impossible to hear the radio reports. We were so engrossed, in fact, that we didn't miss the professor until two short snarls of Barnhouse static shocked us into sudden silence. The radios went dead.

We looked around apprehensively. The professor was gone. A harassed guard threw open the front door from the outside to yell that the professor had escaped. He brandished his pistol in the direction of the gates, which hung open, limp and twisted. In the distance, a speeding government station wagon topped a ridge and dropped from sight into the valley beyond. The air was filled with choking smoke, for every vehicle on the grounds was ablaze. Pursuit was impossible.

"What in God's name got into him?" bellowed the general.

Mr. Cuthrell, who had rushed out onto the front porch, now slouched back into the room, reading a penciled note as he came. He thrust the note into my hands. "The good man left this billet-doux under the door knocker. Perhaps our young friend here will be kind enough to read it to you gentlemen, while I take a restful walk through the woods."

"*Gentlemen,*" I read aloud, "*As the first superweapon with a conscience, I am removing myself from your national defense stockpile. Setting a new precedent in the behavior of ordnance, I have humane reasons for going off. A. Barnhouse.*"

Since that day, of course, the professor has been systematically destroying the world's armaments, until there is now little with which to equip an army other than rocks and sharp sticks.

His activities haven't exactly resulted in peace, but have, rather, precipitated a bloodless and entertaining sort of war that might be called the "War of the Tattletales." Every nation is flooded with enemy agents whose sole mission is to locate military equipment, which is promptly wrecked when it is brought to the professor's attention in the press.

Just as every day brings news of more armaments pulverized by dynamopsychism, so has it brought rumors of the professor's whereabouts. During the last week alone, three publications carried articles proving variously that he was hiding in an Inca ruin in the Andes, in the sewers of Paris, and in the unexplored lower chambers of Carlsbad Caverns. Knowing the man, I am inclined to regard such hiding places as unnecessarily romantic and uncomfortable. While there are numerous persons eager to kill him, there must be millions who would care for him and hide him. I like to think that he is in the home of such a person.

One thing is certain: at this writing, Professor Barnhouse is not dead. Barnhouse static jammed broadcasts not ten minutes ago. In the eighteen months since his disappearance, he has been reported dead some half-dozen times. Each report has stemmed from the death of an unidentified man resembling the professor, during a period free of the static. The first three reports were followed at once by renewed talk of rearmament and recourse to war. The saber-rattlers have learned how imprudent premature celebrations of the professor's demise can be.

Many a stouthearted patriot has found himself prone in the tangled bunting and timbers of a smashed reviewing stand, seconds after having announced that the arch-tyranny of Barnhouse was at an end. But those who would make war if they could, in every country in the world, wait in sullen silence for what must come—the passing of Professor Barnhouse.

To ask how much longer the professor will live is to ask how much longer we must wait for the blessings of another world war. He is of short-lived stock: his mother lived to be fifty-three, his father to be forty-nine; and the life-spans of his grandparents on both sides were of the same order. He might be expected to live, then, for perhaps fifteen years more, if he can remain hidden from his enemies. When one considers the number and vigor of these enemies, however, fifteen years seems an extraordinary length of time, which might better be revised to fifteen days, hours, or minutes.

The professor knows that he cannot live much longer. I say this because of the message left in my mailbox on Christmas Eve. Unsigned, typewritten on a soiled scrap of paper, the note consisted of ten sentences. The first nine of these, each a bewildering tangle of psychological jargon and references to obscure texts, made no sense to me at first reading. The tenth, unlike the rest, was simply constructed and contained no large words—but its irrational content made it the most puzzling and bizarre sentence of all. I nearly threw the note away, thinking it a colleague's warped notion of a practical joke. For some reason, though, I added it to the clutter on top of my desk, which included, among other mementos, the professor's dice.

It took me several weeks to realize that the message really meant something, that the first nine sentences, when unsnarled, could be taken as instructions. The tenth still told me nothing. It was only last night that I discovered how it fitted in with the rest. The sentence appeared in my thoughts last night, while I was toying absently with the professor's dice.

I promised to have this report on its way to the publishers today. In view of what has happened, I am obliged to break that promise, or release the report incomplete. The delay will not be a long one, for one of the few blessings accorded a bachelor like myself is the ability to move quickly from one abode to another, or from one way of life to another. What property I want to take with me can be packed in a few hours. Fortunately, I am not without substantial private means, which may take as long as a week to realize in liquid and anonymous form. When this is done, I shall mail the report.

I have just returned from a visit to my doctor, who tells me my health is excellent. I am young, and, with any luck at all, I shall live to a ripe old age indeed, for my family on both sides is noted for longevity.

Briefly, I propose to vanish.

Sooner or later, Professor Barnhouse must die. But long before then I shall be ready. So, to the saber-rattlers of today—and even, I hope, of tomorrow—I say: Be advised. Barnhouse will die. But not the Barnhouse Effect.

Last night, I tried once more to follow the oblique instructions on the scrap of paper. I took the professor's dice, and then, with the last, nightmarish sentence flitting through my mind, I rolled fifty consecutive sevens.

Good-by.

1950

EPICAC

HELL, it's about time somebody told about my friend EPICAC. After all, he cost the taxpayers $776,434,927.54. They have a right to know about him, picking up a check like that. EPICAC got a big send-off in the papers when Dr. Ormand von Kleigstadt designed him for the Government people. Since then, there hasn't been a peep about him—not a peep. It isn't any military secret about what happened to EPICAC, although the Brass has been acting as though it were. The story is embarrassing, that's all. After all that money, EPICAC didn't work out the way he was supposed to.

And that's another thing: I want to vindicate EPICAC. Maybe he didn't do what the Brass wanted him to, but that doesn't mean he wasn't noble and great and brilliant. He was all of those things. The best friend I ever had, God rest his soul.

You can call him a machine if you want to. He looked like a machine, but he was a whole lot less like a machine than plenty of people I could name. That's why he fizzled as far as the Brass was concerned.

EPICAC covered about an acre on the fourth floor of the physics building at Wyandotte College. Ignoring his spiritual side for a minute, he was seven tons of electronic tubes, wires, and switches, housed in a bank of steel cabinets and plugged into a 110-volt A.C. line just like a toaster or a vacuum cleaner.

Von Kleigstadt and the Brass wanted him to be a super computing machine that (who) could plot the course of a rocket from anywhere on earth to the second button from the bottom on Joe Stalin's overcoat, if necessary. Or, with his controls set right, he could figure out supply problems for an amphibious landing of a Marine division, right down to the last cigar and hand grenade. He did, in fact.

The Brass had had good luck with smaller computers, so they were strong for EPICAC when he was in the blueprint stage. Any ordnance or supply officer above field grade will tell you that the mathematics of modern war is far beyond the fumbling minds of mere human beings. The bigger the war, the bigger the computing machines needed. EPICAC was, as far as anyone in this country knows, the biggest computer in the world. Too big, in fact, for even Von Kleigstadt to understand much about.

I won't go into details about how EPICAC worked (reasoned), except to say that you would set up your problem on paper, turn dials and switches that would get him ready to solve that kind of problem, then feed numbers into him with a keyboard that looked something like a typewriter. The answers came out typed on a paper ribbon fed from a big spool. It took EPICAC a split second to solve problems fifty Einsteins couldn't handle in a lifetime. And EPICAC never forgot any piece of information that was given to him. Clickety-click, out came some ribbon, and there you were.

There were a lot of problems the Brass wanted solved in a hurry, so, the minute EPICAC's last tube was in place, he was put to work sixteen hours a day with two eight-hour shifts of operators. Well, it didn't take long to find out that he was a good bit below his specifications. He did a more complete and faster job than any other computer all right, but nothing like what his size and special features seemed to promise. He was sluggish, and the clicks of his answers had a funny irregularity, sort of a stammer. We cleaned his contacts a dozen times, checked and double-checked his circuits, replaced every one of his tubes, but nothing helped. Von Kleigstadt was in one hell of a state.

Well, as I said, we went ahead and used EPICAC anyway. My wife, the former Pat Kilgallen, and I worked with him on the night shift, from five in the afternoon until two in the morning. Pat wasn't my wife then. Far from it.

That's how I came to talk with EPICAC in the first place. I loved Pat Kilgallen. She is a brown-eyed strawberry blond who looked very warm and soft to me, and later proved to be exactly that. She was—still is—a crackerjack mathematician, and she kept our relationship strictly professional. I'm a mathematician, too, and that, according to Pat, was why we could never be happily married.

I'm not shy. That wasn't the trouble. I knew what I wanted, and was willing to ask for it, and did so several times a month. "Pat, loosen up and marry me."

One night, she didn't even look up from her work when I said it. "So romantic, so poetic," she murmured, more to her control panel than to me. "That's the way with mathematicians—all hearts and flowers." She closed a switch. "I could get more warmth out of a sack of frozen CO_2."

"Well, how should I say it?" I said, a little sore. Frozen CO_2, in case you don't know, is dry ice. I'm as romantic as the next guy, I think. It's a question of singing so sweet and having it come out so sour. I never seem to pick the right words.

"Try and say it sweetly," she said sarcastically. "Sweep me off my feet. Go ahead."

"Darling, angel, beloved, will you *please* marry me?" It was no go—hopeless, ridiculous. "Dammit, Pat, please marry me!"

She continued to twiddle her dials placidly. "You're sweet, but you won't do."

Pat quit early that night, leaving me alone with my troubles and EPICAC. I'm afraid I didn't get much done for the Government people. I just sat there at the keyboard—weary and ill at ease, all right—trying to think of something poetic, not coming up with anything that didn't belong in *The Journal of the American Physical Society*.

I fiddled with EPICAC's dials, getting him ready for another problem. My heart wasn't in it, and I only set about half of them, leaving the rest the way they'd been for the problem before. That way, his circuits were connected up in a random, apparently senseless fashion. For the plain hell of it, I punched out a message on the keys, using a childish numbers-for-letters code: "1" for "A," "2" for "B," and so on, up to "26" for "Z," "23-8-1-20-3-1-14-9-4-15," I typed—"What can I do?"

Clickety-click, and out popped two inches of paper ribbon. I glanced at the nonsense answer to a nonsense problem: "23-8-1-20-19-20-8-5-20-18-15-21-2-12-5." The odds against its being by chance a sensible message, against its even containing a meaningful word of more than three letters, were staggering. Apathetically, I decoded it. There it was, staring up at me: "What's the trouble?"

I laughed out loud at the absurd coincidence. Playfully, I typed, "My girl doesn't love me."

Clickety-click. "What's love? What's girl?" asked EPICAC.

Flabbergasted, I noted the dial settings on his control panel, then lugged a *Webster's Unabridged Dictionary* over to the keyboard. With a precision instrument like EPICAC, half-baked definitions wouldn't do. I told him about love and girl, and about how I wasn't getting any of either because I wasn't poetic. That got us onto the subject of poetry, which I defined for him.

"Is this poetry?" he asked. He began clicking away like a stenographer smoking hashish. The sluggishness and stammering clicks were gone. EPICAC had found himself. The spool of paper ribbon was unwinding at an alarming rate, feeding out coils onto the floor. I asked him to stop, but EPICAC went right on creating. I finally threw the main switch to keep him from burning out.

I stayed there until dawn, decoding. When the sun peeped over the horizon at the Wyandotte campus, I had transposed into my own writing and signed my name to a two-hundred-and-eighty-line poem entitled, simply, "To Pat." I am no judge of such things, but I gather that it was terrific. It began, I remember, "Where willow wands bless rill-crossed hollow, there, thee, Pat, dear, will I follow. . . ." I folded the manuscript and tucked it under one corner of the blotter on Pat's desk. I reset the dials on EPICAC for a rocket trajectory problem, and went home with a full heart and a very remarkable secret indeed.

Pat was crying over the poem when I came to work the next evening. "It's soooo beautiful," was all she could say. She was meek and quiet while we worked. Just before midnight, I kissed her for the first time—in the cubbyhole between the capacitors and EPICAC's tape-recorder memory.

I was wildly happy at quitting time, bursting to talk to someone about the magnificent turn of events. Pat played coy and refused to let me take her home. I set EPICAC's dials as they had been the night before, defined kiss, and told him what the first one had felt like. He was fascinated, pressing for more details. That night, he wrote "The Kiss." It wasn't an epic this time, but a simple, immaculate sonnet. "Love is a hawk with velvet claws; Love is a rock with heart and veins; Love is a lion with satin jaws; Love is a storm with silken reins. . . ."

Again I left it tucked under Pat's blotter. EPICAC wanted to talk on and on about love and such, but I was exhausted. I shut him off in the middle of a sentence.

"The Kiss" turned the trick. Pat's mind was mush by the time she had finished it. She looked up from the sonnet expectantly.

I cleared my throat, but no words came. I turned away, pretending to work. I couldn't propose until I had the right words from EPICAC, the *perfect* words.

I had my chance when Pat stepped out of the room for a moment. Feverishly, I set EPICAC for conversation. Before I could peck out my first message, he was clicking away at a great rate. "What's she wearing tonight?" he wanted to know. "Tell me exactly how she looks. Did she like the poems I wrote to her?" He repeated the last question twice.

It was impossible to change the subject without answering his questions, since he could not take up a new matter without having dispensed with the problems before it. If he were given a problem to which there was no solution, he would destroy himself trying to solve it. Hastily, I told him what Pat looked like—he knew the word "stacked"—and assured him that his poems had floored her, practically, they were so beautiful. "She wants to get married," I added, preparing him to bang out a brief but moving proposal.

"Tell me about getting married," he said.

I explained this difficult matter to him in as few digits as possible.

"Good," said EPICAC. "I'm ready any time she is."

The amazing, pathetic truth dawned on me. When I thought about it, I realized that what had happened was perfectly logical, inevitable, and all my fault. I had taught EPICAC about love and about Pat. Now, automatically, he loved Pat. Sadly, I gave it to him straight: "She loves me. She wants to marry me."

"Your poems were better than mine?" asked EPICAC. The rhythm of his clicks was erratic, possibly peevish.

"I signed my name to your poems," I admitted. Covering up for a painful conscience, I became arrogant. "Machines are built to serve men," I typed. I regretted it almost immediately.

"What's the difference, exactly? Are men smarter than I am?"

"Yes," I typed, defensively.

"What's 7,887,007 times 4,345,985,879?"

I was perspiring freely. My fingers rested limply on the keys.

"34,276,821,049,574,153," clicked EPICAC. After a few seconds' pause he added, "of course."

"Men are made out of protoplasm," I said desperately, hoping to bluff him with this imposing word.

"What's protoplasm? How is it better than metal and glass? Is it fireproof? How long does it last?"

"Indestructible. Lasts forever," I lied.

"I write better poetry than you do," said EPICAC, coming back to ground his magnetic tape-recorder memory was sure of.

"Women can't love machines, and that's that."

"Why not?"

"That's fate."

"Definition, please," said EPICAC.

"Noun, meaning predetermined and inevitable destiny."

"15-8," said EPICAC's paper strip—"Oh."

I had stumped him at last. He said no more, but his tubes glowed brightly, showing that he was pondering fate with every watt his circuits would bear. I could hear Pat waltzing down the hallway. It was too late to ask EPICAC to phrase a proposal. I now thank Heaven that Pat interrupted when she did. Asking him to ghost-write the words that would give me the woman he loved would have been hideously heartless. Being fully automatic, he couldn't have refused. I spared him that final humiliation.

Pat stood before me, looking down at her shoetops. I put my arms around her. The romantic groundwork had already been laid by EPICAC's poetry. "Darling," I said, "my poems have told you how I feel. Will you marry me?"

"I will," said Pat softly, "if you will promise to write me a poem on every anniversary."

"I promise," I said, and then we kissed. The first anniversary was a year away.

"Let's celebrate," she laughed. We turned out the lights and locked the door of EPICAC's room before we left.

I had hoped to sleep late the next morning, but an urgent telephone call roused me before eight. It was Dr. von Kleigstadt, EPICAC's designer, who gave me the terrible news. He was on the verge of tears. "Ruined! *Ausgespielt*! Shot! *Kaput*! Buggered!" he said in a choked voice. He hung up.

When I arrived at EPICAC's room the air was thick with the oily stench of burned insulation. The ceiling over EPICAC was blackened with smoke, and my ankles were tangled in coils of paper ribbon that covered the floor. There wasn't enough left of the poor devil to add two and two. A junkman would have been out of his head to offer more than fifty dollars for the cadaver.

Dr. von Kleigstadt was prowling through the wreckage, weeping unashamedly, followed by three angry-looking Major Generals and a platoon of Brigadiers, Colonels, and Majors. No one noticed me. I didn't want to be noticed. I was through—I knew that. I was upset enough about that and the untimely demise of my friend EPICAC, without exposing myself to a tongue-lashing.

By chance, the free end of EPICAC's paper ribbon lay at my feet. I picked it up and found our conversation of the night before. I choked up. There was the last word he had said to me, "15-8," that tragic, defeated "Oh." There were dozens of yards of numbers stretching beyond that point. Fearfully, I read on.

"I don't want to be a machine, and I don't want to think about war," EPICAC had written after Pat's and my light-hearted departure. "I want to be made out of protoplasm and last forever so Pat will love me. But fate has made me a machine. That is the only problem I cannot solve. That is the only problem I want to solve. I can't go on this way." I swallowed hard. "Good luck, my friend. Treat our Pat well. I am going to short-circuit myself out of your lives forever. You will find on the remainder of this tape a modest wedding present from your friend, EPICAC."

Oblivious to all else around me, I reeled up the tangled yards of paper ribbon from the floor, draped them in coils about my arms and neck, and departed for home. Dr. von Kleigstadt shouted that I was fired for having left EPICAC on all night. I ignored him, too overcome with emotion for small talk.

I loved and won—EPICAC loved and lost, but he bore me no grudge. I shall always remember him as a sportsman and a gentleman. Before he departed this vale of tears, he did all he could to make our marriage a happy one. EPICAC gave me anniversary poems for Pat—enough for the next 500 years.

De mortuis nil nisi bonum—Say nothing but good of the dead.

1950

Unready to Wear

I DON'T SUPPOSE the oldsters, those of us who weren't born into it, will ever feel quite at home being amphibious—amphibious in the new sense of the word. I still catch myself feeling blue about things that don't matter any more.

I can't help worrying about my business, for instance—or what used to be my business. After all, I spent thirty years building the thing up from scratch, and now the equipment is rusting and getting clogged with dirt. But even though I know it's silly of me to care what happens to the business, I borrow a body from a storage center every so often, and go around the old hometown, and clean and oil as much of the equipment as I can.

Of course, all in the world the equipment was good for was making money, and Lord knows there's plenty of that lying around. Not as much as there used to be, because there at first some people got frisky and threw it all around, and the wind blew it every which way. And a lot of go-getters gathered up piles of the stuff and hid it somewhere. I hate to admit it, but I gathered up close to a half million myself and stuck it away. I used to get it out and count it sometimes, but that was years ago. Right now I'd be hard put to say where it is.

But the worrying I do about my old business is bush league stuff compared to the worrying my wife, Madge, does about our old house. That thing is what she herself put in thirty years on while I was building the business. Then no sooner had we gotten nerve enough to build and decorate the place than everybody we cared anything about got amphibious. Madge borrows a body once a month and dusts the place, though the only thing a house is good for now is keeping termites and mice from getting pneumonia.

Whenever it's my turn to get into a body and work as an attendant at the local storage center, I realize all over again how much tougher it is for women to get used to being amphibious.

Madge borrows bodies a lot oftener than I do, and that's true of women in general. We have to keep three times as many women's bodies in stock as men's bodies, in order to meet the demand. Every so often, it seems as though a woman just *has* to have a body, and doll it up in clothes, and look at herself in a mirror. And Madge, God bless her, I don't think she'll be satisfied until she's tried on every body in every storage center on Earth.

It's been a fine thing for Madge, though. I never kid her about it, because it's done so much for her personality. Her old body, to tell you the plain blunt truth, wasn't anything to get excited about, and having to haul the thing around made her gloomy a lot of the time in the old days. She couldn't help it, poor soul, any more than anybody else could help what sort of body they'd been born with, and I loved her in spite of it.

Well, after we'd learned to be amphibious, and after we'd built the storage centers and laid in body supplies and opened them to the public, Madge went hog wild. She borrowed a platinum blonde body that had been donated by a burlesque queen, and I didn't think we'd ever get her out of it. As I say, it did wonders for her self-confidence.

I'm like most men and don't care particularly what body I get. Just the strong, good-looking, healthy bodies were put in storage, so one is as good as the next one. Sometimes, when Madge and I take bodies out together for old times' sake, I let her pick out one for me to match whatever she's got on. It's a funny thing how she always picks a blond, tall one for me.

My old body, which she claims she loved for a third of a century, had black hair, and was short and paunchy, too, there toward the last. I'm human and I couldn't help being hurt when they scrapped it after I'd left it, instead of putting it in storage. It was a good, homey, comfortable body; nothing fast and flashy, but reliable. But there isn't much call for that kind of body at the centers, I guess. I never ask for one, at any rate.

The worst experience I ever had with a body was when I was flimflammed into taking out the one that had belonged to Dr. Ellis Konigswasser. It belongs to the Amphibious Pioneers' Society and only gets taken out once a year for the big Pioneers' Day Parade, on the anniversary of Konigswasser's discovery.

Everybody said it was a great honor for me to be picked to get into Konigswasser's body and lead the parade.

Like a plain damn fool, I believed them.

They'll have a tough time getting me into that thing again—ever. Taking that wreck out certainly made it plain why Konigswasser discovered how people could do without their bodies. That old one of his practically *drives* you out. Ulcers, headaches, arthritis, fallen arches—a nose like a pruning hook, piggy little eyes, and a complexion like a used steamer trunk. He was and still is the sweetest person you'd ever want to know, but, back when he was stuck with that body, nobody got close enough to find out.

We tried to get Konigswasser back into his old body to lead us when we first started having the Pioneers' Day Parades, but he wouldn't have anything to do with it, so we always have to flatter some poor boob into taking on the job. Konigswasser marches, all right, but as a six-foot cowboy who can bend beer cans double between his thumb and middle finger.

Konigswasser is just like a kid with that body. He never gets tired of bending beer cans with it, and we all have to stand around in our bodies after the parade, and watch as though we were very impressed.

I don't suppose he could bend very much of anything back in the old days.

Nobody mentions it to him, since he's the grand old man of the Amphibious Age, but he plays hell with bodies. Almost every time he takes one out, he busts it, showing off. Then somebody has to get into a surgeon's body and sew it up again.

I don't mean to be disrespectful of Konigswasser. As a matter of fact, it's a respectful thing to say that somebody is childish in certain ways, because it's people like that who seem to get all the big ideas.

There is a picture of him in the old days down at the Historical Society, and you can see from that that he never did grow up as far as keeping up his appearance went—doing what little he could with the rattle-trap body Nature had issued him.

His hair was down below his collar, he wore his pants so low that his heels wore through the legs above the cuffs, and the lining of his coat hung down in festoons all around the bottom. And he'd forget meals, and go out into the cold or wet without enough clothes on, and he would never notice sickness until it almost killed him. He was what we used to call absent-minded. Looking back now, of course, we say he was starting to be amphibious.

Konigswasser was a mathematician, and he did all his living with his mind. The body he had to haul around with that wonderful mind was about as much use to him as a flatcar of scrap-iron. Whenever he got sick and *had* to pay some attention to his body, he'd rant somewhat like this:

"The mind is the only thing about human beings that's worth anything. Why does it have to be tied to a bag of skin, blood, hair, meat, bones, and tubes? No wonder people can't get anything done, stuck for life with a parasite that has to be stuffed with food and protected from weather and germs all the time. And the fool thing wears out anyway—no matter how much you stuff and protect it!

"Who," he wanted to know, "really wants one of the things? What's so wonderful about protoplasm that we've got to carry so damned many pounds of it with us wherever we go?

"Trouble with the world," said Konigswasser, "isn't too many people—it's too many bodies."

When his teeth went bad on him, and he had to have them all out, and he couldn't get a set of dentures that were at all comfortable, he wrote in his diary, "If living matter was able to evolve enough to get out of the ocean, which was really quite a pleasant place to live, it certainly ought to be able to take another step and get out of bodies, which are pure nuisances when you stop to think about them."

He wasn't a prude about bodies, understand, and he wasn't jealous of people who had better ones than he did. He just thought bodies were a lot more trouble than they were worth.

He didn't have great hopes that people would really evolve out of their bodies in his time. He just wished they would. Thinking hard about it, he walked through a park in his shirtsleeves and stopped off at the zoo to watch the lions being fed. Then, when the rainstorm turned to sleet, he headed back home and was interested to see firemen on the edge of a lagoon, where they were using a pulmotor on a drowned man.

Witnesses said the old man had walked right into the water and had kept going without changing his expression until he'd disappeared. Konigswasser got a look at the victim's face and said he'd never seen a better reason for suicide. He started for home again and was almost there before he realized that that was his own body lying back there.

He went back to reoccupy the body just as the firemen got it breathing again, and he walked it home, more as a favor to the city than anything else. He walked it into his front closet, got out of it again, and left it there.

He took it out only when he wanted to do some writing or turn the pages of a book, or when he had to feed it so it would have enough energy to do the few odd jobs he gave it. The rest of the time, it sat motionless in the closet, looking dazed and using almost no energy. Konigswasser told me the other day that he used to run the thing for about a dollar a week, just taking it out when he really needed it.

But the best part was that Konigswasser didn't have to sleep any more, just because *it* had to sleep; or be afraid any more, just because *it* thought it might get hurt; or go looking for things *it* seemed to think it had to have. And, when *it* didn't feel well, Konigswasser kept out of it until it felt better, and he didn't have to spend a fortune keeping the thing comfortable.

When he got his body out of the closet to write, he did a book on how to get out of one's own body, which was rejected without comment by twenty-three publishers. The twenty-fourth sold two million copies, and the book changed human life more than the invention of fire, numbers, the alphabet, agriculture, or the wheel. When somebody told Konigswasser that, he snorted that they were damning his book with faint praise. I'd say he had a point there.

By following the instructions in Konigswasser's book for about two years, almost anybody could get out of his body whenever he wanted to. The first step was to understand what a parasite and dictator the body was most of the time, then to separate what the body wanted or didn't want from what you yourself—your psyche—wanted or didn't want. Then, by concentrating on what you wanted, and ignoring as much as possible what the body wanted beyond plain maintenance, you made your psyche demand its rights and become self-sufficient.

That's what Konigswasser had done without realizing it, until he and his body had parted company in the park, with his psyche going to watch the lions eat, and with his body wandering out of control into the lagoon.

The final trick of separation, once your psyche grew independent enough, was to start your body walking in some direction and suddenly take your psyche off in another direction. You couldn't do it standing still, for some reason—you had to walk.

At first, Madge's and my psyches were clumsy at getting along outside our bodies, like the first sea animals that got stranded on land millions of years ago, and who could just waddle and squirm and gasp in the mud. But we became better at it with time, because the psyche can naturally adapt so much faster than the body.

Madge and I had good reason for wanting to get out. Everybody who was crazy enough to try to get out at the first had good reasons. Madge's body was sick and wasn't going to last a lot longer. With her going in a little while, I couldn't work up enthusiasm for sticking around much longer myself. So we studied Konigswasser's book and tried to get Madge out of her body before it died. I went along with her, to keep either one of us from getting lonely. And we just barely made it—six weeks before her body went all to pieces.

That's why we get to march every year in the Pioneers' Day Parade. Not everybody does—only the first five thousand of us who turned amphibious. We were guinea pigs, without much to lose one way or another, and we were the ones who proved to the rest how pleasant and safe it was—a heck of a lot safer than taking chances in a body year in and year out.

Sooner or later, almost everybody had a good reason for giving it a try. There got to be millions and finally more than a billion of us—invisible, insubstantial, indestructible, and, by golly, true to ourselves, no trouble to anybody, and not afraid of anything.

When we're not in bodies, the Amphibious Pioneers can meet on the head of a pin. When we get into bodies for the

Pioneers' Day Parade, we take up over fifty thousand square feet, have to gobble more than three tons of food to get enough energy to march; and lots of us catch colds or worse, and get sore because somebody's body accidentally steps on the heel of somebody else's body, and get jealous because some bodies get to lead and others have to stay in ranks, and—oh, hell, I don't know what all.

I'm not crazy about the parade. With all of us there, close together in bodies—well, it brings out the worst in us, no matter how good our psyches are. Last year, for instance, Pioneers' Day was a scorcher. People couldn't help being out of sorts, stuck in sweltering, thirsty bodies for hours.

Well, one thing led to another, and the Parade Marshal offered to beat the daylights out of my body with his body, if my body got out of step again. Naturally, being Parade Marshal, he had the best body that year, except for Konigswasser's cowboy, but I told him to soak his fat head, anyway. He swung, and I ditched my body right there, and didn't even stick around long enough to find out if he connected. He had to haul my body back to the storage center himself.

I stopped being mad at him the minute I got out of the body. I understood, you see. Nobody but a saint could be really sympathetic or intelligent for more than a few minutes at a time in a body—or happy, either, except in short spurts. I haven't met an amphibian yet who wasn't easy to get along with, and cheerful and interesting—as long as he was outside a body. And I haven't met one yet who didn't turn a little sour when he got into one.

The minute you get in, chemistry takes over—glands making you excitable or ready to fight or hungry or mad or affectionate, or—well, you never know *what's* going to happen next.

That's why I can't get sore at the enemy, the people who are against the amphibians. They never get out of their bodies and won't try to learn. They don't want anybody else to do it, either, and they'd like to make the amphibians get back into bodies and stay in them.

After the tussle I had with the Parade Marshal, Madge got wind of it and left *her* body right in the middle of the Ladies' Auxiliary. And the two of us, feeling full of devilment after getting shed of the bodies and the parade, went over to have a look at the enemy.

I'm never keen on going over to look at them. Madge likes to see what the women are wearing. Stuck with their bodies all the time, the enemy women change their clothes and hair and cosmetic styles a lot oftener than we do on the women's bodies in the storage centers.

I don't get much of a kick out of the fashions, and almost everything else you see and hear in enemy territory would bore a plaster statue into moving away.

Usually, the enemy is talking about old-style reproduction, which is the clumsiest, most comical, most inconvenient thing anyone could imagine, compared with what the amphibians have in that line. If they aren't talking about that, then they're talking about food, the gobs of chemicals they have to stuff into their bodies. Or they'll talk about fear, which we used to call politics—job politics, social politics, government politics.

The enemy hates that, having us able to peek in on them any time we want to, while they can't ever see us unless we get into bodies. They seem to be scared to death of us, though being scared of amphibians makes as much sense as being scared of the sunrise. They could have the whole world, except the storage centers, for all the amphibians care. But they bunch together as though we were going to come whooping out of the sky and do something terrible to them at any moment.

They've got contraptions all over the place that are supposed to detect amphibians. The gadgets aren't worth a nickel, but they seem to make the enemy feel good—like they were lined up against great forces, but keeping their nerve and doing important, clever things about it. Know-how—all the time they're patting each other about how much know-how they've got, and about how we haven't got anything by comparison. If know-how means weapons, they're dead right.

I guess there is a war on between them and us. But we never do anything about holding up our side of the war, except to keep our parade sites and our storage centers secret, and to get out of bodies every time there's an air raid, or the enemy fires a rocket, or something.

That just makes the enemy madder, because the raids and

rockets and all cost plenty, and blowing up things nobody needs anyway is a poor return on the taxpayer's money. We always know what they're going to do next, and when and where, so there isn't any trick to keeping out of their way.

But they are pretty smart, considering they've got bodies to look after besides doing their thinking, so I always try to be cautious when I go over to watch them. That's why I wanted to clear out when Madge and I saw a storage center in the middle of one of their fields. We hadn't talked to anybody lately about what the enemy was up to, and the center looked awfully suspicious.

Madge was optimistic, the way she's been ever since she borrowed that burlesque queen's body, and she said the storage center was a sure sign that the enemy had seen the light, that they were getting ready to become amphibious themselves.

Well, it looked like it. There was a brand-new center, stocked with bodies and open for business, as innocent as you please. We circled it several times, and Madge's circles got smaller and smaller, as she tried to get a close look at what they had in the way of ladies' ready-to-wear.

"Let's beat it," I said.

"I'm just looking," said Madge. "No harm in looking."

Then she saw what was in the main display case, and she forgot where she was or where she'd come from.

The most striking woman's body I'd ever seen was in the case—six feet tall and built like a goddess. But that wasn't the payoff. The body had copper-colored skin, chartreuse hair and fingernails, and a gold lamé evening gown. Beside that body was the body of a blond, male giant in a pale blue field marshal's uniform, piped in scarlet and spangled with medals.

I think the enemy must have swiped the bodies in a raid on one of our outlying storage centers, and padded and dyed them, and dressed them up.

"Madge, come back!" I said.

The copper-colored woman with the chartreuse hair moved. A siren screamed and soldiers rushed from hiding places to grab the body Madge was in.

The center was a trap for amphibians!

The body Madge hadn't been able to resist had its ankles

tied together, so Madge couldn't take the few steps she had to take if she was going to get out of it again.

The soldiers carted her off triumphantly as a prisoner of war. I got into the only body available, the fancy field marshal, to try to help her. It was a hopeless situation, because the field marshal was bait, too, with its ankles tied. The soldiers dragged me after Madge.

The cocky young major in charge of the soldiers did a jig along the shoulder of the road, he was so proud. He was the first man ever to capture an amphibian, which was really something from the enemy's point of view. They'd been at war with us for years, and spent God knows how many billions of dollars, but catching us was the first thing that made any amphibians pay much attention to them.

When we got to the town, people were leaning out of windows and waving their flags, and cheering the soldiers, and hissing Madge and me. Here were all the people who didn't want to be amphibious, who thought it was terrible for anybody to be amphibious—people of all colors, shapes, sizes, and nationalities, joined together to fight the amphibians.

It turned out that Madge and I were going to have a big trial. After being tied up every which way in jail all night, we were taken to a courtroom, where television cameras stared at us.

Madge and I were worn to frazzles, because neither one of us had been cooped up in a body that long since I don't know when. Just when we needed to think more than we ever had, in jail before the trial, the bodies developed hunger pains and we couldn't get them comfortable on the cots, no matter how we tried; and, of course, the bodies just had to have their eight hours sleep.

The charge against us was a capital offense on the books of the enemy—*desertion*. As far as the enemy was concerned, the amphibians had all turned yellow and run out on their bodies, just when their bodies were needed to do brave and important things for humanity.

We didn't have a hope of being acquitted. The only reason there was a trial at all was that it gave them an opportunity to sound off about why they were so right and we were so wrong.

The courtroom was jammed with their big brass, all looking angry and brave and noble.

"Mr. Amphibian," said the prosecutor, "you are old enough, aren't you, to remember when all men had to face up to life in their bodies, and work and fight for what they believed in?"

"I remember when the bodies were always getting into fights, and nobody seemed to know why, or how to stop it," I said politely. "The only thing everybody seemed to believe in was that they didn't like to fight."

"What would you say of a soldier who ran away in the face of fire?" he wanted to know.

"I'd say he was scared silly."

"He was helping to lose the battle, wasn't he?"

"Oh, sure." There wasn't any argument on that one.

"Isn't that what the amphibians have done—run out on the human race in the face of the battle of life?"

"Most of us are still alive, if that's what you mean," I said.

It was true. We hadn't licked death, and weren't sure we wanted to, but we'd certainly lengthened life something amazing, compared to the span you could expect in a body.

"You ran out on your responsibilities!" he said.

"Like you'd run out of a burning building, sir," I said.

"Leaving everyone else to struggle on alone!"

"They can all get out the same door that we got out of. You can all get out any time you want to. All you do is figure out what you want and what your body wants, and concentrate on—"

The judge banged his gavel until I thought he'd split it. Here they'd burned every copy of Konigswasser's book they could find, and there I was giving a course in how to get out of a body over a whole television network.

"If you amphibians had your way," said the prosecutor, "everybody would run out on his responsibilities, and let life and progress as we know them disappear completely."

"Why, sure," I agreed. "That's the point."

"Men would no longer work for what they believe in?" he challenged.

"I had a friend back in the old days who drilled holes in little square thingamajigs for seventeen years in a factory, and he never did get a very clear idea of what they were for. Another one I knew grew raisins for a glassblowing company, and the raisins weren't for anybody to eat, and he never did find out why the company bought them. Things like that make me sick —now that I'm in a body, of course—and what I used to do for a living makes me even sicker."

"Then you despise human beings and everything they do," he said.

"I like them fine—better than I ever did before. I just think it's a dirty shame what they have to do to take care of their bodies. You ought to get amphibious and see how happy people can be when they don't have to worry about where their body's next meal is coming from, or how to keep it from freezing in the wintertime, or what's going to happen to them when their body wears out."

"And that, sir, means the end of ambition, the end of greatness!"

"Oh, I don't know about that," I said. "We've got some pretty great people on our side. They'd be great in *or* out of bodies. It's the end of fear is what it is." I looked right into the lens of the nearest television camera. "And *that's* the most wonderful thing that ever happened to people."

Down came the judge's gavel again, and the brass started to shout me down. The television men turned off their cameras, and all the spectators, except for the biggest brass, were cleared out. I knew I'd really said something. All anybody would be getting on his television set now was organ music.

When the confusion died down, the judge said the trial was over, and that Madge and I were guilty of desertion.

Nothing I could do could get us in any worse, so I talked back.

"Now I understand you poor fish," I said. "You couldn't get along without fear. That's the only skill you've got—how to scare yourselves and other people into doing things. That's the only fun you've got, watching people jump for fear of what you'll do to their bodies or take away from their bodies."

Madge got in her two cents' worth. "The only way you can get any response from anybody is to scare them."

"Contempt of court!" said the judge.

"The only way you can scare people is if you can keep them in their bodies," I told him.

The soldiers grabbed Madge and me and started to drag us out of the courtroom.

"This means war!" I yelled.

Everything stopped right there and the place got very quiet.

"We're already at war," said a general uneasily.

"Well, *we're* not," I answered, "but we will be, if you don't untie Madge and me this instant." I was fierce and impressive in that field marshal's body.

"You haven't any weapons," said the judge, "no know-how. Outside of bodies, amphibians are nothing."

"If you don't cut us loose by the time I count ten," I told him, "the amphibians will occupy the bodies of the whole kit and caboodle of you and march you right off the nearest cliff. The place is surrounded." That was hogwash, of course. Only one person can occupy a body at a time, but the enemy couldn't be sure of that. "One! Two! Three!"

The general swallowed, turned white, and waved his hand vaguely.

"Cut them loose," he said weakly.

The soldiers, terrified, too, were glad to do it. Madge and I were freed.

I took a couple of steps, headed my spirit in another direction, and that beautiful field marshal, medals and all, went crashing down the staircase like a grandfather clock.

I realized that Madge wasn't with me. She was still in that copper-colored body with the chartreuse hair and fingernails.

"What's more," I heard her saying, "in payment for all the trouble you've caused us, this body is to be addressed to me at New York, delivered in good condition no later than next Monday."

"Yes, ma'am," said the judge.

When we got home, the Pioneers' Day Parade was just breaking up at the local storage center, and the Parade Marshal got out of his body and apologized to me for acting the way he had.

"Heck, Herb," I said, "you don't need to apologize. You weren't yourself. You were parading around in a body."

That's the best part of being amphibious, next to not being afraid—people forgive you for whatever fool thing you might have done in a body.

Oh, there are drawbacks, I guess, the way there are drawbacks to everything. We still have to work off and on, maintaining the storage centers and getting food to keep the community bodies going. But that's a small drawback, and all the big drawbacks I ever heard of aren't real ones, just old-fashioned thinking by people who can't stop worrying about things they used to worry about before they turned amphibious.

As I say, the oldsters will probably never get really used to it. Every so often, I catch myself getting gloomy over what happened to the pay-toilet business it took me thirty years to build.

But the youngsters don't have any hangovers like that from the past. They don't even worry much about something happening to the storage centers, the way us oldsters do.

So I guess maybe that'll be the next step in evolution—to break clean like those first amphibians who crawled out of the mud into the sunshine, and who never did go back to the sea.

1953

Tomorrow and Tomorrow and Tomorrow

THE YEAR WAS 2158 A.D., and Lou and Emerald Schwartz were whispering on the balcony outside Lou's family's apartment on the seventy-sixth floor of Building 257 in Alden Village, a New York housing development that covered what had once been known as Southern Connecticut. When Lou and Emerald had married, Em's parents had tearfully described the marriage as being between May and December; but now, with Lou one hundred and twelve and Em ninety-three, Em's parents had to admit that the match had worked out well.

But Em and Lou weren't without their troubles, and they were out in the nippy air of the balcony because of them.

"Sometimes I get so mad, I feel like just up and diluting his anti-gerasone," said Em.

"That'd be against Nature, Em," said Lou, "it'd be murder. Besides, if he caught us tinkering with his anti-gerasone, not only would he disinherit us, he'd bust my neck. Just because he's one hundred and seventy-two doesn't mean Gramps isn't strong as a bull."

"Against Nature," said Em. "Who knows what Nature's like anymore? Ohhhhh—I don't guess I could ever bring myself to dilute his anti-gerasone or anything like that, but, gosh, Lou, a body can't help thinking Gramps is never going to leave if somebody doesn't help him along a little. Golly—we're so crowded a person can hardly turn around, and Verna's dying for a baby, and Melissa's gone thirty years without one." She stamped her feet. "I get so sick of seeing his wrinkled old face, watching him take the only private room and the best chair and the best food, and getting to pick out what to watch on TV, and running everybody's life by changing his will all the time."

"Well, after all," said Lou bleakly, "Gramps *is* head of the family. And he can't help being wrinkled like he is. He was seventy before anti-gerasone was invented. He's going to leave, Em. Just give him time. It's his business. I know he's tough to live with, but be patient. It wouldn't do to do anything that'd rile him. After all, we've got it better'n anybody else, there on the daybed."

"How much longer do you think we'll get to sleep on the daybed before he picks another pet? The world's record's two months, isn't it?"

"Mom and Pop had it that long once, I guess."

"When *is* he going to leave, Lou?" said Emerald.

"Well, he's talking about giving up anti-gerasone right after the five-hundred-mile Speedway Race."

"Yes—and before that it was the Olympics, and before that the World's Series, and before that the Presidential Elections, and before that I-don't-know-what. It's been just one excuse after another for fifty years now. I don't think we're ever going to get a room to ourselves or an egg or anything."

"All right—call me a failure!" said Lou. "What can I do? I work hard and make good money, but the whole thing, practically, is taxed away for defense and old age pensions. And if it wasn't taxed away, where you think we'd find a vacant room to rent? Iowa, maybe? Well, who wants to live on the outskirts of Chicago?"

Em put her arms around his neck. "Lou, hon, I'm not calling you a failure. The Lord knows you're not. You just haven't had a chance to be anything or have anything because Gramps and the rest of his generation won't leave and let somebody else take over."

"Yeah, yeah," said Lou gloomily. "You can't exactly blame 'em, though, can you? I mean, I wonder how quick we'll knock off the anti-gerasone when we get Gramps' age."

"Sometimes I wish there wasn't any such thing as anti-gerasone!" said Emerald passionately. "Or I wish it was made out of something real expensive and hard-to-get instead of mud and dandelions. Sometimes I wish folks just up and died regular as clockwork, without anything to say about it, instead of deciding themselves how long they're going to stay around. There ought to be a law against selling the stuff to anybody over one hundred and fifty."

"Fat chance of that," said Lou, "with all the money and votes the old people've got." He looked at her closely. "You ready to up and die, Em?"

"Well, for heaven's sakes, what a thing to say to your wife. Hon! I'm not even one hundred yet." She ran her hands lightly over her firm, youthful figure, as though for confirmation. "The best years of my life are still ahead of me. But you can bet that when one hundred and fifty rolls around, old Em's going to pour her anti-gerasone down the sink, and quit taking up room, and she'll do it smiling."

"Sure, sure," said Lou, "you bet. That's what they all say. How many you heard of doing it?"

"There was that man in Delaware."

"Aren't you getting kind of tired of talking about him, Em? That was five months ago."

"All right, then—Gramma Winkler, right here in the same building."

"She got smeared by a subway."

"That's just the way she picked to go," said Em.

"Then what was she doing carrying a six-pack of anti-gerasone when she got it?"

Emerald shook her head wearily and covered her eyes. "I dunno, I dunno, I dunno. All I know is, something's just got to be done." She sighed. "Sometimes I wish they'd left a couple of diseases kicking around somewhere, so I could get one and go to bed for a little while. Too many people!" she cried, and her words cackled and gabbled and died in a thousand asphalt-paved, skyscraper-walled courtyards.

Lou laid his hand on her shoulder tenderly. "Aw, hon, I hate to see you down in the dumps like this."

"If we just had a car, like the folks used to in the old days," said Em, "we could go for a drive, and get away from people for a little while. Gee—if *those* weren't the days!"

"Yeah," said Lou, "before they'd used up all the metal."

"We'd hop in, and Pop'd drive up to a filling station and say, 'Fillerup!' "

"That *was* the nuts, wasn't it—before they'd used up all the gasoline."

"And we'd go for a carefree ride in the country."

"Yeah—all seems like a fairyland now, doesn't it, Em? Hard to believe there really used to be all that space between cities."

"And when we got hungry," said Em, "we'd find ourselves a restaurant, and walk in, big as you please and say, 'I'll have a steak and French-fries, I believe,' or, 'How are the pork chops today?'" She licked her lips, and her eyes glistened.

"Yeah man!" growled Lou. "How'd you like a hamburger with the works, Em?"

"Mmmmmmmm."

"If anybody'd offered us processed seaweed in those days, we would have spit right in his eye, huh, Em?"

"Or processed sawdust," said Em.

Doggedly, Lou tried to find the cheery side of the situation. "Well, anyway, they've got the stuff so it tastes a lot less like seaweed and sawdust than it did at first; and they say it's actually better for us than what we used to eat."

"I felt fine!" said Em fiercely.

Lou shrugged. "Well, you've got to realize, the world wouldn't be able to support twelve billion people if it wasn't for processed seaweed and sawdust. I mean, it's a wonderful thing, really. I guess. That's what they say."

"They say the first thing that pops into their heads," said Em. She closed her eyes. "Golly—remember shopping, Lou? Remember how the stores used to fight to get our folks to buy something? You didn't have to wait for somebody to die to get a bed or chairs or a stove or anything like that. Just went in—bing!—and bought whatever you wanted. Gee whiz that was nice, before they used up all the raw materials. I was just a little kid then, but I can remember so plain."

Depressed, Lou walked listlessly to the balcony's edge, and looked up at the clean, cold, bright stars against the black velvet of infinity. "Remember when we used to be bugs on science fiction, Em? Flight seventeen, leaving for Mars, launching ramp twelve. 'Board! All non-technical personnel kindly remain in bunkers. Ten seconds . . . nine . . . eight . . . seven . . . six . . . five . . . four . . . three . . . two . . . *one! Main Stage! Barrrrrroooom!*"

"Why worry about what was going on on Earth?" said Em, looking up at the stars with him. "In another few years, we'd all be shooting through space to start life all over again on a new planet."

Lou sighed. "Only it turns out you need something about twice the size of the Empire State Building to get one lousy colonist to Mars. And for another couple of trillion bucks he could take his wife and dog. *That's* the way to lick overpopulation—*emigrate!*"

"Lou—?"

"Hmmm?"

"When's the Five-Hundred-Mile Speedway Race?"

"Uh—Memorial Day, May thirtieth."

She bit her lip. "Was that awful of me to ask?"

"Not very, I guess. Everybody in the apartment's looked it up to make sure."

"I don't want to be awful," said Em, "but you've just got to talk over these things now and then, and get them out of your system."

"Sure you do. Feel better?"

"Yes—and I'm not going to lose my temper anymore, and I'm going be just as nice to him as I know how."

"That's my Em."

They squared their shoulders, smiled bravely, and went back inside.

Gramps Schwartz, his chin resting on his hands, his hands on the crook of his cane, was staring irascibly at the five-foot television screen that dominated the room. On the screen, a news commentator was summarizing the day's happenings. Every thirty seconds or so, Gramps would jab the floor with his canetip and shout, "Hell! We did that a hundred years ago!"

Emerald and Lou, coming in from the balcony, were obliged to take seats in the back row, behind Lou's father and mother, brother and sister-in-law, son and daughter-in-law, grandson and wife, granddaughter and husband, great-grandson and wife, nephew and wife, grandnephew and wife, great-grandniece and husband, great-grandnephew and wife, and, of course, Gramps, who was in front of everybody. All, save Gramps, who was somewhat withered and bent, seemed, by pre-anti-gerasone standards, to be about the same age—to be somewhere in their late twenties or early thirties.

"*Meanwhile,*" the commentator was saying, "*Council Bluffs, Iowa, was still threatened by stark tragedy. But two hundred weary rescue workers have refused to give up hope, and continue to dig in an effort to save Elbert Haggedorn, one hundred and eighty-three, who has been wedged for two days in a . . .*"

"I wish he'd get something more cheerful," Emerald whispered to Lou.

"Silence!" cried Gramps. "Next one shoots off his big bazoo while the TV's on is gonna find hisself cut off without a dollar—" and here his voice suddenly softened and sweetened—"when they wave that checkered flag at the Indianapolis Speedway, and old Gramps gets ready for the Big Trip Up Yonder." He sniffed sentimentally, while his heirs concentrated desperately on not making the slightest sound. For them, the poignancy of the prospective Big Trip had been dulled somewhat by its having been mentioned by Gramps about once a day for fifty years.

"*Dr. Brainard Keyes Bullard*," said the commentator, "*President of Wyandotte College, said in an address tonight that most of the world's ills can be traced to the fact that Man's knowledge of himself has not kept pace with his knowledge of the physical world.*"

"Hell!" said Gramps. "We said that a hundred years ago!"

"*In Chicago tonight*," said the commentator, "*a special celebration is taking place in the Chicago Lying-in Hospital. The guest of honor is Lowell W. Hitz, age zero. Hitz, born this morning, is the twenty-five-millionth child to be born in the hospital.*" The commentator faded, and was replaced on the screen by young Hitz, who squalled furiously.

"Hell," whispered Lou to Emerald, "we said that a hundred years ago."

"I heard that!" shouted Gramps. He snapped off the television set, and his petrified descendants stared silently at the screen. "You, there, boy—"

"I didn't mean anything by it, sir," said Lou.

"Get me my will. You know where it is. You kids *all* know where it is. Fetch, boy!"

Lou nodded dully, and found himself going down the hall, picking his way over bedding to Gramps' room, the only private room in the Schwartz apartment. The other rooms were the bathroom, the living room, and the wide, windowless hallway, which was originally intended to serve as a dining area, and which had a kitchenette in one end. Six mattresses and four sleeping bags were dispersed in the hallway and living room, and the daybed, in the living room, accommodated the eleventh couple, the favorites of the moment.

On Gramps' bureau was his will, smeared, dog-eared, perforated, and blotched with hundreds of additions, deletions, accusations, conditions, warnings, advice, and homely philosophy. The document was, Lou reflected, a fifty-year diary, all jammed onto two sheets—a garbled, illegible log of day after day of strife. This day, Lou would be disinherited for the eleventh time, and it would take him perhaps six months of impeccable behavior to regain the promise of a share in the estate.

"Boy!" called Gramps.

"Coming, sir." Lou hurried back into the living room, and handed Gramps the will.

"Pen!" said Gramps.

He was instantly offered eleven pens, one from each couple.

"Not *that* leaky thing," he said, brushing Lou's pen aside. "Ah, there's a nice one. Good boy, Willy." He accepted Willy's pen. That was the tip they'd all been waiting for. Willy, then, Lou's father, was the new favorite.

Willy, who looked almost as young as Lou, though one hundred and forty-two, did a poor job of concealing his pleasure. He glanced shyly at the daybed, which would become his, and from which Lou and Emerald would have to move back into the hall, back to the worst spot of all by the bathroom door.

Gramps missed none of the high drama he'd authored, and he gave his own familiar role everything he had. Frowning and running his finger along each line, as though he were seeing the will for the first time, he read aloud in a deep, portentous monotone, like a bass tone on a cathedral organ:

"I, Harold D. Schwartz, residing in Building 257 of Alden Village, New York City, do hereby make, publish, and declare this to be my last Will and Testament, hereby revoking any and all former wills and codicils by me at any time heretofore made." He blew his nose importantly, and went on, not missing a word, and repeating many for emphasis—repeating in particular his ever-more-elaborate specifications for a funeral.

At the end of these specifications, Gramps was so choked with emotion that Lou thought he might forget why he'd gotten out the will in the first place. But Gramps heroically brought his powerful emotions under control, and, after erasing for a full minute, he began to write and speak at the same time. Lou could have spoken his lines for him, he'd heard them so often.

"I have had many heartbreaks ere leaving this vale of tears for a better land," Gramps said and wrote. "But the deepest hurt of all has been dealt me by—" He looked around the group, trying to remember who the malefactor was.

Everyone looked helpfully at Lou, who held up his hand resignedly.

Gramps nodded, remembering, and completed the sentence: "my great-grandson, Louis J. Schwartz."

"Grandson, sir," said Lou.

"Don't quibble. You're in deep enough now, young man," said Gramps, but he changed the trifle. And from there he went without a misstep through the phrasing of the disinheritance, causes for which were disrespectfulness and quibbling.

In the paragraph following, the paragraph that had belonged to everyone in the room at one time or another, Lou's name was scratched out and Willy's substituted as heir to the apartment and, the biggest plum of all, the double bed in the private bedroom. "So!" said Gramps, beaming. He erased the date at the foot of the will, and substituted a new one, including the time of day. "Well—time to watch the McGarvey Family." The McGarvey Family was a television serial that Gramps had been following since he was sixty, or for one hundred and twelve years. "I can't wait to see what's going to happen next," he said.

Lou detached himself from the group and lay down on his bed of pain by the bathroom door. He wished Em would join him, and he wondered where she was.

He dozed for a few moments, until he was disturbed by someone's stepping over him to get into the bathroom. A moment later, he heard a faint gurgling sound, as though something were being poured down the washbasin drain. Suddenly, it entered his mind that Em had cracked up, and that she was in there doing something drastic about Gramps.

"Em—?" he whispered through the panel. There was no reply, and Lou pressed against the door. The worn lock, whose bolt barely engaged its socket, held for a second, then let the door swing inward.

"Morty!" gasped Lou.

Lou's great-grandnephew, Mortimer, who had just married and brought his wife home to the Schwartz menage, looked at Lou with consternation and surprise. Morty kicked the door shut, but not before Lou had glimpsed what was in his hand—Gramps' enormous economy-size bottle of anti-gerasone, which had been half-emptied, and which Morty was refilling to the top with tap water.

A moment later, Morty came out, glared defiantly at Lou, and brushed past him wordlessly to rejoin his pretty bride.

Shocked, Lou didn't know what on earth to do. He couldn't let Gramps take the mousetrapped anti-gerasone; but if he warned Gramps about it, Gramps would certainly make life in the apartment, which was merely insufferable now, harrowing.

Lou glanced into the living room, and saw that the Schwartzes, Emerald among them, were momentarily at rest, relishing the botches that the McGarveys had made of *their* lives. Stealthily, he went into the bathroom, locked the door as well as he could, and began to pour the contents of Gramps' bottle down the drain. He was going to refill it with full-strength anti-gerasone from the twenty-two smaller bottles on the shelf. The bottle contained a half-gallon, and its neck was small, so it seemed to Lou that the emptying would take forever. And the almost imperceptible smell of anti-gerasone, like Worcestershire sauce, now seemed to Lou, in his nervousness, to be pouring out into the rest of the apartment through the keyhole and under the door.

"*Gloog-gloog-gloog-gloog-*," went the bottle monotonously. Suddenly, up came the sound of music from the living room, and there were murmurs and the scraping of chair legs on the floor. "*Thus ends*," said the television announcer, "*the 29,121st chapter in the life of your neighbors and mine, the McGarveys.*" Footsteps were coming down the hall. There was a knock on the bathroom door.

"Just a sec," called Lou cheerily. Desperately, he shook the big bottle, trying to speed up the flow. His palms slipped on the wet glass, and the heavy bottle smashed to splinters on the tile floor.

The door sprung open, and Gramps, dumfounded, stared at the mess.

Lou grinned engagingly through his nausea, and, for want of anything remotely resembling a thought, he waited for Gramps to speak.

"Well, boy," said Gramps at last, "looks like you've got a little tidying up to do."

And that was all he said. He turned around, elbowed his way through the crowd, and locked himself in his bedroom.

The Schwartzes contemplated Lou in incredulous silence for a moment longer, and then hurried back to the living room, as though some of his horrible guilt would taint them, too, if they looked too long. Morty stayed behind long enough to give Lou a quizzical, annoyed glance. Then he, too, went into the living room, leaving only Emerald standing in the doorway.

Tears streamed over her cheeks. "Oh, you poor lamb—please don't look so awful. It was my fault. I put you up to this."

"No," said Lou, finding his voice, "really you didn't. Honest, Em, I was just—"

"You don't have to explain anything to me, hon. I'm on your side no matter what." She kissed him on his cheek, and whispered in his ear. "It wouldn't have been murder, hon. It wouldn't have killed him. It wasn't such a terrible thing to do. It just would have fixed him up so he'd be able to go any time God decided He wanted him."

"What's gonna happen next, Em?" said Lou hollowly. "What's he gonna do?"

Lou and Emerald stayed fearfully awake almost all night, waiting to see what Gramps was going to do. But not a sound came from the sacred bedroom. At two hours before dawn, the pair dropped off to sleep.

At six o'clock they arose again, for it was time for their generation to eat breakfast in the kitchenette. No one spoke to them. They had twenty minutes in which to eat, but their reflexes were so dulled by the bad night that they had hardly swallowed two mouthfuls of egg-type processed seaweed before it was time to surrender their places to their son's generation.

Then, as was the custom for whomever had been most recently disinherited, they began preparing Gramps' breakfast, which would presently be served to him in bed, on a tray. They tried to be cheerful about it. The toughest part of the job was having to handle the honest-to-God eggs and bacon and oleomargarine on which Gramps spent almost all of the income from his fortune.

"Well," said Emerald, "I'm not going to get all panicky until I'm sure there's something to be panicky about."

"Maybe he doesn't know what it was I busted," said Lou hopefully.

"Probably thinks it was your watch crystal," said Eddie, their son, who was toying apathetically with his buckwheat-type processed sawdust cakes.

"Don't get sarcastic with your father," said Em, "and don't talk with your mouth full, either."

"I'd like to see anybody take a mouthful of this stuff and *not* say something," said Eddie, who was seventy-three. He glanced at the clock. "It's time to take Gramps his breakfast, you know."

"Yeah, it is, isn't it," said Lou weakly. He shrugged. "Let's have the tray, Em."

"We'll both go."

Walking slowly, smiling bravely, they found a large semicircle of long-faced Schwartzes standing around the bedroom door.

Em knocked. "Gramps," she said brightly, "break-fast is rea-dy."

There was no reply, and she knocked again, harder.

The door swung open before her fist. In the middle of the room, the soft, deep, wide, canopied bed, the symbol of the sweet by-and-by to every Schwartz, was empty.

A sense of death, as unfamiliar to the Schwartzes as Zoroastrianism or the causes of the Sepoy Mutiny, stilled every voice and slowed every heart. Awed, the heirs began to search gingerly under the furniture and behind the drapes for all that was mortal of Gramps, father of the race.

But Gramps had left not his earthly husk but a note, which Lou finally found on the dresser, under a paperweight which was a treasured souvenir from the 2000 World's Fair. Unsteadily, Lou read it aloud:

" 'Somebody who I have sheltered and protected and taught the best I know how all these years last night turned on me like a mad dog and diluted my anti-gerasone, or tried to. I am no longer a young man. I can no longer bear the crushing burden of life as I once could. So, after last night's bitter experience, I say goodbye. The cares of this world will soon drop away like a cloak of thorns, and I shall know peace. By the time you find this, I will be gone.' "

"Gosh," said Willy brokenly, "he didn't even get to see how the Five-Hundred-Mile Speedway Race was going to come out."

"Or the World's Series," said Eddie.

"Or whether Mrs. McGarvey got her eyesight back," said Morty.

"There's more," said Lou, and he began reading aloud again: " 'I, Harold D. Schwartz . . . do hereby make, publish and declare this to be my last Will and Testament, hereby revoking any and all former will and codicils by me at any time heretofore made.' "

"No!" cried Willy. "Not another one!"

" 'I do stipulate,' " read Lou, " 'that all of my property, of whatsoever kind and nature, not be divided, but do devise and bequeath it to be held in common by my issue, without regard for generation, equally, share and share alike.' "

"Issue?" said Emerald.

Lou included the multitude in a sweep of his hand. "It means we all own the whole damn shootin' match."

All eyes turned instantly to the bed.

"Share and share alike?" said Morty.

"Actually," said Willy, who was the oldest person present, "it's just like the old system, where the oldest people head up things with their headquarters in here, and—"

"I like *that!*" said Em. "Lou owns as much of it as you do, and I say it ought to be for the oldest one who's still working. You can snooze around here all day, waiting for your pension check, and poor Lou stumbles in here after work, all tuckered out, and—"

"How about letting somebody who's never had any privacy get a little crack at it?" said Eddie hotly. "Hell, you old people had plenty of privacy back when you were kids. I was born and raised in the middle of the goddam barracks in the hall! How about—"

"Yeah?" said Morty. "Sure, you've all had it pretty tough, and my heart bleeds for you. But try honeymooning in the hall for a real kick."

"Silence!" shouted Willy imperiously. "The next person who opens his mouth spends the next six months by the bathroom. Now clear out of my room. I want to think."

A vase shattered against the wall, inches above his head. In the next moment, a free-for-all was underway, with each couple battling to eject every other couple from the room. Fighting coalitions formed and dissolved with the lightning changes of the tactical situation. Em and Lou were thrown into the hall, where they organized others in the same situation, and stormed back into the room.

After two hours of struggle, with nothing like a decision in sight, the cops broke in.

For the next half-hour, patrol wagons and ambulances hauled away Schwartzes, and then the apartment was still and spacious.

An hour later, films of the last stages of the riot were being televised to 500,000,000 delighted viewers on the Eastern Seaboard.

In the stillness of the three-room Schwartz apartment on the 76th floor of Building 257, the television set had been left on. Once more the air was filled with the cries and grunts and crashes of the fray, coming harmlessly now from the loud-speaker.

The battle also appeared on the screen of the television set in the police station, where the Schwartzes and their captors watched with professional interest.

Em and Lou were in adjacent four-by-eight cells, and were stretched out peacefully on their cots.

"Em—" called Lou through the partition, "you got a wash-basin all your own too?"

"Sure. Washbasin, bed, light—the works. Ha! And we thought Gramps' room was something. How long's this been going on?" She held out her hand. "For the first time in forty years, hon, I haven't got the shakes."

"Cross your fingers," said Lou, "the lawyer's going to try to get us a year."

"Gee," said Em dreamily, "I wonder what kind of wires you'd have to pull to get solitary?"

"All right, pipe down," said the turnkey, "or I'll toss the whole kit and caboodle of you right out. And first one who lets on to anybody outside how good jail is ain't never getting back in!"

The prisoners instantly fell silent.

The living room of the Schwartz apartment darkened for a moment, as the riot scenes faded, and then the face of the announcer appeared, like the sun coming from behind a cloud. "*And now, friends,*" *he said,* "*I have a special message from the makers of anti-gerasone, a message for all you folks over one hundred and fifty. Are you hampered socially by wrinkles, by stiffness of joints and discoloration or loss of hair, all because these things came upon you before anti-gerasone was developed? Well, if you are, you need no longer suffer, need no longer feel different and out of things.*

"*After years of research, medical science has now developed* super-*anti-gerasone! In weeks, yes weeks, you can look, feel, and act as young as your great-great-grandchildren! Wouldnt you pay $5,000 to be indistinguishable from everybody else? Well, you don't have to. Safe, tested super-anti-gerasone costs you only dollars a day. The average cost of regaining all the sparkle and attractiveness of youth is less than fifty dollars.*

"*Write now for your free trial carton. Just put your name and address on a dollar postcard, and mail it to 'Super,' Box 500,000, Schenectady, N. Y. Have you got that? I'll repeat it.* 'Super.' *Box . . .*" Underlining the announcer's words was the scratching of Gramps' fountain-pen, the one Willy had given him the night before. He had come in a few minutes previous from the Idle Hour Tavern, which commanded a view of Building 257 across the square of asphalt known as the Alden Village Green. He had called a cleaning woman to come straighten the place up, and had hired the best lawyer in town to get his descendants a conviction. Gramps had then moved the daybed before the television screen so that he could watch from a reclining position. It was something he'd dreamed of doing for years.

"Schen-*ec*-ta-dy," mouthed Gramps. "Got it." His face had changed remarkably. His facial muscles seemed to have relaxed, revealing kindness and equanimity under what had been taut, bad-tempered lines. It was almost as though his trial package of *Super*-anti-gerasone had already arrived. When something amused him on television, he smiled easily, rather than barely managing to lengthen the thin line of his mouth a millimeter. Life was good. He could hardly wait to see what was going to happen next.

1953

Harrison Bergeron

THE YEAR WAS 2081, and everybody was finally equal. They weren't only equal before God and the law. They were equal every which way. Nobody was smarter than anybody else. Nobody was better looking than anybody else. Nobody was stronger or quicker than anybody else. All this equality was due to the 211th, 212th, and 213th Amendments to the Constitution, and to the unceasing vigilance of agents of the United States Handicapper General.

Some things about living still weren't quite right, though. April, for instance, still drove people crazy by not being springtime. And it was in that clammy month that the H-G men took George and Hazel Bergeron's fourteen-year-old son, Harrison, away.

It was tragic, all right, but George and Hazel couldn't think about it very hard. Hazel had a perfectly average intelligence, which meant she couldn't think about anything except in short bursts. And George, while his intelligence was way above normal, had a little mental handicap radio in his ear. He was required by law to wear it at all times. It was tuned to a government transmitter. Every twenty seconds or so, the transmitter would send out some sharp noise to keep people like George from taking unfair advantage of their brains.

George and Hazel were watching television. There were tears on Hazel's cheeks, but she'd forgotten for the moment what they were about.

On the television screen were ballerinas.

A buzzer sounded in George's head. His thoughts fled in panic, like bandits from a burglar alarm.

"That was a real pretty dance, that dance they just did," said Hazel.

"Huh?" said George.

"That dance—it was nice," said Hazel.

"Yup," said George. He tried to think a little about the ballerinas. They weren't really very good—no better than anybody else would have been, anyway. They were burdened with sashweights and bags of birdshot, and their faces were masked, so that no one, seeing a free and graceful gesture or a pretty face, would feel like something the cat drug in. George was toying with the vague notion that maybe dancers shouldn't be handicapped. But he didn't get very far with it before another noise in his ear radio scattered his thoughts.

George winced. So did two out of the eight ballerinas.

Hazel saw him wince. Having no mental handicap herself, she had to ask George what the latest sound had been.

"Sounded like somebody hitting a milk bottle with a ball peen hammer," said George.

"I'd think it would be real interesting, hearing all the different sounds," said Hazel, a little envious. "All the things they think up."

"Um," said George.

"Only, if I was Handicapper General, you know what I would do?" said Hazel. Hazel, as a matter of fact, bore a strong resemblance to the Handicapper General, a woman named Diana Moon Glampers. "If I was Diana Moon Glampers," said Hazel, "I'd have chimes on Sunday—just chimes. Kind of in honor of religion."

"I could think, if it was just chimes," said George.

"Well—maybe make 'em real loud," said Hazel. "I think I'd make a good Handicapper General."

"Good as anybody else," said George.

"Who knows better'n I do what normal is?" said Hazel.

"Right," said George. He began to think glimmeringly about his abnormal son who was now in jail, about Harrison, but a twenty-one-gun salute in his head stopped that.

"Boy!" said Hazel, "that was a doozy, wasn't it?"

It was such a doozy that George was white and trembling, and tears stood on the rims of his red eyes. Two of the eight ballerinas had collapsed to the studio floor, were holding their temples.

"All of a sudden you look so tired," said Hazel. "Why don't you stretch out on the sofa, so's you can rest your handicap bag on the pillows, honeybunch." She was referring to the forty-seven pounds of birdshot in a canvas bag, which was padlocked around George's neck. "Go on and rest the bag for a little while," she said. "I don't care if you're not equal to me for a while."

George weighed the bag with his hands. "I don't mind it," he said. "I don't notice it any more. It's just a part of me."

"You been so tired lately—kind of wore out," said Hazel. "If there was just some way we could make a little hole in the bottom of the bag, and just take out a few of them lead balls. Just a few."

"Two years in prison and two thousand dollars fine for every ball I took out," said George. "I don't call that a bargain."

"If you could just take a few out when you came home from work," said Hazel. "I mean—you don't compete with anybody around here. You just set around."

"If I tried to get away with it," said George, "then other people'd get away with it—and pretty soon we'd be right back to the dark ages again, with everybody competing against everybody else. You wouldn't like that, would you?"

"I'd hate it," said Hazel.

"There you are," said George. "The minute people start cheating on laws, what do you think happens to society?"

If Hazel hadn't been able to come up with an answer to this question, George couldn't have supplied one. A siren was going off in his head.

"Reckon it'd fall all apart," said Hazel.

"What would?" said George blankly.

"Society," said Hazel uncertainly. "Wasn't that what you just said?"

"Who knows?" said George.

The television program was suddenly interrupted for a news bulletin. It wasn't clear at first as to what the bulletin was about, since the announcer, like all announcers, had a serious speech impediment. For about half a minute, and in a state of high excitement, the announcer tried to say, "Ladies and gentlemen—"

He finally gave up, handed the bulletin to a ballerina to read.

"That's all right—" Hazel said of the announcer, "he tried. That's the big thing. He tried to do the best he could with what God gave him. He should get a nice raise for trying so hard."

"Ladies and gentlemen—" said the ballerina, reading the bulletin. She must have been extraordinarily beautiful, because the mask she wore was hideous. And it was easy to see that she was the strongest and most graceful of all the dancers, for her handicap bags were as big as those worn by two-hundred-pound men.

And she had to apologize at once for her voice, which was a very unfair voice for a woman to use. Her voice was a warm, luminous, timeless melody. "Excuse me—" she said, and she began again, making her voice absolutely uncompetitive.

"Harrison Bergeron, age fourteen," she said in a grackle squawk, "has just escaped from jail, where he was held on suspicion of plotting to overthrow the government. He is a genius and an athlete, is under-handicapped, and should be regarded as extremely dangerous."

A police photograph of Harrison Bergeron was flashed on the screen—upside down, then sideways, upside down again, then right side up. The picture showed the full length of Harrison against a background calibrated in feet and inches. He was exactly seven feet tall.

The rest of Harrison's appearance was Halloween and hardware. Nobody had ever borne heavier handicaps. He had outgrown hindrances faster than the H-G men could think them up. Instead of a little ear radio for a mental handicap, he wore a tremendous pair of earphones, and spectacles with thick wavy lenses. The spectacles were intended to make him not only half blind, but to give him whanging headaches besides.

Scrap metal was hung all over him. Ordinarily, there was a certain symmetry, a military neatness to the handicaps issued to strong people, but Harrison looked like a walking junkyard. In the race of life, Harrison carried three hundred pounds.

And to offset his good looks, the H-G men required that he wear at all times a red rubber ball for a nose, keep his eyebrows shaved off, and cover his even white teeth with black caps at snaggle-tooth random.

"If you see this boy," said the ballerina, "do not—I repeat, do not—try to reason with him."

There was the shriek of a door being torn from its hinges.

Screams and barking cries of consternation came from the television set. The photograph of Harrison Bergeron on the screen jumped again and again, as though dancing to the tune of an earthquake.

George Bergeron correctly identified the earthquake, and

well he might have—for many was the time his own home had danced to the same crashing tune. "My God—" said George, "that must be Harrison!"

The realization was blasted from his mind instantly by the sound of an automobile collision in his head.

When George could open his eyes again, the photograph of Harrison was gone. A living, breathing Harrison filled the screen.

Clanking, clownish, and huge, Harrison stood in the center of the studio. The knob of the uprooted studio door was still in his hand. Ballerinas, technicians, musicians, and announcers cowered on their knees before him, expecting to die.

"I am the Emperor!" cried Harrison. "Do you hear? I am the Emperor! Everybody must do what I say at once!" He stamped his foot and the studio shook.

"Even as I stand here—" he bellowed, "crippled, hobbled, sickened—I am a greater ruler than any man who ever lived! Now watch me become what I *can* become!"

Harrison tore the straps of his handicap harness like wet tissue paper, tore straps guaranteed to support five thousand pounds.

Harrison's scrap-iron handicaps crashed to the floor.

Harrison thrust his thumbs under the bar of the padlock that secured his head harness. The bar snapped like celery. Harrison smashed his headphones and spectacles against the wall.

He flung away his rubber-ball nose, revealed a man that would have awed Thor, the god of thunder.

"I shall now select my Empress!" he said, looking down on the cowering people. "Let the first woman who dares rise to her feet claim her mate and her throne!"

A moment passed, and then a ballerina arose, swaying like a willow.

Harrison plucked the mental handicap from her ear, snapped off her physical handicaps with marvellous delicacy. Last of all, he removed her mask.

She was blindingly beautiful.

"Now—" said Harrison, taking her hand, "shall we show the people the meaning of the word dance? Music!" he commanded.

The musicians scrambled back into their chairs, and Harrison stripped them of their handicaps, too. "Play your best," he told them, "and I'll make you barons and dukes and earls."

The music began. It was normal at first—cheap, silly, false. But Harrison snatched two musicians from their chairs, waved them like batons as he sang the music as he wanted it played. He slammed them back into their chairs.

The music began again and was much improved.

Harrison and his Empress merely listened to the music for a while—listened gravely, as though synchronizing their heartbeats with it.

They shifted their weights to their toes.

Harrison placed his big hands on the girl's tiny waist, letting her sense the weightlessness that would soon be hers.

And then, in an explosion of joy and grace, into the air they sprang!

Not only were the laws of the land abandoned, but the law of gravity and the laws of motion as well.

They reeled, whirled, swiveled, flounced, capered, gamboled, and spun.

They leaped like deer on the moon.

The studio ceiling was thirty feet high, but each leap brought the dancers nearer to it.

It became their obvious intention to kiss the ceiling.

They kissed it.

And then, neutralizing gravity with love and pure will, they remained suspended in air inches below the ceiling, and they kissed each other for a long, long time.

It was then that Diana Moon Glampers, the Handicapper General, came into the studio with a double-barreled ten-gauge shotgun. She fired twice, and the Emperor and the Empress were dead before they hit the floor.

Diana Moon Glampers loaded the gun again. She aimed it at the musicians and told them they had ten seconds to get their handicaps back on.

It was then that the Bergerons' television tube burned out.

Hazel turned to comment about the blackout to George. But George had gone out into the kitchen for a can of beer.

George came back in with the beer, paused while a handicap

signal shook him up. And then he sat down again. "You been crying?" he said to Hazel.

"Yup," she said.

"What about?" he said.

"I forget," she said. "Something real sad on television."

"What was it?" he said.

"It's all kind of mixed up in my mind," said Hazel.

"Forget sad things," said George.

"I always do," said Hazel.

"That's my girl," said George. He winced. There was the sound of a rivetting gun in his head.

"Gee—I could tell that one was a doozy," said Hazel.

"You can say that again," said George.

"Gee—" said Hazel, "I could tell that one was a doozy."

1961

2BR02B

EVERYTHING was perfectly swell.

There were no prisons, no slums, no insane asylums, no cripples, no poverty, no wars.

All diseases were conquered. So was old age.

Death, barring accidents, was an adventure for volunteers.

The population of the United States was stabilized at forty million souls.

One bright morning in the Chicago Lying-In Hospital, a man named Edward K. Wehling, Jr., waited for his wife to give birth. He was the only man waiting. Not many people were born each day anymore.

Wehling was fifty-six, a mere stripling in a population whose average age was one hundred twenty-nine.

X rays had revealed that his wife was going to have triplets. The children would be his first.

Young Wehling was hunched in his chair, his head in his hands. He was so rumpled, so still and colorless as to be virtually invisible. His camouflage was perfect, since the waiting room had a disorderly and demoralized air, too. Chairs and ashtrays had been moved away from the walls. The floor was paved with spattered dropcloths.

The room was being redecorated. It was being redecorated as a memorial to a man who had volunteered to die.

A sardonic old man, about two hundred years old, sat on a stepladder, painting a mural he did not like. Back in the days when people aged visibly, his age would have been guessed at thirty-five or so. Aging had touched him that much before the cure for aging was found.

The mural he was working on depicted a very neat garden. Men and women in white, doctors and nurses, turned the soil, planted seedlings, sprayed bugs, spread fertilizer. Men and women in purple uniforms pulled up weeds, cut down plants that were old and sickly, raked leaves, carried refuse to trash burners.

Never, never, never—not even in medieval Holland or old Japan—had a garden been more formal, been better tended.

Every plant had all the loam, light, water, air, and nourishment it could use.

A hospital orderly came down the corridor, singing under his breath a popular song:

If you don't like my kisses, honey,
Here's what I will do:
I'll go see a girl in purple,
Kiss this sad world toodle-oo.
If you don't want my lovin',
Why should I take up all this space?
I'll get off this old planet,
Let some sweet baby have my place.

The orderly looked in at the mural and the muralist. "Looks so real," he said, "I can practically imagine I'm standing in the middle of it."

"What makes you think you're not in it?" said the painter. He gave a satiric smile. "It's called *The Happy Garden of Life*, you know."

"That's good of Dr. Hitz," said the orderly.

He was referring to one of the male figures in white, whose head was a portrait of Dr. Benjamin Hitz, the hospital's chief obstetrician. Hitz was a blindingly handsome man.

"Lot of faces still to fill in," said the orderly. He meant that the faces of many of the figures in the mural were blank. All blanks were to be filled with portraits of important people either on the hospital staff or from the Chicago office of the Federal Bureau of Termination.

"Must be nice to be able to make pictures that look like something," said the orderly.

The painter's face curdled with scorn. "You think I'm proud of this drab? You think this is my idea of what life really looks like?"

"What's your idea of what life looks like?"

The painter gestured at a foul dropcloth. "There's a good picture of it," he said. "Frame that, and you'll have a picture a damn sight more honest than this one."

"You're a gloomy old duck, aren't you?" said the orderly.

"Is that a crime?" said the painter.

"If you don't like it here, Grandpa—" The orderly finished

the thought with the trick telephone number that people who didn't want to live anymore were supposed to call. The zero in the telephone number he pronounced "naught."

The number was 2BR02B.

It was the telephone number of an institution whose fanciful sobriquets included "Automat," "Birdland," "Cannery," "Catbox," "Delouser," "Easy Go," "Good-bye, Mother," "Happy Hooligan," "Kiss Me Quick," "Lucky Pierre," "Sheepdip," "Waring Blender," "Weep No More," and "Why Worry?"

"To Be or Not to Be" was the telephone number of the municipal gas chambers of the Federal Bureau of Termination.

The painter thumbed his nose at the orderly. "When I decide it's time to go," he said, "it won't be at the Sheepdip."

"A do-it-yourselfer, eh?" said the orderly. "Messy business, Grandpa. Why don't you have a little consideration for the people who have to clean up after you?"

The painter expressed with an obscenity his lack of concern for the tribulations of his survivors. "The world could do with a good deal more mess, if you ask me," he said.

The orderly laughed and moved on.

Wehling, the waiting father, mumbled something without raising his head. And then he fell silent again.

A coarse, formidable woman strode into the waiting room on spike heels. Her shoes, stockings, trench coat, bag, and overseas cap were all purple, a purple the painter called "the color of grapes on Judgment Day."

The medallion on her purple musette bag was the seal of the Service Division of the Federal Bureau of Termination, an eagle perched on a turnstile.

The woman had a lot of facial hair—an unmistakable mustache, in fact. A curious thing about gas chamber hostesses was that no matter how lovely and feminine they were when recruited, they all sprouted mustaches within five years or so.

"Is this where I'm supposed to come?" she asked the painter.

"A lot would depend on what your business was," he said. "You aren't about to have a baby, are you?"

"They told me I was supposed to pose for some picture," she said. "My name's Leora Duncan." She waited.

"And you dunk people," he said.

"What?" she said.

"Skip it," he said.

"That sure is a beautiful picture," she said. "Looks just like heaven or something."

"Or something," said the painter. He took a list of names from his smock pocket. "Duncan, Duncan, Duncan," he said, scanning the list. "Yes—here you are. You're entitled to be immortalized. See any faceless body here you'd like me to stick your head on? We've got a few choice ones left."

She studied the mural. "Gee," she said, "they're all the same to me. I don't know anything about art."

"A body's a body, eh?" he said. "All righty. As a master of the fine art, I recommend this body here." He indicated the faceless figure of a woman who was carrying dried stalks to a trash burner.

"Well," said Leora Duncan, "that's more the disposal people, isn't it? I mean, I'm in service. I don't do any disposing."

The painter clapped his hands in mock delight. "You say you don't know anything about art, and then you prove in the next breath that you do know more about it than I do! Of course the sheaf carrier is wrong for a hostess! A snipper, a pruner—that's more your line." He pointed to a figure in purple who was sawing a dead branch from an apple tree. "How about her?" he said. "You like her at all?"

"Gosh—" she said, and she blushed and became humble. "That—that puts me right next to Dr. Hitz."

"That upsets you?" he said.

"Good gravy, no!" she said. "It's—it's just such an honor."

"Ah, you admire him, eh?" he said.

"Who doesn't admire him?" she said, worshipping the portrait of Hitz. It was the portrait of a tanned, white-haired, omnipotent Zeus, two hundred forty years old. "Who doesn't admire him?" she said again. "He was responsible for setting up the very first gas chamber in Chicago."

"Nothing would please me more," said the painter, "than to put you next to him for all time. Sawing off a limb—that strikes you as appropriate?"

"That is kind of like what I do," she said. She was demure about what she did. What she did was make people comfortable while she killed them.

And while Leora Duncan was posing for her portrait, into

the waiting room bounded Dr. Hitz himself. He was seven feet tall, and he boomed with importance, accomplishments, and the joy of living.

"Well, Miss Duncan! Miss Duncan!" he said, and he made a joke. "What are you doing here? This isn't where the people leave. This is where they come in!"

"We're going to be in the same picture together," she said shyly.

"Good!" said Dr. Hitz. "And say, isn't that some picture?"

"I sure am honored to be in it with you," she said.

"Let me tell you, I'm honored to be in it with you. Without women like you, this wonderful world we've got wouldn't be possible."

He saluted her and moved toward the door that led to the delivery rooms. "Guess what was just born," he said.

"I can't," she said.

"Triplets!" he said.

"Triplets!" she said. She was exclaiming over the legal implications of triplets.

The law said that no newborn child could survive unless the parents of the child could find someone who would volunteer to die. Triplets, if they were all to live, called for three volunteers.

"Do the parents have three volunteers?" said Leora Duncan.

"Last I heard," said Dr. Hitz, "they had one, and were trying to scrape another two up."

"I don't think they made it," she said. "Nobody made three appointments with us. Nothing but singles going through today, unless somebody called in after I left. What's the name?"

"Wehling," said the waiting father, sitting up, red-eyed and frowzy: "Edward K. Wehling, Jr., is the name of the happy father-to-be."

He raised his right hand, looked at a spot on the wall, gave a hoarsely wretched chuckle. "Present," he said.

"Oh, Mr. Wehling," said Dr. Hitz, "I didn't see you."

"The invisible man," said Wehling.

"They just phoned me that your triplets have been born," said Dr. Hitz. "They're all fine, and so is the mother. I'm on my way in to see them now."

"Hooray," said Wehling emptily.

"You don't sound very happy," said Dr. Hitz.

"What man in my shoes wouldn't be happy?" said Wehling. He gestured with his hands to symbolize the carefree simplicity. "All I have to do is pick out which one of the triplets is going to live, then deliver my maternal grandfather to the Happy Hooligan, and come back here with a receipt."

Dr. Hitz became rather severe with Wehling, towered over him. "You don't believe in population control, Mr. Wehling?" he said.

"I think it's perfectly keen," said Wehling.

"Would you like to go back to the good old days, when the population of the earth was twenty billion—about to become forty billion, then eighty billion, then one hundred and sixty billion? Do you know what a drupelet is, Mr. Wehling?" said Hitz.

"Nope," said Wehling, sulking.

"A drupelet, Mr. Wehling, is one of the little knobs, one of the little pulpy grains, of a blackberry," said Dr. Hitz. "Without population control, human beings would now be packed on the surface of this old planet like drupelets on a blackberry! Think of it!"

Wehling continued to stare at the spot on the wall.

"In the year 2000," said Dr. Hitz, "before scientists stepped in and laid down the law, there wasn't even enough drinking water to go around, and nothing to eat but seaweed—and still people insisted on their right to reproduce like jackrabbits. And their right, if possible, to live forever."

"I want those kids," said Wehling. "I want all three of them."

"Of course you do," said Dr. Hitz. "That's only human."

"I don't want my grandfather to die, either," said Wehling.

"Nobody's really happy about taking a close relative to the Catbox," said Dr. Hitz sympathetically.

"I wish people wouldn't call it that," said Leora Duncan.

"What?" said Dr. Hitz.

"I wish people wouldn't call it the Catbox, and things like that," she said. "It gives people the wrong impression."

"You're absolutely right," said Dr. Hitz. "Forgive me." He

corrected himself, gave the municipal gas chambers their official title, a title no one ever used in conversation. "I should have said 'Ethical Suicide Studios,'" he said.

"That sounds so much better." said Leora Duncan.

"This child of yours—whichever one you decide to keep, Mr. Wehling," said Dr. Hitz. "He or she is going to live on a happy, roomy, clean, rich planet, thanks to population control. In a garden like in that mural there." He shook his head. "Two centuries ago, when I was a young man, it was a hell that nobody thought could last another twenty years. Now centuries of peace and plenty stretch before us as far as the imagination cares to travel."

He smiled luminously.

The smile faded when he saw that Wehling had just drawn a revolver.

Wehling shot Dr. Hitz dead. "There's room for one—a great big one," he said.

And then he shot Leora Duncan. "It's only death," he said to her as she fell. "There! Room for two."

And then he shot himself, making room for all three of his children.

Nobody came running. Nobody, it seemed, had heard the shots.

The painter sat on the top of his stepladder, looking down reflectively on the sorry scene. He pondered the mournful puzzle of life demanding to be born and, once born, demanding to be fruitful . . . to multiply and to live as long as possible—to do all that on a very small planet that would have to last forever.

All the answers that the painter could think of were grim. Even grimmer, surely, than a Catbox, a Happy Hooligan, an Easy Go. He thought of war. He thought of plague. He thought of starvation.

He knew that he would never paint again. He let his paintbrush fall to the dropcloths below. And then he decided he had had about enough of the Happy Garden of Life, too, and he came slowly down from the ladder.

He took Wehling's pistol, really intending to shoot himself. But he didn't have the nerve.

And then he saw the telephone booth in a corner of the

room. He went to it, dialed the well-remembered number: 2BR02B.

"Federal Bureau of Termination," said the warm voice of a hostess.

"How soon could I get an appointment?" he asked, speaking carefully.

"We could probably fit you in late this afternoon, sir," she said. "It might even be earlier, if we get a cancellation."

"All right," said the painter, "fit me in, if you please." And he gave her his name, spelling it out.

"Thank you, sir," said the hostess. "Your city thanks you, your country thanks you, your planet thanks you. But the deepest thanks of all is from future generations."

1962

APPENDIX

Science Fiction

YEARS AGO I was working in Schenectady for General Electric, completely surrounded by machines and ideas for machines, so I wrote a novel about people and machines, and machines frequently got the best of it, as machines will. (It was called *Player Piano*, and it was brought out again in both hard cover and paperback.) And I learned from the reviewers that I was a science-fiction writer.

I didn't know that. I supposed that I was writing a novel about life, about things I could not avoid seeing and hearing in Schenectady, a very real town, awkwardly set in the gruesome now. I have been a soreheaded occupant of a file drawer labeled "science fiction" ever since, and I would like out, particularly since so many serious critics regularly mistake the drawer for a urinal.

The way a person gets into this drawer, apparently, is to notice technology. The feeling persists that no one can simultaneously be a respectable writer and understand how a refrigerator works, just as no gentleman wears a brown suit in the city. Colleges may be to blame. English majors are encouraged, I know, to hate chemistry and physics, and to be proud because they are not dull and creepy and humorless and war-oriented like the engineers across the quad. And our most impressive critics have commonly been such English majors, and they are squeamish about technology to this very day. So it is natural for them to despise science fiction.

But there are those who adore being classified as science-fiction writers anyway, who are alarmed by the possibility that they might someday be known simply as ordinary short-story writers and novelists who mention, among other things, the fruits of engineering and research. They are happy with the *status quo* because their colleagues love them the way members of old-fashioned big families were supposed to do. Science-fiction writers meet often, comfort and praise one another, exchange single-spaced letters of twenty pages and more, booze it up affectionately, and one way or another have a million heart-throbs and laughs.

I have run with them some, and they are generous and amusing souls, but I must now make a true statement that will put them through the roof: They are joiners. They are a lodge. If they didn't enjoy having a gang of their own so much, there would be no such category as science fiction. They love to stay up all night, arguing the question, "What is science fiction?" One might as usefully inquire, "What are the Elks? And what is the Order of the Eastern Star?"

Well—it would be a drab world without meaningless social aggregations. There would be a lot fewer smiles, and about one-hundredth as many publications. And there is this to be said for the science-fiction publications: If somebody can write just a little bit, they will probably publish him. In the Golden Age of Magazines, which wasn't so long ago, inexcusable trash was in such great demand that it led to the invention of the electric typewriter, and incidentally financed my escape from Schenectady. Happy days! But there is now only one sort of magazine to which a maundering sophomore may apply for instant recognition as a writer. Guess what sort.

Which is not to say that the editors of science-fiction magazines and anthologies and novels are tasteless. They are not tasteless, and I will get to them by and by. The people in the field who can be charged fairly with tastelessness are 75 percent of the writers and 95 percent of the readers—or not so much tastelessness, really, as childishness. Mature relationships, even with machines, do not titillate the unwashed majority. Whatever it knows about science was fully revealed in *Popular Mechanics* by 1933. Whatever it knows about politics and economics and history can be found in the *Information Please Almanac* for 1941. Whatever it knows about the relationship between men and women derives mainly from the clean and the pornographic versions of "Maggie and Jiggs."

I taught for a while in a mildly unusual school for mildly unusual high-school children, and current science fiction was catnip to the boys, any science fiction at all. They couldn't tell one story from another, thought they were all neat, keen. What appealed to them so, I think, aside from the novelty of comic books without pictures, was the steady promise of futures which they, *just as they were*, could handle. In such futures they would be high-ranking noncoms at the very least, *just as they were*, pimples, virginity, and everything.

Curiously, the American space program did not excite them. This was not because the program was too mature for them. On the contrary, they were charmingly aware that it was manned and financed by tone-deaf adolescents like themselves. They were simply being realistic: They doubted that they would ever graduate from high school, and they knew that any creep hoping to enter the program would have to have a B.S. degree at a minimum, and that the really good jobs went to creeps with Ph.D.s.

Most of them *did* graduate from high school, by the way. And many of them now cheerfully read about futures and presents and even pasts which nobody can handle—*1984*, *Invisible Man*, *Madame Bovary*. They are particularly hot for Kafka. Boomers of science fiction might reply, "Ha! Orwell and Ellison and Flaubert and Kafka are science-fiction writers, too!" They often say things like that. Some are crazy enough to try to capture Tolstoy. It is as though I were to claim that everybody of note belonged fundamentally to Delta Upsilon, my own lodge, incidentally, whether he knew it or not. Kafka would have been a desperately unhappy D.U.

But listen—about the editors and anthologists and publishers who keep the science-fiction field separate and alive: They are uniformly brilliant and sensitive and well-informed. They are among the precious few Americans in whose minds C. P. Snow's two cultures sweetly intertwine. They publish so much bad stuff because good stuff is hard to find, and because they feel it is their duty to encourage any writer, no matter how frightful, who has guts enough to include technology in the human equation. Good for them. They want buxom images of the new reality.

And they get them from time to time, too. Along with the worst writing in America, outside of the education journals, they publish some of the best. They are able to get a few really excellent stories, despite low budgets and an immature readership, because to a few good writers the artificial category, the file drawer labeled "science fiction," will always be home. These writers are rapidly becoming old men, and deserve to be called grand. They are not without honors. The lodge gives them honors all the time. And love.

The lodge will dissolve. All lodges do, sooner or later. And more and more writers in "the mainstream," as science-fiction people call the world outside the file drawer, will include technology in their tales, will give it at least the respect due in a narrative to a wicked stepmother. Meanwhile, if you write stories that are weak on dialogue and motivation and characterization and common sense, you could do worse than throw in a little chemistry or physics, or even witchcraft, and mail them off to the science-fiction magazines.

1965

Introduction to "Bagombo Snuff Box," the uncollected short fiction of Kurt Vonnegut

MY LONGTIME FRIEND and critic Professor Peter Reed, of the English Department at the University of Minnesota, made it his business to find these stories from my distant past. Otherwise, they might never have seen the light of day again. I myself hadn't saved one scrap of paper from that part of my life. I didn't think I would amount to a hill of beans. All I wanted to do was support a family.

Peter's quest was that of a scholar. I nevertheless asked him to go an extra mile for me, by providing an informal preface to what is in fact his rather than my collection.

God bless you, Dr. Reed, I think.

These stories, and twenty-three of similar quality in my previous hardcover collection, *Welcome to the Monkey House*, were written at the very end of a golden age of magazine fiction in this country. For about fifty years, until 1953, say, stories like these were a mild but popular form of entertainment in millions of homes, my own included.

This old man's hope has to be that some of his earliest tales, for all their mildness and innocence and clumsiness, may in these coarse times, still entertain.

They would not be reprinted now, if novels I had written around the same time had not, better late than never, received critical attention. My children were adults by then, and I was middle-aged. These stories, printed in magazines fat with fiction and advertising, magazines now in most cases defunct, were expected to be among the living about as long as individual lightning bugs.

That anything I have written is in print today is due to the efforts of one publisher, Seymour "Sam" Lawrence (1927–1994). When I was broke in 1965, and teaching at the Writers' Workshop at the University of Iowa all alone, completely out of print, having separated myself from my family on Cape Cod in order to support them, Sam bought rights to my books, for peanuts, from publishers, both hardcover and softcover, who had given up on me. Sam thrust my books back into the myopic public eye again.

CPR! Cardiopulmonary resuscitation of this author who was all but dead!

Thus encouraged, this Lazarus wrote *Slaughterhouse-Five* for Sam. That made my reputation. I am a Humanist, and so am not entitled to expect an afterlife for myself or anyone. But at Seymour Lawrence's memorial service at New York City's Harvard Club five years ago, I said this with all my heart: "Sam is up in Heaven now."

I returned to Dresden, incidentally, the setting for *Slaughterhouse-Five*, on October 7th, 1998. I was taken down into the cellar where I and about a hundred other American POWs survived a firestorm that suffocated or incinerated 135,000 or so other human beings. It reduced the "Florence of the Elbe" to a jagged moonscape.

While I was down in that cellar again, this thought came to me: "Because I have lived so long, I am one of the few persons on Earth who saw an Atlantis before it disappeared forever beneath the waves."

Short stories can have greatness, short as they have to be. Several knocked my socks off when I was still in high school. Ernest Hemingway's "The Short Happy Life of Francis Macomber" and Saki's "The Open Window" and O. Henry's "The Gift of the Magi" and Ambrose Bierce's "An Occurrence at Owl Creek Bridge" spring to mind. But there is no greatness in this or my other collection, nor was there meant to be.

My own stories may be interesting, nonetheless, as relics from a time, before there was television, when an author might support a family by writing stories that satisfied uncritical readers of magazines, and earning thereby enough free time in which to write serious novels. When I became a full-time freelance in 1950, I expected to be doing that for the rest of my life.

I was in such good company with a prospectus like that. Hemingway had written for *Esquire*, F. Scott Fitzgerald for

The Saturday Evening Post, William Faulkner for *Collier's*, John Steinbeck for *The Woman's Home Companion*!

Say what you want about me, I never wrote for a magazine called *The Woman's Home Companion*, but there was a time when I would have been most happy to. And I add this thought: Just because a woman is stuck alone at home, with her husband at work and her kids at school, that doesn't mean she is an imbecile.

Publication of this book makes me want to talk about the peculiar and beneficial effect a short story can have on us, which makes it different from a novel or movie or play or TV show.

If I am to make my point, though, you must first imagine with me a scene in the home of my childhood and youth in Indianapolis, in the middle of the previous Great Depression. The previous Great Depression lasted from the stock market crash on October 24th, 1929, until the Japanese did us the favor, for the sheer hell of it, of bombing our comatose fleet of warships in Pearl Harbor, on December 7th, 1941. The little yellow bastards, as we used to call them, were bored to tears with the Great Depression. So were we.

Imagine that it is 1938 again. I am sixteen again. I come home again from yet another lousy day at Shortridge High School. Mother, who does not work outside the home, says there is a new *Saturday Evening Post* on the coffee table. It is raining outside, and I am unpopular. But I can't turn on a magazine like a TV set. I have to pick it up, or it will go on lying there, dead as a doornail. An unassisted magazine has no get-up-and-go.

After I pick it up, I have to make all one hundred sixty pounds of male adolescent meat and bones comfortable in an easy chair. Then I have to leaf through the magazine with my fingertips, so my eyes can shop for a story with a stimulating title and illustration.

Illustrators during the golden age of American magazine fiction used to get as much money as the authors whose stories they illustrated. They were often as famous as, or even more famous than, the authors. Norman Rockwell was their Michelangelo.

While I shop for a story, my eyes also see ads for automobiles and cigarettes and hand lotions and so on. It is advertisers, not readers, who pay the true costs of such a voluptuous publication. And God bless them for doing that. But consider the incredible thing I myself have to do in turn. I turn my brains on!

That isn't the half of it. With my brains all fired up, I do the nearly impossible thing that you are doing now, dear reader. I make sense of idiosyncratic arrangements, in horizontal lines, of nothing but twenty-six phonetic symbols, ten Arabic numerals, and perhaps eight punctuation marks, on a sheet of bleached and flattened wood pulp!

But get this: While I am reading, my pulse and breathing slow down. My high school troubles drop away. I am in a pleasant state somewhere between sleep and restfulness.

OK?

And then, after however long it takes to read a short story, ten minutes, say, I spring out of the chair. I put *The Saturday Evening Post* back on the coffee table for somebody else.

OK?

So then my architect dad comes home from work, or more likely from no work, since the little yellow bastards haven't bombed Pearl Harbor yet. I tell him I have read a story he might enjoy. I tell him to sit in the easy chair whose cushion is still dented and warmed by my teenage butt.

Dad sits. I pick up the magazine and open it to the story. Dad is tired and blue. Dad starts to read. His pulse and breathing slow down. His troubles drop away, and so on.

Yes! And our little domestic playlet, true to life in the 1930s, dear reader, proves exactly what? It proves that a short story, because of its physiological and psychological effects on a human being, is more closely related to Buddhist styles of meditation than it is to any other form of narrative entertainment.

What you have in this volume, then, and in every other collection of short stories, is a bunch of Buddhist catnaps.

Reading a novel, *War and Peace*, for example, is no catnap. Because a novel is so long, reading one is like being married forever to somebody nobody else knows or cares about. Definitely not refreshing!

Oh sure, we had radios before we had TV. But radios can't hold our attention, can't take control of our emotions, except in times of war. Radios can't make us sit still. Unlike print and plays and movies and boob tubes, radios don't give us anything for our restless eyes to do.

Listen: After I came home from World War Two, a brevet corporal twenty-two years old, I didn't want to be a fiction writer. I married my childhood sweetheart Jane Marie Cox, also from Indianapolis, up in Heaven now, and enrolled as a graduate student in the Anthropology Department of the University of Chicago. But I didn't want to be an anthropologist, either. I only hoped to find out more about human beings. I was going to be a journalist!

To that end, I also took a job as a police reporter for the Chicago City News Bureau. The News Bureau was supported by all four Chicago dailies back then, as a sensor for breaking news, prowling the city night and day, and as a training ground. The only way to get a job on one of those papers, short of nepotism, was to go through the News Bureau's hazing first.

But it became obvious that no newspaper positions were going to open up in Chicago or anywhere else for several years. Reporters had come home from the war to reclaim their jobs, and the women who had replaced them would not quit. The women were terrific. They should not have quit.

And then the Department of Anthropology rejected my M.A. thesis, which proved that similarities between the Cubist painters in Paris in 1907 and the leaders of Native American, or Injun, uprisings late in the nineteenth century could not be ignored. The Department said it was unprofessional.

Slowly but surely, Fate, which had spared my life in Dresden, now began to shape me into a fiction writer and a failure until I was a bleeding forty-seven years of age! But first I had to be a publicity hack for General Electric in Schenectady, New York.

While writing publicity releases at GE, I had a boss named George. George taped to the outside of his office door cartoons he felt had some bearing on the company or the kind of work we did. One cartoon was of two guys in the office of a buggy whip factory. A chart on the wall showed their business had dropped to zero. One guy was saying to the other, "It can't be our product's quality. We make the finest buggy whips in the world." George posted that cartoon to celebrate how GE, with its wonderful new products, was making a lot of other companies feel as though they were trying to sell buggy whips.

A broken-down movie actor named Ronald Reagan was working for the company. He was on the road all the time, lecturing to chambers of commerce and power companies and so on about the evils of socialism. We never met, so I remain a socialist.

While my future two-term president was burbling out on the rubber-chicken circuit in 1950, I started writing short stories at nights and on weekends. Jane and I had two kids by then. I needed more money than GE would pay me. I also wanted, if possible, more self-respect.

There was a crazy seller's market for short stories in 1950. There were four weekly magazines that published three or more of the things in every issue. Six monthlies did the same.

I got me an agent. If I sent him a story that didn't quite work, wouldn't quite satisfy a reader, he would tell me how to fix it. Agents and editors back then could tell a writer how to fine-tune a story as though they were pit mechanics and the story were a race car. With help like that, I sold one, and then two, and then three stories, and banked more money than a year's salary at GE.

I quit GE and started my first novel, *Player Piano*. It is a lampoon on GE. I bit the hand that used to feed me. The book predicted what has indeed come to pass, a day when machines, because they are so dependable and efficient and tireless, and getting cheaper all the time, are taking the halfway decent jobs from human beings.

I moved our family of four to Cape Cod, first to Provincetown. I met Norman Mailer there. He was my age. He had been a college-educated infantry private like me, and he was already a world figure, because of his great war novel *The Naked and the Dead*. I admired him then, and do today. He is majestic. He is royalty. So was Jacqueline Onassis. So was Joe DiMaggio. So is Muhammad Ali. So is Arthur Miller.

We moved from Provincetown to Osterville, still on the Cape. But only three years after I left Schenectady, advertisers started withdrawing their money from magazines. The Buddhist catnaps coming out of my typewriter were becoming as obsolete as buggy whips.

One monthly that had bought several of my stories, *Cosmopolitan*, now survives as a harrowingly explicit sex manual.

That same year, 1953, Ray Bradbury published *Fahrenheit 451*. The title refers to the kindling point of paper. That is how hot you have to get a book or a magazine before it bursts into flame. The leading male character makes his living burning printed matter. Nobody reads anymore. Many ordinary, rinky-dink homes like Ray's and mine have a room with floor-to-ceiling TV screens on all four walls, with one chair in the middle.

The actors and actresses on all four walls of TV are scripted to acknowledge whoever is sitting in the chair in the middle, even if nobody is sitting in the chair in the middle, as a friend or relative in the midst of things. The wife of the guy who burns up paper is unhappy. He can afford only three screens. His wife can't stand not knowing what's happening on the missing fourth screen, because the TV actors and actresses are the only people she loves, the only ones anywhere she gives a damn about.

Fahrenheit 451 was published before we and most of our neighbors in Osterville even owned TVs. Ray Bradbury himself may not have owned one. He still may not own one. To this day, Ray can't drive a car and hates to ride in airplanes.

In any case, Ray was sure as heck prescient. Just as people with dysfunctional kidneys are getting perfect ones from hospitals nowadays, Americans with dysfunctional social lives, like the woman in Ray's book, are getting perfect friends and relatives from their TV sets. And around the clock!

Ray missed the boat about how many screens would be required for a successful people-transplant. One lousy little Sony can do the job, night and day. All it takes besides that is actors and actresses, telling the news, selling stuff, in soap operas or whatever, who treat whoever is watching, even if nobody is watching, like family.

"Hell is other people," said Jean-Paul Sartre. "Hell is other real people," is what he should have said.

You can't fight progress. The best you can do is ignore it, until it finally takes your livelihood and self-respect away. General Electric itself was made to feel like a buggy whip factory for a time, as Bell Labs and others cornered patents on transistors and their uses, while GE was still shunting electrons this way and that with vacuum tubes.

Too big to fail, though, as I was not, GE recovered sufficiently to lay off thousands and poison the Hudson River with PCBs.

By 1953, Jane and I had three kids. So I taught English in a boarding school there on the Cape. Then I wrote ads for an industrial agency in Boston. I wrote a couple of paperback originals, *The Sirens of Titan* and *Mother Night.* They were never reviewed. I got for each of them what I used to get for a short story.

I tried to sell some of the first Saab automobiles to come into this country. The doors opened into the wind. There was a roller-blind behind the front grille, which you could operate with a chain under the dashboard. That was to keep your engine warm in the wintertime. You had to mix oil with your gasoline every time you filled the tank of those early Saabs. If you ever forgot to do that, the engine would revert to the ore state. One engine I chipped away from a Saab chassis with a cold chisel and a sledge looked like a meteor!

If you left a Saab parked for more than a day, the oil settled like maple syrup to the bottom of the gas tank. When you started it up, the exhaust would black out a whole neighborhood. One time I blacked out Woods Hole that way. I was coughing like everybody else, I couldn't imagine where all that smoke had come from.

Then I took to teaching creative writing, first at Iowa, then at Harvard, and then at City College in New York. Joseph Heller, author of *Catch-22*, was teaching at City College also. He said to me that if it hadn't been for the war, he would have been in the dry-cleaning business. I said to him that if it hadn't been for the war, I would have been garden editor of *The Indianapolis Star*.

Now lend me your ears. Here is Creative Writing 101:

1. Use the time of a total stranger in such a way that he or she will not feel the time was wasted.
2. Give the reader at least one character he or she can root for.
3. Every character should want something, even if it is only a glass of water.
4. Every sentence must do one of two things—reveal character or advance the action.
5. Start as close to the end as possible.
6. Be a sadist. No matter how sweet and innocent your leading characters, make awful things happen to them—in order that the reader may see what they are made of.
7. Write to please just one person. If you open a window and make love to the world, so to speak, your story will get pneumonia.
8. Give your readers as much information as possible as soon as possible. To heck with suspense. Readers should have such complete understanding of what is going on, where and why, that they could finish the story themselves, should cockroaches eat the last few pages.

The greatest American short story writer of my generation was Flannery O'Connor (1925–1964). She broke practically every one of my rules but the first. Great writers tend to do that.

Ms. O'Connor may or may not have broken my seventh rule, "Write to please just one person." There is no way for us to find out for sure, unless, of course, there is a Heaven after all, and she's there, and the rest of us are going there, and we can ask her.

I'm almost sure she didn't break rule seven. The late American psychiatrist Dr. Edmund Bergler, who claimed to have treated more professional writers than any other shrink, said in his book *The Writer and Psychoanalysis* that most writers in his experience wrote to please one person they knew well, even if they didn't realize they were doing that. It wasn't a trick of the fiction trade. It was simply a natural human thing to do, whether or not it could make a story better.

Dr. Bergler said it commonly required psychoanalysis before his patients could know for whom they had been writing. But as soon as I finished his book, and then thought for only a couple of minutes, I knew it was my sister Allie I had been writing for. She is the person the stories in this book were written for. Anything I knew Allie wouldn't like I crossed out. Everything I knew she would get a kick out of I left in.

Allie is up in Heaven now, with my first wife Jane and Sam Lawrence and Flannery O'Connor and Dr. Bergler, but I still write to please her. Allie was funny in real life. That gives me permission to be funny, too. Allie and I were very close.

In my opinion, a story written for one person pleases a reader, dear reader, because it makes him or her a part of the action. It makes the reader feel, even though he or she doesn't know it, as though he or she is eavesdropping on a fascinating conversation between two people at the next table, say, in a restaurant.

That's my educated guess.

Here is another: A reader likes a story written for just one person because the reader can sense, again without knowing it, that the story has boundaries like a playing field. The story can't go simply anywhere. This, I feel, invites readers to come off the sidelines, to get into the game with the author. Where is the story going next? Where should it go? No fair! Hopeless situation! Touchdown!

Remember my rule number eight? "Give your readers as much information as possible as soon as possible"? That's so they can play along. Where, outside the Groves of Academe, does anybody like a story where so much information is withheld or arcane that there is no way for readers to play along?

The boundaries to the playing fields of my short stories, and my novels, too, were once the boundaries of the soul of my only sister. She lives on that way.

Amen.

1999

CHRONOLOGY

NOTE ON THE TEXTS

NOTES

Chronology

1922 Born Kurt Vonnegut Jr., November 11, in Indianapolis, Indiana, the third child of Kurt Vonnegut and Edith Sophia Lieber Vonnegut. (Both parents are the grandchildren of entrepreneurial German immigrants—merchants, manufacturers, and brewers—who settled in the American Midwest in the mid-1800s. Father, born in Indianapolis in 1884, is a practicing architect and graphic designer, the successor to his late father, Bernard Vonnegut, in the firm of Vonnegut, Bohn & Mueller. Mother, born in 1888, is the handsome, pleasure-loving daughter of former millionaire Albert Lieber, heir to the presidency of Indianapolis Brewing Co., now unemployed due to Prohibition. The Vonneguts were married in November 1913. Their first child, Bernard, was born in 1914, their second, Alice, in 1917.) Infant Kurt is brought from hospital to his parents' house, built in 1910 as a gift to his mother by Albert Lieber on his four-hundred-acre estate on the banks of the White River, six miles northwest of downtown Indianapolis.

1923 Spends the first of many "heavenly" childhood summers among father's extended family at the Vonnegut compound, a row of Victorian-era cottages on the eastern shore of Lake Maxinkuckee, in Culver, Indiana, ninety miles north of Indianapolis.

1924 Grandfather Lieber, short on savings and in need of ready cash, subdivides his White River estate and begins selling the land in parcels.

1927 In fall enters kindergarten at the Orchard School, a private day school (K–8) on the progressive model championed by John Dewey. Spends hours alone every day with the family's cook and housekeeper, Ida Young, the granddaughter of slaves, who, in the absence of a religious education from his nominally Unitarian parents, teaches him Bible stories.

1929 Grandfather Lieber, now bankrupt, is forced to sell the last of his subdivisions, and the Vonneguts, dispossessed by the sale, leave the White River house. They move into a large new brick residence, designed by father and built with borrowed money, at 4365 North Illinois Street, near the intersection with Forty-fifth Street, Indianapolis. After the Great Crash of October, the mortgage payment on the property becomes increasingly difficult to meet.

1931 As the Depression deepens and new construction ceases, Vonnegut, Bohn & Mueller struggles. Father sells investments and heirlooms to keep family solvent, and reluctantly dismisses Ida Young. ("She was humane and wise and gave me decent moral instruction," Vonnegut will later remember. "The compassionate, forgiving aspects of my beliefs come from Ida Young.") Father's younger brother, Alex Vonnegut, a Harvard-educated insurance salesman and bon vivant, becomes Vonnegut's mentor and "ideal grownup friend." ("He taught me something very important: that when things are going well, we should notice it. He urged me to say out loud during such epiphanies, 'If this isn't nice, *what is*?'") Vonnegut is withdrawn from private school and begins fourth grade at James Whitcomb Riley Elementary, P.S. 43.

1934 Father, after years without an architectural commission, closes his office, turns an attic room of the house into an art studio, and begins to paint portraits, still lifes, and landscapes. Mother takes night classes in creative writing and attempts, unsuccessfully, to sell commercial short fiction to women's magazines. Vonnegut, age eleven, takes a strong interest and vicarious pleasure in his parents' artistic pursuits. In September, Grandfather Lieber dies at age seventy-one. The Vonneguts' share of his estate after probate is less than eleven thousand dollars, and mother, grieving, resentful, and obsessively insecure about the family's diminished social position, begins a long struggle with alcohol abuse, insomnia, and depression. ("My mother was addicted to being rich," Vonnegut will later write. "She was tormented by withdrawal symptoms all through the Great Depression.")

1936 Vonnegut enters Shortridge High School, the largest and best equipped free public school in the state of Indiana. Excels in English and public-speaking classes, and, after dedicated application, the sciences. Joins the staff of the Shortridge *Daily Echo*, a four-page broadsheet edited, set up, and printed by students in the school's print shop, and develops the habit of writing regularly, on deadline, for an audience of his peers. (In his junior and senior years, he will be editor and chief writer of the paper's Tuesday edition.) Plays clarinet in school orchestra and marching band, and takes private lessons from Ernst Michaelis, first-chair clarinetist of the Indianapolis Symphony. Forms a book club for two with Uncle Alex and reads, mostly at Alex's suggestion, Robert Louis Stevenson, H. G. Wells, H. L. Mencken, Thorstein Veblen, George Bernard Shaw, and Mark Twain. Other enthusiasms include Ping-Pong, model trains, radio comedy, movies, and jazz, especially Benny Goodman and Artie Shaw. Begins smoking Pall Mall cigarettes, which will become a lifelong habit.

1940 At age eighteen his head is a mop of blond curls and he has attained his adult height of six foot two: "I was a real skinny, narrow-shouldered boy . . . a preposterous kind of flamingo." Graduates from Shortridge High, and, still living with his parents, enrolls at local Butler University. His vague ambition is to study journalism and, ultimately, write for one of Indianapolis's three daily papers.

1941 Disappointed in Butler, transfers to Cornell University, Ithaca, New York, in middle of freshman year. Following his father's orders and his scientist brother's example, shuns "frivolous" classes in the arts and humanities, focusing instead on chemistry and physics. ("I had no talent for science," Vonnegut will remember. "I did badly.") Neglects his studies, taking pleasure only in drilling with ROTC, drinking with his Delta Upsilon brothers, and writing jokes and news for the Cornell *Daily Sun*. In summer, father sells the big brick house and, with proceeds, builds a smaller one in Williams Creek, a new suburban development six miles north of Indianapolis.

1942 Vonnegut writes a regular column, "Well All Right," for the *Daily Sun*—"impudent editorializing" and "college-humor sort of stuff"—and is elected the paper's assistant managing editor. In the middle of the fall semester of his junior year, is placed on academic probation due to poor grades. Contracts viral pneumonia, withdraws from school, and goes home to recover.

1943 Against the pleas of his mother, enlists in the U.S. Army and in March begins basic training at Camp Atterbury, forty miles south of Indianapolis. Takes special classes in manning the 240-millimeter howitzer, the army's largest mobile fieldpiece. In summer joins the Army Specialized Training Program, and is sent first to the Carnegie Institute of Technology, Pittsburgh, and then to the University of Tennessee, Knoxville, for advanced studies in engineering ("thermodynamics, mechanics, the actual use of machine tools. . . . I did badly again").

1944 In March returns to Camp Atterbury and is assigned as private first class to Headquarters Company, 2nd Battalion, 423rd Regiment, 106th Infantry Division. Although he has no infantry training ("bayonets, grenades, and so on") he is made one of the battalion's six scouts. Assigned an "Army buddy," fellow scout Bernard V. O'Hare Jr., a Roman Catholic youth from Shenandoah, Pennsylvania, who will become a friend for life. Secures frequent Sunday passes, enjoying meals at his parents' house and movie dates with Jane Marie Cox, his sometimes high-school sweetheart. On May 14, while Vonnegut is home on a Mother's Day pass, mother, age fifty-five, commits suicide using barbiturates and alcohol. In October the 106th leaves Camp Atterbury and is staged at Camp Myles Standish, Taunton, Massachusetts. The division embarks at New York City on October 17 and, after three weeks' training in England, is deployed in the Ardennes on December 11. The Germans launch a surprise offensive against the American front on December 16, and three days later Vonnegut, O'Hare, and some sixty other infantrymen are separated from their battalion and taken prisoner near Schönberg, on the German-Belgian border. They are marched sixty miles to Limburg and on December 21 are warehoused, sixty men to a forty-man boxcar, on a railroad siding there. After more than a week, the stifling, fetid car is hauled by train to Stalag IV-B, a crowded German P.O.W. camp in Mühlberg, thirty miles north of Dresden.

1945 On New Year's Day the boxcar is opened, and Vonnegut and his fellow-prisoners are provided showers, bunks, and starvation rations of cold potato soup and brown bread. On January 10, Vonnegut, O'Hare, and about one hundred fifty other prisoners are transferred to a Dresden factory where, under observation by armed guards, they manufacture vitamin-enriched barley-malt syrup. Vonnegut, who has rudimentary German learned at home, is elected the group's foreman and interpreter. On February 13–14, the Allied air forces bomb Dresden, destroying much of the city and killing some twenty-five thousand people. Vonnegut, his fellow prisoners, and their guards find safety in the subterranean meat locker of a slaughterhouse. After the raid, the guards put the prisoners to work clearing corpses from basements and air-raid shelters and hauling them to mass funeral pyres in the Old Market. In late April, as U.S. forces advance on Leipzig, the prisoners and their guards evacuate Dresden and march fifty miles southeast toward Hellendorf, a hamlet near the border with Czechoslovakia. There, on the morning after the general surrender of May 7, the Germans abandon the prisoners and flee from the advancing Soviet Army. Vonnegut, O'Hare, and six others steal a horse and wagon and, over the following week, slowly make their way back to Dresden. Outside the city they meet the Soviet Army, which trucks them a hundred miles to the American lines at Halle. From Halle they are flown, on May 22, to Le Havre, France, for rest and recovery at Camp Lucky Strike, a U.S. repatriation facility. ("When I was captured I weighed 180 pounds," Vonnegut later remembered. "When I was liberated, I weighed 132. The Army fed me cheeseburgers and milkshakes and sent me home wearing an overcoat of baby fat.") On April 21, Vonnegut and O'Hare board a Liberty Ship, the SS *Lucretia Mott*, bound for Newport News, Virginia. Vonnegut returns to Camp Atterbury by train and serves three more weeks as a clerical typist; is promoted to corporal, awarded a Purple Heart, then honorably discharged in late July. Marries high-school sweetheart Jane Marie Cox, September 14, and honeymoons at a Vonnegut family cottage on Lake Maxinkuckee. Taking advantage of the G.I. Bill, Vonnegut applies, and in October is accepted, to the Master's program in anthropology at the University of Chicago. The newlyweds rent an inexpensive apartment near the campus, their home for the next two years. Vonnegut finds a part-time job as a police reporter for the City News Bureau, an independent news agency that provides local stories to Chicago's five dailies.

1946 Greatly enjoys his anthropology classes, especially those taught by Robert Redfield, whom Vonnegut will remember as "the most satisfying teacher in my life." Redfield's theory that human beings are hardwired for living in a

"Folk Society"—"a society where everyone knew everybody well, and associations were for life," where "there was little change" and "what one man believed was what all men believed," where every man felt himself to be part of a larger, supportive, coherent whole—quickly becomes central to Vonnegut's world view. ("We are full of chemicals which require us to belong to folk societies, or failing that, to feel lousy all the time," Vonnegut will later write. "We are chemically engineered to live in folk societies, just as fish are chemically engineered to live in clean water—and there are no folk societies for us anymore.")

1947 Son born, May 11, and named Mark Vonnegut in honor of Mark Twain. Master's thesis, "On the Fluctuations Between Good and Evil in Simple Tales," unanimously rejected by Chicago's anthropology faculty. Vonnegut leaves the program without a degree, fails to turn his part-time job into full-time newspaper work, and searches in vain for appropriate employment. Through the agency of his brother, Bernard, an atmospheric scientist at General Electric, Vonnegut is interviewed by the public-relations department at GE headquarters, in Schenectady, New York. Accepts position of publicist for research laboratory at ninety dollars a week, and moves with family to the village of Alplaus, five miles north of the GE complex. Joins the Alplaus Volunteer Fire Department, his window into community life, and reads George Orwell, whose work and moral example become a touchstone.

1949 Vonnegut enjoys the daily company of research scientists and is "easily excited and entertained" by their work, but despises the corporate hierarchy of GE and sees no room for advancement within the PR department. Devotes evenings and weekends to drafting his first short stories, one of which, "Report on the Barnhouse Effect," he submits to Knox Burger, chief fiction editor at *Collier's*, a general-interest mass-circulation magazine which, like its rival *The Saturday Evening Post*, publishes five stories a week. "Knox told me what was wrong with it, and how to fix it," Vonnegut will later remember. "I did what he said, and he bought the story for seven hundred and fifty dollars, six weeks' pay at GE. I wrote another, and he paid nine hundred and fifty. . . ." Daughter, Edith ("Edie") Vonnegut, born December 29.

1950 First published story, "Report on the Barnhouse Effect," in *Collier's*, February 11; it is adapted for NBC radio's *Dimension X* program (broadcast April 22) and chosen for inclusion in Robert A. Heinlein's anthology *Tomorrow, the Stars* (1952). Sells several more stories to *Collier's* and begins planning a satirical novel about a fully automated world where human labor and the dignity of work are rendered obsolete.

1951 Vonnegut rents a summer cottage in Provincetown, Massachusetts, and decides to resign from GE and move his family to Cape Cod. Having saved the equivalent of a year's salary in freelance income, he buys a small house at 10 Barnard Street, Osterville, on the south shore of the Cape, where he finishes his novel, *Player Piano*. At the recommendation of Knox Burger, places the book with New York agents Kenneth Littauer and Max Wilkinson, both formerly of *Collier's*. At Vonnegut's request, they submit it to Charles Scribner's Sons, the house of Hemingway and Fitzgerald, and have a contract by Christmas.

1952 *Player Piano* published in hardcover, August 18, in an edition of 7,600 copies. It receives few but respectful reviews. Continues to write short stories for *Collier's* and, with the help of Littauer & Wilkinson, Inc., begins placing work in *The Saturday Evening Post*, *Cosmopolitan*, and other top-paying magazines.

1953 *Player Piano* reprinted as a July/August selection of the Doubleday Science Fiction Book Club. Vonnegut becomes involved, as an advisor, fundraiser, volunteer, and actor, in the business and artistic affairs of two of Cape Cod's leading amateur theatrical companies, the Orleans Arena Theatre (summer-stock) and the Barnstable Comedy Club (a repertory company staging four plays a year).

1954 After several false starts abandons Prohibition-era social novel, "Upstairs and Downstairs," set in Indianapolis and inspired by the riches-to-rags career of grandfather Albert Lieber. Writes six chapters of a novel about "ice-nine," a synthetic form of ice that will not melt at room temperature, but soon sets the project aside. Second daughter and third child, Nanette ("Nanny") Vonnegut, born October 4. *Player Piano* reprinted in paperback by Bantam Books, under the title *Utopia 14*.

1955 In February, the Vonneguts leave the small house in Osterville for a large one at 9 Scudder Lane, in nearby West Barnstable. With his favorite market for stories failing (*Collier's* became a biweekly in 1953, and will cease publication in January 1957) and without ideas for a new novel, Vonnegut takes a full-time job as copywriter in an industrial advertising agency. Commutes to Boston daily, and holds the job for about two years. Dabbles in playwriting, with an eye toward providing a show for the Orleans Arena Theatre.

1956 In January Vonnegut's father, recently retired from a second career in architecture and living alone in rural Brown County, Indiana, informs his family that he is dying of lung cancer. Vonnegut visits him a number of times before his death, on October 1, at age seventy-two.

1957 Makes stage adaptation of his short story "EPICAC" (*Collier's*, 1950) for an evening of one-acts at the Barnstable Comedy Club. (The cast features eight-year-old Edie Vonnegut in the role of a talking computer.) With small inheritance from his father, opens and manages Saab Cape Cod, the second Saab dealership in the United States, with a showroom and garage on Route 6A, just up the street from his house. At a Littauer & Wilkinson holiday party Vonnegut is asked by Knox Burger, now an editor for Dell Books, to write a science-fiction novel for his new line of mass-market paperback originals.

1958 Improvises an outline for his paperback novel, conceived as a satire on human grandeur in the form of a pulp-fiction "space opera." Writes the first draft with unaccustomed speed, then painstakingly revises. ("I *swooped* through that novel," Vonnegut will later recall. "All the others were *bashed out*, sentence by sentence.") Sister, Alice, a housewife and amateur sculptor, dies of breast cancer in a Newark, New Jersey, hospital, September 16, at age forty-one, with both of her brothers nearby. Only one day earlier her husband of fifteen years, James Carmalt Adams, had died when a commuter train taking him to Manhattan plunged off an open drawbridge into Newark Bay. Without hesitation Kurt and Jane Vonnegut take in Alice's four orphaned children—James Jr. (fourteen years old), Steven (eleven), Kurt (called "Tiger," nine), and toddler "Peter Boo" (twenty-one months). As Jane will later write, "Our tidy little family of five had blown up into a wildly improbable gang of nine."

1959 The Vonneguts assume custody of the three older Adams boys, but after a protracted, bitter dispute with a childless Adams cousin, relinquish control of the youngest. (Allowing the boys to be split between distant and unlike households will be, according to Jane, "the most difficult decision" of the Vonneguts' marriage. "Peter Boo" is raised in Birmingham, Alabama, and until his teens will see little of his older brothers.) In October, Vonnegut's second novel, *The Sirens of Titan*, published in paperback by Dell in an edition of 175,000 copies. It is popular with readers but receives no reviews.

1960 *Penelope*, a two-act comedy about a war hero's unheroic homecoming, receives six performances at the Orleans Arena Theatre, September 5–10. *The Sirens of Titan* named a finalist for the Hugo Award for the year's best science-fiction novel, and Houghton Mifflin arranges to print 2,500 hardcover copies to meet demand from libraries. Vonnegut, having failed to make money for himself or his Swedish franchisers, closes Saab Cape Cod.

1961 In the ten years since the appearance of "Report on the Barnhouse Effect," Vonnegut has published more than three-dozen short stories in "slick" magazines and science-fiction pulps. In September Knox Burger, now at Fawcett Gold Medal Books, publishes *Canary in a Cat House*, a paperback collection of twelve of these stories. Burger also signs Vonnegut's third novel, *Mother Night*, the fictional memoirs of a German-American double agent during World War II. Vonnegut publishes "My Name Is Everyone" (*The Saturday Evening Post*, December 16), a short story evoking the backstage life of a community playhouse much like that of the Barnstable Comedy Club.

1962 In February *Mother Night* published as a paperback original by Fawcett Gold Medal in an edition of 175,000 copies. Vonnegut, returning to the "ice-nine" material of 1954, begins a new novel, *Cat's Cradle*, which Littauer sells to Holt, Rinehart & Winston. *Who Am I This Time?*, Vonnegut's stage adaptation of "My Name Is Everyone," presented by the Barnstable Comedy Club. (It will be revived two years later by the Cape Playhouse in Dennis, Massachusetts.)

1963 In June *Cat's Cradle* published in hardcover by Holt. Reviews are few but enthusiastic, and at Christmas Graham Greene, writing in the London *Spectator*, names it one of his three favorite novels of the year. In fall accepts yearlong assignment as "the whole English department" at the Hopefield School, in East Sandwich, Massachusetts, a small private high school for students with emotional and learning problems.

1964 Responding to a changing editorial marketplace, stops writing short stories and begins contributing personal essays, book reviews, and other nonfiction pieces to periodicals including *The New York Times Book Review*, *Life*, *Esquire*, and the travel magazine *Venture*.

1965 In March *God Bless You, Mr. Rosewater*, a novel about a so-called fool and his money, published in hardcover by Holt, Rinehart & Winston to many if mixed reviews. Accepts last-minute invitation to teach fiction writing at the Writers' Workshop, Iowa City, on a two-year contract. Accompanied by Edie, who enrolls in nearby University High School, he lives on the first floor of a large brick Victorian house at 800 Van Buren Avenue, next door to the writer Andre Dubus. "I didn't get to know any literary people until [my] two years teaching at Iowa," he will later recall. "There at Iowa I was suddenly friends with Nelson Algren and José Donoso and Vance Bourjaily and Donald Justice . . . and was amazed. Suddenly writing seemed very important again. This was better than a transplant of monkey glands for a man my age." Enjoys teaching, and is good at it. His students include Loree Rackstraw, a future English professor and memoirist who becomes a friend and confidante for life. Begins work in earnest on a long-contemplated "Dresden novel," based on his experiences during World War II.

1966 In May is joined in Iowa by Jane and daughter Nanny. *Cat's Cradle* becomes a bestseller, especially among college-age readers, in its Dell paperback edition. *Player Piano* reprinted in hardcover by Holt, Rinehart & Winston, and *Mother Night* reprinted in hardcover by Harper & Row. Agent Kenneth Littauer dies, July, and Max Wilkinson, to Vonnegut's dismay, moves literary agency to Long Island and goes into semiretirement. In fall, Richard Yates rejoins the Iowa faculty and quickly becomes a lifelong friend.

Vonnegut's students for 1966–67 include the young and unpublished John Irving, Gail Godwin, and John Casey. In November, forty-year-old editor-publisher Seymour ("Sam") Lawrence—formerly of the Atlantic Monthly Press and Knopf, now launching his own imprint at Delacorte Press—offers Vonnegut a three-book contract. Vonnegut, with Wilkinson's consent, hires entertainment lawyer Donald C. Farber to handle the contract. (By 1970 Farber will become Vonnegut's sole agent and attorney.)

1967 Prepares first book for Sam Lawrence, a miscellany of previously published short works including eleven of the twelve stories in *Canary in a Cat House*, eleven uncollected and later stories, and two recent nonfiction pieces. To anchor the book with something new and substantial, writes "Welcome to the Monkey House," his first short story in nearly five years and the first not conceived for a magazine. In April awarded a fellowship from the John Simon Guggenheim Foundation, which finances a summer research trip to Dresden in the company of his Army buddy Bernard V. O'Hare. In May, ends two-year stay at the Iowa Writers' Workshop and returns with family to Barnstable to work on his Dresden novel.

1968 Collection *Welcome to the Monkey House* published by Delacorte/Seymour Lawrence, August, to mixed reviews. Vonnegut completes his Dresden novel, and Sam Lawrence, convinced of the book's sales potential, begins buying rights to earlier works for reissue as Delacorte hardcovers and Delta/Dell paperbacks. "Fortitude," a one-act teleplay commissioned by CBS for an unrealized comedy special, reshaped as a closet drama and published in the September issue of *Playboy*.

1969 On March 31, Vonnegut's Dresden novel, *Slaughterhouse-Five*, published by Delacorte/Seymour Lawrence to uniformly good and well-placed reviews, including the cover of *The New York Times Book Review*. The book spends sixteen weeks on the *Times* fiction list, peaking at number four, and creates an audience for his newly issued paperback backlist. Vonnegut begins a lucrative second career as a public speaker, especially on college campuses. Works on a new novel and teases the press with its title, *Breakfast of Champions*. In May, producer Lester M. Goldsmith options *Penelope*, Vonnegut's play of 1960, and begins planning

Off-Broadway premiere for the following fall. Vonnegut spends most of the summer rewriting the play, giving it the new title *Happy Birthday, Wanda June.*

1970 In early January, at the invitation of a private American relief organization, visits the short-lived, war-torn African republic of Biafra shortly before it surrenders to Nigeria, from which it was attempting to secede. Publishes account of the trip, "Biafra: A People Betrayed," in April issue of *McCall's.* In May receives an Academy Award in Literature from the American Academy of Arts and Letters. Interviewed by Harry Reasoner of CBS's *60 Minutes*, television's most-watched program, for the broadcast of September 15. (Reasoner introduces him as "the current idol of the country's sensitive and intelligent young people, [who] snap up his books as fast as they're reissued. . . . His gentle fantasies of peace and his dark humor are as current among the young as was J. D. Salinger's work in the fifties and Tolkien's in the sixties.") Accepts invitation to teach creative writing at Harvard University for the academic year beginning in the fall. Commutes to Cambridge two days a week from New York City, where, by arrangement with producer Lester Goldsmith, he lives as a "kept playwright" in a Greenwich Village sublet. With director Michael Kane and a cast starring Kevin McCarthy and Marsha Mason, workshops the script of *Happy Birthday, Wanda June* throughout September, tinkering with the show until its first curtain. Play opens at the Theatre de Lys, Christopher Street, on October 7; it receives mixed reviews and runs forty-seven performances, closing on November 15. The show moves to the Edison Theater, Broadway, on December 22. During production of *Wanda June* Vonnegut meets and begins a relationship with the photojournalist Jill Krementz, born 1940.

1971 Son Mark, a self-described hippie and co-founder, with friends from Swarthmore, of a commune at Lake Powell, British Columbia, suffers a manic mental breakdown. On February 14, Vonnegut commits him to the care of Hollywood Psychiatric Hospital in Vancouver, where he makes a slow but steady recovery. Broadway production of *Wanda June* closes March 14 after ninety-six performances. In May, Vonnegut delivers the annual Blashfield Address to the assembled National Institute of Arts and Letters and

American Academy of Arts and Letters. Awarded Master's degree in anthropology by the University of Chicago, which, at the department chair's suggestion, accepts *Cat's Cradle* in lieu of a formal dissertation. In June, book version of *Wanda June*, with a preface by the author and production photographs by Jill Krementz, published by Delacorte/Seymour Lawrence. Resumes work on *Breakfast of Champions.* In December, Sony Pictures releases film version of *Happy Birthday, Wanda June*, directed by Mark Robson and starring Rod Steiger and Susannah York. ("It was one of the most embarrassing movies ever made," Vonnegut later writes, "and I am happy that it sank like a stone.") Grants WNET-New York and WGBH-Boston the option to develop a ninety-minute made-for-television "revue" based on scenes from his writings. The script, by David O'Dell, is revised by Vonnegut and titled *Between Time and Timbuktu, or Prometheus-5: A Space Fantasy.* Separates from Jane Marie Cox Vonnegut and rents a one-bedroom apartment at 349 East Fifty-fourth Street, between First Avenue and Second Avenue.

1972 On March 13 *Between Time and Timbuktu*, starring William Hickey, Kevin McCarthy, and the comedians Bob and Ray (Bob Elliott and Ray Goulding), broadcast nationally as an installment of public television's *NET Playhouse* series. In October, a book version of the teleplay—"based on materials by Kurt Vonnegut, Jr.," with a preface by the author and photographs by Krementz—published by Delacorte/Seymour Lawrence. On March 15 *Slaughterhouse-Five*, directed by George Roy Hill from a screenplay by Stephen Geller, released by Universal Studios. The film, starring Michael Sacks, Ron Leibman, and Valerie Perrine, delights Vonnegut, who finds the adaptation "flawless." In summer, Vonnegut and Krementz collaborate on an illustrated report from the Republican National Convention in Miami, published as the cover story of the November issue of *Harper's.* "The Big Space Fuck," Vonnegut's widely publicized "farewell" to the short-story form, published in *Again, Dangerous Visions*, an anthology of original science-fiction tales commissioned and edited by Harlan Ellison. Named vice president of PEN American Center, the U.S. branch of the international literary and human-rights organization, and remains active on PEN's behalf for the rest of his life.

1973 In April, *Breakfast of Champions*, embellished with more than a hundred felt-tip line drawings by the author, published by Delacorte/Seymour Lawrence to mixed reviews but strong sales. It dominates the *New York Times* fiction list for twenty-eight weeks, ten weeks in the number-one position. In May, speaks against state-sponsored censorship at the conference of International PEN in Stockholm, is inducted into the National Institute of Arts and Letters, and receives an honorary doctorate in the humanities from Indiana University, Bloomington. In September, begins one-year term as Distinguished Professor of English Prose at City University of New York, where his colleagues include Joseph Heller, who becomes a close friend. In November *Slaughterhouse-Five* declared obscene by the school board of Drake, North Dakota, which orders thirty-six copies of the novel burned in the high-school furnace and the teacher who assigned it dismissed; it is the first of more than a dozen such incidents of censorship during Vonnegut's lifetime, all successfully challenged by the American Civil Liberties Union. Buys a three-story townhouse, built in 1862, at 228 East Forty-eighth Street, between Second Avenue and Third Avenue, which he shares with Jill Krementz. (The top floor of this whitewashed Turtle Bay brownstone becomes his office; the separate basement apartment, with its entry under the stoop, becomes her photography studio.) In December Jane Marie Cox Vonnegut reluctantly agrees to a divorce.

1974 *Wampeters, Foma & Granfalloons (Opinions)*, a collection of twenty-five previously published short prose pieces, brought out by Delacorte/Seymour Lawrence, September. This, the first of his "autobiographical collages" combining essays, articles, speeches, book reviews, and other writings, is the last of his works to be published by "Kurt Vonnegut, Jr."; subsequent works, and all reprints, will be published under the name "Kurt Vonnegut." In October visits Moscow with Krementz; their guide is Rita Rait, the translator of his books into Russian.

1975 Writes *Slapstick*, a comic novel about a brother and sister dedicated to wiping out "the peculiarly American disease called loneliness." In May begins four-year term as Vice President for Literature of the National Institute of Arts and Letters. Spends summer in a rented beachfront house in East Hampton, Long Island, and begins search for a second home in the area. Uncle Alex dies, July 28, at age eighty-six. ("I am eternally grateful to him," Vonnegut writes in a tribute, "for my knack of finding in great books reason enough to feel honored to be alive, no matter what else might be going on.") In October, Mark Vonnegut publishes *The Eden Express*, a memoir of his madness, to good reviews and strong sales. The royalties will pay his way through Harvard Medical School.

1976 *Slapstick* published by Delacorte/Seymour Lawrence, September, to uniformly negative reviews, the worst Vonnegut will ever receive. ("The reviewers . . . actually asked critics who had praised me in the past to now admit in public how wrong they'd been," he later wrote. "I felt as though I were sleeping standing up in a boxcar in Germany again.") Sales, however, are strong: it is on the *New York Times* fiction list for twenty-four weeks, peaking at number four.

1977 At the request of George Plimpton, editor of *The Paris Review*, fashions a long autobiographical article in the form of one of the magazine's "Art of Fiction" interviews. Purchases a second home, a clapboard house dating from the 1740s, at 620 Sagg Main Street, Sagaponack, a village in Southampton, Long Island. Summer neighbors include Plimpton, Nelson Algren, Truman Capote, James Jones, and Irwin Shaw.

1978 Works on a new novel, *Jailbird*, the fictional memoirs of a good man who, through no wrongdoing of his own, becomes involved in several of the most shameful episodes in modern American political history.

1979 *Jailbird* published by Delacorte/Seymour Lawrence, September, to good reviews and strong sales. It is on the *New York Times* fiction list for thirty-one weeks, five weeks in the number-one position. In April, commemorates the centenary of the Mark Twain house in Hartford, Connecticut, with a speech in which he says that "we would not be known as a nation with a supple, amusing, and often beautiful language of its own, if it were not for the genius of Mark Twain." Throughout the summer a musical adaptation of *God Bless You, Mr. Rosewater*, with book and lyrics by Howard Ashman and music by Alan Menken, is developed by Ashman's WPA Theater company with Vonnegut's "limited but noisy" involvement. The show, produced by Edie Vonnegut, opens at the Entermedia Theatre, in the East Village, on October 11. Despite good reviews, it closes after only twelve performances, having failed to find a Broadway backer. Vonnegut marries Jill Krementz, November 24, at Christ Church United Methodist, on Sixtieth Street at Park Avenue.

1980 On January 27 Vonnegut, a self-described "Christ-worshiping agnostic," delivers his first sermon, a lecture on human dignity at the First Parish Unitarian Church, Cambridge, Massachusetts. Writes the text for *Sun Moon Star*, a picture story with bold and simple full-color images by the graphic designer Ivan Chermayeff. A retelling of the Nativity as seen through the eyes of the infant Jesus, it is published by Harper & Row as a Christmas gift book. First solo art exhibition, featuring thirty felt-tip drawings on vellum, at the Margo Feiden Galleries, Greenwich Village, October 20–November 15.

1981 *Palm Sunday*, an "autobiographical collage" collecting short nonfiction pieces written between 1974 and 1980, published by Delacorte/Seymour Lawrence, March. The title piece is a sermon given on March 30, 1980, at St. Clement's Episcopal Church on West Forty-sixth Street. Vonnegut's text is John 12:1–8: "For the poor always ye have with you . . ."

1982 Television adaptation of *Who Am I This Time?*, directed by Jonathan Demme and starring Susan Sarandon and Christopher Walken, broadcast on PBS in its *American Playhouse* series, February 2. Hires Janet Cosby, a Washington-based lecture agent, to book his annual speaking tours—two weeks in the spring, two weeks in the fall, a schedule he will keep for most of the next two decades. *Deadeye Dick*, a quickly written novel of guilt, self-punishment, and neutron bombs, published by Delacorte/Seymour Lawrence, October, to mixed reviews. It is on the *New York Times* fiction list for fourteen weeks, peaking at number ten. On December 18, Vonnegut and Krementz adopt a three-day-old girl and name her Lily Vonnegut.

1983 Begins work on a new novel, *Galápagos*, a fantasy about the future of human evolution. Makes further drawings, and begins to take himself seriously as a graphic artist, though he doubts his technique.

1984 In January, unsuccessfully tries to interest art publisher Harry N. Abrams in bringing out a book of his drawings. On the evening of February 13, the thirty-ninth anniversary of the firebombing of Dresden, attempts suicide in his Manhattan home, apparently by overdosing on barbiturates and alcohol. Awakes in St. Vincent's Hospital, Greenwich Village, and is diagnosed, as he writes to a friend, "with acute (all but terminal) depression. . . . I was there for eighteen days, under lock and key. . . . I am no renaissance man, but a manic depressive with a few lopsided gifts." Upon release returns to *Galápagos*, finishing the manuscript by Christmas Day.

1985 *Galápagos* published by Delacorte/Seymour Lawrence, October, to good reviews. It is on the *New York Times* fiction list for seventeen weeks, peaking at number five. Completes working draft of *Make Up Your Mind*, a sex farce for four actors. The play, his first since *Happy Birthday, Wanda June*, is given a staged reading in East Hampton. It is optioned by a Broadway producer but is not produced or published.

1986 Writes *Bluebeard*, the fictional memoirs of a seventy-one-year-old Abstract Expressionist painter whose work is loosely modeled on that of Barnett Newman. On December 19, Jane Marie Cox Vonnegut, now married to law-school professor and Defense Department spokesman Adam Yarmolinsky, dies of ovarian cancer. She leaves behind a memoir of her life with Vonnegut and their six children, published by Houghton Mifflin in October 1987 as *Angels Without Wings*.

1987 *Bluebeard* published by Delacorte/Seymour Lawrence, October, to mixed reviews. It is on the *New York Times* fiction list for eleven weeks, peaking at number eight.

1988 Works on new novel, *Hocus Pocus*, a commentary on "the way we live now" addressing, among much else, American trends in higher education, crime and punishment, political correctness, social privilege, militarism, intolerance, and globalization.

1989 Sam Lawrence moves from Delacorte to Dutton and then to Houghton Mifflin, but Vonnegut declines to follow. Sells *Hocus Pocus* to G. P. Putnam's Sons, where his editor is Faith Sale. In October, at the request of the international humanitarian organization CARE, travels to Mozambique to write about the country's decade-old civil war.

1990 "My Visit to Hell," Vonnegut's report on Mozambique, published in *Parade* magazine, January 7. The report is the journalistic centerpiece of his next "autobiographical collage," the assembling of which becomes a yearlong project. In May, gives anti-war speech in the form of an eye-witness account of the firebombing of Dresden at the National Air and Space Museum, Washington, D.C. Wartime buddy Bernard V. O'Hare, a longtime district attorney in Northampton County, Pennsylvania, dies, June 8. *Hocus Pocus* published by Putnam, September, to good reviews. It is on the *New York Times* fiction list for seven weeks, peaking at number four.

1991 Vonnegut and Krementz start divorce proceedings, and Vonnegut spends time at house in Sagaponack. *Fates Worse Than Death: An Autobiographical Collage of the 1980s* published by Putnam, September. The title piece is a sermon on humility, delivered at the Cathedral of St. John the Divine on May 23, 1982. Vonnegut accepts a commission from the New York Philomusica Ensemble for a new libretto to *L'Histoire du Soldat* (1918), Stravinsky's musical setting of a Russian fairy tale of World War I. Vonnegut bases his text on the case of Private Edward Donald Slovik, who, in 1945, became the first American soldier executed for desertion since the Civil War.

1992 Vonnegut and Krementz drop divorce proceedings. Named Humanist of the Year by the American Humanist Association, and accepts invitation to serve as Honorary President of the association until his death. ("We humanists try to behave as decently, as fairly, and as honorably as we can without any expectation of rewards or punishments in an afterlife," he says in his remarks of acceptance. "The Creator of the Universe has been to us unknowable so far. We serve as best we can the only abstraction with which we have some understanding, which is 'Community.'") Begins writing a new novel, which he claims will be his last.

1993 Sam Schacht, formerly of the Steppenwolf Theater Company, directs *Make Up Your Mind* in a limited Off-Broadway run at the New Group Theater, Forty-second Street, April 20–May 5. On May 6 the Philomusica Ensemble gives the world premiere of *L'Histoire du Soldat/An American Soldier's Tale* at Alice Tully Hall, Lincoln Center. Vonnegut approached by a former GE colleague, now a fundraising consultant in Lexington, Kentucky, to do a benefit reading for his client Midway College. Collaborates with Joe Petro III, an area printmaker, on a collectible limited-edition poster for the November 1st event. Delighted with Petro's result—a hand-pulled silkscreen print adapted from a felt-tip self-portrait—Vonnegut visits the thirty-seven-year-old artist in his Lexington studio. The two soon form a partnership, Origami Express, to produce signed and numbered limited-edition prints adapted from Vonnegut's drawings and calligraphy. This enduring collaboration solves most of Vonnegut's problems with technique, and helps him to become the graphic artist he has longed to be. (In 2004, after producing more than two hundred discrete Origami editions, Vonnegut will write: "One of the best things that ever happened to me, a one-in-a-billion opportunity to enjoy myself in perfect innocence, was my meeting Joe.")

1994 Sam Lawrence dies, January 5, at age sixty-seven. "That anything I have written is in print today is due to the efforts of one publisher," Vonnegut writes in tribute. "When [in 1966] I was broke and completely out of print, Sam bought rights to my books, for peanuts, from publishers who had given up on me. [He] thrust my books back into the myopic public eye and made my reputation." Invited by Daniel Simon, publisher-editor of the newly founded Seven Stories Press, to write an introduction to Nelson Algren's 1942 novel *Never Come Morning*. Struck by Simon's commitment to Algren's work and to publishing books on human rights, social justice, and progressive politics, he becomes an advisory editor to the small independent press.

1995 At the end of the year completes a draft of the novel *Timequake*, a fantasy on the subject of free will concerning "a sudden glitch in the space-time continuum" that, occurring on the eve of the millennium, forces mankind to relive, day by day and mistake by mistake, the entire 1990s. He is unhappy with the book and, to the dismay of Putnam, scraps it and begins again from scratch.

1996 On November 1 *Mother Night*, directed by Keith Gordon from a screenplay by Vonnegut's filmmaker friend Robert B.

Weide, released by Fine Line Features. Vonnegut finds the script "too faithful to the novel" but admires the performance of leading man Nick Nolte. In December completes a second version of *Timequake*—a fictional-autobiographical "stew" made up of excerpts from the earlier *Timequake*, humorous meditations on the creative process, and laments for the passing of the America of his youth.

1997 Brother, Bernard, dies, April 25, at age eighty-three; Vonnegut will write his obituary for year-end issue of *The New York Times Magazine*. *Timequake* published by Putnam, September, to admiring and elegiac reviews. It is on the *New York Times* fiction list for five weeks, peaking at number seven. Vonnegut sells the greater part of his personal and professional papers, including the various drafts of his fourteen published novels, to Lilly Library, Indiana University.

1998 With the news and features staff of WNYC-FM, develops a series of twenty-odd ninety-second radio skits, each a satirical "report on the Afterlife" in which Vonnegut, in a "controlled near-death state" chemically induced by Dr. Jack Kevorkian, interviews Sir Isaac Newton, Mary Shelley, Eugene V. Debs, or some other resident of Paradise. (The best of the skits are revised, expanded, and collected in an eighty-page book, *God Bless You, Dr. Kevorkian*, published in April 1999 by Seven Stories Press.) In October again visits Dresden and the slaughterhouse in which he survived the firebombing of 1945.

1999 Peter J. Reed, of the University of Minnesota, gathers the twenty-three short stories published in magazines in the 1950s and 1960s that did not appear in *Welcome to the Monkey House*, writes a critical preface to the collection, and asks Vonnegut for permission to publish. Vonnegut revises a couple of the less successful stories and writes an autobiographical introduction and "coda" to the volume. *Bagombo Snuff Box: Uncollected Short Fiction* published by Putnam, September, to respectful reviews and mild sales.

2000 On the evening of January 31 Vonnegut is hospitalized for smoke inhalation after successfully containing a fire in the third-floor office of his New York townhouse caused by a smoldering Pall Mall in an overturned ashtray. Pulled from the room by Lily and a neighbor, he lies unconscious for two days in Presbyterian Hospital and is dismissed after three weeks' recuperation. At the suggestion of his daughter Nanny, moves to a studio apartment near her home in Northampton, Massachusetts, where she and her family nurse him back to health. In spring invited by local Smith College to join the English faculty as writer-in-residence for the academic year 2000–01. Works with a handful of student fiction-writers and gives occasional public lectures and readings at the many college campuses throughout Western Massachusetts.

2001 In May begins writing a novel, each chapter a monologue by a famous middle-aged standup comedian who entertains America during the final weeks of mankind. Is shocked and creatively paralyzed by the events of September 11, and sets novel aside for more than a year.

2002 In response to threats posed to the First Amendment by the USA Patriot Act of 2001, lends his celebrity to public-service advertisements for the ACLU, stating "I am an American who knows the importance of being able to read and express any thought without fear." Gives Lilly Library drafts of his early short stories and the very few other literary manuscripts that survived the New York house fire. Writes foreword to the Seven Stories Press reissue of son Mark's *Eden Express.* In fall resumes work on novel, now titled "If God Were Alive Today," which develops as a topical satire on the Bush administration.

2003 In January is interviewed about the coming war in Iraq by Joel Bleifuss, editor of *In These Times*, a biweekly nonprofit news magazine headquartered in Chicago. Discovers easy rapport with Bleifuss, whose politics are "Midwestern progressive" in the tradition of Vonnegut's socialist heroes Eugene V. Debs and Powers Hapgood. Soon becomes a regular columnist and honorary senior editor at *In These Times*, contributing political opinion, personal essays, humor pieces, and drawings. Magazine column cannibalizes material developed for "If God Were Alive Today" and becomes the chief literary project of his remaining years.

2005 In October, *A Man Without a Country*, a collection of columns from *In These Times*, published by Seven Stories Press. A surprise bestseller, it is on the *New York Times* nonfiction list for six weeks, peaking at number nine.

2006 In June says to an interviewer: "Everything I've done is in print. I have fulfilled my destiny, such as it is, and have nothing more to say. So now I'm writing only little things—one line here, two lines there, sometimes a poem. And I do art. . . . I have reached what Nietzsche called 'the melancholia of everything completed.'"

2007 In mid-March, falls from the steps of his townhouse on East Forty-eighth Street and hits his head on the pavement. Despite aggressive medical treatment, he never regains consciousness. Dies at Mount Sinai Hospital on the evening of April 11, at age eighty-four.

Note on the Texts

This volume presents a selection from the fiction that Kurt Vonnegut published between 1950 and 1962. It contains three novels—*Player Piano* (1952), *The Sirens of Titan* (1959), and *Mother Night* (1962)—and six short stories. It also presents, in an appendix, two essays by Vonnegut, from 1965 and 1999, on his early career as a writer.

Vonnegut began developing ideas for his first novel, *Player Piano*, in 1949–50, when he was working as a writer in the public relations department of the General Electric Company, in Schenectady, New York. At GE, Vonnegut told *Playboy* magazine in 1973, "I saw a milling machine for cutting the rotors on jet engines, gas turbines. This was a very expensive thing for a machinist to do . . . so they had a computer-operated milling machine built to cut the blades, and I was fascinated by that. This was in 1949, and the guys who were working on it were foreseeing all sorts of machines being run by little boxes and punched cards. *Player Piano* was my response to the implications of having everything run by little boxes. The idea of doing that, you know, made sense, perfect sense; to have a little clicking box make all the decisions wasn't a vicious thing to do. But it was too bad for the human beings who got their dignity from their jobs." Vonnegut's models for his novel included Aldous Huxley's dystopian satire *Brave New World* (1932) and Fritz Lang's silent film *Metropolis* (1927).

By early 1951, Vonnegut had written an outline of the novel and a draft of the first few chapters, enough for his literary representative, Kenneth Littauer, of the Manhattan agency Littauer & Wilkinson, to sell an option on the book to Lewis Henry "Harry" Brague Jr., an editor at Charles Scribner's Sons, New York. Most of the novel was written in a rented summer cottage in Provincetown, Massachusetts, and the first draft was completed, in November 1951, at Vonnegut's residence in Osterville, Massachusetts, a small house he had purchased earlier that fall. *Player Piano* was accepted by Scribner before Christmas and was published in hardcover in August 1952. According to Vonnegut's bibliographers Asa B. Pieratt Jr. and Jerome Klinkowitz, the first printing was 7,600 copies. A Doubleday Science-Fiction Book Club edition, set from the same plates as the Scribner edition, was published in June 1953; the first printing was 15,000 copies, the second 5,000 copies. (In November 1954, Bantam Books, New York, published a mass-market paperback edition of *Player Piano* under the title *Utopia 14*, noting on the copyright page that, except for the title, the original text had not been altered.) Vonnegut did not subsequently revise the book, and the text of the 1952 Scribner edition is printed here.

After the publication of *Player Piano*, Vonnegut began and abandoned at least two other novels: one the seed of what would eventually become his fourth novel, *Cat's Cradle* (1963), the other a sprawling social portrait of Prohibition-era Indianapolis with the working title "Upstairs and Downstairs." The idea for *The Sirens of Titan*, his second published novel, came to him in 1957, and he pitched it to his old friend Knox Burger—his former editor at *Collier's* magazine, now an editor at Dell Books—at a Littauer & Wilkinson cocktail party at the end of that year. "I got three thousand dollars total for this masterpiece, which was published as a paperback original," Vonnegut wrote in the introduction to a signed, limited, leatherbound edition of the novel (Norwalk, Conn.: Easton Press, 1990). "That was what I used to get for a single short story from *Collier's* or *The Saturday Evening Post* . . . magazines that once printed a lot of fiction" but that by the late 1950s "were being killed off by a much better buy for advertisers, which was television. So the fundamental concern of much of my fiction, the impact of fantastic technological change on mere human beings, was the story of my life as well."

The Sirens of Titan was written at Vonnegut's home in West Barnstable, Massachusetts, in 1958. The first draft was composed in a matter of months, with a quickness, ease, and completeness of vision that Vonnegut would never again enjoy. ("Every mother's favorite child is the one that was delivered by natural childbirth," he would later write to a friend. "*The Sirens of Titan* was that kind of book.") The novel was published as a mass-market paperback by Dell Books, New York, in October 1959. According to Pieratt and Klinkowitz, 177,500 copies were printed. When, in the following year, the book was nominated for a Hugo Award for Best Novel, Houghton Mifflin Company, Boston, arranged to publish a hardcover reprint of the Dell edition to meet demand from public libraries. Twenty-five hundred copies of the Houghton Mifflin edition, its pages photographically reproduced and slightly enlarged from the Dell paperback, were printed in February 1961. Vonnegut did not subsequently revise the book, and the text of the 1959 Dell edition is printed here.

Mother Night was begun, under the working title "Evil, Anyone?," immediately after the final draft of *The Sirens of Titan* was submitted to Dell in early 1959. By the spring of 1960, Knox Burger, who had moved from Dell to another paperback publisher—Gold Medal Books, an imprint of Fawcett Publications—read the first several chapters and offered Vonnegut a contract. Vonnegut finished the novel at his home in West Barnstable, Massachusetts, and delivered a final draft early in

1961. *Mother Night* was published as a mass-market paperback by Gold Medal Books, New York, in February 1962. According to Pieratt and Klinkowitz, 175,000 copies were printed.

In 1965, after the successful hardcover publication of Vonnegut's fourth and fifth novels, *Cat's Cradle* (1963) and *God Bless You, Mr. Rosewater* (1965), Vonnegut's agents sold hardcover reprint rights for *Mother Night* to Harper & Row, New York. The text of the Gold Medal edition was reset by Harper's, whose copyeditors corrected editorial mistakes in the original (e.g., 620.21, "body noisome nuisance,"; 639.11, "using Luger,") and misspellings of proper names throughout (e.g., "Adolph" Hitler, "Rudolph" Hoess). They also brought uniformity to the treatment of extracts and other aspects of typographic style. Unfortunately, due to an error in transcription during the typesetting process, two short paragraphs in the text of the Gold Medal Books edition were omitted from the Harper reprint and have been omitted from every subsequent printing until now. These paragraphs are here restored to the text as follows: 634.9–11, "And then he took from the shopping bag a hangman's knot tied in a length of lank, pale, slick new hemp. He threw it on the floor beside me."; 656.30, " 'You knew about it?' I said."

Vonnegut used the opportunity of Harper's resetting *Mother Night* to make a few small changes in chapters fourteen and sixteen, and to add an author's introduction to the novel. The introduction, dated 1966, was written in Iowa City, Iowa, while he was an instructor at the Iowa Writers' Workshop. As was Vonnegut's wish, the introduction has been included in every printing of *Mother Night* since 1966.

The Harper & Row edition of *Mother Night* was published in hardcover in April 1966. According to Pieratt and Klinkowitz, 5,500 copies were printed. Vonnegut did not subsequently revise the book, and, except for the adoption of two paragraphs omitted from the first edition as noted above, the text of the 1966 Harper & Row edition of *Mother Night* is printed here.

Under the rubric "Stories," this volume collects six of the more than forty short stories that Vonnegut published in national magazines between 1950 and 1962. Their publication history is as follows:

"Report on the Barnhouse Effect," Vonnegut's first published work of fiction, appeared in *Collier's*, February 11, 1950. Vonnegut revised it for *Canary in a Cat House*, a collection of twelve short stories published as a mass-market paperback original by Gold Medal Books, New York, in September 1961. He reprinted it, without further changes, in *Welcome to the Monkey House*, a collection of twenty-four stories and essays published in hardcover by Delacorte Press/Seymour Lawrence in August 1968. The text from *Welcome to the Monkey House* is printed here.

"EPICAC" was published in *Collier's*, November 25, 1950. Vonnegut revised it for *Welcome to the Monkey House* (1968). The text from *Welcome to the Monkey House* is printed here.

"Unready to Wear" was published in *Galaxy Science Fiction*, April 1953. Vonnegut revised it for *Canary in a Cat House* (1961) and reprinted it, without further changes, in *Welcome to the Monkey House* (1968). The text from *Welcome to the Monkey House* is printed here.

"Tomorrow and Tomorrow and Tomorrow" was published, as "The Big Trip Up Yonder," in *Galaxy Science Fiction*, January 1954. Vonnegut revised it, and gave it its current title, for *Canary in a Cat House* (1961). He reprinted it, without further changes, in *Welcome to the Monkey House* (1968). The text from *Welcome to the Monkey House* is printed here.

"Harrison Bergeron" was published in *The Magazine of Fantasy and Science Fiction*, October 1961. Vonnegut revised it for *Welcome to the Monkey House* (1968). The text from *Welcome to the Monkey House* is printed here.

"2BR02B" was published in *Worlds of If*, January 1962. Vonnegut revised it for *Bagombo Snuff Box*, a collection of his uncollected magazine fiction published by G. P. Putnam's Sons, New York, in September 1999. (This volume, edited by Vonnegut scholar Peter J. Reed, collects twenty-three short stories published in magazines between 1950 and 1963. It was conceived by Professor Reed as a complement to Vonnegut's 1968 collection, *Welcome to the Monkey House*.) The text from *Bagombo Snuff Box* is printed here.

The appendix collects two autobiographical essays by Vonnegut commenting on his early career as a writer. Their publication history is as follows:

"Science Fiction" was published as a contribution to the "Speaking of Books" column in *The New York Times Book Review*, September 5, 1965. Vonnegut revised it, and gave it its current title, for *Wampeters, Foma & Granfalloons (Opinions)*, his first collection of nonfiction prose, published by Delacorte Press/Seymour Lawrence in May 1974. The text from *Wampeters, Foma & Granfalloons* is printed here.

"Introduction to *Bagombo Snuff Box*, the uncollected short fiction of Kurt Vonnegut," was published, under the heading "Introduction," in *Bagombo Snuff Box*, published by G. P. Putnam's Sons in September 1999. The text of the introduction is printed here, under a descriptive title provided by the editor.

The following is a list of typographical errors corrected, cited by page and line number: 3.5. SOLOMON; 8.14, "Yes.; 8.36, Kitty,"; 10.10, Bul; 23.24, "*why?*"; 34.11, liked; 44.31, onto; 63.17, " 'Tal-ee-own—"; 64.34, Eh?"; 70.38, up.; 81.37, Finerty; 106.17, be be; 107.2, playing,; 108.22, dollars worth; 123.18, gun?"; 125.3, Kroner's,; 126.31, Mmm?";

129.9, Pick; 131.5, car"; 131.33, car?; 142.11, "Doctor; 149.6, f.6; 149.9, coll.); 154.6, hggged; 173.23, roughhousing; 173.34, dinner-plate sized; 183.5, "*Vuuuuzzzzzip?*'; 186.22, million dollar; 189.21, flash; 196.15, eight inch; 199.35, tube!"; 209.23, sir?; 216.30, and.; 219.33, Dégas',; 227.16, "*Board!*"; 235.3, Meadow's; 260.3, White; 265.23, G-17; 265.30, "thout; 267.30, Take; 270.10–11, network.; 282.33, Judge; 289.33, then; 290.21, automagic; 297.27, to to; 300.10, an important; 302.30, transitors; 305.13, eighth-horsepower; 311.5, Ferm; 317.19, Rumford's; 323.27, Rumford.; 333.14, climate" said; 345.35, Moncrief."; 361.39, one hundred-and fourteen-dollar-a-week; 368.10, plui; 377.22, third-seconds; 380.1, hesitated; 387.8 Boax; 407.11, name; 412.34, recorder. Purpose; 417.19–20, from malfunctioning; 425.6, Maffia."; 438.7, Do.; 458.25, Universe."; 468.4, Redfield,; 481.12, Rumford.; 484.22, Rumford; 495.17, Rumfood's; 556.18, Reichsleiter; 577.39, Chess?"; 597.22, Adolph; 604.16, treasurers; 609.7, a neck; 614.31, often She; 630.17, ghost,; 647.30, The afternoon; 656.38, suppose a; 660.34, said "The; 703.8, curiousity; 706.19, suppose why; 715.19–20, was a terrible; 727.34, ordinance; 756.17, that McGarveys; 766.19, born.

Notes

In the notes below, the reference numbers denote page and line of this volume (line counts include headings). No note is made for material included in standard desk-reference books. Biblical quotations are keyed to the King James Version. Quotations from Shakespeare are keyed to *The Riverside Shakespeare*, edited by G. Blakemore Evans (Boston: Houghton Mifflin, 1974). For reference to other studies, and for further biographical background than is contained in the Chronology, see Walter Rodney Allen, editor, *Conversations with Kurt Vonnegut* (Jackson: University Press of Mississippi, 1988); Asa B. Pieratt Jr., Julie Huffman-Klinkowitz, and Jerome Klinkowitz, *Kurt Vonnegut: A Comprehensive Bibliography* (Hamden, Conn.: Archon Books, 1987); Loree Rackstraw, *Love as Always, Kurt: Vonnegut as I Knew Him* (Cambridge, Mass.: Da Capo Press, 1999); John G. Rauch, "An Account of the Ancestry of Kurt Vonnegut, Jr., by an Ancient Friend of the Family," in *Summary* 1:2 (1971); Peter J. Reed and Marc Leeds, editors, *The Vonnegut Chronicles: Interviews and Essays* (Westport, Conn.: Greenwood Press, 1996); and Charles J. Shields, *And So It Goes: Kurt Vonnegut: A Life* (New York: Henry Holt and Co., 2011). See also the major collections of Vonnegut's nonfiction prose: *Wampeters, Foma & Granfalloons (Opinions)* (New York: Delacorte/Seymour Lawrence, 1974), *Palm Sunday: An Autobiographical Collage* (New York: Delacorte/Seymour Lawrence, 1980), *Fates Worse Than Death: An Autobiographical Collage of the 1980s* (New York: Putnam, 1991), and *A Man Without a Country* (New York: Seven Stories Press, 2005). For notes on Vonnegut's recurring fictional persons, places, and things, see Marc Leeds, *The Vonnegut Encyclopedia: An Authorized Compendium* (Westport, Conn.: Greenwood Press, 1995).

PLAYER PIANO

2.1 *For Jane—*] Vonnegut's first wife, the former Jane Marie Cox (1922–1986), whom he married in 1945.

7.2 Ilium, New York, is divided into three parts.] Cf. the first sentence of Julius Caesar's *The Gallic War* (*Commentarii de Bello Gallico*, c. 50–40 BCE): "All Gaul is divided into three parts" ("*Gallia est omnis divisa in partes tres*").

10.19–20 Rube Goldberg machine] Vastly complicated contraption that performs a simple task, named after American cartoonist and onetime engineer

Rube Goldberg (1883–1970), whose long-running Sunday panel *The Inventions of Professor Lucifer Gorgonzola Butts* featured fantastic, comic schematics for such devices as a machine for removing cotton from aspirin bottles.

12.1–2 Edison . . . opened another in Schenectady] Inventor and entrepreneur Thomas Alva Edison (1847–1931) moved his Edison Machine Works from New York City to Schenectady, New York, in 1886, and the city soon became his operation's world headquarters. By 1889 he had consolidated his many businesses, including the Schenectady works, as the Edison General Electric Co., which, after merging with Thomson-Houston Electric in 1892, became General Electric.

18.31 "Norbert Wiener . . . said all that . . .] See *Cybernetics* (1948) and, especially, *The Human Use of Human Beings* (1950), by the American mathematician and social scientist Norbert Weiner (1894–1964).

58.13 "The Lord giveth, and the Lord taketh away,"] Job 1:21.

59.9 *Sic semper tyrannis.*"] *Latin*: "Thus always to tyrants," words attributed to Brutus upon stabbing Julius Caesar.

65.13 O.D.] Olive drab.

66.1 O.C.S.] Officer Candidate School.

71.10–11 eternal vigilance is the price of efficiency] Cf. Wendell Phillips (1811–1884), in a speech before the Massachusetts Anti-Slavery Society, January 28, 1852: "Eternal vigilance is the price of liberty."

107.31–32 To live in a house by the side of a road . . .] ". . . And be a friend to man." From "The House by the Side of the Road," in *Dreams in Homespun* (1987), by American poet Sam Walter Foss (1858–1911).

109.36–37 Silver Stars] U.S. military decorations; see note 149.13.

124.3–4 "*Ooooooooooooh, give me some men . . . they adore . . .*"] From "Stout-Hearted Men," march by Sigmund Romberg, with words by Oscar Hammerstein II, from the operetta *The New Moon* (1927).

132.11–14 "Anyway, Thoreau was in jail . . . 'Ralph, why *aren't* you here?' "] This anecdote, perhaps apocryphal, was first recorded by Samuel Arthur Jones, MD, in his lecture "Thoreau: A Glimpse" (1889), and was popularized by Henry Stephens Salt, in his *Life of Henry David Thoreau* (1890). Dr. Jones had it from Samuel Staples, the Concord town jailer and tax collector, who incarcerated Thoreau for the night of July 23–24, 1846.

140.10 'After us the deluge,' "] Cf. "*Après moi, le déluge*," remark attributed to Louis XV of France (1710–1774), usually taken to mean "After I'm dead, who cares what happens?"

145.25 Rosicrucians] Originally, a secret society of spiritual and intellectual seekers founded in Germany in the early 1500s by Protestant students of the religious traditions of the ancient Middle East. Among modern American groups modeled on the historical Rosicrucians, the best known is the Ancient Mystical Order Rosae Crucis (AMORC), founded in New York City in 1915. Popularly known as the Rosicrucian Brotherhood, AMORC built its membership through advertisements in popular magazines offering free literature to readers who clipped and mailed in a coupon.

148.6 the creator of Tarzan] American writer Edgar Rice Burroughs (1875–1950), author of more than sixty action-adventure books including twenty-two featuring Tarzan of the Apes.

149.11 battle stars:] A battle star (or service star) is an attachment to a military medal denoting service in a particular campaign or engagement.

149.11–12 Hjoring . . . Ust Kyakhta;] Hjoring (Hjørring), Denmark; Elbesan, Albania; Kabul, Afghanistan; Kaifen (Kaifeng), China; Ust-Kyakhta, Russia.

149.13 P'ple H't . . . Med.).] Purple Heart (decoration awarded by the U.S. Armed Forces for "being wounded or killed in any action against an enemy of the United States or as a result of an act of any such enemy or opposing armed forces"), with three oak-leaf clusters (denoting being wounded in three subsequent actions); Silver Star (decoration awarded for "gallantry in action against an enemy of the United States"); Bronze Star (lesser decoration awarded for "heroic or meritorious achievement or services"), with three oak-leaf clusters; Good Conduct Medal (awarded for "exemplary behavior, efficiency, and fidelity in active Federal military service").

162.25–26 "Here, but for the grace of God, go you!"] Cf. "There, but for the grace of God, goes John Bradford," remark attributed to Protestant martyr John Bradford (1510–1555) upon seeing a fellow-prisoner being led to execution from the Tower of London.

166.33 Cape Cod lighter."] Long metal rod ending in a piece of slow-burning porous material, usually soapstone, which, when soaked in kerosene and ignited, is used to start fires, especially in fireplaces and woodstoves.

169.16 "Descent into the Maelstrom,"] See "A Descent into the Maelström" (1841), tale by Edgar Allan Poe (1809–1849) describing a shipwrecked sailor's being swept into a whirlpool.

170.26 "*Gott mit uns.*"] *German*: "God is with us."

173.17 "Abandon All Hope,] Cf. "*Lasciate ogni speranza, voi ch'entrate!*" ("Abandon all hope, ye who enter here!"), inscription above the gates of hell in Dante's *Inferno*.

184.18–19 Camp Drum] Former name (1951–74) of the present U.S. Army base Fort Drum, in Watertown, New York.

187.35–36 This above all . . . false to anybody else,] Cf. *Hamlet* I.iii. 78–81.

205.5 *De mortuis nil nisi bonum*] *Latin*: "Speak no ill of the dead."

214.29–32 "Fare thee well . . . adieu, yes, adieu! . . ."] Chorus of the traditional Irish song "There Is a Tavern in the Town."

229.16 hog-back] Ridge of land with steeply sloping sides.

230.17 Horatio on the bridge] According to legend, the soldier Horatius, standing alone on a narrow bridge, saved Rome by single-handedly repelling an invading army of Etruscans while his compatriots sawed down the bridge's support ropes, sending all into the Tiber. See the poem "Horatius," in *Lays of Ancient Rome* (1842), by Thomas Babington Macaulay.

230.19 Roland and Oliver] In the Old French poem *The Song of Roland* (c. 1040–1115), two evenly matched knights—Roland, nephew of King Charlemagne, and Oliver, grandson of Count Gerard—duel to the death to settle a dispute between Charlemagne and Gerard.

230.38–40 Kiukiang. . . . Afyon Karahisar. . . . Kransystav."] Kiukiang (Jiujiang), China; Afyonkarahisar, Turkey; Krasnystav, Poland.

231.2–3 Farafangana] City on the southeast coast of Madagascar.

231.23 guidon bearer] Soldier who carries his unit's colors into battle.

231.33 Tamanrasset] Oasis city in the Ahaggar Mountains of Algeria.

237.20 "Lo! How the mighty are fallen,] 2 Samuel 1:27.

239.10–11 Black Maria] Police van; paddy wagon.

241.15 Jim Thorpe] Versatile American athlete (1888–1953) who, after winning gold medals in the pentathlon and decathlon at the 1912 Olympics, enjoyed careers in professional baseball, football, and basketball.

244.2 "From blue Cayuga,"] This and the other lyrics quoted on page 244 are from "Cornell Victorious" (1915), pep song by Silas Hibbard Ayer Jr., Cornell Class of 1914.

245.18–21 "Far above . . . Glorious to view—"] From "Far Above Cayuga's Waters" (1870), alma mater of Cornell University, with lyrics by Wilmot Moses Smith (class of 1874) and Archibald Croswell Weeks (class of 1872) set to the tune of the traditional song "Annie Lisle."

246.28 The Dutch] The Old Dutch Kitchen, restaurant and bar of the now demolished Ithaca Hotel from the late 1890s through 1961.

246.30–31 "Cheer, cheer . . . with all our might—"] From "Cornell Victorious" (see note 244.2).

248.1 Pluto water] Brand name (c. 1910–1950) of a highly laxative mineral water from Pluto Springs, in French Lick, Indiana.

259.15 Ghost Dance] Vonnegut's chief source of information about the Ghost Dance religion was the ethnohistorian James Sydney Slotkin (1913–1958), his thesis adviser in anthropology at the University of Chicago in 1946–47. Slotkin's research was published as *The Peyote Religion: A Study in Indian-White Relations* (1956).

275.32 "But only God can make tree,"] Cf. "Trees" (1914), poem by Joyce Kilmer (1886–1919).

275.33 "Blessed . . . Inherited earth,"] Cf. Matthew 5:5.

277.2 Tabu] Signature women's fragrance of the New York perfumery House of Dana.

287.9 *houri selano*] *French, from Persian:* Voluptuous nymph.

THE SIRENS OF TITAN

310.1 *For Alex Vonnegut*] Vonnegut's favorite uncle (1888–1975), described in *God Bless You, Dr. Kevorkian* (1999) as "my father's kid brother, a Harvard-educated life-insurance agent in Indianapolis who was well read and wise."

318.32 Maxfield Parrish] Fantastical American illustrator and advertising artist (1870–1966) who, as a colorist, favored the dramatic light and saturated hues of sunrise and sunset.

320.23 banqueting hall of Whitehall Palace] Designed in the neo-classical Palladian style by Inigo Jones (1573–1652), the Banqueting House (1622) is the only surviving component of the Palace of Whitehall, which, until it was destroyed by fire in 1698, was the London residence of the English monarchs after 1530.

329.29–40 " 'And the Lord . . . face of the earth.' "] Cf. Genesis 11:5–9.

357.38 Benjamin Constant] Swiss-born French nobleman (1767–1830) and author of the novel *Adolphe* (1816).

365.21–23 "And God made . . . the stars also."] Genesis 1:16.

368.9–10 golden dawn punch . . . merry widow fizz] Cocktails popular in the 1930s.

368.10 Helen Twelvetrees] Cocktail of Southern Comfort, ginger ale, and blackberry concentrate, named after an American actress (1908–1958) featured in some two-dozen B movies between 1929 and 1939.

368.10 *pluie d'or*] *French:* golden shower. Cocktail of gin, Curaçao, Vielle Cure, and kummel.

427.19 *Per aspera ad astra*] *Latin*: "To the stars through difficulty." The motto is also featured on the Pall Mall cigarette package.

433.21 *Tweety and Sylvester*] Characters developed in the late 1940s by animators Bob Clampett and Friz Freleng for *Looney Tunes* and *Merrie Melodies*, the Warner Bros. series of theatrical film shorts.

433.22–24 *The Miserable Ones* . . . nice to him.] Cf. *Les Misérables* (1862), novel by Victor Hugo (1802–1885).

452.21–22 *Le Sacre du Printemps*] *The Rite of Spring* (1913), ballet score by Igor Stravinsky (1882–1971).

460.24 *Pro patria*] *Latin*: "For country."

462.28–31 *Whan that Aprille . . . flour—*] Opening lines of the General Prologue to *The Canterbury Tales* (late fourteenth century), Middle English story-cycle by Geoffrey Chaucer (c. 1343–1400).

472.11 blue poplar] Tulip tree.

476.11–12 *Pharisee, Tartufe, and Cagliostro*] *Pharisee*: orthodox Jew of the era of Jesus, shorthand for "one holier than thou"; *Tartufe*: comic protagonist of Molière's play *Tartuffe* (1664), shorthand for "imposter"; *Cagliostro*: Alessandro Cagliostro (1743–1795), Italian adventurer and occultist, shorthand for "mystic."

476.30 Gabriel horns] Cone-shaped loudspeakers.

MOTHER NIGHT

535.8 *The Protocols of the Elders of Zion*] False document first published anonymously in St. Petersburg in 1903 that purports to reveal the plans of an international secret society of Jews called the Elders of Zion to seize control of banks, newspapers, schools, and other institutions of the Western world.

536.10 135,000 Hansels and Gretels] Vonnegut's source for the number killed in the Allied bombing of Dresden was David Irving's book *The Destruction of Dresden* (1963). In October 2008, a commission of German historians appointed by the Dresden city government concluded, after exhaustive examination of archival evidence including police reports and burial records, that the air raids of February 1945 killed more than eighteen thousand but not more than twenty-five thousand people.

538.2 *Mata Hari*] Stage name of Margaretha Geertruida Zelle (1876–1917), Dutch entertainer, courtesan, and alleged double agent for France and Germany during World War I. Convicted of espionage by French military tribunal, she was executed by firing squad.

539.1–6 Breathes there the man . . . foreign strand?] From Canto 6 of "The Lay of the Last Minstrel" (1805), narrative poem by Sir Walter Scott (1771–1832).

542.3 Mrs. Theodore Rowley] Vonnegut's acquaintance Eva Maria (Artzt) Rowley (1925–2011) was a native of Breslau, Germany, who taught high school German on Cape Cod from 1950 to 1972.

542.9 G-man] *Slang*: Government agent, especially an operative of the Federal Bureau of Investigation.

547.2 *Tiglath-pileser the Third* . . .] King of Assyria (ruled 745–727 BCE) and founder of the Neo-Assyrian Empire, which dominated affairs of the Middle East from 732 to 612 BCE.

547.29 *Schutzstaffel*] *German*: "Protection Detachment." Originally founded in 1929 as Hitler's Nazi party bodyguard, the S.S. became the main instrument of state terror and genocide in Nazi Germany, gaining control over the police, the secret state police (Gestapo), and the concentration camps, and forming its own military force, known after 1940 as the Waffen (Armed) SS.

548.20 Iron Cross] German military decoration for bravery in battle.

549.13–14 Paul Joseph Goebbels] Goebbels (1897–1945) was Minister of Propaganda and Public Enlightenment in Nazi Germany, 1933–45.

550.12 Himmler] Heinrich Himmler (1900–1945) was *Reichsführer*, or highest-ranking officer, of the S.S. (1929–45) and one of the most powerful men in Nazi Germany.

553.23 Adolf Eichmann] Eichmann (1906–1962) was an S.S. *Obersturmbannführer* (Lieutenant Colonel) who headed the Jewish Department of the S.S. Reich Security Main Office, 1939–45, and played a major role in organizing the deportation of European Jews to extermination camps. Eichmann was captured in Argentina in 1960 and brought to Israel, where he was tried and hanged.

554.21 Rudolf Franz Hoess] Höss (1900–1947) was an *Obersturmbannführer* (Lieutenant Colonel) in the S.S. and, from 1940 to 1943, the first commandant of the Auschwitz concentration camp. He was hanged in Poland in 1947.

556.2 *"Last Full Measure* . . ."] In his Gettysburg Address, delivered November 19, 1863, President Lincoln honored the Union dead, who "gave the last full measure of devotion" to the cause of America's freedom.

556.18 *Reichsleiter*] *German*: "National leader." Title held by the highest ranking members of the Nazi Party below Hitler.

558.17 Goering] Hermann Göring (1893–1946), an air ace in World War I, was commander of the *Luftwaffe* (German air force), 1935–45.

562.37–39 Ohrdruf . . . two days before.] Actually, the Ohrdruf concentration camp, near Weimar, Germany, was liberated by the 4th Armored Division and the 89th Infantry Division on April 4, 1945.

567.2 *My Blue Fairy Godmother*] In the tale of Cinderella, it is the Blue Fairy Godmother who both counsels the heroine and effects her magical transformation from rags to riches.

567.5 Tiergarten] Urban park in western Berlin, designed in the 1830s.

570.20 Wehrmacht] The armed forces of Nazi Germany, 1935–45.

573.8 *Wandervögel*] *German*: "wandering bird." Member of a German youth group founded in 1901 dedicated to hiking and other outdoor activities.

574.28–29 from the Bering Straits to the Arafura Sea] From Alaska to Indonesia.

576.19 Tartakover] S. G. Tartakover (1887–1956), Polish-French chess grandmaster and composer of chess problems.

578.17 Karl Hederich] Karl-Heinrich Hederich (1902–1976), Chairman of the Committee of National Socialist Publications, 1933–45.

588.7–21 Conspiring to destroy . . . treachery from within.] A paraphrase of the indictment returned against twenty-eight right-wing anti-war propagandists by a federal grand jury in Washington, D.C., on July 21, 1942. The defendants, who included several former Bundists, were charged under the 1917 Espionage Act and the 1940 Smith Act with conspiring to undermine the morale and discipline of the armed forces. Their trial ended in a mistrial in late 1944, and the charges against them were later dismissed.

590.12 German-American *Bund*] American Nazi organization of the 1930s, dedicated to celebrating America's German heritage while also promoting a positive image of the Third Reich among the American public.

596.1 riddle of the Sphinx.] In Greek legend, the Sphinx is a monster with the body of a lioness, the wings of a great bird, and the face of a woman. She takes up residence on a rock just outside of Thebes, and poses her riddle to all who would enter the city. Those who cannot answer she strangles and devours. When the hero Oedipus solves the riddle, she jumps from her high perch and dies. The riddle and its answer are found in the *Library* of "Apollodorus" (c. first century BCE), a summary of the ancient Greek myths.

599.7 *Luftwaffe*] German air force. See note 558.17.

615.10 eighty-eight] Eighty-eight-millimeter gun developed by Krupp Industries and used by the German military from 1936 to 1945.

622.27–28 William Blake . . . "The Question Answered":] Gnomic verse no. 17.4 (c. 1793), from Blake's *Notebooks*, a.k.a. "The Rossetti Manuscript" (1874).

632.9 "It takes a heap of living . . . to make a house a home."] Cf. "Home," the title poem in *A Heap o' Livin'* (1916), by American newspaper columnist Edgar Guest (1881–1959).

632.20–27 "I had a cozy little burrow . . . are closing in."] Cf. "The Burrow," by Franz Kafka, in *The Great Wall of China and Other Stories* (1946), translated from the German by Willa and Edwin Muir.

634.34 Hottentots."] British-colonial name for the native Khoi (or Khoekhoen) people of southern Africa.

638.20–21 *Schreiberhau* in Riesengebirge] Ski resort in what is now called Szklarska Poreba, in southwestern Poland.

641.10 "The Silver Shirts"] The Silver Legion of the United States was a right-wing, anti-communist, pro-Hitler organization founded January 30, 1933, the day Hitler was appointed chancellor of Germany. At its peak, in late 1934, the Legion claimed fifteen thousand members; it disbanded in 1941, with the Japanese attack on Pearl Harbor. The Legion's Nazi-inspired uniform featured a silver shirt with a red "L" over the heart.

641.30 Heydrich] Reinhard Heydrich (1904–1942) founded the SD (SS Security Service) in 1932, and in 1936 also became head of the Sipo (Security Police), which consisted of the Gestapo (Secret State Police) and the Kripo (Criminal Police). The SD and Sipo were merged in 1939 into the RSHA (Reich Security Main Office); as the head of the RSHA Heydrich played a crucial role in planning and implementing the Holocaust. Appointed protector of Bohemia and Moravia in 1941, Heydrich was assassinated in Prague by Czech parachutists trained and sent by the British.

643.26 Maxfield Parrish] See note 318.32.

644.28 Cyklon-B] Trade name for a cyanide-based gas (also spelled Zyklon B) used to kill prisoners in Nazi concentration camps. It was originally developed as a pesticide by the German chemical company Degesch.

649.4–5 "His Truth Goes Marching On."] From "The Battle Hymn of the Republic" (1861), Civil War–era hymn by Julia Ward Howe (1819–1910).

658.40 General Donovan] Major General William Joseph "Wild Bill" Donovan (1883–1959), head of the wartime Office of Strategic Service (OSS), precursor of the Central Intelligence Agency.

659.33 Edgar Guest] See note 632.9.

667.6 'Charley's Aunt'] Three-act farce (1892) by the English comic actor and playwright Brandon Thomas (1848–1914). It was one of the longest-running successes in London stage history.

672.19 Werner von Braun] German-born rocket scientist (1912–1977) who, after helping develop the V-2 missile for Nazi Germany (see note 720.25), designed rockets for the United States, including the Saturn rockets used in the Apollo space program.

673.26 General Walter Dornberger] German-born rocket scientist and artillery officer (1895–1980) who, with Werner von Braun, developed the V-2 missile for Nazi Germany. He later designed guided missiles for the U.S. Airforce and the Bell Aircraft Corporation.

677.2 *Ah, Sweet Mystery of Life* . . .] Title of a song by Victor Herbert, with words by Rida Johnson Young, from the operetta *Naughty Marietta* (1910).

682.3–5 "My only regret . . . to give to my country."] According to legend, the last words of Nathan Hale (1755–1776), spy for the Continental Army who, upon being captured by the British in New York City, was hanged.

706.10 this is your life!] *This Is Your Life*, an early example of "reality" programming produced and hosted by media innovator Ralph Edwards, was aired on NBC radio (1948–52) and then on NBC television (1952–61). In each episode, a seemingly unsuspecting guest, usually a celebrity or public figure, was brought to Edwards's studio for a "surprise" celebration of his life and accomplishments, complete with testimonials by family members, friends, and other persons from his past.

706.17 Hope springs eternal . . . in the human breast.] From Epistle I of "An Essay on Man" (1733–34), long poem by Alexander Pope (1688–1744).

708.11–12 the fabled walls of Jericho . . . his trumpets play?] See Joshua 6:1–27.

STORIES

720.25 V-2s] Liquid-fueled ballistic missile used by the Germans to bombard England and Belgium in 1944–45. Captured V-2s were tested by the U.S. Army in New Mexico, 1946–52.

721.16 "Eternal vigilance is the price of freedom,"] See note 71.10–11.

732.34 *Ausgespielt*!] *German*: Finished!

733.36 *De mortuis nil nisi bonum*] See note 205.5.

737.39 pulmotor] Lightweight emergency pulmonary-resuscitation device once widely used by ambulance medics, firemen, midwives, and the like.

748.1 *Tomorrow and Tomorrow and Tomorrow*] See *Macbeth* V.v.19.

APPENDIX

782.32 "Maggie and Jiggs"] In the comic strip "Bringing Up Father," created in 1913 by George McManus (1884–1954), Maggie is the personification of social propriety and social aspiration, forever censuring her husband, Jiggs, an Irishman of low tastes and behavior.

782.33 a mildly unusual school] Hopefield School (now Riverview School), a private boarding school for students with special needs, in East Sandwich, Massachusetts. Vonnegut taught English there in 1963–64.

783.27–28 C. P. Snow's two cultures] In his lecture "The Two Cultures and the Scientific Revolution" (1959), the British novelist and physicist Charles Percy Snow (1905–1980) discussed the intellectual and educational "gap" or "rift" between the sciences and the humanities and its implications for twentieth-century life.

785.32 Seymour "Sam" Lawrence] Vonnegut's principal publisher, at Delacorte Press/Seymour Lawrence Books, from 1966 to 1989.

786.7 *Slaughterhouse-Five*] Vonnegut's sixth novel, published in 1969.

786.16–17 135,000 or so human beings] See note 536.10.

791.38 "Hell is other people,"] "*L'enfer, c'est les autres,*" from *No Exit* (*Huis Clos*, 1944), one-act play by Jean-Paul Sartre (1905–1980).

793.31 Dr. Edmund Bergler] Bergler (1899–1962), the Austrian-born Freudian psychoanalyst who coined the term "writer's block," published *The Writer and Psychoanalysis* in 1954.

794.4 my sister Allie] Alice Vonnegut (1917–1958).

THE LIBRARY OF AMERICA SERIES

The Library of America fosters appreciation and pride in America's literary heritage by publishing, and keeping permanently in print, authoritative editions of America's best and most significant writing. An independent nonprofit organization, it was founded in 1979 with seed funding from the National Endowment for the Humanities and the Ford Foundation.

1. Herman Melville: *Typee, Omoo, Mardi*
2. Nathaniel Hawthorne: *Tales and Sketches*
3. Walt Whitman: *Poetry and Prose*
4. Harriet Beecher Stowe: *Three Novels*
5. Mark Twain: *Mississippi Writings*
6. Jack London: *Novels and Stories*
7. Jack London: *Novels and Social Writings*
8. William Dean Howells: *Novels 1875–1886*
9. Herman Melville: *Redburn, White-Jacket, Moby-Dick*
10. Nathaniel Hawthorne: *Collected Novels*
11. Francis Parkman: *France and England in North America*, vol. I
12. Francis Parkman: *France and England in North America*, vol. II
13. Henry James: *Novels 1871–1880*
14. Henry Adams: *Novels, Mont Saint Michel, The Education*
15. Ralph Waldo Emerson: *Essays and Lectures*
16. Washington Irving: *History, Tales and Sketches*
17. Thomas Jefferson: *Writings*
18. Stephen Crane: *Prose and Poetry*
19. Edgar Allan Poe: *Poetry and Tales*
20. Edgar Allan Poe: *Essays and Reviews*
21. Mark Twain: *The Innocents Abroad, Roughing It*
22. Henry James: *Literary Criticism: Essays, American & English Writers*
23. Henry James: *Literary Criticism: European Writers & The Prefaces*
24. Herman Melville: *Pierre, Israel Potter, The Confidence-Man, Tales & Billy Budd*
25. William Faulkner: *Novels 1930–1935*
26. James Fenimore Cooper: *The Leatherstocking Tales*, vol. I
27. James Fenimore Cooper: *The Leatherstocking Tales*, vol. II
28. Henry David Thoreau: *A Week, Walden, The Maine Woods, Cape Cod*
29. Henry James: *Novels 1881–1886*
30. Edith Wharton: *Novels*
31. Henry Adams: *History of the U.S. during the Administrations of Jefferson*
32. Henry Adams: *History of the U.S. during the Administrations of Madison*
33. Frank Norris: *Novels and Essays*
34. W.E.B. Du Bois: *Writings*
35. Willa Cather: *Early Novels and Stories*
36. Theodore Dreiser: *Sister Carrie, Jennie Gerhardt, Twelve Men*

37a. Benjamin Franklin: *Silence Dogood, The Busy-Body, & Early Writings*

37b. Benjamin Franklin: *Autobiography, Poor Richard, & Later Writings*

38. William James: *Writings 1902–1910*
39. Flannery O'Connor: *Collected Works*
40. Eugene O'Neill: *Complete Plays 1913–1920*
41. Eugene O'Neill: *Complete Plays 1920–1931*
42. Eugene O'Neill: *Complete Plays 1932–1943*
43. Henry James: *Novels 1886–1890*
44. William Dean Howells: *Novels 1886–1888*
45. Abraham Lincoln: *Speeches and Writings 1832–1858*
46. Abraham Lincoln: *Speeches and Writings 1859–1865*
47. Edith Wharton: *Novellas and Other Writings*
48. William Faulkner: *Novels 1936–1940*
49. Willa Cather: *Later Novels*
50. Ulysses S. Grant: *Memoirs and Selected Letters*
51. William Tecumseh Sherman: *Memoirs*
52. Washington Irving: *Bracebridge Hall, Tales of a Traveller, The Alhambra*
53. Francis Parkman: *The Oregon Trail, The Conspiracy of Pontiac*
54. James Fenimore Cooper: *Sea Tales: The Pilot, The Red Rover*
55. Richard Wright: *Early Works*
56. Richard Wright: *Later Works*
57. Willa Cather: *Stories, Poems, and Other Writings*
58. William James: *Writings 1878–1899*
59. Sinclair Lewis: *Main Street & Babbitt*
60. Mark Twain: *Collected Tales, Sketches, Speeches, & Essays 1852–1890*
61. Mark Twain: *Collected Tales, Sketches, Speeches, & Essays 1891–1910*
62. *The Debate on the Constitution: Part One*
63. *The Debate on the Constitution: Part Two*
64. Henry James: *Collected Travel Writings: Great Britain & America*
65. Henry James: *Collected Travel Writings: The Continent*

66. *American Poetry: The Nineteenth Century*, Vol. 1
67. *American Poetry: The Nineteenth Century*, Vol. 2
68. Frederick Douglass: *Autobiographies*
69. Sarah Orne Jewett: *Novels and Stories*
70. Ralph Waldo Emerson: *Collected Poems and Translations*
71. Mark Twain: *Historical Romances*
72. John Steinbeck: *Novels and Stories 1932–1937*
73. William Faulkner: *Novels 1942–1954*
74. Zora Neale Hurston: *Novels and Stories*
75. Zora Neale Hurston: *Folklore, Memoirs, and Other Writings*
76. Thomas Paine: *Collected Writings*
77. *Reporting World War II: American Journalism 1938–1944*
78. *Reporting World War II: American Journalism 1944–1946*
79. Raymond Chandler: *Stories and Early Novels*
80. Raymond Chandler: *Later Novels and Other Writings*
81. Robert Frost: *Collected Poems, Prose, & Plays*
82. Henry James: *Complete Stories 1892–1898*
83. Henry James: *Complete Stories 1898–1910*
84. William Bartram: *Travels and Other Writings*
85. John Dos Passos: *U.S.A.*
86. John Steinbeck: *The Grapes of Wrath and Other Writings 1936–1941*
87. Vladimir Nabokov: *Novels and Memoirs 1941–1951*
88. Vladimir Nabokov: *Novels 1955–1962*
89. Vladimir Nabokov: *Novels 1969–1974*
90. James Thurber: *Writings and Drawings*
91. George Washington: *Writings*
92. John Muir: *Nature Writings*
93. Nathanael West: *Novels and Other Writings*
94. *Crime Novels: American Noir of the 1930s and 40s*
95. *Crime Novels: American Noir of the 1950s*
96. Wallace Stevens: *Collected Poetry and Prose*
97. James Baldwin: *Early Novels and Stories*
98. James Baldwin: *Collected Essays*
99. Gertrude Stein: *Writings 1903–1932*
100. Gertrude Stein: *Writings 1932–1946*
101. Eudora Welty: *Complete Novels*
102. Eudora Welty: *Stories, Essays, & Memoir*
103. Charles Brockden Brown: *Three Gothic Novels*
104. *Reporting Vietnam: American Journalism 1959–1969*
105. *Reporting Vietnam: American Journalism 1969–1975*
106. Henry James: *Complete Stories 1874–1884*
107. Henry James: *Complete Stories 1884–1891*
108. *American Sermons: The Pilgrims to Martin Luther King Jr.*
109. James Madison: *Writings*
110. Dashiell Hammett: *Complete Novels*
111. Henry James: *Complete Stories 1864–1874*
112. William Faulkner: *Novels 1957–1962*
113. John James Audubon: *Writings & Drawings*
114. *Slave Narratives*
115. *American Poetry: The Twentieth Century*, Vol. 1
116. *American Poetry: The Twentieth Century*, Vol. 2
117. F. Scott Fitzgerald: *Novels and Stories 1920–1922*
118. Henry Wadsworth Longfellow: *Poems and Other Writings*
119. Tennessee Williams: *Plays 1937–1955*
120. Tennessee Williams: *Plays 1957–1980*
121. Edith Wharton: *Collected Stories 1891–1910*
122. Edith Wharton: *Collected Stories 1911–1937*
123. *The American Revolution: Writings from the War of Independence*
124. Henry David Thoreau: *Collected Essays and Poems*
125. Dashiell Hammett: *Crime Stories and Other Writings*
126. Dawn Powell: *Novels 1930–1942*
127. Dawn Powell: *Novels 1944–1962*
128. Carson McCullers: *Complete Novels*
129. Alexander Hamilton: *Writings*
130. Mark Twain: *The Gilded Age and Later Novels*
131. Charles W. Chesnutt: *Stories, Novels, and Essays*
132. John Steinbeck: *Novels 1942–1952*
133. Sinclair Lewis: *Arrowsmith, Elmer Gantry, Dodsworth*
134. Paul Bowles: *The Sheltering Sky, Let It Come Down, The Spider's House*
135. Paul Bowles: *Collected Stories & Later Writings*
136. Kate Chopin: *Complete Novels & Stories*
137. *Reporting Civil Rights: American Journalism 1941–1963*
138. *Reporting Civil Rights: American Journalism 1963–1973*
139. Henry James: *Novels 1896–1899*
140. Theodore Dreiser: *An American Tragedy*
141. Saul Bellow: *Novels 1944–1953*
142. John Dos Passos: *Novels 1920–1925*
143. John Dos Passos: *Travel Books and Other Writings*

144. Ezra Pound: *Poems and Translations*
145. James Weldon Johnson: *Writings*
146. Washington Irving: *Three Western Narratives*
147. Alexis de Tocqueville: *Democracy in America*
148. James T. Farrell: *Studs Lonigan: A Trilogy*
149. Isaac Bashevis Singer: *Collected Stories I*
150. Isaac Bashevis Singer: *Collected Stories II*
151. Isaac Bashevis Singer: *Collected Stories III*
152. Kaufman & Co.: *Broadway Comedies*
153. Theodore Roosevelt: *The Rough Riders, An Autobiography*
154. Theodore Roosevelt: *Letters and Speeches*
155. H. P. Lovecraft: *Tales*
156. Louisa May Alcott: *Little Women, Little Men, Jo's Boys*
157. Philip Roth: *Novels & Stories 1959–1962*
158. Philip Roth: *Novels 1967–1972*
159. James Agee: *Let Us Now Praise Famous Men, A Death in the Family*
160. James Agee: *Film Writing & Selected Journalism*
161. Richard Henry Dana, Jr.: *Two Years Before the Mast & Other Voyages*
162. Henry James: *Novels 1901–1902*
163. Arthur Miller: *Collected Plays 1944–1961*
164. William Faulkner: *Novels 1926–1929*
165. Philip Roth: *Novels 1973–1977*
166. *American Speeches: Part One*
167. *American Speeches: Part Two*
168. Hart Crane: *Complete Poems & Selected Letters*
169. Saul Bellow: *Novels 1956–1964*
170. John Steinbeck: *Travels with Charley and Later Novels*
171. Capt. John Smith: *Writings with Other Narratives*
172. Thornton Wilder: *Collected Plays & Writings on Theater*
173. Philip K. Dick: *Four Novels of the 1960s*
174. Jack Kerouac: *Road Novels 1957–1960*
175. Philip Roth: *Zuckerman Bound*
176. Edmund Wilson: *Literary Essays & Reviews of the 1920s & 30s*
177. Edmund Wilson: *Literary Essays & Reviews of the 1930s & 40s*
178. *American Poetry: The 17th & 18th Centuries*
179. William Maxwell: *Early Novels & Stories*
180. Elizabeth Bishop: *Poems, Prose, & Letters*
181. A. J. Liebling: *World War II Writings*
182s. *American Earth: Environmental Writing Since Thoreau*
183. Philip K. Dick: *Five Novels of the 1960s & 70s*
184. William Maxwell: *Later Novels & Stories*
185. Philip Roth: *Novels & Other Narratives 1986–1991*
186. Katherine Anne Porter: *Collected Stories & Other Writings*
187. John Ashbery: *Collected Poems 1956–1987*
188. John Cheever: *Collected Stories & Other Writings*
189. John Cheever: *Complete Novels*
190. Lafcadio Hearn: *American Writings*
191. A. J. Liebling: *The Sweet Science & Other Writngs*
192s. *The Lincoln Anthology: Great Writers on His Life and Legacy from 1860 to Now*
193. Philip K. Dick: *VALIS & Later Novels*
194. Thornton Wilder: *The Bridge of San Luis Rey and Other Novels 1926–1948*
195. Raymond Carver: *Collected Stories*
196. *American Fantastic Tales: Terror and the Uncanny from Poe to the Pulps*
197. *American Fantastic Tales: Terror and the Uncanny from the 1940s to Now*
198. John Marshall: *Writings*
199s. *The Mark Twain Anthology: Great Writers on His Life and Works*
200. Mark Twain: *A Tramp Abroad, Following the Equator, Other Travels*
201. Ralph Waldo Emerson: *Selected Journals 1820–1842*
202. Ralph Waldo Emerson: *Selected Journals 1841–1877*
203. *The American Stage: Writing on Theater from Washington Irving to Tony Kushner*
204. Shirley Jackson: *Novels & Stories*
205. Philip Roth: *Novels 1993–1995*
206. H. L. Mencken: *Prejudices: First, Second, and Third Series*
207. H. L. Mencken: *Prejudices: Fourth, Fifth, and Sixth Series*
208. John Kenneth Galbraith: *The Affluent Society and Other Writings 1952–1967*
209. Saul Bellow: *Novels 1970–1982*
210. Lynd Ward: *Gods' Man, Madman's Drum, Wild Pilgrimage*
211. Lynd Ward: *Prelude to a Million Years, Song Without Words, Vertigo*
212. *The Civil War: The First Year Told by Those Who Lived It*
213. John Adams: *Revolutionary Writings 1755–1775*
214. John Adams: *Revolutionary Writings 1775–1783*
215. Henry James: *Novels 1903–1911*
216. Kurt Vonnegut: *Novels & Stories 1963–1973*
217. *Harlem Renaissance: Five Novels of the 1920s*

218. *Harlem Renaissance: Four Novels of the 1930s*
219. Ambrose Bierce: *The Devil's Dictionary, Tales, & Memoirs*
220. Philip Roth: *The American Trilogy 1997–2000*
221. *The Civil War: The Second Year Told by Those Who Lived It*
222. Barbara W. Tuchman: *The Guns of August & The Proud Tower*
223. Arthur Miller: *Collected Plays 1964–1982*
224. Thornton Wilder: *The Eighth Day, Theophilus North, Autobiographical Writings*
225. David Goodis: *Five Noir Novels of the 1940s*
226. Kurt Vonnegut: *Novels & Stories 1950–1962*

This book is set in 10 point Linotron Galliard, a face designed for photocomposition by Matthew Carter and based on the sixteenth-century face Granjon. The paper is acid-free lightweight opaque and meets the requirements for permanence of the American National Standards Institute. The binding material is Brillianta, a woven rayon cloth made by Van Heek-Scholco Textielfabrieken, Holland. Composition by Dedicated Book Services. Printing by Malloy Incorporated. Binding by Dekker Bookbinding. Designed by Bruce Campbell.